I0581889

FATED OR KNOT

Copyright © 2025 by Ella Hendricks

All rights reserved.

No part of this book may be reproduced in any form or by any electronic or mechanical means, including information storage and retrieval systems, without written permission from the author, except for the use of brief quotations in a book review. This book may not be redistributed to others for commercial or noncommercial purposes.

No part of this book may be used for AI training or data mining. Your support of authors' rights is appreciated.

This novel is entirely a work of fiction. The names, characters and incidents portrayed in it are the work of the author's imagination. Any resemblance to actual persons, living or dead, events or localities is entirely coincidental.

Flutterbye Trail Press
797 Sam Bass Road #2541
Round Rock, TX 78681

First edition

Chapter Art by Etheric Tales
Cover Design by Orina Kate
Editing by Red Loop Editing
Hardback Case Design by Enchanting Covers
Illustrated Cover Design by Melody Knighton
Map by Fictive Designs
Published by Flutterbye Trail Press

ISBN: 978-1-954582-46-0 (E-book)
ISBN: 978-1-954582-55-2 (Paperback)
ISBN: 978-1-954582-50-7 (Alternate Paperback)
ISBN: 978-1-954582-51-4 (Hardback)

Feedback: Encounter a problem with this book? Let us know at
ellahendricksauthor@gmail.com

BOOKS BY ELLA HENDRICKS

THE ARCANE ALLIANCES UNIVERSE

House of the Sanguine
with Nicole LaBrocca
Dark Vampire Romantasy (RH)

Thirst

THE FAERIE ARCHIPELAGO
SERIAN
THE AEONIAS BAY
EVER BOROUGH
GRIMSTROM
ONCE ELSE
THE DREAMLANDS
FOXTAIL MOUNTAINS
SORLES RIVER
NESLUNE
MIRROR LAKE
PORT EDRIS
TELIMARR
VAULTOR
LACULI POINT
DORAS SEA
LINFALL
DREY RIVER
LOCH DREYSON
PORT RAINCAP
ILYSNOR
THE SELKIE SHALLOWS
THELIS
THE ETERNAL
SYLVANAIRE
CELA REEF
ETALENZA
THE PIXIE'S LAMENT
THE DRAGONWAKE
OSME FEN
SLEEPING CALIARD
AQUANAAR
LANDIS
FURIGOR

FATED OR KNOT
THE OMEGA MASQUERADE

ELLA HENDRICKS

CONTENT OVERVIEW

This is a fantasy omegaverse RH romance, meaning that the main female character does not need to choose between love interests. There are graphic sex scenes (some including more than one partner) between consenting adults. This book does not contain MM content. You will find omegaverse dynamics in these pages, including scenting, nesting, knotting, etc. *Fated or Knot* is a standalone novel with a guaranteed HEA!

As the book is inspired by Cinderella, you will find a highly abusive stepmother character and a golden child/scapegoat relationship between the girls she's raised. Also contained within are brief descriptions of sexual assault from the members of an antagonist pack, plus mentions of torture, blood, and death. While the main characters discuss breeding in detail, this book does not include a pregnancy for the FMC.

If you find anything in the contents of this book that should be added to this page, please let me know at ellahendricksauthor@gmail.com.

1
LARK

THE CARRIAGE WOBBLED up the busy street on ancient wheels. Each time its interior swayed, there was an accompanying sound of straining wood that had icy nerves skittering down my spine. I tried to distract myself from my worries of the whole thing collapsing by sneaking peeks out the window, barely letting in a sliver of light to see Ilysnor decorated for the spring festival.

Forest elves and dryads worked in harmony to cultivate the woven garlands of flowers that lined every roof and railing on the buildings we passed. The blooms were fresh and alive, glowing with essence lining each petal and leaf. It made for a riot of colors, all to celebrate the warming of the sun and the shifting of nature's eternal balance back to Seelie hands for our seasons, spring and summer.

What had me gawking, though, was the sheer number of fae going about their day outside. A generous mix of races and designations traded coin and goods. A diminutive pixie girl stood at the intersection of two busy streets, waving fistfuls of silvery masks by their ribbons and calling out in a voice too small to reach me.

If I had to guess, she was shouting, "It's not too late to buy a mask for tonight!"

My heart ached when I spotted the child's mother, an omega with an intricate pack mark between her brows, watching her daughter with a mix of affection and caution.

I leaned forward, eager to see more of the city, just as a flash of teal fingers took hold of the curtain and snapped it over the window. Cymora cleared her throat. "Lark, you are testing my patience. If you can see them, they can see you. And you are not to be seen."

Like all mermaids, she had a voice like liquid silk, designed to flow and mesmerize. But her tone was acidic, and I hunched away as if it could burn me.

"Yes, Stepmother," I muttered.

A musical snicker sounded from Laurel. I could feel my stepsister's gaze on my face as I fixed my gaze on the floorboards and the thin, mud-stained rug beneath our feet.

"Our time here is all about appearances," Cymora stated.

"Appearances, yes, I know!" Laurel put in. We'd heard the lecture until Cymora's already blue-toned skin was a deep shade of sapphire.

From the moment we transferred from the roomier traveling coach to this creaking, swaying box, the only thing that mattered was how we *looked*. The outside of the carriage was gorgeous, lined with abalone-inlaid wood and swirls of pearl and seashell. The surface glittered with silver and diamonds when it caught the sun.

Only the absurdly wealthy would commission such a gaudy thing, but it was all a part of the charade. For one eventful night, Cymora was a mermaid alpha, Laurel her omega daughter, and I their dutiful human servant.

It was an elaborate falsehood completed by my illusions. Cymora wanted me to save my magic until we reached our quarters in the richest side of the city. I couldn't ruin things by peeking out of the window as we headed for the shadow of the castle, not even to see the preparations before the main event of the evening began.

The Omega Masquerade.

My stepfamily's one chance to avoid financial ruin...and my glimmering window of hope to escape them forever.

All I had to do was endure. *Just a few more hours.* How much heavier could a little more time weigh after so long spent at Cymora's whims?

It would be easy if she ignored me, as she did now. Her green eyes were fixed on her daughter as they went over the plan yet again. Laurel answered with the kind of whiny tone that would earn me a switching, but Cymora gazed at her like that omega on the street had with her tiny girl. Pain bloomed in my chest again at the sight.

I'd once had a father who looked at me like that. And my mother, had she lived for long past my first breath, may have as well. I'd never know for sure.

In my stepmother's eyes, Laurel could do no wrong. If she returned from the masquerade having not tricked a pack into claiming her tonight, I was sure to be blamed. All of my stepsister's faults were made my own failings one way or another.

I studied our feet until the carriage came to a halt. I lifted my chin to see both betas looking at me expectantly. With a flex of my fingers, essence glowed over my skin. Magic erased the wings on my back and blunted the points of my ears to the unpracticed eye. I reached out and touched Laurel first, giving her the illusion of wings and the more delicate build of a pixie omega. My fingertips brushed Cymora's proffered wrist next, and my magic gave her muscles and height so she would appear to be a rare female alpha.

Only when our disguises were complete did I exit the carriage, nearly tripping when I stepped out on my crippled foot first. Laurel followed, nose lifted, and I helped her to the ground with a gruff, "Watch your step, my lady." I'd never met a human, but I imagined their voices were deeper and more confident than my small, higher-pitched voice.

Cymora stepped down on her own, barely sparing me a glance. "Get our things," she ordered.

"Yes, Stepmother," I said, suppressing a sigh.

The carriage pulled away to wait for early evening with a line of other similarly overdecorated coaches, leaving me with three bulging bags. They were mostly stuffed with nonsense, considering how we would stay at this upscale location for the shortest period possible.

This is the last time. Once I enacted my plan, I wouldn't have to carry anything for my stepfamily again. Discomfort twinged up my right leg after I lifted the weight and began to walk, but I soon forgot the pain as I trailed behind my stepfamily, goggling at the grounds.

The path snaked along through a garden of spring blooms held at the peak of their life and vibrancy with only the most subtle glow of essence. A rainbow of a meadow surrounded the individual cottages here, and I wanted to pluck one of the purple flowers and tuck it behind my ear. Instead, I did my best not to tread on any greenery.

I followed my stepfamily to the cottage we'd rented for the night, sweat beading down my back and sticking to my invisible wings. A couple of servants helped my stepfamily while sneering my way as I stumbled past with the bags. Humans were allowed in Seelie lands, but our relationship with the magicless was still frosty at best. Still, the naked dislike aimed at me had me suppressing a whine that'd give away my true designation.

"We will not be requiring any extra help," Cymora was saying to them as I passed her and stepped into our cottage. She slammed the door shut a moment later and became a flurry of blue ensuring every curtain was closed throughout the dwelling.

Only once we could be assured of our privacy did she turn toward me and nod. I dropped the illusions on us with a huff of relief.

Cymora's truth was revealed as the layer of my magic faded off her body. She was a curvy beta with extra weight in the length of her thighs. She liked to emphasize her blue and teal hues by wearing gauzy dresses and too many gemstones along the finned lengths of her ears. Pearl clips studded the wild waves of her hair.

She'd spent enough time in her land form, preferring two legs to the fin of a mermaid, that her scales were nearly invisible. A faded mark still made a purple arch on her brow. It was all that remained of the magical tattoo she'd gained when she'd mated with my father. It was honorary now, with his passing, as was her title, Lady of Osme Fen. The money that'd once graced the name was gone, scraped out to buy her fine things and a lavish lifestyle.

She eyed my smock and plain servant's dress, their worn brown patchwork setting off the dull gray of my pixie wings and pale skin. I hadn't always been this color. As a girl, I'd been vibrant too, blessed with fae coloring that wouldn't look amiss in the meadow outside this cottage. But that'd been before I'd made a childish vow to Cymora and ruined my life.

Something dark creased her face when she finished her inspection. I took heart in one thing: I was the true omega in this cottage. No matter what else she took from me, she could not pluck out my designation and give it to Laurel. But if she could rip off my pixie wings and sew them onto my stepsister's back, she would.

Through her scheming, she'd devised the next best thing. If Laurel was bitten into a wealthy pack tonight, it would be through trickery of her design. And my magic would be to blame for the illusion.

I swallowed a lump of guilt. Pixies, the only Seelie fae with the omega designation, were rare enough that I knew some desperate alpha would claim Laurel. And then they would be soul bonded for life, dooming that pack to the grasp of my stepfamily.

Cymora beckoned. "Come, Lark. It's time for you to be of use."

Haven't I been already? I asked myself bitterly. If she had any inkling that I was anything other than an obedient servant at her beck and call, she would punish me severely, so I pushed down my feelings to speak in a bland voice. "Yes, Stepmother."

2

LARK

I'D ALREADY COMPLETED the more unsightly prep work on Laurel the night before we left for the capital, so grooming her today wouldn't require any more waxing or plucking. Tending to her when Cymora wasn't around was like wrestling a wet fish. She was slippery and very much wanted to sulk in the nearest source of water rather than face any sort of work or pain.

With my stepmother hovering nearby, Laurel didn't shift her legs into a mermaid tail and splash me for my firm treatment of combing, brushing, and scrubbing her body to get her ready for the evening. Thank the stars for small miracles. After Cymora dismissed the last of our servants, this set of duties had fallen to me, amongst other tasks.

"I don't understand why you can't just illusion me perfect," Laurel complained while I pinned locks of her hair into curlers and pulled them tight. She winced. Maybe I'd tugged a little too hard on that last one.

"My magic only works on sight," I said, suppressing a sigh. How many times had I explained this to her? "You don't want a handsome alpha running his fingers through your curls just to feel straight hair or a snarl of knots."

"Hehe. Knots," she repeated.

Cymora, who was applying purple stain to her lips, shot her a pointed look in disapproval. "Her magic has its limits and does its best work on enhancing what's already there. It's already going to be hard work to hide this." She reached over and pinched the side of Laurel's belly, causing her to squawk in protest.

"Mom! It's not so bad!"

Cymora scoffed. "You're beyond lucky the modiste could alter your dress so it still fits."

I ducked my head and bit my lip to stifle any hint of a laugh. On the inside, I was bent over with mirth.

Laurel's love of rich food clashed with the style of dress pixies traditionally wore to the Omega Masquerade. It wasn't her fault mermaids carried extra weight on their bellies and thighs, but she was *finally* getting some kind of consequence for stealing food off my plate.

"Well, she could've put an illusion over the dress," Laurel muttered.

Cymora caught her cheeks between her hands, and I got back to work with the curlers. "No, baby. All of her effort is going to make you stunning. *Stun-ning.*" She gave my stepsister a little shake for emphasis. "Every alpha in that room will be salivating to leave their mark on you. There is no chance you'll leave the party without a new pack."

Unless the alphas get a moment to talk to her first, I thought.

Cymora released her so I could finish preparing her makeup. Laurel replaced her pout with a smug smile through the powdering and painting to get her face as flawless as possible. She hadn't been in her full mermaid form ever since my stepmother had hatched this plan, which meant the scales that usually lined her cheeks and neck were small and soft. I hid them under a layer of paste that matched the blue of her skin. The scales on her arms and legs received the same treatment.

"She's ready for the scent, Stepmother," I said, not quite meeting Cymora's eyes.

"Step back." She bustled to the bag filled with her things to retrieve the bottles I wasn't allowed to handle.

Our local apothecary had taken a sample of sweat from my neck and a touch of my essence to make the jelly and perfume spray Cymora was about to apply to my stepsister. He'd called his creation "concentrated pheromones" and guaranteed it would make Laurel smell like me. As soon as Cymora opened the bottle and rubbed jelly between her fingers, a sugary scent wafted through the air.

My omega smell was of chocolate and honey crackers. It was a faint scent that clung to my skin, and while I was nose blind to it most of the time, I knew every nuance of my own pheromones. The recreation my stepmother rubbed vigorously over Laurel's wrists and neck had an undertone of sickly-sweet chemicals. I secretly hoped an alpha would pick up on it too and this lie would be exposed—once I was safely away from Cymora's wrath.

She snapped her fingers at me. "Bring the dress."

"Yes, Stepmother."

Stars, *the dress*. It was a unique torture to retrieve it from our things and undo the garment bag to reveal it in a waterfall of deep green fabric. I ran my fingers over the velvety soft material, reverent with the silken ties and decorative bells that tinkled from the tiniest touch. It was a traditional omega dress, two scraps of cloth a female had to be tied into. As the style was meant to be cinched tight, it left little about the body to the imagination.

Also tucked in the garment bag was a set of cloth pixie wings. I set them and the decorative lantern that was part of the presenting ceremony on the vanity and started lacing Laurel into her exquisite dress. If she had real wings, the fabric would fit right under the base of the lower pair, with an extra tie to fit in between her top and bottom wings to ensure the dress wouldn't fall off.

The style left her shoulders bare, and the fabric stopped after covering a few inches of her thighs. The silken ties crisscrossed down her sides, tied off at the ends with a set of three bells that rested just past the hem of the dress.

I handed her the fake wings, and she shrugged them on while I inspected her from top to bottom. Yes, she looked like a mermaid beta wearing a pixie's dress.

She was ready for the final touch. Cymora tied a decorative mask onto Laurel's face and nodded toward me. "Remember, Lark. Stunning," she warned.

"Yes, Stepmother," I repeated.

I'd imbued their masks over the last few weeks, flooding them with my essence until raw power stuck in every fiber. When I reached out to touch the edge of the feathers decorating one side of Laurel's mask, I was really tapping into that power to give it a purpose. As long as she wore the mask, the illusion I spun over her would remain in place no matter how far apart we were.

The cloth wings brightened with an inner glow, twitching occasionally like real pixie wings. My magic smoothed her curves and embedded sparkles in her skin, erasing any lingering evidence that she was a mermaid. I even changed the beta mark that'd come in low on her back when she hit adulthood to resemble an omega symbol instead.

I tried for stunning. As numbness threaded up my arms, starting from my fingertips, I brushed away any blemishes to make Laurel as pretty as possible. Not exactly stunning, but as close as I could get.

Save some essence. Don't use everything.

Once it was done, I hunched and rode a wave of vertigo with my eyes tightly shut. Judging by the tinkling of bells, Laurel must've turned around to see her reflection in the mirror. She gasped and exclaimed, "Look at me! I make such a beautiful pixie. I bet you wish you were this gorgeous, huh, Lark?"

A cool hand gripped my shoulder. I opened my eyes just a crack to make sure the room wasn't still spinning, just for Cymora to jostle me. "An adequate job. Finish my illusion now," she said.

She gestured toward the master bedroom just through the door, adding something about being allowed to sleep there, rather than on the floor, until they returned from the event tonight. *So generous.*

I took a few shaking breaths. Their voices were like white noise, an undercurrent of disdain woven into the melody of my life. Laurel's illusion had needed more essence than I'd already placed into her mask. If I ran out of magic now, I would fall into an exhausted sleep for days, long enough to close my eyes here and wake up in a coach bringing us back to Osme Fen and the looming threat of Pack Ellisar.

Stars, I couldn't let that happen. I blinked away the bleariness of fatigue and refocused on Cymora, whose lips were still moving. She released me before I registered what she said, and tied a matching mask to Laurel's onto her face. The decorative feathers rose on the opposite side, but I'd painted them with the same swirls.

Just a little more. You can do this. I pictured the freedom I'd have if I managed to stay awake after casting this spell.

Her illusion wouldn't be as difficult. I didn't need to alter the cut of her dress, just increase her size and lengthen the points of a couple of her teeth to make proper alpha fangs. I touched the side of her mask and used the essence already imbued there, shaping and molding this illusion more carefully so it didn't require any of the limited magic I had left.

Numbness crept up to my elbows, but I was upright, and Cymora seemed pleased.

She shoved me toward the bed. "Rest up." It looked very soft, with heaps of sheets and pillows. I wanted to test the plushness of the pile, imagining for a moment a nest made with all this. But if I lay down, I wouldn't have the energy to get back up. "Maybe your heat will *finally* arrive. Wouldn't that be lovely?"

I grimaced for half a moment, barely a flinch. *Oh yes, so great,* I wanted to say in a biting tone. A response like that would have me punished severely, but she'd already turned away, gathering up Laurel and everything else they'd need tonight.

"Good luck," I croaked.

Laurel glanced back at me and scoffed. "I don't need it." She sashayed out the door.

I stood by a window and combed my short hair to pass the time. The simple motion kept me awake, and feeling slowly circulated into my arms again.

I didn't dare sneak a peek outside, afraid Cymora would spot me. I just listened for the telltale clop of hooves and the creak of wooden wheels to let me know my stepfamily and the wealthy visitors who'd rented the other cottages were off to attend the Omega Masquerade.

Only then did I draw a new bath. It was time for me to prepare to go to the event, too. When Cymora began plotting Laurel's place in a wealthy pack, I'd planned as well. Waiting for this moment.

I had one night to change my fate.

I cleaned the grime of travel from my skin and inspected the magical tattoo right under my belly button. It was a small set of concentric circles painted in enchanted ink by the most discreet essence spinner in Osme Fen. Already, lines of skin threatened to split the whole thing in half... As I'd been warned, the longer I pushed off my heat, the less time the suppressant tattoos would last. I'd only gotten this one reapplied three months ago.

I paid dearly for the magical charm, trading anything of value I could take from the estate to cover the essence spinner's fee. It was worth it, especially when his magic had helped me stave off my first heat for four years. Pack Ellisar was prepared, breeding contract in hand, to claim me when it finally arrived, but the trio of barkfolk would wait fruitlessly once I escaped tonight.

The thought of them waiting for me in Osme Fen drew a shudder through my wings. I wouldn't go back. They'd never grab me in the market again. Never force another kiss on my lips. Never pull my hair to expose my neck to another slimy lick and to whisper lewdly in my ear about chocolate and honey crackers for dessert. Cymora may have agreed to sell me to them once I went into my first heat, but they'd never see that moment to claim me permanently.

I finished cleaning myself and limped over to view my reflection in the mirror. My determination faltered as I inspected what I saw there. Four years ago, I thought I'd rather die than see myself bitten into Pack Ellisar, but...I was fading.

My essence, the purple hue I'd once carried in my wings and hair, was almost gone. The shoulder-length strands hanging down around my face were a snowy white, my wings ashen. Even now, I regretted how naive my six-year-old self had been for not realizing Cymora was going to trick me into a deal after my father's funeral. And now I couldn't tell anyone why I was fading, since she'd forbidden me from speaking of it.

I had to get away from her and her orders before she destroyed me for good. There was still a chance I could start over in a sanctuary city, where only omegas and betas were allowed to live. But first, I had to hide the dark circles under my eyes and the fact I didn't have a traditional dress to wear to the Omega Masquerade. I used the makeup spread across the vanity to cover up what I could and to put some color back on my lips.

I donned my newest servant's dress and put my smock back on. Then I dug around the bags until I found what I needed—a pair of Laurel's amethyst studs and the spare mask I'd snuck into a side pocket.

The mask was the first one I'd designed for my stepsister, but she'd turned her nose up at it. I'd kept it and poured my essence into it when there was some to be spared. The fabric was designed in the shape of leaves around the eyeholes, with a butterfly made of genuine silver on the brow, large enough to cover the skin where a pack mark would rest.

Travel, or Laurel's rough handling, had warped the butterfly's slender wings and bent its little wire antennae, but this mask was still the key to my freedom. I tied it to my face and activated the essence imbued within it. In the mirror, I adjusted myself. I changed my servant's clothes into a purple and silver pixie dress hugging the curve of my waist. Soundless bells rested against my thighs.

There was still a bit of magic left in the mask to complete the illusion. I used it to alter the color of my wings to match the amethysts earrings. Numbness returned to my arms, creeping swiftly from my fingertips this time, but I cut off the magic before I grew too dizzy.

A lavender pixie glowed in the mirror, chest rising as I gasped. "It's not real," I whispered to ground myself.

However, I couldn't help a shimmy to admire the fake dress and the washed-out purple coating my wings. There was nothing I could do for my hair color, but that was okay. For a few short hours before I ran, I'd have one of the things Cymora didn't want for me: the chance to be myself, an omega. I would be *seen*.

I'd meet the same wealthy alphas as Laurel. Maybe even let them get close enough for a sniff so my scent would distract them. I'd been practicing my pickpocketing skills, after all. How else was I going to get the coin required to leave Ilysnor before my stepfamily recaptured me?

3
LARK

THE SUN SET while I walked to the castle through noisy crowds of beta revelers around each street corner. Even though I cringed at every touch, both accidental and not, I didn't have any essence to spare to fly to my destination. Besides, I needed to slip in after the presenting ceremony, where each and every omega walked in on the arm of their guardian while the attending alphas looked on.

Cymora had been planning for this moment meticulously. That was the only reason I knew the presenting ceremony existed. My lack of an introduction shouldn't matter—I had to focus on what did. I was going to steal enough valuables to afford a magirail ticket and the services of an essence spinner before my journey away from Ilysnor. I might enjoy the attention of a few alphas, but soon I was leaving to start my new life in a place my stepfamily and Pack Ellisar wouldn't find me.

My foot dragged painfully after blocks of dodging the celebrating fae, and my anxiety was at an all-time high. There were so many fae here. I was an omega on her own. A number of things could happen under the anonymity of a crowd, so I kept as alert as possible for potential danger.

Don't bring attention to yourself. I tried not to jump from every shadow and motion of those around me. It only earned me glances and perusals of my illusioned-on dress.

Any drunken, grasping fae that noticed me were typically reaching for my body, not my mask. I checked the edges of it often, making sure it was still secured. By the time I made it to the closed gate in front of the castle grounds, extra tendrils of fatigue were pulling at my limbs.

Still, I kept my voice light for the pair of guardsmen standing sentinel behind the gate. "Am I too late for the Omega Masquerade?" I fluttered my lashes with a forced laugh. "I, um, took too long getting ready."

The pair of betas exchanged a glance. They had the power to turn me away and ruin my plan without cause or remorse. The seconds passed with excruciating sluggishness as they spoke behind their hands and gestured before coming to a decision.

"Right this way, miss," the one on the left said, opening the gate long enough for me to slip inside.

Not all betas are like Cymora and Laurel, I reminded myself in relief. The guard seemed cordial. He even offered his arm with a friendly smile.

I wavered, unsure why he'd extended his elbow my way. I'd seen other females rest a hand on the forearm of their companions. I placed my hand on his arm before he gently took my fingers and fixed them to rest in the crook of his elbow. Then he steered me up the path to the event.

The stone walkway was lined with spring blooms glowing from within. Most of the castle grounds around us were well-lit from patches of luminous flowers, with the figures of couples occupying some of the darkness in between them.

"You've missed the presenting ceremony, I'm afraid. I could still try to announce you, if you'd like?" the guard offered. He slowed his stride, shifting to accommodate a particularly bad limp that sent fractals of pain up my right leg.

"No," I puffed out. "That...that's okay."

He peered down at me, face creased with concern. "Where is your guardian, miss?" Once we entered the castle, I saw that he was a forest elf with strands of gray shot through his leaf-green beard. He had kind eyes, though I suspected he saw more of my secrets than I would've liked. I hadn't expected anyone to care enough to ask that question.

In an unguarded moment, I said, "I am without one." Like any fae, I couldn't lie, but I still kicked myself a moment later for telling the whole truth to this stranger.

His brows rose past the visor of his helmet. "In that case, at least let me escort you to the royal pack."

"No...I don't..." I stammered.

"It's protocol, miss. The queen greets every omega who attends the masquerade." His face smoothed into a comforting look. "She's the kindest female I've ever worked for. You have nothing to worry about."

He led me through a couple of corridors, to a spiraling staircase that took us a while to climb. My cheeks burned like little suns as I puffed and struggled. The guard became one of my favorite fae by providing his support along the way and not commenting.

Eventually, we made it to the top of a railing overlooking a ballroom in full swing. We were on eye level with a chandelier dripping with specialized essence that glimmered in crystalized drops and provided gentle illumination for the sight below us. The ballroom was gigantic, lined on all sides by massive windowpanes adorned with ornate drapes.

The crush of fae below reminded me of the meadow outside of my stepfamily's rented cottage. The gemstone brightness of glowing pixie wings stood out here and there in pops of color. No one would notice a faded bloom slipping in amongst this number of vibrant souls.

As we descended slowly so I wouldn't trip down the stairs, I took in the setup of the room. Guardians milled about with drinks in hand, mostly gossiping and sitting at the round tables to the side of the ballroom. Several couples danced, following the melody of a soaring, upbeat song played by a live orchestra. I couldn't see the musicians, but I felt the vibrations of sound through the worn soles of my slippers.

A fine mist hazed over the whole event, smelling like...well, nothing. Given that my nose wasn't assaulted by the mixed pheromones of hundreds of alphas plus at least fifty omegas, it had to be a cloud of scent blocker. How was an omega supposed to find a scent match with this much mist hanging in the air?

By the time my feet reached the end of the stairs, I was sure I'd made a terrible mistake. There were more fae here than the entire population of Osme Fen, and I had no idea what to do in such a large crowd.

From listening to my stepfamily plot, the whole point of the event was for omegas to meet alphas from across the kingdom. But was I supposed to meet *this* many alphas? I made a shy cringe at the notion. My earlier desire to be seen as an omega felt like utter foolishness. I needed to get in and out of this event as quickly as possible.

"This way," the guard said, interrupting my thoughts. He led me around the edge of the dance floor. The far side of it had a set of five raised thrones for the royal pack, though each high seat was empty. "When an alpha offers you his hand, what do you do?"

"Huh?" I glanced up and saw the set of his jaw. He was still a little worried. "I shake his hand?"

"In any other situation, yes. But at this event, he will kiss your fingertips and take a *brief* smell of your wrist. You don't have to let every alpha here do this, miss. Only the ones you like."

"Oh, for scent matching," I said. My stepfamily hadn't talked about this part of the masquerade.

"This is the biggest crowd of alphas we've hosted in a long time. You're going to have some that will try to insist you're a match when you're not," he continued. Now he was simply sounding almost... fatherly. "Since you are without a guardian, I strongly suggest you don't leave the castle grounds with an alpha you meet tonight. Any guard would be happy to escort you home if you're feeling unsafe."

Emotion choked up my throat. I managed a wobbly little "Thank you."

"And here we are." He jerked his chin, drawing my attention to an omega dancing nearby. Her long blonde hair flowed behind her like a pennant in the wind, along with her deep blue skirts and the pretty pink and yellow of her pixie wings. We stopped nearby and waited as the music came to a high point, suggesting the song would finish soon.

This far into the room, the light was a romantic suggestion from garlands of glowing flowers and a few decorative lanterns on the tables and pillars behind us. Still, I'd need to be blind to miss that the queen was an omega of impeccable grace, and the alpha who danced with her met her in a choreographed whirl of their bodies.

His skin was such a vivid shade of red that I blinked in surprise. Only a dragonsblood salamander, a rare type of Seelie shifter, would be such a color. As the music came to a brief pause, he wound his arm around her waist and dipped her, lifting his mask to kiss the breath off her lips. I blushed, feeling like I was intruding, and dropped my gaze with an all too familiar hunch to my shoulders.

The guard must've gotten their attention, as the next thing I knew, the queen and her crimson king were heading our way. I fumbled into a curtsy and held it. "Oh, a late bloom? I'm so glad you could make it." The queen's voice was coming closer, and the next thing I knew, her slender fingers were tilting up my chin. She took my hands in hers.

I was absolutely stunned this was happening. The salamander alpha and the guard started chatting a few feet away as if nothing was out of the ordinary. My mind had chosen to freeze, thoughts stuttering. This was...*the* queen? Queen Alora? Touching me?

"Welcome, dear," she said warmly. "Tell me about you. Where are you visiting from?"

I cleared my throat, willing myself to rally and not make a fool of myself. "I...I'm Lark." And I couldn't help the nervous quake in my body. She was still the queen. "I'm from Osme Fen. It's a little...tiny farm town?"

Her painted lips pursed thoughtfully under her glittering sapphire-dusted mask. "Oh, yes! I just met your sister, I think. Laurel?"

"Step," I said a little too fast. "Um. Stepsister. Yes."

"Well, how delightful that you both could make it. We're always happy to have citizens from across the Kingdom of Thelis attend, but especially those from so far away. Don't let me hold you back from enjoying your evening."

"Thank you, Your Majesty." My shoulders loosened with relief. I could start achieving what I'd come here for rather than dare to stand in front of the queen while wearing an illusion over plain servant's garb. She wouldn't have been so quick to touch me if she'd known. Or maybe she still would've. I'd never know for sure.

I started to skulk off in shame. "Oh, and Lark?" Queen Alora added. I turned back to look at her. The guard was gone, and she was resting her hand on her alpha's arm. "If you happen to run into my daughter, Glory, will you let her know I'm looking for her? Her wings are this shade of red. You can't miss her."

She patted the salamander king, and I nodded, mustering enough nerve to say something else while they were both looking at me. "Yes, Your Majesty. That guard...the male who brought me to you. He is very kind." I hoped the clumsy compliment would help him in some small way.

Both of them smiled. "Loren has been a loyal member of our household since before I was born," said the king, his voice a deep rumble. "I'm glad he continues to treat our guests well."

"Enjoy the festivities," Queen Alora added brightly.

I went the opposite direction they did, heading for the tables laden with food at the back of the room. Stars, this was already not going how I'd expected it to. All I'd known about Queen Alora and her pack before now was that she had one child, the omega crown princess. The folk of Osme Fen gossiped about her lack of fertility.

They were afraid, maybe, but that fear had made them cruel. They compared her to the Queen of Serian, who was rumored to be pregnant yet again. The Unseelie had more than secured their next generation, while the Seelie continued to wait for Queen Alora to birth a pack of princes.

Maybe she didn't want to. Maybe one was enough, despite the impatience and worry from her subjects and the weight of responsibility Crown Princess Glory must feel as the sole heir.

I entered the line for a turn in front of the refreshments, behind a pixie with beautiful evergreen wings. Her blonde hair was up in a braided coronet on the back of her head, exposing the slender golden column of her neck. The dress clinging to her curves was embroidered with a leaf pattern.

I was still admiring her dress when an alpha came over and wedged between us. "Ladies," he rumbled. First, he offered his hand to her and took a breath of her scent. Looking disappointed, he released her and did the exact same thing to me. Muttering, he turned his back, leaving me to exchange a glance with the other pixie.

"Some of the males here are so rude," she declared with a huff. Her mask was small and white, with painted flowers dotting it for pops of color.

"You look very pretty tonight," I blurted before I could second-guess the compliment.

Her wings fluttered as she smiled. She fell into step beside me as the line inched forward. "So do you! I'm Poppy of Etalenza. This is my first time at the Omega Masquerade."

"I'm Lark of Osme Fen. And this is my first, and hopefully last, time," I murmured.

She giggled openly. "That's the spirit! Are you hoping to find a solo mate or a pack tonight?"

"Um…" Neither, honestly. I wanted a ticket out of the city, a new heat suppressant tattoo, and a leisurely night's sleep, not necessarily in that order. "My parents were a couple. I think one male would be plenty for me."

"Well, don't be afraid if you do get a pack of scent matches. I come from a happy pack with five alphas and two omegas. I've got more siblings than I know what to do with," Poppy declared. "I'm half dryad, but my brothers are orcs, dryads, and selkies. Never a dull moment at home."

That was common in a pack of mixed fae races. Pixies, as omegas, had more pixies for their daughters and sons that reflected the race of their fathers. Had my parents lived, I would probably have at least one alpha wind sprite brother. Couples were frowned upon and considered an incomplete pack. Omegas were so rare that the collective sentiment was that they needed to be shared by more than one alpha or, at the very least, a mixed pack of alphas and betas.

"I'm half wind sprite," I told her. "And, well, I'm an only child."

"How lonely! Where'd you say Osme Fen is? I couldn't imagine not having a big family." Poppy fluttered her lashes. "I'm here with my best friend, but I don't know where she's gone. I'd better get her a sticky bun. She'd hate having to stand in this line."

"I just hope there's some food left." My belly grumbled in agreement.

As we chatted, we attracted attention from the alphas roaming the edges of the ballroom. Several stopped and offered their hands with barely a word of hello. I didn't tell anyone no, letting myself get used to the ritual of strangers brushing their lips over my fingertips before they scented my pheromones.

Most breathed a sigh that sounded something like defeat. "It seems we are not a match," more than one alpha said before he went about his evening.

No one asked to dance, which was just fine by me. If they passed too close, I took the opportunity to sneak my fingertips in their pockets or over wrists and belts. Poppy didn't notice, too happy to gossip and giggle as we waited in line.

Anything I stole, I quickly dropped into the front of my invisible smock to sift through later. No alpha noticed their rings or coin purses disappearing... Stars help me if they did. I'd practiced as much as I could so tonight would go off without a hitch.

"Oh, there's my friend. Coral!" Poppy pointed out a petite, blue-winged pixie with soft gray skin and thick black hair, who waved on her way by.

"Get me something!" Coral called back.

Poppy pointed at her, then raised her thumb and brow at the same time. The other pixie flashed a thumbs-up back. "Tell you later," she added. She was being escorted between two alphas who appeared to be arguing over top of her head.

Poppy shook her head with a playful sigh. "She's always getting herself into something. It looks like they're going out to the balcony, so I'll check on her later."

I nodded. The event seemed relatively safe, but I hoped the balcony had guards. It was always potentially dangerous for an omega to spend alone time with two unknown alphas. They were so much larger and stronger than us.

It was soon our turn with the table of food and beverages, and I was momentarily dazzled as I took in everything alongside Poppy. Towers of pastries and pyramids of tiny sandwiches were piled up next to little serving tongs. We noted everything that looked good, eager to start filling our plates. Goblets of sparkling wines and juices were also displayed and neatly marked for whether they contained hallucinatory fae fruit.

I reached for a plate, just to turn and startle since an alpha had snuck up on me and put his big hand right in my path. I was of half a mind to tell him to leave me alone since the food was *right there*, but I'd already gotten used to this ritual and put my palm in his.

He was a wind sprite, tall and turquoise with an artfully tousled mass of light blue hair. Instead of wearing a suit like most of the other alphas here, he was in plain everyday clothes and took a much longer sniff of my wrist than any other alpha had. His gaze flew to mine as he said, "You smell exquisite, little lady. See for yourself that we're a match."

With a tug on my arm, he tripped me forward into his chest, and trapped my head against his shirt. I smelled wood and smoke, and it threatened to choke me. My eyes watered from how unpleasant his pheromones were up close. I may not have dreamed of meeting my scent matches, but even I knew any fated alpha of mine would smell lovely. Most mated couples called their scent matches "irresistible," even. The newly mated in Osme Fen were always trying to sneak in sniffs of one another.

It was something about compatibility that made a scent match smell incredible to the nose of their mate or mates alone. This alpha wind sprite was just trying to force something that wasn't there.

"What do you think you're doing?" Poppy exclaimed at him as soon as she turned to see me trying to push away from him.

"No—" I protested.

"Let's take this next dance, and I can tell you about my pack," he said, ignoring us both. He swept me off my feet without so much as a grunt of effort.

I reached for the delicious-looking pastries with a longing swipe of my hand as he carried me away from them.

4
LARK

I KICKED and shouted in the wind sprite's hold. The orchestra finished its song, and in the resulting pause, a female voice exclaimed, "Hey! Put her down!"

There was a flash of essence before flaming embers scattered in the air nearby. He hastily placed me back on my feet, and another omega was in his face the next moment. "You should be ashamed of yourself. I heard her no from here—" she scolded.

"I'm sorry, Your Highness. Forgive me," he interrupted.

This had to be Crown Princess Glory. If the title wasn't enough to give it away, she had wings as bright red as a dragonsblood salamander and wore a mask with a tiny crown set above her brow. Her orange-tinged skin glowed with health and a generous dusting of pixie sparkles, and her high ponytail of ruby hair swung with her quivering wings as she angered further.

"Perhaps you should have your ears examined," she continued in a barbed tone. "What is your name?"

"Willis, Your Highness." He held his hand out to her.

Glory must've signaled a guard, as one materialized by her side. She pinched Willis's fingers and placed his hand in the guard's gauntlet. "Be a dear and ensure Willis doesn't handle another female without her permission," she instructed him.

"Yes, Princess Glory."

I watched them leave the dance floor, my lips parted in awe. Even though a new song was well underway, a cluster of fae had stopped to watch the exchange, several alphas chuckling at Willis's expense. More than one admired Glory as she stood there with her fists propped on her hips.

"Thank you for that, Your Highness," I said. Though I'd liberated Willis of his timepiece, which was payment enough for trying to force me into a dance, I couldn't have gotten him to back off like she had.

She turned her gaze toward me. Her eyes were pink with specks of gold, and soft as only an omega's could be. "Don't mention it. Us omegas have to stick up for one another."

"I met the queen, and she wanted me to tell you—"

She held up her hand hastily. "Ah, no, don't."

I wavered, confused.

"If you don't tell me, then I have deniability that I never heard the very predictable thing she wants you to say." She swung around as if just noticing the gathered observers. "Well? We're here to party, aren't we? I need a dance partner, and so does this lovely lavender omega."

My eyes widened. I'd just wanted something to eat...but now I had my choice of partner as Glory let herself get swept back onto the dance floor. Five masked males approached with their hands extended in offering. There was really no reason to pick one over the other, and I'd probably be seen as peak *rude* if I said I didn't want to dance with any of them.

Just one dance to embarrass myself over, then I'll get out of here. I'd probably stolen enough at this point.

I picked the male with the most expensive-looking mask. The other four shuffled away with the equivalent of a shrug. The forest elf who now held my hand bowed over my fingers in an elegant sweep before standing to his full height, over a head taller than me.

"Not going to test my scent?" I asked, a little surprised.

"I can smell you just fine, my lady." He spoke with a touch of an accent I didn't recognize. In the low light of this area, his hunter-green hair seemed almost black, as did the hint of his eyes from within his mask. He had an athletic build, lean and trim in the silver-filigreed suit he wore.

The alpha drew me closer, resting a hand on the small of my back. Our bodies didn't touch, at least a foot of propriety between us as he tried to move me into the next step of the dance. *Well, might as well get this over with.* I stood there like a statue, cheeks flooding with heat. "I, um, don't know how to dance."

His brows may have risen, but the mask he wore covered his face to mid-forehead. It glittered with gemstones, a merry rainbow of them placed in an intricate design. He had to be a wealthy lord of some kind. Maybe I'd get an opportunity to pick his pocket while he scorned me.

I braced myself, but he merely cocked his head to the side, his fine mask framing a mischievous smile. "Is that so? It's not difficult. Here…" He positioned my hand on his arm. "Relax. Just move with me."

He took a step, and I did too, mirroring him. Before long, he had me dancing, though at a fraction of the pace of the couples around us. *This isn't so bad,* I decided. But the song ended soon after, and my patient partner released me to bow. Other omegas were curtsying to their companions around me and I echoed the motion off sync.

There were more alphas without a partner than omegas, and I didn't need to look over my shoulder to know others were staring. I had to move quickly to escape the dance floor before I ended up cornered for another song. "Thank you for the dance," I said.

"Don't leave yet. I don't even know your name." There was a lightness to his tone, as if he was teasing me.

"Well, I don't know yours either," I said, trying for the same levity.

In response, he beckoned for me to dance with him again, offering his long, graceful fingers in a showy flourish as the orchestra started up another tune. I bit my lip, tempted. I needed to leave, but one more dance wouldn't hurt. I let him take the lead in showing me the steps again.

"I'm Falindel, by the way," he said once we were moving together. "I prefer Fal. It's less stuffy." He pronounced it like the season, fall.

"Hi, Fal. I'm Lark."

His smile included a hint of fang. All alphas had a pair of them, but his seemed particularly sharp.

"You're good at this," I noted. Fal had seemed to notice my right side wasn't as strong as my left and compensated for it somehow. To say *we* were dancing was a laugh, though. It was about ninety percent him, with me along for the journey as we traveled further onto the dance floor.

He shrugged. "Practice, though I shouldn't downplay it too much. My father insisted I dance until the dark of night some days."

"Oh, I'm sorry." That didn't sound pleasant.

"No need to be. I mostly enjoyed it, and now I get to dance with you, so surely I'm doing something right." He winked, a flash of tanned skin.

I ducked my head with a flattered giggle. I was nothing special, just a servant wearing illusions. My goal was to steal a bit of wealth and run, not give any alpha a false sense of my interest.

And it wasn't as if we were scent matches. He'd barely smelled me and hadn't drawn close enough for me to breathe him in either with all the scent blocker misting over us.

"May I ask you a question, Lark?" He broke through my concentration, my brow knit as I tried not to step on his toes.

I missed some cue and nearly stumbled into him, but he caught me without trouble. "Um, sure." Stars, I was so clumsy.

"Tell me a secret." Fal's voice was a low purr. It felt like an invitation to lean in. "Why did you come here tonight? Truly."

My gaze darted away as my wings flattened defensively to my back. I hadn't...no, I'd been too distracted by dancing to steal anything from him. Maybe it wasn't a serious question. Maybe he was flirting and I'd been about to overreact.

There were hidden depths I couldn't say to answer his question. But I still offered him a glimmer of myself with something that qualified as a secret. "I wanted to be seen," I murmured. *And to have the freedom to be like the other omegas here, dressed to be desired and able to choose mates for love. Not here to take and run.*

I didn't think I'd share any of this aloud with anyone, but why not with Fal? He'd probably forget it by tomorrow, just a throwaway comment from one of the silly omegas he'd met tonight.

"Did you?" He had a teasing tone again, but I wasn't quite sure he *was* flirting, with how his gaze suddenly seemed intent on me.

"That was before I noticed how many fae were here," I continued in a lighter tone.

"So many souls here, and yet only one scent match, if a member of your future pack even attended. Did you expect to find yours tonight?"

"No. Did you?"

He dipped his chin. "I came a very long way hoping to find my one true mate."

"Well, I hope you find her," I said sincerely.

Fal's smile held a hint of mischief. "I see you, Lark." I doubt he realized how much I wanted to hear something like that. My wings fluttered with my happiness. "But I want to know so much more. You seem tired. Perhaps we could sit and chat once this song is finished?"

I should've told him no. I really did need to leave, and he should've stopped wasting time with me, a graceless swan, and gotten back to searching for his scent match. But the song in question was already nearly done, and as it concluded, his hand tightened on my back.

He swung me toward the ground, dipping me like Glory's father had with the queen. For a moment, his face was close enough to kiss, but I was too busy yelping.

Blood flooded straight to my head and back as soon as I was on my feet. That was...thrilling. And stars, what was that incredible smell?

I lidded my eyes and inhaled. It was dreamy, a bright and fresh scent, like crisp grass and sunshine. I pictured lazy summer days out on the lawn with nothing to do but play games with my family and the neighbor's kids. I'd lie out on the green, living carpet with my face raised and wings spread to bake in the sun.

Before Cymora, before Laurel, before I'd learned how much life could hurt. Yearning filled my chest to be that summer child again and redo my life with different decisions. Perhaps I wouldn't be here under false pretenses if it were possible.

"You have a lovely smile," Fal murmured.

I blinked back to reality. He watched my face as I drew in a deep breath to catch more of that smell, and his lips took on a knowing curve. His gaze flashed toward another alpha approaching, and he shook his head with a brief baring of his fangs to get the other male to leave. I was still leaning toward him for more—it was *his* scent that smelled like my childhood.

He offered his arm to lead me off the dance floor. We avoided other couples starting to sway together to a slower tune.

"Are *we* scent matches?" I asked in disbelief. I'd never had such a strong reaction to another fae's pheromones before.

His nostrils flared as he scented me back. "I strongly suspect so. You smell decadent. Seems I didn't come all this way for no reason. Of course, we won't know for sure until you meet my brothers, but I'll be more than happy to introduce you."

So the omegas wouldn't be overwhelmed, each alpha here was a representative of his pack. But the mention of meeting brothers was as effective as a slap. I couldn't meet his brothers. I couldn't have *scent matches*! I was going to be on a magirail tomorrow to a sanctuary city.

"I'm the lead for a pack of four," Fal continued, not realizing my change in mood. "My brothers will love you. We've been searching for our omega for several years."

I couldn't tell Fal why I couldn't meet his brothers or join their pack. My tongue was still bound up in a foolish vow. Stars, this was my fault. I could've made money another way. I didn't have to stoop to Cymora's level and steal from others to get by.

"Can we get a bit of air?" I asked. It was so hot in this room all of a sudden, and the crush of fae around us didn't help.

"Of course." His presence was enough to dissuade anyone from approaching, and his height helped him cut through the crowd.

He led us to one of the massive windows, which was set ajar. I hadn't realized it coming in, but it was one of several doorways leading out to a stone patio. It was significantly cooler outside, and I pinched the edge of my dress, unsticking it from my skin and venting in a little cold air.

A cramp seized my middle. I bit my lip to keep a curse from escaping at the sudden pinch. My body told me it was going into pre-heat about as subtly as a fist closing around my stomach. I'd put off my heat for so long that the warning signs were sudden and painful.

"Here, have a seat for a moment," Fal said, nudging me. I was half blinded by the pain in my middle, but he guided me around the shapes of other fae and potted plants to the edge of a carved stone bench. It was blessedly cool against my thighs.

Closing my eyes, I rode out the waves of discomfort until the cramp dissipated. They would only get worse from here, too. My suppressant tattoo had to have gotten a new crack, and I suspected it'd happened the moment I'd caught Fal's alluring scent.

His concerned face swam into view, framed by a starry sky when I opened my eyes and took a ragged breath. My gaze focused on his jeweled mask glittering from the light of an essence lamp hovering over the patio. I had an *insane* idea.

I took a glance around. Our bench was in relative privacy, guarded by a large fern in an oversized pot. Other couples murmured on the patio in different nooks. There was a raised stone rail behind the bench, overlooking the castle garden from a dizzying distance. We must've been on the second story, which certainly made my new idea risky.

However, there was one surefire way to dampen Fal's view of me. That mask he wore...the number of gemstones alone would be enough to buy me the magirail ticket to my new future.

"How are you—" he began to ask.

Before I could second-guess myself, I grabbed him and planted my lips on his. He made a surprised "mmph" but didn't hesitate or balk for a single second. Instead, his lips softened, parting, and his tongue tested the seal of my mouth. He deepened the kiss, flooding my taste buds with the essence of sunny, grassy days, and for one dizzying moment, my worries eased.

A soft noise lifted from my chest. I didn't recognize it until his fingers ran through my hair and stroked down my cheek. He repeated the motion. I was *purring* for him. Stars, I'd never purred for anyone, yet he coaxed it free with a gentle touch.

Remembering why I'd kissed him in the first place, I reached for the knot tying his mask to his face and loosened it with one quick jerk, tugging the fabric off him.

I pulled away first and gasped. My eyes darted from the mask in my hand, which practically vibrated with the essence of a powerful illusion, to the magic unraveling down his hands and unveiling fingers tipped with claws. His eyes were lidded from our kiss, lips pursed around his extra-sharp fangs.

It was still Fal, and he was still an elf. His complexion turned a striking shade of blue with deep gray undertones, unlike any forest elf I'd met. His suit was different, too, the fabric navy and its silver markings twisting into an unfamiliar style embroidered into the collar. The straight, green hair down his back sprang into loose waves, turning black with a sheen of blue in the light.

His long ears went from unadorned to being pierced with silver chains and several hanging stars. And the pack mark on his brow... I caught a glimpse of it as I stared at his transformation, stunned. It was framed by glowing sapphire ink tattoos in motifs of winter, swirls of air and snowflakes that trailed down his temple to frame his high cheekbones. He was... But he *couldn't* be...

Fal drew me closer to nuzzle against my neck and mark me with his scent, a low alpha rumble in his chest. "Why did you do that?" His accent was thicker. No wonder I didn't recognize it. It was from another *kingdom*.

"You're Unseelie," I breathed. The magical forces that shaped our kind had long cursed the Unseelie fae to be known by the evil of their ancestors. They were forced to carry a permanent animal feature so the descendants of the fair Seelie fae knew them on sight.

And he wasn't just any Unseelie. By the identifying magic in his pack mark, he was the eldest son of the Unseelie royal pack. A dark elf prince of vile tricksters and wicked malcontents. He looked at home in the night, practically a being of cold winter shadows.

Now that I knew the truth of him, the roguish angle to his smile and the razor-sharp fangs made more sense. He finally looked at me, his eyelids lifting from his animal feature: eyes like a cat's, dark blue and slitted. And I remained frozen like a quivering mouse before him.

"I am. Now, it's only fair I see you unmasked as well," he said in his teasing tone. He pulled the ribbon attaching the mask to my face.

"Wait, no!"

He already had it in hand, and the beautiful lie of my illusions dissipated into lavender sparks. My depleted wings flattened on my back with my distress.

His lips parted in surprise. That feline gaze was pointed at my real dress and the front pocket of my smock, which bulged with everything I'd stolen tonight.

Well, now he knows. No prince, Unseelie or not, would want a common servant to complete his pack. There'd be no introductions to his brothers, no more talk of scent matches. I was as good as rejected.

And stars, that truth hurt worse than I thought it would.

Standing with a jolt, I shoved his mask in with the rest of my ill-gotten gains. "Unseelie!" I shouted, hoping to catch a guard's attention.

Then I leapt onto the stone railing overseeing the two-story drop to the garden and jumped.

5
LARK

Wind whistled past my ears, whipping back my hair. Yet I still heard Fal's exclamation. "Lark, what are you doing? There are stairs!" He sounded...amused. There was definitely an edge of surprised laughter there.

I called upon the meager lining of essence I still had within me and flapped my wings, lifting in the air with a scattering of magical sparkles. I glided further into the gardens and away from the ridicule I'd find with Fal if I'd stayed. Had I seen his full reaction, it would've turned to mockery, something I fully deserved for pretending I should be here.

I wasn't permitted to chase fanciful ideas like fate and scent matches when I was sold to Pack Ellisar. And why would I want a twisted bond with an Unseelie? He and his brothers would steal me away to Serian, their homeland, to meet the fate all Seelie did at the hands of their cursed kin. Better to evade them and find sanctuary in a city away from alphas of all kinds.

My gaze blurred for several reasons as I descended from my glide. I was running out of essence. Fatigue was less of a suggestion now and more like an iron weight secured around my neck. I hiccupped a sob and tried to blink hard to clear my vision, only to succumb to unconsciousness for one vital moment.

When I came to, I was falling. I had time to scream before landing in a patch of grass in an ungainly tangle of limbs. My smock smacked the ground with a metallic *clang* I felt to my bones as I vibrated with the force of my reacquaintance with the earth.

I lifted my head to take inventory of my new aches and scrapes but gave in to self-pity instead. I curled up into a ball and cried, keening like only a wounded omega could manage. Everything hurt now—my ankle and foot as always, but notably, my heart and the inside of my head throbbed together. And it was all my fault. I should've known coming here under false pretenses would only get me hurt.

I cried myself out. After nearly two decades under Cymora's thumb, it didn't take longer than a few minutes. I cracked open my swollen eyes and found urgency as I remembered: Fal had said there were *stairs*. Stars, he could be right behind me. I'd be much easier to kidnap to Serian from the gardens, as opposed to still being at the Omega Masquerade. Or he could simply come by to mock me for my graceless fall and the resulting pity party. Either way, I didn't want him to see me like this.

With a huff, I leveraged myself to a seated position and brushed dirt and grass off my clothes. The world fuzzed in and out of focus as I tried to note what was wrong with me.

I pinched myself to shake off the lethargy clawing at my body. *Don't go to sleep!* There was no telling what I'd wake up to if I succumbed to my lack of essence.

I couldn't just sit around; I had to move. As I pushed up, the scrapes I'd acquired from my hard landing pulsed with the more dangerous pain lancing up my leg from my crippled foot.

"You can do this," I said through gritted teeth as I stumbled a few steps. I ran my knuckles under my eyes and the lingering wetness making chill tracks down my cheeks, smudging the thick coat of my makeup. More tears followed, my eyes still leaking as I struggled to take a deep breath and calm down.

I dragged myself to a garden path that was illuminated by a few sparsely placed essence lamps. With my sight wavering, I just picked a direction at random, and I walked headlong into something.

It felt like a wall, except no stone had a give of softness or jiggled when it rebounded a crying pixie. Strong arms caught me before I could tumble to the ground. "What's this? A sad little omega?" a male asked.

Except he had a thick accent, so it sounded more like, "Wuh's dis? A sad li'l omehga?"

With the nearest lamp behind him, I only had the impression of a broad fae bending down to envelop me. He was hard with muscle but cushioned with extra padding, especially around the middle. And giving off a radius of heat that I appreciated in the evening's chill.

Another sob wracked my body while this stranger cradled me against him. He stroked my hair and left his broad hand cupped over the back of my head. "There, there. No need for sad," he murmured. "Omegas most blessed ladies. Li'l and sweet."

He coaxed a sound from his chest, loud and resonant, and it vibrated through every bone in my body. He inhaled deeply, and on his exhale he made the sound again. My crying weakened, tears receding like he used some kind of magic on me. I'd heard that an alpha's purr was soothing, but it was amazing how comforted I felt as I laid my cheek on his chest and snuggled in. He smelled so nice, like mallows toasting over an open flame. I savored his scent, caramelized sugar mixed with a bit of smoky char.

For a few minutes, I let myself be soothed. I could give in to the weight of fatigue wrapped around my limbs and simply fall asleep here in his arms. This alpha was everything I needed on a level my body recognized and reacted to.

I wished I could stay as he lulled me, just "li'l" and protected in the circle of his arms. But my stomach cramped with vicious intensity and the stark reminder that my heat was coming with a vengeance.

I sighed, clamping my eyes shut in denial. "I need..." I stopped when I heard the croak in my voice and cleared my throat. "I need to go."

After his next inhale, instead of purring again, he asked, "Go where?"

"Away from here." I tried to tug myself free of his hold. He let me go with slow reluctance. I stumbled a couple steps back before picking a direction and trudging that way.

"But where are you going, wee pixie?"

I stopped under the halo of an essence lamp and craned my neck up at him. He was a salamander, I think, with dark red hair and brass-toned skin marked with a sprinkling of brown freckles. He had a well-manicured beard and mustache to match the fluff of hair on his crown, which was cut short along the sides.

Stars, he was a giant, possessing a height that would tower over most alphas. His attire resembled traveling clothes, with the exception of a vibrant scarlet cloak secured under his chin with a gold ring. His gray gaze roamed over my expression, and his generous mouth formed a frown.

Those eyes were small in the crag of his face and made tiny by how he squinted at me. His accent sounded suspiciously like Fal's, just a lot more concentrated. It'd make sense that an Unseelie pack would send the member who spoke Theli the best to the Omega Masquerade.

Two Unseelie in one evening. I shouldn't just be standing here looking at him, but I had the strange sense that I could trust him. Besides, I didn't have the energy to run.

When I still didn't say anything, he shifted closer to me. He pinched the edge of his cloak and lifted it to my face, rubbing away the wet smudges of makeup down my cheeks. I didn't flinch away from the tender touch.

"Li'l omega does not know where to go?" He put a little more pressure on a spot under my eye.

I should've been terrified of this male...but if he was Unseelie, he was unlike every stereotype so far. He smelled like a scent match and hadn't seemed to notice or care about my grass-stained servant's attire and the dimness of my wings.

I could *probably* trust him to get me to an inn. "Do you know the way out of the castle grounds?" I asked him.

"Aye."

I didn't know what he meant, but he nodded, so I took it as a yes.

"I just want to find a place with a room for the night," I murmured.

He swung a heavy arm over my shoulders. "I will take you somewhere safe."

We made it a few steps before I trembled. The sweat that'd clung to my skin from the last wave of pre-heat was swiftly chilling now that my body was cooling. The big alpha paused and unfastened the hook holding his cloak over his shoulders. He draped the blanket of warm fabric over me, his meaty fingers working the gold ring closed again under my chin. I tugged on the sides of the cloak, putting pressure on the semiflexible base of my top wings to lower them so the cloth rested over my shoulders properly.

"There." A moment later, he added, "Nay."

"Nay?" I echoed, confused.

He dropped to one knee and withdrew a knife from his boot. The edge went into the beautiful cloak before I could protest, cutting off the bottom third so it wasn't dragging on the ground.

"There," he said again, putting the knife away.

What was done was done, but I didn't know how to respond to him mangling his own cloak for me. Even with the bottom removed, it was still voluminous around my frame. I pulled it closed around my front, taking a moment to breathe in his scent clinging to the fabric.

Well, waste not. I picked up the length he'd cut away, folded it into a rectangle, and stuffed it into my smock.

He steered me down the garden path once more. His shirt barely had sleeves, revealing his arms, both thick with muscle and cushioned from plenty to eat, with more brown freckles dotting his exposed skin. A gold, ruby-gemmed armband engraved with maple leaves was wrapped around his bicep.

"I am Tormund. What is your name?" he asked.

I told him, and he grinned. He had a charming smile, wide and toothy. I guessed what he was about to say in my head before his lips formed the words. "Lark, I like. Li'l bird."

"Where are you from, Tormund?"

His big smile faded, replaced by a thoughtful squint. There was no answer for a long pause, before he finally said, "I tell you a secret. But it is between you and me, okay?"

I nodded. "Okay."

He angled his hand over his lips. "I am from Neslune, capital of Serian," he whispered. "My brothers didn't want me to tell anyone. But the li'l bird should know."

Well, I'd figured him out pretty quickly. He wasn't exactly a subtle member of the Unseelie. He didn't seem to possess even a sliver of the deceitful nature they were known for.

Or maybe he's an excellent *liar.*

"Where's your animal feature?" I asked, hoping that wasn't a rude question.

"Oh, it's hidden. You want to see?"

"Um, sure."

He tugged his armband off, and an illusion faded from his face. We were walking through the part of the garden illuminated by essence-filled flowers, so I saw the change immediately. He had the same pack mark as Fal, which suggested they were both princes and half brothers born of the same omega.

His Unseelie trait poked from his hairline. They were a pair of dark gray horns, pointed triangles about three inches long. I saw why he had his hair cut short on the sides, as the longer middle rested perfectly in between his horns.

"Thank you for showing me. You might want to put them away before a guard sees," I suggested.

"Aye, smart." He put the armband back on, erasing all signs that he wasn't a salamander. I didn't know what race he was, only that he and Fal couldn't be more different.

We passed the front gates of the castle, which were propped open now that a stream of partygoers was leaving the masquerade. I kept my head down and my shoulders hunched just in case the kindly guard from before was still at his post.

When we reached the street, Tormund murmured, "This way, li'l bird."

He steered me in a different direction than the cottage my step-family had rented. As long as we weren't heading toward it, I didn't care where we went anymore. I was bone tired, my belly was aching and empty, and I'd never see this Unseelie again after tonight. I'd take comfort in his presence and scent for the limited time I could.

Many of the street revelers had turned in by this point. The ones that remained were well into their cups. I was glad of the giant beside me and the big cloak hiding my pixie wings, as no one dared to bother us.

My limping steps forced Tormund to slow a few times before he glanced down, made a throaty sound like *ach*, and bent. He picked me up under my knees and behind my back, carrying me secured to his chest as if I weighed next to nothing. I looked up at him, confused but not exactly unhappy to be off my feet.

"Why did you do that?" I echoed his brother after a different baffling action.

He gave me a squeeze. "You are hurt and tired. I'm strong for you."

I told myself it wasn't like Willis dragging me onto the dance floor without permission. He probably wasn't taking me to a magirail. *This isn't a kidnapping. He has good intentions.* I searched within for the reason I trusted this Unseelie so much and disregarded the answer with a flick of denial. He'd put me down if I asked him to.

I just didn't ask. He carried me for several blocks, humming an unfamiliar tune and smiling to himself all the while. We passed by a few inns before he turned toward one and scented the air with a long inhale.

I did the same, mostly picking up the caramelized sugar that represented him with an undertone of other, less interesting alpha scents. Now that I knew what a scent match smelled like, other males simply couldn't compare.

"I can take it from here," I told him.

He shook his head. "Let me get your room. No one questions an alpha."

"If you insist."

He nodded like it was settled and didn't put me down until we were inside. My feet protested their acquaintance with the ground, and my sight grew hazy at the corners. I propped myself against a wall and rode out a wave of dizziness.

Tormund marched up to a desk where a couple keys hung on hooks behind a tired-looking barkfolk. He slapped down a couple extra coins and pointed to the key he wanted. My gaze slipped longingly toward the taproom, where a mixed crowd of fae were still celebrating and the ale was flowing. Although, I was more interested in the sandwiches and pretzels being passed around.

"I got you the last room on the third floor." Tormund announced his presence right before he picked me up again. I couldn't help a surprised squeak, though I had no complaints as he bounded up the stairs two at a time. If anything, I envied his energy.

"How much did it cost?"

"It's okay."

"I'll pay you back. How much?"

He gave me a big smile. "Not too much. No worries. Small price to pay for a safe room."

I frowned in return. Now I was just taking advantage of him.

Tormund squinted at me. "Don't be sad again. No omega should be sad."

He set me on my feet and handed me a key attached to a small wooden tag that read 312, the same number carved into the door.

"I'm not sad," I assured him. "I'm just not... Nobody buys things for me." Maybe he'd missed how I was dressed earlier. I shrugged out of his mangled cloak and passed it back to him. My top wings popped back up without the weight of the cloth.

"Be right back," he declared, walking off without waiting for a response.

I released a tired sigh and let myself into the room. The first thing to go was my smock. I'd count the contents tomorrow before setting off to find a pawn shop. *If* I woke up tomorrow, considering how low my essence level was. There was nearly no glow coming off my wings.

Hopefully my fall hadn't damaged many of the goods within. As soon as I was free of my smock, I stripped the cushions off the small couch and checked the tiny closet for spare pillows and blankets. There was an extra set of sheets, so I grabbed them and started arranging everything on the bed.

My inner omega wouldn't stop to let me rest until it was just so. But once my nest was in place, with a small space in the center for me to curl up, there was still something missing. I made a whimper of denial when I realized what I needed to add.

A firm set of knocks stopped me from lying down anyway. Tormund waited for me to answer before he hung a token on a hook by the door. "I ordered you dinner. It's on the way!"

It was such welcome news that I teared up. My belly had grumbled the whole trip to the inn. Tormund only saw the crying, though, and opened his mouth with a draw of his brow. I launched at him before he could say anything, putting all my gratitude into a hug.

He hugged me back and I buried my face in his chest, breathing him in. For a moment, I hoped he'd hold me for a long time and pet me with those huge hands of his. But he drew away with a gentle look. "Good night, li'l bird. I will see you tomorrow."

If fate was merciful, he wouldn't. But I didn't know anymore if that mercy would be for him or me.

"Good night, Tormund." I lifted a hand in farewell as he walked away.

When the food arrived, it came with its own table. My eyes widened as a pair of fae passed plate after plate into my room. There were nibbles with dipping sauces, pull-apart breads, pretzels with cheese cubes, so many different variations of sandwiches...and the desserts. I could've simply started there. A slice of chocolate cake, moist and dense. Brownies with chilled cream, berries and foam, and, perhaps cheekily, toasted mallows in their own separate bowl.

I thanked the pair who'd delivered all this and stood there with my lips wobbling. All this was for me?

I ate more than my fill and cradled my stomach with a content sigh as I headed for my nest to pass out, just to stop short. It smelled clean, but it was still missing two key components.

I told myself I couldn't have the males I'd just met, even while doubling back to pick out Fal's mask and the piece of Tormund's cloak from the things I'd stolen. I snuggled into the soft bed and tucked the two items close to my heart so I smelled grassy days and mallows roasting over a fire. My scent wove into theirs with perfect harmony.

But they weren't actually here, and my most familiar companion, empty loneliness, came to settle with me instead. The ghosts of Tormund's resonant purr and Fal's leading hand on the small of my back lingered. I ached for more, my omega side craving to be gentled by positive touch.

How was it possible that two Unseelie were my scent matches anyway? I pictured them on either side of me in my nest and loosed a rusty noise that startled me. My purr wouldn't be amiss from a kitten's, a weak and roughened sound. Once it escaped, it flowed from me without pause, no matter if I was breathing in or out.

The part of me that was all instinct knew I needed them. Their skin on mine...but not only that. I blushed with a heady wave of pre-heat. I needed their knots, too. With my heat built up and denied for four years, I needed their knots over and over and over so I didn't burn myself to a stifled cinder.

My fingers drifted to my pussy and the slick that coated my folds. My scent leaked out, made richer by the nearness of my heat. I circled my clit with my thumb, then inserted my fingers one at a time to stretch my aching core. All the while, I pictured Tormund and how gentle he would be with my body. And Fal too...whispering teasing words in my ear while he knotted me with just the right amount of pressure. My toes curled as I found release, but it was a hollow and brief high.

What did a knot even *feel* like? I'd been too afraid to dally in Osme Fen. One curious encounter could trigger the point of no return with my heat, and then it would be Pack Ellisar biting me when I couldn't tell them no and soul bonding us until the end of our days.

I huffed in disappointment, but just thinking about the trio of bark-folk who'd purchased my first heat was enough to dampen any sort of afterglow. *What if I could have something else?*

"I see you, Lark."

No. I refused to entertain the impossible. If I veered off the path of my plan, I was doomed. It didn't matter that neither Unseelie had seemed as monstrous as the stories. I had to leave Ilysnor before my stepfamily tracked me down. No exceptions.

Still, their lingering scents were a comfort. *Dessert after a warm summer's day. Mmm...*

I was asleep as soon as I closed my eyes.

6

FAL

THE OTHER FAE on the patio turned to stare, alerted by Lark's breathy cry of "Unseelie!" I jumped to my feet after Lark's leap from the balcony, my call into the night following the gray blur of her wings.

What a situation this had become. Some might even call it a *fiasco*. I worked to fix a semblance of my princely dignity back into place after a simple kiss from a pixie had obliterated it. Her taste lingered on my tongue, sweeter than any dessert. I adjusted my clothes to hide the arousal that'd flooded me at witnessing her daring.

I headed for the stairs to go into the garden after her. That didn't seem like a steady flight, and I wasn't about to let my future mate escape me so easily.

"Unseelie aren't allowed at this event," a male said as I passed the bench where he sat.

I paused, my gaze slipping toward him and the two others who shared his bench. "Two alphas from the same pack aren't allowed, either," I responded coolly. They had a blue-winged pixie between them.

"We're not from the same—"

I strode past them with a scoff, uncaring of what they had to say for themselves and, frankly, tired of listening to Theli. The burr found in the Seelie tongue was starting to get on my nerves…except when spoken by a certain shy omega who smelled like she was already mine. Lark could talk to me in Theli all she wanted with her higher pitched, musical voice.

Suppressing a growl, I took the stairs down to the garden two at a time.

There was no way word of my presence didn't filter to the ears of the Seelie royalty, but the deed was done. I'd found my scent match. The repercussions of *who* she was would be interesting, to say the least. But I'd still managed to pass as Seelie long enough to pick up on her indulgent scent of chocolate and honeyed dessert crackers.

I craved another taste as I strode through the castle's garden, looking for her or Tormund. He had insisted on coming and waiting outside the event, just in case I needed rescuing. An eye-rolling sentiment from my baby brother.

As the eldest of my pack and the one to come up with the idea of meeting Seelie omegas, I'd practically been forced to attend this event. The first hours were dreadful, as the scent blockers in the air were not enough to dampen my sense of smell completely. I'd worried that all the less interesting pheromones of those attending the event would dull my nose.

But then Lark had tiptoed right past me on a guard's arm, and I'd loosed an unpracticed purr as the wake of her scent made my skin tingle. There was no hiding how potent our compatibility was. It'd only been a matter of time before I would've gotten her alone. I'd observed her, guessing the reasons for her every quirk.

And while she'd been stiff and unsure face-to-face, she'd certainly left a favorable impression on me. She'd reacted like a scent match to my pheromones, too, and let me catch a glimpse of her true self when she'd let down her guard. That smile had been as radiant as starshine.

I had too many unanswered questions about her. Why had she come to the event late and without supervision? Why did she take in the crowd of potential doting mates with the chagrin of someone who'd rather be anywhere else?

And most importantly, why had she stolen from nearly every alpha who'd passed by her?

I didn't disapprove. If anything, the fact that she was a tricksy little thing who'd pulled off a surprise on me too was better than foreplay. I was so rarely shocked, but it turned out Lark was hiding her identity the exact same way I was. How incredibly invigorating.

Now I wanted to steal *her*. We'd be on the first magirail to Serian tomorrow morning if she hadn't run from me.

The trail of bitter chocolate scent she'd left behind tempered my excitement some. Especially when I found a concentrated circle of it mixed in with the smell of bruised grass and freshly disturbed soil. She must've crashed at this spot. I circled out from there, picking up the ghost of her fear and pain with an agitated snarl.

This was my fault. This harsh smell had come from her, startled free by our joint identity revelations. I should've immediately started explaining myself when I felt her removing my mask. She was a flighty pixie, not some dalliance used to my particular kind of teasing. Many Seelie still believed my kind to be "cursed" when there was no such thing.

The fae people had split long ago to populate the island nations of Thelis and Serian. Thelis enjoyed more temperate weather and nurtured milder Seelie, with their primary population consisting of sweet woodland fae—forest elves, pixies, gnomes, and dryads included. Meanwhile, Serian, situated further to the north, invited any race hearty enough to survive its harsh winters to live under the label of Unseelie. This included most of the bestial fae races. It was no surprise that most of my people carried at least one animal trait under those conditions.

As for Lark's true identity, I didn't care that she was a servant—and why was she dressed like one anyway? Omegas were the most precious and rare fae. The rest of us were plucked from the stars to serve *them*.

I stopped below an essence lamp, drawing in a deep breath. Unsweetened chocolate wove in with my brother's familiar scent. It grew more honeyed as the wind picked up a chill gust.

Oh, good. She'd run into Tormund. My lips relaxed, and I slid my fingers into my suit pockets as I followed the trail they'd left behind with less urgency. This was the best possible outcome. If anyone could gentle a frightened and potentially wounded omega and see to her needs, it'd be that lovable oaf.

I tracked their scents straight to the inn my pack was staying at.

Somehow, I beat Tormund to my inn room, where Marius and Kauz waited for us with one of their never-ending card games.

"Finally!" Marius exclaimed in our mother tongue, throwing down his hand and jostling the piles of coins heaped between them.

Kauz looked me up and down, then raised a brow and asked, "Where's your mask?"

I flashed my usual mischievous smile. "Our tricksy omega stole it." I was glad to switch back to Serri after suppressing my natural accent for so long.

Kauz narrowed his eyes of violet-threaded starlight. He'd worked hard on making the illusion airtight. We'd wanted to avoid the inevitable litany of uncomfortable questions when the Seelie royals contacted our mother and accused us of some kind of wrongdoing.

My brothers and I had been on our best behavior for the trip here and our stay in Ilysnor. Some of it was for our own sanity, as traveling for so long on a magirail while carrying on with a sibling feud would be absolute misery, but for the most part, it was for the Seelie around us. Inevitably, the Seelie always found some fault in our actions, no matter how polite we were or how benign our common trickery had become of late.

Well, when it happened, I would handle it.

"*Our* omega," Marius echoed. He crossed his arms, his denial already leaking into the pack bond.

"I know you didn't want to consider that fate would give us—"

Tormund burst into the room behind me with an exclamation of "Brothers!"

His presence blotted out Marius's doubt with a heaping cup of joy drenching our pack bond. He crushed me in a big hug, lifting me to the tips of my toes.

Marius sighed. "What happened to your cloak?"

"I met the most perfect omega," Tormund said, ignoring him and denying me another breath at the same time. "She's just a wee little bird, but she smells like a dream. And she's only two rooms down from this one."

"She couldn't possibly be our omega." Marius emphasized his words with a growling undertone.

"Tor," I managed, pulling on his wrist. He released me with an apologetic glance, smoothing out some of the new wrinkles in my suit with a couple brushes of his broad palm. He was the youngest out of the four of us, and sometimes I questioned when he'd gotten to be the biggest and strongest as well.

"Yes, our omega!" he exclaimed.

"I'm going to need more of a description than 'wee little bird,'" Kauz remarked. "And 'tricksy' while you're at it."

Tormund and I sat at the table and took turns explaining Lark. I went first, and my brothers noticed she'd vexed me a bit by the shift of amusement in our pack bond. I hated unfinished puzzles, and Lark was one I hadn't figured out yet.

While Tormund described how he'd calmed her down, shooting me a scowl for causing her distress, I met Marius's gaze. We stared one another down in a contest of wills and dominance. He'd had a bad attitude about this whole venture, but he wouldn't ruin it now that we'd found Lark.

"Then I bought her something to eat," our redcap brother concluded. "So, we're going to steal her away to Neslune tomorrow, right?"

For the Unseelie, nothing was quite so romantic as a well-meaning relocation. Mother still swooned over how our fathers had stolen her from her childhood home in the dark of night for their first date.

But for a skittish Seelie who'd already bolted once? Maybe not the best strategy to win her heart.

"With a few extra steps," I hedged, pulling out Lark's mask from my pocket and sliding it across the table to Kauz.

He picked it up, spinning his starlight essence around it with a thoughtful hum. "This is hers?"

"Aye."

His dark purple lips pressed into a line. "How unusual." No one interrupted as he inspected the tarnishing surface and made a pinching motion above it. A misty layer of magic lifted from the mask, resembling a fold of the fake dress Lark had been wearing. "Creating something as easy as a layer of clothes shouldn't have taken this much essence. Not to mention, illusion is an unusual skill for a Seelie to possess." Kauz flipped the mask between his fingers, seeming troubled. "Did you want me to visit her dreams tonight?" he asked me.

I nodded. "Something is amiss with her."

He murmured in agreement and went back to working magic over the mask.

"Perhaps her subconscious will tell you her troubles. Imagine if we swept away all her worries before we steal her to meet Mother. We can earn her trust quickly and elevate her to where she belongs," I reasoned.

"Our pack princess," Tormund said with a broad smile. He smacked the table and stood, trailing red fibers from his ruined cloak as he bid us good night and went to his room. I shook my head with a chuckle, now that I knew why he'd butchered the cloth. He'd hand out the family fortune if given half a chance.

As soon as the door closed behind him, Marius said, "No Seelie will ever trust us. And our people will never accept a Seelie princess. Stars forbid, a Seelie queen."

I put on my practiced politician's voice. "There will certainly be consequences for Lark being our omega."

"We've met countless nixies that would fulfill the role beautifully without *consequences*." He gestured widely. Kauz leaned back to avoid being grazed by a flying fin. "And this female was disguising how she was dressed like a servant. She will have no idea what to do when tossed into the piranha pit Mother navigates with ease every day!"

I sighed to myself. I knew what this was really about. Marius was willing to settle for any halfway-suitable female. For some reason he wouldn't divulge, he was sure his mate—and thus, our mate—had died when we were still children. Why bother looking? The pessimism grated on my last nerves.

"We will teach *our* mate everything she needs to know," I stated.

Marius turned to Kauz. "This is insane, right?" he demanded.

Kauz was the neutral arbiter of the pack, as eerily serene as always. He didn't lift his gaze from the mask in his hands. Starlight glittered over his fingers and along the patterns painted over his leathery wings as he spun essence for some unknown spell.

He spoke after some consideration, sounding distracted. "We've met every unmated nixie in Serian. Shaking the hand of one of the princes is practically a rite of passage for our kingdom's omegas. So, Fal guessed that she had to be a pixie instead. And he was right."

I smirked over at Marius, whose ear flicked as he glared back.

"Our search is finally over," Kauz concluded. He'd taken on that soothing tone that lulled most fae into a sense of calm. "We should be celebrating."

I let his reasoning sink in for a moment before adding, "Give her a chance. See if she's so bad when she realizes you're one of her scent matches and starts to consider you for a mate."

Marius released a distinctively equine snort that matched his kelpie form. Judging by his side of the pack bond, he remained unconvinced. "Do we control fate, or does it control us?" he asked.

"Smarter minds than ours have been asking that since the dawn of Faerie," Kauz remarked.

"All I'm asking is that you *try* before you dismiss her." I resisted the urge to roll my eyes. "If not for your own happiness, then for Tormund. His rages have been getting worse."

Marius stood with an irritable grumble. "I know."

"One day, our pack bond will not be enough to call back his sanity," I pressed.

"I *know*," he growled.

"And," I added with the intentionality of a finishing blow, "his fated mate will always be able to soothe him."

Marius scoffed and headed for the door. "Not fate. Some quirk of redcap biology at best."

"He needs her."

"Good night." He slammed the door behind him.

Stubborn as a kelpie wasn't a saying for nothing. He'd have fought this trip tooth and nail if he'd realized we'd really come here for his sake first and foremost, not for Tormund's. Hopefully meeting Lark would inspire a sense of purpose in Marius and give him a reason not to turn wild. We were almost out of options to reverse his condition.

I gnawed on my worries as I waited for Kauz to finish his intricate spell work.

"She sleeps," he murmured eventually. "I must go do the same to dream with her. You only wish to know of her troubles?"

I itched to know a lot more about her. To turn her past out and shake all the skeletons loose with the dust, to learn why she limped—and if someone was to blame for her injury, their identity so I could ruin them utterly.

I wanted to know the things she wished for at night so we could grant them. Locations she dreamed of visiting so I could steal her away to them.

But most urgently, I had to understand why her blue eyes had been shadowed with darker emotions when she'd said she'd wanted to be "seen" at the Omega Masquerade tonight. It'd felt like a cry for help, and I *would* answer it once I knew what she needed from me.

"Her troubles will suffice."

He lifted his brow with a knowing look.

"For now," I added.

If he could tell me *everything*, it would save me time and effort. But I would eventually learn it all myself once she trusted me enough to confide in me. No matter how long it took, I'd show her that fate had crossed our paths for a reason.

I looked forward to seeing her again. No masks, no illusions, and fewer secrets between us.

7
LARK

My feet dropped onto the cobbled road I'd seen from a carriage window. Now, instead of a pixie child trying to sell masks, there was a busker on the street corner, strumming a tune I'd heard played by a full orchestra only hours ago. I twirled on cue and stumbled with no Fal to catch me, falling to the ground. My smock burst at the seams, and out tumbled coins, rings, timepieces, and a few jeweled bracelets.

Faceless fae stooped to pick at the bounty of gold and silver while I scrambled for what I could reclaim and dropped it into the ruined pocket, holding it closed with one hand.

"No! It's mine!" I grabbed the band of a timepiece, trying to tug it from an equally determined shadow. The leather snapped, and I ended up holding an empty strap.

"Don't you understand?" My eyes welled as my future was taken by grasping hands. "I need all this!"

"More than the ones who bought it all fairly?" asked a fae weighing a coin purse in her hand.

"More than us, who beg for scraps every night?"

The faceless forms stood when I did, surrounding me on all sides with accusing fingers pointed square at me.

"At least you have a home."

"At least you'll have a pack, no matter what."

I clutched at my middle, holding my diminished fortune to my chest. My throat was in a vice, my air closing off as I looked for some kind of escape from the waves of accusations.

"You still have magic."

"You're still an omega."

"A waste of pixie wings."

"Thief!" the crowd screamed.

I bent, ducking my head to shield my face from the words, each of them falling like blows. "I'm sorry, I'm sorry!" I wailed. I deserved all of this and more.

Phantom hands seized my arms, and panic further gripped my chest. My headspace was all shrill noise and overstimulated nerves.

A whisper threaded under the ringing in my ears. *"Hmm, guilt. Interesting."*

Then there was silence. Figures frozen in time, their pointing fingers and clenched fists turning into wavering lines, and then nothing at all. Just a nightmare...something I should have shaken awake from but didn't. I blinked, and my dream continued on as if nothing had happened. My ill-gotten gains returned to me, and I went through the motions of finding a pawn shop willing to buy everything from me with no questions asked.

The details were hazy at best. I haggled with a faceless fae standing in a misty box, then headed to a magirail station that looked like I suspected one to look. It was a fanciful place with a sleek silver snake of a machine waiting to board travelers.

"Does this train go to Zemosia?" I asked an attendant. That was the furthest sanctuary city from here, on a tiny island all its own. I fancied going there since my stepfamily was incredibly lazy. They might try to search the closer sanctuaries for me and give up from there. I would have time to settle and make a life for myself in a city only occupied by betas and omegas.

And I would be a citizen protected by the law if Cymora and Laurel found me anyway and tried to take me back to Osme Fen.

The attendant gave me a long look before gesturing behind him. Three familiar barkfolk emerged from the train, Ellisar and his brothers. They were fae of the wood, growing shingles of bark that they wore instead of clothes. Ellisar, the eldest, had the largest plates, which resembled a tunic that rattled with each of his steps. He took me in with cold, moss-green eyes that matched the vines growing from his scalp in place of hair.

"Here she is, as you suspected," the attendant said, gesturing to me.

I shot him a look of betrayal as Ellisar stepped forward and seized my shoulder. "You thought you could get away from us just like that? We *own* you, wretch."

I trembled where I stood, a fearful whine sticking in my throat halfway. The scene froze again, as if my sleeping mind rejected the idea that Pack Ellisar would know to wait for me on the train to Zemosia.

They're not here. They wouldn't follow my stepfamily to Ilysnor in the first place.

A misty figure wafted around Ellisar, inspecting his grip on my shoulder. *"Who are these fae?"* it whispered.

I tried to glance at the figure, but it was like looking at a warped mirror. All I saw were shapes and colors that didn't match what it seemed to be. "Pack Ellisar," I answered in a humiliated hush. "I had to agree to a breeding contract with them..."

"And so they think they own you." A scoff of disgust lifted from it before a translucent hand waved.

My dream rearranged, and I blinked, now standing in front of a female attendant. She picked up where the last attendant had left off. "This is the rail to Zemosia, yes. Right this way."

I shook off the oily feeling of what could've occurred here and followed her into a little room set with plush seating and a window overlooking the train station. As soon as I sat down, the seats across from me filled with two males and their alluring scents.

"Alphas aren't allowed in Zemosia," I said guilelessly.

"That's not where we're going," Tormund said, his words weighed by his thick brogue. He reached over and locked the door out of the chamber.

I dry swallowed as the haze over their faces cleared. The shadows in the room deepened as I quaked with fear. Tormund eyed me as if I were his next meal, while Fal sat with his hands laced under his chin. The latter's naturally mischievous features were well shaped for casual cruelty, and his harsh smirk was exactly what I'd expected from the unmasked Unseelie prince.

They were wearing the same clothes I'd seen them in last, complete with the roughly cut cloak tucked under Tormund's thighs. What else would they wear?

Tension pulsed thick through the air as I waited for what they would say. Something told me they had worse in store for me than Pack Ellisar. Fate was unkind to tie us together as scent matches. They were princes, after all, and I was next to nothing.

"You are a disappointment," Fal finally said, his teasing tone turned cutting. "But you are still ours. We're taking you to Serian."

"Even a servant can fulfill her purpose for our pack." Tormund scented the air and rumbled deep in his chest. "Your heat is soon. Time to do your duty."

"N-no," I whispered, as if my wants mattered. As if they'd listen.

Fal chuckled darkly. "Now for the key question. Which of us will breed her first?"

My hands clenched on my thighs, and I lowered in the chair with a whimper of denial. Of course they'd use me for breeding. That was exactly what Pack Ellisar had bought my first heat for. To have a soft omega to fuck and impregnate.

The figure of warped air was back, standing beside my seat. *"I can't watch any more. This is not them at all."*

The two princes and their comments fuzzed into white noise. Shutting my eyes tightly, I willed them away. They weren't right. Tormund didn't seem to know enough Theli to speak so clearly, and Fal... I was pretty sure I'd dreamed his features incorrectly. These weren't the males I'd met. At least, I sure hoped this wasn't a glimpse at their true intentions.

When I opened my eyes, I was standing before the nice attendant again. "It goes to all places, dear. Zemosia included," she said.

I glanced side to side, palms sweating as she led me onto the train once more. *Here we go again.* What other horrors could she possibly seat me with? My stepfamily?

She showed me to a seat straight from my favorite childhood restaurant. Upon a worn wooden table was a feast of my favorite foods from there: roast boar, herb-stuffed mushrooms, cheesy potatoes, and apple tartlets decorated with thin slices of apple folded into a rose shape on the top.

"We're prepared for a long trip. Enjoy, and once evening comes, we have special beds prepared for our omega guests," the attendant said in a sweet voice.

She disappeared the next moment, and I dug into the food without a second thought for her. It tasted just how I remembered, and I settled into my chair with a soft sigh as memories sharpened every detail. The scratchiness along my back was the aging stitching on the chair, with its innards poking out.

It smelled a bit like Osme Fen; the row of shops and restaurants that served the locals had a particular odor from the animals kept at the local farmsteads. Even the estate sometimes received a rank wind. But that was just home. And though I could lie to myself, I wouldn't. I missed my home. Especially how it used to be, when Father would take me to dine here, just him and I.

I have to leave this behind. Forever.

If I escaped to Zemosia, I would never see my stepfamily again, or Pack Ellisar. But I would never see everyone else, too. All the common fae who had become my friends when I became a house servant. Even the sharp-tongued ones who always told me their opinions on the state of the kingdom and its politics. I'd never visit this restaurant again. I had not acknowledged what I would lose for a chance to venture into the unknown alone. I'd only wanted to flee the bad instead of saying goodbye to the good.

I can do that. Life in Osme Fen would move on without me. I'd make new friends in a sanctuary city free of alphas. My heat, once I finally stopped suppressing it, would make me cry out for an alpha, any alpha, to alleviate the pain, but there had to be a way of easing it that didn't require their knots. Surely the omegas that already lived in Zemosia could teach me how to ride out my body's urges.

There was a sudden jolt underneath me. The platform outside was slowly moving to one side as the train lurched into motion. I watched Ilysnor tug by as the train picked up speed along the magirail, gliding along on essence-infused metal. These trains could go *really* fast, I'd heard, and with that thought, the scenery blurred further.

The hair on the back of my neck rose, and I turned to look at the seat across from me. Someone sat there, a fae far more solid and real than the others I'd dreamed up. He smelled of... well, I didn't recognize his scent, but it was pleasant. And—thankfully—he was a stranger. I still braced for what might come next.

His nostrils were flared from scenting me back. A flicker of shock passed over his face. He picked up an apple tartlet and took a testing nibble. "Oh, that's really good," he murmured.

I looked out the window again, but there was nothing to see anymore, just a blur of colors streaking by outside. When I settled to eat more of my meal, the male across from me somehow had a basket full of apple tartlets, but they were small, and he popped them into his mouth with casual flicks of his wrist.

"Excuse me," I said after watching him go for a minute or so. "Who are you?"

He startled, looking at me. At least, I think he did, since he had no pupils. The orbs of his eyes were full of the starry night sky and threaded with a gleam of violet where light reflected off them. They were his most notable feature, seeming oversized amongst the other angles of his face. I stared, fascinated by their odd beauty.

"You can see me?" he asked. Something about his voice seemed familiar, but I wasn't sure what. His tone was calm and smooth, making me feel more relaxed.

"Yes."

The dark leather cloak behind him stirred and shifted. Actually, those were *wings*, marking him as an Unseelie of some kind, but that was a detail my sleeping mind slid right off of. He had sharp features and pointed ears that stuck out on either side of his face as if he were part bat. His clothes were a confusing blur, something gray that offset the soft purple tones of his skin well.

He had white hair like me, though his was cut short and shot through with starry pinpricks. I wished I could touch his hair and see if it was as velvety as it looked. Though I rarely got to indulge myself, my omega instincts loved checking the textures of certain things.

"Well, this is unusual," he said in a musing tone. "But you'll forget me when you wake, as I have ensured you won't remember your worries. No guilt, no fear of Pack Ellisar, and certainly nothing about the versions of Fal and Tormund your dreaming mind assembled." He shuddered and shook his head. "I'm nearly afraid to ask what other things trouble you."

"Then don't," I blurted, then realized myself and softened my voice. "I mean, this is nice." I gestured to our surroundings.

"I wanted your dream to provide you with something better for the rest of the night. I hate when my questions draw forth a full nightmare from others," he explained. I nodded along, as if having someone guiding the path of my dreams was perfectly reasonable.

"But...who are you?" I repeated.

He tilted his head back and forth. "A dreamer, just like you. A student of Ever and Always, and sometimes Never when it calls to me."

I cracked a little smile. What a silly answer. "That doesn't make sense," I giggled.

He smiled back with two rows of flat teeth. A beta. My mind relaxed some, thinking we were heading to Zemosia after all.

"Many things don't make sense in dreams. When we all carry our own yearning, guilt, and lives into one vast space, strange things are bound to happen," he said.

"Like what?"

"Hmm. What's your favorite fabric?" he asked. I set my lips at an angle, confused by the question. "Like, for your nest?"

For several seconds, I struggled to find an answer to his question. I was barely allowed to have a nest in the waking world. What was Laurel's pixie dress made of?

"Lavir spidersilk," I said once I remembered.

He looked at me with something like concern and, for a moment, seemed a lot like Fal in the set of his features. But then he gestured, and the seat behind me became plush and coated with a layer of buttery soft silk. I settled back against it, wishing I could rip the cloth free and nest with it in my waking life.

"Without magic, dreams are molded by your desires. Your deepest yearnings can clash and turn to nonsense," he explained.

"Can you make me a blanket, too?" I asked shyly.

"More spidersilk? Expensive taste."

I thought he might be teasing. "No, just something soft and warm. Something for comfort," I murmured.

The next thing I knew, I had a blanket folded in my lap. It was softer than fur and as thick as I imagined clouds were, practically a pillow that I spread and burrowed into until it was fully wrapped around me. I sank my fingers into it, petting the material. I was growing so desperate for positive touch and soft materials that even the slightest comfort was a blessing.

The stranger watched me, his expression softening. "I'm glad you like it."

I wanted to give him something in return for this. "My name is Lark."

He nodded, unsurprised. "What kind of lark were you named for?"

"I don't know. I don't think I was named after a specific type."

"No shame in that. I am rather partial to the"—he said a word I didn't quite catch—"that fly through the dreamlands. Maybe I'll show you one day."

"Implying I will see you again." I drew my new blanket tighter around me, already knowing I wanted to meet the star-eyed stranger in another dream.

He flashed a surprisingly tender smile. "I don't think that will be much of an issue. But our time together tonight draws short. Tell me something before you wake. Why do you want to go to Zemosia? What's waiting there for you?"

It was just a dream. There was nothing stopping me from revealing things I'd left unsaid for so long. "Freedom. It's a place I could go, free of everyone who wants a piece of me. I can open a shop or find some other job for myself. And only betas and omegas live there, so I don't have to worry about being forced into a pack or made to do…other things against my will."

His growl was soft and unpracticed. "You won't be forced into a pack, ever," he said firmly.

"The ink is dry." I ducked my head, staring at my lap out of old habit. "Running is my only option."

"No, Lark." He knelt beside my seat, taking my hands in his. He'd moved to this spot abruptly, bending some kind of dream logic. "You can trust your new pack to free you of anything that would get between you and us."

I tried to tug my fingers free.

"What new pack?" I asked in despair.

Reality leaked in, smudging the edges of the dream. I was waking up to the day after I'd stolen from a scent match and fled. There was no pack to turn to, only a disaster to continue running from.

The stranger shook his head. "Promise me you'll hear out Fal and Tormund tomorrow. Let us take you to Serian, li'l omega."

THE LAST OF his plea was an echo of a memory as I jerked awake with a gasp. The sun was high in the sky, casting full bars of light over my face as I lay there in my makeshift nest, heart thumping hard in my chest.

What a wild dream...

"Let us take you to Serian, li'l omega."

The accented voice lingered in my mind. A noble Unseelie asked before he whisked a pixie away to his homeland, I guessed.

What else had happened in the dream? My brow crinkled as I struggled to remember anything else past a feeling of incredible softness against my palms.

8

LARK

"You survived the Omega Masquerade," I told myself after scooting to the edge of the bed and hanging my legs over the edge. I hesitated, knowing exactly what was waiting for me the moment I stood. "You can do anything, which means you can—ow!" The moment I put weight on my feet, I nearly fell as sensation returned and lanced up both legs.

It was going to be a bad walking day. The pre-heat symptoms had only worsened overnight, making my skin feel tight and sensitive all over. I couldn't believe other omegas enjoyed going into heat. Maybe the sex made it worth it. For me, it would be torture until I found an essence spinner to give me a new suppressant. The sooner, the better.

I inspected the grass stains on my dress and made a pledge that, if I had any money to spare after buying my magirail ticket, I'd get a change of clothes. With the heat spreading from my core out to my limbs, I was liable to sweat through the material by the end of the day. *Gross.* I wasn't at the point of no return, though, not yet perfuming or dripping slick. I could still push my heat back.

Before I left the room, I ate as much as I could of the cold leftovers from last night's feast. Tormund has bought me at least four meals' worth of food, and it felt so wasteful to leave a lot of it behind, but I had to move. I donned my smock, tucked in Fal's mask and the piece of Tormund's cloak into the pocket, then checked the hall with a poke of my head out the door.

There was no one in the hall, so nobody witnessed my limping, which was worse than usual. I regretted agreeing to dance last night. My crippled foot was not made for that kind of motion, and it ached. I reached the stairs and gulped a swallow. I checked the level of essence within me, finding it was still dangerously low but not quite as depleted as yesterday.

I no longer had to worry about Cymora demanding illusions with little warning, yet I still took a guilty look around as if I were doing something wrong. Cupping the railing with one hand, I flapped my wings and loosed tiny shimmers of essence as I floated down one staircase at a time. By the last one, where the innkeeper and the few patrons at the bar could see me, I hobbled to the ground floor the traditional way.

"Stairs are the worst," I muttered. I bet Zemosia, utopia that I'd built it up to be, didn't have stairs.

After turning in my room key, I felt eyes on me. A handful of alphas were eating and talking in small, animated clusters. One sat alone, tracking my progress toward the exit over the rim of a copper mug. He was distinctly merman blue, with a shaggy mane of cerulean hair shot through with green highlights.

That was about all of him I needed to see. I gritted my teeth and increased my stride to put distance between myself and the too-interested merman. Hopefully he was just a disappointed suitor from the masquerade, due to return home at any hour.

I picked a direction and joined a flow of other fae heading straight into the busy market I'd glimpsed yesterday. I rested my hand over the front pocket of my bulging smock, picking my steps carefully to avoid being jostled by passing folk of all sizes and designations. My mouth hung open as I took in both the variety of fae and the storefronts while I tried to locate a pawn shop.

Now that I was hyperaware of it, I noticed Unseelie here and there. I guess it wasn't as big a deal as I thought? No one seemed surprised. There was some dissonance in my head as I compared the peaceful Unseelie minding their business with the wicked and downright evil fae I'd grown up hearing about.

Thelis and Serian hadn't been at war even in my parents' generation, and it seemed more than a handful of Unseelie had made their way across the sea to the Seelie capital. Just seeing a curvy scaled naga slithering along with a basket of eggs and a pair of dark elf alphas laughing together arm-in-arm nearly had me tripping over my own feet, though.

This was definitely not Osme Fen.

I liked the anonymity of the crowd and the sight of so many varied shopfronts. I walked several blocks and lingered to look at jeweled bags and elaborate garments positioned by the windows of stores for the wealthy. Restaurants wedged in between them, using their window space to host elaborate banners illusioned to look like freshly prepared meals sizzling enticingly.

The hair on the back of my neck rose. I looked over my shoulder more than once, but no one seemed to be following me.

Stars, don't be so flighty, I admonished myself after my third glance back at the peaceful market.

The costliness of the displayed items diminished in the direction I walked until I happened upon my first pawn shop. It was a small box, full of display cases lit by specialized essence lamps to cause their contents to sparkle.

I caught the attention of a dryad alpha who looked to be an honored elder, if his seven-foot-tall stature and the thickness of the mossy greenery and blooming flowers coating his shoulders and scalp were any indication. Many members of the Seelie had plant features or power over the natural world, more traits that set us apart from our Unseelie cousins.

He hulked behind the counter, narrowing his pupilless green eyes at me. "See something you want, kid?" he grunted.

"I wanted to sell something, actually." The fingers I had in my smock shook as I took out a few items. It would seem rather farfetched if I tried to offload twenty-one timepieces sized for males at the same shop, so I put two timepieces in front of him, along with three jeweled bracelets and the pair of amethyst studs I'd stolen from Laurel.

The dryad didn't say anything for several seconds. I was already sweating from my pre-heat, but he was making my anxiety so much worse. A justification for why I had these items perched on my tongue before he lifted the first bracelet and ran it through his branch-like fingers.

"Fourteen fulls for this," he rumbled.

He worked methodically through the items, naming a price for each. Given that I could see a timepiece for sale at two hundred and ninety-nine full moon coins in his case, I knew I was getting a raw deal when he said fifty each for the two I was offering him. But I nodded at all of his named prices, pretty sure a magirail ticket couldn't cost more than five hundred full moons. That price would've been outrageous anyway.

I might've stolen a lot more than I needed to. I picked at my fingernails, overcome with a rush of guilt. It wasn't as if I could return the excess items I'd taken.

After counting out the money and handing it to me in a small sack, the dryad alpha gestured toward my front pocket, which was still full of lumps. "Got anything else?"

I opened my mouth to respond, just to sneeze into my elbow. "Sorry." I gave him a fluttery smile. This persistently unamused male wouldn't appreciate me mentioning being a little allergic to the pollen he was putting off.

The bell on the door jingled behind me. I was weighing my options before saying, "I do have more." I started lining up more items of value, rings and bracelets and a third timepiece.

"That's clearly not all." The dryad circled his hand. I hesitated before stacking up a couple more of my ill-gotten gains onto the counter. He picked up one of the rings, tilting it so it sparkled. "Hmm. Did you steal all this from somewhere, kid?"

My wings flicked before flattening to my back in a defensive posture as he fixed me with a steely green stare.

"Every time there's a big event, the thieves come out the next day with goods they shouldn't—"

"If you don't buy her things, I will," interrupted a deep and annoyed voice.

I whipped around, having missed someone else entering the shop. He loomed behind me, scowling at the dryad. My eyes rounded to the size of saucers as the lilt this stranger spoke with hit me at the same time his pheromones did. *Water. Danger.* Cymora and Laurel's domain.

He carried the fresh, green scent of waterlilies and the kind of wild mint that grew close to the lake and streams around Osme Fen. And he was the alpha who'd watched me leave the inn. Now that I saw the rest of him, I noticed the signs that he was only a merman as an illusioned disguise. He wore fashionable clothes, cut and dyed in what appeared to be an expensive style. They hugged his muscular torso in a way that left little of his sizable strength to the imagination.

Unlike Tormund, who'd been husky as well as naturally large, this alpha looked like he'd never tasted a sweet in his life. The frizzy waves of blue and green hair hanging to just past his jaw may have been the only thing soft about him. That jawline was chiseled perfection and coated in the cerulean shadow of an unshaved beard. Though one of his arms was covered by a half cloak that draped over his shoulder, the other that he placed on the counter around me had large, contoured muscles.

He met my eyes for a moment before staring at the dryad, and a shiver went down my spine. That yellow gaze was not particularly friendly. But at least it was leveled at the shopkeeper for now in some alpha dominance match.

"I could take them somewhere else," I suggested to keep the peace.

"No," they said at the same time.

"How much are you going to pay her?" the prince, I assumed, asked. His Serri accent was mild yet present.

"How many items does she have?" the shopkeeper countered.

The prince gestured at me impatiently, and I set out another time-piece. "All of it," he ordered.

My knees got a little weak. I didn't think he'd put the full force of his alpha presence into the words to bark at me, but he might've been close. I started lining up each and every item I stole from yesterday's masquerade.

Bowing his head slightly to the prince, the dryad began rifling through the goods. "I wasn't going to report her," he grumbled. "Thieves are good for my business. There's always some put-out noble sauntering around, looking to replace something they lost."

The prince merely growled. His gaze slid back to me, flicking up and down in a perusal so fast I could've blinked and missed it. I crossed my arms over my belly, turning partially away from him. I suspected this was the maw of some Unseelie trap swinging closed around me. Even if I could bolt with most of my stolen valuables laid out, one of the other males from his pack could be waiting to intercept me.

"Five hundred thirty-two fulls," the shopkeeper said.

"Double it," the prince ordered.

He raised a mossy brow. "Seven hundred."

"You're taking advantage of her."

"Need I remind you that she's a thief, sir?"

"Seven hundred is fine," I put in tentatively. More currency than I'd ever held, for certain. The most Cymora entrusted me with were a couple half-moons, usually slivers and chips for my trips to the market.

The prince released a most unprincely snort. He sounded somewhat like an irritated horse. "You have no proof she stole anything. Nine hundred."

"Deal." The dryad began counting out coins.

Wow. I guess I really was getting taken advantage of on my own. I turned to the prince and worked up the nerve to thank him. He cut a forbidding form—arms crossed, brow knitted in a scowl—and watched the shopkeeper with intense focus. Was it to avoid looking at me? Maybe I wasn't in danger of a trap after all. If this was how much interest he had...

Well, it was within the Unseelie princes' rights to reject me as a potential mate and bite a more suitable princess into their pack. It just made me feel a little small and then annoyed at myself at the same time. I didn't need them. But my core tightened with another wave of unbearable warmth at the end of that thought, as if to say *yes you do*.

I sneezed again. "Blessings," the prince said, offering over a kerchief.

I was already dabbing my nose on my sleeve when I accepted it and felt the velvety material it was made of. No way was I blowing my nose into something so nice. I covertly rubbed it against my cheek, then took in the concentrated scent of him with the stirrings of a purr.

His smell triggered another cramp to seize my middle, insistent and somehow different than the others I'd suffered on and off for four years. It felt final. I clenched my eyes shut in denial, dreading the reaction building within me as heat spread into my veins like liquid lava. No matter how tightly I pressed my thighs together, I still perfumed, wafting the final sign of my pre-heat in a cloud of the sweetest chocolate and honey crackers.

When I peeled my eyelids up, I had the prince's full attention. His jaw was tight enough to grind his teeth to powder, but his nostrils were flared and the yellow of his eyes reduced to the merest ring as his pupils expanded.

"You're going into heat," he stated, his deep voice coarse with lust.

"I... I need..." I stuttered, backing away a step that he matched. My wings hit the icy metal edge of a display case, and I whimpered. He answered with a low growl, easing into the last inches of space between us. I was giving off a furnace but still felt the heat of his body, hyperaware of the way he stopped without actually touching me. His hands were braced on either side of the case, boxing me in.

"I need..." I tried again. The air smelled too much like him, waterlilies, mint, and male musk becoming a heady mix I couldn't get enough of. Desire wrapped around my spine. I wanted to feel his skin against mine more than anything. Those strong hands belonged on my curves, and *I needed his knot inside me.*

No. No, this couldn't be happening. I clenched my fingernails into the pads of my hands and blurted, "I need...an essence spinner! Now!"

He startled, then recoiled, giving his head a shake. The sheer panic in my words must've woken him from the spell of my pheromones. "Now?" he demanded.

"Right now!"

Pivoting on his heel, he grabbed the dryad shopkeeper by the shoulder, who was watching us as if we were his afternoon entertainment. "I will be back." The prince had a growling undertone in his voice. "And you will have her nine hundred full moons ready for me. I will be counting each and every one."

"Of course," he replied dryly.

Releasing him, the prince frowned at me. "If it's *right now*, you walk too slowly." It sounded like he was reasoning with himself before he lifted and tossed me over his shoulder as if I were a sack of grain. I squeaked a short protest. His hand closed around my thigh, and his arm became a band holding me in place as he strode out of the pawn shop.

He took off running down the street, announcing himself with a shout of "Out of the way!" I bounced on his shoulder, watching different fae's reactions to the scene we made after we had already passed them by.

My cheeks were so hot I couldn't tell the difference between heat and embarrassment. Stars, it was a good thing I was leaving Ilysnor as soon as I could—I'd never be able to show my face again, just in case anyone recognized me as the pixie who'd been run through the marketplace in a mad dash and left a trail of perfume in her wake.

He picked up speed somehow, racing around and through the crowd. I tried to focus on not going into heat. The process was a lot faster, I'd heard, if an omega surrendered to it, preferably in the comfort of her nest with her chosen mates already marked with her scent. My body didn't want to hold back any longer.

No. No no no.

I'd clenched my muscles and eyes shut again, noticing when the sunlight dimmed behind my lids. We bounced up several flights of stairs, and he jostled my too-sensitive body the entire way up, drawing a full-blown moan from me. The prince rumbled low in his chest, sounding more like thunder than an alpha, and it was the hottest thing I'd ever heard. I perfumed again for him.

A few moments later, he was knocking furiously on a door. "Kauz!" he roared.

I fluttered my wings, trying to get a look over his shoulder, but I was well and truly stuck in this compromised position. His grip on my thighs felt like a vice. But at least I recognized where we were—the same inn I'd just spent the night in. Just figured that Tormund would take me to where the rest of his pack was.

The hinges on the door creaked, and a much calmer male said, "It's unlocked, you barbarian—"

There was one last whirl of air as I was rushed into the room and plonked in a seat. Now upright, I reeled, dizzy with the sudden movement.

"There. She needs you," my would-be savior said before running back out the door and slamming it behind him.

I turned to the male he'd left me with, Kauz. He had a heavy set of bat wings that nearly swept the ground when he turned and looked at me. His large eyes were unusual, resembling the starry sky and rimmed by icy white lashes. He looked familiar, though I had no idea how. I'd never met anyone with such a striking feature.

"Are you an essence spinner?" I asked.

"I am. You have need of me, hmm."

His nostrils flared, and the set of his mouth softened. As he spoke, I caught no sign of sharp fangs. He must've been an Unseelie with wings like that, but I didn't care. He was a beta and could weave magic, so the stars themselves had sent him. Only a beta could ignore the pheromone cloud I was putting off as I sat there holding my thighs as tightly pressed together as I could. My breath came in short pants, and my pupils had to be blown.

"My heat," I managed to say before yet another cramp had me in its grasp.

"Finally, I've found a force that can make Marius turn tail and flee." He chuckled as he raised a hand, summoning essence that began to spin between his fingers. The magic matched his hair, white with a sprinkling of glimmers like stars. "His mate's heat."

Oh no. Not the *m* word. Calling these males scent matches was enough; *mates* implied a sense of intimacy we definitely didn't have. "Suppressant," I gasped. "Please."

Kauz's face etched in concern. At that moment, he looked exactly like Fal; they had to be brothers. He spoke in a low tone, mostly to himself. "Suppress this? I can give it a try. I'll go get the ink."

9
LARK

THE WORLD SWAM in a feverish haze. Kauz returned to sit across from me, a table between us. He had a kit containing a grid full of tiny bottles open on the surface. "Any color preference?" he asked.

I inhaled through my teeth, but I was beyond words. An inferno was eating me from the inside out, and I felt so empty, my pussy clenching on air. I was mentally undressing this poor beta while it happened, imagining how good his cock would feel inside me even though he didn't have a knot.

No. Stop that. Bad Lark.

I shook my head, and he nodded, lifting a brush and selecting for me. He shook the bottle and infused the liquid with his magic in a swirl of starlight. If I were in my right mind, I'd mention the ink on my lower belly, where I preferred to hide the tattoo. But I would probably succumb to full-blown heat if I took my dress off right now.

Kauz drew the brush's bristles into a point by placing them between his lips. I imagined them pinching the little cherry at the apex of my legs, and slick escaped the seal of my thighs, dripping onto the bottom of my dress.

I was slicker than a fish in the sea, my whole body aching to be filled. I needed…a knot. *No.* A bath. I needed a long, hot bath.

The first line of ink brushed the inside of my wrist and shimmered with the starlight of Kauz's essence. The tremors wracking my body eased.

"Come back, Lark," he was murmuring, spinning essence with one hand while the other drew another line next to the first. By the third stroke of his brush, he'd taken hold of my fingers, running starry magic down my arm and straight to my core. It tingled over my skin, cool and soothing, and the temperature in my body fell, giving way to chilled shivers. A bit at a time, my muscles relaxed and my skin loosened.

He dipped the brush in the ink pot and ran the tip in a delicate pattern over the back of my wrist, his eyelids narrowed in concentration. I watched him work with fascination that had nothing to do with how horny I'd been moments ago.

His essence felt right in the places where it entwined with mine, as if it belonged there. My body responded to his power and obeyed his spell work without a fight, going dormant once more and shoving my heat away.

I caught a whiff of his scent through my overpowering cloud of perfume. It was a hint of something nice, tickling my nostrils and disappearing when I tried to get another sniff.

"Would you like a fertility blocker?" he offered. He flashed a reassuring smile. "To prevent conception when you inevitably go into heat."

"Such a thing exists?" The essence spinner in Osme Fen had never offered me something like this, and I would've gladly paid extra for it.

"Of course." He squeezed my hand between both of his, careful of the wet brush. "You should always have the freedom to choose."

I practically wilted with relief. He had no idea about Pack Ellisar and the way they'd promised to breed me. They wanted a baby from the heat they'd purchased, and I shuddered with a spike of fear just at the reminder.

They're not here. You're going to be on a magirail to Zemosia as soon as possible.

"No one's going to force you into anything, Lark," Kauz said gently. It was like he'd read my mind. He brought me back from the spiral of my thoughts and lanced through the heart of my fears all in one go.

"How do you know my name?" I wasn't suspicious... I'd told him, hadn't I? Silly me, forgetting that detail while my mind cooked from heat-driven fever.

"Fal mentioned it last night."

My cheeks pinkened. Of course Fal had talked about me. He'd probably sat his whole pack down to tell them what a disappointment I was. Some scent match, flying away the moment he was revealed as an Unseelie.

"I did," confirmed the dark elf himself. Gasping, I nearly fell out of my chair, but Kauz caught my arm when I startled hard. Like the cat Fal halfway resembled, he'd slipped into the room on silent feet and caught the latch behind him to ease the door closed.

He was dressed down from the fancy suit he'd worn to the masquerade yesterday, but his navy getup and the glittering chains and earrings along his long ears still screamed *prince*. My heart just about galloped out of my chest to see him again.

His feline gaze gleamed with interest even from several feet away as his nostrils flared.

Kauz's face twisted with a severe look he turned toward the dark elf. "You scared her."

"Apologies, my lady," Fal said, nodding my way. "It was simply impossible to miss Marius panicking. I *had* to investigate."

I swallowed with a dry click. If I didn't need to stay for another magical tattoo, I'd be bolting out the door right now. So, I nervously told Kauz, "I want the fertility blocker, please." The quicker he applied it, the sooner I could leave. Maybe with him present, Fal wouldn't lay into me for leaving him unmasked last night.

Kauz retrieved a second brush from his kit and shook another bottle of ink. I took my eyes off Fal to see the new suppressant tattoo and cooed from how unexpectedly pretty it'd turned out. He'd given me a bracelet of silver ink with tiny gemlike designs threaded through it. I wanted to inspect his handiwork when he wasn't turning my hand over and posing his brush over my pulse point.

"What're you thinking for this one?" Fal asked. He'd moved soundlessly to the chair beside Kauz, and I sucked in a smaller startle.

The summery scent that wafted from him would smell even better mixed with the waterlilies and mint from Marius. It was unfair a pair of alphas could smell so nice and yet be Unseelie. I couldn't trust them. Right? Maybe I shouldn't allow Kauz to give me a second tattoo, even though he'd clearly suppressed my heat as requested with the first.

"Don't make the lady ask you to leave," Kauz said.

Fal leaned down to rest his forearms on the back of his chair. "Please. I'm just here for the ambiance. I can shut up." He flashed me a quick wink.

"You? Never," Kauz stated.

I ducked my head, glad to feel the cool tingles of Kauz's magic as he started drawing the fertility blocker on my skin. Just the act of perfuming so hard for a stranger was bad enough before adding in how Marius had dumped me here and left. Now Fal and Kauz would smell my sweaty body after the last vestiges of my perfume faded. How mortifying. Fal's alpha instincts probably wouldn't let him leave until I disgusted him with my body odor.

I looked around at anything but these two males. This was a bigger suite than the one I'd slept in last night, with this table that sat four. Kauz had his chair flipped around to account for the leathery wings he had mantled to either side of his lean body.

I clenched my free hand in my lap. "I hope Marius is okay," I mumbled.

Both of them laughed. I peeked through my lashes, catching Fal's graceful fingers forming a lewd gesture. "Oh, just give him a moment. He'll be fine."

"He dropped her and ran as if a raging redcap were chasing him," Kauz said, still chuckling.

"Did he? I'm going to give him so much shit for that." Fal then switched to Serri to add something else to Kauz, the language earthy and lyrical in its own way. His every inflection made him sound like he was up to no good, his teasing edge verging on lustful.

Stars. I imagined him being in the pawn shop with me rather than Marius. Fal probably would've taken me back here to seat me on his knot. A stirring of heat pooled low in my belly, but I pushed it away. *I'm very fortunate to get another suppressant tattoo. Not the added complications of a full-blown heat.*

Kauz responded in Serri, but his tone was of warning. The shift of mood the dark elf experienced was immediate. He schooled his expression as Kauz lifted my wrist and blew on the drying ink.

"Sorry, li'l pixie," Fal said. He sounded nearly serious, the mischief placed aside for a moment. It was interesting that he couldn't fully pronounce *little* either. Like Tormund, it seemed his tongue was trained to flick the top of his mouth mid-word. "Not to make light of the moment. I'm sure no omega wants a suppressed heat triggering in a public place."

"No," I murmured.

My inner omega perked up. *Surely he isn't angry about last night if he's apologizing.* That bundle of instincts wanted me to be held by my scent match. It was only natural for an alpha-omega pairing to bond over touch and comfort.

I can't ask him for that. Maybe I'd get a chance to apologize, at least, before I left for Zemosia. I'd also give him his mask back, despite wanting to hoard it.

"How long has it been since your last heat?" Kauz asked. He lifted my fingers to brush a kiss over my knuckles before releasing my arm. A shiver of awareness passed up my skin from just that little touch of his lips.

I turned my wrist over. He'd picked a sparkling purple ink to make a separate tattoo that was attached to the first by a stylized swirl and a pretty knot that all seemed interconnected. The most prominent lines formed an X, and I imagined that was the point. No babies for this omega.

I was so grateful that I answered his question. "I've never had a heat."

I looked up. Both males were staring at me. "You don't have an omega mark, then?" Kauz asked in surprise.

Fal whistled low. "And how old are you?" he asked.

They were way too interested in this, and their intensity spooked me. "How old are *you*?" I countered nervously.

It was easier to respond to Fal rather than admit I'd purposefully made myself packless for four years. Without my first heat, the omega mark wouldn't manifest on my body and I couldn't be bitten and soul-bound into any pack against my will.

Alphas and betas simply had their mark appear when they hit adulthood. I'd pushed the moment mine came in as far back as I could. I'd find my freedom in Zemosia before I was forced to become a breeder for any alphas, especially the likes of Pack Ellisar.

Fal's brow rose. "Old enough to recognize a deflection."

"I...thank you," I said to Kauz, gesturing to my wrist as I drew to my feet. "I don't know what I would've done without your timely intervention. If you need a favor or money, just let me know—"

I was edging toward the door, ready to declare a "none of your business" if they pressed any harder. I'd try to run to the magirail station, not that these males wouldn't follow me. After the moment in the pawn shop, it was clear the Unseelie pack wanted something from me. They hadn't done anything yet to convince me they had darker intentions, but they couldn't help their nature as the tricksters of the fae race.

Kauz opened one of his wings to stop me, creating a living barrier that I nearly bumped into. His wingspan was huge, but what caught me off guard were the patterns of silver ink that were exposed while it was extended. The tattoos popped against the purple-black hue of his wing.

The bottom half of the leathery span looked like the night sky full of falling stars and shimmering, misty clouds. An incredibly talented essence spinner had inked these tattoos.

Wow. I just wanted to touch him. Maybe see if he'd let me lie on his wing like it was a blanket and trace every sparkle and glimmering trail. I wondered if he could fly, *really* fly. If so, he could carry me into the sky, and I could experience more than a few short glides on my comparatively tiny wings.

You can't have him either, I reminded myself. This sudden neediness was unsettling. All he'd done was touch my hand and wrist, and my inner omega wanted to jump straight to him hugging me with that impressive span.

"Just answer one question. How long have you pushed off your heat?" Kauz asked. The concern in his tone had my insides tying themselves up. He was being way too nice, considering the circumstances.

"Four years," I breathed.

Kauz gasped and Fal growled. I backed away from the unspoken aggression that rose from the alpha's chest. "Why?" the dark elf demanded.

"I need to go." I stumbled around the edge of Kauz's wing.

"Tell me why you're endangering your health. Lark!" As predicted, Fal followed me out of the room, his tall stride keeping up with my hitching gait effortlessly. "Has someone intimidated you into suppressing yourself this long?"

"It's not that."

"Give me a clue," he beseeched. "Help me see you."

I stopped before the stairs. *Fuck. We're on the third floor again.* Turning to face Fal, I tried to swallow the lump in my throat. He wasn't going to let this go. I saw his determination but also far more tenderness in his expression than I'd expected. He hadn't laughed off my desire for freedom as omega silliness, either.

After all my imagined versions of him returning to his brothers and laughing about the pathetic pixie who didn't have a dress for the masquerade...maybe that didn't matter to him. Not like this did. In my wildest dreams, I'd never expected this male to *care*.

"Lark." The way he said my name had my wings quivering. "No omega pushes off a heat for four years willingly. Tell me what's wrong. My brothers and I would fall over ourselves for a chance to help you." Closing the distance between us, he cupped my cheek. I nearly whined, torn between how much I wanted to be touched and how little I could open up to him. Cymora had ordered my silence on too many occasions.

Tilting my head, I leaned into the warmth of his presence and lidded my eyes. It felt so nice to be caressed. I couldn't remember the last time someone had gentled me, and I ached for more. It'd be too easy to get lost in his enticing scent of sun and grass.

"I'm leaving," I murmured.

"You're fleeing," he corrected.

"Is there a difference?"

"Aye." His free hand combed through my hair.

Do not purr, I hissed at my inner omega.

He's Unseelie. He's going to use what I say to trick me later.

"I..." Just opening my mouth released a soft sound, a bubbling pre-purr that threatened to deepen. Despite my misgivings, I wanted to trust him. I guess I was a moth this afternoon, daring to fly closer to a fire. "I'm going to a sanctuary city."

"Are you?" Those sharp fingernails grazed my scalp just so. Oh, that felt amazing.

"Yes."

"Then why haven't you left yet?"

His lighthearted tone was back. I looked up at him and the quirk of his mouth. I wanted him to hold me, and he probably knew it on instinct. Yet he wasn't merely joking; he was challenging and prompting me to leave. Right now.

What I wouldn't do to have his brand of confidence.

"It's the stairs," I answered, hoping to catch him off guard. I was second-guessing my whole plan, and that would get me stolen away by a pack of Unseelie after all.

The side of his lips lifted further. "What?"

"The stairs," I repeated. "Going down them hurts."

His gaze dropped to my feet, and I saw his moment of clarity. He smoothed my hair before drawing back enough to bow. "It would be my infinite pleasure to assist you with this part of your journey, my lady," he said with a dramatic flourish of his hands.

I fidgeted, blushing again. "I'm not a lady. I'm...a servant." Like he didn't have eyes to see it for himself.

"Not anymore," he said smoothly. "No matter where you go from here, you are *my* lady."

Oh no. I could feel my defenses fizzling away. My fingertips tingled. This prince was claiming me as his. So unlikely a true reaction and so clearly a trap, but...I wanted to believe it so badly.

"There's that lovely smile. I mean it. Please let me carry you."

I hesitated another moment before nodding, and he bent, lifting me as Tormund had, one arm around my back, threaded between my upper and lower wings, and the other under my knees. The moment he secured me against his body, I couldn't help it anymore. I snuggled into the strength of his chest and inhaled with a purr. He descended the stairs slowly, careful not to jostle me too much.

"Neither of your brothers asked."

"No accounting for manners, hmm." He nuzzled my neck, leaving the mark of his warm scent on me again and inhaling with a possessive growl.

"Hmm," I echoed, part agreement and part enjoyment.

His lips brushed my skin, featherlight. I tilted my head for more, an unconsciously submissive gesture.

"You keep purring for me like that, and I'll carry you straight to the next train to Serian," he said.

"I can't help it," I mumbled in a weak protest.

His hold tightened around me. "That's fate, my lady. You belong with me."

Belonged *with* him, not *to* him. I flushed, sensitive to the distinction. Stars, if he didn't stop talking soon, I'd go right back into pre-heat.

"Who caused your leg injury?" he asked.

I stopped purring. His tone hadn't shifted, so it wasn't quite the change of subject that it seemed. "Huh? No one. I mean, I was born like this."

"Hmm." This hum sounded disappointed.

Now that the moment had passed, I wished there were more stairs for him to carry me down. "Hey, Fal. I'm, um, sorry about last night," I blurted before I lost my nerve.

His smile returned, pure mischief glinting in his eyes. "Oh aye, about which part?" he teased.

Stars, all of it. "About tricking you," I said carefully, trying to get to the heart of the matter.

He released a deep laugh, burying his face in the crook of my neck again. It was a wonder we didn't crash down the rest of the stairs. "Don't be sorry. I *loved* it."

I practically tingled with disbelief. He couldn't mean that.

He moved his mouth to my ear, giving it a nip with those extra-sharp alpha fangs. I shivered, feeling the sensation down to the end of my toes. He whispered against the pointed shell, "Try doing it again, tricksy li'l pixie. I'm certainly going to return the favor."

This had to be an Unseelie thing. Or a dream. I couldn't imagine conjuring a more perfect male willing to look past both last night's illusion and my station. It was simply too good to be true.

Perhaps that's why Laurel called out in the next moment, "It's Lark!"

My heart dropped, and my nerves stood on end like I'd been submerged in icy water. We'd reached the hall leading out of the inn, and there was my stepfamily, as if the stars themselves had decided I'd had too much freedom and wanted to put me on a crash course with reality.

Fal glanced up when I tensed, an aggressive rumble rising in his chest.

For one beautiful moment, Cymora looked bewildered to see me carried in the arms of an obvious noble male. As I'd come to expect, though, she recovered first out of all of us. "Lark, there you are!" she exclaimed, hand resting overtop her heart. "I've been *so* worried!"

10

LARK

"Who are they?" Fal murmured.

I met his gaze, torn. Who could I trust more, the Unseelie I'd just met or my stepfamily?

He was putting me down. My right foot twinged upon coming in contact with the ground. Just another dose of reality as the surge of panic in my chest settled into resignation. It was over. Already.

I came to a decision and hoped, somehow, Fal could become the unlikely ally I needed. "The clue you wanted. So you could see me," I mumbled back.

Stars, they'd found me so fast. I'd thought they wouldn't bother to search Ilysnor all that hard, and that was my fatal mistake. A keening tone rose in my head, screaming out a silent denial. I couldn't go back to Osme Fen. I would rather die than have Pack Ellisar touch me, even more so now that I'd met my scent matches, Unseelie or not.

My hand covered the new tattoos on my opposite wrist, hiding them under an illusion with a bit of essence. I stood in a servant's obedient pose with my face inclined toward the ground, bracing for whatever came next.

"Lark, who is this handsome male?" Cymora simpered.

It wasn't a direct order, but I responded like it was so Fal could hear who she was. "Yes, Stepmother. This is Prince Fal...uh." I'd forgotten his full name.

"Crown Prince Falindel of Sorles, second only to Pack Serian," he supplied, picking up seamlessly from where I'd left off. I felt his attention on me and dared a peek through my lashes. His gaze was probing as it flashed from me to my stepfamily and back. Practically demanding an explanation. "Lord heir and leader of Pack Sorles."

Cymora rushed to curtsy, stomping on Laurel's foot until she stopped gaping and did the same. "It's an honor to meet you, Prince Falindel. I am Cymora, Lady of Osme Fen. And this is my daughter, Lady Laurel. Thank you for finding Lark for us. We lost her after the Omega Masquerade."

"Indeed." I must've been imagining the suspicion in that single word, as Fal sounded warm afterward as he gestured to the taproom. "How lovely it is to meet you both. Let's have a seat. I'll call my brothers to join us through our pack bond. We have something to discuss."

"We do?" Laurel asked. She made a soft yelp as Cymora must've dug her heel in.

"We certainly do," he said cheerfully, sweeping me in that direction with his arm around my shoulders. I tried not to despair as he hauled two tables together, moving chairs so there was enough room for all of us. This was about to be humiliating. I didn't want the princes to see me under Cymora's thumb, but I didn't have a choice.

I glanced her way, and my heart sank further at what I saw. My stepmother was scheming so hard it was a wonder she wasn't blowing hot steam from her finned ears.

"Please, sit," Fal said, drawing the first chair on one side. "I have joyous news to share once we're all here."

Cymora eased into the second chair, gesturing for me to sit across from Fal and for Laurel to flank her other side. "I am quite eager to hear it, especially if it concerns my dear Lark."

I hid any sign of a flinch under a practiced mask, going as blank as possible. She had a habit of punishing me for any public reactions later, in private, and I didn't need to make her wrath any worse than it already was.

A barmaid came by, and Fal had her leave, passing her a coin. He wasn't planning on this being a long conversation, it seemed. Kauz was the first of his pack to arrive, keeping the chair beside Fal empty and turning around the next one in line to account for his wings.

"Prince Kauzden of Sorles, magician heir," Fal supplied while introducing my stepfamily to him.

Laurel murmured in awe when Kauz smiled and offered his hand to each of them. The sunlight leaking into the taproom caught his unusual eyes to make them shine with ribbons of purple nebulae. I wanted to gaze into them to see more, and so did my stepsister, it seemed. A flash of jealousy hit me that she was the one across from him, able to look at her leisure.

Whoa there. What was that? I'd rarely cared so much about such a small thing before.

"A pleasure to meet Lark's family," he said.

"The pleasure is ours," Cymora replied.

Next to arrive was Marius, who had a brief exchange with Fal in Serri before shrugging off his half cloak and the illusion making him look like a merman. It unveiled his Unseelie animal feature first. Fins stretched from just below the knobs of his wrists to his elbows, folded close to his skin with multiple sharp-looking points at the ends.

His facial structure changed in several subtle ways, starting with his nose flattening from a blade to a more subtle ridge with a golden ring glinting on his right nostril. Two emerald studs lined the end of his right eyebrow. His ears reshaped from merman fins into long fae points that sported a wavy outside edge.

The most striking change was the long scar bisecting his face at an angle, lending him a look more roguish than handsome. It was thick and silvery, crossing over the bridge of his nose and cutting through his brow close to his pack mark and the top of the opposite cheek.

The oblong shape of his face reminded me again of a horse. *Kelpie,* my mind supplied. A breed of aquatic Unseelie shifter known for feasting on flesh and having loyalty only to their nixie mates. He was

short with my stepfamily, practically grunting his way through introductions.

"Marius is a male of few words," Fal added, earning a nod from the
kelpie. "It comes with his role as protector heir."

"Where's Tormund?" Marius asked. His ear flicked in an impatient
gesture.

"Enjoying Ilysnor, I'm sure," Kauz answered.

The longer it took for the last prince to arrive, the more time
Cymora had to scheme. I fidgeted with my fingers under the table,
picking at the skin around my fingernails until it hurt, as I wondered
what new terrors she was coming up with. My belly was full to the brim
with queasy nerves. No matter what she decided to do, I had no power
to stop her. And she was sure to try to ruin how the princes saw me.

It was almost comedic how when the illusion of choice was taken
away, I realized what I wanted. With the exception of Marius, who had
caught me in such an embarrassing moment, I *liked* what I'd seen of the
Unseelie princes. If I ended up stolen away to Serian...

Well, if my stepfamily hadn't been standing in the way, I'd have let
Fal carry me to the magirail station. I'd never see Pack Ellisar again, not
even spare their breeding contract a second thought if I were soul-
bonded into a nicer pack. *Amazing. What happened to wicked tricksters
and vile malcontents? It hasn't even been a day.*

The four princes weren't like the stories. They'd been kind to me,
despite my lower station. They were simply just like any other fae I'd
met. Maybe I was wrong, and maybe it was too soon to write off Fal's
mischievous face, Marius's clear dismissiveness, and Kauz's unreadable
starry eyes. They could've already misled me about their intentions or
any evil plots they had until I was shut inside a train with them.

But Tormund...I thought of him as having the purest intentions of
the four of them. We all knew when he arrived, as he exclaimed, "Hello
again, li'l bird!" He came into the taproom from behind me, announced
by the inn's door closing.

He'd changed cloaks, wearing an intact one that was orange and
edged in gold embroidery. "I bought you something," he said as he bent
way down and pressed a kiss to my cheek.

My face warmed, and I blinked up at him in surprise. He'd really
kissed me, no hesitation, and I released a giddy laugh in response.

Tormund wore a big smile as he whispered behind his angled hand, "I'll give it to you later."

The table had gone silent during this exchange. I was aware of Cymora's focus next to me, watching with a hawk's unerring gaze.

"Okay," I said, wondering what he'd gotten me. Hopefully it wasn't anything too nice, or my stepfamily would take it away.

Fal came to my rescue again, introducing Tormund as he took the last seat, next to Kauz. The brothers edged out to give him room. After a murmur from Kauz, Tormund took off the ruby and gold armband he wore, revealing his horns. All four males had the same pack mark, a three-pointed crown between their brows.

"As you may be aware, every royal pack has a member that sees to the queen's household. Tormund is the heir to her needs," the dark elf explained. "Now that we're all here, let's cut to the chase. Lark is the scent match of Pack Sorles."

"Yes," Cymora breathed. "What great news indeed."

I didn't like the sound of *that* at all. Nor her hand coming down on my knee and squeezing it firmly under the table. "You met at the Omega Masquerade, then?" she added.

Laurel stirred. "But Unseelie—" she began to whisper before Cymora elbowed her.

Fal nodded. "As my brothers will tell you, we've met every eligible nixie in Serian. We've taken our duty to find our princess quite seriously. I suspected our mate would be a pixie instead, and I was rewarded last night after crossing paths with Lark."

"You are certain?" my stepmother asked with a dry chuckle.

The only reaction on their side of the table came from Tormund, whose brow knitted.

"She is our scent match. Our fated mate," Fal stated.

"Well, how interesting. I'm not sure I can approve of such a match. Lark is a wallflower, I'm afraid. And untrained for a princess's duties. Perhaps another can fulfill that role for you," Cymora said.

My cheeks burned, and I clamped down on a whine of denial. Stars, this was exactly what I was expecting. The next thing in her book of tricks was to recommend that Laurel take my place because she was *so superior.*

She wasn't going to give me a direct order in front of the princes, but she did tighten down on my knee with a vicelike grip until I winced and ducked my head again without a word. A growl rose from Tormund's direction.

"You can't fault me for telling the truth to spare us some trouble," she said to him. "I'm not sure she will be a good princess for you, fated or not."

"We are not ones to judge her lacking in any regard, Lady Cymora," Fal said. "There is protocol to observe before she joins our pack officially, but we've already recognized her as our princess and intend to begin fitting into her life with the roles we've been raised in since birth."

My eyes widened with shock. My stepmother wasn't wrong. How, exactly, did they expect me to perform as a princess—no, a future queen—of a kingdom I'd never even visited? This went beyond scent matching. They needed someone to fulfill a specialized role other omegas were trained to step into.

But he'd said *recognized her as our princess* with that confidence I'd been admiring in him earlier.

Cymora reacted quickly, patting my knee as permission to stop stooping. The princes had to be looking at us with suspicion, which was why I didn't straighten or speak up yet. It was the only thing I could do to signal that there was something off about the situation.

"Princess Lark. I like the sound of it," Fal added with an edge of mischief. That seemed to be his more casual tone.

"*Our* princess. Even better," Tormund said.

They waited, probably expecting me to say something.

"Let's give her a moment. This must be overwhelming," Kauz suggested.

Cymora cleared her throat, probably reeling from my sudden change in fortune. "Well, in the meantime, if you don't mind me asking... Prince Kauzden, I couldn't help but notice..."

"That I'm a beta?" Kauz supplied wryly.

"Only a curiosity for the other betas in the room," she said.

"Of course. My race defies usual breeding rules for designations. There are no alphas with powers such as mine, and nixies are rare outside of a couple lucky bloodlines. My many-greats grandfather was selected to be a mate of the first Queen of Serian for his talent in essence spinning, which I have thankfully inherited to be of use to Lark."

"I see. Thank you for sharing that."

Though she was polite on the surface, I could tell she was a little sour about his explanation. I glanced up with a mousy lift of my lips, figuring it had to be in response to how he'd tied it back to me.

"Will you tell us about Osme Fen? We're not familiar with small Seelie settlements," Kauz offered. Calling it *small* was accurate, but he was sure to rankle Cymora further. By the shape of his eyelids, he was looking my way and cracking a little smile.

While she replied, Fal caught my attention. He gazed into my eyes for a long moment, before he blew me a kiss with one of his elaborate hand flourishes. I hid a giggle behind my fingers.

"Why don't I send you and one of my brothers off while we finish up here?" he suggested in an undertone.

Cymora was busy talking about herself and Laurel, so I nodded and murmured, "I'd like that a lot."

"Lark's father passed away when she was only six years old, leaving me with the estate in Osme Fen and Lark's care. I've anticipated this moment for us," Cymora was saying. She rested her fingertips on my shoulder as if she had some kind of affection for me. Again, I held in a flinch, used to her touch being a prelude to pain. "To think you are so... eager to have her. What are the next steps, then? You mentioned a protocol, Prince Falindel?"

Fal had a practiced face too. He erased any sign of his emotions as he blinked and turned back to my stepmother. "She must be presented to our mother, the queen, for approval. Then we will be permitted to court her before she meets our fathers in a formal dinner. After that, we will take her into our pack bond. Finally, she will be introduced to the Unseelie Court. It's tradition for her to be named princess at the autumn festival so our people can celebrate her together."

"I see," Cymora stated thoughtfully.

The dark elf flashed a playful look my way. "It won't take too long. Our parents have been eager to see us bachelors properly mated."

"Do you think they—" I began to say.

"When do we leave?" Cymora said over me.

Fal raised a brow. "We, Lady Cymora?" he echoed.

She placed a hand over her heart. "As Lark's only remaining family, I must insist that Laurel and I accompany you all back to Serian. Who else will look after her honor before she earns the royal pack's approval? And if she doesn't...we wouldn't want her to be left all alone and unwanted, now, would we?"

My breathing shallowed out. Stars, *unwanted* dug into my mind with vicious talons.

Tormund's hands clenched and flexed. Something in his small eyes shifted. I caught a glimpse of his pupils turning orange red before he shuttered them and took a deep breath. That looked like *fire*. He must've been a fire fae of some kind. Kauz patted his arm, murmuring something in Serri.

"We were only intending to take Lark with us," Fal said.

Cymora gripped my knee again. She stared me down, somehow promising every pain in the known world if I tried to exclude her and Laurel. The palpable threats shooting out of her expression were so potent that I feared I'd start bleeding then and there.

"If it's possible, I would like them to come too," I said. *Don't hurt me. Don't hurt me again,* I silently pleaded.

Fal took a moment to consider my stepfamily and then me, his pupils narrowed to feline slits. Marius, who'd barely said two words this whole time, muttered in Serri to Fal. The dark elf responded with a noncommittal hum.

"If your things are in order, *we* can leave as early as this evening," Fal answered. "If such a short timeline is okay with Lark."

"Of course it's okay," my stepmother said.

Fal pursed his lips and turned my way, waiting.

"Yes," I rushed to say. "This evening will work." It was infinitely better than returning to Osme Fen, knowing what awaited me there.

Fal smiled slowly. "Excellent. Well, no time to waste. We must do some shopping for you, and then we'll be eager to head home with you as our prize."

"Why do you need to shop for her?" my stepmother asked.

"It is a long trip, Lady Cymora, and Serian is still frozen this time of year."

"Lark already has things," she deadpanned.

Fal's courtly mask slipped and revealed a hint of derision. "You must be—"

Tormund blew out a plume of smoke from the side of his mouth. He stood abruptly, stomping toward the stairs.

"He's going to pack," Kauz said, putting his palms up. "Nothing to worry about."

"We would love to buy her the newest and best items Ilysnor has to offer," Fal added smoothly, having recovered during the distraction. "Perhaps we can entice you with a gift of coin to buy yourself and your daughter something as well?"

This melted any of Cymora's lingering protests. Her face lit up at the prospect of free things.

11

LARK

"Kᴀᴜᴢ, will you accompany Lark into the city while I finish speaking with her charming family?" Fal invited. Cymora and Laurel smiled at the flattery.

The winged Unseelie stood with a relieved sigh. "It would be my honor."

I made to stand too, just for Cymora to band her hand around my forearm. "Before you do anything else, go retrieve our bags. We had to leave them outside the cottage while we went looking for you."

Her melodious voice didn't have its usually acidic edge, but there was a gleam of malice in her eyes as she delivered the order.

I swallowed to keep from frowning. It'd take me ages to find the cottage and return with our bags. No time for the princes to buy me anything if I was kept busy. With no other choice, I bobbed my head in agreement. "Yes, Stepmother."

Marius also stood, shrugging on his cloak and his merman illusion as he went. "I have errands in the city," he growled, sparing my step-family a brief glance before striding away.

Kauz offered me his arm, and we walked out together. I didn't release the pent-up breath I was holding until the inn's door shut behind us. Stars, it wasn't a complete disaster, but now my stepmother had a chance to influence the events to follow. My mind buzzed with all the implications of what could happen next.

"Hey. Are you all right?" Kauz asked, resting his free hand over mine. He drew me to the side of the inn for a bit of privacy.

"I don't know."

I didn't even know if I could answer the question. An honest fae response would prompt a negative comment about my stepmother, something she'd forbidden me from doing years ago.

"I know they're family to you, but we could trick them into boarding a different train tonight," he offered.

I pictured it, especially Cymora's face when she realized she'd been fooled halfway to the wrong destination. I giggled, and Kauz laughed with me.

"No, really," he said.

"My stepmother is too smart for that. She'd notice." I sounded distant even to my own ears. It felt like pouring cold water over the moment. I'd found her next to impossible to fool and considered whether I was a simpleton for thinking my trick at the masquerade would end any differently than this.

Maybe if I'd managed to board a train to Zemosia earlier today. Then I'd be out of her grasp for good.

"I have to go get those bags," I said, letting reluctance bleed into my voice.

"Are you truly in the habit of being such a doormat?"

I startled at Marius's gruff question. He crowded the little alleyway we'd ducked into and looked down at me with a probing expression.

"Doormat?" I repeated meekly.

"Marius," Kauz said, a warning in his tone.

"You were there. You saw it too," the kelpie said to him before his attention returned to me. "You allowed that beta to belittle and talk over you in front of your potential pack, and all you did was take it. Why?"

My cheeks stung as my mouth parted, but try as I liked, I couldn't get more than a few sounds out. I couldn't share that I'd once been a foolish, heartbroken child who'd rushed to promise, then *vow* to her stepmother that she'd be good and do everything she was told.

Cymora had implied that if I was disobedient, I'd be heading for an orphanage with "all the other unwanted brats," and I'd bawled at the implications. I'd given away my freedom for the chance to avoid the truth: I'd been unwanted from the moment my father died from a sudden heart attack and left me in the hands of his second mate. In the years that followed, I'd taken a lot worse than what they'd seen at that table.

But again, I couldn't tell Marius any of that. All I could do was break eye contact and hunch like a good little servant. Kauz freed his arm from my hold and wrapped his wing around me. He switched languages, the earthy Serri rising and falling in a furious cadence.

Marius reared back in surprise, then snorted like a pissed-off horse and replied in kind. They were definitely arguing about me, and Kauz's wing only tightened around my shoulders as their verbal duel grew more heated still.

It felt like an eternity before Marius switched back to Theli. "Fine! Where is this cottage?" he demanded.

The lingering anger on the kelpie's face turned me into a trembling creature. I made a small whimper before saying, "I...I'll go. She told me to get the bags."

"Ridiculous," Marius sighed. "I'm going to do *my duty*—" His gaze cut pointedly toward Kauz. "—and retrieve them for you."

"She didn't say your name. Technically, any one of us could fulfill her request," Kauz murmured.

"No...I have to," I insisted.

Marius hadn't stopped staring at my face. "It would be no trouble for me."

I shook my head. "That's okay. My legs work."

The kelpie's lips pressed into a tight line.

"Mostly," I added in a mumble.

"I see what you mean." His expression shaded with understanding. Kauz nodded. I wonder what else they'd said in Serri during their argument, because I was a little lost.

"Look, Lark. I will get the bags, and your stepmother will be none the wiser. The bags can stay with the innkeeper, and I'll give him coin to say you brought them. Will that work?" Marius asked.

This seemed like the most he'd actually said to me at one time. He'd also lost the air of alpha aggression that had my chest pinched so tight with fear. I uncurled from my frightened posture, rapt by the sound of his voice. Without the growling undertone, it was deep and rich, full of princely authority.

"Marius won't do anything else before he retrieves the bags," Kauz added.

I guess I felt like looking this meat-eating horse in the mouth. "You'd do that for me?" I asked.

One of Marius's ears flicked. Even illusioned to look like a merman, that tell of his remained. "If you would give me a hint as to where the cottage is," he said irritably.

I flinched away from him. The rumbling anger was back. Well, he wasn't doing this to be nice; Kauz had somehow forced him into it.

I told him the name of the rental cottages and the general idea of where they were. That was apparently enough information for him, as he strode off without another word.

I'd missed my chance to more heavily imply that there was a vow between Cymora and me. Maybe one of the princes knew of a way I could break it. I'd never figured out if it was possible, other than if Cymora willingly released me from it. Something she'd never do.

Instead of interrupting my thoughts, Kauz waited for me to resurface from my musing. His eyes sparkled with stars, glimmering this way and that as his gaze roved over me. They really were pretty. I'd already lost any unsettled feeling at looking at his lack of pupils.

Since he was a beta, he was only a few inches taller than me. While his brothers had alpha height and muscles, he was lean, with the impression of being broader than he was due to his wings. I wondered how heavy they were since he kept them furled tight like a trailing cloak of leather and stars.

"Kauz," I murmured, mustering my nerve to ask to see his wings again. I hoped it wasn't weird. Maybe he got the question a lot and would handle it with the same grace he had when talking about his beta designation with Cymora.

"Aye," he answered, shifting his weight. "Ready to go? I only have a few hours to spoil you." He was serene again, calm in a way that had me relaxing too. I think it was just something about him, despite the fact I'd seen he had a temper even Marius respected.

My mind blanked. "Uh...spoil? No," I protested. Once Cymora noticed anything of interest in what he bought me, she'd demand it for herself or Laurel.

"Come along." He smiled, motioning me out of the alleyway. "I have my brothers to answer to if we don't return with more bags than I can carry."

We walked into the midday crowd, swinging around to the expensive side of the market I'd walked through earlier in search of a pawn shop. "First stop should certainly be clothes," he said, heading into one of the shops before I could talk him out of it.

If the beta who greeted us was surprised to see an Unseelie, she kept it under a bright smile as she greeted Kauz and then side-eyed me and what I was wearing. She modeled clothes from this shop, bright colors offsetting her light brown skin. They were altered to fit her form perfectly.

"We have a train to catch this evening," Kauz said. "I know it's short notice, but is there a seamstress here who can alter clothes for pixie wings within the next few hours?"

"Of course, sir," she simpered. "If you'll follow me, we have some ready-made clothing for omegas that may be of interest."

Kauz fell into step with me. "We're going to get you a set of winter wear. Serian, especially the capital city, Neslune, will still be cold for another month or more. Plenty of time for us to have lighter clothes tailor-made for you. There are a few designers who would murder for a chance to dress the next princess."

I fidgeted with my fingers, releasing a nervous laugh. "Oh, but I'm a pixie. That must be a big change for Unseelie tailors."

"The good kind of challenge. Do you know how many different slits and folds there have to be in nixie fashion for all their flashy fins?" He rested a reassuring hand on my shoulder.

I didn't know, actually. I hadn't met a nixie, but I'd heard they were vicious and toothy, the beastly opposite to the ethereal charm most pixies possessed.

The beta showed us to a section of the store lined with ready-made clothes. She hovered a polite distance away. I waited and eventually turned to Kauz, who mirrored the movement.

"If you don't start trying clothes on, I'm going to buy every single thing here that fits you," he said mildly.

That spurred me into action. I looked at every tunic and dress in the first row. These were clothes for noble omegas, made of buttery soft fabrics I'd never worn but wanted to rub against my cheek the moment they were between my fingertips.

The steep prices for each item glowed on their sleeves or collars in enchanted ink. In reality, Kauz shouldn't buy me any of them. I didn't pick anything off the rack before moving to the next one.

I browsed the whole section and turned, empty-handed, to tell Kauz that we should shop at a more affordable store, just to do a double take. He'd slung several items over one arm and reached past me to pick up the cloak I'd just barely restrained a purr over. It was charcoal gray on the outside, with a snowy lining of responsibly harvested fur. I'd snuck a covert rub of it against my jaw while I'd longed to wear something so soft.

"The changing rooms are over there," he said, pointing.

The beta jumped forward to prepare a room for me, sweeping away the chosen clothes. I followed, shaking off my daze. The changing rooms were split by designation, with a couple sectioned off for omegas. There were complimentary heat supplies beside a three-fold mirror, and I helped myself to them once I was shut away for a moment of privacy.

I dressed down, pulling my smock and dress off, then used some sanitary wipes to clean away the spots where my perfume and sweat remained, not wanting to get any offensive odors on the clothes. With care, I peeled my panties off, hissing at how wet and oversensitive my folds were when exposed to the air. I'd come a hair's breadth from my heat, and my intimate spots still felt it.

I sighed and used more wipes to clean off the lingering slick, grateful to wipe it away even as I frowned at my panties. Guess they had to go back on, soaked as they were.

"Lark? You know I want to see you model the clothes, right?" Kauz called.

"One moment," I called back. Then I poked my head out of the changing room to catch the attention of the beta assisting us. She came over when she noticed me. Though my cheeks heated, I whispered in her ear about underclothes, and she went off to retrieve some.

It was another ten minutes at least before I emerged in a new ensemble. Kauz glanced up from where he'd been waiting in a chair built large enough for his wings, which he had half spread behind him. He had his chin resting in the cradle of his hand but sat up with a jolt when he noticed me.

"Well, look at you." His tone lit warmth in me, unrelated to any kind of pre-heat.

I felt pretty, and my wings fluttered under his admiring inspection. Most of the clothes on offer were neutral colors, designed to make pixie hues pop. They even made the dim glow of mine look nice. This tunic was a light brown, with fawn-colored pants that went with it. It'd be good traveling attire, though the decadent fabric felt odd against my skin. If I was given such a nice outfit, I'd be afraid to exist in it and potentially stain it.

We'd acquired a second assistant, apparently, as Kauz signaled to a beta male. "The lady requires new shoes as well," he said.

"Right away," he answered, taking a good look at my worn slippers before heading further into the store.

Kauz sent me off to change into a new outfit. He didn't say whether he liked any of the various things I ended up modeling for him, though on occasion, he asked if I did, especially if something needed tailoring to fit me correctly.

After the hitch in starting the process, I had fun, enjoying the feel of some of the clothing that swished just right against my skin. He'd picked up everything I'd spent more than a couple moments touching and admiring, and I was grateful for the chance to try it all on.

And the fur-lined cloak... I modeled it last, with the gray pants and amethyst-toned tunic Kauz wanted me to wear out of the store. It was huge on me, as some of the clothes were, but that made it easier to close around my body and sink into like a wearable blanket. The fur gave it enough weight to put the right amount of pressure on my top wings; their bases bent until the fabric rested on my shoulders properly. It even had a hood... I loved this thing.

"That was everything?" Kauz asked. Once I nodded, he stood and took the edge of the cloak, brushing my cheek with its ultra-soft lining. He smiled, adding his fingertips as he held the side of my face for a too-brief moment. I leaned into his touch as he withdrew it and reached for the clasp holding the cloak around my shoulders. "You're going to over-heat if you wear this right now."

I whined as he pulled it off my shoulders. Out of habit, I suppressed the sound before it got too loud or annoying. His starry eyes flickered, and something unknowable passed over them. "I know," he murmured. "I'll carry it for you."

"Oh, wait, you're going to buy it? It's a lot." I figured he hadn't looked at the hood's edge, where the price was inked. Over a thousand fulls, probably because of the fur.

"Why don't you rest your leg a moment while I finish up here?" He didn't even look at the cloak's price before leaving with it.

I sank into the big chair he'd left behind with a sigh. The clothes I wore, plus the cloak, shoes, and underclothes, were already a pricey gift. However, getting to this point had taken a lot more time than Kauz probably expected. We had maybe an hour before the sun would start setting.

The act of taking clothes on and off, twisting to get my wings through some of the holes, trying on different pairs of shoes until Kauz insisted I walk out with the fur-trimmed boots I now had on... I'd aggravated my foot at some point along the way. He'd noticed that, too.

Instead of feeling worried, as I probably should've been with an Unseelie able to perceive my inner thoughts, I was flattered. I thought I just might like Kauz and the smell of pine he'd left behind on this chair. It had to be a soap, since betas didn't naturally have scented pheromones.

There was something else too, a smell more alluring, and fleeting, underneath. What *was* that?

He returned after a short while with the fur-lined cloak thrown over one arm. "I've been given leave to spritz you," he said, showing that he had what looked like a perfume bottle in his hand.

"Oh no, I smell that bad?" I asked in a small voice, mortified that I'd gotten my scent on all the clothes I'd tried on after all. The female beta attendant had offered to dispose of my old clothes, but I'd insisted on keeping them, so they rested in a bag by my side. My smock still had my limited funds and the tokens from my scent matches.

His snowy lashes fell in a long blink. "No, sweetheart," he said gently. "It's a potion to remove the prices. See?" With a little shuffling, he showed me the damp edge of the cloak's hood, which no longer had luminous numbers.

I nodded, glancing down as I rode out my embarrassment. Kauz sighed as he knelt and took my wrist, spraying away the price on the tunic I wore. "You must feel overwhelmed by my family and our personalities all at once," he said in that same tone. "No one expects you to change overnight. But what you're doing right now, hiding your face and reactions...we've got to break you of the habit."

"Sorry," I murmured.

He took hold of my chin, forcing me to meet his gaze. "You have nothing to hide, li'l omega. Not from your mates."

"It's a little early to call me a mate, isn't it?" I protested, though it didn't have much teeth. Not while he was touching me even this little bit.

His fingers drifted down my jaw, and this time, he let me lean into it. He cupped my face, his thumb caressing my cheekbone. Stars, even something so basic had me fit to melt.

His striking eyes remained unreadable, though they seemed to soften. "Perhaps, but look how you respond to my touch. When you're in the pack bond... Shall I clue you in to a secret?" His lips took on a conspiratorial slant at the abrupt change of subject. "Hmm. Maybe after I take you to the next store. I paid one of the attendants to do some minor shopping for us, by the way. There's a place I have to take you to before we return to the inn."

"Oh, you *have* to," I echoed curiously.

He returned to spritzing off the prices of my new clothes. "See, that's the kind of reaction I want to hear. Don't hold yourself back so much."

"I'll try," I promised. Though that also didn't have much teeth. We were going to be traveling in an enclosed space with my stepmother. Candid moments would be dangerous.

He offered a hand up and led me out of the store, passing the perfume bottle back to an attendant on our way out. "We will have the items delivered as soon as possible, sir," she said.

He nodded and turned his sparkling gaze toward me. "The store isn't far. This way."

We entered a thinning crowd, with him slowing to stay by my side. His hand bumped mine, and a moment later, our fingers were entwined.

I wondered what kind of store it had to be for him to seem excited. We were heading away from the pawn shop, toward a section of the market I hadn't visited yet. It wasn't too long before he pointed with his free hand. "Have you been to an omega store before?"

We were coming up on a shopfront with a hanging sign that was just the horseshoe-like omega symbol. "Um, no," I admitted.

"Hmm. Osme Fen just keeps getting smaller in my estimations." He released me to get the door.

"It is very..." I drifted off as I took a look around. My eyes widened. Most, if not all, of the items on display were for nest building. Mattresses, pillows, blankets, and more.

Kauz nudged me in encouragement. "Go ahead. We have time."

Next thing I knew, I was face down on a display mattress, vividly imagining taking a nap on it. It had just the right amount of give without engulfing my body, and its outer fabric was thick enough that no quills poked up from the feathers within. Would Kauz buy it for me?

How will you get it onto a train? a more reasonable part of me asked. There probably wasn't space to haul an entire mattress on board.

Though my body had decided to weigh a hundred extra pounds in my reluctance to leave the mattress, I turned my head looking for Kauz. He'd intercepted an attendant, and the two of them were talking over a basket the prince held.

I stood before I could really fall asleep and decided to leave the mattresses alone, just in case I encountered an even nicer one. I went to the pillows and bedding section, losing myself to feeling each and every display item. My inner omega was going crazy, wanting to arrange everything anew as the logical lines and stacks didn't fit her style.

Kauz interrupted the process by asking, "Do you have a favorite fabric?"

This completely derailed my train of thought. I tilted my head up at him. Hadn't he asked me that before? But wait...when? We'd just gotten to the omega store.

"Lavir spidersilk," I answered uncertainly, itching all over with a sense of déjà vu.

He rifled through the blankets with a hum, producing a folded bundle that was exceptionally thick. "Try this one."

I took it and squished it against my chest, my fingers roaming over the material. Stars, it was so nice. I'd felt it before...last night...

I looked up at Kauz, who was waiting with a kind of knowing expression as hazy memories clicked into place. No wonder he'd seemed so familiar. He was the star-eyed stranger I'd met last night.

"You were in my dream," I practically accused before sucking in a breath. I couldn't talk like that to a prince. "Sorry, I mean, I had this dream and..."

"You can trust your new pack to free you of anything that would get between you and us."

Ah, stars. I remembered a quarter of last night's dream, if not less.

"Let us take you to Serian, li'l omega."

I was struck breathless by the implications. Had he somehow spelled me into trusting him and his brothers subconsciously? If it was Unseelie trickery, I didn't know what to do. My eyes darted cagily around the store, seeking some escape. I should've known he was too good to be true.

"Lark, it's okay." He dropped his voice to a soothing murmur. "All we did was talk. I swear it." Oh, he *swore*. That meant the ring of truth in his voice was obvious fae to fae. I didn't know why or how he'd infiltrated my dream, but that was a boundary we needed to discuss.

He unfolded the blanket and draped it over my shoulders, pillowing me in its softness. "By the way, this is fleece."

I nodded, not trusting my voice as I wrapped the material around me more. I was seconds from rolling around in this blanket if he would just look away for a moment.

"I have a theory, if you would indulge me." He held out his arms for a hug.

More trickery? Or just a kind offer?

I barely hesitated. I let the blanket drop before walking into him, resting my cheek on his chest while he held me tight. "You need this, don't you? You're a little touch starved," he whispered.

Since I couldn't remember the last time I'd been held like this, other than Tormund's soothing last night, he was probably right. I whispered back, "Was my dream why you already know me so well?"

His muscles shifted as he shook out his wings and added them to the embrace. Starry leather made a boundary between us and the outside world, and I succumbed to a purr that rattled my whole frame from how snug and safe I felt. This was no trick.

"Being observant isn't magic, sweetheart," he said just loud enough for us in this cocoon of comfort. "I just want you to know...if your step-mother turns out to be the reason you're touch starved and have pushed off your heat for so long, I *will* ensure she has nightmares for the rest of her days."

That was possible? I couldn't wish ill on Cymora due to my vow, but I could purr even more at the idea.

12

LARK

"Weren't you going to tell me a secret?" I asked Kauz once we left the omega store. He'd held me for an extended period of time, yet I still mourned the loss of his wings when he decided we needed to go. We had to make it back to the inn in time to catch a train to Serian's capital, which would launch when the first stars appeared in the sky.

"From my pack bond, yes. Well, I bought this soap for a reason."

He carried my fur-lined cloak and the bag of purchases from the omega store. In it was the fleece blanket and an additional pillow for the trip, but also several bars of scent-blocking soap. I'd figured those were to keep my smell contained when my pre-heat returned.

"It's for my brothers. We share strong emotions through our pack bond. Over the last day, I've felt an echo of their attraction to you, and it is *potent*. I smelled our compatibility too...last night. Things are different in dreams." He gave a vague wave. "In the enclosed space of a train, I believe my brothers will bend to their alpha instincts if you remain smelling so tempting."

My cheeks warmed to a rosy glow. That was how they already felt? I mean, the scent-led attraction was mutual, considering their pheromones had triggered the onset of my heat. Maybe I was too easy to mislead, but the extended hug in Kauz's wings had gone a long way to convincing me that them being Unseelie wasn't so bad after all.

I wanted to ask if he meant to include Marius, but I didn't dare. The kelpie thought I was a *doormat*. How mortifying. A burning sensation lingered in my belly every time I thought about it and acknowledged with shame that he was probably right.

"But our honor is on the line. If we don't deliver you to the queen, our mother, untouched by us for her approval, we're breaking a long line of tradition. Forgive me, but we've assumed you are intact, considering the situation with your heat," he added.

Stars, the lingering humidity in the air had gotten so much thicker all of a sudden. I murmured, "I am."

He chuckled. "It's like asking foxes to guard a henhouse. If their scents prompt your heat's return, you won't leave the train unclaimed. I'm going to touch up your heat suppressant daily, but given how powerful your body's needs are..."

"Right. I'll use the soap."

I also didn't want to tempt the alphas and end up in emotional agony later if they rejected me as a mate. As much as I wanted to be touched and held, I didn't want to get too attached before their mother's appraisal. Too many things stood in the way of me becoming their pack princess.

I also should've mentioned Pack Ellisar.

Later. I'd do it later, after we put a sea between us and them. I didn't want to kill any potential interest because a pack back in Osme Fen had a piece of paper Cymora had forced me to sign.

"In the meantime, let me tell you about my family," he said, distracting me from that threat to my happiness.

We returned to the inn laughing together as he finished telling a story about his big sisters. He talked like I'd soon call these fae my family too. I didn't dare allow myself to hope for it yet.

Before he told me their birth order, I hadn't realized just how many siblings he had. After Fal and Marius were born thirty-some years ago, two nixie sisters came along and treated toddler Kauz, born fifth, like an accessory to tea parties and game nights before another sister was born. Tormund followed, but the Queen of Serian had since birthed a fourth daughter and was now about halfway through her ninth pregnancy.

"She's as clever as ever, our mother," Kauz said fondly. "Our next sibling hasn't slowed her down at all."

This was the female I had to impress if I truly wanted to be a part of Pack Sorles. If I followed in the queen's footsteps, I may also have to birth seven children before making the required four male heirs for the next generation. Maybe more, depending.

That was a hair-raising number of babies. More babies than I had ever imagined carrying, whether I had a pack of supportive males or not. My sight swam at the requirement.

But then I thought of Queen Alora and her single child. When placed under similar pressure, she'd given her kingdom one fiery omega to inherit everything.

Maybe I could do that too.

Or maybe I could find my way to Zemosia after all and never have to worry about babies. I could have the freedom I'd planned to grab...only, my belly tugged with yearning for what I'd leave behind. I reminded myself yet again that I couldn't have everything I wanted. I could leave for true freedom, or I could pick the princes.

If I went with the route of claiming my scent matches, it would be a fight. Cymora was scheming, and I *had* to outmaneuver her this time with a foolproof plan. Else I'd lose everything.

She was there in the inn as we breezed in, watching us with narrowed eyes. My laughter cut short, the joy fading under her judgment. The stars in Kauz's eyes dimmed as he noticed, and I gave him an apologetic look. *I still have to protect myself,* I wished I could tell him.

Cymora stood with Fal and Laurel to one side of the inn's front hall, with Tormund, Marius, and a cart loaded with several bags on the other side. To my relief, the three belonging to my stepfamily and me were in the pile.

Fal said something in Serri, which Kauz responded to. He lifted my hand and brushed a kiss over my knuckles before we parted, with him going to the dark elf, leaving me to be swept up by Tormund in a hug. "He took his time returning you, li'l bird," he grumbled.

I savored his toasted mallows scent, lamenting that he needed to cover it up soon. "We made the most of the time."

Tormund glanced up and said something in Serri to Fal. The brothers smiled, except for Marius, who stood with his back to a wall, serious faced.

"He said well done to Kauz and that you look very cute. I agreed," Tormund said to me in a loud whisper. My wings gave a little flutter at the unexpected compliment. "Though he also used a word that's not for li'l omega ears."

Oh? I considered what word that could be and came to only one conclusion. "I've heard profanity before, Tormund," I whispered back.

"It's not right for a noble male to swear in front of a lady."

"Before she gets the whole chivalry lesson, we should go," Marius muttered.

Tormund cleared his throat. His gaze flashed toward Fal, then back to me. "May I assist you to the train station?" he asked with stiff formality.

I considered my aching feet and the throbbing pain up my right leg. It seemed so much worse when I stood still and acknowledged it. I hoped he meant that he wanted to carry me, even if it made me spoiled to nod and release a soft sound of delight when he scooped me into his arms.

By the sneer Cymora shot in my direction, I knew there would be another thing for her to chastise me about when we next spoke in private. I could practically hear it already. *Pretending to be weak so an alpha carries you. Don't you know how pathetic you look?*

Fal herded my stepfamily out of the inn first. As Tormund and I followed, Marius snatched away the bag with my old clothes that I'd been carrying. Before he placed it atop the pile on the cart, he pulled a coin purse off his belt and dropped it inside with a heavy thud. "All nine hundred fulls."

I thanked him with a sigh of relief. He'd taken care of returning to the pawn shop after all, and the money could still be useful later.

Tormund fit in between Kauz and Marius while Fal coaxed my stepfamily into an animated conversation ahead of us. "They told me all your new things arrived ahead of us," Kauz told me.

"We put it all in four luggage bags for you," Tormund said.

"Four," I echoed.

"That's right. All for you." The giant sounded gleeful.

"Not *all* of it," Marius said before I could protest. "We filled at least one with new books and other entertainment for the trip."

As we walked down the market road, curious and wary faces turned toward us amongst the clusters of Seelie fae heading home this evening. I'd expected fear and hostility when it came to spotting an Unseelie in Ilysnor, but I only saw hints of negativity when there was a whole pack of them moving toward the magirail station.

"How long will it be?" In retrospect, I should've asked earlier. All I knew was that we'd be heading north, crossing the sea between the Seelie and Unseelie island nations. It'd once been called the Sea of Strife, as the first meetings between our people were the merfolk and undines warring with the nixies and kelpies.

Now that we'd met humans and allied briefly to fight them, in our truce with everyone, the sea was renamed the Doras Sea for the short-lived King Doras. The human monarch had brokered the sometimes-uneasy three-way peace we all maintained to this day.

Marius released a weary sigh. "Eight days. But it will feel like an eternity."

"We will be in the same room. It is already agreed," Tormund said.

Raising a brow, Kauz asked something in Serri. The three of them had a short conversation as I reeled. Eight days in a compact space with both my scent matches and my stepfamily. That *would* be an eternity.

"The only way Fal could get Cymora to agree to the arrangement we had in mind was for her to have extra room." Marius switched languages and lowered his voice to a mere growl. "There are four fae to a room, so one will be Fal, Cymora, and Kauz. The rest of us to another."

Stars, they'd made special arrangements and split us up? They could have easily put Laurel and me with Cymora and had a room to themselves. This was such a huge and unexpected kindness that my lip wobbled with emotion.

"Trade you," Kauz remarked.

"No," both Marius and Tormund said at the same time. The latter snuggled me tighter to his chest.

"We'll rotate places during the day. Give us all some respite from one annoyance or another," Marius added in a mutter.

He didn't look my way, but for a sensitive moment, I figured I was one of the annoyances to dodge. Given that I was a doormat and all.

Kauz tilted a smile toward me. "Now that, I insist on. I'm going to need more time with Lark."

My lips tilted up in a shy echo. "I would like that."

"You've had your time with her. Now it's my turn," Tormund groused. "I have your gift ready once we're settled, li'l bird. You can have it after the launch."

I shifted in his hold, looking over at the pile of bags. They'd already bought me so much. What could possibly be in the four bags in this mix that were now mine? And he wanted to give me *more*. Tormund's nostrils flared, and his brows drew in to form a line through his pack mark. "Your smell changed. No feeling guilty. We all wanted to buy you things. Kauz just got to buy you the most."

I covered my face. That was definitely not helping. "It's just—I don't know if I can—"

"Accept that we're going to spoil you?" Kauz interrupted.

"Just wait until we're home, Lark. You're going to be the happiest omega in Serian." Tormund ran his hand down my back, teasing the sensitive membranes of my wings with his broad palm.

The giant watched my wings as they opened and closed of their own volition, tilting his head. "Don't pixies have sparkle dust?"

"Pixie dust, yes. I just don't have much," I said, hoping he wasn't about to ask why my wings also weren't a gemstone color.

Most pixies were dazzling from the diamond-like powder they shed from their wings. It was made of spare essence, and I rarely had enough to shed more than a mote here and there. I saw it as a blessing in disguise, since the sparkles got over everything.

Tormund quizzed me about pixie dust while we slowed and joined a line of fae catching the evening trains out of the city. He seemed fascinated by my wings and gave one of the top ones a curious tug after I told him about their semiflexible bases. "Pixies with better wing control than me can move them up and down"—I gestured between the sky and ground—"as well as flap them. In the air, they kind of angle themselves."

"They're pretty. Like you." He had a jolly laugh when they wiggled from my happiness at the compliment. From my vantage in the big alpha's arms, I watched one of the trains launch along a magirail with a deep, vibrating hum of essence.

Magirails weren't physical. They were gigantic cords of mostly transparent essence, twisting and weaving off from the straight lines in and out of the massive stone platform ahead of us. The trains floated over the rails they were on, coasting like they repelled their rails by magnetic force.

"Do close your mouth, dear stepdaughter. You don't want to catch flies." Cymora hadn't quite wedged herself between our cart and Tormund, but she was trying.

"Yes, Stepmother," I muttered, shuttering the awed expression I had. Our group inched forward.

Tormund breathed a low growl I felt more than heard. Cymora's tone softened, as if she'd felt it too. "And perhaps you would spare this poor male's arms and walk on your own."

He blew a curl of smoke out of his mouth. "*Ach.* She weighs nothing," he practically rumbled. "I could carry her anywhere."

"Carry her to my arms?" Fal suggested.

He shook his head. "It's my turn with her."

Fal flashed a cheeky grin and responded in Serri. Tormund leaned down and whispered, "He called me…" He drifted off and glanced at the dark elf, saying a single word in Serri.

"Greedy," Fal supplied in Theli.

"Right." Tormund nuzzled into my neck and scented my skin. "He's right. I am *very* greedy for more of you."

Face flaming, I opened my mouth to reply.

"I'm sure we're all going to spend *plenty* of time together," Cymora interjected.

"I can't wait to get to know you all as my new family," Laurel added.

Fal, who had his back to them for a moment, let his smile become brittle. His sapphire cat's eyes fixed on me, and he mouthed *save me* before putting on his polite face again. "Of course! What better time than on a magirail over the Doras Sea? You haven't lived until you've felt the saltwater breeze between cars—"

Marius coughed and cleared his throat over the sound of him possibly saying, "Avoiding others."

"—and seen the sun set over the waterline," the dark elf finished.

"It sounds quite lovely. I am looking forward to the trip, and seeing Serian, of course," my stepmother said.

Fal nodded. "I suggest you brush up on your Serri. Many Unseelie do not bother to learn the tongue of the Seelie."

Stars, I needed to do that too. I wanted to at least have an idea of what the princes were saying to one another during their asides in Serri.

"I'm sure we'll get by," she said dismissively.

"Hmm." He kept smiling. "Well, I'll go buy our tickets, as promised." He strode ahead of the group to speak to a forest elf on one side of the counter in front of the station. The travelers behind us headed to the other side, where they flashed tickets and were waved on.

Call me a brat, but I wondered if we could buy more space. How popular could a train between capital cities be? Maybe we could spread out more and put Cymora in her own room.

Fal gestured for us to follow, fanning out our newly acquired tickets. I had my answer pretty soon as we wove between platforms, heading for a sleek silver train at the back of the station. It was shorter than the others by a few cars, with a nose shaped more like a needle point than a blunt triangle.

I was being stolen away by the Unseelie after all, and a little flowering bud of awe bloomed in my chest as Tormund ducked inside with me still in his arms. This was all a new experience. I kept looking around, taking in the details.

"Latecomers get the end of the train, I'm afraid," Fal said, leading us to our rooms.

The first car we passed through had several tables on either side of the main row, with savory scents lingering in the air. We ducked outside onto a metal railing wide enough for two fae standing side-by-side. The next four cars were for passengers, with six rooms per car, three to either side.

Slowly, we made our way to the fourth car, where our rooms were.

Other travelers were arranging their bags and rooms around us. More fae than I'd expected, and only about half of them Unseelie. Once we reached our car, Laurel, Marius, Tormund, and I were in the first room on the left, and Kauz, Fal, and Cymora were in the last room on the right.

"I'll get our stuff into storage," Marius said. "Grab what you want now."

He passed me the bag containing my old clothes and the pouch of money he'd snuck inside it. Tormund put me down to take a bag for himself and picked one at seemingly random for me. He checked its contents before nodding in approval.

Kauz passed me the strap to the bag he'd been carrying for me from the omega store. We stepped aside for a semiprivate moment in front of the door to my room. He unfurled the fur-lined cloak and wrapped it carefully around my wings and shoulders, securing its clasp with a twist of his fingers. "There. The evenings get chilly once we're out over the sea."

The starry galaxy in his eyes glittered as he took the edge of the cloak and brushed its softness over my cheek, resting it there with the edges of his fingertips. I tilted my head into his touch, smiling for an unguarded moment.

"See you tonight, okay?" he murmured.

"Okay." I hoped he meant in my dreams. Maybe then he'd tell me how he could appear in them.

His expression softened, and he ran his thumb down the curve of my cheek ever so slowly. He eased forward until I felt the heat of his chest nearly pressed to mine. My breath caught when I realized what he was about to do.

"Hey, are you two kissing?" Laurel asked loudly. "I don't think Mother would be very happy about that."

He and I startled apart, and his wings shifted with a rustling sound. My heart beat at twice its usual pace as I looked past her to Cymora, but my stepmother was busy lugging a pair of bags into her room.

"Certainly not, Lady Laurel." A hint of a flush darkened his purple cheeks. "It will simply be a while until I see Lark again."

She wrinkled her nose and pointed to the other room. "You're just going to be over there."

"Indeed. Farewell for now." He nodded and headed in that direction.

I sighed and turned toward where I'd left my bags, just to notice their absence. They were already in my room, delivered to one corner courtesy of either Tormund or Marius. The kelpie stood by the doorway, arms crossed and brow furrowed as he took in the setup of the furniture.

There was a small desk between two couches that had sheets peeking out from under the cushions. A metal ladder was flat against the wall above each couch, attached to a mechanism that would fold down a second bed also pressed to the wall when the ladder was pulled out. A dimly glowing essence lamp was placed in the ceiling.

Laurel brushed past me, and I teetered, nearly losing my balance. "I call this bed!" she exclaimed, heading for one of the couches.

Marius stuck out his arm to stop her, the razor edges of his fin causing her to rear backward. "No," he growled, then started pointing and naming who would be going to which bed. He and Tormund would be on bottom, while I'd be above Marius and she'd be in the other bunk.

"I guess," she said, deflating.

"For now, sit. We have to secure our things for the launch." He then left to store our extra bags.

While he was gone, I rifled through one of my bags, making sure I still had Fal's mask, Tormund's cloak piece, and Marius's kerchief. My fingers brushed the coin purse the kelpie had passed me, and it slumped over oddly. I glanced up at Laurel, who was attempting to make small talk with a disinterested Tormund, and decided she was suitably distracted. I peeked in the purse and found a squashed box underneath the weight of all the full moon coins.

I kept my hands in the bag as I pulled the top off the box and held in a gasp. There was a pair of hoop earrings inside, silver with tiny white crystals along their loops. They were no bigger around than my fingertip, dainty and pretty.

I closed the box and picked up the slip of paper that'd escaped when I'd lifted the lid. It had to be Marius's handwriting. Each word was a slanted slash in bold ink.

Saw this and thought of you. He hadn't signed his name.

I tucked it into the bag for now. I couldn't wear this gift. It would replace the tarnished silver studs I'd worn since my ears were first pierced under my dad's watchful eye. They were the last thing I had left from him.

Marius didn't strike me as a male who apologized for anything, yet the gift seemed like one. I was too nervous to ask him about the earrings when he returned to the room. I assumed this was over the insult, but it could've also been for picking me up and practically throwing me at Kauz when I needed a new suppressant tattoo.

I breathed a tired sigh. That'd only just happened earlier today. What a long day this had been.

An attendant in a tight skirt tapped on our door, saying that the launch was imminent. Dinner would be served shortly afterward if we wanted to head to the dining car once the train was leveled out. She insisted we remained seated and secured our things for the duration of the launch.

I ended up next to Marius on the couch, across from Tormund, while my stepsister pouted on the edge of her seat. My bags were wedged between my legs for now so they wouldn't go flying.

Tormund drew back the blind, revealing a rectangular window looking out at the station. "This is my favorite part," the giant told us, smiling broadly.

A vibration began below our feet, resonating through the whole train. The table, bolted to the floor as it was, rattled, along with the rest of the furniture over our heads. It increased in frequency as the train car lurched, lifting off the magirail with a groan of metal. I tensed, wings flattening to my back. The launch I'd watched looked as effortless as a bird taking flight, but it was completely different inside this car, feeling the essence shake faster and harder.

Just as it reached a pitch I could barely hear, pressure jolted through the train, and it lurched backward.

"Here we go!" Tormund whooped.

A magical force shot the train like a stone out of a slingshot, and we hit the portion of the magirail that twisted and turned, jostling us along with it. Tormund and Laurel laughed.

The car jolted fast enough to give me whiplash, and I hunkered down with a fearful whimper, shutting my eyes tight. A strong arm banded around my back, drawing me closer to the clean scent of waterlilies and mint. I hid my face in Marius's chest, calming from his smell. His solid presence kept me from getting whipped around until the train leveled out, speeding us along on an ethereal rail of magic.

13
LARK

ALL THE RATTLING in the furniture settled to a dull hum. I was protected against Marius. I snuggled closer and purred for a split second, just for him to push me away with a rumble of warning deep in his chest.

His scowl was as unfriendly as ever. *Oh, I guess he wasn't trying to comfort me...* I wilted and pressed closer to the wall to put a couple more inches between us.

Gravity tilted me back in my seat, and once I looked out the window, I saw it was no wonder. We were climbing up and away from the shadows of Ilysnor's outskirts at dizzying speed. The pinpricks of stars dotting the sky were mere smears of light.

"Finally! I've been waiting for too long," Tormund said, his hands coming together for a definitive clap. He removed a long, mostly flat box from a pocket secreted in his cloak and offered it to me over the table.

Oh, right, the gift. One of the gifts. They'd already given me a staggering number of things...but Tormund was so excited for me to open this one. His meaty hands rested on his knees, and he leaned forward, alpha fangs on display with his eager expression.

I opened the box and couldn't hold in my gasp. A silver chain necklace was nestled inside, with a small pendant shaped like a bird with two outstretched wings. Its tiny eye was a little white gemstone.

"Yes? You love?" Tormund asked.

"I do," I promised him, picking it up with reverent fingers. "Thank you, Tormund."

"Let me guess," Marius muttered. "A li'l bird for the li'l bird."

"My big brother knows me so well," Tormund said cheerfully. "You are welcome, Lark. Just wait until we get to Serian. I'm going to spoil you next."

My gaze slipped from him to my stepsister. She was wearing a look I recognized with a tickle of dread at the bottom of my stomach. That was an envious pout, her eyes narrowed on my new necklace and her fingers clenched in the fabric of her skirts.

Any time she coveted something of mine, she would inevitably receive it. I'd given up on trying to keep anything of true value after acknowledging that my stepfamily wouldn't change their ways. They took and took.

The princes, by giving, were only providing new things for Cymora and Laurel to take. I...couldn't get attached to this gift or any of the other items packed away for me, whatever they might be.

Tormund seemed to miss my inner turmoil, distracted by his belly rumbling. He slapped its curve with a laugh. "Let's go eat."

"Great idea," Laurel chirped.

"Stay right there, Lark. I'll get us a table and come back for you," he promised before heading out to do just that.

We waited well into the evening for a table, as most of the train's patrons had the same idea as us. The dining car was like a restaurant, with a short menu to order from, and we ended up at one of two curved booths with just enough room to fit all seven of us. I was wedged between Fal and Tormund in the middle of the booth. The dark elf was a buffer between Cymora and me.

The most she said in my direction was, "I hope you do everything you can to charm these noble males."

Not an order, but close. I nodded to acknowledge I'd heard her. I saw the end goal of her scheming from just that suggestion but not how she would maneuver for it yet. It soured my belly some, though I was starving. The leftovers from this morning felt like a meal enjoyed a much longer time ago.

Dinner was uneventful, with the conversation slowing over time. I must not have been the only one tiring at the end of the meal. Though the bunk bed setup seemed a little precarious, I looked forward to making as much of a nest in it as I could and resting after this.

Fal insisted on sharing a dessert first, and I pressed a little closer to his side as we considered the options. My nostrils flared, but I didn't detect even a hint of his grass and sunshine scent. He must've taken a quick bath while we'd been waiting for our table. My inner omega keened at the loss.

It's temporary and necessary, I thought. I needed to bathe with scent-blocking soap before turning in for the night as well.

Half the group left, uninterested in dessert. Fal and I settled on a slice of berry pie with a side of chilled cream, and Tormund and Laurel remained too, waiting for their own sweets. Without my stepmother around, I relaxed, smiling more openly. I could do eight days of travel if this was an example of how it'd go.

Of course, I thought this as Fal fed me spoonfuls of pie and snuck his arm around my shoulders so I'd lean against him. I fed him back, taking simple pleasure at watching his lips curl around the spoon I offered him. He watched me with a kind of intensity too, something like desire on his elfin features. His clawed fingers toyed with a lock of my hair.

Soon, we weren't eating, just gazing. A hint of mischief tugged at his lips. "Sliver for your thoughts?" he whispered.

I'd just been admiring his handsome features and noting how they differed from those of the forest elves I knew. But saying *"You are a shade of blue and gray I've never seen before"* would certainly ruin the moment, even if I also told him I liked it.

"Did Kauz draw your tattoos?" I drew a circle midair around my forehead and cheeks.

He mirrored the motion playfully, circling his ink, and nodded. "They're temporary. I'm fickle with such things. I had these done for Yule while I was performing as the Prince of Winter. They'll last another couple of months before they'll need to be touched up. Do you like them?"

"They fit you," I said.

I saw the inspiration. The Prince of Winter was a character in a common Yuletide play, a male of bitter frost who had to be convinced to let a child into his palace and out of the cold. The glowing sapphire ink looked like swirls of cold air and falling snowflakes, framing his alluring cat eyes that were nearly the same hue.

Stars, in such a short time, his Unseelie features had gone from *alarming* to *alluring*. Even without his appealing scent, I felt drawn to him.

"I should've made them silver; they'd stand out more. Alas. I have a different motif in mind for my next set."

"Oh?" I asked curiously.

He offered me another spoonful of dessert. "Feathers." This was accompanied by a wink.

"Shouldn't the li'l bird have those?" Tormund suggested, and I nearly startled. I'd forgotten he and Laurel were still sitting with us.

"Nay. I was thinking she should have a guiding star." Fal flicked one of the hanging earrings between the chains strung along his long ears. It, like the others, was an eight-pointed star with tiny, sharp points.

"That's his symbol," Tormund whispered to me behind his hand.

Fal rolled his eyes. "Thank you. I wasn't just about to tell her that."

Ignoring the edge of sarcasm in his voice, Tormund said cheerfully, "You are welcome. Mine is a knot of promise, li'l bird. You should get one of those too."

"What are the other two prince's symbols?" Laurel put in.

"You'll have to ask them," Fal answered. It was a chill response, and Laurel stiffened at it.

She finished her dessert and left in a huff. It was a relief to have her gone, even though she was in a bratty mood and I would see it again when we were stuck in our room together.

"I have a question for you, Lark," Fal said, withholding his spoon and dripping cream back onto the plate.

"Okay."

"Do you think my brothers and I are cursed?" He tilted his head toward Tormund, who laughed when he heard the question.

"Um..." I supposed we needed to talk about this sooner rather than later. "Well, you're Unseelie. So, yes?" It came out as a question, and Fal's expression creased with amusement.

"That's a common misconception for those who've never met an Unseelie," the dark elf said.

"Made up when our countries were at war," Tormund put in. "Easier to hate the other side, thinking they're all born evil."

"I don't think you're evil," I blurted. I had at first, but the more I spent time with these males, the more I'd assumed they were an exception to the stories about their kind.

They spent a few minutes explaining the origins of their bestial traits, the so-called curse born of generations of mixed breeding with the more animal-like fae that lived in Serian, like satyrs, naga, and grimalkin. It made a lot more sense that the traits were natural rather than a lineage curse once they were done.

Fal finished the meal by scraping our plate and offering me the last of the pie and melting cream before we all walked back to our car. I turned down Tormund's offer to carry me, dragging along at my own pace. I wanted more of the fresh air between the train cars. It rushed by at a rapid clip, but the ends of the cars were designed to keep it contained so travel up and down the train was safe. If it weren't dark out, we could stand at one of the railings and watch the world pass by far below us.

We bid Fal good night and found Marius stretched out on one of the couches, reading a book. His expression hardened into displeasure as he looked at us over the edge of the page he was on.

He read for leisure? That was a surprise to me. Not that I knew enough about the kelpie to jump to conclusions about how he passed his time.

Marius sat up, and we gathered to discuss an evening schedule since we'd sleep after we turned off the overhead essence lamp. To my relief, we agreed to turn in for the evening after going to the baths. There were two cars behind ours, one for hygiene, with bathrooms and laundry, and the last one for storage.

I discovered the bag packed for me had toiletries, a fluffy towel, and several changes of clothes. I took my bath and scrubbed away any hint of my scent, then helped bathe Laurel and brushed her hair, falling back into my servant role like it'd never stopped.

After we were ready for bed, I started the process of preparing my cot with only a small sigh as I eyed the ladder up and down from my bunk. It'd be much easier, with my crippled foot, to sleep on the ground bunk, but the alphas would be really cramped in the little corner of space I had between the ceiling and the too-thin mattress.

I shimmed into my new space and leaned over the edge to look at my bags a couple yards below.

"What do you need?" Marius asked, glancing up from where he was seated on his cot.

He handed up each item I wanted. First, the fleece blanket with its bold swirls of color and the oversized, fuzzy pillow from the omega store. I arranged the blanket under me as best as I could and then peeked down at him again. "And in the other bag... You can just hand it up to me."

He held it by its underside and lifted it to a height where I could rustle around in it. One of his blue brows rose when he noticed me slipping out the three items that still bore the unique scents of their original owners, but he didn't comment. Once I was settled, he snuffed out the essence lamp for the evening with a tug on its hanging cord.

I snuggled in under my new blanket, putting my arms around the fuzzy pillow and trapping the mask, kerchief, and piece of red cloth up against me. Their scents had faded some, but they wove together into a suggestion of an outdoor day. Sunshine, grass, smoky toasted mallows...all by a lakeside with waterlilies and wild mint in bloom.

It smelled perfect.

"What's that sound?" Laurel whispered in the dark.

"The best one," Tormund answered quietly.

It was coming from me, a sweet and warm omega's purr flowing from my chest steadily until I slipped into sleep.

MY REST WAS blissful darkness before it became a full-blown dream. I was back in the omega store, but this time, no one stopped me from dragging all the blankets and pillows I wanted to make an epic nest atop the mattress I'd nearly taken a nap on.

Though when I looked at how empty the huge nest was, I released a long, lonely whine. I lay down on it and sank into the comfort I'd arranged. As always, there was no one there to hold me. My eyes watered as I watched the ceiling, waiting for time to pass.

"You're not alone anymore," a male murmured.

I blinked, and he was there, standing a few feet away from the nest with his hands folded before him. "Kauz?" I asked.

"Last I checked."

I breathed out in relief and beckoned for him to join me. He took the invitation and lay down next to me, his dark wings spilling out to either side of him.

The comfort around me seemed fuzzy, and not because of its softness. But when I rested a hand on his wing's edge, he was solid. "You can still see me," he said.

"We're dreaming?" As I asked, a bit of the realism in the moment faded. I *was* dreaming and knew it.

He looked at me as if I'd hung some of the stars personally. It was the kind of expression I'd seen between mates and lovers, but this was the first time it'd been aimed at me. He shifted, pulling the wing between us behind him so he could rest on his side, then held his arms out. "Come here."

In a jump of some kind of dream logic, one moment, I was scooting toward him, and the next, he was holding me. His chest was firm muscle under what felt like a soft sleeping shirt.

"Lark," he said, nearly reverent.

I was slow to realize his affection, my response a delayed catch in my breath. It wasn't just how he looked at me. It was in his voice, his touch, and maybe even the pleasant haze over my dream.

"Kauz," I murmured back. What'd changed? I hadn't done anything to warrant such tenderness. Was he just more open in dreams?

"You are the first fae who's seen me in your dream and remembered it the next day, besides other dream wardens like me. Do you know what that means?"

I didn't know what it meant, but my curiosity piqued. "Is that your race? Dream warden?"

"Aye. I'm a dreamlander. My people are from a piece of land in Serian where the space between sleep and waking leaks into the real world," he explained. "Dreamlanders weren't originally Unseelie, but crossbreeding many generations ago with our Unseelie neighbors gave us designations and fae blood. Only those close to the royal family know that my line can walk into dreams. Ordinary dreamlanders cannot be both essence spinners *and* dream wardens."

"But you're not ordinary," I said.

A teasing smile crossed his face. "Oh, you think so? I'm flattered."

Even in a dream, I wasn't able to stop the heat of a blush. "Yes, actually."

He was an approachable face amongst his brothers, and I felt a draw to him that had nothing to do with how he smelled. Even though... I leaned forward to nuzzle against his neck, trying to pick out any scent. My nostrils flared when I found it, the same note that'd been coming in and out of my nose in a more concentrated form.

He smelled amazing and unlike anything I could put a word to. Like a feeling or a concept, but not something tangible like with his alpha brothers.

"I don't think you're ordinary either, sweetheart." Once I was done investigating his mysterious smell, he nuzzled me back and inhaled just like an alpha would.

I closed my eyes with a sigh. "Oh, I really am, though."

"Don't hide from me." He gently caught my chin between his thumb and forefinger. We were lying so close, face-to-face now, tucked together. "All the males in my line have had to accept the scent-matched omega their brothers select. Sometimes, chosen princesses aren't the dream warden's mate too. It's part of the burden of being the pack's beta."

He stroked my cheek, cupping my face as his expression softened, searching mine with a whole galaxy of stars glimmering in his gaze. "But here, in my domain, you smell like Always and the promise of eternity. The stars have blessed us. No matter what happens in the waking world, know that I am yours and would follow you anywhere. We are fated to be."

He kissed me. That was really the only way to keep me from pestering him with dozens of questions, and I melted into him like his next exhale was the breath I needed. We tangled further, wings and arms and the heat of him growing hard between us.

He tasted like he smelled. Like Always, whatever he meant by that. It was dreams and potential and something more nebulous still, like the sparkling stardust that made up his magic. I wondered if I would've tasted this if he kissed me in reality, or if it was only for the time beyond our waking hours.

Warmth lingered on my tongue as I woke abruptly, clutching my fleece blanket. I cracked my eyes open to the light of early morning warming the room and made a mewl of denial at being awake.

"I am yours." What a gentle male. Any ordinary alpha would turn it around and say *"You are mine."* Maybe it was a blessing in disguise that I'd woken when I did, else I might've told him the truth: that I wanted to be his, too.

So much for not getting too attached. It was time to acknowledge it; I was ready for the fight to come. I would scheme against my stepmother and try to become the best potential princess in the week I had before I met the Queen of Serian. Only then could I keep these princes and let myself be their omega.

14
LARK

SNORES AND SNORTS PERMEATED the other side of the room, most of them coming from Laurel, who was splayed on her side with her mouth wide open. I stirred as I caught another, lower sound and looked over the edge of my bunk.

Marius grunted and puffed on the floor, shirtless, his blue skin coated in a sheen of sweat as he performed pushups with one arm. His defined back muscles flexed, holding my admiring gaze. Males didn't get as strong as him without significant discipline and focus.

My nerves quavered as I mustered up my nerve to talk to him. *If anyone is going to be brutally honest, it'd be him,* I reminded myself.

"Marius," I whispered.

He paused before his next pushup and cracked his neck, standing with a slow roll of those muscles. He looked up at me. Most of the impatience and anger I'd seen mark his yellow eyes yesterday was absent. From this vantage, I had a straight view down at his ridged abs and the gold bars piercing his nipples. Most of the thoughts populating my mind vanished. I wanted to ask him...about how much it hurt to get those piercings? No, that wasn't it.

"What is it?" he muttered, drawing my attention back to his face. Oh, he was going straight back to being annoyed with me.

I willed myself to rally. "What do I need to do to improve?" My inner omega trembled when his gaze sharpened with predatory focus. I really should've just asked him about the piercings; that'd be a more pleasant conversation. "To...to be more like a princess? And to impress your mother?"

His answer was about as blunt as I'd expected. I retreated into my little nest to think while he finished his stationary workout.

Amongst the items the princes had gathered for the return trip was a primer on Serian's language and a blank journal for me. I pulled these items out after Laurel and Tormund woke.

We pressed the top bunks back into their places and stacked the couch cushions over the lower cots. Laurel went to eat breakfast right away, leaving me with the two princes. Marius sat to my left, closest to the door. Tormund tried to talk to him in groggy Serri. It sounded like a one-sided conversation, as the kelpie responded with the occasional low noise or grunt.

On the first page of the journal, I put a charcoal pencil to the immaculate paper and marked it with my untidy scrawl.

Things to improve on:

1. Learn Serri.

2. Guard your true self.

3. Be charming, strong, intelligent, and cunning.

4. Don't be a doormat.

To be fair to Marius, he'd only suggested the last point by saying being passive woke the aggressive instincts in alphas. The Queen of Serian was a tough female who could put most of her subjects in their place without the help of her kings. If I wanted her to approve of me as her successor, I needed to be more like her.

The other thing I'd learned about the royal pack was that the kings supplemented her. They were trained in the same roles as the princes traveling with me. The lord was her charmer. The protector was her strength. The magician was her dreamlander and guarded her sleep.

And as for cunning...she passed ideas back and forth with her comfort, as Tormund was officially titled.

But the takeaway there was *supplemented*. The kings only started where she left off. I had so far to go and so little time.

I read over the list again and blew out a sigh. I could do this, right?

Reaching over, I tapped Marius on the arm. I had my journal in hand, ready to ask him a question, when he rounded on me with his fangs bared.

"Don't *touch* me." His tone was extra deep, undercut by a growl. "Who do you think you are?"

Wings flattened to my back, I pressed as far away from him as I could go. The train's metal siding was icy cold over my back. I opened my mouth to apologize, but what emerged was a fearful whine as I crumpled in the face of his anger.

He took in my reaction, and his sudden rage vanished as he cringed. He pressed his fingertips to his chest with a gasping breath. An ominous sound emerged from across the table, akin to a growl but lower still, accompanied by an *ach*. Tormund said something else in Serri that Marius responded to, though the kelpie and I were still making eye contact. Not quite a staring match, as I had no chance in matching his dominance as an alpha. More like...awkwardness.

I bowed my head. "S-s-sorry," I mumbled to empty air as Marius turned and bolted from the room the moment I looked away.

I curled up where I sat and rode out a spike of pain in my chest. It wasn't a pre-heat cramp; I'd had plenty of those over the years. This was higher in my torso, wrapping around my racing heart and squeezing.

A bit of rejection, maybe. A taste of the agony that awaited if my scent matches found me unsuitable and mated with another omega. I bit down on my lower lip, stopping the flow of soft whimpers rolling out of me. *It's not so bad. I'll just avoid him.* Easier said than done when we were sharing the same room for eight days, but I had no better plan.

A large set of fingers entered my field of view. "It's okay. Come here, li'l bird." Tormund leaned over where Marius had been. I took his hand, and he pulled me away from the wall. It was only when I felt the heat of his skin that I realized how I'd been trembling.

I held my arms out, and he effortlessly scooped me up into his cushioned torso. He sat down, still holding me, and murmured soothing nonsense in a mix of our languages. The gentle tone of his voice mattered more than what he was actually saying.

Eventually, he replaced his words with his rich purr, and chased away my lingering fear and pain with sweeps of his giant hands. He kept his touch chaste, warming my wings, back, and arms. I clung to him for all the gentling he could provide.

"Careful. I release heat through my back." He leaned away from me when I looped an arm around him. The scratchy material of his sleeping shirt was burning hot where it pressed to his skin. I withdrew that arm and tucked both of my hands under my chin, resting my head against his chest and taking in the solid drumming of his heartbeat.

"This is like sitting next to a fire," I said. His body heat was welcome with the drafty air that circulated our room.

"You like?"

"I do. Could you..." I mustered up my nerve. He squinted at me with a curious tilt of his head. Stars, I barely knew this male, but he was an expert in making me feel more secure. "Just hold me for a while?"

He nodded and gave me a squeeze. "I'm not a fool, like a different male we know. I'll hold you for as long as you like." And he purred again now that we were done talking, lulling me into a boneless sense of peace. Though he'd washed with scent-blocking soap, he still emitted enough smoke from his back and mouth to smell halfway like his pheromones. It was soothing in its own way.

The stars had blessed me, to give me Tormund as a scent match. If only we didn't have such a steep language barrier between us. It'd be worth it to study hard, to more easily have conversations with him. Even if my conviction to have *all* the princes was damaged, Marius was just one of four. He'd change his mind...maybe. I'd cling to his kinder brother in the meantime.

I reached over to retrieve the journal and language primer. "Want to help me learn Serri?"

His smile widened to show its full, toothy charm. Those pearly whites gleamed like the dull metallic shimmer suffusing his brassy skin. "I would love to."

I smiled back shyly. *Blessed, indeed, to have a warm giant looking out for me.*

LUNCHTIME ARRIVED, and I worked through it in an empty room. Starting my learning with Tormund had given me a boost, but on my own, getting the hang of a whole new language seemed like an insurmountable task. I copied the Serri alphabet and tried to get my tongue around the painstakingly spelled-out sounds that accompanied each letter and foreign accent mark.

The way this was going, the queen would never be impressed with me and my stumbling attempts at her language. Maybe she'd laugh and I could be her court jester instead.

I was holding my face in both hands when the door opened, letting in the sound of the princes laughing and speaking Serri so effortlessly out in the hall. Tensing, I braced myself to see Marius again.

Someone wafted a baked treat under my nose. "How're you supposed to learn on an empty stomach, hmm?" Fal teased.

I peeked between my fingers. To my relief, Fal had slipped into the spot next to me, and Kauz had his wings spread across the couch on the other side of the table. The dark elf wiggled a chocolate chip-studded muffin at me enticingly while the dream warden set down two glasses, one filled with pink juice and the other with chilled water. He also placed down his box of ink, which he'd secured under one arm.

"Oh, hi," I said.

Kauz flashed a knowing smile. Our dream, the kiss—it all flashed before my mind's eye. I wondered if he was thinking about it too.

I was certainly reliving his confident declaration right before he kissed me. *"We are fated to be."* My belly filled with warm flutters.

I took the muffin and eased a little closer to Fal while I ate it. He flipped through the first couple pages in the Serri primer I'd been poring over. The alphabet practically sounded like music when he said it, before he repeated it back with the clunky pronunciations given in the primer. His shoulders shook with laughter all the while. "Is this what the Seelie think we sound like?"

Kauz chuckled. "A good thing Lark has four dedicated tutors."

"Three at best. One of us has to make sure she has fun." The dark elf glanced my way and patted his thigh, motioning for me to come over to him. I hesitated for only a moment. My inner omega would not be denied more cuddles after so long without. I scooted over, and he pulled me into his lap, scenting my neck, just to sigh. "Your soap idea is going to be the death of me, Kauzden."

He seemed to roll those starry eyes. "It's to help keep us honorable, Falindel."

Strong arms banded around my middle, brushing the sensitive edge of my top wings. Fal tucked me into the line of his body. "Not an inch to the north or south. Our etiquette tutor will be so proud."

"It's only day one. And how are you going to ensure she 'has fun'?"

Fal smacked his lips. "Such doubt on my honor. From the same male who suggested our omega might be a little touch starved?" He nuzzled my cheek, and my wings fluttered in his hold. My sudden, thrilled purr was all the answer he needed.

My next reaction was embarrassment, but then I wondered if Kauz hadn't done me a favor. I just wanted to be touched without it being treated as an oddity or a chore. Tormund had already done an excellent job at helping, but as an omega, I needed all the attention they could offer.

Before Cymora had ordered me to stop, I'd been the type of child who sought out any positive touch. Hugs, cuddles, companionable leans, squeezes... my omega instincts craved it all. Even unreciprocated hugs with the prickly mermaid were better than the nothing I'd gotten resigned to as an adult.

So, having Fal hold me tight and rest his chin atop my head was bliss. The vibrations of his voice sent a pleasurable shiver up my spine. "We're going to fix that."

"I'm watching you," Kauz remarked before his expression softened. "Would you like a memory charm for your studies, sweetheart?"

"Say yes. They're very helpful," Fal whispered.

"Yes," I said. Anything that'd help me learn their complicated language, I'd take.

I went back to work, jotting down information with my right hand while Kauz kept the left occupied. He promised he'd give me ink I wouldn't have to hide.

He pinched away the illusion I'd set on my wrist and dismissed it with a flick of his fingers.

"How'd you do that?" I asked in surprise.

"I can also make illusions."

"As an essence spinner?"

"No, it's part of my natural magic as a dream warden. What are illusions but dreams given form in our waking hours?" he said with a shrug. "You'll also be able to save some magic not having to hide your suppressant tattoo. Your essence levels seem awfully low." He looked at me curiously for an explanation I didn't give. Fulfilling Cymora's wishes had depleted my essence to a dangerous degree, and it never seemed to recover.

Kauz painted the memory charm on my wrist, and a tingling surge of his magic traced up my arm when it was completed. That ticklish feeling made its way to my scalp, and I felt smarter in a way I couldn't describe. Especially because I went back to stumbling over their language, earning a few laughs and corrections along the way.

The afternoon passed pleasantly and thus quickly. Kauz didn't let me have my arm back for hours. He stopped spinning essence but continued painting, his brushes running over my hand, wrist, and upper arm. When I stole glances at his work, all I saw was a shimmer like a heat mirage as some magic kept me from seeing what he was doing.

Fal held me the whole time, and while his hands didn't drift, as promised, his mouth did. As his brother and I were distracted by our own pursuits, he would steal a nip on my ear or a kiss on my neck. He took every opportunity to whisper Serri in my ear with his talent in making it sound a little naughty.

When it was dinnertime, Kauz stole my workbook and journal. "You'll get them back tomorrow," he said in response to my protesting mewl.

"Tonight, you're doing something else." Fal nuzzled me one last time before we headed to the dining car. I sat between Kauz and Tormund, starting to catch on that the princes were arranging some kind of rotation. Marius sat with Cymora, and I avoided looking at either of them. She spoke to him at length about Osme Fen and Laurel's pedigree.

I rested my left elbow on the table and looked at what Kauz had inked on my skin. My eyes watered, and I covered my wobbly lips with my other hand. The only way to describe it was *art*. He'd obscured the heat suppressant tattoo with a bracelet of vines, leaves, and flowers that spilled out from my wrist. A tiny hummingbird had its long beak up the bell of a flower, while mini butterflies and bees were caught mid-flight around the scene.

He'd added another, larger bird to the inside of my arm. I traced the open wings of an unusually colored lark poised to fly further toward my inner elbow. Its feathers were indigo, with starry pinpricks scattered across them. The little spots under its chin were lavender, but it had the white belly and beady little eyes of any other lark. Kauz had captured the details down to the grains of its feathers. Its feet were curled around a ribbon with a single sentence in Serri written upon it.

"Do you like it?" Kauz asked, holding himself still as I took in his work. I nodded, still teary. "If you don't, it's temporary. I can remove it if—"

I forgot Cymora and Laurel were at the table with us, flinging my arms around him for a tight hug. "I *love* it," I enthused. "You're so talented."

His murmur was in Serri as he hugged me back.

"He said—" Tormund began. Kauz interrupted with something else in Serri. "He said to tell you in private."

"Not that there is much privacy to be had around here," Cymora stated.

I caught the hint of her acidic tone bubbling to the surface and focused on Kauz. A doormat would notice her displeasure and let go of the male who'd painted her with art. I didn't want to send that kind of message to him.

Once we ate, I spent the evening with Kauz, Tormund, and Laurel. The males taught us a Serri card game, and we played a few rounds. Laurel leaned on Kauz while giving him moon eyes. "Could you tattoo something on me, too?" she asked. Even from the warm comfort of Tormund holding me again, I felt a territorial growl rising in my chest.

He withdrew the wing she was touching. "No. Not unless you're willing to pay for the ink. It's rather expensive."

My stepsister glanced at me, shock rounding her lips. He'd told her *no,* denied her something I'd already received. I saw the thoughts rolling around in her head before one clearly came to the fore.

Did he make me pay for my tattoo?

She eyed me and the colorful ink on my arm. The question was poised on her tongue. Laurel always got to be the brat in our family, poking and prodding in ways that'd get me lashed. But she had some self-awareness, apparently, as she let it go and focused on her hand of cards in an attempt to win the complicated game we were trying to play.

She lost again. So did I, even more spectacularly, but it was a fun distraction. Kauz eventually left to trade places with Marius so they could rest in their own cots.

I fell asleep with ease, but as pleasant as my dreams were, I didn't think the dream warden visited them.

THE NEXT THREE days passed in much the same way. Every morning, first thing, I limped past Marius to cuddle Tormund and soak in his warmth and resonant purr. Enjoying the giant's cheeriness was the best way to start every day. He told me stories, practicing his Theli, especially when one of his brothers was around to help translate a word or two.

I studied and spent time with one or two of the princes on a rotation. I endured two afternoons with Cymora, who gave me no direct orders in the presence of the princes, though I could tell she was chafing more and more at their constant presence.

She also wasn't sleeping well. By day four, purplish bruises were appearing in the hollows under her unhappy eyes. They grew more displeased each time she saw me having fun with the Unseelie males. We saw each other in the baths, and while she was short with me and had me arrange her hair, groom her nails, and apply her makeup, her only direct orders were to hear how "wooing" the princes was going.

She coached Laurel on how to win over Marius first, as their foot in the door to Pack Sorles. Both mermaids had noticed how I avoided him.

He'd shown no signs of thawing toward me. Though, occasionally, when we were in the same room, the hair on the back of my neck would lift. I'd look up from what I was doing to see the kelpie watching me. The intensity in his expression would be softened by something like longing.

I didn't know what was going on with him. He didn't do much talking, and his brothers seemed unconcerned by his behavior. But he wasn't interested in me like the other princes were; that was clear.

I sympathized with him more as the trip went on. The hours grew longer for no particular reason. I was rarely alone in any space, including the baths. What I wouldn't give for the privacy to read a book in peace, too.

He thumbed through his while I studied in the afternoon, making the occasional reaction. Usually an amused puff of air, the closest thing he uttered to a laugh.

"What are you reading?" Laurel asked.

"A war memoir," he answered.

"Oh." She considered for a few moments. "What's a memoir?"

He ignored her. Thus began her clumsy attempts to woo him, in accordance with Cymora's directions. "Hey, Marius," she would begin. The kelpie's snorts of annoyance were only getting louder with each interruption of his reading time.

Tormund, who was passing the time with a book of poetry, chuckled under his breath. He wore a new addition today, a tiny pair of reading spectacles that stopped him from squinting at the words. He also had me in a cuddle and snuggled me tighter to his chest. "Better him than me," he murmured. I nodded in agreement, trying not to pay attention to those two.

Marius eventually snarled and left the room. My stepsister looked... genuinely upset. That was not the face of a girl just following directions. She made up an excuse to follow him about five minutes later. I watched and shook my head, hoping my first thought was just a wild guess. Laurel wasn't actually developing a crush on him, was she?

She came back with a pout a little later. "He's reading in the hall and wants to be alone. Can you believe it?"

Oh stars. She does have a crush.

Nothing about this was going to end well.

15
LARK

I HAD A CRUSH, too. Three of them, to be exact.

I think they liked me back, even though the shadow of their mother loomed overhead. They didn't allow one male to be alone with me. And when Cymora and Laurel ended up rotating to my room together, the male beside me was a scowling Marius.

It made every interaction a touch awkward when they'd check each other's behavior at the first sign of slipping. Not that we didn't all slip at one point or another. My body wove in and out of the first stages of pre-heat with Kauz restoring my suppressant tattoo as often as he could. With my heat as tightly bound as it was, I couldn't blame the hollow longing in my gut on anything but my own feelings.

I noticed every time Tormund hesitated, his fingertips drifting lower on my belly before returning to the safe band around my middle that was not an inch too far to the north or south. He never tired of cuddles, though, and eased my yearnings to be touched and gentled one caress at a time.

When Kauz tilted my head up in the hall one evening, a tremble of restraint and frustration creased his expression right before he pressed his lips to my forehead. He said the Serri phrase inked on my wrist, in the ribbon the purple bird carried. None of the princes would tell me what it meant or what kind of bird Kauz had drawn, and I was itching to find out.

Fal would always note who was in a room with us before keeping any touch chaste. He implied he wanted time alone with me, but it never happened. And as for Marius, well, we were good at avoiding one another.

I missed their scents. Sleep didn't come so easy now that the tokens I had from the alphas had mostly lost their scent. Kauz hadn't returned to my dreams, either, where we could kiss without consequences. Three interested males and zero kisses... It was disappointing.

Even though I knew why it was all happening, it didn't feel great. The foxes were guarding the henhouse most efficiently despite the initial concern about us spending eight days in this train together.

Cracks showed in our routine by day five. Marius looked at the open pages of his book like he was going to harm someone if he heard "Hey, Marius" one more time from Laurel. Fal hadn't settled this afternoon, pacing the limited space in the room and eventually out in the hall.

Laurel had asked me to brush out her hair, which I was doing when Fal returned. He took one look at Marius and said something in Serri that had the kelpie snarling at him. Fal bared his teeth back with a growl.

I'd come along enough in my studies to string basic Serri phrases together, but I didn't know what they were about to fight over except there was a lot of "fuck" being thrown around. In Serri, it was *"foc,"* a snappy replacement I'd picked up on after they switched languages enough to mask the curse.

I stopped mid-brushing with a whimper, terrified of alpha anger, especially when it was between the princes. Marius stood, spiking the aggression in the room when they were nose to nose. The dark elf's athletic frame seemed small this close to his brother. Marius had a couple inches on him and the bulk of muscle. I thought they'd really come to blows, and I feared for Fal.

With a dismissive snort, Marius left the room. Fal settled on the couch across from us, his muscles still tensed.

"What was that about?" Laurel asked. She was just as wide-eyed as I was.

"He was in my seat." Fal's usual measured voice was much deeper with a growl underlying it.

It seemed like a lot more than that, but he wasn't in the mood to explain further. He took us in while I worked the brush through a knot in Laurel's hair. "I didn't realize you required special assistance," he commented toward her.

"This is her job," Laurel said.

Fal's lips thinned. "What *job*?" He was clearly still pissed off and narrowing in on a new target to take it out on.

Some of her self-preservation instincts kicked in, and she stammered, "Uh, in our family...she picked up what the help used to do after we fell on hard times and had to dismiss them all. She likes it. Right, Lark?"

I didn't answer, too nervous in the presence of an angry alpha. He stood, snatched the hairbrush from my hand, and shoved it into Laurel's chest. "Let's cut this off at the quick. My lady is not your servant. Your hands work just fine, so brush your own starsdamned hair."

She staggered back into me. "You can't talk to me like that," she said in a low, teary voice.

Oh no. She was going to run to Cymora, and then I'd have a serious problem. "It was no bother," I put in. "We were bonding."

He wore an unimpressed expression, which didn't change a flicker to acknowledge me. "Laurel, I need you to leave. Right now." Fal mustered a tight smile. "I want a few minutes with my omega. Could you find somewhere else to be?"

"I...I guess so," she said with the beginnings of a serious pout.

"I'm glad you understand." He gestured for her to go, and she fled. The door closed behind her with a clatter. I wondered how long it would take for my stepmother to hear about this short conversation, exaggerated to make Laurel look as innocent as possible.

When Fal held his hand out, I flinched and inched away from him. There wasn't far to go before my wings brushed against the opposite wall.

"Come here, please." He offered both hands now, palms out. "I'm sorry. I'm not angry at you... I'm angry *for* you. The nerve of that girl, and her insufferable mother too. And add on to that something Marius did that I noticed earlier today. I'm about to lose my mind if I have to be stuck in here with all of them without saying something."

He softened his stance and I put my hands in his, letting him tug me toward him. He rested his forehead against mine; I breathed out and relaxed as he started to purr. The sound was pleasant, if shaky at first.

I offered a little smile to show I was okay. Maybe better than okay. It sounded like he was trying to protect me, and having an alpha stand up for me was new.

"You purr like an omega," I noted. Where Tormund rumbled loudly with his alpha purr, Fal sawed in and out with a more subtle vibration.

He choked on the noise and took a moment to clear his throat. "No. Like a grimalkin." Pointing at one of his slit-pupiled eyes, he clarified, "As in, I'm part cat fae, thanks to my grandfather. I can't believe this hasn't come up sooner."

"Oh, of course. It's nice." I said this hoping he'd purr again, which he did with a playful slant to his lips.

He soothed me for a while, until eventually he let the thrumming taper off and said, "I can tolerate a lot of things from my family, but this is not one of them." He took my journal and flipped back to the first page. His finger came down on the fourth line hard enough to embed his claw tip in the paper. "He will not speak to you like this."

4. Don't be a doormat.

"He didn't," I said, eyes widening. "I asked him for advice and paraphrased what he said."

"He admitted he called you this earlier," he growled. "Don't make excuses for him. It's bad enough that he's more interested in that stars-damned book than the beautiful omega sitting next to him."

He took my thoughts straight off the rail they'd been on. My wings fluttered happily. He thought I was beautiful. He'd said it with full conviction.

"Not to mention how you practically hurt yourself to get away from him," he added. "Tormund told me about what he did. We're going to fix him. Today."

We were? My lips and brow pulled into a dubious look.

He reached over to pick up my charcoal pencil. "And before you say anything, I'm not overreacting. I'm tired of his..." He circled his hand for a moment and then gave up. "I'm so tired of his shit."

I snorted a laugh before I could muffle it behind a hand, surprised that this was what broke the barrier of polite speech between us. He smiled at my reaction before turning the pencil on my list and writing underneath it. "Not that I was privy to this particular conversation, but I assume it had to do with meeting my mother. Here is what you should work on."

He turned the page so I could see what he'd written in an overly elegant, looping script.

New steps:

1. Learn Serri.

2. Be yourself.

Everything else, we can teach you.

"Contrary to what my raincloud of a younger brother thinks, I *know* our mother is going to love you." Fal drifted his knuckles down my cheek. "Wholly because she's going to see that we adore you."

My breath caught. "You do?"

"Our whole pack bond lights up brighter than a Yuletide bonfire when you're around." His touch trailed to my neck, encircling its column gently to guide me as he leaned forward. "Can't wait to feel how jealous this makes them."

If I thought my surprise kiss with him had been amazing, it was nothing compared to the one he led me into. It tasted like sunny, grassy days, bursting into my mouth like drinking from a stream of pure joy after a long drought. I threaded my fingers into his silky blue-black hair, holding on to him for more. Our tongues brushed and swept in a tender dance, then his fangs caught my lower lip and tugged just right.

His growl rippled through me as his fingers closed around my hips. Tipping backward, he pulled me down with him onto the nearest couch. I naturally settled in his lap with my thighs spread to either side of his legs. I liked that he was just as turned on by my taste as I was by his, as he ground a growing bulge in his pants against the needy ache rising in my pussy.

The door flung open, and in prowled Marius. Fal slowed and parted from me with an impish smile on his kiss-swollen lips.

Oh stars, was this what we were going to do to "fix" Marius?

"I can't trust you with her *at all*, can I?" the kelpie demanded.

"You came back awfully fast," Fal teased. He licked up my neck with a rumble that had me clenching my thighs. "It's okay to want a taste too."

Marius loomed over us, crossing his arms. "Don't forget we're stuck here for three more days. If I decide to chase you, you have nowhere to run."

"Hmm." Seeming unconcerned, Fal dragged his fangs ever so slowly down the path he'd laved. I moaned, tilting my head for more. "Why don't you show her the benefits of the famed kelpie loyalty instead?"

"You know I can't." Marius's answer sounded hoarse.

"Still in denial, then." The dark elf tsked. "I don't understand why you're being so stubborn about this."

Marius answered in Serri.

Fal spoke in Theli without missing a beat. "Nay. This concerns her, so she will hear it. We've found our mate, Mar. If she's mine, she's yours. And she's right here." His feline gaze flashed from his brother back to me, and his eyelids fell in a smoldering look.

I didn't dare glance up at the kelpie, too afraid of what he'd say next. What I expected was another, more vicious rejection. Fal nibbled on the edge of my collarbone and ran his hands over the curve of my waist. I focused on him instead, hoping for another kiss.

The dark elf leaned in, and air flowed over my skin as he scented me. His low rumble was all alpha. I was slick, my core clenching on air as my pre-heat threatened to return with a vengeance. I inhaled too, smelling warm sunshine cutting through the scent-blocking soap.

The dark elf took hold of my chin, gently turning my head. "Look at him, li'l omega," he whispered in my ear. "If I can smell your arousal, he can too."

Marius watched us with his fists clenched at his sides and heat blazing in his dilated eyes. I'd seen that expression before, when he'd nearly pinned me to a pawn shop's display. "Stop. You have no idea what you're doing." His voice was roughened into a rusty growl.

My eyes widened. After the last few days...*this* was how he felt? I thought he couldn't stand me.

"He desires you too. He just doesn't want to admit it. All the self-control of the protector heir mixed in with the anxiety of an unmated kelpie. How very...tedious," Fal continued. His lips dragged to my earlobe, tongue teasing and flicking the stud I wore.

My breath came in uneven shudders, a needy mewl rising in my chest. I was so flushed with longing and yet paralyzed with indecision. We couldn't do this, right? They had to leave me untouched. No matter how much I wanted more as he teased the kelpie and me both. Each soft noise he wrung from me increased the tension in Marius's body another notch. He would snap at any second.

Fal's other hand found the apex of my thighs and rubbed circles over the fabric covering where I needed him most. "Strip all that aside, and he wants you just as badly as I do. Don't you, Marius?" he challenged.

The kelpie's face warred between temptation and steely determination before the latter won. "Stop fucking around."

Fal stilled his hand and withdrew his fingers. He gave my thigh a pat. "You notice he didn't deny it," he whispered to me.

"You notice he's just toying with us both," Marius echoed.

The dark elf smirked at him. "Someone has to tell her the truth about you. Here's a novel idea. Talk to her. Tell her why you're terrified of what you might feel if you two touch. If you don't do it soon, I will." Fal cupped my cheek and delivered one last kiss, swift and breathtaking.

"Terrified." The kelpie's echo was low and dangerous, practically radiating alpha fury. "I will show you—"

"No, you won't," Fal interrupted, his tone turned cutting. He disentangled from me with care. When he rose to his feet, he subtly adjusted the front of his pants before going nose to nose with Marius for a second time today. "Who do you think you are? Consider the feelings of someone other than yourself for once. You're ruining this for all of us."

I was no longer worried for the dark elf. Despite his smaller build, both of the males postured as if Fal was the more dominant alpha, with him leaning in, clawed finger poking Marius's chest. "Get your shit together. That's an order from your pack lead."

"Aye, pack lead," the kelpie answered through gritted teeth. Though he was forced to lean back, his expression was twisted with ire.

"I'll leave you to it, then." Fal blew me a kiss with an elaborate flourish of his hand before he left the room.

Silence followed in his wake, hanging thick in the air. Marius sat on the couch across from me. His gaze became unfocused, his pupils slowly retracting back to normal. I had to wonder if he was reeling from that conversation, because I certainly was, and I hadn't even been on the receiving end.

"Are you all right?" I finally asked. That look on his face was becoming unnerving.

He sighed heavily and shook out his mane of hair. "Despite the show, Fal doesn't know the first thing about kelpie loyalty," he muttered. "Surely you know the stories. My kind bond with our mates very deeply. Our loyalty is our most sought-after trait."

"Have you already bonded?" I could barely breathe. It would explain so much about him.

"No. It's not..." He clenched his eyes closed, forcing out his words. "I'm not bonded. I had... Well, I thought I had someone, once."

"Oh, I'm sorry."

"Don't be. She's dead." His forbidding tone drew a flinch from me. He'd slammed closed that window of insight before I caught more than a glimmer of understanding. "When it comes to a potential mate, every other female I've met so far has been unsuitable."

"You think I'm unsuitable too," I said with a sinking feeling of dread and understanding.

He didn't answer for long enough that I wondered if he hadn't heard me. When he opened his eyes, he had the focused, predatory look that made my instincts quake. "You are half my size and a fraction of my strength," he said in a low growl. "How are we to mate when you're so tiny and frail?"

"We're still scent matches." A puzzling fact, since he was right. He was a big male compared to me. But his giant of a brother was even larger, and I'd never had a problem seeing him as a potential mate.

"Besides, if my mother decides you are not tough enough to be her heir..." This felt like a change of subject he was forcing, sidestepping any talk of our scent matched compatibility. "If even one of us bonds with you, the rejection will be messy for all five of us."

"I understand. The pain would be immense."

"What do you know of pain?" he muttered. I loosed a little growl, a defensive comment on my tongue. But it seemed that was a remark he didn't mean for me to hear, as he continued more clearly, "If it happens, the four of us must decide whether to remain together as Pack Sorles and rule one day with a different omega or to leave the royal family to mate with you. There's a good chance my pack gets torn apart. Everything I—we—have trained for will have been for nothing."

My omega instincts told me to put my offense aside. Forget his behavior; he was masking something else underneath it.

My alpha is in distress.

Stars, I hoped my instincts were right about this one. I sucked in a steadying breath and got to my feet. My heart flipped in my chest, beating harder the closer I came to Marius. He stiffened, leaning back when I eased onto his leg and pressed myself against his chest.

This was exactly what he'd told me not to do. But he didn't push me away or snarl or use all that considerable muscle and bulk to intimidate me. All he did was whisper, "What are you doing?"

I forced a purr, throaty and high at first. Trying to soothe an immovable wall of muscle was harder than I thought it'd be. But I was going to comfort him; he needed it. "It'll be okay." If I said it confidently enough, I had to believe it too. "It's fate. What will be will be."

He scoffed. "Fate. If such a force were real, it has been too cruel to earn my trust." He traced the ridge of the scar crossing his face.

Okay, so I'd found the one fae who didn't feel secure in fate's guiding hand. "Your pack will remain intact," I promised instead, though fear quivered in my belly at what awaited me if I had to return to Osme Fen. "If the Queen of Serian finds me unsuitable, I'll leave. I wouldn't ask any of you to give up everything because of me."

His growl rippled over my skin, and I shivered at the sensation. "It's not your choice, li'l omega."

"I guess not," I conceded. There wasn't a lot that *was* my choice from here. Until my heat overwhelmed me and my omega mark manifested, no pack could claim me with their bites and their mark between my brows. I gave a hollow little laugh, no humor there. "What's life without a little uncertainty?"

His frown deepened, a line forming through his own pack mark. My breath caught as he tucked me into a hug and curled his body around mine, even angling so his back was pointed toward the door. Like he would shield me from whatever could walk in on us.

"Marius—"

"Shh."

He hid his face in my hair and took a deep inhale. I couldn't hush completely, as a new purr vibrated from me at just how protected I felt while he held me like this. He nuzzled just behind my ear and listened. Tension eased from him on a long sigh.

We stayed like this for far longer than I thought he had the patience for. I soaked in his solid presence and what comfort he was willing to provide. This was safety, a feeling I'd chased since I was just a kid. This unpredictable male had no idea how much I'd longed for it.

When he broke the silence, it was a mere murmur in my ear. "I'm a danger to you, broken in half on the inside. It would be for the best if you stayed away from me."

My purr faded as I considered what he was trying to say. "What do you feel?"

He made a sound somewhere between a growl and a confused grunt.

"We're touching. What do you feel?" I repeated.

"Something I don't have the words for, li'l omega."

He straightened but still didn't push me away. Instead, he lifted his fingers and halted them a couple inches from my face, as if he wasn't sure what to do. I leaned into his hand in encouragement.

The texture of his fingertips skimmed my cheek, and I blinked at the unfamiliar rasp of his calluses. He withdrew his touch, and I nearly whined. "They make this look so easy," he muttered.

Determination creased his face, and he resumed his efforts. He tried stroking my hair and neck, then his fingertips sank to my wing. Those same calluses felt amazing against the sensitive membrane.

Laurel walked in, saw me in his lap, and made an ugly face of jealousy. I stiffened, and the kelpie stopped touching me, glancing toward her with a low sound, like something an animal would make. Fal popped his head through the threshold before she could leave again, grinning when he spotted where I was.

"I got my shit together, pack lead," Marius growled.

The dark elf continued to beam. "Finally. In the meantime, I promised the lady a game after she gave us so much privacy. No, don't move, Lark. It's a team game, and Marius is actually good at this one."

The kelpie scowled, muttering under his breath, "He's such an asshole."

THE NEXT MORNING, I worked on a writing lesson from the Serri primer. I wasn't pressed against the wall while sitting next to Marius, so that had to amount to some progress between us. It seemed he couldn't avoid correcting me, though, stealing the pencil from my hand a few times to modify mistakes and apply accent marks in their proper places. He slid the journal back and forth, writing with his left hand while I sat on his right side.

He was mid-explanation when Laurel came in, fresh from a bath, and pulled out her first "Hey, Marius" of the day while she sat down next to Tormund. The giant's nostrils flared, and his face scrunched like he smelled something rancid.

"Aye?" the kelpie grumbled. He was reacting the same way as Tormund. I didn't smell her quite as quickly, but her clean skin carried notes of...

Oh, that was *my* scent. Kind of. She'd applied the jelly and perfume spray the apothecary had created from my pheromones. I sure hoped they were reacting to its chemical undertones.

"Good morning." She hit a melodic note like only a mermaid could and smiled sweetly at him.

Unimpressed, Marius released a kelpie's snort and turned back to me. He resumed his explanation of Serri verb tenses and the relevant accent marks.

Laurel canted her lips to the side and bid Tormund a good morning next, a little less musically. He nodded and adjusted his reading spectacles, hardly looking up from his poetry book. When she was around, he pretended he didn't understand Theli much at all to keep their conversations shallow to nonexistent. In reality, he'd gotten his own memory charm from Kauz and was slowly lightening his brogue as he practiced his Theli in idle moments.

I was in the midst of asking for clarification when she interrupted. "Hey, Marius."

His teeth ground together before he responded with a flat, "What?"

"How did you get that scar on your face?"

Oh stars. Talk about a lack of tact.

"Training accident," he answered shortly.

A few moments passed before Laurel asked, "Like, what kind of training accident?"

"That's not your business." A noticeable growl had entered his voice.

Her full lips framed a pout. "I'm just curious."

He ignored her and gave me the pencil to continue the lesson. I'd forgotten my question after witnessing that exchange, so I sipped from a mug of tea to wake myself up more and filled the rest of the page with my unsteady script.

Marius took a moment to inspect my work. "Good job," he said in Serri.

"Thank you. I'm working hard," I said in kind.

At least, that's what I wanted to say. By the way he chuckled, it may have gone awry. "Cute accent," he remarked, switching back to Theli.

"You too." Though all four of the princes sounded attractive rather than cute with theirs, in my opinion.

I turned the page to see another writing exercise and sighed, getting back to it. He had the pencil again and was correcting my work ten minutes later when Laurel said, "Hey, Marius."

"I'm busy."

"I just want to talk."

"No."

"Won't you tell me the story about your scar?"

There was a brittle *snap* as his fingers clenched on the pencil. He turned a look of wrath on her, so potent I cringed away, and stared for long enough that she squirmed.

"You," he finally said from between his teeth, "*stink*. Why don't you go bathe that foul concoction off rather than pester me?"

"You think Lark stinks?" She asked this with her full bratty entitlement. But as Marius snarled and Tormund loosed a low, furious growl, her smug expression turned into instant distress.

"She smells amazing. As a scent match should," Tormund put in.

"And natural, unlike you." Marius kept his fangs bared as he motioned toward the door. "Leave. And bring back whatever fake scent you're wearing so Tormund can burn it."

"Fine. So rude," she muttered, getting up and slamming the door behind her. I could still hear her stomping footfalls in the hall. It was gratifying, for a moment, that they thought the recreation of my pheromones was that terrible.

But then sinking dread wormed inside my belly. I knew where she was going, and it wasn't to take another bath.

"That girl, she likes you," Tormund remarked.

The kelpie's ear flicked in annoyance. "I know. It's ridiculous."

"Maybe not anymore. She called him rude," I said. That was usually the prelude to her running to Cymora to make the situation right. *Again*. Now my stepmother would undoubtedly hear about Fal, Marius, and maybe even Tormund. I didn't doubt that it'd been Cymora's idea for Laurel to wear the fake pheromones.

"She's the rude one," the giant said, shrugging. "Coming in here wearing your scent, but fake. *Ach*. And it's not our fault she doesn't want to learn with you. She didn't bring a book or anything else instead."

"She doesn't read."

"Mortifying." Marius tapped the page to suggest I return to my studies. He fished out a new pencil from somewhere to replace the one he'd broken. Tormund settled in, content to listen to us and say the occasional word or phrase in Serri for me.

With the memory charm inked on my skin, I was retaining what I'd learned well enough to make simple conversations. I wouldn't be completely flatfooted in Neslune, unlike my stepfamily when they realized they couldn't get by on finding Unseelie who spoke Theli.

We spent another hour at this before Tormund's belly started to grumble. "Lunchtime," he announced. "I'll bring you something, li'l bird?"

I patted my belly, considering. Usually, I could get by on a nibble or two, but today I was feeling hungrier than usual. "Maybe a sandwich. I'll come with you—"

"No, it's no trouble," he interrupted quickly. "Don't bother your foot any worse."

Marius stood with a sigh. "I suppose I'll go with him to make sure he doesn't bring you one of every sandwich they offer."

"Thank you."

They left, and I considered returning to my nest. I'd been working hard, so maybe a nap was in order. It'd be pleasant to wake up to the smell of whatever kind of sandwich Tormund decided to bring.

I stood and pulled on the ladder, easing my bunk down from the wall. I was just fitting my foot in the bottom rung when Cymora walked in, followed by Laurel and her cloud of fake pheromones. "Lock the door," my stepmother said.

"Okay," Laurel said, sniffing. She still sounded teary. I made a face at the wall, imagining she'd been forcing herself to cry for the hour or so she'd been gone from the room.

Now I was stuck in here with them. I should've expected this to happen. Lunch was the only time I really had to myself, and they were bound to notice and take advantage. I eyed my distance from the door, calculating if I could get it unlocked and stumble into the hall before Cymora ordered me to come back inside and sit down.

I'd probably just get myself hurt and drag out whatever punishment she already had planned. Laurel's tears usually became mine, and I knew being on a train to Serian didn't mean there were any exceptions made to the unspoken rules of my life. I bowed my head, hoping my stepmother made this quick.

"So, you think you're someone, hmm, now that you're the whore for a pack of princes?" Cymora sneered. "It seems you've forgotten your place. Let me remind you what we do to servants who disrespect their betters."

16

LARK

When I was younger, I used to argue with Cymora's statements. I'd thought I wouldn't need to be punished if I just proved to her that I didn't actually say or think the things she accused me of.

But I'd learned since then. She was justifying her view of events out loud. Arguing only deemed me "combative" and made the pain to come that much worse. The best thing I could do was hunker down and take it. So, I didn't tell her that I wasn't a whore and hadn't disrespected Laurel. I didn't reply at all.

"Laurel tells me you're nesting," Cymora stated. I tensed, waiting for the order to come. "Throw everything in your nest out."

"Yes, Stepmother." I climbed the rungs up to my bunk ever so slowly and tossed down my fur-lined cloak first. I was using it as an extra layer to ward off the early morning chill that seeped in from outside. Next went the fleece blanket and the fuzzy pillow I snuggled at night.

Marius's kerchief fell next, then the bright streak of color from Tormund's cloak piece, and finally a glitter of gems as Fal's mask sailed after them. This was all Cymora wanted to see, my comfort items, but I fulfilled the whole order and tossed out the pillow and blanket that'd already been here.

"They gave all this to you? Such comfort for the omega," she cooed.

I climbed down the ladder and watched Cymora nudge items aside with the tip of her shoe. My palms were clammy already, nerves churning as she took her time looking at it all.

I'm going to lose these things. Telling myself what was to come sometimes helped. Back home, I was allowed a couple of blankets and a pillow, no more than any other fae. I'd trained myself to accept it, as nests led to the heat cycle and succumbing to it meant a trap with a trio of males who would then own me.

I knew I shouldn't have gotten attached. I *knew* I couldn't keep these things for very long. From the moment Kauz started buying, I'd thought about what my stepfamily would do with the gifts. My eyes still watered. In finding value in these things, I had given Cymora power.

"Fold it all up and stack it neatly," she ordered.

"Yes, Stepmother," I murmured. I knelt and started with the blankets. While I folded, Cymora put the bunk back into its place against the wall.

Laurel stood over me, watching with her arms crossed. Our eyes met, and I pleaded with her silently, softening my expression. I'd ask the princes to be nicer, to include her more rather than treat her presence like a burden. I *was* sorry.

My stepsister's lips pressed together, and she slid her gaze away from mine. Through the fake pheromones she wore, I caught a whiff of sour shame haloing her.

Cymora made an impatient gesture when I finished my task and remained kneeling by the neat stack of bedding I'd made. "Bring all that. Let's go," she stated.

"Yes, Stepmother." I didn't hold in my resigned sigh, and in response, she tripped my bad foot, sending me sprawling. I released a choked scream as agony coursed up my leg.

"Smile," she barked. "Be happy. You did this to yourself, so you have no reason to act moody."

"Y-yes," I managed through a grimace forced upon my face. She hadn't quite realized she couldn't order me to feel differently about a situation than I already did, but I could be made to look happy through most pains. I gathered up the items that'd scattered when I fell and limped after her and Laurel.

They looked both ways up and down the hall before gesturing me onward. We went through the bathing car and stepped out onto the last observation platform easily accessible without an attendant's help. The storage car was usually locked, requiring a staff member to be present to deter thievery. Wind shrieked beyond the platform. We stood under an arc of metal that protected us from the worst of it.

I gulped a swallow even while wearing a forced smile. The sweat on my palms soaked into the fleece blanket at the bottom of the pile I held.

"Layer an illusion over the window to make it look like no one is out here," Cymora ordered.

"Yes, Stepmother." I turned toward the door leading back into the bathing car and considered the window. They were almost as tricky as mirrors, reflecting light at odd angles depending on the time of day and the cleanliness of the glass. To use the least amount of essence possible, I frosted the window with a layer of icy mist.

"Good enough. Now stand right here." Cymora indicated the middle of the platform.

I went to where she'd pointed, looking out over the sea. It was a dizzying distance below, any waves or disturbances on its surface smoothed to a glasslike finish. "Yes, Stepmother... *Please.*" I felt like I was a teenager again, hopeful that she would simply stop if I was contrite enough. "Please, don't do this. Let me show my regret. I can make things right."

Ignoring me, Cymora lifted most of the stacked items from my hands, leaving the fleece blanket on the bottom resting atop my palms. "Tell me what this means to you."

"It was a gift from Prince Kauzden," I answered. New tears sprung to my eyes. "He saw that I loved how it felt and bought it for me to nest with."

"Oh, *very* sweet," she said in a cloying tone.

I turned toward her, but the plea on my tongue shriveled to nothing at the malice I saw reflecting back at me. Nothing I could say would deter her from the next order. Like every other punishment, it was as inevitable as my next breath. I could either let it happen or have it shoved down my throat.

With a smile of pure glee, Cymora ordered, "Drop it into the sea."

For a moment, my fingers tightened around the soft fabric. I wanted to scream, to wail. *No, it's mine!* But all that'd accomplish would be her further satisfaction. I was always going to lose this blanket. If not now, then tomorrow or later, whenever Cymora decided I needed to be put in my place. Fighting only made it worse.

I lifted the blanket past the safety rail and let go of it, watching it unfurl like a multi-colored sail on its way down, pinwheeling to its inevitable saltwater demise. A single droplet fell from my cheek to join it down below.

The train-assigned blanket and pillow followed it. "Don't need this or this..." Cymora muttered. She handed me the fuzzy pillow, and we restarted the process. I told her about the gift and where it came from and was forced to release it off the side of the railing.

"Prince Kauzden is going to be so disappointed you threw his gifts in the sea," Laurel giggled as it became a speck behind us.

Cymora smirked. "Like he's even going to notice."

My belly hollowed out. The princes had no reason to notice my nest, so it probably would go overlooked once she ordered me to keep this punishment a secret. All I had to look forward to for the next couple nights was a bare mattress.

"All right, what's all this?" With my cloak thrown over one of her arms, she was inspecting the three tokens I'd collected.

"They have the alpha's scents. A kerchief from Marius," I began. She handed it to me and ordered me to throw it away. "Part of the cloak Tormund was wearing when we met." It went flying next. "And...the mask Fal was wearing at the Omega Masquerade."

Cymora tilted it, letting the light glitter off its encrusted gems. "No, I'm keeping this," she muttered, pocketing it. "You know what's been the most offensive thing to me, Lark?"

I held my tongue, sucking down heaving breaths. My nest was gone, and the last of the alphas' scents too until they stopped using the scent-blocking soap. Even with my stepfamily out here with me, I'd never felt so alone.

She answered her own question with a sneer. "What you've been wearing, these clothes the princes bought for you. Like your old dresses weren't enough. I've kept the peace while you've frolicked and pretended you're good enough to join their pack. Like *you* could ever be a princess." She and Laurel's melodious mermaid voices harmonized their mocking laughter.

She shook out the cloak, admiring its snowy fur lining. "Someday, another will wear this, if I allow you to keep it," she mused, mostly to herself. "On your knees, Lark."

"Yes, Stepmother." I held on to the railing as I went down, my whole body trembling with the vibrations of the train.

I shook with nerves too, knowing one nudge would send me over the edge of the platform and to my certain death. I didn't have enough essence to fly back to the train or to the closest section of dry land. I'd either die upon impact with the water or drown shortly after from exhaustion. Such a death might be a mercy compared to what my stepfamily had planned for me.

Cymora stood over me, her eyes flashing. Scheming, always scheming. Her gaze was on me kneeling on the platform, my body swaying with each jostle that ran through the train. A hint of white teeth met her lip as her attention turned to the sea below us. She considered the deadly drop with a thoughtful tilt of her head before making the same hum she always did when she decided against something.

A little spark flared in my chest. *The princes would miss me.* If I only endured a little longer, I would see them again. Like Kauz kept telling me, I was not alone anymore.

She can't have what she wants if I die now. I was sure that she'd seek to fool the princes later by ordering me to illusion Laurel as myself. If they bit her mark, that was it. Cymora would have a princess for a daughter and access to endless wealth, plus a royal pardon for her crimes, courtesy of Laurel. What else could she possibly want from them?

She stuck her leg out. "You know what to do," she said.

Yes, I did. She wanted to know that her punishment worked, that I was hers forevermore. I lowered myself further, until my lips pressed to the top of her shoe. Then I said what I thought she wanted to hear. "I'm sorry, Stepmother. I have remembered my place as your servant and ever-dedicated stepchild. I won't disrespect you or Laurel again."

"Very good," Cymora said. "You will not say a word of this to the princes."

"Yes, Stepmother."

"Hand me your necklace."

My fingers flew to the little silver bird charm. Tormund's gift. *No, not this too!* My omega instincts wailed in my head.

It was an order, though. I unlatched it and placed it in her waiting palm. She gave it to Laurel. "It's probably from one of the princes. You should hide it until we deem it safe."

"Okay," Laurel answered.

"And the earrings too, Lark." My stepmother held out her hand again.

I was taking out the tarnished silver studs before the order fully registered. "Yes, Stepmother...but they were a gift from my father."

She'd once loved him, enough to mate with him and carry his pack mark on her brow. But even the mention of him wasn't enough to move her to sympathy. She inspected the old pair of earrings, probably wondering if there was any worth left in them. With a careless flick, she tossed them off the side of the train. "They are not suitable for your charade."

My eyes welled with tears. I fought not to spill them and give her the satisfaction of seeing my pain. I was already stripped down before her, just as she liked it.

"As I was saying...if the princes ask where any of the jewelry went, you tell them you took it off," she instructed.

"Yes, Stepmother," I mumbled. Numbness stole through my insides. At least with her closing the loopholes that may reveal her power over me, the punishment was over.

"You may stand."

She took my face in firm grip, forcing my gaze up to meet hers. We stared at one another, truth to truth. I hated her and her control over me with all that I was. And she liked that, relished in it, because she hated me too. She'd hated me since before I knew what hate was.

She glanced away, eyeing the platform under us. Before I realized what she had planned, she flattened my cloak over a piece of sharp metal sticking out of the walkway. I gasped and reached for the fabric, pulling it as her foot came down between us. The *rip* sent an unpleasant roll of static down my spine.

"Oops." Cymora let go of it. "Tell the princes you tripped...if they even notice. Come Laurel. It's lunchtime."

They left me there with the finality of a closed door. I took in the damage, the hanging fibers of ruined cloth and the sullied print in the fur where she'd put her shoe. The rip couldn't have been longer than a foot, but it was all I could see, bisecting the fur cloak. An ache seized my chest.

I bundled it to me and wailed, releasing a keen that was pure wounded omega. I made other sounds I didn't realize I knew, feral and anguished. It'd been the gift I'd loved above the others, even over the blanket and the old earrings. The one thing I would've dove off the train to save. And now it was *ruined*.

Still clutching it, I fumbled for the door, heading inside half blinded by pain. I just had to get back to my room. Tormund would come back with a sandwich and hold me, and everything would be okay.

But willing myself to rally wasn't working like it usually did. I sobbed into the cloak's soft lining all the way back. When Cymora kicked me, she'd aggravated my limp, so the trip was slow and agonizing.

Yet when I twisted the knob, my room was still empty. Not all that much time had passed at all for the princes to still be at lunch. They might even be lingering over their plates, thinking they were giving me more private time. I released a bitter whine and lay across one of the couches, face down on top of my ruined cloak.

I could take a few minutes to pity myself before I *had* to stop crying. If they came back now and started asking questions, it'd only make everything worse when I was compelled to lie or sit in silence.

Better they not know I'd been punished at all.

17
LARK

Only moments after I had that thought, Tormund came in, announcing himself cheerfully. "Hello, li'l bird! I have your sandwich. And a triple berry cookie. I know they're your fav—what's wrong?"

A plate clinked against the table, and fingertips landed on my shoulder. I released a helpless sob. Stars, there was no avoiding more unpleasantness, was there?

"Nothing's wrong." I was muffled by the fur I'd soaked through with tears.

"*Ach.* Tell me," he insisted, rubbing little circles over one of my wings. "Was it Fal? I tell him he has to be more polite. He goes too far sometimes, thinking he's funny."

I sniffed and wiped at my face, trying to make my eyes stop leaking. "No, Fal didn't do anything," I mumbled.

Tormund shifted uneasily. He scented the air and growled. "I smell fish. Cymora was here."

My heart lurched at the anger underlying his words. I sat up and forced a dubiously convincing smile on my face, just for it to evaporate the moment I saw Tormund's furious expression. One of his eyes twitched before twin flames ignited in his pupils. Heat and humidity poured from him in a thick wave.

"Did she say something to you?" His low voice was full of menace I would've thought was unlike him.

"It's okay," I said. "I...will be okay."

In sitting up and swinging my legs to the floor, I'd exposed the rip she'd made in the bottom of my cloak. The afterimages of light in his gaze streaked toward the stretch of ruined fibers, and a series of twitches spasmed through his fingers and face.

"Tormund, are you all right?" I asked in a frightened hush.

What kind of question was that? He clearly wasn't. His muscles shifted and swelled under his skin, stretching the seams of his clothes and revealing the yellow glow of an ignited furnace in his chest. The light filtered through the brassy cast of his skin, making it look like molten metal.

I backed away as his fingernails and horns grew several inches spontaneously, developing dangerous points. He opened his mouth, revealing similarly elongated and sharpened teeth. Steam and plumes of smoke escaped his mouth as a guttural roar ripped from him.

I flinched in terror. This kind of transformation was unique to only one kind of fae, and I'd read about it in one of my adventure books. The description paled in comparison to the burning menace of the male before me. I'd wondered what kind of fire fae he was, but he and his brothers had never been forthcoming. Stars, no wonder. He was a *redcap*, and this was the beginning of a rage. He snarled, "What did she do? Where is she? I'll kill her!"

I did the only thing I could think of: I dove onto the couch and curled up into a ball at the end of it. They say if you keep yourself quiet and still, a raging redcap may overlook you by mistaking you for already dead. As he maintained this monstrous form, he would burn hotter and his form would swell further, exposing more of the white-hot heat inside of him.

He swung toward the door as Marius flung it open and rushed inside. He pivoted around the redcap's body and grabbed his arms, restraining them while pressing his knee to the small of Tormund's back. His skin sizzled on contact.

"Calm down," he ordered in a full bark. The hefty force of his alpha dominance slammed into my stomach, even if I wasn't the intended recipient.

"She hurt Lark!" Tormund roared, crackling power filling his voice. He bucked and slammed his skull into his brother's jaw. Marius reeled and lost control of one of his arms.

"I'm sure there's a perfectly good expla—" Fal cut off as he side-stepped a clumsy swing of Tormund's claws.

The redcap lurched for the door, where Kauz stood in the threshold, hands twisting as he directed starry essence into a spell between his fingers. Tormund snarled and raised one meaty arm to slash him. I covered my eyes with a fearful wail.

"I don't want *explanations*. I want *blood*!" the redcap boomed. "Let go!"

I peeked between my fingers. Fal had caught Tormund's arm, but without Marius's trained strength behind his trembling restraint, those long claws were still descending toward Kauz in steady jerks.

"You can't go shouting about blood on a public magirail," Fal said from between his teeth.

Kauz finished his spell, which hardened into a shackle of essence that closed around Tormund's wrist. He listed to the side with a *thud* as if the shackle weighed a ton. Despite the flexes and pulls of his bulked-out arm, he couldn't lift it. He snarled and snapped his teeth like a rabid creature, straining against Marius to free his other arm.

Fal's face entered my line of sight, his pupils panicked lines as he leaned over me. "He needs you," he murmured before scooping me up. I'd made myself into the smallest ball I could, ripe for the plucking.

"What are you... Fal! Ahh!" I protested, my teary voice hitting a high, terrified octave as he jumped over Tormund's grounded arm and pushed me into his chest. The redcap freed his other arm and swung it around, claws extended, just as Fal released me and stepped away.

Tormund's limb closed around my torso, crushing me to the hardened muscles bursting out of his tunic. Heat sweltered over me. Just being this close to his chest was so hot it was unbearable, and I soaked my clothes with sweat. The flames in his pupils swung down and fixed on my face.

I'm going to die. I stared into the face of death, petrified to see it belonged to a male I trusted. It'd take one bite for him to liberate my throat. Or a single blast of fire.

What? It's still Tormund! Somewhere underneath this monstrous form was the gentle giant who'd dusted me off after my fall in the castle gardens. Who held me like I was precious and purred like a champion, without a hint of embarrassment for wanting to comfort me. The same one who took glee in making sure I had access to more food than I could eat and loved to warm me up first thing in the morning.

Now, somehow, he needed me to call him back from this rage.

"T-Tormund," I managed, lifting shaky fingers to cup his cheek. It was like touching an overheated plate, and my skin stung with the promise of a burn. "This isn't you. You have to calm down."

Vibrating with unchecked fury, Tormund still tilted his head into my touch. He closed his eyes and breathed out a gust of smoke and stinging embers. His body deflated and cooled, and his newly sharpened bits shrank until the only edged teeth in his broad mouth were his alpha fangs. Tormund cradled my sweaty body one-armed, nuzzling into my hair.

"It worked," Fal said with wonder.

"You bastard," Marius snarled. Behind Tormund's back, there was a heavy thump and the sound of someone choking.

That was it for me and my composure. I bucked, trying to escape the cage of Tormund's arm. I scrabbled against his broad chest, feeling trapped as he struggled to keep a hold on me. "Sorry, li'l bird. So sorry."

Kauz had his hand on the door, drawing it closed. "Yes, everything's fine," he was saying in a tense voice. He winced when I shrieked and clawed, going increasingly feral. "We have it handled!" He shut the door and locked it with that exclamation.

"I knew it would be..." Fal wheezed.

"You handed our mate to a raging redcap! You endangered her with no heed to what Tormund could've done," Marius seethed.

Tormund finally released me, and I backed away from all of them. "Sorry," he kept whispering over and over.

There was nowhere to go. The walls of the room closed in, and pressure mounted in my chest as I looked around frantically for an escape.

"She soothed his rage. There's no need for this." Kauz spoke more calmly than anyone else in the room.

"*Our* mate?" Even now, Fal managed to sound smug. "Was that what it took for—" He cut off with a grunt of pain.

Marius rumbled, "How fucking dare you—"

I clutched my head and keened, sharp and shrill. Several cries erupted from me, as I was used to my distress going unanswered.

The males all froze. Tormund, who held his hand as Kauz's shackle spell dissipated, made an anxious sound back. Marius had Fal trapped against the wall with a forearm, his razored fin extended just enough to secure him in place. His other arm was cocked back to punch. Kauz had a hold on the kelpie's wrist and was in the middle of trying to tug him away.

They turned toward me, eyes dilated, while I had my breakdown. I kept to the edge of the room and pulled at my hair while I paced, trapped. My nest was gone, my males were fighting—everything was wrong, *wrong*. A scream began to coil in my chest like a snake poised to strike.

The next thing I knew, Kauz was there. "Sweetheart," he murmured, enveloping me in his wings.

I clung to him and took a ragged breath. When the scream came, it was muffled against his shoulder while I blindly clawed at his clothes. He didn't restrict me fully, enduring the scratches without a sound of pain.

The other males' voices faded to masculine whispers. Tormund begging me to stop, Marius demanding a chance to talk to me, and Fal murmuring words of comfort and trying to touch me through the barrier of Kauz's wings. The dream warden hissed warnings, telling them to back off, that they were only going to make it worse.

I sagged eventually, exhausted and hoarse. Beyond the star-flecked leather of my safe haven, the alphas growled and snapped at one another. Instead of being distressed by it, I had finally found a bubble of peace where nothing else could bother me other than my own actions.

I'd lost myself and let my instincts take control. Gone feral. It was... *inevitable*. It'd been something I'd felt forming inside of me in Osme

Fen, during the long nights alone with my own thoughts. My inner omega threatened to take over and find me a pack that would treat me right. I'd fought the pull of my instincts, called myself needy and bratty, but the urges to turn wild and leave civilization behind never fully went away.

"Lark?" Kauz whispered. I answered with a soft mewl, too embarrassed to look at him. My nails were short, and I'd still ripped his tunic. He was probably bleeding.

"You're safe. I have you," he murmured, stroking my hair. "Everything's going to be all right. Tormund is calm."

"I am. Very calm," the giant reported, sounding miserable. "I am very, very sorry, li'l bird."

I shook my head in denial. He was a redcap all this time, and they hadn't breathed a word of it. I would've never suspected it either, had he not succumbed to a rage right in front of me.

Kauz tucked me closer and leaned back, supporting me so I could raise my foot and relieve some of the pain still throbbing up my leg.

"Marius and Fal are getting along."

"Opposite sides of the room," Fal said, his voice coming from over my right shoulder.

"Not as far as Fal wishes it were," Marius said from over my left shoulder.

Both of them were using gentling voices, calm and soothing, but there was definitely still an edge to their words.

"I don't want to be anywhere but here with you, lovely," Fal rushed to add.

Marius switched to speaking Serri. If they were arguing, at least I didn't have to listen. I shifted, picking up the mysterious but amazing scent of Always drifting from Kauz. Like dreams and promises, faint but present. He tilted his head and made a sound of pleasure when I leaned up and nuzzled against his neck, hoping to catch more than a fleeting hint of his scent. In the half-light filtering from his wings, starlight glimmered on his fingertips. Little pinpricks of light rested on my skin and hair, soaking into me.

"I'm trying to give you some of my essence," he said in a low voice.

My gaze flicked upward. Kauz had reddened scratch lines over his collar, but he seemed fine. "It smells nice," I whispered back.

His lips lifted. He seemed to know exactly what he was doing when I nuzzled him again. "My brothers are going to search the room now. We're looking for anything amiss. What can you tell us?"

"You will not say a word of this to the princes."

I whimpered, feeling my tenuous peace slip. Kauz seemed to take that as answer enough. "Do you want us to switch languages so you don't have to listen to us talking about you?"

I shook my head, clutching him harder. I wanted to know what they were saying, even if they figured out nothing. Then they could smooth out the last ragged edges roughing up my inner omega.

"I'm not going anywhere. I'm going to hold you for as long as you need," he promised.

"Well, let's start with the obvious." Fal said, keeping his voice low and gentle. "What set you off, Tormund?"

"I come in here, and Lark is crying, face down. Very odd." The redcap tried to also have a low and gentle tone, but he just sounded deeply upset. "I smelled that the fish was here recently and saw the damage to Lark's cloak. Then I lost control."

"I tripped," I mumbled. Though I was compelled to say it, it wasn't a lie. Cymora had tripped me in this room earlier.

There was a rustle of fabric, and Tormund released his signature *ach*. "Does that print match Lark's?" Kauz asked. He loosened the seal of his wings, peeling one back over my right side.

"Bend your knee, Lark." This came from Marius, who tsked when I did. Fabric rustled again. "The print doesn't match. Also, it looks like she was helped to the ground. She has a bruise forming right above her ankle."

The room was filled with repressed rumbling from the three alphas. "So, Cymora tripped her and damaged her cloak," Fal stated.

"That can't be all. Not with her having a feral moment there," Kauz murmured.

"I thought she did that because of me," Tormund said guiltily.

"That's not how it works. All you did was scare her," Marius growled. "That was clearly a trauma response."

The dream warden stroked my hair again. "He's right. She has to have suffered a wound to her instincts, and recently. Hmm...try checking her things, and her bed."

He closed his wing back around me. I waited, stunned he'd thought to check my nest so quickly. I also braced myself for the reaction of the male who climbed up there as the bunk creaked with its descent.

There was a single, sharp "*foc*" from Marius less than a minute later. "It's empty," he said.

"Empty?" Fal echoed in disbelief.

"Just a fucking mattress. See for yourself."

I scrunched my face and hid it in Kauz's tunic, whimpering.

"We'll build you a new nest," he whispered. My inner omega perked her ears.

The ladder creaked as an alpha went up and down from my bed. Then a third time, punctuated by a dangerous-sounding growl.

"Easy there, big guy," Fal said.

"One with all our scents and a real mattress. Plus all the fleece we can layer on top. It'll be your epic dream nest come to life," Kauz was still promising.

I pictured it and yearned to see it filled. "Would you sleep there with me?" I asked in a small voice.

"Every single night, sweetheart."

"I'd end her in a heartbeat," Marius's harsh growl countered Kauz's tender tone.

"I think we all can agree the fish is a frigid bitch. However, we can't just murder her," Fal said. "Not without a legal reason. We *are* representatives of the new Unseelie order, after all."

A charged silence fell amongst the males. Kauz shifted, withdrawing his wings, and I looked up to see two of the alphas staring at him. Tormund was seated at one of the couches, looking down at his hands.

"I thought it was a mistake to entertain her minutes after she introduced herself," Marius continued. "We could dump the fish's body in the Doras. No one but the fishling would notice."

Fal's lips twisted as he considered it. "Unless she met a similar fate," he reasoned.

I hadn't heard *fish* and *fishling* from the princes before, but it was clear they were talking about Cymora and Laurel. I felt compelled to say, "Please don't kill them."

Fal and Marius exchanged a glance. "She probably doesn't mean that," the dark elf said.

"I do," I said woodenly.

"See?" he said.

Marius responded with a kelpie's snort, looking unconvinced.

Kauz helped support me as I limped toward the couches. Three sets of hands reached out in invitation. I needed to sit in someone's lap to make this work. I looked between the three alphas, weighing whose comforting I wanted most right now.

Tormund, who I would've gone to first without hesitation if it weren't for his surprise transformation. Fal, who'd given me a fright by pushing me into a raging redcap. Or Marius, who used to be my last choice of the four males, except he'd said "our mate." And yesterday, he'd made me feel *safe*.

I picked Marius because I needed to feel safe again. He sat me across his lap. "Could you get the wound salve from my bag?" he asked Kauz. While the dream warden went rooting around Marius's luggage, the kelpie turned over my hand, inspecting the reddening skin on my palm.

"It's fine," I murmured.

"It's not," he answered in a tone that invited no argument. "If we took care of Cymora and you never saw her again, would that really upset you?"

I nodded once, compelled by some order made long enough ago that I'd forgotten the wording.

His ear flicked. "Kauz is convinced she's controlling you through a spell or a vow."

I dropped my gaze, unable to talk about it. "The 'yes, Stepmother' thing she does any time Cymora gives her an order," Kauz said. My head snapped back up. He was in the midst of handing Marius a small wooden pot. "It's beneficial to be observant. And there's no one I've paid closer attention to than you."

Marius unscrewed the lid from the pot and gave it a brief sniff. It was fragrant with herbs and florals. Almost overpoweringly so. "Let's let it go for now. We have a problem to solve. Fal's plan didn't work."

The kelpie scooped up a dollop of salve and rubbed it into my burned palm. It stung at first, before cool tingles soothed the skin. The redness visibly receded in moments. I murmured in wonder since it had to be magic at work.

"It was going so well, too," Fal said.

"Plan goes well until it doesn't. Like every other plan," Tormund grumbled.

"We didn't understand the situation as well as we do now. It's not as if anyone told us what was going on between our Seelie guests when they invited themselves along for this trip," the dark elf remarked.

Kauz made an annoyed sound. "I told you. Lark *can't*. Depending on the vow, she may even be forced to mislead us."

I hadn't realized he'd figured out the situation between Cymora and me so quickly. My chest warmed with gratitude.

Fal blew out a sigh. "Right. Well, we're displacing the fishling from this room. I'll take her place."

"I'm moving in as well," Kauz said. "Lark can sleep with me."

The other three males protested at the same time.

"We can decide that part later," I ventured. I was just relieved they'd be coming here, leaving no room for my stepfamily. Even though two more days of being crammed together like this may be less fun soon, I was tentatively excited. Two days of nonstop cuddles awaited...as long as we could all get along.

Kauz and Fal started searching the room for Laurel's things, putting them into her bag haphazardly before they left the room. As soon as Marius applied the magic-infused salve to his own burns and set the pot aside, he held me curled up against his chest. I dozed against him in the quiet that followed, breathing in trace amounts of his waterlily and mint scent. It sent me straight to sleep.

Sometime later, I awoke still secured against the kelpie's solid frame. He had one arm around me and held his book open with the other. There was no way he was actually reading it. His eyes were dilated too much.

Tormund stared at the ceiling beside us while Kauz and Fal whispered intently in Serri on the other couch. Somehow, the sandwich and cookie Tormund had brought earlier were still on the table, untouched.

"Welcome back, lovely. I have something for you," Fal said in Theli. "Hold out your hand."

I did so, and he dropped silver into my palm. My lips parted in surprise to see the silver necklace with its bird charm. I put it back on with a bittersweet feeling, happy that he'd somehow retrieved it but sad knowing my earrings were still gone. "How?" I asked.

"I noticed you were missing your favorite necklace, with the li'l silver bird. As I was moving out of the other room, I told Laurel that you were missing your jewelry. She went to search the female's bath and, lo and behold, found the necklace. No earrings yet, though."

"They're lost," I murmured.

He read my expression and frowned.

"It's okay. I should've replaced them a long time ago." Before I ended up shedding more tears over them, I wiggled out of Marius's hold, limped to my luggage, and dug around inside. "My stepfamily didn't mind you changing the room assignments?"

Fal's feline gaze was still focused on me, but his expression was unreadable. "I don't give a single shit if they mind or not. You will never be alone with them again if any of us can help it. We're going to make sure the female's bath is closed when you need to use it. We'll be a little uncomfortable for a couple days, but we'll soon be in Serian. Things will be different there."

I nodded, my dry eyes stinging as my lip wobbled. "Thank you. It means so much that you'd do all this for me."

I found the squashed jewelry box containing Marius's gift that'd seemed like an apology. I fixed the little silver hoops in my ears.

"You're worth it," Fal said, giving me a warm look. We gazed at each other for a long moment before he clapped his hands. "Well! I don't know about you all, but I'm ready to play one of Kauz and Marius's endless card games."

The kelpie finally seemed to acknowledge the conversation by asking in a roughened voice, "Which one?" He motioned for me to come back to him, and I did. His yellow gaze lowered to my ears, and instead of saying anything, he tapped one of the hoops and set it to swaying. He nodded in approval.

"Let's teach the li'l bird Liar Liar. It's my favorite," Tormund suggested.

"I'm the best at that game. Have the trophy to prove it, too," Marius said to me as Kauz fished out a deck of cards and began dealing five piles. The kelpie explained the game efficiently while we waited. We split the deck evenly between us, except for the last card, which was flipped over. The objective was to put up to four cards from our hands face down on that card and suggest whether they matched its suit or color.

If no one challenged them, the cards were flipped and the next fae had their turn. But if they were challenged—called a liar—they flipped their cards on the spot. If the cards didn't match what they'd suggested, they took every card in the pile except for one. But if they weren't lying, the accuser took the pile instead. The fae who had no cards left in their hand won.

I saw how someone like Marius, with his usual stony countenance, could be a champion at Liar Liar. But I also agreed with Fal. This game was designed to never end. The fewer cards one had, the more likely one would need to lie when putting a card down.

It was a nice way to pass a few hours, and with each male taking a turn holding me, I eventually relaxed into a point of almost purring contentment. My anxiety over fibbing got me poked on the nose and called a liar pretty much every time I tried to pass off a few cards that didn't match, though.

The brothers were all much more invested in this card game than I'd expected them to get. It would've been just as fun to sit back and watch them play without me. No one ended up winning, though Marius and Tormund got within a few cards of it.

They got dinner one at a time while I stayed in the room and ate my sandwich and cookie. When it was time to sleep, my mood dipped as I remembered there would be no warm nest for me, just a decision to share a cot...though all four males seemed welcoming.

I wished I didn't have to choose, but I ended up in Kauz's arms, trusting the dream warden to guard my sleeping body.

18

KAUZ

Most dream wardens worked in the fourth stage of rest, when dreams formed. They manipulated dreams by night and illusions by day. My line was a rarer, stronger version that could start poking around others' heads at the second stage of rest, when the mind abandoned idle thoughts and descended toward a maintenance-and-repair stage. Sleep was vitally important, and to interfere with the delicate process could cause irreparable memory damage or worse.

I'd spent many long hours with my father, snooping around in various volunteers' minds, learning how the process worked so I could be the strongest possible defender of the future queen's psyche. I had to understand her at a level deeper than my brothers. All the better to protect her at night from others with similar powers to mine and to know her needs practically before she did during the day.

As a boy, I'd thought my parents were just being gushy when they hinted they spent most nights joint dreaming. Who'd want such a lack of privacy? Especially after they'd been mated for decades. I couldn't imagine desiring such a constant and intimate connection with anyone when I could simply pass the nighttime in blissful unconsciousness.

But after smelling the promise of Always wafting from Lark and ending our first dream together on my knees, I was rapidly understanding the appeal.

I thought I'd get through this train ride without trouble as a beta, not detecting the same desirable pheromones off her that my brothers did. Instead, I'd ended up drawn to her light, melodic voice and smart conversations. And stars, how sweet she was. She captured my heart almost immediately and made it look effortless. I'd gone to sleep tonight painfully hard for her, my pelvis shifted away so she wouldn't notice.

Any night, I could've entered her dreams and seduced her. She'd be presented to Mother untouched, yet on the inside, she would already intimately know me. I yearned for time with her, to master her body and show her pleasure. But she needed my help far more than nocturnal lessons in making love.

The amount of pain and disorientation in the recesses of her psyche was staggering. It was cluttered with memories. *Forcefully forgotten* memories, shorn raggedly and scattered before they could enter a space of long-term storage. They knotted and tugged at one another, sure to cause her agony if anything jogged her waking mind to call upon one of these forgotten moments.

It was difficult to linger in her mind outside of a dream. *My* head hurt before I even began to pick up lost memories, taking a peek inside of them for a hint as to what had happened to her. All I'd received for nights' full of work were bits and snatches of her past, mere slivers of understanding.

One day, I would heal these ragged edges, and we could visit her memories together. I just had to figure out the root cause of her forced forgetfulness...and I had a good hunch for where it was coming from.

I waited for Lark to enter the third stage of rest and reached out to halt her short-term memory. My magic sorted through the individual strands, nudging along some things until I had one specific event wrapped around my fingers.

I squeezed just right to relive it, plunging into a vivid replay of the time my brothers and I missed earlier: Cymora tormenting our mate. Though I didn't truly want to see it all, I owed it to Lark to bear witness.

During my training, I'd relived memories of the worst of faekind and the traumas that could happen to the mind. Torture, intrusive thoughts, severe depression, the murderous rage of redcaps, and more... The empathy it instilled in me had others calling me "wise beyond my years." Or, as Fal liked to put it, "eerily calm."

That was before I found the one bound to me by the magic of Always and heard her hopeless thoughts while she was forced to throw away items she loved.

I knew I shouldn't have gotten attached.

The best thing I can do is hunker down and take it. Fighting only makes it worse.

Death might be a mercy compared to what my stepfamily has planned for me.

She won't push me off the train. She can't have what she wants if I die now.

I gritted my teeth through the whole thing. None of this would've happened had I been there. One intrusive thought lingered past the recollection as I returned to myself.

Better the princes not know I'd been punished at all.

I was ready to tear Cymora from her bed and force her to grovel before my mate. This memory, this *abuse*, had happened while we'd assumed Lark was safe. She hadn't even locked the door... She was so used to us coming and going with no efforts for privacy.

We'd been far too kind to Cymora. I'd suspected something was off, but the flat cruelty I'd just witnessed in her was breathtaking. Worse still, the way Lark had immediately folded in despair. This had been their dynamic for a long time. Too long.

Since Lark could not fight back, I would get revenge in her name. Cymora would understand firsthand why Unseelie had a healthy fear of dream wardens at their most vengeful. I would snap her sanity with the ease of breaking a twig.

Breathe, I reminded myself, slowly letting my fingers uncurl. I'd almost destroyed the memory just by holding it too tightly. I let go of it, and the strand whipped out of my grip, joining the rest of Lark's memories of her day. It wasn't my place to snip it loose, no matter how much I wished it'd never happened.

There was a lot of valuable information in what I'd just seen. Cymora had ultimate power over Lark, able to command her. Now that I had that confirmed, it seemed my theory that Cymora had ordered Lark to forget an egregious number of events was true. After viewing the mess of her memories, it was the only thing that made sense.

Lark was also sure that Cymora was seeking an opportunity to trick us into taking Laurel as our mate. Trick *us*, a whole pack of Unseelie. Fal was going to laugh his ass off when he heard this one.

And in the tiniest chance one of us did accidentally lay a claiming bite on the fishling... well, we weren't above carrying a damaged pack bond if Laurel then died, not if it meant we would have our correct mate. I'd eventually be able to repair the fractures to our psyches. Laurel was doomed by her own mother's ambitions.

Now to get Lark to accept that she wasn't alone anymore. We would fight her battles and respond to her whims until she found her strength. She would be magnificent in her own right once we coaxed her to fly free of the cage her stepfamily had shoved her into. It would be the honor of my life to pry open the cage door.

Just like it'd been my pleasure to dispatch a spy I knew I could trust —a winged dreamlander like myself, skilled in stealth and speed—to Osme Fen to investigate this Pack Ellisar Lark feared from her first dream. She wouldn't have to worry about them anymore.

Light and color formed around me, the first hints that Lark was entering the fourth stage of rest. I wanted to stay and comfort her in her upcoming dream, tempted, as always, to see if she'd let me pleasure her. But it was time to go. I whispered the promise of Always, "Fate has bound us forever in the depths of time." By the time her dream took shape, it would be soaked in my starlit magic, invoking true rest in pleasant nonsense.

I stepped out of her mind, waking in the cot I shared with her. It was the dark of night, and her slight form rested in the crook of my arm. She hugged me tight around my chest as her substitute pillow. Her dim gray wings fluttered open and shut slowly, like a butterfly's might, a sign of content rest that I watched for a few minutes.

Stars, she was so cute. Those wings always gave away what she was feeling, more so than her expressive blue eyes. If the touch wouldn't potentially wake her, I'd trace the faded patterns in her wings and idly paint my skin with her pixie dust.

If she had pixie dust. Another odd little fact about her that worried me. No dust meant no extra essence to shed, and her essence level seemed concerningly low. I sighed, acknowledging I had more work to do tonight. Fal had wanted me in Cymora's dreams since we met her, sure she would incriminate herself in a space free of consequences. It was the Unseelie way, to hang criminals with the rope they handed the law, woven of their guilt and regrets...or lack thereof.

I assumed the fish's mind would give me the latter, especially once I cracked her psyche for fucking with my mate. I *had* been taking my time, as Cymora's mind was more resilient than most, resisting my halfhearted attempts to pay her dreams a visit. I'd left her with unsettled sleep, the creeping onset of nightmares, weakening her defenses over several nights while I spent most of my time with Lark.

Closing my eyes, I cast out my senses. I needed to hold a possession from another person to accurately locate their sleeping mind, especially in a crowded area. Little as I wanted to admit it, I *was* holding one of Cymora's possessions. The train's enclosed space helped me identify her in moments after sifting past minds in various sleep stages.

Cymora was already dreaming. What a terrible coincidence for her. I slipped through her mind's awareness, no more than a mirage of shadows taking shape behind the dreaming manifestation of her body. She was with a male, a broad, gray-skinned alpha wind sprite with a tousle of white hair. He was seated in an armchair before a fire, and she was about to crawl into his lap.

This dream smelled of Ever. This was something she remembered happening long ago, but she probably didn't expect her wind sprite to become me as I supplanted her memory of the male.

"Cymora," I said, startling her before she could have a seat.

She jumped backward. "Prince Kauzden? This isn't how..."

I made a chair appear behind her, and she tripped into it. In a blink,

I had her seated across from me. Dreamers were often confused when I showed up, since they usually weren't thinking about me.

But the familiarity of us sitting across from one another had her mind relaxing. It reset her expectations for her dream. Our surroundings bled from a nicely appointed sitting room into the more familiar atmosphere of the train.

"How are you this evening, Prince Kauzden?" she asked. Her resting smile rekindled the embers of my rage, as did the falsely sweet tone she took.

Soon. I couldn't punish her before she told me some vital information.

"We're going to talk about Lark tonight." My voice had an undertone of magic that seeped into her psyche. If I'd done my job correctly over the last few nights, she would simply take over from here and start talking.

"Oh, that ungrateful whore's daughter." She scoffed. "Now one in her own right. I'm sure you all took turns with her tonight."

My jaw tightened, but I remained quiet. I'd only speak to direct her if she drifted off topic.

"She should have died with her mother, but the illness curse wasn't quite fast enough. I wanted Kellam without any baggage from his first mating. But no, the little half-breed was born, and with that *face.* Exactly like her mother's," Cymora seethed, balling her fists in her lap. "She looks at me with that face, and I simply cannot stand her."

"You hate Lark because she looks like her mother?" I asked to confirm.

Her face creased with bitterness. "That's right. Just like that male-thieving whore, Dorei. He goes off to 'see the world' and doesn't return for me. He only comes back with her on his arm and, a couple years later, his baby in her belly. While I suffered through an arranged mating of my own. At least I got my darling Laurel from it."

"All right," I sighed. I didn't want to hear another word about Laurel. She'd tried pitching the fishling to me more than once, and I couldn't see the appeal. "We're talking about Lark. Who looks just like Dorei."

"Indeed."

"And Kellam was an alpha wind sprite?" I guessed. She nodded in agreement. He must've been the male she'd just been about to seduce when I arrived. "How did he die?"

"I poisoned him," she said with her usual false sweetness.

My heart leapt, throbbing in my chest. Here was her confession, a dusty crime that we could still use to imprison her. It was the *new* Unseelie way to confirm wrongdoing before going straight to capricious punishment. Mother would be so proud.

"Why?" I was genuinely curious. Such intense hatred of Lark's mother for the slight of mating with Kellam. All to murder him later?

There was only a fleeting hint of regret suspended around Cymora as she answered with a dreamer's lack of guile. "He never let Dorei's death rest. He questioned it and revisited it until, one day, he was too close to the truth. To protect my name and my daughter's future, he had to go."

Ice cold. Exactly what one could expect from a fish, but the lack of remorse showed me this mermaid needed to be far, far away from my mate. Lark likely didn't even realize the great injustice Cymora had committed upon her family.

"Killing them both wasn't enough for you," I stated slowly. "You set out to torture Lark next."

"Oh, don't make it sound so dramatic. I took her in with good intentions. Secured her loyalty."

"How?"

"A vow, of course. But even with her doing everything I told her to, every time I looked at her, I couldn't stop seeing Dorei staring back at me." She shuddered violently. "So, I did what I had to."

Cymora's dreaming mind resisted. "What?" I pressed, scattering starry essence to keep her in the dream with me. Whatever it was, she *knew* it was bad.

"I had to," she echoed.

"What did you do to my mate, Cymora?" I asked in a dangerous hush.

For the first time, her eyes focused. She pursed her mouth in disapproval. "Are you making demands of me in my own dream, Prince Kauzden? My family's matters are none of your business. You won't get another word out of me."

"Is that so?" I snapped my fingers. As if her stubborn chin lift was enough to defeat me in my own realm.

She flicked her hand dismissively. "Begone. Leave me to my privacy."

I chuckled and stood, leaking shadows and starlight as I loomed over her. With my magic coating my features, I took on the visage of a night terror as our surroundings blurred and changed around us. "To think you have any power here. How rich," I mocked.

Cymora startled when she turned her head and watched a second version of herself walk by, hissing at a beta dryad who couldn't have been older than a teenager, "I'm not paying you to run your mouth."

The manifestation of her dreaming mind turned back to me, mouth agape. "That's right. If you won't tell me, your memories will," I said.

I lifted my hand, directing starry essence to weave into rope. I bound her hands behind her and stuffed her mouth with the magical equivalent of a gag. She made muffled sounds of protest as her dream officially became a nightmare, with her tethered to me while I followed the path of her memory.

It was early evening inside of an old but well-maintained manor. Cymora's memory wore a floaty dress which rasped against the mermaid scales patterning her thighs. She looked the part as the lady of this house, with her blue and teal hair filled with pearls and ears lined with spiky abalone.

The dryad teen sweating beside her was an essence spinner. If I was meeting him face-to-face, I'd know because I could sense the excess magic in him and the telltale way it spun through his body. It was just an educated guess from this memory, as his arms were covered in shaky tattoos of leafy vines.

I'd covered myself in poorly rendered art when I was just learning. It seemed this boy did the same thing. He was carrying a large briefcase and had a dodgy look about his glowing green eyes.

"I'm just saying, missus," he muttered.

"Relax. The device will be *temporary*. She just needs to be taught a lesson in discipline," Cymora said breezily. "You were able to buy it, right? It's not illegal."

"Sure, but it was made for magic-wielding anim—"

"Exactly," she said over him. "And you reviewed the spell?"

He sighed as only a teen could. "Yes, missus."

"A device and a spell," I remarked, not that either person in this memory noticed me talking behind them. I turned to the dreaming Cymora and raised a brow. "Here's your chance to confess before we see the truth." She stared back at me, eyebrows slanted. With my starlight magic sealing her lips shut, she could've nodded or shaken her head in response. She chose to glare.

It didn't matter. I was going to witness her guilt firsthand, whether she admitted to it or not. "Suit yourself," I said.

The memory of Cymora led the dryad to a door missing a handle. It gave way with a push of her palm, revealing a bedroom and a girl lying on a cot at the center of it. She was resting on her belly, wings halting their contented fluttering as she looked up from an open book.

"Oh, hello, Stepmother." There were obvious nerves in the greeting, and her gaze darted toward the dryad.

I held up one finger. The memory froze in place. For a moment, the dreaming Cymora breathed a sigh of relief. That was before I willed the ropes of essence binding her hands to multiply, some sticking to the floor to anchor her, others winding around her ankles so she'd remain in place.

"Hello, baby Lark," I murmured, crossing the room to the girl. She couldn't be more than ten or eleven, her body all sticks and elbows. Even now, she was dressed in drab colors, her only adornment a familiar pair of studs in her earlobes and the silver swirls glittering through her wings. They were stunning, indigo and oversized, looking like they'd carry her away with one flap.

Her cringing expression bared her teeth and a pair of tiny fangs. The longer I looked at her, the more details were different than the Lark I knew. Stars were frozen mid-wink in the whites of her eyes, and a purple sheen glittered over her blue eyes. Her hair was a washed-out purple, heading for the transition to stark white most of my people made as they came into their powers. *Dreamlander,* my instincts screamed.

Lark was in the process of tucking her hands, hiding the exaggerated membranes between her fingers and the needle-sharp claws most nixies kept refined to demure points. My gaze flicked to her neck and the suggestion of gills tucked under her ears. Most of the breath left my lungs.

Lark was half Unseelie.

Not only that, but she was a dreamlander like me. Our magics were one and the same. I should've felt joy that I had the opportunity to teach her about our people, but all I could grasp was a growing sense of injustice at all she'd lost. All because of the hateful female who'd orphaned her.

"Dorei was a nixie," I said. Cymora stared at me in defiance, tugging fruitlessly at her bonds. "It's all right. I don't need another word out of you. I imagine this memory will show me everything else I want to know."

I placed my hands behind my back, lacing them under the curve of my wings, and took a leisurely look at Lark's bedroom. There wasn't much to see, as it had been stripped of most things of value. The ghosts of larger furniture made bright spots against the wallpaper. She had a generous bookshelf, I supposed. Most of the volumes looked well-loved. I read the spines, wondering how many times she thumbed through each one by the time she was an adult.

What a tiny, miserable box for a young omega. She didn't even have any special extra-soft or colorful bedding to account for her budding nesting instincts. No stuffed toys, either. At this age, my sisters' nests were mostly toys and blankets. Cymora's earlier torment took on a new edge.

Lark had never had a true nest, going by what I saw here. No wonder she had a little feral in her. It was a miracle she hadn't completely lost her mind to her instincts before she crossed paths with Fal.

A soft growl rose in my throat. I would soon set such terrors on Cymora's mind that she would cry out for mercy. There wouldn't be any, just like how she never listened when Lark begged.

With a gesture from me, the memory continued where it'd left off. I stood close to Lark, watching from her side and ignoring the dreaming Cymora, who struggled and stamped her feet.

"Sit at the edge of your bed. I have something for you," Cymora's memory said, pointing to a specific spot.

"Yes, Stepmother."

I grated my teeth together. That obedient, forced response raised every hair on the back of my neck.

The dryad teen opened his briefcase, revealing a glint of gray and a dusty spell book. I looked over his shoulder as he flipped to a dog-eared page and read the title of the spell he was about to perform. Stars, I felt ill. Cymora couldn't possibly expect such a green essence spinner to perform an *olcanus* correctly.

Lark trembled with a soft whine. Even at this age, she tried to muffle the noise by closing her lips tightly. "What's going on?"

"I've had enough of your nighttime visits." Cymora's acidic tone drew a flinch from the girl. "Last night was the absolute last straw."

"I'm sorry, Stepmother. I can't help it." Lark hunched her shoulders and fiddled with her fingertips, picking around the nail beds. The habit was even less endearing as I watched her claws draw blood immediately.

"That's all right, dear. I've secured a device that will help you. This boy is only here to place it on you." The mermaid explained it was temporary while the dryad picked up a length of metal studded with spikes from his briefcase.

It was a silencing band, designed to suppress magic and, once activated, hide its existence at all costs. Serian had it listed near the top of a list of forbidden magical items by labeling it an *olcanus*, along with the other spells or devices designed to control the magic, will, or body of another fae. The teen had suggested it was made for magical animals, but it shouldn't have existed at all.

I watched with rising dread as Cymora ordered Lark to keep still. The teen consulted his book again and threaded the metal links around her ankle. *This idiot.* He had to wrap it twice, as it was built to be a slave collar. Because that's what our forefathers used silencing bands for— suppressing their enemies, turning them into weakened husks. The band could only be removed with magical force, if uncovered, or by a key tuned to the band's location.

"Please, Stepmother. I won't enter your dreams anymore," Lark begged as the teen pick started to spin glowing magic around the metal as he read off the spell book's page.

Cymora framed Lark's face, watching the girl panic when the band tightened, its spikes sinking into her skin. She whimpered from the first hints of pain before yelping as beads of blood welled around the wounds encircling her ankle and calf.

The dryad slowed his spell work, looking at what he'd done. His eyes widened in alarm.

"Keep reading!" Cymora barked. "Don't worry—this is part of the process. It's *temporary*."

"Stepmother, please don't do this. Make him stop! Please!" Lark shouted, shaking from the pain of the band embedding and tightening further.

My hands balled into fists as Lark's begging became screaming. I trembled violently. This was only a memory, a glimpse at the distant past. There was nothing I could do to stop it.

She seized and fell backward, thrashing on her cot as the silencing band activated. Cymora whispered instructions, which the teen added to the spell. She wanted Lark's Unseelie side hidden and her magic bound. He had to be reassured again that it was only going to be in place temporarily before he unhooked the key from the device that would unlock and remove it. She traded him a jingling sack of coins, and soon he was on his way.

Lark lay sprawled on her side, keening a wounded omega's call. The sounds of her distress dug at me to *do something*, to reach through time, strangle her stepmother, and set her free. Because this device was anything but temporary. It had to be the source of her limp and her "crippled foot."

The color rained from her wings in a shed of pixie dust, and her claws receded to the naked eye. The band would use her magic to hide itself, layering on an illusion so thick that it would continually require most of her essence.

Cymora wasted no time in brushing back Lark's hair and meeting her gaze. "Forget receiving this device. You were born this way. Damaged. You'll think of some explanation." She waved dismissively.

The stars in Lark's eyes winked out, one by one, as the light behind them dimmed. "Y-yes, Stepmother," she rasped.

Shadows of nightmares wove around me as I swung to look at the dreaming Cymora. Sheer wrath darkened my snarl, and the whites of her eyes flashed in terror.

I stopped the memory and skipped it back in time to the moment where the teen started placing the silencing band on Lark's ankle. Then I raised my hand, and the dreaming Cymora was there in a blink, my fingers digging into her neck. "See how *you* like it," I growled.

In a blip of dream logic, it wasn't Lark sitting there anymore. It was Cymora having the same band installed into her flesh.

Her sudden scream followed me into waking, but it wasn't nearly enough.

My eyes opened to reality and the first dim rays of early morning. Lark had hardly twitched, still clinging to me, but now her washed-out wings vibrated from a pleasant dream.

"I'm sorry. I didn't know," I whispered, leaning over to kiss her pert little nose.

I didn't deserve so much as a moment of her attention until I removed her silencing band, even if I had to somehow pry it off with my bare hands. It was my mistake to underestimate the depths of Cymora's depravity. I should have inspected Lark's foot and ankle more closely. She was too sweet to bend the truth too far, so I'd assumed she *knew* her truth when she told me she had a crippled foot.

With a murmur of magic and a press of my index finger from her temple down to her lips, I left a glittering line of essence as a sign of a gentle sleeping spell. She'd be dead to the world for several hours while I shared what I'd learned with my brothers.

Marius was already awake. I could sense Tormund's troubled sleep and Fal's wet dream from here and envied the latter. He'd be dreaming of Lark, of course. He was absolutely lovestruck by her, not that the rest of us were very far behind.

I climbed out of the bunk, dragging Lark's limp form with me. I couldn't stand the idea of leaving her alone, even while she was out cold.

Marius cracked his eyes open. After all his military training, he never slept too deeply. "Still in control?" I whispered.

He was fighting a losing battle with his instincts, like always. But I trusted him, no matter what his answer was. He just needed someone to ask the question, as an acknowledgment of how much effort he was expending on his self-control.

His throat bobbed with a dry swallow. "Barely."

"Hold her. I'll be right back."

He helped support her weight as I cradled her ankle on her way into his arms. It looked and felt normal, but that was the evil of a silencing band at work. Lark may even look down and see a twisted, misshapen lump instead of her foot, proving to herself that she was right to call it crippled. Whatever we all had to believe to leave the band in place to guzzle on her essence.

Marius seemed ready to ask a dozen questions, but I was already at the door and barely caught the latch before it slammed. This wouldn't take long.

There was a single lock between Cymora and me. I flicked it open without trouble, using a magic trick on the other side of the door. She and Laurel were in the bottom bunks. While the fishling slept peacefully, Cymora's sheets were in disarray. She'd tossed and turned while being forced to endure her own actions.

I laid a fingertip on her forehead while she muttered in her sleep, jerking, caught in the loop of feeling the pain of a silencing band closing around her ankle. This sleeping spell I placed on her was larger, meant to hold her in unconsciousness for a day, maybe longer. I planned on keeping it refreshed so she slept through the rest of the trip. Lark would not have to tiptoe around in fear of her stepmother a second longer.

The air around Cymora's head darkened as I switched the type of magic I was wielding. It was a simple matter to spin essence and put her to sleep, but the terrors came from the depths of a dream warden's skills. I suggested that her sleep be full of her worst nightmares, and her mind took it from there, supplying the fears and shadows that haunted her psyche.

I pressed a little harder. She grimaced and sweated as the magic took hold.

That would do for now. I'd visit her mind tomorrow night to make sure the nightmares were to my satisfaction. Maybe I'd have her replay every interaction she'd had with Lark from the other side to browbeat a shred of empathy into her.

I turned to Laurel, whose sleep patterns were petering toward waking. I cast the same sleeping spell on her before she could become aware of my presence, then considered whether she deserved the full nightmare treatment her mother received.

Hmm. Maybe a taste. She wasn't quite an innocent here. I gave her troubled rest and left them to it, making sure to relock the door behind me.

I returned to my brothers to find Tormund rousing, Fal still asleep, and Marius angled over Lark's back protectively. He breathed in her scent with his nose buried in her hair. Her white hair, which should sparkle with dreamlander stars just like mine.

She was like me. Eventually, it would sink in and I would celebrate her. But first, there had to be a reckoning on her behalf and an unleashing of her true form. Then we could embrace the next Queen of Serian for who and what she was.

"Wake up," I announced, prodding Fal's dream for good measure.

He groaned from the other top bunk. "You better have a good fucking reason for waking me at this starsforsaken hour."

"Only if you care about Lark," I responded in a heated tone.

As an angry Kauz meant nightmares and disrupted sleep, all eyes were on me. Though I didn't abuse my powers unnecessarily, my brothers had all suffered at some point from what I could do between pranks and childhood feuds.

"Of course I care," Tormund said, sleepy but upright. He tidied up his cot and put the couch cushions back so a rumpled Fal could come down and sit next to him.

I took Lark from Marius so he could do the same with his cot. "Will you need restraints?" I asked Tormund. His side of the pack bond was still not quite right after his earlier rage. "Lark is spelled for a long nap. She won't be able to calm you."

He tensed. "That depends on what you have to say."

"He could hold her," Fal suggested.

"Aye, good idea. Give me the little bird."

Though I felt Marius's disapproving stare on my back, I carefully transferred her into Tormund's arms. It'd help keep him calm, to see her safe and mostly whole. The last thing we needed was for him to erupt in a new rage and go kill Cymora before we had a chance to find the key to the silencing band.

We'd also need his help if Marius had one of his wild fits at the news I was about to share. Stars help us if they lost control at the same time.

For now, Tormund cradled Lark tenderly, while Fal rested a hand on her calf. Both of them seemed to relax just from touching her.

I began with, "I've had a fruitful night in Cymora's psyche…"

I told them everything I'd seen, inciting dangerous alpha growls and a unifying of murderous thoughts in our pack bond.

Before anyone could lose their cool, the conversation softened as our attention turned to our omega. She snoozed on, blissfully unaware of the unspoken tension draining from Fal as he murmured, "She has Unseelie blood. She's one of us."

I knelt in front of Tormund, holding Lark's damaged foot in my palms as I worked on finding the magic that rendered the silencing band invisible.

"Her wings were dark purple, you said?" Marius emanated a sweeping wave of mixed emotions. Before he closed himself off from the pack bond, the potency of his reaction had me feeling a little ill to my stomach.

I shot him a concerned look, but he didn't meet my gaze. "That's right. And she had gills and a few other nixie features," I said.

"What a relief. I thought I would drown her trying to finish a kelpie bond with her," he muttered.

Fal smirked. "How romantic."

Marius rounded on him with a snarl. "I'm still going to kick your ass once we're off this train, Falindel."

The dark elf mimed rubbing a shiver from his arms. "I am absolutely shaken by your continued postponement of my ass-kicking."

Marius chuffed in exasperation. "So Lark doesn't notice."

"*Our* mate will see the bruises when she strips me," he said with a flippant toss of his hair.

I rolled my eyes as Tormund exaggerated a groan. I'd found a thread of essence and was working with it. If they'd just quiet down, I could concentrate…

Lark's magic felt like my own, like calling to like. I'd tried giving her some of my essence earlier to help her recover from her depleted state, but it'd been like pouring water into a cracked cup. If the band drew on much more of her magic, it would kill her, so I only sought to work with the illusion on her ankle to move it aside for a couple of minutes. Seeing was believing, and I wanted to know how this improperly placed device had shifted in a decade.

If it was as bad as I thought it was, I needed professional help. I had to get her to the only other essence spinner I trusted with such a delicate matter.

I worked my finger under the illusion, which was a solid mesh of essence strands, and tugged at it with a few bits of my own starry magic. It was as delicate as a negotiation, and I tuned out my brothers' continued banter to focus on doing it correctly.

Success smelled like rotten essence. The alphas in the room gagged, as the smell was so much worse for their sensitive noses. Magic left to sit too long had a certain odor, like sulfur mixed with the vilest black mold. It came from the spell masking the silencing band, disturbed when I lifted it.

Either that or from the purplish fluid that oozed in goopy clots like sap from the wounds circling Lark's ankle and lower calf. The bruise on her leg from Cymora's kick matched a line of dried blood. She'd managed to hit Lark right over an embedded spike.

The silver metal was tarnished from all its exposure to time and wear while Lark was none the wiser to its existence. She had to feel those points jabbing her with every step she took.

I burned with the desire to rip it free, but this was a deeply enmeshed *olcanus*. It had to remain on her for a few short days. But no longer than that. I couldn't bear the thought of Lark suffering further.

Since the wounds it caused weren't quite physical, other than where she'd been kicked, she'd never gotten an infection and lost this foot. Thank the stars for small concessions…I guessed. It also hadn't shifted much as she grew older, only embedded in her flesh more tightly.

"What the *fuck*," Fal said, pinching his nostrils closed as he leaned over and inspected the band.

I smacked his hand away before he could touch it. "Pulling on it will only hurt her worse," I warned.

"Why are we even looking at it?" Distress leaked from Tormund into our pack bond. "We have to get that thing off of her!"

"We will. I have a plan." I began the process of settling the spell I'd lifted back into place. "For now, we keep Lark as comfortable as we can and steal the band's key from Cymora while she's incapacitated."

"And we cannot discuss the band with Lark. Or…anything else we've just learned," Marius said, more a statement than a question.

"Only if you want to cause her more pain. And if you do…" I took a steadying breath and said succinctly, "Nightmares."

Marius released a kelpie's snort. "Noted."

I peered up at her sleeping face, longing to kiss her. She needed pampering and that epic nest she'd dreamt of. More importantly, she had to know how we were coming together to defend her, our mate.

And she would have me Always. *Fate has bound us forever in the depths of time.*

19
LARK

I HAD the sense of time passing as I came in and out of the darkness of deep sleep. There was a gentle weight keeping my eyelids from lifting. It was like a soap bubble stretching around me when I reached for wakefulness. That thin barrier wouldn't allow me to rouse completely, but sometimes I got close.

There were voices speaking in Serri, mostly indistinct. The door opening and shutting more than I was used to. Tormund's sudden exclamation of, "I found it!"

Kauz whispering at him to keep his voice down. His warmth was wrapped around me...his hand cradling my back, gently rocking me to return to resting.

And so I slept until the soap bubble popped on its own and I cracked open my eyes. The light from the shaded window was slanted like it was already afternoon. I smelled the princes all at once: a summery evening by a lake flush with wild mint and waterlily blooms. Completed by roasted mallows and the sprinkling of stardust I was starting to associate with Always.

I sighed out a brief purr and shifted, realizing I was snuggling with my arms around three thin pillows. The blanket under me was actually Kauz's wing. He lay next to me, one hand splayed over his stomach, the other curled around my hip. The shape of his eyelids changed. Even without pupils, he was looking at me, and I looked back. Stars glimmered and winked in his eyes, dancing under the diffuse purple sheen they'd taken from the shaded sunlight.

This is better than stargazing. The night sky was static and remote compared to the warmth of his gaze. Even the frame of his white lashes glittered with the occasional starry mote set free after each blink.

The rest of the room was still, absent of shuffling clothes or the whispers of others keeping quiet below our bunk. Maybe they'd gone to lunch. They'd given me their pillows, and the combination of their fresh scents had me filled with a fuzzy kind of peace. I still set them aside, dropping them off the edge of the cot, to shift closer to Kauz.

We were nearly nose to nose when I was satisfied, my head resting on his shoulder and my arm banded around his torso. "Hi," I breathed.

"Hello, sleepyhead," he teased.

I narrowed my eyes in suspicion. "Why'd I sleep so late?" That soap bubble feeling was probably magic, meaning he'd cast it upon me with his fancy essence spinning.

He shifted me with his shrug. "You must've needed it. This many days stuck on a train, with present company, is stressful."

Well, he wasn't wrong about that. It wasn't that I'd forgotten Cymora's punishment and the breakdown I'd had afterward, but for a few blissful moments, it hadn't been important. I needed to relieve myself. That meant figuring out whether my stepfamily was already in the female's bath. I'd also have to leave his warmth, which I didn't want to do yet.

"But if I had used magic on you," Kauz continued. He brushed hair out of my face, tucking it behind the point of my ear. "It would be worth any ire you have to share this moment alone together."

Ah, stars. With a tender noise in the back of my throat, I leaned in and kissed him. I hoped I wasn't misreading him and going too far, but the opportunity was too good to pass up.

His lips yielded to mine, and he cupped my face as our mouths melded. I longed to taste Always on him like the blast of pheromones from an alpha's kiss, but it wasn't like that. Kauz was still a beta, his own unique individual compared to his brothers.

Essence tingled on my lips, making the pressure of his mouth and tongue feel incredible. It had to be a deliberate trick, as he wasn't spinning magic, though my skin felt extra sensitive in the path he traced up the curve of my waist.

Kauz hadn't touched up my suppressant tattoo since before yesterday's events. Warmth built at my core, and I released a needy mewl for more.

What am I doing? This was a mistake. He had to feel my body heat swelling against him. In a moment, he'd stop kissing me and go for his ink kit to restrain the need building in my body.

Kauz lifted one hand, and a thread of starry essence curled through his fingers. He flicked it away, and the door locked a moment later, its bolt sliding into place with a *click*.

His fingertips drew up the hem of my shirt, letting in cool air. He spoke between kisses. "And it would be worth my whole pack's ire to give you some relief."

"Kauz, what—" I cut off with a moan. He'd caught the curve of my neck in his blunt teeth, and I stilled, my inner omega submitting by instinct with one last flutter of my wings. My breath came in short, heated bursts as he pawed my back blindly until he found the buttons keeping my sleeping shirt closed. The material loosened significantly.

His touch lingered as he tunneled his hands underneath my shirt to rub my bare skin. He used that same essence trick, leaving tingles in the wake of his fingertips. He traced circles up my back, teasing the base of my wings, which trembled the more he touched me. I was slick and needy for him, my core pulsing to the fevered beat of my heart.

"Kauz," I murmured, reluctant to stop him. "We can't."

He released my neck to reply. "'Untouched' has many definitions, but only one that matters."

He caught my hips and rolled until I was lying on my back, wings out flat on either side of me. I was loosely caged, his weight braced between my top and bottom wings. My pussy fluttered and clenched as I considered how easy it'd be to pull him the rest of the way on top of me.

"Not touched."

"By a penis. In a very specific place." He watched my face as he eased his fingertips under the front of my shirt. He tilted his head, asking for permission.

I nodded back. "So, you're not going to, um..." I didn't want to say *touch your penis to my specific place.* I was twenty-two, for stars' sake. But I missed my chance to say *fuck me* instead. It just didn't seem like Kauz's style.

"Nay," he chuckled. "But you could touch it, if you liked."

He nudged my thigh with his erection, and I gasped. My body flamed with need, and I reached for him. Did I know what I was doing? No. But he sucked in a hiss of pleasure when I felt the outline of his cock through his pants. It pulsed through the cloth barrier between us.

He traced the curve of my belly and squeezed my breast just right. "More," I moaned. The whisper of my feral side suggested ripping his clothes off to feel his skin against mine. I settled for reaching under his shirt to feel the flex of his muscles as he drew me closer.

"More," he agreed. With some shuffling, we worked together to free me of my shirt. My nipples pearled under the appreciative gleam in his gaze. The backdrop against that starry night had darkened with lust, losing its purple sheen.

He palmed one breast, rolling the sensitive orb between his fingers, while he lowered his mouth to the other. The brush of his tongue nearly undid me as he pulled my nipple into his mouth and *sucked.* My toes curled, and my hips bucked from the wave of pleasure.

I stopped clutching him to run appreciative fingers over his body, exploring it through touch. His lean figure concealed hard muscle, especially in his shoulders and abs. Everything connected to his massive bat wings was strong and firm to the press of my fingertips.

I wanted to take my time and see the planes of his chest for myself when there wasn't a threat of someone interrupting us. He had his other hand down the front of my pants, his fingertips gliding through the slick coating my lower lips. I trembled and clenched on air.

"Kauz," I whined.

He rewarded me with the press of one fingertip. It sank in easily until my core clamped with another wave of pre-heat to soak his hand. He growled against my breast, his hips jerking, grinding his cock against my thigh. Against all better judgment, I wanted him inside of me. I spread my legs further with a new sound, a lusty trill.

He worked a second finger in my channel while I reached under his clothes and grasped his erection. It was velvety to the touch with an unyielding core, wet with precome at the tip. I spread the bead of liquid over his shaft and rubbed back and forth, grinning when I felt his breath quicken.

Maybe we couldn't join bodies yet, but surely this felt nearly as good. His thumb circled the swollen bud of my clit, and he pumped his fingers in and out of my soaked pussy. My moans hit a higher pitch as the pressure mounted, promising the kind of peak I'd never achieved with my own hand.

Someone tried the knob into our room, then knocked on the door. I froze, and Kauz released my breast from the seal of his mouth and muttered a soft "*foc.*"

He caught my face with his free hand and kissed me hard, then twirled and pressed his thumb down, reminding my body just how close it'd been to coming. With our lips locked, he muffled my moans as he drove his fingers into my needy slit and curled them. He brushed a hidden spot that set me off with a detonation of bliss that radiated through me like a sunburst. His mouth caught my scream.

"Kauzden," Fal sing-songed from the other side of the door. He jiggled the doorknob. "I can smell her from here. You'd better let me in now..." He let the thought drift off meaningfully.

I panted in an utter daze, watching the slightest hint of concern cross and fade from Kauz's face as he broke our kiss with one last gentle brush of his lips.

"One second," he called. With a shift of his shoulders and a great rustle, he folded his dark wings to his back. He licked clean the fingers gleaming with my slick, looking entirely too pleased even with the raging erection he sported.

"Next time, we won't be interrupted, sweetheart," he vowed in a low voice.

My pussy clenched at the thought. *Greedy thing.*

I just hoped there was a next time. I'd never felt such pleasure in my life, and he'd given it to me with only three fingers. "I look forward to it."

At the sound of a key turning in the lock, I went grabbing for my shirt. I dove behind the bulk of Kauz's folded wings and shoved it over my torso.

Fal slipped in with a question in Serri.

"Nay. She's still untouched," Kauz answered in Theli.

The dark elf breathed a sigh of relief. "I must point out the utter irony."

Kauz grumbled under his breath.

"My little beta brother, so worried about the smell of our pheromones!" Fal exclaimed with dramatic flair. "The one who bought special soap so the rest of us could control ourselves. He who was so concerned about that alpha-omega connection taking over."

"I know, I know."

"I am losing my starsdamned mind over this turn of events, Kauz. After all that, *you're* the one to break first and pleasure our omega."

"Like you wouldn't do the same," Kauz remarked.

"I've been *dying* to do the same. You couldn't wait until we could share her? Honestly," he tutted.

I peered around Kauz's side, surprised at how unsurprised I was at Fal's lack of anger. He stood just inside the door, nostrils flared as he scented the air. With his jeweled masquerade mask in place, his illusioned evergreen eyes were dark with promise as they met mine. "It's too bad Tormund and Marius are on their way back from lunch, else I wouldn't call this a missed opportunity," he growled.

My cheeks heated further. Now that I'd come, my scent must be suffusing every nook of the room. There'd be no hiding what we'd just done from the other two males, not with the sugar-kissed promise of my pre-heat woven into the smell of my pheromones.

"We could prop the door," I suggested. The charged air weighed down around us, and I knew we had to change the subject.

Fal chuckled. "Nay, sweet thing. I think Kauz gets to explain himself while I take you to the female's bath."

"Fine," Kauz said.

I imagined Marius and Tormund being much less relaxed about the whole thing. "Sorry," I whispered.

He shifted and put an arm around me, pressing one last kiss against my cheek. "It was worth it." There was still lingering heat in his gaze as he stroked his fingers through my hair.

My heart leapt. I think I fell deeper for him then and there, and it had nothing to do with my pre-heat or any post-orgasm high.

He handed me down to Fal, who already had a towel and my bag of toiletries in hand. The dark elf scooped me up and carried me out of the room.

"What are you doing?" I protested. "I can walk!"

"Then Kauz didn't do a very good job." Something hit the other side of the door with a *thump* after it closed behind us, and he snickered.

"He..." Oh, talking about this with his brother was weird, even if they were packmates.

Fal raised a brow behind his mask, his grin playful. "He what?"

I cleared my throat, grasping for another change of subject. "Why are you wearing that?" I pointed at the mask.

"I found it and figured you should see my Seelie disguise in the light of day."

The illusion on it had changed him into a forest elf, sure, but there was no mistaking his Unseelie mischief or the lilt in his words. Now that I knew better, all I saw was Fal overlaid with tanned skin and green hair and eyes. It was eerie.

"Why? Do you want it?" he teased. I started to smile, hopeful to have at least one of my tokens back for a future nest. "You know what to do to get it back, tricksy li'l pixie."

Well, darn. I might as well stop coveting it. How was I supposed to steal it from him again when he was expecting it this time?

He set me on my feet before the female's bath with a wink, offering over the towel and toiletry bag. I glanced over my shoulder, wary Cymora or Laurel were having a long soak in one of the tubs, waiting for me to show up.

"They're not in there," Fal said. I blinked at the sudden seriousness in his tone. He'd bared the edges of his fangs, just the beginnings of a snarl. "You won't have to worry about them anymore. Trust me."

I did. Trust him, that was. Despite the way we'd met—and the reminder of it he wore—he'd earned my trust with the rest of his brothers by caring for me after my feral moment yesterday.

"Okay." I tilted my head, flashing my throat to show that trust. He released a pleased rumble that I felt to my core.

I walked into the female's bath and found that he was right. I *was* feeling weak in the knees.

20

LARK

A CHANGE of clothes was folded and waiting for me just within the threshold of the female's bath once I was cleansed. Tormund waited for me to emerge, a hopeful little smile crossing his face. "Hi, li'l bird," he said in a way too gentle voice.

He offered his arms for a hug with the slow movements of an alpha to a frightened omega. But there was no need. He wasn't raging, nor did more straightforward alpha anger waft off of him. I limped into his embrace and melted into him and the deep purr rumbling from his chest. I'd missed this.

He scooped me up and began to carry me back to our room. I huffed into his shoulder. "I can walk."

"I just want to comfort you," he answered in a low voice. "Show that I am more than what you saw yesterday."

My alpha is in distress.

Ah, stars. There was no need for him to continue beating himself up for his rage. We had to talk about it. "Could you stop here for a moment?" I asked when we were between cars.

"Of course. You want to look at the sea?" He turned so the sun was at his back, though it still cast a glare over the water far below us. Sunlight haloed him, bringing out the dull shine in his freckled skin and the red tones threaded through his short hair. "Soon we'll be over Serian. I can smell it."

"What does it smell like?" All I could scent was salt water and dust.

He smiled wistfully. "The cold. The more north we go, the colder it gets. And I can smell the chill from here. We'll be home tomorrow."

I hummed. The alphas seemed to have stronger noses than me, but I doubted "cold" was such a distinct smell.

"Hey, Tormund," I said tentatively.

"Aye?"

"I, um. I didn't know you were a redcap."

Any happiness at the proximity of Serian's smell vanished from his expression. "I am so sorry you saw that part of me," he murmured.

"It's not—" I cut myself off, shaking my head. He'd been asking for forgiveness since I'd had my feral moment, and I'd failed to acknowledge it. "You don't have to apologize for who you are. It was just...a lot."

"Sorry."

I lifted a finger to rest over his lips. "And unexpected. If it hadn't happened, were you planning on telling me you're a redcap?"

He didn't reply until I took my finger off his lips. "Eventually. I wanted you to *know* me first." His mouth twisted into a troubled frown. "My brothers agreed to let me be the one to tell you. And I did in the worst way possible. Just say 'redcap,' and watch others go pale. We have a reputation, especially alpha redcaps."

My throat clicked with a dry swallow.

"I can't get a hold of my rage. My brothers have to restrain me each time," he muttered miserably. "I was trained to be your comfort, to help you keep a household and manage a nation. Mother wanted to prove a point. By raising me as the future queen's comfort, she tried to show that redcaps deserve to be treated like any other fae. That we can choose a life other than delivering bloodshed and death."

"Tormund." I waited until he squinted down at me. "You would be terrible at delivering bloodshed and death."

His squint only became more pronounced. "What?"

"You are a generous, snuggly bear of a male, *and* you need to wear your spectacles more. You hold most things way too close to your face," I said, happy to see a little smile tugging at his mouth.

"I do not! I see just fine," he protested.

"The spectacles are really cute," I added.

"Fine...I'll wear them for you," he hedged. "Just to see your face better. That's all."

"You're a sweet male. I'd say your mother proved her point already. You just needed someone able to calm your rages. Your ma—" Oh stars, I almost said the *m* word. It seemed to be on everyone's lips lately except for mine. I barely wanted to acknowledge something when I still didn't know if I could keep it.

He gave me a squeeze. "My mate," he said for me, expression softening. His shoulders fell as if he'd dropped a heavy weight off them. Hopefully that was his lingering guilt and self-hate tumbling into the sea below. "May I kiss you?"

My heart raced with excitement. After two kisses with his brothers had gone out of control, one would think I'd be worried this would end the same way, but I'd loved the kisses from his packmates too much to hesitate. "Yes."

"And..." He scuffed his foot, glancing away for a moment. "I know I am not a beautiful male like Fal or Kauz. But I would give you pleasure any time you asked, li'l bird. Don't forget I was built for...ah. For all your needs."

Heat rose in my cheeks. "I will. But just a kiss for now. We should stop there."

"*Ach.* Of course. I'm honorable," he promised. I leaned up, and he cupped my cheek, the two of us meeting in the middle.

His beard and mustache were scratchy against my face, but I didn't dislike the rougher texture of his kiss. Not when he tasted like dessert, caramelized sugar with its sweetness cut by a satisfying edge of char. We made identical hums of enjoyment.

His big hands were gentle as always. He held me aloft one-armed, my face cradled in a broad palm, while his mouth moved like he could devour me. Our tongues tangled, and his fangs didn't so much as graze my lips.

When the kiss faded, he held me close enough that he didn't have to squint to look at me. He wore a look of such genuine joy that I had to return it, and his gray eyes took in my expression and kiss-swollen lips with an intensity that showed he had to be committing this moment to memory.

Stars, I was doing the same thing. Falling more for this sweetheart, too, while I was at it.

My belly rumbled. "Think you could take me to the dining car?"

"Of course. I'd be happy to feed you," he declared.

When we returned to the room a while later, I was absolutely stuffed. Tormund had bought the train out of its last triple berry cookies, as they were running low this late in the trip. Since he insisted, he carried me, and I held the half dozen cookies in their little paper wrapper.

Tormund announced us at the door and earned an ear flick from Marius and a sleepy sound from Fal. They'd sprawled out over the couches. Marius was reading with a fist curled under his nose, while Fal had been napping face down. He still wore his mask. *Damn.* I could've snuck it away from him if Tormund was quieter.

"Li'l bird's fed and happy. Where's Kauz?" the giant asked.

Fal muffled a yawn. "Laundering our bedding, presumably."

"*Ach.* Still?"

"It's being washed to Marius's satisfaction. Most sensitive sniffer in this room." The dark elf poked his own nose.

Marius made a wordless grumble. Not quite a growl, but close.

"Oh, I see," Tormund said. He headed for the couch with Fal and plopped down once the dark elf made room for us. I stayed with the giant for now, cozy against his padded chest.

"See what?" I asked.

Tormund angled a hand over his mouth to tell me in a loud aside, "He's almost done with his book. He gets very mad if anyone interrupts him."

Marius grunted, sounding annoyed.

"Relatable," I whispered back. If I was a big, angry kelpie, I would do the same thing to get to the end of a story undisturbed.

We sat quietly until he closed the book and placed it aside. He sat there with a faraway look in his eyes.

"Well, was it any good?" Fal asked.

"It was...unexpected. I thought I was reading about a Seelie female's firsthand account of the last war, just for it to become a fictional romance between her and a human alpha."

"Wait," I blurted. "Have you been reading *The Battle of Marsh Hill* this whole time?"

Marius glanced at me. "Aye."

"I've read that book!" With a title like that, it'd been one of the last books left in my old home I'd picked up rather than reread one of my dog-eared favorites. "It really gets you in the first third, doesn't it? You think it's a gritty war memoir, and then Sylvie meets John."

"John?" Fal echoed with a little laugh. "What kind of name is *John*?"

We both ignored him. "Yes, it tricked me too," Marius said. "This was one of the only books written in Serri at the bookshop. I wanted the tale of war."

"Oh, I skip that part on a reread."

He snorted, though it was a gentle one. Amused, perhaps. "Of course you do. What was your favorite part, then?"

I stroked my chin. "When they kissed behind the waterfall. No, wait. When they kissed on their *wedding* day."

"What is a wedding?" Tormund asked.

"It's a human thing. It's very romantic." My wings fluttered with my giggle. "A human couple or pack throw a party after exchanging vows to love one another for their whole lives in front of their families and friends."

"Vows?" he echoed, eyes widening. "That sounds dangerous."

"Humans aren't bound to their word like fae are. And I guess they don't have pack bonds either."

"Oooh."

"The kisses were your favorite part?" Marius asked in disbelief. "Not the saucy bits?"

"Did you like the saucy bits?" I countered.

"They didn't strike me as particularly well-written. I think John had three hands in the cave scene. However, that could be the fault of the translator."

"I think he accidentally had three in the Theli version too." I scrunched my brow as I tried to remember.

"Well, it was some entertainment. I bought another for the trip. I believe it was titled *Tides of Treason*."

I gasped. "*Much* better story. You should've started with that book! The crew is so much fun, and even though the author says it's a romance, that part is really second to the swashbuckling."

Marius's expression brightened. I caught my breath at seeing an actual smile on his face, made lopsided by the pull of his scar. "I'll have to get started, then. Maybe I'll get far enough in that we can talk about it—*what*, Fal?" He cut a sudden glare at the dark elf, who was posed with his chin on his fist, grinning broadly.

"I can hardly believe it. You two book nerds are flirting." He affected a swoon with a grand gesture of his free hand. "Are you going to start a book club? I'll join if we read the saucy bits out loud."

I turned pink at the thought. Of course Fal wanted to read those parts out loud. I was also feeling a little flush all of a sudden. The pulsing in my belly that preceded a cramp was coming on, and I held my middle in anticipation of it. In the day's events, Kauz still hadn't refreshed my suppressant tattoo.

"No," Marius said flatly.

"Don't be so hasty. The li'l pixie looks like she likes the idea," Fal teased.

I blushed a little harder. "Only if you're the one to read them."

The dark elf looked positively gleeful. "Do I smell a deal?" He offered his hand to shake.

My eyes narrowed. Any Seelie would be suspicious when an Unseelie offers a deal, but this one seemed benign enough. What were the chances Marius wanted to start a book club with me anyway?

"I'll shake on it if you give me your mask," I said.

"Ah. If you're adding to the deal, then so am I. I want to hear this scene with the human alpha and his three hands. Read by you, *mo stór*." His expression was pure mischief as he continued to offer his hand.

I leaned back, whispering in Tormund's ear, "What did he call me?"

"My darling or my treasure. Same idea," he whispered back.

"Treasure," Fal confirmed with a wink. "A prize I've stolen from Thelis."

Oh. That was sweet, actually. My fluttery wings definitely gave away how flattered I was as I shook his hand.

And that was how I was partway through reading a Serri translation of a poorly written sex scene out loud when Kauz walked in with a basket overflowing with freshly washed bedding. He paused in the threshold, head tilting as he took in the fascinated way his brothers listened to my off-kilter delivery.

Fal gestured for him to join us. And Kauz did, settling in the space next to Marius, his expression shading from confused to amused as I kept going. I pitched my voice higher for Sylvie and lower for John, pausing at a few unexpected points when my audience burst out laughing. Usually followed by them urging me to read more.

Eventually, I hit the end of the chapter, and Fal was still egging me on. I said, "I think that was the whole scene."

"Oh yes, pages ago. I just love listening to you. You're going to speak Serri beautifully." He waited for a moment before adding, "Someday."

I tossed the book at him. He caught it, laughing, before I even realized the audacity of what I'd done. A week ago, I would've never dreamt of throwing something at a prince, Unseelie or not. My stepfamily would've admonished me for even thinking about it.

Well, they weren't here. My whole day had been blessedly free of Cymora and Laurel, and I wasn't going to let the specter of their disapproval ruin anything.

"And, as promised." Fal untied the mask from his face and offered it to me. I scented it with a purr of approval, sure to press it to my nose later when no one was looking. It smelled strongly of him after he'd worn it for so long. Plus, now that he'd taken it off, his forest elf disguise was replaced by his real features—his handsome coloring and striking feline eyes.

Silly lovestruck omega, I sighed at myself.

I was four for four today, loving Fal a little more for his teasing and holding on to some hope of gaining more positive attention from Marius now that we'd connected as book lovers.

Fal cleared his throat. "Now, where are the other saucy bits? I promised *mo stór* I would read them to her."

21

LARK

WHEN IT WAS time to sleep for our last night on the train, I chose to rest with Marius. I don't think anyone was more surprised than the kelpie himself, who pointed to his chest to confirm.

"It's not a good idea, li'l omega," he warned in his low growl.

That wasn't enough to change my mind. I'd picked him to sidestep any more chances to fool around, as I knew he wouldn't try to touch me intimately. Plus, he'd keep me safe. Since Kauz had touched up my suppressant tattoo before bedtime, I was in the right mind to make a sound decision.

Once we'd turned off the essence lamp, Marius avoided touching me by keeping most of the cot's space between us. His back was essentially flush against the wall.

I held my pillow and drifted off. I had Fal's mask for his scent. Tormund also gave me his cloak to sleep with—the undamaged one, its fabric orange with gold accents—which was like a fireproof blanket. It was heavy and scratchy, but I burrowed into it for the trace smell of smoke and mallows clinging to it.

I woke up early to a dim gray sunrise, feeling a rare sort of contentment. It was earlier than I usually roused, and by the soft snores and heavy breaths around the room, the princes were asleep. Waterlily and wild mint were the dominant scents in my nostrils, and I made a pleased hum. Marius really did smell amazing. And he put off a lot of heat, chasing away the chill hanging in the morning air. I was pressed up against his chest.

Wait.

I cracked open my eyes, wondering how this had happened. At some point in the night, I'd discarded the pillow, mask, and cloak and was under the covers with Marius instead. We'd met in the middle of the cot. His thighs trapped my legs, and his arm melded to my waist and held me against him. I'd curled into the embrace, my palms resting over his steady heartbeat.

This position also pressed the length of his cock, harder than a metal bar, right up against my belly. My face flamed. Alphas were supposedly bigger, but I hadn't realized just how large that actually meant.

Hello. Stars, I was certainly awake now. As was Marius. He was nuzzling my hair and scenting me with deep breaths through his nose.

"You're awake." He spoke in a rusty growl. Marius had many different growling tones, I'd learned, but this one had a particular rasping texture that I'd only heard a couple times. Most notably when we'd met in a pawn shop and he'd scented my impending heat. The little hairs on the back of my neck lifted of their own accord.

I tilted my head up to catch a glimpse of his face. His pupils were extra dilated, swallowing up all but the smallest rim of yellow. He gazed back at me without any of his usual scowling anger. In fact, it was the opposite. He beheld my sleepy face with an expression full of emotion. I should've been elated to see him more open, but unease ate into my sense of peace and safety. My omega instincts wiggled at the back of my mind, sure there was something *different* about him right now.

"So soft," he whispered, lifting the weight of his arm. He traced the curve of my cheek with the smooth backs of his fingers. "So small and fragile. I've been afraid. Worried I'd harm you." He retrieved his other hand and began to gentle me, using his knuckles to rub my cheeks and jaw, and tugging on my ears just right.

Then his fingers drifted into my hair and I leaned into his touch. He made a sound like an animal would, deep and low. And somehow, I knew he was saying, "*Mine.*"

I'd leaned enough into his hands to expose my throat. His hot breath washed over my skin before the points of his fangs pressed to the curve where my shoulder and neck met. I stilled on instinct, submitting the moment he applied pressure there.

He eased me onto my back so I was pinned beneath his bulk. My breath caught in a stutter of fear with how much this position put me at his mercy.

Realization hit me, swift and stunning like a bolt of lightning. *"I'm a danger to you, broken in half on the inside."*

He'd been speaking literally with his earlier warning. Of course he had. Marius had never been anything but straightforward and blunt in his fae honesty. He'd just about told me this secret without saying it outright.

He was *feral.*

Every fae knew about the perils of losing themselves to their instincts, even in a farm town as small as Osme Fen. Trauma, especially sustained and repeated forms of abuse, created a wedge between instinct and reason and caused fae to go feral. It could happen to anyone of any designation, and there were levels of severity.

There was me, a touch feral, prone to the occasional fit. But then there was Marius, who...well, was clearly at the stage of feral behavior where he was losing his mind, since he was acting like an animal. Dangerous, indeed, when combined with his alpha size and strength.

As I lay there with my heart pounding a frenzied cadence, I took in how he had me pinned and, despite that, how he wasn't hurting me. My inner omega told me to keep submitting, not that I had much of a choice with his fangs at my neck.

This is about dominance, not sex, said my own instincts.

Though his arousal was heavy and pulsing against my hip, he wasn't trying to disrobe me or shove my thighs apart. He wasn't even restraining me with his whole weight. His knees were on either side of my legs, and he'd braced his forearms away from my wings. The wet brush of his tongue replaced the pressure of his bite, slowly swiping along my neck.

He's tasting my fear. If I struggle, he'll taste my blood too.

Even without his fangs at my throat, I continued to hold myself as still as possible. Feral alphas were known to be unpredictable. I wasn't sure calling for help and startling him was my best course of action.

"Sweet prey," he murmured. He nuzzled either side of my neck, long brushes of his cheeks and jaw. He'd shaved last night, leaving his skin smooth against mine. "Don't be afraid. I can't stand it anymore." He met my gaze. There was just something so earnest about him... maybe he wasn't so dangerous after all, now that he'd established his dominance.

"You have me pinned."

He rumbled a content noise and grinned, the very image of a predator who had his prey exactly where he wanted her.

Also, he didn't take a hint well. "Maybe you should get off of me?"

The glimpse of his happiness faded. "Nay. The last time I let you go, you disappeared. Where have you been?" He sounded almost hurt. "I've waited for you. I've been loyal."

I crinkled my brow. "What?"

If I thought his feral side would explain, I was wrong. He dipped his head to nip along the side of my ear and down my neck.

"Marius," I prompted, stifling a moan. Each gentle bite felt better than the last.

He stopped at the crook of my neck after putting the pressure of his teeth against my pulse. "I didn't mean to give you a fright earlier. I should've told you." He lifted his arm briefly to tap under his right eye. "This is damaged. Always approach me from the left, li'l omega. Other-wise, I startle."

I took another look at his facial scar. It crossed over his right brow, which meant it was probably a wonder he had the eye at all. "I didn't realize," I murmured.

"I hide it. It's my secret." He winked, which was an odd thing to see him do. With his ultra-serious demeanor, he barely smiled, but here the feral version of him was going and sharing what had to be a guarded weakness without worry.

Well, if I was stuck here and he was in a sharing mood... "What happened to hurt you so badly?" I asked.

"So much. But I wouldn't burden you." He eyed me with concern. "What happened to *you*? You're so..."

"Tiny and frail?" I supplied a little dryly.

"Stifled. No magic. No color." With an unexpected yank on my collar, he exposed the stretch of bare skin above my left breast. He pressed his finger over top my racing pulse as I yelped in surprise. "And where is your mark?" he rasped.

He traced the horseshoe-like omega symbol starting where his fingertip had landed. Every omega manifested their mark in a different place, though it tended to be in an easily bitable location. Did Marius's instincts sense where mine would manifest?

"It's not ready," I whispered.

His answering rumble sounded uneasy. "When we bond, you'll claim me first anyway. My mark is here, mate." He took hold of my hand and pressed my palm to his hipbone.

He jerked the moment I made contact with the barrier of his clothes. His eyes clenched closed with a pained gasp. When he looked at me again, his pupils were shrinking back to their proper size. He took in how he had me pinned.

His nostrils flared and his breathing shallowed. "You smell like...ah, fuck. Did I hurt you?"

"No, it's okay. We mostly talked—"

"I told you," he growled out. He batted away the covers tangled around him with a desperate air. "All it takes is a moment of lost control. I could've snapped one of your delicate bones or..." Shaking out his mane of hair, he muttered what had to be a streak of Serri curses. He pulled away from me and straightened, beaming his head off the cot above us and snarling as he stalked out of the room.

Tormund growled with fiery menace as he sat up in his cot. *Stars, he was going to rage.* I launched at him with a flap of my wings.

"Don't rage. Please," I said, clinging to his torso.

The redcap, still bleary from his wakeup, put his arm around me. "I'm not going to rage, li'l bird. What is happening?" he whispered.

"More of Marius's shit," Fal grumbled from his bunk above us. "Let's go back to sleep."

I DIDN'T GO BACK to sleep. And I had no idea where Marius hid for the last few hours of our trip, because he didn't return to the room. At first, I waited and watched the door, wanting to see if he'd explain some of the things his feral side had said.

The longer he was away, the more his words niggled at me. I chewed on them without satisfaction as I spent the morning with Fal and Tormund. Kauz had left the room after breakfast to check on the kelpie and hadn't returned either.

"The last time I let you go, you disappeared. Where have you been?"

It wasn't as if I could ask him what he'd meant by that. But there was someone else who might tell me, and it was the dark elf who held my hand while we waited to arrive in the Unseelie capital, Neslune. I was otherwise snuggled into my fur-lined cloak. Ripped or not, it was heavy enough for the winter chill, and one of the males had cleaned off Cymora's shoeprint.

We rolled up the shade over the room's window and watched Serian whoosh by as the train descended toward our destination. The further north the train traveled, the more snow and ice coated the land and the pointed roofs of houses below.

I turned my gaze from the window to Fal, whose slitted eyes read my expression. "What's on your mind?" he asked.

"Marius is feral."

"Oh, aye. Very. I'm surprised it took you this long to figure it out."

Maybe I should've, considering his behavior. It was certain the princes wouldn't tell me since they hadn't mentioned that Tormund was a redcap, either. The giant was seated across from us, flames flickering briefly in his pupils. He blew a curl of smoke from the corner of his mouth.

"Is he...dangerous?" I asked.

Fal chuckled. "Lark, give us some credit. We wouldn't trust him around you if he was."

"He's just mean," Tormund muttered.

"As a snake," Fal said in agreement. "But I will say, I don't blame him. The event that led to his condition was entirely out of his control. He's still a part of the pack, as you will soon be, *mo stór*."

I managed a tense smile, reminded that today was the day. I'd meet the queen tonight, after I settled my things and changed clothes. Stars, I wasn't ready.

In the worst-possible scenario, I could use my bare understanding of Serri and the full moon coins stashed in my things to get a magirail ride to Zemosia after all. I wasn't completely without options. However, I *had* gotten complacent with how easy it was to spend time with the princes.

The ghost of mermaid laughter haunted me. *"Like you could ever be a princess."*

I had to prove Cymora wrong. Somehow.

I replaced her voice in my mind with the roughened growl of Marius's feral side. *"Mine."* It helped. I was smiling as the train glided into the magirail station in Neslune, secure in one thing: the princes wanted me too. No matter what happened next, I had that.

"Stay here for now, Lark. Back of the train disembarks last. Plus, we have to secure transport for all our things," Fal said. He exchanged a meaningful look with Tormund before leaving the room.

The window looked out over a stretch of the station platform. I watched the semi-familiar faces of other passengers file off with their bags. Among them was Fal, who hurried out of sight, just to return ten minutes later with four alphas dressed in police uniforms.

"Is something else happening?" I asked, stiffening as they boarded the train. Were they here for me? Was all this some Unseelie trick after all?

"No?" Tormund tried to say innocently, his tone pitching up.

It wasn't long until we heard shouting. "How dare you! I have done nothing wrong! Arrest the nightmare monster that assaulted me in my sleep instead!" It was Cymora, her voice getting louder. "I want to speak to my stepdaughter. Lark—" She cut off with a sudden choke as I went board-straight and tensed, awaiting an order.

"Maybe something is happening," Tormund said with a wince. In the silence that followed, Cymora must've been dragged away before she could give me an order. "Please don't ask any more. We'll tell you everything when we can."

I sighed and whined at the same time, earning an unhappy look from Tormund. "It is a happy day, li'l bird. We're home! I can't wait to show you your new nest. We will fill it together with all the things you love."

My inner omega perked up. I wanted a nest again...a space that was my own. I wouldn't have to share it with anyone else unless I invited them. "That sounds like a lot of fun," I said.

"It will be. We could stop at an omega store on the way—"

Fal poked his head back into the room. "I have terrible news," he interrupted. "We're *expected*."

The royal pack had sent a small army of servants to meet us at the station, it turned out. Several betas and a handful of alphas, most of races I'd never seen before, came into the train to get our things. Tormund carried me out with the group, much to my chagrin until he stepped off the train and the Serian winter enveloped us. The air was dry and frigid, biting at my exposed skin.

I wrapped my cloak tighter around my body and snuggled back into Tormund's fire fae warmth. He took a deep breath and exclaimed, "There's the wonderful smell of Serian cold!"

All I scented was the fur lining of my drawn hood and the nothingness of a frozen nose. "How can you smell anything?" I asked with chattering teeth.

He released a jolly laugh. "You'll get used to it. Would you be okay sharing a horse?"

I lifted my hood to spot the horse in question. It was waiting with a beta holding the reins, nickering happily upon seeing Tormund approaching. What a beautiful beast. It was huge and shaggy, with fur the blue-white color of aged ice and broad hooves like snowshoes.

"I have some experience with horses," I ventured.

"I will buy you one, then. But this is my girl."

He placed me back on my feet to take the mare's reins and coo while he rubbed her nose. She nuzzled his palm thoroughly and stamped a front hoof. "I know," he murmured in Serri, along with more I didn't understand.

I accepted a boost into the saddle and scooted forward when Tormund squeezed in behind me. He guided the mare into motion. I sat straighter and relaxed my back out of old habit. "Did you ride often?" he asked.

"I used to," I said wistfully. "Osme Fen didn't have a lot to do, but we certainly had horses. We'd race them for fun on quiet days."

"Would you win?"

I twisted my lip as I thought. "Stars, it was a long time ago now. I can't remember."

We were at the heart of a procession through the street leading away from the magirail station. I felt eyes on me as the fae of Neslune parted for the princes and their servants. My fingers closed around the side of my hood, prepared to draw it further over my head if anyone tried to approach us.

At first glance, it seemed a lot like Ilysnor, only with significantly colder weather. We displaced many of the Unseelie residents, who stopped going about their business and stared as we passed them.

"Hmm. We should race once you train your new horse, li'l bird. But don't be surprised if you win—you are so lightweight," he teased.

"Oh, you don't actually have to buy me a horse," I hedged.

"No, I want to. I'll get you one of those wee li'l half-unicorn horses that leave sparkles behind them. You would look very cute on one!"

"Cute on what?" Kauz had dropped back to bring his mount next to ours. To keep warm, he wore a vest over his chest and a cloak stretched to wrap around his furled wings and back.

Tormund explained in rapid Serri, and Kauz nodded. "Aye, she would look adorable on a horse like that. Let's buy her one."

"Not you too," I protested.

The dream warden grinned. "Don't you remember me telling you how much we're going to spoil you, sweetheart?"

"If this evening goes well. And..." I said under my breath.

Somehow, Kauz still heard me. "And what?" he prompted.

"It's nothing."

"Tell me," he invited with that calm, soothing voice of his.

"Just...Marius." I fiddled with my fingertips under the folds of my cloak. I still didn't feel like I had an explanation for this morning, and the kelpie wasn't part of the procession.

Kauz hummed. "I can't wait for you to meet my mother. It's going to be wonderful to watch you blossom once you see how excited she'll be that we've found our mate. Marius will also have to acknowledge that he gets to keep you. Just hold on a little longer. His kelpie loyalty is as solid as faesteel."

"He would know. Marius and Kauz are best friends," Tormund told me, whispering behind his hand. "Most of us don't spend a lot of time together like we did on the train. We have lives, duties, and friends outside of being brothers. But we'll become a more unified pack with you at our center, li'l bird. All four of us will want to share your nest."

Kauz nodded, murmuring in agreement.

"There it is. Home." Tormund pointed. Up ahead, built on a high hill overlooking the rest of the city, was Serian Palace. I'd read somewhere that it'd once been a fortress stronghold built to withstand anything war could bring, and I believed it.

The palace was squat and plain at its core, two stories that were thick and unadorned. More artful wings and towers had been sculpted into its sides. It wasn't pretty like the Seelie royal castle, but it had its own charm under a glistening coat of ice and snow.

"Home," I repeated in a hopeful murmur.

We passed by the last of the shops and homes closest to the palace and wound around to the front gates, which were already open for us. "Why was Fal nervous about being expected?" I asked Tormund.

"Mother, or one of our fathers, is probably waiting for us."

I felt the color in my face drain away. Stars, he couldn't have told me this earlier? I gulped a nervous swallow. Well, it may be a joyous thing. The princes were returning together from a long trip to Thelis, after all.

The train of servants we'd brought with us started to head around to enter through the side of the palace while we crossed its frozen grounds. Special flowers and plants stuck out of the snow and ice, blooming in silvers, grays, and light blues like camouflage. I wondered if they would melt at the barest touch. We rode straight past them and dismounted before a short and narrow staircase leading into the belly of the palace.

Once a set of servants took the horses' reins, Fal turned to us and said, "We'll go inside together once Marius gets here." He fidgeted with his clothes, uncharacteristically anxious. I matched his energy by wringing my fingers under my cloak while we waited.

Marius arrived with a clatter of horse hooves, dismounting from another hearty, furry steed. I wondered if it was weird for a kelpie to ride a horse—not that I was going to ask. Now that I knew he was feral, I saw the signs. His fluid prowl of a walk. The piercing, predatory stare. And, as the other princes had a short conversation in Serri, the way he grunted and growled rather than spoke.

Yet when Fal went up the stairs and the others followed, it was Marius who turned to me. "Would you like assistance?"

I'd barely used my legs the last couple of days, despite complaining most of the times I was picked up the moment I limped. Tormund and Fal were in the habit of carrying me without asking. Kauz and Marius hadn't, not even once. The former didn't have alpha strength, and the latter, well...

I still didn't understand him. But he didn't hate me, as I'd originally assumed.

His ear flicked as I overthought the offer. "I'm in control. I won't bite you," he said irritably.

"I didn't think you would."

"Make a decision, li'l omega."

I took a hitching step toward him. "Yes. Please help me." *Stars-damned stairs.*

He scooped me up before I could put my weight on my right foot again. A pair of guards opened the double doors leading inside and announced something in Serri. Once we were through the threshold, the guards closed the doors behind us. Marius set me down and strode ahead of me.

The area was heated by a large fire crackling at the back of the foyer. It was a smaller space than I'd expected, barely more than a large room, though richly appointed with rugs, upholstered chairs, and essence lamps. Several doorways branched off from it, most of them shut with what looked like metal doors lined with seals. Another gift from the palace's fortress days.

A female no taller than me stood across from Fal, her fists propped on her hips as she took in the four princes. She *had* to be the queen. Her dress was beautiful, black but shimmery, reflecting light like liquid silk. It was tailor-made to hug her figure, with room for the baby bump rounding her middle. The color set off her light gray skin tone and icy blue eyes well.

I shuffled in slow, steady movements so I didn't draw her attention and hid behind Tormund's bulk. He glanced back with a little smile. "That's our mom. She is asking where we've been," he whispered behind his hand.

I nodded but didn't emerge from his shadow. The last thing I needed was for her to notice me and have our first meeting happen while I was fresh off the magirail.

Queen Nemensia was the first nixie I'd seen in person. She had claws for nails and small, needle-like fangs. Several rings lined her fingers when she gestured, and she seemed to lack the webbed membranes between her fingers that nixies were said to had. But it was still obvious she was a water fae from the trailing fins that lay down her back like several sets of pseudo-wings.

They snapped behind her with a whip-like noise as she drew in a deep breath and started saying their names, exaggerating them angrily. "Fal*und*el." She pointed at Marius. "Mar*ee*us." Her accusing finger hesitated a moment before landing on Kauz. "Kauz*uh*den." She shook that digit at Fal. "*Mo leanbh*, Tormund." Her tone softened while she clasped her hands and smiled at him. He preened a bit.

Then he whispered to me, "She is very mad. She forgets our names when she is this mad."

"What's happening?" I whispered back. And watched in fascination as the other three princes shrank in the face of the queen's tone. That was until she spoke Serri too rapidly for me to follow and they exchanged confused looks.

"She's asking where Princess Glory is," Tormund explained as quietly as he could. "The Queen of Thelis wrote to her and said the princess was missing and that Fal was seen at the masquerade. He's explaining that we didn't steal her—"

"What do you mean, you stole a different pixie?" Queen Nemensia demanded, switching to flawless Theli. "Is she here? I want to see her *now*."

Tormund stepped aside, gently nudging me forward. I barely had time to panic before the Queen of Serian was taking my measure across the room. She looked me over top to bottom, and I braced myself for her reaction.

She drew herself up and gasped, eyes sparkling with delight. As she bustled over, her fins fanned out like a gossamer train undulating behind her. Their translucent blue lengths glowed throughout with gray lines and spots, sure to seem brighter in the dark or underwater.

Fal followed in her wake. "Mother, I'm happy to introduce you to our mate."

Queen Nemensia put a hand to her chest. "Oh, my heart. Finally, my sons bring me a new daughter."

Someone else spoke up in Serri from one of the armchairs by the fire. I was so pulled in by the queen's presence that I hadn't even realized he was there, even though a gold crown gilded his head. One of the kings—Queen Nemensia took hold of my cheeks before I could figure out whose father he was. Her fins slowly settled along her back as she took me in more closely.

Every greeting I'd practiced slipped straight out of my head. I curtsied, and my cloak parted with the motion. "Take that off for a moment. Let me see those wings," she said before I could stumble over a hello.

I unclasped it, and Fal took it from me. My anxiously flicking pixie wings popped back into place without the weight of the fur pushing them down. She hummed, tilting her head. "You'd fit right in with the Serian winter. Tell me your name, dear."

I swallowed thickly. "It's Lark. Um, of Osme Fen. It's a ple—"

"Lark of Osme Fen!" She took hold of my shoulders, and my eyes widened at the sudden exclamation. "Are you a ghost?" With strength I would've never expected, she spun me around to face her sons and pointed at me, speaking Serri, presumably asking the question over again.

Kauz looked baffled as he shook his head. Marius, next to him, had an expression of grim concern.

"*Because*," Queen Nemensia said heavily. "I remember the awful day when I read your father's letter detailing your sudden passing. You were still a babe. Six years old, if that."

So many questions piled up in my head, one on top of the other. Was this somehow a dream? There was no other explanation I could think of as I watched the queen's eyes well with tears.

"Mother, there's something else we need to tell you—" Kauz began.

She waved dismissively. "Not now, Falindel."

"It's Kauzden," he corrected patiently. "And it really can't wait—"

"Not now," she repeated in a hiss. "I know who you are. My errant son that leaves me to worry with no word for nearly a *month*."

"You knew my father?" I whispered.

She sniffed and shook her head, scattering her azure-colored curls. "Oh, I knew him. How could I not? He was mates with my best friend, Dorei. Stole her from Serian and the beauty of Once Else to live in a farm town in another kingdom. She said it was *true love*, and I still think she was crazy. She died there, without me." A tear leaked down her cheek as she reached up, cupping my face. "But here you are, in her spitting image and back from the dead. What happened to you, *mo stóirín*? You were purple. And a seamless mix of pixie and nixie."

Her voice fuzzed into a ringing in my ears. "What...what did you say?" I mumbled.

"You don't remember me? I'm your godmother. I took you to my nest like my own child," she continued. "I need every answer you have, Metalark!"

My full, forgotten name hit me like a blow to the head. I reeled, dizzy, and stumbled back from her. Colors washed out to gray, covering my sight in lines so bright that I saw them behind my shuttering eyes. Air kissed my wings as I fell into the arms of unconsciousness.

22

LARK

I came back to the waking world in completely different surroundings. My cheek was pressed into Kauz's padded vest, swaying as he carried me at a fast walk through a corridor. I shut my eyes again with a groan. It felt like someone had buried an iron spike in my head. It hurt to even think.

"Welcome back," Kauz whispered.

"What happened?" I croaked.

He hesitated. In the meantime, we passed by several fae that greeted him in Serri. It sounded like he was asked several questions, none of which he responded to.

I viewed the world through a crack in my lids. The hallway he strode down was more open than the former fortress, lined with windows. They let in streams of cold light that played across the purple reflections in Kauz's eyes. His brow was drawn and his teeth bared, giving him as unapproachable a visage as he could make.

I whined. Was he unhappy with me? I couldn't remember what I'd done to upset the calmest prince.

"I'm taking you to someone who is going to help you, sweetheart," he murmured.

Hopefully someone who could heal away the headache threatening to split my skull.

"Wait...the queen?" I asked. I'd just met her, right? Yet the more I tried to recall what she looked like, the worse the pain behind my eyes became.

"Don't worry about her right now."

I sighed and bared my throat in a sign of trust. Though it probably looked like my head was lolling. Kauz would talk to me about what'd happened when he was ready.

He stopped before an ornate pair of doors with no visible handles. There was a pattern in raised gold swirls across it, though it was cut through by a circle over both doors that was several feet long. The pattern was shifted upside-down inside of the circle.

Kauz set me on my feet and supported me with a wing around my back as he started making gestures with both hands. Essence wove through his fingers and into the circle, which jerked with the squeal of metal brushing metal. It began to turn, then stuck. He cursed under his breath and jabbed his right hand forward.

The circle jerked again before righting itself with the ticking of rotating gears. A heavy lock slid open, and the double doors parted for us. Kauz shifted, peeling the cloak from his wings and offering it to me. I wrapped it around my body with an appreciative smile and sank into its lingering warmth. My fur-lined cloak was...somewhere else. I was trying to puzzle out what'd happened to it when he picked me up again and carried me into the room he'd opened.

He closed the door behind him with a kick of his heel, and the lock reengaged. "He never remembers to oil that thing," he muttered.

I was too busy gaping at our surroundings to reply. The room was an observatory of some kind, dominated by a giant telescope in the center. It was two stories at least, built with an open concept. Painted canvases covered most of the wall space, some faded with age. There were several balconies lining the walls too and items scattered *everywhere.*

"Who's there?" a male called from somewhere above us in Serri.

Kauz called his name back, and a face leaned over the side of one of the top balconies. "Kauzden!" he echoed with a big smile.

He took a leap down to us, spreading a pair of black bat wings at the last minute to break his fall. The markings on the inside of his wings were unique, a jumble of brightly hued, abstract lines that looked as if they were designed by a distracted mind.

He was a little taller and slimmer than the prince holding me, with a heavy pair of glasses hanging on a chain around his neck, forgotten or dropped from his face. His pack mark was similar to that of Pack Sorles, painted over with small, ornate details. He also had starry night eyes, and while he was clean-shaven like Kauz, he kept his white hair long and drawn back in a thin tail.

"Dad, this is my mate, Lark," Kauz said in Theli.

The king glanced at me, and his excited expression faded to concern. He cleared his throat and switched languages too. "I'm not supposed to meet her until later. Though." He smiled and dipped his head. "Don't get me wrong, I'm glad to make your acquaintance. Call me Thalas. No need for fancy titles."

I managed a pinched smile, while Kauz held me to him a little tighter. "It's an emergency," he stated.

"It is?" I murmured.

He squeezed me but didn't answer. They switched languages again, and Thalas gestured for Kauz to follow. Thalas unfurled his wings and took flight with a leap and heavy flap, heading for one of the larger balconies overhead. Kauz waited until he'd landed before crouching. My heart lurched at the weightless feeling that followed as he carried me into the air.

He powered through the observatory with ease to take me to the balcony his father had picked out. It had an extra-large upholstered chair built for a winged dreamlander and a table covered with various tools and implements, none of which I recognized. The tiled floor was a maze of more tools, and many of them looked sharp.

Kauz picked his way through them with care and set me in the chair with a brush of his lips over my forehead. "What's the emergency?" I asked.

He replied with only a look, tightened lips, and eyes more night than stars. He wasn't going to tell me. I just had to trust him, even though anxiety tightened my skin.

Thalas rummaged through the things on the table, muttering under his breath. He'd donned his glasses, magnifying and blurring the stars in his eyes, and eventually picked out what he was looking for. It looked like a wooden stick, which he held out to me. "Put this under your tongue."

I loosened Kauz's cloak and took the stick, turning it over.

"It's an essence meter. I just want a quick reading," he explained.

I took in his encouraging smile and echoed it shyly. The stick had a flattened end, which I pushed under my tongue. Symbols and lines lit up its length, which he read upside-down with a troubled hum.

"All right, then. A couple more tests while I confer with my son. Nothing to worry about." He patted my shoulder and plucked the stick out of my mouth. He handed it to Kauz, and the two of them chatted away in Serri. Just like earlier, with the queen...they naturally spoke too quickly for me to follow.

And trying to remember what happened earlier was bringing my headache back to full blast. I bit my lip to suppress a whine.

The king's next test involved getting a different reading by tying a leather strap around my wrist. He'd produced a sheaf of loose paper and a clipboard from somewhere in the clutter of items on the floor and noted down the reading the strap took.

"Did you know butterfly wings have scales?" he asked me while searching for a third tool. "They are wee flecks of color to our eyes, but they help the little bugs stay dry and fly properly."

"I didn't know that," I said, wondering why he mentioned it.

"Your wings have the same property. Though pixies are much larger than butterflies, so your scales are also bigger and mostly made of essence."

Oh, that *was* interesting. "Is that what pixie dust is?"

"Aye. We're going to inspect your wings to find a loose scale for a test."

"I don't really shed dust." I felt an embarrassed blush coming on when he looked up and tilted his head. He was writing with one hand and handing Kauz a magnifying glass with the other.

He started asking questions rapidly. "Do you have trouble flying? Do they get cold before the rest of you when you're outside? Do they soak through quickly in the rain?"

I nodded along.

"Were they once a different—"

"Dad," Kauz interrupted, nudging him.

"Right, right. I just don't get to study pixies very often." Thalas straightened. "Well, there's got to be a speck of dust on you somewhere. If you would stand for a moment, please."

I eased to my feet and left Kauz's cloak behind on the chair, immediately shivering. The observatory wasn't as cold as outside, but it was drafty. I was covered in goosebumps under my long-sleeved blouse.

The males stood behind me with magnifying glasses, inspecting my wings while I tried not to flutter them anxiously. They were deep in discussion over something they didn't want me to understand while they looked. Thalas repeated "need one" more than once as they moved to my sides and looked at the front of my wings instead.

"Aha!" Thalas said in Theli. "I see a scale. Get me the..." He made a pinching motion with his fingers.

"Where?" Kauz asked.

"Over there."

Kauz went over to the table to start looking. "When's the last time you organized this part of the workshop?"

"I know where everything is. Organizing only ruins it," Thalas answered.

Kauz rolled his eyes and returned with a pair of tweezers.

"This may sting, Lark. The scale is in a sensitive spot." He pulled it free before he was even done explaining, catching me by surprise when the pinch came from the tender inner curve of my lower wing.

I yelped, and Kauz growled, showing his teeth for a moment. Thalas glanced around me. "Did that come from you?" he laughed.

Kauz drew his brow in. "Is this the last test?"

"It should be before we view... Let's call it *the item*. And look how pretty this is." He showed Kauz the scale and tilted it toward the overhead essence lamp. All I saw was a shimmer of gray before he placed it on a metal disc.

I sat and bundled myself in the cloak again, watching them pour over the magical reading. Thalas wrote and wrote, soon setting aside a page to start fresh with another. A magical formula covered the bottom half of the first page, full of unfamiliar symbols and mathematical equations. He spoke to himself all the while.

"It seems the item has ninety percent, while she has ten," he was muttering to Kauz, who had his pointed ears perked. "Give or take a margin of error of less than point one percent, she's holding this many units right now. To keep her stable, we want her at about fifty percent, and that's an easy enough equation..."

"I'll donate," Kauz murmured back.

Thalas hummed and handed over the same leather strap and wooden stick he'd tested me with. Kauz noted down his own results on a separate sheet of paper.

"What in the stars required so much magic?" Thalas grumbled. "You have just enough."

"She can have it all, as far as I'm concerned..."

Thalas glanced over at me, lips twisted with worry. "Be right back."

After he launched himself off the balcony to circle around to a different part of the workshop with a few flaps of his wings, Kauz came around the table to kneel before me and take my hand between both of his. I looked up at him, hopeful he'd give me some kind of answer for what was going on.

He picked his words with care. "We're going to fix a problem you didn't know you had. It's related to your foot, and it's going to hurt. But you will feel a lot better once it's done."

"My crippled foot?" I asked, more confused than soothed by this explanation.

"You're going to understand so much better once it's done. And you *have* to do it." He squeezed my hand between his for emphasis.

"I trust you." Though my voice shook with nerves as I spoke.

His expression softened. "What'd I do to earn such a sweet mate?" He let go of my hand to cup my face. I leaned up to meet his lips, sighing happily even from a tender, controlled kiss. His father could be returning any moment, after all.

Kauz pulled away first, though he didn't go far, resting his forehead on mine. "Can you trust me to go a little further with one more thing? You can't watch what we're about to do with your foot."

"You're not going to take it off, are you?" I asked with a jolt of fear.

His eyes widened in horror. "No! Most certainly not. It's just..." He shrugged helplessly. "We'll use my cloak's hood. You could lift it if you feel unsafe, though I *really* don't suggest it."

The snap of Thalas's wings warned us of his arrival, though Kauz barely stirred until boots thudded on the floor. His father glanced between us, his eyes creasing at the corners. "Are we ready to begin?" he asked.

Kauz reached behind me and pulled the hood of his cloak free, lowering it over my face until all I saw was its fuzzy lining. This was fine. I could do this.

Probably.

"Let me lift it," Kauz said. Lift...what? Implements and tools clinked together as they were brushed out of the way. One of them took hold of my right leg and unlaced my shoe, working it carefully off my foot. A warm hand wrapped around my heel, offsetting the chill in the air.

The next thing I knew, a truly vile smell hit me straight in the nose. I gagged and pinched my nostrils closed, but it was too late. The stink, like rotten eggs and mold, was so strong I could practically taste it.

"*Olcanus*," Thalas said grimly.

Kauz hushed him, though I wasn't sure why. I didn't know what that Serri word meant.

"I will keep this lifted. Go," Thalas added.

More items were moved around, and someone took my hand, dangling it off the chair's armrest. "I'm tying our wrists together, just in case," Kauz told me. He laced his fingers with mine before he ran smooth leather around my wrist and a buckle clinked.

"Just in case of what?" I murmured, not expecting an answer. My hand trembled in his, even with the way he pressed his thumb in soothing circles over the skin between my thumb and forefinger.

Tingles ran over my palm, and the starry glow of his essence lined the side of the hood over my face. The fleeting, wonderful smell of Always pushed out the molding egg stink from my nostrils. I relaxed as his magic started to weave into mine; his raw power pushed into my body in a trickle to wet the dried riverbeds of my essence channels.

"We're ready, Dad," he said.

Kauz squeezed, pressing our palms together as tightly as possible. In the next moment, there was a *clink* like a key turning in a lock, followed by a metallic rattle.

Dozens of pain points erupted around my foot and ankle, but what felt worse was the draining sensation of my essence gushing out of me in the wake of what Thalas had done. I wavered at the edge of consciousness, gray oblivion leaching through the corners of my vision while the king cursed viciously in Serri.

Kauz poured his essence into me through our connected palms. The trickle became a flood, our laced hands like a lifeline as everything I was *shattered*.

A change took over top to bottom, my body mutating while I jerked and screamed. I thrashed, immediately feral from whatever was happening, clawing at the air and screeching. I tried to fight, but all I ended up doing was kicking out at Thalas.

The king locked one of his arms around my knee, holding it with bruising force. He pressed a finger into each individual hole in and around my ankle and twisted. At least, I thought that's what he had to be doing, as the wounds burned worse once he was done. I tried to struggle, but his grip was unforgiving.

"It's okay, Lark. It's going to be okay," Kauz was saying. I could barely hear him. In fact, the sudden burst of sensations was dying off and...

I was weightless. Free. Cut adrift from the limitations of my body, my mind flexed mental muscles I'd long forgotten it had.

Whatever this was, it wasn't pain. It was *bliss*.

"Lark, stop!" Kauz shouted.

The hood lifted from over my eyes. I was floating amongst a cloud of little gadgets and tools. The table followed suit, though its battered surface flickered with uncontrolled illusion magic. Confused colors and patterns fought to dominate it while it slowly tipped on its side. I watched it happening with detached awe.

"She's using up too much essence," Thalas said urgently. "Knock her out."

I turned my head. My body was tethered by two forces. Thalas, who had my ankle wrapped in his essence, like a black scarf threaded with silver stars, and Kauz, who tugged me downward toward him by our entwined hands.

His thumb landed in the middle of my forehead and left a glittering trail down my nose and over my parted lips. I dropped into sleep with the same lack of grace as all the tools that smashed to the floor with sudden gravity, followed by the table landing face down on top of them.

23
MARIUS

When Lark asked Mother, "What did you say?" in her little flute of a voice, she wavered on her feet. An unfocused look entered her eyes. I saw what was about to happen and launched into motion before anyone else.

Mother continued on, unaware of Lark's troubles. "You don't remember me? I was your godmother. I took you to my nest like my own child. I need every answer you have, Metalark!"

I lunged the last few feet between us. Lark dropped like a stone and fell into my arms.

As I took in her slack face, I lost my starsdamned mind. My brothers all reacted, shouting in surprise. I growled at them, crouched over my mate's body with my fangs bared.

Mother stepped back on instinct. "What did... Why did she... I didn't mean..." Now that the one person benefiting from us speaking Theli wasn't listening, she switched back to Serri and made a sound of distress. She backed into my father, Elion, who'd abandoned his chair by the fire. He drew her behind him.

Kauz stepped forward and knelt as close as anyone dared come. "Marius?"

The ever-present cloak of calm he carried with him threatened to settle over me. Usually I welcomed it as one of the only things that helped me keep my feral impulses under control. But not right now.

Defend mate.

I chuffed at him in warning.

"Niall, then."

It'd been his idea to name my feral side, to speak with it more personably when it took over. *"You're like another person when he's active, so he deserves a distinct name,"* he'd reasoned.

It wasn't that I was two people in one body, even though it seemed that way from the outside. I was simply always in conflict: Marius the prince versus Niall the feral beast.

"She's going to be okay, Niall," he murmured. "She's experiencing some mental backlash from Mother triggering something she was forced to forget."

I snorted, unimpressed with the explanation. Too many words. "Stay back," I said in a feral rasp.

"I need you to give her to me. The only way she's going to get better is if I get that silencing band off her." He held out his hands.

I stood with Lark still in my arms. Her limp body was so light in my hold, too fragile to be believed. I glanced around and scented the air. *Home.* I could take her to my rooms to recover.

She wanted to feel safe, my instincts whispered.

And she would be safe in my bed—no. I shook my head sharply.

"We have a plan, remember?" Kauz was saying.

"I remember," I gritted out.

I had to be strong for her. I had to give her to Kauz. But I didn't want to.

P'nixie.

No, I said to Niall. I didn't speak to him as forcefully as I had been for the last week and a half. Shouting at him, at *myself,* that Lark was not the p'nixie. My true mate was dead. Gone! She'd become a star and left me behind when I was a boy. No hopes, wishes, or so-called fate could impose her on this omega we'd stolen from Thelis. It just didn't make any fucking sense. Yet my instincts fought back with ferocity, sure that Lark was *her*.

My feral side hadn't been subtle when I'd met Lark in a pawn shop. The smell of her perfume had just about caused me to come undone. The only thing that'd stopped me from bending her over a display case was how small and frail she'd seemed shrinking away from me. Innocent, sweet prey who wouldn't choose to be bred viciously by someone like me.

Niall and I had a full-blown fight about what to do over her perfuming. He'd tried to seize control. It was *her*, and she was in *estrus*. I'd held him off and done everything I could to ensure that her heat didn't fully develop. It was the only right thing to do.

Stubborn, foolish animal. How long will you ignore the obvious?

Mother had just said Lark's secret identity aloud. *"A seamless mix of pixie and nixie."*

Kauz had seen what she'd looked like in the past. Her wings had once been dark purple.

Then there was how right it felt to protect her. How easy it was to call her my mate.

And how full my heart had been this morning when Niall had forgone any space between us and drawn her into my arms. For the first time since I'd lost my true mate, I'd felt...content. But she couldn't be the p'nixie. I wouldn't let my feral side bully me into delusion, no matter what Lark made me feel.

She wasn't the same girl I'd lost. Before I'd ever gone feral, my instincts were strong enough to know my true mate on sight. And I had been what, seven? I'd bonded so deeply with that girl that I still felt the ragged edges of her loss. *That* was the tragedy of kelpie loyalty.

Word of her death had led to my scarred face and the damage in my right eye. The adults in my life had mourned her and moved on, but I never could. I saw the evidence of the pixie-nixie's death on my face every time I looked in the mirror.

"Marius," Kauz prompted. Everyone else was looking at me with shades of pity. I was still standing there, dissociating from reality while staring at Lark.

I breathed a low, "Thanks." He always knew what to do when Niall took over. I passed her into his arms, helping arrange her limbs to make it easier for him. He didn't have alpha strength, but he wasn't a slouch either. I'd helped him develop his muscles to rein in those wings, after all.

"I'll get her back to you as soon as possible," he whispered.

I answered with a grunt of acknowledgment. When my feral side was this active, words were a challenge to form.

Kauz turned and carried her away. His steady presence faded from our pack bond as he shielded his emotions. I did the same a moment later, as did my other brothers. The last thing we needed right now was to multiply each other's feelings, as the empathy of the pack bond could make Tormund or me unstable and violent in the worst circumstances.

The mood in the room was awkward as the rest of us exchanged glances. "All right. Someone else had better explain," Mother demanded.

"Perhaps it would be easier to show you?" Fal suggested, raising a brow in my direction. We still had something to do while Kauz sought out Thalas for help removing the *olcanus*.

I considered, then nodded.

"Your answers are waiting in the dungeon," Fal said to our mother.

"Then we'll go to the dungeon," she said, tugging on my father's arm. "We'll all go together."

"As you wish, my heart," Elion murmured back.

That settled it, then. Tormund went to get our stuff arranged, as he knew he couldn't watch what was about to happen without triggering a rage. But the rest of us headed toward the back of the palace, where the underground prison wing was situated. Mother was uncharacteristically quiet on the way there, walking by my father's side.

Fal and I fell in step to go over our plan one more time. Well, Fal spoke. I just made the appropriate sounds in the right places. These were our trained roles, and we did them well enough. I was simply distracted.

He walked by my left side, where I could see him clearly. But I wasn't seeing much of anything right now, the world just as blurry on one side as the other.

My mate...

I was heading in the wrong direction. I should've gone with Kauz, even though his essence-spinning bullshit only became more incoherent with his father around. Thalas was a genius by all accounts, but he lacked the awareness that not everyone without magic could understand the advanced terms and mathematics he worked with daily.

There's nothing I could do to help her there. My presence in the Magician King's workshop would only increase the anxiety in the room.

But the dungeons. More specifically, the interrogation rooms. I could help Lark there.

My daze lifted as we descended into the freezing nightmare that was the palace prison. The underground wing was hewn straight from the stone, including the rough-cut stairs to and from the blocks of cells. Though the frigid air helped cut down on the smell, nothing could stop my nose from picking up on the lingering stench of piss, blood, and death. Enemies of the more capricious queens of Unseelie infamy had died down here, and their suffering still haunted this place.

My father was the lord of the current royal pack, Serian's beloved Wave King, a male of refinement and poise. Fal had trained with him extensively to one day take his job. Neither of them came here much, and when they did, they always wore the same expressions of barely restrained disgust. I was more used to it as the apprentice of the male waiting for us to arrive.

We did questioning and torture in the first few enclosed rooms, acts Theodred, the Blood King, specialized in. All of the kings were half brothers, like my pack, and shared fatherly duties to the point I could say I had four dads. When more than one king was present in a room with us, like now, we referred to them by first name to head off miscommunication.

"The guards say the mermaid awaits the tender mercies of our sons. I was not aware they'd finally returned," Theodred remarked.

He was so large that his voice was a bass rumble that our more skittish citizens mistook for growling. Until they felt the absolute menace that was his *real* growl, something I'd endured enough in my training until I no longer flinched away from it.

Mother grimaced. "You're going to interrogate a mermaid? Swear to the stars, boys, you had better not create an even bigger fiasco for me than Princess Glory's disappearance."

"We really had nothing to do with that, Mother," Fal said, holding up his hands. "I swear it."

"I swear it as well. We don't have Glory," I echoed.

If we were scent matches with Glory, we'd know it by now. Our parental packs had collectively taken a fancy to uniting our nations for a short spell and tried to push us together, but we repelled like magnets. Her fiery nature matched the abrasiveness of her cinnamon. My pack needed someone a lot sweeter than cinnamon girl.

"But you stole away a mermaid too?" Mother pressed, drawing me out of my thoughts about the red pixie.

"Two, actually. In our defense, they insisted on tagging along," Fal said.

Elion turned to Theodred. "Do you get the feeling there is just…" He held his hands out at his sides. "…a massive gulf of things they're not telling us?"

"I wonder where they learned that from," the huge redcap replied.

They considered for half a moment. "Rennyn," Theodred said, naming Fal's father.

"Definitely Rennyn," Elion agreed.

"I'm *dying* to know what's going on here," Mother put in with an impatient gesture. "Go do what you have to do. If it's not informative enough, I'll send in Theo."

The redcap cracked his knuckles with an eager smile. On him, that barely looked like a lift of his lips.

"We'll do our best," Fal remarked before heading into the first interrogation room. The rest of us followed, crowding the small observation area. It was dominated by a solid sheet of essence-treated glass serving as a one-way view into the sights and sounds of what happened inside the room beyond.

Cymora was tied to the single chair in the room, her head listing to one side. She was dirty and unkempt, her clothes torn from struggling her way off the train. There was probably a sizable bruise forming from when I'd elbowed her in the gut to prevent her from shouting an order at Lark during her forceful disembarking.

All told, she already looked like shit. The hollows under her eyes were deeply shadowed from two days of Kauz's dream tortures. The occasional gasp and paranoid dart of her eyes as she jumped at nothing showed he'd left his mark in her mind.

Not enough, my instincts insisted.

"May I borrow your sword?" I asked Theodred. He was always armed, today with one of his favorite swords. Usually, I was the same way, but weapons weren't allowed on public magirails. He unsheathed his weapon and offered me the hilt without hesitation.

Thankfully, it was one of his shorter swords, so it didn't look comically large in my grip like some of his weapons. I nodded at Fal and followed him into the room. He burst in, exclaiming in Theli, "Hello, Cymora!"

The mermaid startled so hard she nearly tipped over her chair. It was the newest thing in this room, as the walls were lined with torture implements in various cruddy states, stained with rust and blood. Most of them were there for ambiance, not that our guests realized that.

"Prince Falindel." She sounded hopeful until her gaze found me next and she cringed. She already realized I despised her after throwing her off the train, but Fal had kept his true feelings about her concealed behind a courtly mask. "And...Prince Marius. I wish I could say I was glad to see you both. Where is my daughter?"

Fal raised a brow. "Which one?" he asked coldly.

This gave her pause. "Laurel. I know you've probably brought my stepdaughter to your chambers already," she snapped.

Fal flicked his fang with his tongue and jerked his chin at me. Even with our pack bond shielded, I understood. My role was to provide aggression, so I needed to respond, else we would go off script. He couldn't let her see him flinch.

I ignored Niall's suggestion to use Theodred's sword on her. *Not yet.*

The mermaid was watching us carefully, a calculating gleam in her eyes. I grabbed the back of her chair, pivoting it toward me with more force than necessary, and leaned into her personal space. She tilted back with a sharply drawn breath.

"Laurel is fine. She will be given proper hospitality until we figure out what to do with her." I pitched my voice lower, going for the forceful tone Theodred pulled off with ease. "As for Lark, where she is and what she does is no longer your concern. Understand?"

Her throat clicked in a dry swallow. "It seems there's been some kind of mistake," she said with less venom.

"What mistake is that, hmm?" Fal prompted.

I drew back and pulled a kerchief out my pocket, feigning disinterest as I rubbed away any smudges on Theodred's sword. In the process, I flashed its edges in the dim light of the essence lamp above us.

"Your brother, the…" She wheezed with a bit of remembered fear. "Prince Kauzden seems to believe I made some kind of confession about my darling Lark. In my sleep, no less."

I rode out a spike of fury. Since fae couldn't lie, there was more to it when she called Lark *dear* or *darling*. Her dear slave? Her darling servant? I sensed the falseness behind her platitudes each time, and it pissed me off immediately. She used that pleasant mermaid voice to hide an ocean of malice in plain sight.

"Oh, interesting." Fal circled her chair. She shifted to track his movements, but he stopped just out of her line of sight and let some malice creep into his tone. "We Unseelie trust our dream wardens to discover the darkest of acts in others. Fae are at their most forthcoming when they're unconscious. But you know what, Cymora?"

"What?" she echoed.

"Dreams are short. Kauzden only shared one with you, so we're all pretty sure there's more to your deeds than what he discovered." He leaned over, lowering his voice to a hissing whisper. "Are you willing to make a deal and tell us what you've done?"

"Or do we have to cut it out of you piece by piece?" I growled on cue, twirling the sword and pivoting. Its tip rested just under her chin, and I turned it so she would feel the edge nicking against her skin.

She gasped and tilted her head back. "I…I have done nothing wrong!"

A bead of sweat rolled down Cymora's temple. Her eyes were still fixed on the blade I held near her throat, and her breathing was shallow. I was tempted to slide it closer, until she felt the point at her neck.

Make her bleed.

Fal made a patronizing hum. "Oh, really. Yet we put you under a little pressure, and you forgot that you should be concerned for Lark's welfare too. Is it going to be *so* hard for you to admit that you haven't treated her as a stepmother should? Go ahead. Justify yourself."

"I'm not *justifying* anything," she said out of gritted teeth. "If you want me to talk, I need a vow from you both first. And that sword away from my neck. I am a *lady*, and I deserve to be treated as such."

"Marius, does a lady put a silencing band on anyone, let alone her stepdaughter?" Fal asked.

I made a show of thinking about it. My response took longer to piece together, as I had to swallow down a snarl. "I don't know. Does a lady force her stepdaughter into a vow of obedience?"

Much of the anger churning within my chest was self-directed. I'd thought Lark was spineless upon seeing how she acted when seated next to her stepmother. I hadn't stopped to consider whether her spine had already been snapped and crushed under a caregiver's heel.

Fal smirked. He was enjoying this game of words, while I very much wanted to move on to the part where the fish felt real pain. "Ooh, that's a hard one. How about this? Does a lady make her stepdaughter dump out her entire nest off the side of a—"

"Stop! Stop. I get it," Cymora blurted. Thank fuck.

Fal made a motion between his fists like he was snapping a branch. He'd been sure this would be easy. Kauz had already softened her up for us.

"I will make amends with Lark. Just...just take the weapon away," she continued.

"Oh, we don't want amends from you, Cymora." Fal walked two fingers up the side of her head, letting her feel the points of his claws. She twitched, but there wasn't anywhere to go between the two of us. Fal plucked out a pearl-studded hairpin that'd survived her trip here. He left a lengthy pause for her to endure as he turned it over, tossed it aside, and repeated the motions until he'd found and discarded all four decorations remaining in her hair. "Just a confession. I hope you know you're not leaving here until you end every vow Lark's ever made to you."

"I want a vow from you both that you won't harm me and that I *will* be leaving here when we're done. Then you can have your precious omega," she spat.

"She is quite precious," Fal said more pleasantly. He nodded at me, and I lowered the sword, angling it toward the ground. She let out a sigh of relief.

Only a short reprieve. It was getting harder to focus on our end goal here. *Torture?* No. This was about breaking the vow of obedience and uncovering any other nasty surprises we could've missed.

Fal had already devised the wording for our vows to put Cymora at ease while leaving gigantic loopholes for any other fae to manipulate. Considering the fish didn't know the queen and two of her kings were listening in, we were fairly sure she wouldn't try to amend them.

"In exchange for breaking every one of Lark's vows, I vow to you, Cymora of Osme Fen, that I will do you no physical harm from this moment into my last moment. When we are satisfied, you will walk out of this room," Fal said without a hint of concern.

"In exchange for cooperating and answering our questions with the whole truth, I vow to you, Cymora of Osme Fen, that I will do you no physical harm from this moment into my last moment." I spoke my practiced oath grudgingly and continued to keep a hold of the sword. Its heft felt right in my hand.

"Do these terms satisfy you?" Fal asked.

She considered for only a few moments. "They do," she answered.

Magic tingled through my body as the deal was officially struck between us. It wasn't essence, but something older, woven into the very fabric of the fae race. Seelie, Unseelie, we were all held to our word, or else we owed grievances. And the aggrieved or their family, in the case of their death, could ask for almost anything. The fae who'd broken their word would be compelled to fulfill the request.

One side of her mouth lifted, like she thought she'd won. She had no idea she was trapped prey. The Blood King was on the other side of the door out of this room. My feral side hummed with a sense of satisfaction.

"We'll start with the vows. End every vow you have over Lark," Fal said.

"Ah, there's only the one. In her case, I didn't need multiple vows." A hint of her usual bluster was returning now that she thought she wouldn't come to harm. "I've never released one before."

"It starts 'I hereby revoke,'" Fal prompted.

She cleared her throat primly. "I hereby revoke the vow Metalark of

Osme Fen made to me, Cymora of Osme Fen. She vowed to be a good and obedient stepdaughter and do everything she was told with a perky 'yes, Stepmother' and no attitude. That is no more."

Fal and I eased up with relief to know our mate wouldn't be compelled to answer to Cymora's every order and whim. She was a servant no longer.

The mermaid smirked as she added, "I also hereby revoke all demands I made of her while she was under the effects of this vow."

I tensed and snorted while Niall stirred within me, no longer so relaxed. "What the fuck does that addition mean?" I demanded.

She batted her lashes up at me. "I ordered her to forget a number of things. An essence spinner I used to dally with warned me to stop. He said if she ever received those memories back all at once, it would prob-ably break something in that silly little head of hers."

Fal and I exchanged a glance over her head. He gave me a warning look. "It's bluster, Mar," he said, switching languages.

"I did mean what I said, Prince," she continued. "You can have your dear Metalark...however she turns out."

My lips peeled back in a slow snarl that wasn't just for show. With one lunge and bite, I could crush her windpipe.

"She's with Kauz. You know he can get her through something like that," Fal countered.

This malicious trick of hers could only be answered with blood. Maybe she wouldn't feel so smug if I broke a few of her fingers. Or her ankle. See how *she* fared when her every step was agony.

"Hit a nerve, did I?" Cymora taunted, though I only heard it distantly. I listened through a morass of feral instinct as Niall gained control and fixed her with a predator's unblinking stare. "You're the ones who wanted a full confession. My misdeeds, as related to Lark?"

Fal was still trying to reason with me, urgency entering his tone. "Put the sword down, Mar."

Cymora mouthed off with malicious glee. "I'll tell you everything you need to know, starting with the vow. She made it when she was six, right after her father died."

Niall caught the real significance of what she'd just said. "You wrote the letter telling us *she'd* died, not her father," I rasped.

"I did." She had the audacity to sound proud.

My breathing shallowed out. *The letter.* The turning point in my life. Mother's anguish at reading about the sudden death of her godchild had hit her pack bond while I'd been in a practice fight with Theodred. The all-encompassing grief from his mate had triggered his rage and blinded him for a single swing, and that's all it'd taken for him to smash my face in.

"My first order for her was a test. I made her forget her full name, and it worked. The letter wasn't a lie. She did die in a way. There was no longer a Metalark of Osme Fen," Cymora said.

She's alive. She's been alive this whole time.

I clenched my eyes closed on a quiet feral noise of denial. The last *no* I would allow myself. It was true. I was just a stubborn and foolish animal after all.

To think I needed Cymora to spell out her deception to me. I'd believed the p'nixie was dead because we had it in writing. Another fae had given their word that she'd died, and there was no magirail fast enough to deliver us from Neslune to Osme Fen in time to see the body before it dissolved into stardust.

"You are ill in the head, aren't you?" Fal was saying to her in Theli. I was barely in the room with him and Cymora anymore. Pain overwhelmed me as my surroundings disappeared in all-encompassing light.

I'd placed more truth in this deceitful female's words rather than my own instincts, and that was *wrong*. I had fought it and denied it, but in the end, I had to accept it: the p'nixie and Lark were one in the same. My chest burned like my heart was on fire.

When I'd startled and scared Lark on the train ride here, I'd felt this same sort of agony. I'd rejected her a little bit and damaged something between us that I hadn't recognized. Now, I knew what it was. That innate, steadfast magic my kind called kelpie loyalty. We loved and cherished friends and family on a level other fae could barely grasp.

I had harmed what little remained of my childhood bond with her. It was unthinkable that I could fuck up this badly, not only as her mate, but as her protector and down to my roots as a kelpie. I was just a waste of air that called himself the Wave King's son.

The light warped, beckoning. Inviting me to let go, to become Niall permanently and leave this all behind.

It'd never been more tempting. I wouldn't have to face the worst moments I'd created. Like when I dealt a blow to the rawest nerve my mate carried by asking her, *"What do you know of pain?"*

As if she hadn't been carrying an *olcanus* on her ankle this entire time.

I didn't deserve my title as protector heir. I hadn't protected her at all. Not in Osme Fen, nor on the journey here. I couldn't even protect her from myself. She'd suffered right in front of me, and instead of proving I was worth my fangs by taking Cymora's head, I'd chosen to blame the victim. *"Are you truly in the habit of being such a doormat?"*

The pressure in my head was only growing. Cracks sinking deeper, eroding what little reason remained.

"How are we to mate when you're so tiny and frail?"

I was the fool who would end up mateless and alone.

"No," I growled, so guttural I didn't realize I'd spoken aloud. If I gave in to my impulses, all that awaited me was a swing of the executioner's axe. A fate I'd only avoided so far by my father's grace and my own willpower.

And if I turned wild now, I'd never get to have Lark. Yearning tightening my chest. *P'nixie...*

She didn't know how much I'd craved her companionship the whole journey here. I'd hung on her every musical word and giggle while she talked to my brothers. I'd dreamt I'd never thrown a golden opportunity away and had taken her straight to my inn room after she perfumed not for either of my alpha brothers, but for *me*.

Yet I'd held myself back and pushed her away. I was too afraid of breaking her. Too worried my feral side would overpower her. And too stupid to realize that every time I looked at her, my instincts quaked with the desire to defend her to the death and nothing less.

"I wouldn't ask any of you to give up everything because of me," she'd whispered.

Fuck. I would give up *anything* for her.

I roared, releasing a fraction of my pain and grief. The light retracted just enough so I could see, though as always it left me disoriented as the fit faded.

Fal hadn't moved. He watched me with his lips pressed together in a grim sort of worry. His voice faded in and out of my ears as he said my name.

I glanced down. In my left hand was that familiar heft. I stared at the sword without really seeing it. Getting run through by it would probably hurt less.

I bared my teeth at Cymora. "You have no idea what you've done." I could've screamed at her, but I didn't see the point. Her actions with the letter had led to unintended consequences, yes, but I'd fucked up my life all by myself from there.

She was bracing herself. She thought her words would lead to bloodshed. But I hadn't forgotten my vow. I hadn't forgotten any of the stupid shit I'd said recently.

The sword dropped to the ground with a clatter. I turned away, not trusting myself in this room anymore. I couldn't make things right with the p'nixie if I owed Cymora a grievance for harming her. Who knew what she'd ask for—though I suspected it would be whatever would cause Lark maximum pain.

No more. I'll stand by Lark's side, where I belong.

The door opened as I took an unsteady step toward it. Theodred came in and offered his arm. "I'm proud of you, son." The rare affirmation soothed a few of my chafing nerves. "I can take it from here."

I nodded, and we clasped forearms like warriors. I squeezed with all my strength. It felt good to have some outlet, however brief, and in return, he slapped me on the back with the kind of force that probably made Fal wince.

I left the room, flush with shame to be part of the reason Mother was upset. It was rare for me to hear her whine, as she had to keep her omega reactions in check outside of private spaces. I didn't like the sounds she was making at all, but her mates had it handled. My father had his arms around her, purring and rocking her, while Rennyn had found us and was petting all of her fins.

Theodred wasted no time in taking over where I'd left off. "I'm not going to hurt you. But I will make you no vow." His bass voice and presence were usually intimidation enough when I'd seen him work other interrogations. "Let us start from the beginning. We are about to be very well acquainted."

Good. He'd wring every secret from her hide. I turned to skulk off and find a safe place to recover alone.

"Marius, wait," Mother said tearfully.

I didn't want to turn and look at her when I was like this. She already mourned the boy I used to be, when I was *wild* in the innocent sense, and now even more of him was gone.

Rennyn came to my rescue by saying, "Hey, wild boy. Thalas sent a page earlier. He needs a strapping alpha lad like yourself for help in his workshop."

I straightened from my defensive hunch. Had something happened with Lark? Was she okay? Were her memories harming her as they returned?

I took off running.

"Nice to see you," the dark elf king called after me. "Missed you, kid!"

I grunted and dashed out of the underground prison as if my fins were on fire. Since he was comforting his mate as I left him behind, surely he'd understand that I had to return to mine.

And if I was trying to outrun my emotions, so what? The vulnerability in my chest hardened and became what it always did: fury. Anger and violence were my old standbys when life was too hard to bear.

I had half the palace to cross to get to the observatory slash workshop slash clutter box Thalas practically lived in. "Out of my way!" I shouted more than once, scattering clusters of courtiers and servants. The echoes of gossip whispered behind me. So be it. Lark's identity as the next princess wouldn't be a secret for long, especially with my pack-mates all acting erratically after an unexpected shared absence.

Speaking of them... I unshielded my pack bond to find it quiet. Fal was still withdrawn from it, and the lack of anything from Kauz suggested he was either asleep or unconscious. Tormund was present, boredom and anxiety his only contributions. He may have fared better than me if we'd swapped places.

Who was I kidding? Tormund would never hold a sword to a female's throat willingly, not even Cymora's.

His side of the bond perked up when he sensed me. He sent a questioning feeling toward me, and I sent him back the mental equivalent of a thumbs-up. Anything else would cause him unnecessary panic without me there to explain what I meant.

I reached the workshop and breathed a sigh of relief to find the magic-sealed door already propped open. Thalas paced on the ground floor, fiddling with his glasses on their long chain.

He puffed in frustration. "About time Rennyn sent help. Hello, Marius. Your mother's emotions are spikier than your fins. I have no idea what in the stars is going on, but I cannot go to her until I have help moving Kauz and Lark to the infirmary."

The *infirmary*? "What happened to them?" I demanded. My roughened voice bounced in the empty space between the many balconies above us.

He put his palms up. "They're fine. Only sleeping off their ordeals. Kauz depleted himself to the barest edge of essence to get Lark through the removal. Did I mention the silencing band?"

My ear flicked impatiently. "I know about the silencing band."

"It's off now. The magical outburst that occurred afterward was quite fascinating. Now that's a rare phenomenon I am eager to study in further depth—"

Good news about the band, but too many words. "Where are they?" I interrupted.

He pointed upward. "I can fly them both down, but you will have to carry Kauz while we head to the infirmary."

I prodded my pack bond with a quick thought. Tormund would feel it and come to where he sensed I was.

"And while we walk, perhaps you could fill me in on a few things?" Thalas suggested.

I made a noncommittal sound.

"Let's get started, then, shall we?" he said in his gentle way. I tried to take in the sense of calm wafting off him and nodded.

He flew up and retrieved Kauz first, the two of them landing in a less-than-graceful tangle of extra limbs. My brother's skin was ashen. I checked under his eyelids and...yes, he was that depleted. The whites were showing. I rumbled a soft approval of his sacrifice for our mate before arranging his wings closed and picking him up with a grunt.

Thalas returned shortly afterward with Lark in his arms. "Here's your omega. Just resting. See?" He angled her toward my left side. A sleep spell's glitter trail crossed from her forehead to her lips.

P'nixie.

Both sides of myself, prince and feral, acknowledged her for who she was. Stars help her, but she was *mine*.

She had a new addition that I fixated on: the shadow of closed gills along the side of her neck. Inhaling, I caught the first hints of her natural scent returning, plus an extra-sweet note. *Estrus.* Niall estimated it'd arrive in a couple days. Just being able to sense her impending heat was a terrible sign that had me looking at her wrist and doing a double take at the ruin of smeared ink that circled her forearm.

"Have you gotten a good enough look?" Thalas was asking. I blinked, becoming aware that I'd been staring at her quite fixedly for several minutes.

I nodded, and we started walking. The infirmary was at the center of the old fortress, now the heart of the extended palace. I avoided it unless absolutely necessary, as the smell of it was enough to send me back almost two decades to the time I was trapped there in endless-seeming recovery.

Working my jaw, I managed to ask, "What happened to her arm?"

"Oh, that's part of the phenomenon I was mentioning. Taking off the band unleashed so much magic at once that it warped all existing magic on and in her body. I imagine it's harmless. A little ink remover will rub it out," he said with a careless wave.

I released an uneasy growl. "She had a few charms..."

"I'll reapply them for Kauz. He probably won't be spinning any essence for weeks." He shook his head. "Lovestruck lad. Both of you are, actually."

I snuck another look at her in his arms. *P'nixie...*

"Now, will you tell me what's going on?" he asked, disrupting my thoughts before I could place myself back into the loop of regrets threatening to choke me.

"Do you remember Mother taking a godchild to her nest?"

The specks of light in his eyes flickered. "Of course. Sweet Dorei's baby. They're both resting in the stars now. The girl had traits of both a pixie and..." He drifted off. "No, it can't be."

"It is."

"My bonus child. I didn't even realize," he murmured.

I was trying to tell him, using the fewest words possible, about the vow Cymora broke and the memories Lark might be stuck in when Tormund finally found us. He angled for Thalas. I shouldered in the way, placing Kauz into his outstretched arms.

"But—"

"I need to be greedy," I told him.

He must've checked our pack bond, because he didn't argue. I didn't hide the heady relief that rushed through me when I took her into my arms. As long as I held her, she was safe. When she woke, I'd give her a new definition for that word.

Bands of black and silver essence were woven around her right foot, obscuring what it looked like now that that awful *olcanus* was removed. There'd be time to inspect her wounds later. She needed someone to tend to her during her recovery, and I was already volunteering.

"Well, as I was saying," Thalas spoke up once the three of us were back in motion. "I'll check in with Kauz and Lark in their dreams tonight. He'll help her with her memories, but if the situation is severe enough, I'll keep them under for extra time. As many days as it will take for her to wake with her psyche intact."

However long it took, I would look after her while she slept.

Thalas was in the midst of saying something, though. "Bye, Dad," Tormund said.

Oh, he was leaving. I made an approximate sound to goodbye and nodded to the dream warden king. At the next juncture where the halls split, he went one way, and we went another.

I could scent the infirmary from here, and my skin crawled. It only got worse when we arrived. It was the same white tunnel, with its sectioned-off areas for different levels of triage. Spotlights of essence lamps showed where the doctors were working, while patches of darkness in other places suggested resting patients or empty beds.

That *smell*. The sting of pure alcohol mixed with stale sheets and surgical tools, plus undertones of blood and sickly-sweet illness. It made me want to vomit.

We spoke with the squat goblin nurse who'd been one of my primary caregivers while I was bedbound here. She smiled with all her sharp teeth and greeted me warmly by name. Once she saw her new patients were a prince and an omega, she bustled to the back of the infirmary and slid the curtains around until we had a private area with two beds.

I placed Lark in the bed against the wall while Tormund got Kauz situated.

Then we looked at each other. "What now?" he asked.

"The worst part," I answered in a low growl. I angled the chair next to Lark's bed so I could see her with my good eye, laced my fingers through her limp hand, and waited.

And waited some more.

Time bled away. There was no telling the hour when Thalas visited to apply a powerful sleeping spell on both my brother and my mate. He wiped away the ruin of ink on her arm, painted a fertility blocker and a heat suppressant on the inside of her wrist with essence-infused ink, and left.

Day two, he kept them under with the same spell.

I refused to move from her side. I was more of a guard dog than anything else, growling and posturing next to her bedside when anyone tried to get too close. Maybe they tried to talk to me, but nothing got through the feral haze.

After the third day, someone arrived and approached me, not Lark. He drew up a chair beside mine and didn't flinch at my snarling. The sound of his voice, and the subtle influence threaded through it, eventually pierced the thick fog of my instincts.

"...wanted to visit sooner. I've been worried about you." It was my father. And instead of pity in his voice, he seemed proud of me, even now at my lowest. He'd placed aside his crown and waited for me to recognize him.

"Dad," I mumbled. Only then did he open his arms and invite the crushing hug I pulled him into.

"I heard you kids had quite the adventure."

I nodded and worked my jaw, still barely able to speak. "Dad, it's *her*."

As a fellow kelpie, he understood exactly how devastating the p'nixie's death had been. Well, her "death." But he didn't know how I'd already ruined everything.

"I'm so happy for you," he was in the midst of saying.

"I already… I messed up."

I let him go before I squeezed all the air out of him, bowing my head in shame. He waited, again. One of the worst parts of my condition was an inability to speak at length whenever I wanted to. I managed to tell him, "I scared her away. She won't want me. Just my brothers."

My father had perfected a special kind of alpha bark that wove his emotions into his tone. He couldn't conceal his feelings when he spoke with it, but he did reserve a few emotions for when they were needed. So when he answered, "It'll be all right, Marius," he said it with a tide of comforting warmth. It flooded my spiral of self-doubt before it could burrow any deeper. "Perhaps this is the miracle you needed to finally equalize."

Ah, yes. The moment our whole family waited for with bated breath: when I would stop getting worse. Most feral fae removed themselves from the situations that'd caused their trauma. Afterward, there was a sweet spot where instinct and reason stopped separating and balanced out to an even fifty-fifty. They could speak and reason better and lead mostly normal lives.

I made a sound of anguish. I'd turn wild without Lark. Leaving her side now was out of the question.

"You know, denying yourself sustenance and sleep won't do much to help her," he said. Though he eventually left me to my vigil, I had the sense he talked to someone just out of earshot first.

The infirmary remained my nightmare. No windows meant no true understanding of day or night. Some time passed before I nodded off out of sheer exhaustion, just to wake to a concentrated whiff of the smell around me. For an incoherent moment, I feared I was a boy again, trapped in some nightmare.

No, it was all real. And if Lark never woke up, I'd never have the opportunity to apologize.

Wake up, Lark. You have to wake up…

The next time Thalas visited, he reached over unexpectedly to apply a sleeping spell to me, too.

24
LARK

THIS WAS NOT the normal darkness of rest. I didn't feel the wind, but somehow, I knew I was falling. My mind traveled down.

And down.

And down some more.

Flashes of color and sound whirled by. Snippets of the past... though no past I could remember. They fell around me in a sharp-edged rain, and I felt something from each one. They were all mine, fractals of different times. Times I was loved, times I was victorious, times I was hurt so badly it was a mercy to forget. There were so, so many of them.

I looked down to see a jagged bed of forgotten memories. They awaited my inevitable crash, ready to tear me apart in a buzzing cacophony of everything all at once.

I tucked myself into a ball and braced for impact, just to land in another's arms. "That was too close," Kauz murmured.

We rose and fell with the powerful flaps of his wings. The dark purple span seemed impossibly huge in this space...wherever we were.

"Kauz, what's going on?" I clung to him. "Is this a dream?"

He lifted his head, watching the last shards of memory fall around us. They passed right through him on their way by. He surged up the tunnel I'd fallen into, twisting to keep me away from their sharp edges.

"No, it's not a dream. I just put a sleeping spell on you, so you're in the second stage of rest right now."

I was so confused. But he found an alcove of sorts to land on and sat, dangling his feet over the drop. The details were fuzzy at best, like any dream.

"We have a lot to talk about." He patted the space next to him. I eased onto it and leaned into him when he put an arm around me.

He began to explain that we were in my head, watching pieces of broken memories get cycled toward long-term storage. They were fragmented because I'd been forced to forget them by Cymora, who'd always had the power to order me to forget things.

"She must've abused this a lot," I muttered.

"Undoubtedly. You also have to consider the ripple effect of a careless order. You're told to forget one thing, and you forget every instance of it before or since that order. Take the metalark for example."

"The what?"

"The purple bird I drew on your arm," he answered patiently. "You asked my brothers and me about it several times."

My brow wrinkled. I couldn't remember doing that, but I should've. I'd admired the ink tattoo of the purple lark with its star-flecked feathers and idly traced my fingers over the curve of the ribbon it'd clutched in its claws.

"It's a metalark, a bird from the dreamlands that you were ordered to forget," he explained. "No matter how many times we talked about the metalark, the moment I said what it was, you would go quiet and forget what we were talking about. I guessed that it might be your full name."

I glanced down at the basin of memory shards far below us as something stirred. My father's voice echoed up to us. Kauz tilted his head to listen in.

"Metalark, my baby bird."

"You'll fly too someday."

"Your mother wanted to name you after one of her favorite things."

"Tweet tweet, little Metalark."

A baby girl's giggle. *"Tweet tweet!"* she echoed.

Glimmers of light shot back up the tunnel past where we sat.

My eyes welled with tears, and my shoulders shook with a sob. I'd forgotten what he sounded like. The love he spoke with was nearly too much, and I couldn't speak for missing him. What I wouldn't do to see him again one more time.

I buried my face in my hands, and Kauz pulled me closer.

He tilted my chin up and wiped away the tear trails on my cheeks. "You never have to hide your pain from me." He continued his explanation while still cradling my face between his palms. "My brothers forced Cymora to break her vow to you, which is why your memories are returning. It was part of the plan for when we got here. I just didn't expect the memories to fragment this much."

"They did? There was a plan?" I asked.

"A rather successful one at that. My father and I removed the silencing band, Fal and Marius probably wrung the fish dry of any moisture left in her, and now you're on the verge of getting your memories back."

"The what? They did what?" I was trying to follow along, but there appeared to be a lot I'd missed. "When did you—wait. You all planned this when I was sleeping late, didn't you?"

Kauz smiled with a bit of mischief. "Now you're catching on."

I leaned up and kissed him, glad he was as solid as ever in this corner of my mind. He kissed me back slowly, sighing as we broke apart.

"It may be easier to get started rather than continue trying to explain. We have a lot of memories to cover." He took in the pit below us again. "It's going to be hard, but I think the only way to do this is to relive these moments. That way, they'll become your memories again."

"So, do I just jump in?" I asked.

"*Nooo*, don't do that. We'll call individual ones to us. I think I know where to start." Kauz had a sad sort of smile as he reached out over the pit, and a memory flew into his waiting hand. He held his other palm out to me. "Just remember, I'm here. I'll be here with you no matter how bad it gets."

As I took in the shard and the color that radiated off it, then his offered hand, I had the feeling this was the beginning of an ordeal. I literally didn't know what I didn't know, but I was about to find out face-first.

I put my hand in Kauz's. We entered the memory he held together, and I was hit with an immediate sense of dread. My stepmother and a teenage dryad entered my room back at the manor in Osme Fen. I watched as an observer, a floating ghost re-experiencing what was about to happen to my eleven-year-old self.

"I saw this memory in Cymora's dreams," Kauz said. He preemptively put his arms around me. "That is a silencing band. An *olcanus* designed to suck on your essence until almost nothing is left."

I trembled in his arms but didn't look away. Not when my past self screamed and begged and Cymora watched her writhe in pain with poorly disguised satisfaction.

I remembered how much it hurt to have the band bite into my flesh. The worst pain of my life as it settled in and drank deeply of my essence. I'd keened for hours, calling and calling, but no one came to help me.

We returned to the alcove, and off went the memory, restored to my mind. Dozens followed it. The voices of the fae of Osme Fen, filled with mocking. Even from some I thought were my friends.

"Look at her faking that limp."

"Is she trying to get extra attention? Hey, Lark! You're not crippled!"

On and on. Others spoke about my Unseelie side, asking where my gills had gone. Why was I different now?

I touched my neck, feeling the sealed ridges that hadn't been there before. What the fuck? My fingers were tipped with super sharp nails too. I looked at my hand and screamed, flicking it away as if I could get rid of the extra membranes that extended between my fingers.

Kauz looked bewildered. "What's wrong?"

"I'm—" I nearly barked out "I'm Unseelie!" like it was some kind of horror but caught it just in time. My heart hammered as I twisted to look at my wings. They seemed normal, except individual pinpricks of purple were starting to form on them. My color was returning!

I was tugged between great unwanted surprise and a surge of excitement, two reactions that did not blend well. I inspected myself for any more changes.

Kauz watched me until he must've figured out what I was doing. "You're half nixie, sweetheart."

"How is this possible?" I mumbled. I returned to staring at my hand, watching the webbing ripple up and down my fingers depending on how I flexed them. If I did this long enough, I hoped to figure out how to get them to recede completely.

"You just forgot," he said gently. "C'mon. Let's see if we can find a happy memory."

We couldn't. Kauz picked out random memories from the pit. I remembered the day Cymora had sold my aging mare, Meya, after we'd won a third-place prize together at the blossom festival. I'd *loved* that horse. My stepmother made me forget her, though my affection for horses remained despite her cruelty.

I'd also forgotten taking long, luxurious swims in the lake. In my younger years, I was a more athletic swimmer than Laurel, who'd been awkward with her mermaid tail. As I was not allowed to be better than her at anything, Cymora ordered a creeping dread of water into me.

I wasn't allowed to be better than Laurel at singing, either. An order had silenced my budding talents and trapped my perfect pitch in my spoken voice. Since then, I'd never felt compelled to sing along when others carried a tune. Shortly after hearing a song, it'd slip from my mind, disappearing into the breeze.

Each order whittled me down to the silent, head-bowed servant I'd become by adulthood.

Between memories, I sagged. I was exhausted on a bone-deep level. "She just...erased anything about me she didn't like. Who does that to their stepdaughter?"

Kauz was quiet next to me. He wavered where he stood, looking just as tired as I felt, with bruises forming under his eyes. I followed his line of sight to a cloud of black threaded with silver appearing in the tunnel of memories. It unfurled with the spreading of another pair of bat wings. Thalas flapped them hard as he gained his bearings and circled downward with a string of muttered Serri.

"It must be nighttime," Kauz mumbled.

I hoped this meant we were going to take a break and sleep. Except, what was this, other than sleep? My head hurt.

We made room in the alcove for Thalas, though it was a tight fit when he landed. He drew me in for a hug and murmured, "You're Dorei's girl. I can't believe I didn't recognize you."

I didn't quite know what to make of his sudden affection. He was a stranger to me, though I may not have been one to him. Maybe this was buried in my lost memories somewhere. Thalas eventually let me go and hugged Kauz next. "And my boy. You were absolutely right. This is an emergency."

"What's been happening?" Kauz asked.

Thalas sighed heavily. He didn't answer until we negotiated the small space and ended up on either side of him. It seemed strange to be pressed close like this, and I was too rigid to relax. "Too much for one discussion, I'm afraid. I caught the end of an interrogation yielding results that've left your mother nestbound. The grief and rage she's feeling..." He shuddered. "I'm glad she's resting. As should you both."

Thank the stars, we were going to take a break.

"I'll help repair your mind while you dream, Metalark. You will have to stay asleep until your memories are fully restored," he continued. "And Kauzden, you're too depleted to continue on here for much longer."

Kauz lifted his chin. "I'm not leaving Lark to do this alone."

"Then rest." Thalas gave him a little nudge. The other winged fae disappeared in a puff of essence, and I whimpered at how quickly he'd been dismissed. "I'll guide him back to you once you rest as well. Do you remember me, Metalark?"

"Maybe not like you remember me, Your Majesty," I answered.

He blew out a scoff. "I hope you never feel the need to call me that again. I'm going to give you a specific dream so you remember your first trip to Serian." His gaze glimmered with a constellation of gentle stars. "You were three. But trust me, no one in my pack has forgotten you."

Before I could ask how that was possible, he nudged me too and sent my mind into the relief of dreaming sleep.

25
LARK

"First, you should see this," Thalas whispered as the dream formed.

It was one of his memories. Somehow, I could sense that, like his presence in the room was a little firmer than the other fae. I stood behind his seat at a circular table, where seven individuals shared a generous dinner. Queen Nemensia gave her full attention to another nixie seated to her right. She was a dainty omega, but considering how Queen Nemensia's presence commanded a room, it wasn't hard to seem little compared to her.

Next to this other nixie was a younger version of my father, Kellam. Well, maybe not *too* much younger than what I remembered. Just a more carefree version of him. I spent a moment just looking at him and re-remembering every small detail. He was a broad-shouldered male with warm gray skin and white hair that never stayed orderly for long. Even indoors, there was a slight breeze that rippled over his clothes and hair.

He looked at the second nixie as if she'd hung the moon. No wonder —she had his cloud-shaped pack mark between her brows.

I circled the table to get a better look at her, Dorei, my mother. She had a sweet, tinkling laugh, and her fingers twined with my father's. Her hair was braided behind her head in a fancy style, the white strands glimmering with stars. She was a dreamlander, then, made more obvious by the specks twinkling in the whites of her eyes and the blue of her irises.

She had light purple skin, and resting on her back were trailing fins glowing with indigo swirls and motifs of comets.

"You're so beautiful," I murmured.

Then she coughed. A deep, nasty cough that cut through the hum of conversation in the room.

"Oh dear. Should we call for a healer?" Thalas asked.

"No, no. It's okay," Dorei said past the napkin she held over her mouth.

"She's picked up an allergy or something." My father glanced over at her with concern tightening his mouth.

The queen tutted. "She's allergic to that farm town you stole her away to."

"The whole town?" asked the dark elf sitting next to Thalas. He didn't look familiar, with his dusky skin, ruby-red eyes, and backswept horns, but his smile sure did. I'd seen that level of Unseelie mischief on Fal's face every day.

"The *whole* town," the queen echoed in agreement. She rubbed her stomach idly, and the fabric of her dress pulled, revealing the curve of a baby bump half hidden under the table.

"Or it could be..." My father drifted off, and Dorei met his gaze while she finished dabbing at her lips.

As she smiled, I noticed something. That button nose, the shape of her mouth and the apples of her cheeks. I looked in the mirror every day and saw my mother in my features. What an unexpected blessing.

Stars, she seemed so kind. She'd passed away before my memories even started, ended as I began. This dream was a gift. A chance to see her as she was.

"We came here to tell you something special," she said. She was practically glowing with happiness as she and my father announced together, "We're expecting!"

Queen Nemensia purred with happiness and grabbed her in a big hug. "It's about time!"

"Ah, first-time parents," the dark elf king remarked, tilting his head toward Kellam as the two nixies held one another. Queen Nemensia rubbed her own belly again and said something that had Dorei giggling. "Just a bit of advice. The female is expecting. There's very little 'we' to the whole matter."

My father hummed. "Sure, Ren."

"Congratulations," rumbled the gigantic redcap. He nearly knocked the dark elf from his seat slapping the back of it in an unsubtle gesture.

"Okay, here's the plan," the queen was saying. "You sell your farm town and move into the palace with us. We have room and an entire puddle of children to raise your baby with!"

My parents exchanged an amused glance. This wasn't the first time Queen Nemensia had suggested they do something like this, I bet.

"I believe it's more of a lake at this point, my heart," remarked the last king, a kelpie with half his blue and green hair shaved down to stubble. The other half was partially braided, making him resemble his second form even more strongly when combined with his oblong face shape. His name for her was in Serri... They'd been speaking it this whole time, and I'd understood them perfectly.

"More to come," the queen said. She whipped her head toward her redcap mate. "Right? Even more? You still owe me a son."

He gave her such an intense look of promise that I blushed and glanced away. "Then a son you will have," he rumbled.

"Anyway," Dorei put in with a musical laugh. "Before we leave, I was hoping to ask...ah, you all must get this a lot." She fidgeted with her fingers. "We spoke to an auracle and learned we're having a little girl. I just can't imagine a world where we'd leave her, but—"

Another terrible cough wracked her frame. The queen frowned, and she wasn't the only one. Everyone at this table looked like they were worried for Dorei.

"Go on," Queen Nemensia urged.

Dorei took a sip of water and cleared her throat. "Sorry. I was hoping you would be her godmother, Nemensia. And one of your males could be her godfather?" She glanced across the table with a hopeful look. "Thalas, perhaps? She will be part dreamlander. Maybe she'll have my dream warden magic."

Thalas sat straighter in surprise. "Me?"

"Don't leave the rest of us out," the dark elf murmured. He, along with the other kings, had turned to Queen Nemensia, waiting for her decision.

She stood, walked to the space between my parents' chairs, and put an arm around either of them. "I wouldn't dream of taking any bonus child to my nest except for one born from you two," she said.

"Then I'll speak for the rest of my pack in saying, what our omega does, we wholeheartedly echo. We will be the child's godfamily," the kelpie king declared.

As my mother cried tears of joy and my father beamed and thanked them all, I stood behind them, gaping in shock. I had a whole godfamily?

Where have they been?

THE DREAM TRANSFORMED into a retelling of my own memories. These recollections were crisper than one would expect a three-year-old's to be and I lost myself to a pleasant haze of innocence as I relived them.

Dad and I had taken a magirail ride! I'd smushed my face on the glass to watch the world go by, only getting bored when I realized there was mostly water between the fae nations.

Then we'd taken a long walk with my hand in his, up to the biggest building I'd ever seen. It was late springtime, and the Serian winter was finally gone, revealing a field of growing grass and flowers on the path to the palace.

"Remember, Metalark. You want to be on your best behavior," Dad prompted.

"Okay," I giggled agreeably.

I was meeting my godfamily, and Dad was nervous. We reviewed what best behavior meant, because he knew I was about to meet the most powerful Unseelie fae in Serian.

Once I'd promised to be polite to anyone I met, he lifted me up above his head and let his wind magic ruffle my wings as I flapped them eagerly. I couldn't fly yet, but someday!

We met Queen Nemensia in the entry foyer. Dad tried to introduce us formally. I practically vibrated at his side, fascinated by the pretty nixie and her glowing fins that flowed behind her when she moved.

There were more subtle instincts at play. Little omegas wanted the safety and comfort of their mother's nest and the softness of their hugs. I'd yearned for these things without knowing what I was missing, and she had the right kind of milky smell that said *Mom*.

I wandered from my father's side mid-introduction and toddled over with my arms out. She dropped to her knees and swept me up. "Hello, baby Metalark," she murmured. Unshed tears glimmered in her eyes as I snuggled into her.

That was all it took for her to work at convincing Dad to let me sleep in her nest during our stay. We were spending a fortnight here, a rare vacation for Dad and an opportunity for me to meet my godfamily. She became Mama Nem, as my tongue didn't have the agility for the full grandeur of "Nemensia" yet. Though I often forgot and just called her Mom. She never corrected me.

Her nest had seemed beyond massive. It had multiple levels and was full of soft materials I loved. The ground floor had been designed for kids, while the queen disappeared upstairs if she ever needed a break or a moment with her males. Someone always stayed below to watch us. There were three of their kids still young enough to sleep in the nest, and they tossed me in with them without hesitation.

The youngest was Tormund, who was an energetic and playful tot with a tendency to grab and hold on to things with his full strength. He became a lot gentler after he'd grabbed one of my wings and I'd screeched. He'd pet it in apology.

There was also Eletha, a tiny purple nixie with white markings on her fins. She was my age and cuter than most dolls, with wide eyes that took up most of her face.

The last kid still in the nest was Kauz, who, at four, was mostly wings. He had almost no control of them, so they dragged behind him and tangled with everything, including his other limbs. He sported a wavy mop of purple-black hair at this age.

At night, the royal pack would carry us to the biggest bed I'd ever seen, and I slept in various spots. Along with Mama Nem's instant acceptance had come that of her mates. They called me their bonus child, and each spent some time with me.

Dad had raised me bilingual, but at that age, everything I said was a jumble of two languages that required some finesse in interpretation. The best at understanding me was Papa Rennie, also known as the dark elf king Rennyn, who ran the palace for his mate. I followed him like a duckling, "helping" him if I found him. Which wasn't very often, considering how he was always in motion and I was usually in the gaggle of the royal pack's youngest kids.

He'd hum or whistle and snap his fingers, walking to his own rhythm in the halls and trailing a number of servants and officials. Every day, he covered a lot of ground, going to and from what were likely serious matters the queen didn't have time to address personally. He had a lucky coin he'd flip, which, with a little sleight of hand, would become a candy or a shiny chocolate made from a beetle-shaped mold that he simply called a bug, conditioning me to say "Yes, I want a bug!" I was more than a little peeved when he handed me a real bug once.

The Unseelie called him the Clever King, and even at that age, I noticed that many of the adults he interacted with were overly polite when he was around. He tried to teach me some cleverness in idle moments, little cheats and card tricks or just the subtlest of word changes for hiding inconvenient truths. I failed at following his lead each time, and he'd ruffled my hair, saying, "We'll wake the Unseelie in you yet. Maybe in a few years, p'nixie."

P'nixie was shorthand for my race after a lighthearted discussion of what exactly to call a pixie-nixie hybrid. As far as they knew, I was the first one so clearly possessing traits of both omega fae races.

I met the royal pack's other, older kids mostly in passing. There was Fal, who, at eleven, was a tired boy clearly sick of being the eldest kid of a gigantic family. He avoided the little kids when he could, so he and I barely interacted. He was deep in study with various tutors to be the next queen's lord.

The next eldest, Marius, more than made up for his disinterest. He was seven, almost eight, at the awkward in-between phase of early childhood and the start of his training as the next queen's protector. With little to do until he got bigger, he was the family's wild boy, always up to something. By day two of my stay at Serian Palace, he'd presented me with the biggest flowering weed in the garden—roots, dirt clots, and all.

"Want to be friends, p'nixie?" he'd giggled.

This had been before he'd gotten his scar. He had a chubby, often dirt-streaked face, and fast feet to avoid the gaggle of servants assigned to keep him clean and safe. I was too small for some of his mischief, but we sought each other out whenever possible. He quickly became my best friend, the one with all the fun ideas and the extra set of hands to help when I needed it, especially on beach day.

Oh, beach day. Marius and I built sandcastles, chased crabs and sandpipers, collected shells, and, of course, played in the sea. His father lurked underwater in kelpie form while we floated around, surfacing at random under one of the royal pack's kids to send them into the air from a gentle toss of his snout. My wings had been saturated with water and sagged into fins, but I still attempted to flap them with a gleeful giggle each time he launched me before I fell back into the sea with a splash.

The kelpie king, Papa El, was a very busy male. However, every time I was with him, I sensed his fatherly affection on omega instinct. It was a good thing Dad wasn't around when we first met, though, because I broke the news to the kelpie king that he resembled a horse. He reminded me of a noble animal that was both strong and graceful, with his distinctive face shape and long ears. Plus, his gray skin was dappled like a horse's coat.

Which was great, because I loved horses! Dad had the gentlest mare, Meya, and we went for rides together. He promised I'd get to ride Meya on my own when I was older!

He listened to my whole speech with an amused expression before saying, "I'm glad you like horses so much, p'nixie. I hope you never lose that."

I mostly saw him at night and during his morning walk, as he was usually hearing petitions, hosting meetings, or conferring with the queen to solve important problems. He was nothing like his son, neither the wild boy nor the feral male I knew, possessing easy charm and open affection. Of all the kings, he treated me the most as if I were his child.

The morning walk with him was a favorite of mine since that was one of the only times Papa Theo wasn't working either. The redcap king wore shorts and a sleeveless vest most days, plus some of the largest weapons forged, strapped to either his back or hip. The clothes did nothing to hide the tattoos wrapped around his limbs like chains of stylized knots. He was the biggest male I'd seen before or since, a mountain of muscle with one expression carved deep in his craggy face, but I'd taken one look at him and lifted my arms up to be held.

I spent the morning walk on his shoulders, holding the Unseelie's fearsome Blood King's ears for balance while flapping my wings and looking around at the world from a seven-plus-foot vantage.

He'd carry me to the workshop, where my last bonus dad had a daily story time for the littlest kids, plus the other girls in the family, Siora and Tanith, who weren't too old for it yet. Marius joined us too and sat next to me, though he'd fidget from sitting still for too long.

Papa Thas—I couldn't fully pronounce his name either—took the dreamlander kids aside weekly for an extra talk about dreams. We'd sit in the circle of his wings and discuss topics like Never, Ever, and Always.

Never, the path of nonsense at best and insanity at worst. The dreams of lost opportunities, of events that were yearned for but never occurred. These things and their inherent darkness had to be trimmed from the dreamlands.

Ever, dreams focusing on events that had already occurred, were harmonious. They could be beloved memories or terrible ones. The only commonality they needed to have was that they'd happened. Our brains tended to remember things for a reason, even if it was only to remind us not to fail in the same way twice.

And then Always. Thalas smiled to himself as he got to that part. "The rarest of them all, the path of fate. Some say our lives are already written and stamped into the dreamlands as Always. Fate smells incredible, little ones. It will lead you down the path you're meant to walk or to the one you're meant to be with."

"Like you and Mom?" Kauz asked.

Thalas's secretive smile only got wider. "That's right, my boy. I still smell Always from her every night we dream together."

It was a story time session that marked the end of my time with my big, affectionate godfamily. A fortnight had passed in the blink of an eye, full of fun and new experiences. Dad gathered me up and we said an extended goodbye to the Unseelie all the way to the train station.

I hadn't realized it until looking back at these memories, but the adults were putting some pressure on Dad. "We will visit again soon," he promised the queen as we stood to one corner of the station, waiting for our train to arrive. "But Metalark's place is in Osme Fen."

"P'nixie!" a boy exclaimed. I glanced away from Dad and Mama Nem, brightening as little Marius wove through the legs of the travelers around us. We'd already said goodbye, so it was nice to see him again already. He had a gap-toothed grin as he offered me another flower; this one was properly trimmed, a silvery bloom with a light blue center. His father stood a few feet away, watching us with a soft, knowing kind of look.

Dad was still talking. "I intend to court a widow who has a young daughter. Metalark would do well to grow up with a sister of her own age."

"Be that as it may..." The queen dropped her voice to a hush.

Unfortunately, as a child, I only cared about the pretty flower and my friend, not what the adults were discussing. As I became aware that this was a distant memory, a dream within a dream, Dad was gently tugging me away from Marius's second hug goodbye.

I cherished this last gift until it wilted and faded away.

I woke from the spiral of memories with a wistful mewl. I wasn't awake-awake, but I took in the pile of fragmented memories waiting for me in the pit below with a new sense of purpose.

I wasn't alone in this world, not anymore. Those had been my memories, my godfamily, and my future mates before we'd grown up and developed our designations. I was *loved*. I'd just forgotten it for a while.

"No one in my pack has forgotten you."

I intended to find that out for myself and rebuild from there. Kauz joined me when I was in my second memory of the day, his face pinched with worry before relaxing at whatever he saw in me.

"I have to wake up," I told him.

He nodded and stayed by my side. Though he faded in and out on the edge of depletion, he remained with me for nine grueling days as I restored the rest of my memories one at a time. Half of my newfound strength came from having his calm presence at my back. He got me through the ordeal and endured some of my darkest moments with me, all while keeping his silence unless I needed a few words of reassurance to keep going.

Most memories came with a sense of surprise from learning more about myself than I'd realized existed. Hidden depths added nuance to my past and experiences. Like when we stepped into a moment from when I was eighteen. Cymora had taken me and my least favorite trio of barkfolk to the nearest city to sign a couple of contracts. I remembered one contract...but the other...

"Oh. I signed the lands of Osme Fen over to Cymora," I narrated to Kauz while the memory played out in front of us.

The courthouse was empty except for the male overseeing the paperwork across the table from my younger self. She bent to sign her name several times throughout a sheaf of paper while Pack Ellisar leered at her ass. Her cheeks heated with humiliation all the while, tears pricking the corners of her eyes.

"I was her ward until this moment," I mumbled. "She was my guardian until I came of age. Father had put it in the will."

"Of course he did," Kauz answered. His fingers laced with mine. "The title is yours by birthright. My brothers and I noticed Cymora didn't have a reason to be Lady of Osme Fen from the moment you clarified your relationships. This is *theft*."

I nodded, clutching his hand tightly when the memory continued to play out. No wonder she kept me alive until this moment—she wanted the title and the wealth behind it. But then she'd had me sign away my adulthood to Pack Ellisar. That should've washed her hands of me, had I had my first heat on schedule.

Cymora and Ellisar, the eldest of his brothers, crowded close to my past self while she looked over the second contract. I remembered reading it as closely as I could as...

Kauz breathed a low growl while Ellisar groped this memory of me. Shadows darkened the air around him, shivering with promises of nightmares and terror, as the stars in his eyes sparked like lightning strikes. My heart leapt to see him truly angry.

My past self had gone rigid and bitten down on a whine so the bark-folk wouldn't take her reaction as any kind of arousal. The official was too busy congratulating Cymora as the new Lady of Osme Fen to notice what else was going on.

The memory wasn't going to cut off until we saw everything up to the inevitable order by Cymora to forget signing over Osme Fen to her. I remembered and dreaded the other contract, the one I still hadn't told the princes about.

"Kauz, I should've mentioned this. I just..." I fumbled for some kind of explanation, knowing it was way too late now.

"What are you waiting for, girl? Sign it," Cymora snarled, unknow-ingly interrupting me.

"Yes, Step—"

The shadows wrapped around Kauz dissipated. He tugged me to turn away from the scene, pressing little kisses over my face. It was only when he murmured reassurances that I even noticed I was crying. A burning sensation gripped me hard. Growing up, I was rarely allowed to be angry, and expressing it was dangerous anyway, so when it came forward, the strength of my fury left me weeping rather than yelling.

But I was so breathtakingly angry at my stepmother, and yet all I could do was cry and curse myself in frustration. I wanted to go into the memory we'd just left behind and rip the contracts into confetti. Then I would tell the meek little omega I'd been to forget Cymora's lies about Unseelie and head to Serian. But it was the past, and I could do no such thing.

Kauz's voice broke through my thoughts, bringing me back to the present. "So, this is the pack you wanted to run from. I already know you were forced to sign a breeding contract. You told me during our first dream together."

"I did?" I asked.

"Aye. It was your strongest reason for running away to a sanctuary city. If this is how they treated you in public, I can't blame you."

Well, knowing about them hadn't seemed to dampen his opinion of me. And if he knew, that meant his brothers did too, and they hadn't said a word. My sudden influx of anger was flooded with humiliation.

"They're also why I held my heat back for so long," I said. "They bought access to it and always threatened to breed me and make me their omega."

Sparks darted across Kauz's starlit eyes. "They will never touch you again, sweetheart. If they dare to show themselves in Serian, they'll swiftly lose their heads," he said through clenched teeth. "Breeding contracts are *very* illegal."

It was such welcome news that I succumbed to relief and clung to him between memories. I peppered him with questions, and yes, his brothers knew already, and none of them considered Pack Ellisar a threat to our future mating. Kauz had even sent off a spy to be sure they wouldn't meddle with me joining Pack Sorles.

Stars, Kauz was incredible. I... needed him. Like a caged lark yearning for the sky or a night sky awaiting its stars, I *wanted* him. He could lay me down and help me forget the clarity of what we'd witnessed in my memories.

But by the end of our time together, he was so exhausted he could barely speak. He'd pushed the end of his limits and supported me when I needed him most. And I was hopelessly in love with him for it.

Thalas arrived to send us away from this corner of my mind when the last of the memory shards were gone. He turned his head aside to give us privacy when Kauz cupped my face. We kissed once more before we went our separate ways. I'd go up to wakefulness, and he'd go down into rest to recover his essence.

"Come visit me," he murmured.

"I will," I promised.

"Visit my dreams," he clarified, tapping me lightly on the nose.

I hesitated. It wasn't as if I knew how to use any dream warden magic I'd inherited from my mother, but... "I'll try. And Kauz?"

"Mmm?" He was losing definition, fading out of my mind.

I should've told him how I felt. I had the opportunity, but it didn't feel like the right time. Not with his father crammed into our little alcove, his hearing still bat-sharp even with his head turned.

I settled for saying, "Thank you for setting me free." I put as much affection into those words as they could hold.

He attempted to form a knowing smile and dipped his chin. The next moment, he was gone, dropping into a much-needed sleep. And the heartbeat after that, I was opening my eyes to the start of my new life.

26

LARK

The ceiling was gray. At some point, it may have been white, but that'd been a long time ago. I stared up at it in a hazy headspace between reality and memory. After nine days, I wasn't sure whether I'd finally woken up.

The mingling pheromones of several alphas and a couple omegas hung in the air, though I picked out my scent matches from the mix and focused on those. Waterlilies and wild mint were the strongest fragrance, and my belly twisted as I thought of the little Marius I used to know. My best friend, lost to time and feral instinct.

"Kauz will need up to an additional week to rest, but Metalark should wake any minute now." This was from Thalas, speaking Serri with a groggy weight. I didn't understand him perfectly, but my ordeal had the unexpected benefit of advancing my knowledge of the Unseelie language. I now remembered the bilingual practice of my first six years in magic-enhanced clarity.

"And she's healed?" Fal sounded worried. "Her mind is okay?"

I stirred, stretching muscles gone stiff from my long rest. I'd barely pushed myself to sit up before Nemensia was by my bedside, fingers laced over her baby bump. Hope glittered in her light blue eyes.

She was still the pretty omega that'd adopted me on sight and fit as much love as possible into my visit here. As an adult with restored memories of that distant time, it was clear to me that she'd wanted to be the mother I'd lost. I was confident I wasn't about to make a misstep as I said, "Hi, Mom."

"My baby girl," she said in Theli. She pulled me into a hug, and it was everything I imagined a mother's warmth to be, including the soothing but complex scent of her and the not unwelcome sensation of her soft purr. I purred with her in harmony, relaxing into the embrace. She still had that milky note that'd first drawn me to her.

As a mated omega, she represented her pack by carrying the scents of her alpha mates with her, and the combination tugged on my memories of being warm and safe. Her nest had smelled like this. What wasn't an echo of my past was the sob that wracked her as she clutched me harder.

"I didn't know you were still alive, Metalark. Had I known, we would've rescued you long before now. Your fathers would've burned that cursed farm town to the ground."

I tried to rub her back, pausing when my hand ruffled her silky fins. That was going to take some getting used to. "It's okay. Osme Fen isn't worth your time."

"Blasted place," she muttered.

"Besides, I'm here now," I said, and grateful for it too. "By some miracle."

"Aye, my sons. Who I've forgiven for disappearing since they brought you back." She released me and straightened, stepping aside.

The first thing I noticed was Marius out cold in a chair by my bedside, his muscular bulk leaned back against the wall. Black and silver magic glimmered on his forehead and over the scarred ridge of his nose. I wondered what that was about, but with him asleep, I turned my attention to the others in this space.

Fal and Tormund waited at the foot of my bed. The dark elf was a touch disheveled, his hair in disarray like he'd run his hands through it more than once. The redcap just looked excited to see me up.

I smiled and lifted the covers piled on me to swing my legs toward the ground. The right one felt like it weighed double, and I gasped to see a thick cast encasing it from the knee down. Thalas rustled from where he stood off to the side, closer to the other bed in this space. "Don't stand just yet, Metalark," he instructed.

I nodded and let the princes come to me. Fal bent down and hugged me tightly, then caught my chin between his clawed fingers. "It must be called beauty rest for a reason, for you to wake up more stunning than ever," he said, admiring what he saw in me. I felt my cheeks pinken. "Your eyes are sparkly."

"Like a dreamlander's?" I asked. Like Dorei's, I hoped.

"Aye. Not as many stars as Kauz has. Which, I'm glad. Those baby blues of yours haven't hidden a secret from me yet." He winked, stole a quick kiss, and shuffled aside for Tormund to lean in next.

As I expected, he crushed me in the biggest hug he could manage from this angle. "I'm so happy you're awake, li'l bird. We've been worried!" he exclaimed.

"Sorry it took so long," I murmured.

Nemensia spoke up, fists on her hips. "No, dear. Don't you dare apologize for what you've been through."

Tormund nodded in agreement. I soaked in his presence and the caramelized sugar note in his smoke and mallows scent. "Mom has good news to share soon," the redcap said in a loud whisper before he, too, let me go.

It was Thalas's turn. He stepped forward and rested a hand on my shoulder. "You will need to keep your weight off your foot until we're sure you've made a complete recovery. The *olcanus* gave you a magical wound, and those don't seal the same way as ordinary ones."

"How long will it take?" I asked, eyeing the cast. I bit my lip, worried I'd never walk properly despite the silencing band's removal. I still preferred the cast to the band in every possible scenario.

"We'll check it when Kauz wakes up. How about that? A week or so," he offered, glancing over at the other bed and the figure lying motionless under its sheets. It was Kauz sleeping serenely, his complexion more gray than purple.

Hopefully he was having pleasant dreams. A week without him, though? I suppressed a little whimper.

Thalas retrieved a pair of crutches from the floor. They were wooden, carved with pretty flourishes, and padded over the ridges at their tops. "Have you used crutches before?"

I hadn't, and they required more finesse than I expected, so I wobbled like a newborn fawn between Fal and Tormund in the infirmary's main hall while I practiced. Despite how they dug into my armpits even with the padding, I had the sense that they'd make moving around easier than the limping gait I'd gotten used to.

"I wouldn't mind carrying you," Tormund offered for at least the fourth time.

"No. I can do this." No one in this palace would take me seriously if I let the princes carry me around like they had on the train. I crutched along with a determined furrow appearing between my brows. I went back and forth down the hall, to the occasional word of praise from the nurses going about their rounds.

By the third lap, when I was really getting it down, a furious roar echoed from the end of the hall. I startled with a distressed whine and lost my balance. Tormund caught me and the crutch that threatened to slip out from under my arm. Fal whipped around, growling.

I walked myself behind Tormund's protective bulk and peeked around him as the curtains at the end of the hall were thrust aside. Marius emerged, the barrel of his chest heaving and his eyes dilated. He prowled toward us with a fluid turn of his heels.

"Marius, now's not the time," Fal said.

The kelpie replied with a snarl, only stopping when Fal shifted to intercept him. They paused nose to nose in another dominance match while Tormund shielded me, also growling, but with a redcap's menace. Heat warped around the giant as his fingers flexed, claws growing and retracting as he struggled to keep his rage at bay.

"Get your shit under control," Fal hissed.

Marius worked his jaw. "I have to see her," he gritted out.

Both of them had switched to speaking Serri. I hadn't mentioned my improved understanding of their language and kept the information to myself now.

"You're not getting any closer to my mate while you're throwing a wild fit."

"Get out of my way."

"Nay. You're too unstable. We had to put you to sleep because you wouldn't stop posturing over Lark and snapping at the rest of us like an animal," the dark elf said, exasperated.

They did? Stars. I took a deep breath, trying to calm my racing pulse.

Marius's growling deepened and ended with a chuff of warning. "I would destroy you if it comes down to—"

"Cut it out," Nemensia ordered. Even as their mother, she didn't get too close to these pissed-off alphas. I'd been considering crutching away and seeing how far I could get. It was the same omega instinct at work.

The kelpie's ear flicked in irritation. "Let me see *my* mate...please," he said grudgingly.

Neither Fal nor Tormund budged at the request. It was clear they wouldn't with me taking shelter behind Tormund.

I straightened my nerves. "Don't fight. It's not worth it," I said in Theli and crutched into full view.

Marius looked me over from my crown to the new cast, scenting the air with a flare of his nostrils. He reached for me, though everything else about his posture was still poised for a fight. He had that intense, feral expression. *Unpredictable.*

I flinched away from him. Fal shifted again, preventing his brother from coming any closer.

Marius shuttered his countenance. His voice became just as impenetrable as his hand dropped to his side. "I'm glad you're all right," he said in Theli.

He cast his gaze away pointedly, the Marius equivalent of saying the conversation was finished. Before it could get too awkward, I turned with a little hop on my crutches to be sure Tormund was okay. He wasn't showing any more signs of a rage and tilted a smile my way.

"I think I got the hang of this," I said.

"Time to take you to your new rooms, then." He gave Nemensia a questioning glance.

She nodded. "Yes, let's."

We made our way slowly to this new destination, as I set the pace.

Nemensia walked beside me, her hand on Thalas's arm, chatting away about how much I'd love my rooms. Plural. They were moving me straight into a princess suite. A mix of hope and nerves danced in my belly as I wondered if that meant what I thought it did.

Tormund lumbered at my other side, while Fal and Marius hung back. They weren't at each other's throats again, but the tone of their heated whispering wasn't much friendlier. When there was a lull in conversation, Tormund rushed to fill it. "And you have a few starting items for your nest. We'll start filling it with things you like from there," he promised.

"It's customary for the new omega to receive an item from the nests of all the family's omegas," Nemensia said.

"That sounds great." I yearned for the comfort of my new nest as my muscles tired quickly. I'd need to practice with the crutches more if I wanted to be ambulatory. And, actually, I was just low on energy. All that time sleeping, yet it felt like I'd gotten little to no rest.

We passed out of the old fortress into one of the palace wings. The transition was obvious from the widening of the halls and the addition of windows overlooking a snowfall outside. The foot traffic around us decreased the further we walked, though most fae saw the group around me and moved out of the way well in advance.

There was a stretch of hallway where we were quiet, other than the clacking of my crutches striking the marble floor. The broad caps at the end of them prevented me from slipping, though I saw the potential for it happening in my mind's eye. Every new surface and movement I used to take for granted was another opportunity to fall.

This was the royal wing, where the royal pack's children lived. There were several spacious suites on each floor, and they showed me to the last one in a row of rooms, past the four occupied by the four princesses.

My crutches hit the rug past the boundary of the door into my new rooms, and I nearly face-planted. Tormund caught me and laughed. "Clumsy li'l bird," he teased.

"Yeah. Thanks, Tormund." The gentle giant was getting cuddled as soon as I took a bath. Thalas had assured me that my cast was made with a waterproofing spell, so I could take it into...well, he'd called it a "rain room" and told me I was in for a treat if I didn't know what that was.

Once I took my first glance around, I thought they were being too generous. Having one room to myself was a kindness, but this was just the start, a full-on receiving room. I stopped two crutch-lengths past the door, trying not to gape.

"Sorry it's so plain," Nemensia said. "If my sons had told me you were coming, we would have at least put some art up."

I completely missed the brief change in tone aimed at the three males behind me. "No need. It's great," I said in quiet awe.

A princess of the past had removed any signs of wallpaper and left bold swirls of neutral colors swooping up the walls. The back wall had a lit fireplace crackling away, set with red brick. There were two long, overstuffed couches set at an L shape close to the fire. A coffee table fit between them, and a tea service rested on a platter atop it, awaiting use.

Nemensia urged me to explore, and the princes trailed me. I pulled back a curtain on the left wall, just to uncover a private nook with tall windows and a well-varnished table set to serve six fae. The windows had a film on them, suggesting it was a one-way view. When it wasn't wintertime, I hoped I had a view of the gardens.

"They're here!" an unexpected, squeaky voice announced in accented Theli. I turned to see an unusual Unseelie fae beckoning to another, the two of them lining up and curtsying to the queen.

Nemensia smiled and gestured between me and them. "Metalark, these are your handmaidens, Jani and Lon."

The two handmaidens spotted me and gasped with excitement. They were dressed identically in the palace uniform of sorts, dark blue dresses trimmed in silver. And considering they looked the same too, I was worried I'd end up switching their names immediately. They were betas, some kind of moth fae, and didn't even scrape five feet tall, with huge red eyes and rounded, fuzzy bodies. Their black fluff poked out from the cuffs of their dresses.

"I'm Jani," announced the female on the left. Her antennae had streaks of white through them.

"And I'm Lon," said the other female cheerfully. I tried to find an identifying feature about her and ended up noticing the brown leaf-like patterns on the inside of her moth wings.

"We're here to help you with anything you need, Princess!"

"A pleasure to meet you both," I said, a little bemused. After so long being a servant, I guess I wasn't expecting anyone to be assigned to help me. Especially Unseelie I immediately found adorable. Though I didn't dare say anything about it. I'd made the mistake of trying to pet a shifted grimalkin the last time I'd been in Serian Palace, and that hadn't ended well *at all*.

The moth betas stayed behind to talk with Nemensia and Thalas while I toured the rest of the suite. There was a study in the next room that I could see myself spending a lot of time in. Its bookshelves were empty, but that could be fixed. It had comfortable armchairs and a writing desk stacked with neat rows of paper and writing utensils.

Next was the bedroom. I flopped face-first on the giant pack-sized mattress, as was customary for me now. It was *very* nice. I could see myself sleeping here even without covers. "Where are the things to start a nest?" I asked Tormund.

"Oh, this isn't your nest," he said with a grin. He encouraged me to go through an alcove in the opposite wall. I drew its privacy curtain aside and entered another room, gasping when I took in what had to be my new nesting space. It was built into the back of the suite.

The bottom floor was dark and enclosed, with another pack-sized mattress set its own nook. On it rested a note and five different items already smelling of other omegas: two blankets, a pillow, what looked to be an essence lamp, and a stuffed toy. I purred with delight, leaving those things for when I had a moment to inspect them without the princes waiting for me. They wouldn't enter unless invited.

There was a plush rug underfoot that I did my best not to slide on, as I didn't want to fall in the privacy of my nest. Stars, I had a nest, and it had my nemesis, *stairs*. The beginning of the staircase was on the other side of this floor. From the ground, I had the sense that it opened into a large space on the second floor, complete with waning light leaking in from some windows.

I weighed my options and decided to leave exploring the upper level for later. My omega instincts wanted dark and enclosed right now anyway, with my pre-heat looming over my shoulder.

I headed for the privacy curtain and paused, catching a quiet conversation on the other side, spoken in Serri.

"I just want a few minutes to speak to her without you two listening," Marius was saying, sounding defensive.

A redcap growl answered him. "Not a chance."

"No drawing her aside today, at least. She's exhausted," Fal said more calmly. "I suspect I know what this is about. But Mar, she's not ready for another round of your shit, and quite frankly, you will have that fight you keep threatening if you upset her one more time—"

"I won't," Marius interrupted, punctuating it with a snort.

"She's been through a lot," the dark elf continued.

Stars, they were talking about me. I wondered if they realized I was listening in, or if they even cared. They didn't realize I could mostly understand them now.

"I know," the kelpie murmured.

"Nay, you weren't there. It's much worse than you think," Fal sighed. "She deserves a chance to recover in peace. Can we at least agree not to add to her—"

He cut himself off as I shifted forward, no longer wanting to eavesdrop. I emerged from the nest upset, and Tormund was building to echo that energy when he saw my face.

"The nest is great!" I blurted to give us all a change of topic. "I just noticed the art Kauz gave me is gone." I awkwardly pointed at my arm and its slightly rolled cuff. I'd checked my wrist to see how my heat suppressant tattoo was doing, lifting my long sleeve to reveal two circular tattoos on my inner wrist and nothing else.

It was Marius that answered. "Thalas can explain it better, but it was all ruined by the amount of magic released when your silencing band was removed."

"Oh. I wanted to see the metalark," I mumbled.

"You're going to see plenty of metalarks soon, *mo stór*," Fal answered.

But they wouldn't be Kauz's art, nor the phrase he'd left on a ribbon in the bird's claws. Now I wouldn't know what it said, even with my improved understanding of Serri. *So unfair.*

"Speaking of which, do you want us to call you that? Metalark?"

"Probably as much as you want to be called Falindel," I answered. "Maybe less. It doesn't sound like my name."

"Lark it is, then," he purred. "Do you know what else is calling your name right now?"

"A bath," I said with longing.

"No, that one's for Marius," he deadpanned. The kelpie slanted a dirty look at him. "I was going to say dinner."

"Oh, I'll have it delivered!" Tormund exclaimed, cutting into the more flirtatious tone his brother was trying to take. Now Fal was the one shooting over an annoyed glance at the redcap. "They say the first custom meal from one of our chefs is earth-shattering. Are you ready to have your life changed, li'l bird?"

"Only for the better," I said with a tired sigh.

Tormund offered to carry me again and looked fit to burst when I told him I was okay. Instead, he showed me to the last part of my suite, attached to the opposite side of the bedroom. It was the bathroom of my dreams, with creamy tile set into the floor and a claw-foot tub big enough to fit two fae. There were also human inventions: the rain room and a toilet. Two things the giant promised would also change my life for the better.

He'd distracted me while the other two alphas finished their conversation. I turned around to see Marius nodding in agreement with something and Fal smiling. For a moment, there was peace between them.

We returned to the front room together. My handmaidens waited by the door and listened intently to Tormund when he approached with instructions about dinner.

Nemensia and Thalas were still here, and the queen beckoned us over with a big smile. "Well, what do you think?" Since she couldn't take my hands, she rested hers on my shoulders instead.

"Everything is incredible. I can hardly believe it." I was used to a fraction of this amount of space and no nest. If I wasn't careful, I *would* become quite spoiled.

"It is all yours. We'll start your training once you settle in and—oh stars, I didn't tell you. Falindel and Tormund already know, but you and Marius have been asleep." She gave my shoulders an affectionate squeeze. "I've approved you to be my sons' mate. You're going to be my heir, Metalark."

I gasped. Though I'd been halfway expecting the news, given the rooms, I thought she was going to make me earn it. There were no tests? Just straight to the training? My wings fanned in place, practically vibrating.

Fal touched the small of my back, meeting my gaze with a slow smile full of Unseelie mischief.

"She said yes," I whispered to him, gleeful and teary all at once.

"I *told* you," he said in a singsong. "I knew she'd adore you."

"I already did," the queen confirmed. "Hold still. We're going to figure out hugs even with this cast situation." She hugged me around my middle while Fal repositioned his hand so I didn't lose my balance.

"Thanks, Mom." When I mated into Pack Sorles, I'd be expected to call her that. I had double the reason to now. As for her males, though, I'd have to figure it out. "And...Dad?"

Thalas flashed a tranquil smile. "Aye, if that's what you prefer to call me. Your situation is unusual, Metalark. I wouldn't be surprised if you 'run into' the rest of my pack early and reacquire your godchild status."

"That would be breaking protocol," Fal pointed out. "Which, not that anyone has asked yet, we followed. Lark is untouched."

"I am." And more than a little chagrined that neither of the older fae seemed to care.

The queen patted him on the arm. "Good job." She then bid us farewell for the evening, passing hugs all around, though she had to chase Marius with a "Hold still, my wild boy. You're not too tough to get a hug from your mama."

I watched them go, muffling a giggle behind my hand. He eventually relented and gathered her up, fins and all, for a big hug. Stars, I hadn't even turned his way when she'd told us of her approval. Had he at least cracked a smile? I guess I wouldn't know now.

Behind me, Thalas whispered to Fal in Serri, "She's really untouched?"

"It nearly killed us, but yes."

Thalas snickered, and I tried not to twitch and give away that I was listening to them.

"Great to see how much you all care about protocol," Fal grumbled.

The other male only laughed harder. "No, you don't understand. Elion owes me so many full moons. I can't wait to see his face when he hears the news."

27
LARK

DINNER *WAS* LIFE-CHANGING. Everything they served me tasted incredible. I had a moment with the herb-and-breadcrumb-stuffed chicken, wondering how they got all that flavor under the skin. Fal and Tormund ate with me, while Marius left unannounced at some point.

"All he eats is raw meat and sadness anyway," Tormund had muttered.

They left me for the evening with reluctance, but I wanted a bath so badly at that point. Jani and Lon helped me to the rain room, which they called a "shower." They happily told me that since it was a human invention, no magic went into summoning the warm water that washed down on me. Yet it felt truly magical.

I dried off and practically begged my handmaidens to go and rest. They'd done everything to help me get around and redressed in sleeping clothes short of getting in the shower with me.

"It's an honor to be picked as a handmaiden," Lon told me with a fluttery giggle.

"Especially when a princess needs extra hands. We could stay by your nest in case you need anything tonight?" Jani offered.

"Please, go take time for yourselves," I said again.

They walked me all the way to my nest before promising to be back in the morning with breakfast. They turned off the essence lamps as they went, leaving me with one, a ball of light that floated over my shoulder as I made my way to my new bed.

Before I inspected the items, I opened the note left for me.

Dearest Metalark,

Welcome back to the family! Please accept this nestwarming gift from us.

Ambriel gave you her favorite stuffed kelpie. She knows he'll guard you in your sleep.

Eletha gave you a reading faelight. "Everyone should have a light and hope in the dark of night." She is something of a reader and hopes you are the same.

Siora gave you one of her pillows. She wishes you comfort and support as you settle in.

Tanith gave you the dark blanket. It may not look like much, but it will keep you warm in the Serian winter.

And I have given you the silk blanket knowing dreamlanders appreciate having their stars a little closer to home.

Love,

Nemensia

My lips wobbled in appreciation. Here in my nest, I could be as vulnerable as I wanted, so I finally wept with joy as I decorated my bed with the gifts. I shook the faelight first, eager to see it in motion. It leapt up several feet and lit like an essence lamp, but its light compacted into the form of a butterfly that circled overhead.

I inspected the kelpie toy with a curious eye. It was clearly already loved by a small omega, with extra stitches in the fabric on its tail and legs.

I laid the blankets on top of the sheets the bed was already set with and rested my head on the soft pillow from Siora. My fingers explored the texture of the blankets in quiet approval. The one from Tanith was a dark neutral color, but it was dense and trapped my body heat.

My fingertips froze mid-stroke when investigating Nemensia's gift. I recognized what it was by feel alone. The same material as the finest traditional pixie garments, lavir spidersilk. This blanket shimmered with patterns of stars painted over a black background, sure to be stunning in the light of day. It was ludicrously expensive, and here I was, nesting with it.

I thought of Kauz and drifted to sleep with a purr, the stuffed kelpie hugged to my chest.

Alas, just thinking of him didn't plonk me straight into his dream. I woke to an itch I couldn't get to under my cast and a cheerful pair of moth fae calling from the privacy curtain that it was time to get up. Jani and Lon were just as excited to see me as yesterday when I emerged from the nest.

"Good morning. Can you two keep a secret?" I asked.

"Anything that will help us serve you better, Princess," Jani squeaked.

I switched languages, telling them in their native Serri that they didn't have to struggle with Theli while I was the only one in the suite. Their antennae shot straight up before quivering. I took that as surprise and excitement, respectively.

"You can also help me practice," I continued. With my bilingual childhood still a fresh memory, I didn't butcher the words with a heavy Theli burr, either. "But no one else needs to know about this right now."

"Of course, Princess," Lon said. Both of them nodded along.

They guided me to my new closet. My new...walk-in closet. I'd thought Kauz had bought me a lot of clothes, but seeing them all hanging up neatly and arranged by color put it into perspective. There were racks and racks of room to expand.

A particular cloak hung separately from the rest. I balanced on my right crutch and turned it on its hanger, gasping when I saw it'd been repaired. An embroidery of snowflakes and curlicues for eddies of wind were added to the bottom in white thread. The designs completely hid the seam of where it'd once been ripped.

The cloak's clasp had also been replaced. Instead of a simple metal ring, it was a silvery medallion with four symbols etched into it. After recognizing the guiding star on top and the knot of promise beside it, I memorized the last two. Marius's symbol was of a horse's head with a mane of water swirling around it, and Kauz's was a pair of bat wings shrouded by a cloud of mist and pinpoint stars.

This was a not-so-subtle claim and something only an alpha would think of. It had to be Fal's doing, marking me as claimed by Pack Sorles. Their future pack princess.

Once we picked out an outfit for the day and I put the cloak on overtop it, I caught a strong whiff of his sunshine and grass scent. I needed to go kiss him in thanks.

I had a nice conversation in Serri with Jani and Lon over breakfast, and only stumbled over the language a few times when a Theli word slipped in here and there. They corrected me with just as much cheer as before.

I made to set out for the day. I was going to explore the palace; I just had to get around the door. After fumbling the knob a few times, I nudged it open and adjusted my hold on the crutches when they clicked on the marble outside.

Standing just past the alcove that sheltered my door was Marius, who swung around with raised brows when he saw me. He moved his big body in my way. "Do you need something?" he rumbled.

I came to a stop and wobbled before finding my balance. "Not particularly," I said.

He tilted his head in clear confusion.

"Um, why are you out here?" I asked.

He blinked slowly, and his pupils expanded for a moment. He worked his jaw, a sign he might've been struggling to speak.

"Never mind. Could you move?" I lifted my left crutch and motioned toward the side.

His nostrils flared, and he didn't budge an inch.

I frowned at him. "Get out of the way, Marius."

"You need to rest," he finally said.

"I'm okay. I'm bathed and dressed and want to see my new home." Plus, I hoped some exploring would bring back more pleasant childhood memories.

This might've been a good time to mention what I'd seen of him in my recollections of the past. But...I didn't know how he'd react, and it was so long ago. I doubted he remembered any of our old summer friendship.

He considered for a few more moments before nodding. "Fine. Where are we going?"

I swallowed a lump of nerves with a sinking feeling. I'd intended to be alone for my wanderings. "This is not a 'we' kind of outing."

Scowling, he leaned in and dropped his voice. "You are clearly an injured and unclaimed omega. Every outing is a 'we' kind of outing. My brothers are busy, either recovering or working, so you're stuck with me as your escort. No one would dare put their starsdamned hands on you if I'm around. So, tell me where *we're* going."

My belly quivered; betrayal at its finest. I took a deep breath to recenter myself. A bit of a mistake, as I breathed in a heady sniff of his scent. He was very minty today. And leaning in so close, I could try to press my lips to the unforgiving line of his.

His stare only seemed to grow more intense as he waited for me to speak. He was in full form as a predator, sure to go for the throat when presented with a hint of weakness. I wasn't sure if he ever relaxed from that feral state.

I packed away everything I really wanted to say and went for levity. "Have you considered a lip ring?"

His ear flicked twice. Stars, that question must've really annoyed him. "What?" he growled.

"You have what, five piercings? You could have a lip ring too. Or maybe pierced ears," I continued.

Marius shook his head, straightening. "Are you trying to distract me?"

"Is it working?"

"Aye. Go on. I'll follow." He stepped aside so I could pass. My crutches clacked loudly as I steered myself into the hallway and looked right and left. My new suite was at the end of the hall, across from a marble stairwell leading to more rooms on the second floor. I turned in the direction I wanted to go, picking up momentum as I caught my stride, so to speak. Crutching around wasn't exactly pleasant or quick, but it was already faster than what I was used to.

Marius kept pace, slowing his gait to remain beside me. "They're not piercings for decoration. They're kelpie tags, designed to identify me in my shifted form."

I hummed. "Do they get bigger when you shift?"

"They'd be worthless if they didn't."

Oh, that was an interesting bit of magic. "Will you tell me more kelpie facts?" I invited.

"Only if you tell me where we're going."

A small price to pay if he'd answer questions. Maybe it'd transition to Marius facts instead. "I don't know. I just wanted to explore. And... you know..." I let my response drift off to a mumble to avoid mentioning how I'd been here before.

"Hmm. Let's go to the library and see Eletha. You'll like her," he said.

I perked up. After her gift of the faelight, she'd been the princess I'd wanted to reconnect with first. "All right."

"What kind of facts were you hoping to hear?"

"Just anything. I don't know much about Unseelie races," I admitted.

"The basics, then. We're called a nixie's favorite companion because we're ideal mates due to being water fae, predominantly male alphas, and faithful due to the kelpie bond. This way."

We'd reached a hallway more filled with fae, uniformed servants and other officials going about their day. Eyes turned toward us, and the closest fae acknowledged him and his status as a prince. I resisted the urge to bring my shoulders up when I realized most of these strangers were inspecting me like I was an oddity.

Marius wore a hard, unfriendly expression and stayed alert. He bared his fangs in warning at anyone who drifted too close to me. Just his presence was enough to scatter groups. Servants and courtiers alike took pains to remain at a safe distance. He didn't say anything else on our trip to the library, past the occasional acknowledgment toward other males he knew.

I had the impression we crossed most of the palace, heading across a main artery that we'd accessed toward the back and side of the massive building. I was tired by the time we reached a set of doors labeled "Library Tower."

Marius's nostrils flared once we were inside, and he relaxed his guarded stance. "This is one of my favorite places," he murmured.

"I'm going to be right there with you." We were surrounded by books. Osme Fen was too small to have a library, so most of the books in my room had been keepsakes from my father's travels or bartered goods I'd gotten by trading less-beloved novels for a chance to read something new.

I just hoped they had a section with books written in Theli. Otherwise, I was going to study written Serri day and night until my eyes blurred to take advantage of the Library Tower. I made my way around slowly, taking in how everything was set up.

As it was a tower, the room was circular, with stacks full of books set at an angle to form a fan around the heart of the first floor. A handful of fae wandered about, picking out books. Curved bookshelves lined the walls as well, floor to ceiling, with rolling ladders available at regular intervals. There was a spiraling staircase up to the next level, which I noted with an internal sigh. I was to be limited to the first level, then.

Marius tilted his head, indicating I should follow him. We headed to the center of the room and the two desks set below two different floating signs. The desks were shaped like half-moons, with a small divider in between. One was a pristine arc of empty wood with a librarian, a beta naga, coiled up on her tail and waiting with a friendly expression.

The other was another story. There were papers and books scattered all over the desk in haphazard piles, and the librarian in charge of it was bent over a journal, scribbling. Her white-streaked fins twitched, then extended around her in a billow of gossamer. "That's a *great* idea," she said to herself.

"Eletha," Marius said.

Her pen scribbled its way right off the page as she jumped. She was an adult nixie now, but a lot about her hadn't changed, only sized up. She still had big blue eyes that sparkled with stars, made huge behind a thick pair of glasses. Fine-boned and petite, she matched her full brother, Kauz, with light purple skin and white hair that she'd thrown atop her head in a messy bun. When she spotted Marius, her face lit up. He cracked a smile in return.

"Hey! It's about time you came to visit!" she exclaimed in Serri.

She got up and jumped at him. He caught her for a big hug and swung her around before he set her down next to me. "I've been meaning to. I read everything you gave me for the trip, plus a terrible book I bought from an Ilysnor bookstore," he said.

"Tell me the title, and we'll ban it from the library," she offered.

He nodded and cleared his throat, switching back to speaking Theli. "Eletha, this is Lark—"

"Oh my stars," the nixie squealed, switching too. "*The* Lark?"

I giggled. "Hi. Thank you for the faelight. I'm eager to use it once I find something to read."

She wiggled her shoulders in a little dance. "I knew you'd be a reader! Marius needs a mate who can keep up with how many books he chews through."

"I'm going to try," I said, glancing at him curiously. "Do you have a section of books written in Theli?"

"Do we ever. Fourth floor." She adjusted her glasses higher on the bridge of her nose. "Hmm, if we can get you there right now. I only heard a bit about what happened. You'll have to tell me what put you in that cast."

"It's a lot," I warned.

"The best stories are!"

"I'll carry you, Lark," Marius offered.

Stars, I'd barely made it a day before running into a situation where I needed to be carried. "It's fine, we can come back later," I sighed.

"But"—he raised his brows and gave me a meaningful look— "books you can read."

I folded with that argument and the sight of him being a little less serious. He took me up the stairs carefully, given that I was holding my crutches and they were likely to clip someone or the wall on our spiraling ascent. Eletha skipped ahead of us. She must have amazing calf strength.

Each floor had fewer books and more nooks to read them in, the space narrowing closer to the top of the tower. On the second floor, every seat was occupied, though by the fourth, there were several spots open. Marius put me on my feet and held my waist as I maneuvered the crutches back into place. I wouldn't admit it out loud, but it'd been nice to take some pressure off the sore spots forming under my arms.

"So, what do you like to read?" Eletha asked brightly.

We chattered about books, and she pulled several titles off the shelves to recommend. It was easy to talk to her. I found her soft voice and scent soothing. She told me she was a writer, mid-revision of a book she'd been working on for quite some time, and promised to tell me all about it later.

Marius stood a safe distance away, holding a column of books that grew taller every time she recommended one. Eventually, he said, "I think she has plenty to read now." The stack was well past his head. He'd been fitting new recommendations in at the bottom.

She turned and laughed when she saw how many books he was balancing. "Lark, why don't you browse a bit and see if there's anything else you want to check out. Our Theli language titles aren't all that popular, so no one's going to miss them if you take a bunch."

I grinned. I could definitely make some books disappear, especially if no one minded when they went into my new study. She'd stacked up so many recommendations that I probably wouldn't get through them all in five years, but I still wandered the room to see what else was here.

Marius sat on a couch toward the center of the room with his sister, the two of them chatting quietly in Serri. I toured the room and ended up spotting and pulling a book I'd loved back home. As I wandered over to place it on one of the two stacks he had split my acquisitions into, he was saying, "This is real life, not a story. I can't fuck this up too."

Though I burned with curiosity, I went back to the bookshelves. I was starting to feel bad for all my eavesdropping.

I picked out two more books I recognized, and caught Eletha holding his hand between both of hers and saying, "It *will* work out."

Her nails were cut short and rounded, which reminded me that I wanted to do the same with mine. Partially so I didn't poke holes in any pages, but mostly because I wasn't used to having needle-sharp nixie nails nor the webbing that still rippled up and down my hands with little control.

Marius looked doubtful. I'd seen that expression way too much when his brothers were talking about how fast their mother's approval of me would come. Whether it was pessimism or worry at work was anyone's guess.

"Wait, Lark, don't sit down," she said once I started to settle into a chair nearby. "Marius is going to take you to the library nest for a bit."

"Your nest?" I asked, shocked she would invite me to it so casually.

"Oh, no, it's more of a comfortable group space. We made it with Siora, Kauz, and Thalas to have a room for quiet time in a group," she giggled. It was a bit of a surprise to hear her mention her father by first name, though I had vague memories of the kings trying to teach me their names since there were four of them. It was easier that way. "It was nice to meet you! Hope to see you again soon."

I hoped so too. We waved farewell, and she took the majority of my new acquisitions with her, promising to get the rest and send them along to my new rooms. I picked out a single book to delve into and let Marius carry me again, as the library nest was at the very top of the tower.

"I fucking hate stairs," I muttered.

The kelpie glanced down at me. "I think that's the first time I've heard your curse. Why at stairs, of all things?"

"They're the worst," I informed him.

His brow knitted. We spiraled up and up, passing a fifth and sixth floor that mostly resembled study spaces, and came to a door locked with a magic sigil rather than a knob. He pressed his hand to it, and it unlocked.

"Thalas or Kauz can add your palm to the spell if you like it up here," he murmured.

There wasn't a chance I wouldn't after I got a glimpse of the room beyond.

28

LARK

THE LIBRARY NEST was curved like the inside of an oversized bulb. It had three triangular windows overhead, covered in icy patterns from the weather. Wind whistled outside audibly at this height. A swarm of faelights circled just out of reach, all designed as different bugs, birds, or bats that flew around aimlessly.

An essence lamp hovered in the dead center of the room, emitting more heat than light. It was clear this space was half owned by omegas and half by big males that wanted to sprawl. One side had blankets, pillows, cushions, and an unfolded sofa bed—perfect for getting cozy. The other side had a couple of tables and huge armchairs made either for the alpha holding me or the winged dream wardens.

Eletha and Thalas's presences were clear from the way board games, puzzle pieces, and decks of cards were scattered at random. Marius released an annoyed snort and placed me atop a pile of blankets before he started picking up after them. I felt the fabrics, tugging one out from under me and muffling a squeal of happiness against it because it was fleece.

I maneuvered the crutches under my arms and stood with it, just to pause from how Marius had turned to stare with dilated eyes. "Do you...want to keep that?" he asked with effort. "I doubt anyone would mind."

"Maybe." *Definitely*. Once it had Kauz's scent on it, it'd be perfect for my nest. I dragged it behind me as I tried to get to an armchair. I tripped within two paces, and he rushed to catch me.

"I would've helped you, p'nixie," he said in his scratchy feral voice.

"What?" I mumbled.

He carried me to a chair and tucked the blanket in around me. Then he knelt before my legs, smiling and open. He didn't have to answer. I'd heard him clearly enough. His feral side had said *p'nixie*.

He gave me a lopsided grin and took my hand, placing it against his unscarred cheek and nuzzling my palm. "I've missed you more than anything," he rasped.

My heartbeat thudded faster. This was *definitely* his feral side in control.

He blinked a few times and muttered a curse. There was a change in the texture of his voice, and I knew he'd shoved his instincts back. "I usually have better control than this."

"It's all right," I murmured, fully expecting him to recoil when he realized he was holding my hand to his face.

His fingers loosened. My touch ghosted over his jaw as I pulled away, and his breath shuddered as he exhaled. "Distract me. Please," he said.

"You didn't give me many kelpie facts," I ventured.

"Ask me anything."

"Will you tell me how the whole loyalty thing works?"

He pinched the scarred ridge of his nose. "Of all the questions you could've asked..."

"Sorry, never m—"

"My kind are known for two things," he interrupted, closing his eyes. He looked like he was concentrating, and he spoke without a feral rasp. "Our loyalty and our bonds. Besides shifting into an aquatic form, most of our magic involves bonding. Like dream wardens have their illusions and dreams, or redcaps have their fiery forms, kelpies form attachments.

"Kelpie loyalty is for any fae we feel close to, friends or family. Along with having a horse-like second form, we operate on herd mentality. Once a kelpie feels loyalty to you, you have a friend for life. It's technically a magical bond, but it's mostly one-sided. The only time another fae feels the loyalty bond is when it's damaged or breaks."

"Oh." It was all I had to say for him to look at me with such guilt that it dulled the vibrancy of his yellow eyes.

That was the feeling of rejection early in our reacquaintance. Even after so long... Stars, our bond must've been *strong* to last as long as it had with us growing up apart. I doubted he'd intentionally broken it, but I frowned at the loss all the same.

"And then there's the kelpie bond. It's a cornerstone of Serian culture at this point." He inspected the rug below, tugging on loose threads. "It's different than loyalty. The kelpie bond is only for a mate, and it's permanent. It creates an additional connection outside of regular pack bonds, mind to mind. It used to be for communicating underwater, but we don't live in the sea anymore. Instead, it's become an intimacy thing."

"I see. Thank you for explaining it to me," I said.

He blew a heavy breath from his nostrils and continued, "Once mated, my kind shave half their heads and grow the rest long. We braid mementos from our mates into our hair, which transition with us into our second forms. It's a proud, ancient tradition. The unmated and the unlucky few who've survived the loss of their other halves don't do this."

I had seen a few kelpies today sporting that look. Combined with the piercings, they were notable even in a crowd. Marius would look striking if he styled himself the same way.

He fixed his predator eyes on me again. "I used to resent all of this. It was just a visual sign that so many of my people had something I was denied. As I've despised the very concept of fate." He scoffed bitterly. "Some invisible force deciding who is a scent match, or a fated mate, and who loses said mate before they ever get to know them."

"Because I...left?" I asked in a small voice.

"*No*," he said with such anger and force that I leaned back. "You're not at fault. I failed you! I've wallowed in self-pity for over a decade while you—" He cut himself off with a furious snort. "I knew I'd fuck this up."

He bent, deliberately making himself smaller before he bared his throat. My mouth dropped open. "Let's start from the beginning. I have been monumentally selfish, and..." His jaw tightened. "...I'm sorry, Lark."

My breath caught. That wasn't a pose of trust; it was submission. Something an omega rarely saw from an alpha, if ever.

He maintained his deference as he said, "I didn't realize it until recently, but we met as children. From the moment I looked into your eyes, I sensed that you were mine. It wasn't intense back then. I just wanted to be your friend, to be close to you if you needed me."

"Oh, I should've told you. I remember it. Thalas jolted my memories of the visit." I smiled to myself.

"You should tell me about it. I mean, if you want to."

"I do," I assured him, gentling my voice. "I remember it being a great time, and you were in almost every memory. We were instant best friends."

Marius glanced up at me, brows raising. "I wish... I don't remember much of the time, just how right it'd felt to be by your side. You were the p'nixie. *My* p'nixie. The most unique omega who'd ever visited here.

"Then you never came back...and then word reached us of your death. I was in a practice spar with Theodred when Mother read the letter. Her sudden grief at losing a child hit their pack bond. His famed self-control slipped, and he hit me with his full strength." He ran a finger over the silvery scar crossing his face. "I came a hairsbreadth from death and returned with this. The best team of healers and human doctors around restored the shape of my face, but my disfigurement and damaged eye were the trade-off."

I swallowed a secondhand sense of guilt. I hadn't realized I was involved, even this indirectly, with his training accident. My lips pursed around a question before I thought better of asking.

He must've seen my hesitation. "What is it?"

"It's not my business."

"Ask anyway."

"Doesn't he have the job you've trained for? You've had to work with him ever since..."

He tipped his head further as he considered. "I don't resent him, if that's what you're getting at. He gave me the best apology of my life. Not empty words, but actions. He vowed to correct his mistake and helped me through extensive extra training to hide how off-balance I was. Most everything I knew, he taught me to do again with my left hand.

"Anyway, I got out of my infirmary bed a different boy, an angry one. I hated the world and everyone in it, and most of the fae in the stars too, including you. *Especially* you. My face was a constant reminder of your death. It wasn't fair... Other kelpies never had to know the pain of losing their fated mate so young."

My heart ached for him, and my eyes pricked. "Marius..."

He growled softly. "Let me finish. My beast never believed in your death. I began fighting with it, furious it, too, had turned on me. It urged me to leave my life behind and find you. The older I grew, the stronger the urges were. It has wanted you and no other. *My p'nixie.* Kauz named it, as if I have some split personality. It is a 'he' now and answers to Niall."

"Niall," I repeated, mostly to myself. Something told me I would need that name.

His eyes began to dilate before he shook his head, jaw tightening again. "Don't call him. He's already too eager. He recognized you when I didn't."

My inner omega urged for me to go to him, as he was so clearly struggling. But he still wasn't done talking, though now he had to force his words through gritted teeth.

"Like an absolute fool, I believed Cymora's written lie that Metalark of Osme Fen died. I thought my true mate was gone, which made you seem like a frail imposter when we met again. I forced space between us because... what you don't know is that Niall tugs on my self-control every time I look at you. For a while, I didn't understand what he wanted, but I was afraid it was to overpower and claim you, no matter what. The more I denied my instincts, the more violent the urges became. To the point I was certain all I'd do was hurt you.

"Then Niall actually took control. You probably remember that morning. He just wanted to reassure you that he still adored you. And I realized he'd been trying to set me straight the whole trip here. He was spurring me on to protect you and make you my bonded female. So, I drove you away..." His breathing shallowed out, stealing his air so he couldn't finish the thought any louder than a whisper. "...for no reason."

He made a feral noise full of exasperation. His emotions were causing his pheromones to sour, rot lacing his green scent.

My nose wrinkled at the odorous sign of his contrition. Our scents never lied, and all I wanted to do now was to comfort him until he smelled like waterlilies and a patch of wild mint again. "It's okay. We can move on. There's no sense in dwelling in the past."

The scent of his regret was only becoming more acrid as he stubbornly continued his apology, working the words out. "In truth, I failed at being your protector from the moment I accepted your false death. With that in mind, I throw myself on your mercy. I do not deserve to be your mate. I'm sorry I did not rescue you. I'm sorry I pushed you away. I'm sorry I blamed you for your reactions to your abuser. I'm—"

I couldn't take it anymore. Letting the blanket cushion my landing, I slid out of the armchair and onto my knees. I flung my arms around him, hugging the hard lines of his torso, and kissed his exposed throat. My lips landed right next to the parallel impression of his closed gills.

He sucked in with a surprised growl. "I wasn't done," he said gruffly.

"You are," I assured him, reaching up to touch his face and the shadow of stubble gracing his cheek. Only when my thumb brushed the dense end of his scar did he wince and lean away. "I forgive you, Marius."

He looked at me in disbelief for several long moments before he pulled me into his lap and helped me curl in my limbs and cast. It was the kind of hug where he shielded me from the outside world with the bulk of his body. Nosing into my hair, he took a hitching breath. Then another. He released his grief one small sob at a time, and I teared up with him.

"I don't deserve such easy forgiveness," he mumbled after a while. "All I offered was words, not what I was going to do to fix it."

"Maybe all I want is more of the Marius I saw in my forgotten memories. I need my best friend back," I answered.

"Do you think I... But I've been a terrible friend so far."

"That's where the fixing it part comes in." I reached up and tapped him on the nose playfully, like we'd done to one another as kids.

He blinked a few times, leaning back in surprise, though his lips twitched upward. "I think I know how to repair the bond."

"Oh?"

"Touch me. I mean, you have my permission." He loosened his hold, though he tensed when I lifted my hands. His rejection had come when he'd told me not to touch him, so it made sense that he was asking for the opposite. Yet he winced again when I took his hand.

"Has it been a while?" I asked.

"Has what been a while?"

My cheeks pinkened. "Since you've been with someone."

That look of disbelief was back. "I *just* told you my kind mate for life. I've been loyal to you," he said without hesitation.

Stars, he was probably more touch starved than I'd been before I met Tormund.

"I considered settling to fulfill my duty of mating with Serian's next queen. But in truth, Niall has never found another female acceptable. It has been either you or no one, p'nixie."

"No one?" I echoed.

He released a harsh chuff. "Not that I'm much of a prize," he muttered. "I'm just a broken, ill-tempered feral male."

I whined, petting his arm to soothe him. "But..." This went beyond loyalty, a level of faithfulness that'd only hurt him. "We were kids. And you thought I was *dead*. You still deserved to be happy."

Pain shadowed his face. "And so did you. But you have nothing to fear anymore."

I made a noncommittal hum.

He growled, his voice a feral rasp again. "I'll protect you from anything. You are *safe*. And if we were ever parted again, I would tear the world apart to get you back. No force short of death could stop me. I swear it." The ring of truth hung in the air between us, fae to fae, after he swore.

"You won't have to, stars willing."

He was still so tense, going more rigid when my fingers drifted and brushed the joint of his fin where it began just below his wrist. I didn't want to touch him more if he disliked it. I knew how overwhelming it was to have positive touch after so long without it.

"Do you still want to hear what I remember of my first visit here?" I offered, if only to see him smile. He considered, before nodding. "When we first met, you gave me a weed. It was an impressive one. Big and flowering, and you'd pulled up the roots and some dirt along with it. You said, 'Want to be friends, p'nixie?'"

He breathed a little laugh. A real one, not a feral puff of air. The rare sound was deep and rich and had me leaning forward a bit for more.

"That sounds like something I'd do. Well, did you accept my noble offering?"

"I did," I giggled. I shared more of my memories of that time, and he started to relax, just as I'd hoped he would. His shoulders loosened and he gave me his full focus, not interrupting even once.

And while he glanced down a couple times, he didn't pull away when I touched him further up his arm and pressed soothing circles into his sea-blue skin. He wore short sleeves as if he was immune to the chill in the air, and the fabric served as a boundary for my fingers.

He drew in a sharp breath while I was toward the middle of my story and talking about the beach. I felt a sudden lightness in my chest, like something invisible had mended within me.

"That was so...easy," he remarked. Then a big and roughened purr rattled from his chest, startling us. He coughed, striking his sternum with a fist.

"Not everything has to be a fight," I said.

He was trembling. I wondered if it was a consequence of the mostly one-sided loyalty bond as it solidified, maybe just as strong as it used to be. His usual stony expression was a play of complex feelings before it settled into a hopeful smile. "Some things are simply meant to be. Like this, between us. Niall is right...I'm yours. I have been this whole time. I want you to have my kelpie bond, Lark."

I wanted to shake my head. I couldn't just take his one permanent bond, at least not now. The rawness of his emotions were probably affecting how he was seeing our budding relationship.

"When you're ready to have me as a mate," he added. "You were telling me about the beach. By the way, do your illusions not work?"

I flexed my fingers, calling upon my magic. Threads of magic answered my command swiftly. "They do."

"Kauz usually uses his magic to show me things from his dreaming. I figured you could do the same."

It took a bit of work, but I was able to show him the rest of my memories from the visit with illusions that stretched between my palms. We relied on still images since creating moving scenes was beyond my current skills. I completed the story of the visit with an image of the flower he'd handed me.

"I kept it alive as long as I could," I murmured.

He gave me an odd look before he started asking to see specific things. He was fascinated by the images of himself and his siblings as kids. Because of Thalas's dream warden magic, each memory was crisp with detail, despite how long ago it'd been. I flicked through what I remembered out of order, giving him a good view of everyone.

The image of a young Fal was striking in how disinterested he'd been in meeting me, yet another small child underfoot, at the time. That polite, aloof face was difficult to put up against my adult scent match, the prince who'd seen me.

Marius's mouth twisted. "We used to be close around this age. Back when he'd still get his hands dirty."

"What changed?" I asked.

He shrugged and didn't answer for several moments. "Our interests diverged. And after I was disfigured, things just weren't the same."

I spoke without really thinking about it. "You're not disfigured. I think you're handsome, especially when you smile."

By the way he stilled, I figured I'd messed up. But then he cupped my face with a callused hand and regarded me with dilated eyes. His feral side growled *"mine"* before grabbing a fistful of my hair and slanting a possessive kiss over my mouth. The illusion disintegrated into a shower of sparks.

He kissed me harder until I parted my lips and tasted his mint and waterlilies on my tongue. The pressure relented, and he stroked his fingers through my hair, petting it as he slowed to explore my mouth. His other hand wavered before closing around my hip.

He'd certainly been enthusiastic, but he kissed exactly like a clumsy beginner who was figuring out what to do as it happened. That just meant we could kiss more, in the name of practice...

There was an insistent knock on the door. "Oh, Marius," Fal practically sang through it in Serri. "Your emotions have been going crazy over the pack bond. What's going on?"

The kelpie parted from my lips with a frustrated groan. "It's like we're back on that fucking train," he muttered. He got up and opened the door, switching to Serri. "Everything's fine."

Fal scented the air, and his expression creased briefly with concern. "Sure." His gaze landed on me, and he blew me a kiss with a flourish of his hand. "You took Lark to the book nerd loft. That didn't take long," he remarked.

"I'd prefer to have her here rather than anywhere near court."

"Indeed."

"She forgave me. Just like that." He snapped his fingers.

Fal smirked. "Oh. That explains why I thought you might be dying. You were *apologizing*."

I fidgeted and glanced around, feeling weird about eavesdropping on their conversation.

"Shut the fuck up," Marius grumbled. "You knew this was coming."

The dark elf rolled his eyes skyward. "Aye, but I didn't expect to feel such a concentrated dose of your anxiety and fear while in a finance meeting."

"So you're just here to get out of a meeting."

"Hmm. If you don't want me coming to check on you, shield the pack bond from your emotions next time. She's far too sweet, by the way. I would've drawn out your suffering a lot longer," the dark elf remarked.

The kelpie bared his teeth in the beginnings of a snarl.

"What are you two talking about?" I interjected to cover for myself and hopefully stop another aggressive encounter between them.

As always, Fal had a quick, smooth nonanswer as he switched languages to say, "I'm wondering if I'll be labeled a book nerd for staying with you here. Most of the time, I'm not even allowed through the door. I talk too much, allegedly." He rattled his earrings with a toss of his hair. "Shall I pluck you from this nest and return you to yours, *mo stór?*"

29
LARK

Since I hadn't wanted to return to my rooms yet, Fal stayed in the "book nerd loft" with us. I opted to lie down in the pile of blankets and cushions on the omega side of the nest, meaning to read.

However, Fal and Marius were far too distracting. The dark elf promised not to talk too much but made himself comfortable next to me and ever so slowly inched his lips across the curve of my shoulder. And the kelpie pressed in on my other side to surround me with warmth.

Fal encouraged me to nap when I'd yawned one too many times. "I'm not tired," I murmured.

He responded with a smooth, feline purr. *Oh, he's been practicing…*

Next thing I knew, I was stirring in a post-nap haze of tingling warmth, still sandwiched between them. For as little as Fal and Marius seemed to get along, their scents were perfectly harmonious, like an outdoorsy, sunshine-drenched day. I inhaled with a purr at the pleasant wakeup.

I cracked my eyes open to find Fal resting his, our faces close enough for a kiss. The cold caress of Serian's late winter sun brought out the gray tones in his sharp cheekbones and the navy strands in his glossy black hair. His lips were quirked, though closed. A rare moment indeed.

I admired him openly while he wasn't looking, wondering what fate felt it owed me to have such a striking and clever male be my scent match.

Marius had his face buried in my hair again, nuzzling occasionally. His arm was draped over my middle, his fingertips curled over my hip in a possessive hold I felt through the blanket I'd burrowed into.

Fal stirred and spoke to me in an undertone. "Before you look, Marius is gone right now."

"Gone?" I echoed.

"His feral side is in control. He hasn't turned wild, he's just... briefly indisposed. It's the real reason I'm here. I sensed him pushing the limits of his condition." His features slanted with mischief. "Good thing I talk enough for the both of us."

I turned my head to see what he meant. Marius was molded to my side, also close enough to kiss. Niall looked back at me from his dilated eyes and relaxed, open expression. He lifted a hand toward my face. When I didn't flinch, he fidgeted with one of the silver hoops I was wearing.

"He's not dangerous," I said. For as poor a reputation as feral fae had, I understood Niall had never been a threat to me.

"I've been trying to convince the greater Unseelie Court of that since before his designation manifested. They've never seen him with you, obviously," Fal remarked. "You get the puppy-dog eyes, while everyone else gets the teeth."

I pictured the exact snarling expression he was referencing and shuddered. Marius seemed to mistake this for something else, as he tucked me further into the blankets. It was so cozy I purred, and then so did he in a rusty rumble.

Fal exaggerated a sigh. "He's also never done that before. So fucking sweet. What's next, though? I assume you don't want to spend the whole day up here."

"Well, I set off today to see the palace. And, actually, I should visit Thalas too."

"All right. We'll visit him, eat dinner, and retire to your nest tonight, then," he said. "Think Mar will bite me if I try to carry you out of here?"

FAL DIDN'T GET BITTEN, but Marius was the one who carried me down the spiral staircase when I was ready to leave the library tower. The three of us made our way to Thalas's workshop. It was in another wing close to the royal wing, where my rooms were. I ended up in a seat on the first floor while Thalas ran a few tests on me and inspected one of my wing scales.

Fal idly played with a potentially priceless magical tool he'd found on the ground. Marius stood behind my chair and watched Thalas, making the occasional growl while the king poked and prodded.

Thalas didn't seem all that worried about the feral male and worked his tests as if the kelpie wasn't making threatening noises each time I flinched. "Your wings should start glowing lavender shortly," he eventually informed me.

"Not a darker purple?" My wings had been more of an indigo as a kid.

"The scales seem like they're growing in half purple and half silver. There's an iridescence that suggests...hmm." He stroked his chin thoughtfully. "Could you do this for me?" He swirled his hand in a classic essence spinner gesture, summoning a coil of black magic studded with stars.

I mimicked him and nearly fell out of my seat with a yelp. Out of my palm whirled familiar white and silver magic in chaotic threads. Kauz's essence.

Thalas adjusted his glasses. "Oh, fascinating."

"What was that?" I asked breathlessly.

"Nothing to worry about. A temporary effect, I believe." Though as he spoke, he took frantic notes at a nearby table. "Kauz dumped just about every ounce of his essence into you during the *olcanus* removal. It was necessary, as you bled out of your own magic. The lingering essence from him may be affecting the color of your wing scales."

I glanced back at my wings. They had splotches of purple forming on them, something I'd noted with pride today in the mirror. "We could try having you expel his magic to darken your wings to their natural color," Thalas was saying.

"No, no. It's fine," I blurted. Maybe it was temporary, but I wanted the sign of Kauz's influence on me. He'd saved my life. I loved Kauz, and I wish I'd told him earlier. If he was willing, maybe I could keep the change of color as a sign of affection.

"I just wanted help with learning how to use my magic better," I reminded Thalas.

"That's a complicated subject for a quick visit. Is there something in particular I can help you with today?"

"Well...how do you willfully pick someone else's dream to visit?" I asked.

The king brightened. "It's easier than you might think. As long as you go to sleep holding something that fae owns, you will be able to sense their sleeping mind and also whether they're dreaming. Dreams occur off and on over the course of a night. So, if they're not actively dreaming, all you have to do is stay awake for a while and try again."

That did sound easy enough. "Thanks, Dad."

He smiled and nodded. "I look forward to teaching you more when the time comes."

I was too. He seemed like he'd be a patient tutor. When it came time to leave his workshop, he gave me a quick hug, wings included. I missed Kauz all the more acutely a moment later.

"You're coming to my dream tonight, right?" Fal purred on our way back to my suite. "I'll make it worth your while, *mo stór*."

Heat spread from my cheeks to the tips of my ears, but I held my tongue on telling him that I intended to find Kauz's dream. "I don't know. I need to practice," I said.

"Aye, practice. Practice visiting me."

Marius, who kept pace on my other side, turned to growl at his brother.

"Oh, please. What's she going to see in your dreams anyway?" Fal answered as if the kelpie had spoken.

A figure clothed in red waited for us outside of my suite. There was a flutter in my chest as he turned his big smile our way and waved. "Tormund!" I exclaimed.

Such an excited reaction earned me an exuberant hug from the gentle giant. He pulled me off my feet, crutches and all. "Sorry I was away today, li'l bird. Work never ends."

He told me about it after ordering us dinner, including some "raw meat and sadness" for Marius. It seemed Tormund was a beast master, overseeing the care of the various creatures that served the palace. And to my disappointment, he didn't want me going outside and to see them until there wasn't a risk my crutches would slip on some ice or an irregular surface.

Dinner was amazing, again. I snuck a curious look over at what the kelpie was having. It *was* mostly raw meat, cubed to bite-sized pieces, and a broth full of bone pieces that he cracked open to feast on the insides. I felt a little green about that part.

He met my gaze, and his feral stare softened. He opened another bone, offering it to me.

"Oh, um, no thank you." I didn't want him to think I was judging his dietary choices, but I didn't have it in me to eat bone marrow. He shrugged and went back to his feast.

I chatted idly with Fal and Tormund until dessert arrived. It was pretty, served in a clear glass dish to display several colorful layers. I tried a spoonful and made a sound of enjoyment as the flavors of custard, berries, and cake hit my tongue. Stars, that was incredible. I went for another bite and glanced up. All three alphas had stilled and turned to stare at me.

I covered my lips with the spoon. "Sorry," I practically yelped.

"If you wouldn't be sick of it fast, I'd get you a berry trifle every night," Fal remarked. "Don't mind us. Just enjoy it."

It must be an alpha thing.

The moment I was done eating, Tormund slapped the table. Marius snorted angrily at the loud noise. "I will show the li'l bird to her nest now," the redcap announced.

"What if I told you I was planning on showing her to her nest?" Fal asked with a playful lilt.

"It should be me. I give better cuddles. She's even said so," Tormund argued.

"Just cuddles?" I asked. It'd been a long day. I was too tired to consider doing any more than that tonight.

"Aye, of course. I'm still honorable."

Fal leaned his chin on his fist, tongue outlining one of his fangs. "I'm most certainly not, at least in this regard. Perhaps it's your night then, Tormund."

I nodded. That settled, I kissed Fal good night, then Marius. Their pheromones lingered together pleasantly on my tongue. While the dark elf coaxed the kelpie away, Tormund came around to lift me effortlessly with one arm, carrying my crutches in his other hand.

I should've protested, but it was a short trip to the privacy curtain in front of my nest. "May I enter?" he asked.

"Yes. It's just...it's not really..."

He carried me inside and set me on the bed with care. Nests were supposed to be full of things omegas loved, but mine was new. Sparse at best. It wasn't a fit space to present to a future mate.

He spared the room a single glance. "I've gotten everything sorted out for tomorrow. We're going to decorate and make this a home for you. You're going to love it. I swear it."

There was a vague ring of truth to his words, even though it was unusual for him to swear on my happiness. I smiled, still excited to make this suite of rooms mine and perfect the presentation of my nest.

"Tonight...is it okay if I stay?" he asked while wearing a grin full of his usual charm.

I had to think about it, but not for the reasons he probably suspected. I just didn't want to embarrass myself any more past showing him to a nearly empty nest. "You're going to see me struggle with basic tasks if you do."

He made a dismissive wave. "*Ach.* No struggling while I'm here. What do you need?"

I told him, and he left the nest, returning with my nightclothes. He looked the other way as I changed into them and said, "I broke my leg a long time ago. I was maybe twelve? Recovering from that took so long."

"Oh no," I gasped. "What happened?"

"I fell into a…" He made a gesture of a downward slope over his shoulder. "A li'l valley?"

"A ravine?"

"Maybe. I wasn't on my own, at least. It was a hunting party with my dad and some of our clan members. We'd gone past the forest I knew, and it was near dark when I slipped in the ice and fell."

"I'm changed," I put in.

He came over and sat with me on the bed. We were like magnets, always cuddling up when close to one another. I appreciated his natural warmth and settled into his bulk.

"I'd just met some of these other redcaps for the first time. And then they had to save me," he continued, shaking his head. "It was so embarrassing. But I needed their help to come home, and afterward…" He tilted his head toward me with less than subtle meaning. "I had to accept more help than I wanted to from my family and friends while I was on crutches."

I picked up his meaning with a sigh. "That's right."

"I learned who cared about me while I was healing, though. And you wouldn't guess who helped me most."

"Who was it?"

"Fal. He cares a lot, you know?"

I wasn't all that surprised at his answer. I'd just seen Fal show up to help Marius post-apology, after all.

Tormund and I negotiated where on the gigantic pack bed we'd sleep. He thought the center, but I wanted the edge, just in case I needed to visit the bathroom in the middle of the night. It'd be a lot of space to scoot across otherwise.

He agreed but insisted I wouldn't need any blankets. With my back pressed to his front, his heat soaked into my wings and clothes to keep me pleasantly warm. He caressed me with those giant hands, spreading heat over my arms, belly, and neck. We whispered in the dark, mostly nonsense while I fought to stay awake just a few minutes more to enjoy this moment.

I started purring, lulling off to dream land. When he purred too, I was gone in moments, only remembering in that split second before unconsciousness that I hadn't gotten anything of Kauz's to share tonight's dream with him.

I woke up before Tormund in the darkness of my nest. He had me clutched in his arms as if I were an oversized stuffed animal, snoring away in the early hours of morning. For the first time since...maybe my early childhood, I had the luxury of dozing.

Back in Osme Fen, I'd be expected to be up with the sunrise and have breakfast prepared for my stepfamily after *they* had a leisurely rest. I couldn't help a bolt of bitter anger through my chest, though I tamped it down out of habit.

Cymora had never treated me like family, only as someone she could use down to a cinder. I didn't know how nice a lot of things were, let alone sleeping in with my gentle giant. This moment was cozy and painless; I attributed a lot of it to his warmth and the give of his body against mine.

When he woke, he helped me turn in his hold until we were lying face-to-face. I accidentally bumped what had to be an erection in the process. "Sorry," we said at the same time.

"That always happens in the morning. Don't mind it," he added.

"Wait, really?"

"Aye. It's not for you. But—" His eyes widened with sudden panic. "—it could be! I didn't mean..."

I giggled at his reaction. "Are you untouched?" I asked curiously.

Tormund had a rosy hue across the top of his beard that spread to the tips of his pointed ears. "It's obvious, then."

"I am, too. I've stopped at kisses." Any more than that, and I doubted I would've been able to hold off my heat for as long as I have. I was glad I'd waited, too, since now I knew at least two of my future mates were also untouched.

He squinted at me. He'd left his spectacles somewhere to rest without them. "You're such a beautiful omega. You could have anyone you wanted."

Something I loved about Tormund was his earnestness behind statements such as this. He only meant it as a compliment, not as a means to shimmy me out of my pajama bottoms. I answered him with a kiss, savoring his smoke and mallows scent as it lingered on my tongue with its hint of caramelized sugar.

All I wanted was him right now. I tugged at the fabric of his clothes, exploring his chest with shy strokes of my fingertips. It was a wonder Tormund was untouched, actually. I couldn't be the only female to look past his redcap heritage and know he was a sweetheart.

I asked between kisses, fitting the words through our increasing sense of urgency. "Tormund, do you want to..."

His lips slid from mine, and for a moment, desire kindled little flames in his eyes and a wave of heat rolled from his skin. The beginning of his transformation extinguished as he gasped. A flicker of realization and worry crossed his face. "What are we doing? It's a big day, li'l bird! C'mon." He picked me up in the next moment, dragging me out of my comfortable nest.

I caught a flash of unexpected movement in the next room and yelped. Two warning growls hit the air at the same time. The first one resonated through me from Tormund. The other came from Marius, who was reclined on the other bed outside of the nest. One of his arms was behind his head, and he was in the same outfit he'd been wearing yesterday.

"Marius? How long have you been here?" I asked.

His eyes were back to normal, though his response was sluggish. "All night."

"Why?" I hadn't invited him to sleep outside my nest. There was no need. Nor did it look comfortable that he'd done so. The bed was a bare mattress.

He sat up, rolling his neck. "Loyalty. The feral urge to be as close to you as possible. Maybe both."

There was no arguing with instinct, what was done was done. I glanced up at Tormund. "We're going to get sheets for this bed today, right?"

The giant was still scowling at his brother. "Aye. Unless you want it removed. Some omegas prefer to sleep outside of their nests or keep their males in a separate bed. Your choice."

"Let's keep it for now. Is that all right?"

"Definitely! Whatever you like. The omega decides!" Tormund

exclaimed. "How about I leave you with your handmaidens to clean up, and get us breakfast?"

My belly growled in agreement. While I took a visit to the rain room, both males left, and Jani and Lon came in to help me once I was cleaned off.

"May we see to your hair, Princess?" Jani asked. Her oversized red eyes inspected the wet strands.

"I was trying to grow it longer," I said.

"Of course! You would look nice with long hair. Just a trim, maybe? We can get rid of those pesky split ends before they become a problem."

I agreed and hoped they wouldn't remove too much. I'd only just gotten it to grow a little past my shoulders. Lon retrieved a chair for me to sit in before the mirror. The two moth fae chatted away while Jani trimmed and shaped my hair until it was free of split ends and about to my chin in length. Lon saw to my makeup in the meantime, and we giggled together.

Spending time with them felt like hanging out with my friends in Osme Fen. Back then, we'd all been servants. I wondered if I could even have that kind of friendship with the fuzzy pair of betas, considering they'd been assigned to help me and called me Princess.

Well, a question for another time. Once I was dressed for the day, I went to the dining nook at the front of my suite. Tormund and Marius had also seen to their morning routines and returned. The redcap had gotten a breakfast spread ready. He ate with me while Marius was silent company.

The kelpie sat next to me, but I was on his right where I could easily startle him. I murmured his name and got his attention before I took his hand in my free one. He didn't flinch, but he tilted his head as if wondering what I wanted. I circled my thumb on that sensitive patch of skin between his thumb and forefinger, just a casual touch.

He worked his jaw. "I think we need to teach you lessons on common Unseelie races. You need to know more than just kelpie facts."

"That's a great idea," Tormund put in. His enthusiastic response drew a wince from Marius.

"Sure. But do you have any more kelpie facts first?" I asked.

His lips quirked with a hint of amusement. "Always. Our brightest scientific minds call this a *coevolution* with nixies." He released my hand

and flexed his, unfurling membranes between his fingers that looked identical to the webbing nixies had.

I leaned in, fascinated. I had no idea he had those too. He made a playful grab for my face, and I ducked back, giggling. "Can you show me how you tuck those in?" I asked. The webbing between my fingers still lifted up and down with little control, depending on how I curled my fingers.

He nodded and straightened his hand, folding in the webbing without trouble. He signaled to Lon and said to her, "Lark requires a nixie's manicure."

"Yes, Prince. Right away!" she exclaimed.

As the moth fae left to retrieve something, Tormund stood as well. "I'm going to get some fabric swatches for you, li'l bird. Once we have a color scheme in mind, we'll go from there and move furniture in and out."

I smiled, excited to see what we could do with the suite. "Thank you, Tormund."

"It's going to be great," he said before he left.

I turned back to Marius. "I was thinking of having my nails rounded," I said.

He made a disapproving rumble. "Next thing you're going to say is you want to illusion over your gills."

Well, yes, I had considered doing that. I was quite self-conscious of my new gills and the small pair of fangs I'd grown once I no longer had an *olcanus* hiding them. The only changes in myself that I loved so far were the stars flecking the whites of my eyes.

"I just—"

"It's all right. Just know that this"—he stroked his thumb over my palm just right to fully unfurl the webbing between my fingers—"and your gills aren't monstrous. I rather like them, p'nixie. And these"—he curled my fingers in so my needle-sharp claws were extended—"mean that you have some natural weapons to defend yourself. You cannot put your claws through an attacker's eye if you have them rounded."

My mind stopped somewhere around him liking my webbing and gills. He looked at me with a hint of affection as my wings fluttered. Stars, I couldn't cover up my Unseelie changes now. He, as a water fae, didn't find them strange. It was our coevolution.

"Then I won't hide them," I said.

"Good." That being addressed, he kept rubbing his thumb back and forth along my palm until I felt the muscle that controlled my hand's webbing. I retracted it all for the first time since waking up in the infirmary and then let my handmaidens cut and scrub my claws, reducing them to the standard triangle shape and shortened size most nixies liked.

They were finished when Tormund returned with the fabric swatches. My inner omega went a little nuts for the squares of fabric secured on a wooden loop, each a different texture and pattern. Someone who understood omegas had designed this. I quickly fell in love with three different swatches even though I didn't know what the fabrics actually were.

Tormund had acquired an assistant, a young naga, who he sent slithering away to see what the palace had on hand that matched the samples I'd picked. As Marius began to give me Unseelie fae facts, he heartily joined in.

I learned that Jani and Lon were mothkin. Jani said, "You didn't know? Oh, sorry! Most everyone calls us house moths."

"They're the favorites of two of our kings. Beta mothkins make excellent house fae," Marius said. The mothkins fluffed up proudly. "And alpha mothkins defend the skies over the palace. With their thick fur, they can stay outside and alert even in the worst winter storms, and they can see in the dark."

"They're also much bigger than the li'l house moths," Tormund added, patting both my handmaidens atop their heads. Their antennae pointed askew, maybe in displeasure.

We were talking about the size of grimalkin shifters in their feline second forms when Jani went to answer a knock at the door. Fal came in a minute later, holding a clipboard. His shoulders and arms were tangled up in a measuring tape.

"Morning, *mo stór*," he said, bowing with a cheeky smile. "I have detailed instructions from the Threadmistress to get your measurements."

"Even with the cast?" I asked.

"Aye. She's rather eager to find you a personal tailor." He passed the tape and clipboard on to Lon, then helped me up and stole a quick kiss.

"Designs you wear will become fashion, so the competition is going to be fierce."

"Do you all have a different tailor?" I asked. I'd noticed the quality and style in his and Marius's clothes, especially.

"That's right. We have new wardrobes made every year or so, and the tailors make off with a fortune. It's a win-win."

Tormund helped support me so I could stand straight while Fal measured me from the shoulder up, where my handmaidens couldn't reach. The house moths wrote down every measurement, taking great care to note the shape and dimensions of my wings. All the while, we talked about more Unseelie facts. There were a lot of races to learn and things to know about them. This session didn't feel very deep.

"We'll quiz you later," Tormund said. His assistant had returned and whispered something in his ear. "First, we should go to the supply rooms and tag what you want to bring in."

"Can't we have servants bring them to her?" Marius asked with a displeased flick of his ear, switching to Serri for the question.

Ignoring him, Tormund added, "And you will want to see the supply rooms for yourself, li'l bird. It is like we have a whole omega store here for the wee blessed ladies." He lit up before I did, probably knowing that was the kind of place I *had* to visit.

"Where are my crutches? Let's go now!"

I convinced Fal and Marius that we'd attract a lot more attention if I had three princes following me. Tormund had the biggest grin as he held the door for me to leave my suite. "I tell them we don't all have to be around you at the same time. At least you agree."

My crutches clicked on the marble as I maneuvered myself toward the exit of the royal wing. "You did say earlier that you all don't usually spend a lot of time together."

"Aye, but you have a nest now. I guess this is the new normal." He walked in slow paces to stay beside me. "When Kauz wakes up, he'll be here too."

Stars, I'd forgotten to even attempt to visit his dreams last night. "He promised to sleep in my nest with me every night," I said in a quieter voice.

"I'm just going to tell you now, if he moves into your suite, the rest of us will try to as well. Do you want to prepare your rooms for that?"

I considered saying that it seemed premature. Yet I'd had him in my nest last night and couldn't imagine a future where I didn't want him there every night that followed. The same with Kauz. They both had my heart, and I hadn't told either of them yet. Something I needed to do soon.

As for Fal and Marius, they had a place there too, if they wanted it. Fal…his flirting gave me a belly full of butterflies. I kept avoiding spending a night with him, though, and hoped that wasn't sending the wrong message. I just knew I'd fall short of past lovers, and a male like him had to have several to compare me to. And Marius wanted to protect me, so I should give him that chance.

"Yes, let's make room for all of us," I said.

Tormund grinned. "I can't wait."

Neither could I, really. No more restless nights alone with my fears—

"Lark, there you are!" I startled out of my thoughts and lost my balance as Laurel, of all fae, popped out of an alcove.

30
LARK

WE WEREN'T FAR from the exit of the royal wing. Tormund had just bid the two guards on duty a good morning as we'd crossed to one of the smaller hallways leading further into the palace.

Tormund caught me and one of my crutches before I could go toppling over. He righted my balance, and then I was face-to-face with my stepsister. I cast a wary gaze past her out of old habit. But it was just Laurel, dressed in a heavy winter cloak that looked new. Her hair was up in a messy ponytail, and the soft teal oval of her face was unadorned.

She looked me over with puffy eyes, dark blue circles shadowing them. "Hi, Lark. I've been trying to see you." She'd been crying and looked as if she was on the verge of shedding more tears. "Did you have surgery or something? Did they fix your foot?"

Next to me, Tormund shifted uneasily. "You shouldn't be here," he said.

I squared my shoulders as much as I could while leaning on crutches. *I'm the future princess here. She no longer has any sway over me.*

"I never had a crippled foot. They removed the silencing band around my ankle," I answered.

"The what?" she asked.

"The *olcanus*?" I ventured. She still seemed confused. "You didn't know about it, did you?"

"What's an *olcayus*?" Her tongue slipped over the foreign word.

Her green eyes glazed over, and a moment later, she said, "I'm happy they fixed your foot. But did they tell you? They're going to execute Mom!"

"Execute?" I echoed in shock. Tormund released a warning growl full of crackling menace.

Laurel reached for me, panic etched in every line of her body. "She said it's your fault, so you have to do something! You have to make this right!" she demanded with her full entitlement.

A blast of heat radiated off Tormund as he shouldered between us. His fingers were tipped with growing claws, and visible steam lifted from his back. Laurel screamed as the transformation into his fiery form took hold.

"She doesn't have to do *anything* for Cymora. Or you, for that matter," he snapped. "Stay back."

"W-what...no, I have to..."

I crutched around to Tormund's side, laying a hand on his arm before he became too hot to touch. Laurel cowered several paces away.

"It's okay. This is how she is," I said to him. I carefully balanced while petting his swollen arm as he became broader and stronger with the transition into his monstrous form.

He rumbled deeply in warning at Laurel before glancing down at me. Twin fires danced in his pupils, magnified by the spectacles perched on his nose. Curls of smoke and steam escaped between the jagged points of his teeth. They receded as I calmed him from his rage as if we'd gone through this dozens of times rather than twice. I wasn't nearly as afraid of his transformation now that it wasn't a surprise.

"What is he?" Laurel hadn't bolted as I'd expected. She stood a few paces away, gaping at us both. "Anyway, as I was saying—"

"*Shut. Up.*" Tormund had managed to extinguish the flames in his eyes for a split second before they reignited. She closed her mouth with a frightened squeak.

Several fae were running our way. The two guards, plus Fal and Marius, who must've felt Tormund's sudden spike of rage through their pack bond.

"Why is it you cannot go more than ten minutes—" Fal was griping behind us.

Marius interrupted him with a snarl. "What the fuck are *you* doing here?"

The kelpie appeared to my left, scowling at Laurel, while the dark elf flanked Tormund's other side. The moment Fal's gaze landed on my stepsister, his tone turned chilly. "More importantly, how'd you escape your fishbowl?"

I held up my hand. "Wait. Just...hold on a second." I turned to Fal, the most likely male to know what was going on. "She said Cymora is going to be executed."

When his answering smile held an edge of cruelty, I knew it was true.

"You can't just kill my mom," Laurel said in a shaky voice.

Fal pressed his lips into a tight line and jerked his chin. "Marius."

"On it," the kelpie answered. He took my stepsister's elbow in a none-too-gentle grip. He also signaled to the guards to go back to their posts before dragging a protesting Laurel away. She shouted my name, reaching out to me with her free hand. I probably could've helped her, but I didn't. As she had done countless times when I'd been on the receiving end of Cymora's punishments, I simply looked the other way.

Doesn't that make you just as bad as her, with the tables turned?

I tried to ignore that inner voice of reason. "So," I prompted. There was a scratchy sensation in my chest as I met Fal's gaze again. "It seems I've missed a few things."

"I have to take your measurements to the Threadmistress. Why don't we walk together for a while?" he suggested.

The sense of discomfort within me was only growing more chafing as we walked, with either male flanking me. It seemed the princes were going to continue keeping me in the dark about certain things. Maybe in the name of "protecting" me.

"I thought we were giving the li'l bird comfort while she recovered,"

Tormund said in his too-gentle voice, now that he'd come down fully from his rage.

"Aye, that's what I wanted. We were going to tell you, *mo stór*. Eventually," Fal said. I shot him a look colored by how I was feeling, and his lips twitched before his face settled into a practiced, neutral expression. It was only betrayed by the worry in his feline eyes. "There are some things that occurred before your childhood deal with her that I don't think you know. I'd prefer for us to sit down for this conversation."

"And those things are why she's to be executed?" I lowered my voice as a larger group of fae skirted around us.

"Part of it. The other part is the abuse she shamelessly admitted to." He shook his head with a sigh. "Look, the only thing that concerns me is that you're upset. Over her? Really?"

"She's still my…" This was a kneejerk response, not how I really felt. A shade of compulsion that bid me to say Cymora was still my mother. But she truly wasn't anything but a hateful female who'd been forced to keep me around. "No. I just don't need you all keeping something this big from me."

"Oh, Lark," he murmured. He slowed to a stop at a junction where the hallway split in two directions. When he leaned down as if to kiss me, I shied away. I wanted an answer, not a distraction.

He shuffled closer anyway, so I turned my face away to make my opinion clear. His lips skimmed my earlobe instead, before he whispered into the pointed shell. "The only one withholding information from you is me. The others don't know everything she's done. I only wanted you to have at least a few days free from the unpleasantness that is your abuser."

I bit my lip, torn on what to feel. "Yesterday was nice," I murmured back.

He hugged me, careful of my balance. "You're going to have plenty of nice days. She's going to be out of your life soon, but not before she pays for what she's done. And if you truly wish to know…"

I leaned into him, taking in his grass and sunshine scent. "Tell me," I insisted in an undertone.

"I will." He drew back enough to look into my eyes and cocked his usual mischievous smile. It was a little forced. "In private. Until then, won't you have some fun? Enjoy some time with your comfort." He inclined his head toward Tormund, who was blowing curls of smoke from his mouth while watching us with a furrowed brow. "Heal a little. That's what our whole pack wants for you."

"Okay. I can try. And...what about Laurel? Is she going to be..."

Fal rolled his eyes. "That brat was supposed to stay in her new room. Don't worry, she's being cared for. Another magirail ride back to Thelis is in her future."

That seemed reasonable. "Someone does have to look after Osme Fen."

"Sure, but why give it to her? It's *your* tiny farm town. Sell it." He exaggerated a shrug.

My eyes widened. It wasn't... Actually, I guessed it was mine. I was the true Lady of Osme Fen.

He chuckled and pressed a gentle kiss to my crown. "Good omega," he purred, maybe just to see my face turn pink. "See you soon."

Fal left me with Tormund and hummed to himself as he headed down one hallway. We needed to go down the other to get to the palace's storage.

"Are you okay?" the redcap asked quietly. "I'm sorry I raged. This was supposed to be a good day."

I didn't know. Even now, I had that scratchy feeling in my chest, but also a void where...something else was missing. An emotion that wouldn't quite come, like it'd gotten stuck somewhere inside me. "It's okay. It's still going to be a good day." If the words came out of my mouth, they had to be true.

"I want to tell you a secret, li'l bird. A happy one."

Another secret? "Okay."

He angled his hand over his mouth. "You're going on dates soon. Now that Mom approved you, it's the next step. One date with every prince, just you and him. We were going to start them after you're walking again."

I shook off my lingering funk with record speed. "Really? Oh stars! I can't wait!" Real one-on-one dates with these males. That was going to be amazing.

"Me neither. But...I will probably be last. As the youngest and all," he added in a grumble.

"You should tell me what you're thinking. We could plan it together," I suggested, still full of bubbles and sunshine.

"I'm supposed to surprise you with something amazing," he protested.

"Just a hint?" I added a little begging whine.

The giant squinted, despite his tiny spectacles. "Why are you so cute?" he countered. "It's not fair. I want to tell you everything, but I shouldn't."

"You could. Tormund, please." I gave him my best puppy-dog look and watched his resistances crumple as he looked back at me adoringly.

His lips were parting to reply when a two-toned whistle sounded behind us. Tormund slowed to a stop, and I did as well, turning on my crutches.

"Yoo-hoo," a dark elf called. He was trailing four palace workers, who hung back as he approached. "I heard there was a new omega click-clacking around my palace, so I had to see her for myself."

Tormund gasped. "Hi, Dad!" He went over and swept the other male up in a big hug, lifting his feet off the ground.

I gaped a bit. It was one thing to see full-grown alphas as a child, when they all seemed like ancient trees with their heads way up in the clouds. But in reality Rennyn was short for an alpha, maybe six feet tall, though his crown of black, backswept horns added the illusion that he had more height when he wasn't being held up by a jolly redcap.

"Oof, Tor-Tor! Don't break my spine," he laughed. He spoke Theli with the lightest of lilts, practically accentless.

"Sorry, Dad." Tormund put him down and dusted off any imperceptible wrinkles in the king's scarlet tunic.

"No apologies necessary. At least you *said* hello, unlike some other sons I know."

He turned to me, flashing an impish smile. Fal was a blue echo of his father, who had a dark elf's more traditional dusky gray skin and red eyes. Rennyn's raven-black hair was long and lustrous, held back from his face by his horns. His elfin ears were only pierced once; miniature daggers dangled from his earlobes.

"So, anyway, more than one fae has come up and whispered, 'Your Majesty, have you met the omega walking around on crutches? I think she's...'" He gasped dramatically. "*Seelie!*"

I giggled, though my wings flattened to my back self-consciously. Stars, the fae in the palace were already talking about me. I figured it wouldn't be long before someone approached to ask who I was and why I was always with at least one of the princes. It'd be my luck to encounter a jealous ex-lover, a thought that filled me with utter dread.

"That's me. Not quite Seelie," I said shyly.

He cut through the awkwardness of one of my worries by saying, "You remember your Papa Rennie, right? Because *I* remember a tiny p'nixie who was determined to help me around here."

I was sure I did a poor job of hiding my relief. "Yes, of course. You were my favorite bonus dad."

"Hah! Elion would murder me if he heard that. You and your father visited during one of his busy seasons. Was it the tricks? I've had to retire a few with less kids around."

"The bugs?" I guessed.

He cracked his knuckles and brushed his sleeves back one after the other. With a flick of his hand, one of the shiny, small beetles appeared between his fingers, though it was a bright yellow. "No, but they're cheese now. Our youngest, Ambriel, inherited that kelpie palate. Not a single sweet tooth to be found." He tsked and handed me the bug, which I ate without hesitation. It was a nip of cheddar after the crunch of the candy shell. "I'm hoping I can entertain our next kid too, or I'm going to have to retire as the fun dad."

He beamed after a brief pause. "Who am I kidding? I'll never retire. I've got plenty of adult kids to bother. Speaking of which, what are you two up to?"

"We're getting Lark's rooms set up," Tormund answered cheerfully.

"Fantastic idea. Someone get Lark a *chair*. Watching her balance there with a cast on is doing all kinds of terrible things to my instincts." Rennyn had an equally bright tone.

"Sorry," I said, surprised.

"Come along. Dozens of very nice chairs this way." He switched languages with a careless wave behind him. "Clear my afternoon schedule. Say something urgent came up or something."

The four palace workers that'd been following him shrugged and moved on. We continued walking to the supply rooms, now with Rennyn flanking my other side.

I kept trying to guess which tricks he'd retired, which appeared to be none of them. He still had his lucky coin, which was worn down to a flat gold disc after being handled so often. He still had all kinds of things up his sleeves: playing cards, a small flower, an even smaller throwing knife, and a piece of jerky wrapped in a twist of colorful paper as if it were a candy.

I must've found him plenty distracting, because the next thing I knew, I was settled in the first supply room, on a chair made of velvety, dark green fabric.

Rennyn tilted his head. "Hmm. Small purr of approval."

"We can do better," Tormund agreed before wandering off. From my seat, I had the impression that the room was a maze of furniture, cleaning tools, and repair equipment.

The dark elf king leaned on the wall beside me, one leg bent to brace his foot on the surface. He flipped his lucky coin idly. "So, I'd ask how you've been, buuuuut..." He drew out the word. "I was there for the questioning. Don't worry, li'l p'nixie. We're going to make sure you're well cared for here."

My smile slipped. "What questioning?"

"What questioning," he echoed with a sigh. "I knew the lads wouldn't tell you. We had an extended get-to-know-you session with a certain mermaid when you all first arrived."

A bolt of dismay hit me square in the chest. "How much did she tell you?"

An "extended" session with her would probably be all it took for an experienced questioner to pry out every moment of my childhood. Much as I remembered loving my godfamily, that this was their first impression of me as an adult was mortifying. Hopefully they didn't assume I was weak, like Marius initially had.

"Mmm, plenty." He gave a vague wave. "She's in a jail cell, for now. We've written to Queen Alora to inform her of Cymora's upcoming execution and why it's happening to one of her subjects in a foreign land. Usually we are more diplomatic, but you kids returned with quite the situation."

Tormund announced himself before plonking another chair in front of me to try. It was a dove gray and made of soft material that gave just right when I transferred to sit on it. The armrests were also at a perfect height, and I sank into it with a smile despite myself.

"Looks like a winner, Tor-Tor. Why don't you tag the whole set for her?" Rennyn suggested.

He waited until the redcap left to do just that before he turned back to me. "Look, I know the scent of shame when I smell it. Stop that. *We're* ashamed that we were fooled and that you were taken advantage of so cruelly. You could ask my mate for the moon right now, and she'd figure out how to give it to you."

My eyes pricked with tears. I didn't want anyone to feel obligated to give me anything.

"It's not out of pity. Helping you is one of the only things we can do to make up for lost time," he said, as if reading my conflicted thoughts. "My son—Falindel, I mean—was there for the questioning as well. He listened to it all without flinching. That's love, kid."

Oh stars. No wonder Fal knew something the rest of his brothers did not.

"I want to talk to Cymora," I blurted.

Rennyn's brows drifted toward his hairline. "Why?"

That void in me was no longer empty. I grasped a flicker of what I should feel. Unmitigated fury. "Before she joins the stars, she owes me an *explanation*," I said through gritted teeth.

"She owes you a lot more than that. I'll see what I can do to get something set up."

"I don't think it's a good idea," Tormund put in. I startled, not realizing he'd returned and listened to at least some of the conversation.

"I'll let your pack work it out," Rennyn commented.

"Thanks, Dad," I sighed. Stars, my vow to Cymora was broken, yet her mere presence in the palace was causing a mess. And I've always been the one to clean up after my stepfamily.

There was something else I was missing, something Fal didn't want to tell me. The royal pack knew what it was too. It had to be another wicked secret, and I was starting to dread that upcoming conversation.

Tormund cleared his throat. "I want to drop you in the middle of the nesting supplies now, li'l bird."

31
LARK

Tormund meant it literally, because he scooped me up and trotted off to the next room over. He set me atop a pile of blankets I immediately started inspecting by touch.

He stood nearby, ready to help when I needed it. "Supplying nests is hard sometimes. Most of these things were requested by the palace nixies, then they didn't like them. So, you can take anything you want."

My first thought was *I'll take all of it*, but he hadn't lied when he suggested they could stock a full omega store. The room was full of so many options for basic things like blankets and cushions that I could color-coordinate my nest.

What a turn my life had taken. I could have any kind of nest I wanted. No one would force me to destroy it, because it was *mine*. It could be designed down to the grain or as eclectic as my heart desired.

Tormund sat on the pile of blankets, causing me to slide into him.

He tilted my chin up and kissed me. I loosened the seal of my lips and let his tongue in to play with mine, savoring the smoky taste of him all the while.

Once we'd kissed for a while, he nuzzled against my cheek and neck. I giggled at the scratchiness of his beard. He said as quietly as his voice went, "Sorry I pulled you from your bed so soon this morning. We could've stayed in and missed Laurel."

"It's okay. I'm glad to know what's going on." Even if it hurt. As any talk with Cymora hurt. I just thought it could be different, one last time when she didn't have power over me. If she didn't give me answers, she could receive a piece of my mind instead. "And now we're having fun. I get to decorate my nest. I get to *have* a nest."

He nodded, some of his usual cheer returning. "That's right. We'll make it perfect!"

Since we'd left my crutches behind, he helped me to the various piles in the room. I was soon picking out acceptable nesting materials in shades of grays and cool colors. There wasn't much conscious thought behind most of the picks. Some fabrics felt *right*. They had to hit my instincts just so, or they were left behind. I still probably picked too much, but there were several items I had to have.

"And what were you thinking of doing with the second floor of your nest?" Tormund asked once it was all put aside in a neat pile.

"Um...I haven't even looked up there yet." Though I wondered if I could use that space to coax my males to spend more time with me. Especially after we were all bonded and some of the newness wore off. *I don't want them to get tired of me.*

But we haven't even mated yet, I whispered back to that insecure little voice in my head.

I smiled past my worries. "Any chance we can remodel the nest so it doesn't have stairs?"

Though Tormund laughed, his craggy face creased with confusion. "I don't understand."

"Just joking." But I wasn't. Stairs were the worst.

He accepted that and picked me up to view some of the artworks in storage. I snuggled in with him, and we took our time admiring several pieces for longer than was absolutely necessary. I didn't end up picking many paintings. I didn't want to clutter my new space.

Tormund carried me back to my crutches, which Rennyn held upright while he was turned toward the door and a liveried guard. They spoke in hushed voices; then the king gestured the other male off.

"All ready to go?" Rennyn asked.

"Lark has gotten enough things to start her nest," Tormund said proudly.

The dark elf king nodded. He leaned up and sandwiched me in a hug between him and the redcap. Then he tousled my hair. "Great to see you again, p'nixie. Work calls, as it always does."

"I'm glad we ran into each other," I said. I hoped we crossed paths again soon.

"Bye, Dad!" Tormund added. After the king left, Tormund looked at the pair of crutches Rennyn handed me and then at my face.

"I'm going to fly back." I was already tired of crutching around. Marius had prompted me to use my magic yesterday, and it'd come easier than it ever had before. Maybe flight would be the same way.

I flapped my wings and gained some lift. A couple motes of pixie dust drifted off of me as I floated out of Tormund's hold and hovered a few inches above the ground after another flap. Without many colored scales on my wings, that was the best I could do. It wasn't *flight*, but it was good enough to keep my cast from bashing on the ground.

The redcap eyed my feet, then shrugged. "Let's go. I need to visit my brothers' rooms too," he declared, and we set off. I was able to propel myself a lot faster than I could walk with the crutches. "No nest is complete without your mates' scents."

He was right about that. I still had Fal's mask...somewhere. But having freshly worn clothes from my males layered into my nest would be so much better. Tormund produced a master key off his belt to pay their rooms a quick visit.

When we returned to the royal wing, Marius was standing guard at my door, his face blank until he spotted us. He nodded to Tormund, who went upstairs for the moment, then the kelpie frowned down at my feet. "You should be using your crutches, p'nixie."

"It's a lot faster to fly, though. You won't have to shuffle anymore to walk with me."

"It's not a hardship. You're injured," he murmured.

"And I can do this now." I fluttered a little faster to have the height I needed to press my lips to his.

He caught my hips and kissed me back. Then he asked, "What was that for?"

"Practice," I answered playfully. "Don't take it the wrong way. I also really like kisses."

His lips twitched, hinting toward a smile. "Good to know. Let's get you comfortable for now." He carried me into my rooms rather than letting me fly.

Some servants were tagging the furniture. Marius paused and set me down, helping me balance while I spoke with a grimalkin alpha. The unfamiliar male sported a pair of large cat ears high on the sides of his head and a plush feline tail. He'd be getting my new furniture set up.

Our conversation was interrupted by a territorial growl from Tormund, who approached with a stack of clothes in hand. The grimalkin took a healthy step away from me and bowed his head.

"Here. For your nest. If you want to get started setting it up, the rest of your new nesting materials should be here any moment." Tormund's eyes creased with fondness. "Take all the time you need, li'l bird."

I smiled too and watched as he left. I had the clothes in one hand and my crutches held in the other. And Marius behind me, who made a disapproving rumble when I fluttered my wings. He carried me into the bedroom. Jani and Lon were busy making up the pack bed outside my nest with a new set of covers and a gray bedspread with pops of red in raised, flower-like rosettes that I'd selected earlier.

Marius placed me in front of the threshold of my nest but observed the unspoken boundary and left me to crutch-walk inside. I stripped the bed down to its sheets for now and arranged everything into piles. With a hum, my instincts took over in mixing in the shirts and what I'd already had for my nest.

Tormund had retrieved one plain undershirt from each male, which carried more scent than the fancier tunics they wore. Navy for Fal, black for Marius, gray for Kauz, and orange for Tormund. The latter didn't match anything, and it bothered me just a little, but I'd find a place for it since it belonged to my gentle giant.

When the new supplies arrived, Marius delivered them. He peeked into the nest, watching me hop around on one crutch, and his nostrils flared with an equine snort. "Let me in."

"It's not ready yet."

"You're guaranteed to trip over something. I just want to help."

He wasn't wrong. I considered the blankets and pillows he'd placed just within the nest and sighed. "Okay, come in. But I'm not quite running the show here." My inner omega was going to want things moved back and forth and back again along the rectangular first floor of the nest until it was absolutely perfect.

He tipped his head with a sardonic lift of his lips. "Neither am I. Perhaps you need Niall's help. But first..." He ducked into the other room for a couple minutes and returned with a small decorative pot painted in a motif of swirling seawater in blues and greens. The soil within nurtured a single flower. Its budded tip was only just starting to unfurl, revealing silver petals and a light blue center.

I gasped, recognizing the flower he'd once given me when we were kids.

"It's a Serri moonbloom. When it's a goodbye gift, it means 'remember me fondly by moonlight.' As a living plant and a courting gift, it means, well..." He offered the pot to me, cradled between his palms. "I want to give you something worth cultivating."

"Oh, that's so sweet. Thank you." But I wasn't focused on the gift so much as his face. His smile was nearly boyish, echoing the energy of his younger self, who'd grinned from the simple joy of giving a pretty flower to his friend. Warmth filled my chest from us finding this moment again.

I took the flower and sniffed its faintly sweet fragrance before placing it aside in favor of Marius. He bent to meet my kiss midway. It was a slower, more exploratory meeting of our mouths. His technique was already improving.

"I'm going to do my best to keep the moonbloom alive, but I don't have the best track record with green things," I said once we drifted apart.

"I'll help," he promised. "Shall we set up your nest now?"

I nodded, and he hesitated, resisting whatever had to happen to bring out Niall. But then he surrendered to his feral side, judging by the change in his eyes and the softening of his stance. He glanced around and released a soft rumble of approval.

I got to work, starting with the faelights, setting a couple stray ones loose to illuminate more of the first floor and its low, intimate ceiling. I layered in my mates' scents on the bed and then pivoted on my heel, gazing longingly at the pile of pillows.

Marius wordlessly grabbed two armfuls of them and came over to me. I plucked out a pillow and, after testing its filling, tossed it aside with a disapproving growl. *Unacceptable.* He puffed out a laugh. We didn't say a single word as I continued to build, communicating mostly through body language and sounds.

He may not have realized it, but he was reprising his old role as my extra set of hands. At least he seemed to be enjoying it, as he was extra attentive and homed in on my every need as I built this nest on pure instinct.

Once the bed was properly arranged, I set out cushions and the rest of the blankets for a cozy resting space in the alcove beside the stairs. With no kids planned, this spot could be for visitors or used as a place to laze around as an alternative to the bed. I fussed over placement and second-guessed the blankets on the bed, swapping a few out with the kelpie's help.

After I nodded in approval, he pressed to my back, nuzzling my neck. With my omega side so close to the surface, it felt right to tilt my head further for him in both trust and submission. His fangs pressed into the sensitive column with a possessive noise that was Niall saying, "*Mine.*"

"*Yours,*" I agreed, a soft mewl by comparison.

Feral instincts were not something to tease. He picked me up and crossed the room, placing me down so I was flat on my back on the soft cushioning of the nest I'd made. And then we were kissing again, but this time, he took the breath from my lungs with what could only be described as animal passion, a clash of lips and teeth. I was pinned by his weight, his legs on either side of mine and his hold on my hair inescapable.

My inner omega was still in control and had no inhibitions about this moment. My heart raced at the thrill of being pinned beneath my mate. He stopped kissing me abruptly. "Still think I need practice?" he asked in a roughened feral voice.

Chest heaving, I considered him and where we were. "If I said yes, would you kiss me like that again?"

His eyes hooded. "Tell me you're mine again. Because I'm yours, regardless of whether you've claimed my kelpie bond yet."

My lips parted, but I couldn't say it. My inner omega vanished, letting my worries rush back in. In the quiet that followed, his ear flicked, and he glanced away with a growing frown. "It's fine," he said gruffly.

"It's your one permanent bond."

His gaze lifted back up to meet mine, focusing with predatory intensity. "Tell me what you really mean."

I stumbled over the words a bit. "It just seems...fast? I don't want you to regret..."

"Regret," he echoed in a low growl. "No. Claim me today or in twenty years, and I will have no regrets either way. I have one bond to give to my only mate. You. I've never been more certain about such an important decision."

My instincts popped back up, doing an excited little shimmy in my head. "If you're sure."

He answered with a soft rumble. Somehow, I knew it meant *"I'm sure."* And I didn't question it, not when he leaned down to nuzzle and layer little nips down my neck.

I pressed my fingertips into his chest, over his heartbeat through the shirt he wore. His feral affection stilled, and he held his breath.

"Not yet. If you can't bear my touch, how can we go further?" I said as gently as I could.

He released a tense sigh. "Aye. But...touch me more. I want it. I want *you*."

"Only if you enjoy it. There's no rush."

"I do enjoy it. It's just too much of a good thing."

"I know what you mean. That does get better once you get used to it."

He nodded and settled his forehead against mine. Keeping me underneath him had to be a feral instinct, a not-quite-logical drive to prevent me from disappearing on him again. He trembled while I explored the hard planes of his chest. I accidentally tweaked one of his nipple piercings, forgetting in the moment that it was there. He bared his teeth, his hissed breath saying, "*More.*"

I hoped if we did this a bit at a time, he'd find pleasure rather than overstimulation at the brush of skin on skin. That's how it'd worked for me, at least. I touched the bare skin of his arms since he was in short sleeves again. The tremors through his body became a rumbling purr, and his eyes slid closed.

He only flinched when I reached for his face. "That's enough. Thank you. Actually..." He kissed me again, just as fiercely as before, even as he grabbed my wrists and held them over my head in one hand. He ground his growing hardness into my lower belly. Warmth pooled between my thighs, and he took an obvious inhale, growling into my mouth.

Our lips parted, and he stood. "Shall we finish your nest, sweet prey?" he suggested, going to the last pile of bedding left as if nothing had happened. But for a moment, I'd been held at his mercy. Now my slit felt the chill from the absence of his body heat first.

My nest. Right. I got back to work and relied on my now-smug helper to move around the room for me while I balanced on one crutch. When I couldn't possibly get everything more perfect, I regarded the empty space between the bed and lounging corner with a whine.

Something big was missing. Marius and I turned to one another, then back to the empty spot. He left the nest abruptly.

There was a distant cluster of surprised sounds from a group of strangers before Marius returned half carrying and half dragging a divan into the nest. He placed it in the empty space, where it fit perfectly at a diagonal from the bed. It was made of the same gray material as the chair I'd approved of earlier, and as I lay down on it to try it, I purred with strong support of its placement in here.

Marius picked out a blanket and draped it over me before handing over two pillows that hadn't quite found a place anywhere. I arranged them under my head and smiled up at him. He took me in, then went and retrieved one last thing: Kauz's tunic.

"You miss him," he murmured.

"I do. But how did you know?"

His nostrils flared in a gentle snort. "I know my mate better than she thinks." He didn't hide the longing that tightened his expression, though he took a step away when I reached for him again. "Dream with him. I'm sure he wants to see you, too."

I couldn't argue, not when I wanted Kauz so much my chest ached. "Thank you for helping me."

He nodded and left my nest with a murmur of "P'nixie."

I settled in and held the tunic to my chest, scenting only laundry soap from it. It may have been clean, but it was Kauz's, and even though I didn't need a nap, a short one to visit him wouldn't hurt. I closed my eyes and reached out for his sleeping mind.

32
LARK

I STOOD behind a dining room chair, watching a younger version of Kauz. He listened as a tutor explained the setup of the numerous cups, plates, and cutlery set out in front of him. Next to him, Eletha hid a book under the table and turned the pages ever so slowly so she didn't attract unwanted attention.

They had piping-hot bowls of soup and pieces of bread in front of them. The tutor was explaining the etiquette of passing butter when Kauz shifted to look back at me. The sound of the instructions faded out.

"This is complicated enough that I review it regularly," he said.

I wasn't sure whether he knew I was here. It seemed so, but I had to be sure. "Kauz, it's me, Lark. You're dreaming right now."

"Aye. You took your time coming to visit. I've been making do with memories of your voice."

I opened my mouth to respond, then closed it. *Aww.* If I knew how to do the same thing, I probably would. The way he spoke always calmed me. "Could you change to be yourself? You look like a child right now…"

"Ah. You shouldn't alter dreams formed of Ever, so let's go somewhere else." He stood and offered his hands, palms up. I placed my fingers in his and felt the tug of us leaving the memory-created dream behind. Colors dissolved into darkness, replaced by a scene I recognized.

This was once my dream, when I'd created a nest of everything inside of the omega store in Ilysnor. There was nothing here but Kauz and me and the epic dream nest already constructed and plumped up invitingly. He'd become his adult self, his short white hair grown out a bit like it was in reality.

I reached up to run my fingers through the texture of it and kissed him. He met me with all the bottled-up passion of the days we'd been apart. His mouth tasted of Always, of the ecstasy of promises fulfilled and love meant to be. It lingered on my tongue even as it faded in a fleeting tease.

He laid me down on the nest and burrowed his forearms under my top wings to brace his weight above me. The press of his lips traveled to my neck, and I arched into him from the hint of his teeth on my skin.

"I missed you," I murmured.

"I missed you," he echoed.

"Kauz…"

His tongue brushed the hollow of my throat, and I lost all my coherent thoughts. "I was going to tell you something…" Oh, right. I'd wanted to confess my feelings, but now that we were reunited, he didn't seem all that interested in talking. Still, he humored me, leaning up and fixing me with his gaze. I gasped. "Your eyes!"

He fluttered his snowy lashes. The sheen of stars and magic was gone, revealing the whites of his eyes and the silvery irises that must've been hiding underneath. They were still beautiful, just not the purple-threaded nebulae I expected. After a moment, he said, "Just a sign of depletion. My body doesn't have spare essence right now."

Right. The same depletion he'd tangled with to see me through my worst forgotten memories. Something he absolutely hadn't had to do.

He was the kind of mate I'd dreamed of having for so long, and here he was and... "I love you."

He flashed his knowing smile. Of course he already knew. But I was glad I finally got to tell him. "I love you too. I have for some time."

I lit up, framing my mouth with loose fists in absolute delight. This was probably the best dream of my life. And even though a tiny part of me feared that it was *just* a dream, the crispness of the details that formed Kauz made it impossible to deny that it was him taking in my reaction with a soft groan.

"No one warned me that my mate would be the sweetest thing I'd steal away to Serian."

There wasn't another place I'd rather be than here with him, in the palace he and his brothers "stole" me away to.

Those silver eyes searched my face. "Are you still untouched?"

"Um, yeah..."

His laugh was a disbelieving huff. "That's a miracle. Wait, Mother immediately accepted you as her heir, didn't she?"

"Oh, yes."

He rolled onto his side and took me with him so I was enveloped in the circle of his wings. I relaxed against his chest while he traced the lines of my face with slow sweeps of his fingertips. "The whole journey to Serian, I wanted to sneak into your dreams and coax out your pleasure. To show you what Always and the bindings of fate mean for mates."

"Why didn't you?" I would've let him in and embraced him as a lover, had he entered my dreams at all past the first night on the train.

"Mostly what you know now. Your psyche was damaged. It would've been selfish to walk past all your broken memories just for a moment of pleasure. But it was more than that. You used to take every kindness with suspicion and a certain look." He shifted his eyes left to right, an echo of caginess I recognized. "Trying to find the catch or trick. Or, perhaps, an ulterior motive."

I'd been away from Kauz just long enough to forget how perceptive he was to the smallest of things. "It wasn't personal."

"Oh, I know. You were raised to fear anything Unseelie. So, I waited for you to see that my pack's affection wasn't a trick. That this..." He nuzzled against my cheek and kissed a tender spot against my jaw. I tilted my head for more. "...is real, despite the dream."

"I do know it's real," I murmured.

"You're so untouched. I can hardly believe it." Our gazes met, and he caught my wrists and placed my hands on his chest. His heartbeat, a steady rhythm, pulsed between us. "Everyone needs someone to show them what to do for their first time. Do I get the honors of being that person for you?"

"Yes," I breathed. "I wanted it to be you." I had feelings for his brothers, too, but this gentle male had to be first.

He flashed a grin as he sat up. "As I promised you last time, we won't be interrupted." He gestured to our surroundings. "There's no better place to experiment than your dreams."

I followed his lead and sat cross-legged on the nest, hyperaware that I *was* dreaming and would remain physically untouched no matter what he did. Especially when he became shirtless in a blip of dream logic. His chest was a map of strength with ridges of muscle. The tight buds of his nipples were a darker purple than the rest of him, matching the hue of his lips, which were curved in amusement as he caught in my admiring reaction up and down his bare skin.

"There's no rush. Come closer." He beckoned with a curl of his fingers, and since there wasn't much space between us, I ended up in his lap. I straddled his waist and made a soft gasp when his cock twitched against me. But he made no move to release it from his pants. Instead, he leaned back on his palms and watched me with half-lidded eyes.

I took his invitation and explored his body. At first, tentatively. "Does flying give you a physique like this?" I asked. His solid muscles were sheathed in the softness of his unblemished skin.

"I had to do a lot of training before I could fly. My father likes to joke that I have alpha-sized wings on a beta-sized body." While he responded, I touched him more, watching the way his expression shifted when I found a place he liked. He released a soft moan when I finally touched one nipple and circled it with my thumb.

"I thought dream wardens couldn't be alphas."

"We can't. But give us a few more generations to further mix with omegas and…" He shrugged and regarded me tenderly. "Perhaps our son would be so lucky one day."

My cheeks heated. I fought my first instinct to duck and look away. Kauz didn't want me to hide my reactions from him, and there wasn't much else to hide. He already knew my fears and the darkest corners of my mind.

"I like that you're a beta. You're the pack's voice of reason. I mean, not that any son we had would be a copy of you or anything."

"My brothers only listen to me because they know I'll give them nightmares if they don't," he said mildly. I just about choked on my next swallow.

"Is *that* the secret?" I explored his wings next, running my fingertips over the dark, leathery surface and the tattoos of stars and mist that I'd admired so much. The lines of ink were smooth to the touch.

He extended out the wing I focused on, letting me feel its inner curve. A shiver passed through it in a whisper of sound. "Not for you, sweetheart. You barely have to ask. You have all four of us wrapped around your li'l finger."

I made a noncommittal sound, which was enough for him to catch my hand and thread his fingers through mine. "You doubt me?" He skimmed his lips over my knuckles, brushing a featherlight kiss over each. Then he pressed my hand between us, cupping the hardness of his cock through his pants. "Don't you know what this is?"

"An erec—"

"Control. Four of the most powerful males in Faerie are yours by fate." He moved our joined fingers, showing me how to hold and tease him. "You may feel small and unassuming alone, but you're—"

"Not alone anymore," I said with him. It was still so reassuring to hear.

"That's right. And there's a reason every Unseelie generation is marked by the reign of its queen. I may have been born a prince, but I was raised to elevate and serve my fated mate. *You.* My Always, my brothers' scent match." As he spoke, the rest of his clothes disappeared. When he let me go, I had my fingers curled around his throbbing shaft. He released a shuddering breath as I stroked him. "And now that we've elevated you, I have never wanted to serve more."

Well, he had me convinced when the evidence was in my hand. His cock was as heavy as I remembered and darkened by a couple thick veins. I caught the bead of liquid weeping from the slit at its tip and tasted it. Salt and male musk burst on my tongue. I stroked him again, this time reaching for the sack hanging just underneath his cock.

"Careful. No nixie claws there," he teased, taking my fingers in his again to show me how to play with his balls. He watched me with lusty eyes darkened to a stormy gray. "Are you ready for me to return the favor?"

I didn't think I could be shy while I was fondling him. After I nodded, he rid me of my clothes from the waist up with a flick of his fingers. My breasts rolled free, and he caught them, plucking and twisting their peaks just right to wring a breathy moan from me. I released his sensitive sack before my claws could do it any harm.

"I've wanted to play with these for a while." He traced the sensitive outline of my wings and grasped one, pulling it up and down with a curious hum. "This doesn't hurt?"

"About as much as this does." I folded over the tip of my ear. "The base of my wings bends and angles with the wind, while the rest is stiff."

He nodded and pinched the side of my wing. I bit down on a cry from the electric jolt of pleasure. He released me and rubbed my dust between his thumb and forefinger. "You're designed for pleasure. I want to hear it when I do something you like."

"Sorry. Habit."

"A bad one I'll break you of eventually." His tongue darted out to taste the dust, and he smiled, licking the rest off. "As sweet as you are. Don't be surprised if I wear your dust like war paint. You're starting to put off a lot of it."

I didn't think I needed to apologize when he began rubbing the planes of my wings, coaxing a quiver through my body, especially while he touched the more sensitive undersides. He caressed the inside of the second, smaller pair with his thumbs before cupping my ass. As he kneaded, he trailed kisses over my jaw and licked my new gills.

Everything he did with his mouth felt so much more intense. I should've tried exploring his body with my lips and tongue to see what kind of sounds he made. *Darn it.* Well, there was plenty more time to do that soon.

He sucked harder on my neck, and my answering moan was much closer to his sharp ears. His wings shifted, making that shivery sound. It seemed like he enjoyed hearing me nearly as much as his own pleasure.

"You're ready," he said. Air hit my slick-soaked pussy a moment later as he left me without a stitch on in a split second of dream logic. He ran his fingers through my wet folds and pressed his thumb down on the rim of my pussy.

He'd found and tugged on a part of me I didn't have a name for, giving it a testing stretch. It felt incredible but woke a needy ache straight to my core. I flapped in place like a pinned butterfly and loosed a lusty trill.

"You'd take a knot right here," he murmured in my ear. "I don't have one, but this is my dream, so I *could*."

It was only when he eased the pressure that I realized he was offering, and I shook my head. "I want you as you come. Standard Kauz."

"As you desire. I have plenty of fun things to show you later." He nudged me onto my back, climbing on top like how we'd started this part of our dream.

This time, I didn't distract him by trying to talk. I busied my mouth by kissing up his jaw and giving one of his forward-facing ears a testing lick from the lobe to its sharp point. His gasp and the shiver through his wings had me feeling victorious. I thought they'd be extra sensitive, considering how strong his hearing seemed to be.

He nudged my thighs further apart. The heat of his cock dragged through my slick, teasing the swollen petals of my sex without actually penetrating. I whined when he did it again.

He caught my jaw between his thumb and forefinger and tilted my head. Our gazes met. A hint of his magic was there, glittering amongst the intensity of what I saw in his eyes. Love, tenderness, and devotion all mixed together, emphasized by the slow brush of his fingertips up my cheek.

I hoped he saw the same emotions looking back, or maybe my moment of discovery as my breath caught. My heart nearly burst. I understood this wasn't just about feeling good. We were building something, entwining feelings just as much as our bodies. Once he took me, we would truly be mates, intimate partners as fate intended.

I tilted my head more into his touch, showing my submission with a peek at my throat. His wings loosely blocked out our surroundings. I was enveloped in him, but I ached to be filled by him too and trilled with that need.

He took himself in hand and ran the crown of his cock through my slick one last time before pressing the heat of him where I needed it most. My pussy stretched as he sheathed himself in me one slow inch at a time. The pleasure was edged in a little pain from his size, yet oddly, that only made it feel more incredible.

He watched my reaction with a trembling breath. My expression became slack, lips parted on a gasp and then another needy noise when he paused, throbbing within me. With one last touch on my cheek, he guided my leg up and around his hip, and I mirrored with the other.

He withdrew, just to thrust back in at a slightly deeper angle. I was filled by him just enough to satisfy my greedy pussy. I looped my arms around his shoulders, holding on to him as we rocked together, skin to skin.

We tried an open-mouthed kiss, panting, tongues dueling at the pace of his hips greeting mine. The kiss was short-lived when little noises fought to escape my lips from every change in sensation. He buried his face in my neck, soaking in my sounds with his forward-facing ears. He moaned and gasped too, but his reactions were understated compared to the symphony that spilled from me.

"That's right, sweetheart. Let me hear you," he whispered.

When I moaned his name, it drew a shiver out to his wings. I cracked my eyes open, filled with a whole new surge of playful wickedness. I wanted to figure out everything he liked, to really press my thumbs into those spots to get him to come so hard he saw his own stars. Being vocal, not hiding my pleasure, and screaming his name felt like a good step one.

But I knew my inexperience when he played with my body like a fine instrument, touching me everywhere I needed him to. He licked my neck and pinched the skin there between his blunt teeth. My back began to arch, only bending more when he pressed my clit between two fingers. I came in a sudden blast, my eyes rolling back as my breath emerged in a choked gasp.

"K-Kauz!"

He groaned and spilled his seed, grinding his hips against mine as it emerged in heated pulses deep in my pussy. I didn't realize how much I'd love the sensation and how it prolonged my bliss to feel him come too. When he sagged with a satisfied sigh, his weight overtop me wasn't too much, because I felt the same way.

Boneless, blissed out, gratified. No longer untouched. I didn't think I'd ever look at the princes the same way, knowing *this* was the kind of pleasure they wanted to share.

Kauz shifted off me, lying back so I was on top of him instead. He played with a lock of my hair, his knowing smile having a new, intimate angle as I recovered in a daze of bliss.

Sensations that didn't have anything to do with this dream rushed in—the softness of a pillow on my cheek and fabric bunched up against my chest. "I'm waking up." I whimpered in denial.

"I didn't realize this was just a nap. I almost lost you when you came," he teased.

I soaked in the open affection in his gaze. If only this were my real nest, where we could continue to spend a leisurely afternoon in one another's arms. He still had days of recovery sleep ahead of him. "I'll come back tonight," I promised.

"Please do. There's so much more I have yet to show you. And remember..."

He switched to speaking Serri, saying his words in a devoted, lyrical hush. "Fate has bound us forever in the depths of time. You are my Always, and I will return to you soon."

My eyes pricked, and I pressed my lips to his. That had to be the saying he'd drawn to go with the metalark, the mysterious detail he'd included with such care. Thinly disguised words of love that I hadn't been ready to hear until after he'd set me free.

I faded out while kissing him and woke up with my lips firmly pressed into one of my pillows in some half-aware attempt to continue making out with my mate. I slumped into the divan with a mewl of denial. As incredible an experience as it was...it was still just a dream.

33
LARK

I DIDN'T HAVE a sense for how much time had passed, except the sounds of moving furniture had ceased outside of my nest. Wiping away the grogginess on my face, I gathered up my crutches and left the nest, just to stop and admire a new jumbo dresser added to the attached bedroom. It wasn't the only unexpected addition.

Fal was seated at the foot of the bed in a pose of elegant boredom. It was the kind of perfectly crafted arrangement of his limbs and expression that suggested he had a while to sit there and get it just right. "Did you have a nice dream?" he asked.

I slid a little closer to him, though it was hardly a subtle motion with the crutches. "It was good. Did I keep you waiting long?"

His face creased with amusement. "Nay, my tricksy p'nixie. I could soak in the smell of your slick for hours. It must've been a *very* nice dream."

I turned red so fast I could feel the heat rushing over my skin. Any thoughts of laying a clumsy seduction attempt on Fal transformed into embarrassment. Stars, I could've simply retreated back to my nest to hide, and I wavered on my crutches as I considered doing just that.

"Don't fall. Come here," he said, layering a bit of his alpha presence into the order.

Unlike Marius's bark, which hit with the force of a punch, Fal's was a thread of authority. Subtle but meaningful. The kind of power he could wield unnoticed if he wanted to. The fact that he didn't hide it had me yielding without a struggle and closing the space between us. He propped my crutches beside us and pulled me up onto the bed, tugging my legs until I was straddling him. It reminded me intimately of my dream, especially since he was already hard and pressed against me through the barrier of our clothes.

"Kauz must've shown you pleasure in your dream."

My pussy fluttered and clenched. His nostrils flared, and he gained a knowing smirk.

"Yes," I answered anyway.

For a moment, I expected some kind of disappointment from him. There was no sign of it, though, as he asked, low and intent, "Did you like it?"

"Y-yes." I was breathless, caught by the intensity of his gaze.

"I've heard omegas are even more insatiable than alphas in the bedroom. It seems like a requirement, with multiple mates. One of us just had to show you what it's like. Now it won't be long before the rest of the pack"—he tapped his knuckles against my shoulder—"comes knocking."

"If you want, we could—"

He pressed a finger to my lips before I could finish the thought. "Some advice for the inexperienced. Don't invite an alpha into your bed unless you have hours to spend there. Which you don't."

"What do you mean?" He was saying no? I could hardly believe it since his cock was throbbing between my thighs. I rocked my hips against him, and his breath hissed between his fangs.

"I know, I know. I've been hard since a certain omega stole my disguise at the Omega Masquerade. And I intend to see if you'll open up for me soon."

I would if he asked, a certainty that fluttered my insides. My nerves and excitement collided as his lust-darkened eyes hooded with intent.

"Anticipation makes the moment to come all the sweeter," he added in a low purr. He thrust back at me, just once, and I made a needy whine from the friction between us. A wicked smile crossed his face before he cleared his throat.

Somehow, he regained his usual poise while I remained seated on his erection, neither of us grinding for more as he spoke. "Alas, this evening, I'm only here as a messenger. My sisters have invited you to a nixie night. Only one of the four has met you so far, which is a *travesty*. As I have come to understand, every omega needs to clad herself in pajamas and gather in a pile with other omegas to gossip about anything and everything. And since you haven't...had a chance to meet them yet, I accepted the invitation on your behalf."

Maybe he wasn't in full princely form, since I caught the hesitation in what he'd been about to say. My aroused flush disappeared, leaving me cold as I filled in what he'd almost implied. He knew I didn't have any omega friends. Cymora had made sure I was raised without any close contact with the few other pixies in town.

"Falindel was there for the questioning as well. He listened to it all without flinching. That's love, kid."

Fal was distracting me for the evening. If I went to this nixie night, then we wouldn't have to talk about Cymora's execution. I could have a nice night free from the unpleasant secrets about her that he was withholding.

What was I going to do about this? Ask about it anyway, or...

I went with a kneejerk second option and kissed him. Not with the kind of passion I'd just shared with Kauz, but gentler appreciation that said I understood what he was trying to do. He kissed me back briefly.

"An impulsive kisser, hmm?" Though his tone was husky with desire, he was only teasing.

"You have a very kissable face." I smiled at him with shy affection. He cared about me enough to forego his own needs so I could have something new. We could talk about more unpleasant truths... tomorrow.

He swept my hair back behind my pointed ears, his knuckles

brushing my cheek in a slow glide. "You have no idea how many fae disagree with you."

"Well, they're not your omega. Their opinions don't count."

"I wholeheartedly accept this. I'll become even more insufferable in the eyes of the Unseelie Court by wearing your view of me as armor."

I giggled, more than tempted to kiss him again. "When's nixie night, then?" I forced myself to ask, even though I wanted to stay with him instead.

"Right now," he answered.

I startled and flapped my wings, though he held me securely to him. "Right now!" I echoed. "Stars, I'm not ready. Let me down. I should rinse off, at least."

"Now seems like the time I should tell you we dismissed your house moths for the evening. If you need anything, I'd be happy to assist." He helped me stand and handed me my crutches.

I was glad to have their solid lengths under me, because my legs couldn't be trusted to bear my full weight right now. "I can handle it. Do I need to bring anything?"

"Just a blanket and pillow to make a cute little joint nest for the night." He sighed as he watched me maneuver to close the bathroom door. "Reconsider letting me help you, *mo stór*. You don't need to struggle."

"I'll be okay," I tried to assure him.

"Of course. I have no doubts." He gave a vague yet graceful twirl of his hand. "But I'm your pack lead, and I'd like to dote on you."

On the outside, I probably gave him an odd look, somewhere between longing and fear. For the longest time, I had thought Ellisar would be the male I'd answer to as my pack lead, once he and his brothers forced themselves on me. I'd come to equate the intricacies of a pack bond with fear and a lack of control.

But fuck Pack Ellisar. They weren't here, and Kauz had promised their deaths if they tried to come for me. It just hadn't sunk in yet that Fal had already taken over the role properly. I thought of how he'd put himself between me and various dangers, and how he always seemed to show up if one of his brothers needed him. And, of course, how he put me ahead of his own desires.

That made him a solid pack lead in my eyes. "My single shoe gives me the most problems," I said, shuffling aside so he could join me in the bathroom.

Fal knelt and unlaced it while I leaned against the nearby counter and stripped off my tunic and underclothes. My nipples were pearling from their exposure to the cool air when he glanced up. His pupils dilated until they were round, and I shivered as his gaze skimmed my curves.

"I should dismiss your house moths more often," he said under his breath.

"I can get it from..."

He already had my pants undone and down around my knees before I could finish the thought. I hadn't even felt his fingers against my waistband. He worked the right leg off around the cast and then drew down my soaked panties. My chocolate and honey crackers scent was sweeter than ever, warmed by the edge of heat that always seemed to follow me.

"You're gorgeous." He scented the air and groaned, breathing a soft "*Foc.*"

"Fal..." I didn't know if I was going to apologize, ask him to leave, or see whether he'd join me in the shower. He shook his head and rolled to his full height in a fluid motion. With his help, I was inside the rain room and under a shower of hot water in moments.

He released a held breath as humidity began to fog the glass box around me. "May I head into your nest to pick out the things you'll need?" he asked.

"Yes. Consider yourself invited in."

I caught the impression of my favorite smile of his before he left. I took two palmfuls of soap and delved straight between my legs to clean away the evidence of my recent naughtiness. My folds were swollen and tender to the touch.

Being this aroused by your mates is perfectly normal, I reminded myself. *Right?* I had the impression that it was only a taste of what I was capable of when it came to lusting after my princes.

When I was done rinsing, Fal was waiting with a change of under-clothes and my pajamas. He'd filched a folded blanket and pillow from the top of my nest's bed.

"Presentable for nixie night," he declared once I was clothed.

I crutch-walked through the rest of my rooms and took in the changes with some awe. Swapping out the furniture and rugs had really transformed the space. I could see myself reading in the study, with its new overstuffed armchairs and extra-large writing desk. My mostly forgotten Serri primer and journal had appeared on the desk.

Tormund was still in the receiving room, adjusting a couch by lifting it fully off the ground and then setting it back down at a different angle. With his redcap strength, he made it look effortless. Turning, he adjusted his spectacles and beamed when he spotted me. "Li'l bird! What do you think? Does it look more like home now?"

I made my way over to him, and Fal hung back to give us a moment. "It's perfect, Tormund. I'm amazed you got everything swapped around so fast. It must've taken a lot of work."

He shrugged. "I'd do it over again tomorrow if you didn't like it."

"It feels like home," I said, answering his earlier question. "Because you're here."

He breathed a soft "aww" and picked me up, crutches and all, for a hug. "When do you get the cast off again? I'm tired of worrying about breaking these twigs when I want to hold you."

"Soon, I hope."

I snuggled in, and we purred in harmony for a minute, until he set me down with a pat on the wing. "Enjoy your nixie night," he said.

"I'll try. And you should go eat something. My rooms really are perfect."

"Okay, okay." He waved me off playfully. "I'll get them extra perfect and go."

I headed for the door and only fumbled the knob for a second before it opened on the other end. Marius held it for Fal and me before letting it slip from his fingers. The dark elf continued walking down the hall until he was out of earshot.

Marius resumed his post a few paces from the door, back straight as a rod, though his lips quirked as I took him in. He had a recent addition tied to his belt, a mace just big enough to do serious damage to any alpha who crossed him.

"What is it?" he asked.

"You don't have to guard my door."

His ear flicked. "We've been over this, p'nixie. You're injured and unclaimed. There's no chance I'll leave you vulnerable."

"Have you repelled many threats?" I sighed.

"Do you remember what I said about the best apology I've ever received?" he countered. "Words are empty air. I want you to feel safe here in your new home." He gestured down to where he stood. "I'm doing my job."

"You can do your job closer to me. More comfortably," I suggested.

Maybe he felt he couldn't be far from me. Add in the feral anxiety that I was going to disappear again, and here he was, standing guard against enemies that would probably never get this deep in the palace.

His expression softened. "Maybe." Well, it wasn't his usual response, a hard no.

"It'd make practicing easier too," I offered.

"More kissing?"

"Getting you used to touch."

His response was subtle, a little sucked-in breath. I held myself still as he reached between us, hesitated, and then skimmed his fingertips down the side of my face. Tipping his head, he acquiesced with a low growl. "Go to your thing with my sisters, all right? Before I sweep you off those crutches and back to your nest."

I maneuvered around and began to crutch down the hall. He followed at my pace, saying, "By the way, the guard presence along this wing doubles at dinnertime and continues throughout the night. I do trust those alphas so I can rest."

"Marius trusting someone?" Fal made a dramatic gasp. He fell in on my other side when we passed by where he was waiting. "Name a rarer occurrence."

"Shut the fuck up," Marius muttered, switching to Serri. "I trust you with my mate, don't I?"

"You have that backward. I've been trusting you with my mate, despite my better judgment," Fal replied in kind.

I sighed heavily. Could these males not go five minutes without picking a fight? It made the small blue nixie waiting for us down the hall an even more welcoming sight when she waved with both arms.

"Hi! Are you my new sister?" she called. She was practically a doll in a bright pink set of pajamas, with an eager smile through a mop of navy curls.

Stars, how adorable. I waved back, opening my mouth to reply, just to close it again. I couldn't switch to speaking Serri to answer her without tipping off my new language knowledge to the two males.

Fal answered for me. "She sure is. Head inside so we can get her settled; then you can meet her, Happy Fins." She nodded and ducked into the nearest room. Tanith's suite, I assumed.

Fal turned to me and switched back to speaking Theli. "That's Ambriel, the current baby of the family. Fully blood related to this male, if you can believe it." He hooked his thumb toward Marius, who scowled at him. "She's a ray of sunshine. You'll love her, *mo stór*."

"Is that Fal I hear?" an unfamiliar nixie asked, leaning into the hall. She switched to Theli too as she shook out her wild mass of wavy crimson hair. "Stars, the newly mated, though. Did it really require two of you to escort her over here?"

Eletha stepped out behind her. "Lark! You made it."

A third adult nixie peeked around the first and flashed a shy smile. "We didn't have to pry her away from our brothers after all," she murmured.

Fal smacked his lips. "Implying you all could *pry* anything from me, especially my mate."

All three of his sisters rolled their eyes at nearly the same time. After a few hugs, Eletha took my blanket and pillow from Fal, and the other nixies shooed my males out and threatened them with pelted pillows when they tried to delay. Fal didn't even make introductions before he took the hint and left, with Marius following after one last, lingering glance in my direction.

34
LARK

TANITH'S RECEIVING room was built similarly to mine. A merry fire crackled in her fireplace, and most of the furniture was arranged to shelter a block of space in the center of the room, where the joint nest was. Eletha tucked my things into an empty section on top of a mound of cushions.

"Right, now you're suitably pried away from our brothers," the redhead said, tilting her head as she looked me over. She was tall, freckled, and elegant even in sleepwear embroidered with fluffy sheep. Her fins swished behind her as she considered, flashing red and gold coloring against her peach skin tone. "You're cute. I'm Tanith. Half redcap, if you couldn't guess. C'mon."

She jerked her chin, and I followed her, settling as cross-legged as I could manage in my corner of the joint nest. "You've met Eletha." She nodded to the bespectacled purple nixie, who'd settled on a dotted blanket next to mine. "And...Siora? Where'd you go?"

"Getting the snacks," the other nixie called from beyond the joint nest.

My belly took that moment to sound off, and I covered it while we all giggled. Tanith continued, "Siora's somehow Fal's full-blooded sister, though knowing their personalities, we don't know how that happened. So, Lark, I have to ask. Mothkin talk, and your handmaidens have suggested you know Serri better than you let on."

"Oh, uh..." I should've realized Jani and Lon were gossips. I'd been a servant. I knew everyone talked to everyone else except the lord or lady in charge.

"And we'll keep your secret if you'd switch over to talk to Happy Fins." Tanith gestured to the small nixie, who quivered with excitement from her corner of the nest as she waited to be introduced. "Ambriel doesn't speak Theli yet."

I cleared my throat with a flutter of nerves. To my relief, I didn't butcher my second language, though I spoke with slow care. "Hello, Ambriel. I'm Lark, your new sister."

"I've been waiting so long to meet you," she squeaked. "Mom said I had a new sister, but then you were sick for a while, and my brothers tried to keep you all to themselves and..." She took a gasp of breath.

"It's nice to meet you. How old are you?" I asked curiously.

"Five and a half." She sounded rather proud about the half.

"Incoming," announced the last nixie, Siora, as she stepped into the nest holding some goblets and a bottle of wine. She tunneled out a space in the center of our blankets for the half dozen house moths following her with food, more drinks, and a large, unmarked box. Everything except the box went on a platter in the middle of the nest.

"We can handle it from here. Have a nice evening, ladies." Siora waved to the gaggle of mothkin as they bowed and left.

She was a thickset, curvy nixie with extra-long, showy fins that flashed gray, red, and teal as they settled around her body. I could see how she was Fal's sister when she was the same gray-blue hue as him, though the aquamarine hair that framed her delicate features was an unexpected pop of color.

We made introductions while Siora poured the wine and started passing around goblets. "Juice or water, Happy Fins?" she asked Ambriel.

"Juice!" the little nixie exclaimed.

"Aww, a little grownup today," she teased, reaching for the carafe of reddish juice amongst the platter of snacks and pouring some into the last goblet.

In the meantime, Eletha passed me a cup of wine. Tanith was already drinking deep of hers, so I took a cautious sip. The drink was more akin to fruit juice on my tongue, though it became the familiar dry burn of wine as it slipped down my throat.

Wow, that's really good. I nursed it as Ambriel bounced over to the unmarked box, rummaging through it.

"Feel free to get cozy, Lark," Tanith said, gesturing to the food. Eletha had picked up a plate and was loading it up from the piles of delicious-looking delicacies and sweets. "We just wanted to get to know you."

"Our brothers can't hog up *all* your time," Siora agreed with a roll of her eyes.

"Though they're sure to be part of the conversation. They always are," Eletha added.

Knowing their big personalities, that wasn't a surprise.

Ambriel popped her head and arms out of the box, holding a folded board game. "Let's play this one!"

The other nixies smiled fondly as she returned to the nest and began setting it up. I watched after retrieving a plate of food. The board would need to move between us to make this work, but it seemed we would all have a single token to keep track of, so it was doable.

I also wasn't the full center of attention, which was a relief. Tanith and Siora chatted about work while we ate. Tanith didn't say what she did, exactly, only shared idle gossip she'd overheard while spending time around the palace.

Siora traveled, modeling clothes for a few designers, and occasionally posed as an artist's muse. "Still no scent matches from my last trip," she sighed. "I wish a pack would swoop in and steal me away! Like, hello. I'm so available for that."

Tanith shrugged. "All in good time. Males are more trouble than they're worth anyway."

"Spoken like someone who's never been in love," Siora sing-songed.

"*Pfft*. I agree. Too much bother in real life. They're better in books," Eletha said over the rim of her goblet.

"Oh, please. You were *just* talking about your—wait. Let's save that talk for later." Siora's gaze flashed to Ambriel and then back to her adult sister, who nodded in agreement.

"It's ready," Ambriel declared. When I asked what the game was, she gasped and gathered up her blanket, relocating to my lap to snuggle in with me. "It's okay. We can be a team. Team Happy Fins."

I'd frozen with surprise when she'd sat across my thighs without hesitation, but she was a kid. I just hadn't been around an omega this little since...well, I was her age. No one seemed to find it odd, so I relaxed and petted her soft blue curls. She started purring like a kitten, which set me off too.

"Why Happy Fins?" I asked.

Ambriel wiggled hers on cue. "That's what Dad calls me." She tilted her head back to look up at me with wide yellow eyes and added, "All my dads. And everyone else. You should too!"

I smiled down at her. This little omega was going to have me wrapped around her littlest finger by the end of nixie night. My belly was already feeling warm from the wine, and the room was brighter and more colorful around the edges as she and her sisters explained the board game.

Ambriel mostly played for me while I chatted with her sisters. Siora had batted her lashes and asked, "So, Lark, how *did* you meet our brothers?"

This launched into a huge story, which I narrated with increasing style as they kept my goblet topped up.

The princesses howled with laughter when I told them about stealing Fal's mask and spooking when his Unseelie nature was revealed. "She jumped off the balcony," Siora parroted.

Tanith swiped at the corners of her eyes. "I don't think anyone's done that to escape him before."

They didn't seem all that surprised to hear that I wasn't dressed appropriately for the event. I kept my former servant status quiet, though I'd bet full moons on them already knowing something about it.

Still, they had a good time hearing about Tormund's surprise kindness after my balcony flop, Kauz eating the apple tartlets in my dream that night, and Marius's panicked run with me thrown over his shoulder when "he smelled something, uh, off about me." With a kid as part of my attentive audience, I didn't dare say more than that.

By the time we finished the game, said child was starting to nod off. Tanith got up and tapped Ambriel on the shoulder. "Does little Happy Fins want my nest or her own?" she cooed.

Ambriel gave her a sweet, sleepy look. "Yours, please."

The older nixie scooped her up off my lap while I watched the colors in the room dance with a goofy little smile. Siora reached over to top up my goblet again. "It's time for the real nixie night," she said gleefully. "Starting with Eletha and her grimalkin."

"No, no," Eletha giggled, sounding about as drunk as I felt. "Why do you want to talk about him? I don't even know who he is."

Siora laughed and leaned against me, whispering, "She's got the biggest crush on a heat helper. And his textured cock!"

I sputtered out the sip of wine I'd been about to take back into my goblet, then choked on a few errant droplets. "What?"

Eletha blushed so hard her cheeks turned indigo. "I swear, one of them is the same male each time. I can tell by the...you know."

"What's a heat helper?" I asked Siora.

"Oh, you poor sheltered farm town girl," the curvy nixie exclaimed. "It's a real profession for male alphas. Those with the stamina and without a bonded female help us unbonded omegas through our heats."

"They come in when the heat haze has already set in, do their, um, business, and leave before you even know who they are," Eletha mumbled. "I wish the grimalkin would stay. He helps me twice a year and never waits around to say hi or anything."

"Unrequited love." Siora sighed and splayed against me.

Tanith returned without their littlest sister, goblet in hand. "What, Eletha and her grimalkin?"

The librarian nixie covered her face. "Not you too!"

"Maybe he's shy because you're a princess?" I offered.

"Maybe he knows Eletha would *combust* if he asked her on a date," Siora added.

"Speaking of combusting. I've heard you haven't had your first heat yet?" Tanith asked me. Eletha and Siora turned identical looks of horror my way.

I showed them the heat suppressant tattoo on my wrist. It seemed to curl and loop in on itself, changing colors as I watched. Odd. A lot of patterns, like the ones on our blankets, were starting to do that. "Yeah, it's been four years. There weren't any heat helpers in my farm town. Just a disgusting pack that bought the rights to my first heat."

Siora hugged me. "Oh *giiiirl*. Your heat is going to set your nest on fire."

I took a messy sip of my wine while trying to hug her back. "I *knooow*. I'm scared."

"Don't be. It's going to be amazing, even if you'll barely remember more than half of it."

"About that other thing you just said," Tanith put in.

She only asked a couple questions, and I spilled the whole sordid truth about what my stepmother had done. Pack Ellisar and the silencing band were behind me, but it still felt like a relief not to let them lurk in my shadow, unspoken of, as if they were a threat. And I still had an opportunity to get answers from Cymora soon.

My new sisters were a sympathetic audience, throwing in the occasional insult at my past enemies. We were all way too drunk for most of this to be remembered tomorrow, especially me. The walls pulsed around us as if they had their own heartbeat.

"Say, what's in this?" I finally thought to ask, voice slurring, as I raised my goblet.

"Only the finest fae fruit wine. Are you seeing colors yet?" Siora giggled.

I was seeing *a lot* more than that, but I just said, "Yeah!" since this was the first time I'd drunk any fae fruit wine. It was hallucinogenic, and the rest of the night fragmented as the wine soaked into my head.

We talked and laughed in a surreal reality, slowly forming a purring pile until we passed out one after the other.

Tomorrow came with unrelenting force when I woke. The light of day was too bright, sounds too loud, and the lingering smell of fae fruit wine unpleasantly saccharine.

I reclaimed my arm, which had been dangling, and covered my face as I groaned in agony. *Too much wine... Never again...*

"What the fuck did you do to my mate?" Fal hissed from somewhere below me.

Wait, below?

I peeked between my fingers to find the joint nest from last night several yards under me, since I was floating at the top of Tanith's vaulted entryway. A pastry drifted past my line of sight while my heart doubled the speed of its pattering as I, too, wondered what the fuck was going on.

Fal stood next to a disheveled Tanith, both of their faces turned up to look at me. Though their hair stirred from some unseen, indoor wind, he looked as impeccable as ever in one of his dark blue outfits, while she was groggy, her sleepwear lumpy and askew.

"I don't know," she grumbled. They were both speaking in Serri. "She hasn't done this before?"

"No!" he exclaimed in disbelief.

"Could you keep it down?" Eletha's sweet voice requested from somewhere in the mound of blankets I thought I'd fallen asleep in.

The dark elf pinched his brow but lowered his voice. "All right. It's magic of some kind, and uncontrolled at that. We need an essence spinner."

Tanith put her hands together. "Please keep our parent pack out of this. Can't you just climb up and get her?"

"That worked so well for Jani," he said dryly.

I peered around before spotting my handmaiden soaring a couple feet below me. Her wings were spread, and she seemed content amidst a mass of floating food, plates, and dripping goblets slowly circling on an invisible current. Occasionally, she reached out to catch and eat something sweet. By the items—and house moth—the disturbance of air was about a ten-foot diameter of...whatever this was.

"Help," I whined. Somehow, I was responsible for this by the tug of essence within me, but I didn't know how to stop it.

"Try flapping your wings," Tanith called to me in an urgent whisper.

I did, and I made it far enough down to collide with a floating confection that felt cold and slimy against my wing. The wind pushed me back up to the ceiling. My head tapped the hard surface, sending another spike of pain shooting behind my eyes.

"We may have to..." Fal drew off and tilted his head, brows furrowing. "Kauz is awake."

"Thank the stars." Tanith breathed a sigh of relief, which I echoed. He'd know what to do. And...I'd get to see him again. I couldn't even remember whether I'd tried to enter his dreams last night through the fog in my mind.

"We'll see if he can help. Otherwise, it's time for a ladder," Fal said.

I closed my eyes to shut out how bright the world was. What I wouldn't do for a glass of water to float up here, as my tongue was practically stuck to the roof of my mouth. As we waited, the dark elf occasionally checked in with me. All I could make back were noises.

He also tried to coax Jani out of the circle of wind. "I'm fine up here, Prince! This is fun. Besides, if she falls, I'll catch her," she said cheerfully.

Someone give this house moth a raise.

Eventually, there was a knock on the door. "I got it," announced a different mothkin.

I peeked through my eyelids to see Kauz enter the room with princely dignity. He sagged the moment the door closed behind him.

"You're going to the nearest bed after you help us," Fal said to him.

"Mine, preferably." The dream warden sounded exhausted. He tilted his face up and chuckled as he took in my predicament.

"Too much fae fruit wine," Fal explained.

"Ah." Kauz nodded. His color had mostly returned, except his eyes seemed stark white outside of his dream. Dark bruises bloomed under his gaze, making it look as if he hadn't slept in weeks.

He motioned for Tanith and Fal to lean in. They whispered together and spared me a couple glances before the dark elf nodded and went rummaging out of my line of sight.

"Sweetheart, look at me." Kauz addressed me in Serri, but I did as he said anyway, cracking a little smile. He may have been in rough shape, but he was awake. "You have self-control lessons for your magic in your immediate future."

I tried to lick my dry lips to reply, but motion caught my eye. Fal stood with one of his arms cocked like he'd thrown something and a glass hit the ceiling a few yards from my head. It'd just barely missed getting caught in my magic. The sudden shattering sound had me flinching away from it.

The startle ended my uncontrolled spell, and I fell, clawing at the air. I was already landing in Fal's arms by the time my sluggish mind processed that I might've wanted to flap my wings. He brushed a bit of icing off one while I made an embarrassed mewl.

"I'm going to take care of you," he murmured in Theli. "But I hope you know you're never living this down, *mo stór*."

35
LARK

Fal relocated me to a bathroom, presumably in his suite. He gave me a vial full of murky, greenish-gray liquid rather than some water. "This'll fix you right up."

I trusted him and drank it, then re-regretted all of my decisions last night as the potion hit my stomach, churned it, and turned it inside out. I threw up in the toilet while he held my hair back. Shockingly, I did feel a lot better once I was done, though I yearned for the ground to swallow me whole as clarity returned to my mind.

"I take it you had a fantastic nixie night," Fal said, not even teasing.

I studied the white tiles in his bathroom. "Yes, it was great. This wasn't." My voice was little more than a dry croak.

He knelt next to me. "You have to be careful with fae fruit wine. Those hallucinations hit before you realize you've drunk too much, and you start wondering how you never noticed you have twelve fingers." He turned his hands over, pretending to admire them.

I watched him out of the corner of my eye and cracked a shy smile. "The walls were breathing."

"Then you drank *way* too much wine. Were you trying to keep up with Siora?"

"She was pouring."

"Of course she was." He shook his head with a playful tsk. "This isn't how I thought you'd first arrive in my bed, but I'm going to put you there to rest for a while. Thalas can train your magic once that hangover fades."

"Thank you."

He had a sizable bed. It had a dark canopy supported by four posts, the fabric already drawn to block out most of the sunlight from a nearby window. He helped me rehydrate first while I sat on the edge of his comforter. I glanced over my shoulder and then gave him a curious look. Kauz was asleep on the other side of the bed.

"I ordered him to go back to sleep. It's a pack lead thing," Fal explained quietly.

My eyes widened. "You can do that?"

"I only use it if it's necessary. He was in no shape to be awake. He'll either wake up spitting mad and give me nightmares for a week or forget his anger in about five minutes." He shrugged.

"That sounds like him." I was reminded again of why I was glad to have Fal as my future pack lead; he wielded his influence with care.

"Well, that's my thing." He circled his hand vaguely. "Figuring out others and their secrets." He tilted his head, considering me. I saw the hesitation before he added, "Perhaps it's not the time, but I want to ask you a question."

I fidgeted with my fingertips until I accidentally poked a cuticle with a sharp nail point. "Um, okay."

"Do you understand me?" he asked in Serri.

Icy surprise chilled my belly. Had he overhead the house moths talking about this too? Or maybe I'd given myself away while blinded by my hangover.

"I understand you better than I used to," I answered, also switching languages.

His brows rose. "Listen to you. Not even a Theli burr. Restoring your memories gave you Serri, then?"

"Please don't be angry," I added with a hunch of my shoulders.

He corrected my word choice, since I'd said *hot* rather than *angry*. "I'm not. How could I be? You know I love to be tricked." Though his lips downturned. "I'm wondering why you kept this a secret. In a void, I would assume you don't trust us."

"It hasn't come up," I said apologetically.

He tilted his head back and forth. "So, you trust my brothers and me? Your pack?"

"Aye." Though that wasn't the whole truth, so I added on, "Mostly."

"Mostly," he repeated, chewing the word like a tough piece of gristle.

Guilt was about to eat me alive. "You all somehow planned the removal of my silencing band and, um, the thing with my stepmother without me knowing, and we were stuck in a train together while you did. I just wondered what you all talk about while I'm right there in the room with you." My pleading tone faded as I added, "And there's the matter of Cymora's execution."

His gaze softened with understanding. "In our defense, it was an unusual circumstance. If your full name was enough to knock you unconscious, imagine what hearing us discover the *olcanus* and your stepmother's part in it would've done to your health."

"I know," I murmured.

"What I'm taking from this is that we need to do a better job at communicating. I intended to tell you about Cymora eventually." He shifted his weight from foot to foot.

There was that evasive word. Eventually. "When she was already dead?"

"Nay. I wanted you out of your cast, at the bare minimum. I needed to see that lovely smile of yours more before your abuser's actions robbed it away again." He tugged at his face, blowing out a sigh. "It's wrong to withhold important information about your family from you. I apologize for that. But once I share what I know, perhaps you'll understand.

"Also, no one in your pack is plotting against you. You came to us with a head full of nonsense about how Unseelie act, but we've always had your best interests at heart."

Tears pricked my eyes, and I drew in a little sob. He was right, of course. The princes, and now our family, had been nothing but kind to me. "Hey, don't cry. You're barely hydrated," he said in his usual teasing tone. "You eavesdropped on us for a couple days, and what did you really learn?"

I considered and shrugged. Not too much, actually. "You and Marius don't get along."

"And you didn't need to know Serri to realize that. Or to know that we're siblings and needling each other is what we do best."

"I'm sorry." I was still in a heavy mood while he was trying to make light of the moment. My head hurt, and I worried this would come back to haunt me more than waking up with my magic sticking me to a ceiling, however that had happened. "I didn't *really* think you were plotting anything or that it was about you being Unseelie while I'm not. I was mostly curious and feeling a little left—"

He sat on the bed beside me, and I slid into him. He took my fidgeting hands in his, separating them. "It's all right, my treasure. Look at me," he coaxed. I met his gaze, which was still full of the same kind of affection I'd admired last night. "You're Unseelie too."

"Half."

He shook his head. "There's no such thing. Your mates are Unseelie, your new family is Unseelie, and if any of your mother's birth family are still alive, they're Unseelie too. Aspects of your magic—the illusions, at least—are designed to trick and disorient. Which is..." He gasped dramatically.

"Unseelie," I supplied, feeling a crisis coming on. How was that possible? I'd been Seelie since...

Well, since Cymora had hidden away any attributes to the contrary. She'd been the main voice in my head to suggest Unseelie weren't to be trusted. They were vile and cruel...

But the princes weren't that way. *I* wasn't that way.

"Serri is beautiful on your tongue. Tormund is going to be so happy when he hears the news." He switched to speaking in his usual Theli purr. "But I think I'll continue on with this a while more. Until my accent doesn't make you blush."

I reddened on cue. "What gave me away?"

"The way you light up every time I speak?" he teased, making an offhand gesture after releasing one of my hands. "Or the faces you've started making when you're eavesdropping? Hmm, or perhaps it was Kauz sweet-talking you in Serri while you were on a ceiling and you not misunderstanding a word."

"I guess I wasn't subtle." And I hadn't realized he'd watched me this closely.

"Subtle," Fal scoffed. "Also, after all this, I doubt you'll be able to rest. Why don't I send a message to Thalas and we get your training sorted?"

I started to nod, then winced. "Okay," I said aloud instead.

He left the room for a few minutes but didn't go far. The murmur of his voice mixed with the higher, enthusiastic tone of a house moth. I sipped from my glass of water and tried to relax.

When Fal returned, he wiggled the glass out of my hand and took my fingers in his instead. "In regards to Cymora, I do have something to share. We had her arrested and taken to the dungeons," he began. "It was supposed to be just Marius and me questioning her. Our goal was to force her to break the vow that put you under her control and remove anything else she had over you. It became a full-on interrogation with the entirety of Pack Serian watching. Marius couldn't handle hearing about your abuse, so Theodred questioned her in his place. The things she said..."

Most everything she could've told him, I'd lived through. And instead of looking at me with pity, his face hardened from what he had to be remembering. "All of it was terrible. I'm glad she managed to worm her way onto the train ride here, because on Serian's soil, her death will be as painful as she deserves. Now, my father is the worst gossip in the palace and has already sent a message that claims you've said you want to talk to her one last time."

What possessed Rennyn to do that? "That's right."

"*Why?*" He punctuated his question with a low growl.

My heart faltered for a moment, and I breathed a little whine. He wetted his lips and composed his expression so I didn't shrink away from his alpha aggression.

"If she's going to die..."

Fal tilted his head as he waited for me to finish my thought. He flicked his fang with his tongue. "That doesn't mean you have to see her again. She is nothing anymore. Not worth your time or your feelings."

"I'm not sad she's going to be punished for what she's done. But... she's still my stepmother." And, much as I hated to admit it, that meant something. The years we'd lived together under one roof couldn't be waved away like they were "nothing."

Fal groaned, but I had the feeling he was exaggerating it for effect. "That's the reason no one is going to prohibit you from seeing her. But I don't mind being the first to strongly advise against it. All she's going to do is *hurt you*. That's all she's got left."

"Maybe. No, definitely, she's going to try. Just remember that she no longer has power over me. I'm not just going to sit there and take everything she wants to dole out. I'm not a doormat anymore—"

"Going to go back in time and strangle Marius before he says that to you," he muttered.

"—I can do this. It's an opportunity to give her a piece of my mind before she returns to the stars."

Fal's worry changed, retreating behind his usual smirk. "Have you ever given anyone a piece of your mind before?" I used to think his diplomatic expression was his armor, but I was wrong. His wit was what he hid himself behind.

Instead of being offended, I saw through it. "I'm going to be okay, Fal. There's a first time for everything." I forced a smile and a small purr, letting go of his hands to ease closer and rest my head against his shoulder. He put his arm around me, tucking me into his side.

He let the smirk go, all the more open without it. All the more *upset*. "Stars, Lark. I'm not done sharing what I've learned about her. See if it will change your mind."

"I'm listening."

He frowned at the floor, where a bar of over bright light was slowly sliding across the carpet. "Cymora is not well in the head. Put a little pressure on her, and you start to see the fractures. She's one step away from qualifying as completely cracked, in my opinion."

"I could've told you that," I said in an undertone. Her cruelty seemed to do the decision-making for her. She'd go out of her way for it.

Fal took a grounding breath, then forced out, "She admitted to murdering both of your parents."

Cymora occasionally talked about the freedom that came with being mateless. Her wording was subtle, though her order not to repeat what she said about the matter was not. I'd assumed she'd poisoned the tea of Laurel's father in dissatisfaction with their arranged mating. His death had come at the perfect time, in the scheme of things.

"She loved my father. They mated," I said from numbed lips.

"She was obsessed with him. There's a difference." He tightened his hold around my waist. "She poisoned him because he continued looking into the circumstances that lead to your mother's untimely death. When he was too close to the truth, she removed him rather than face any consequences."

So, when she bragged about freedom...it wasn't just Laurel's father she was talking about. It'd been my father, too. Fire ignited in my belly, but with the warmth of indignation came a rush of other emotions too. I sobbed and buried my face against Fal's tunic. He rubbed my back, but now that he'd opened up the past, he wasn't finished making it worse.

"Because of that obsession, she always saw your father as hers. She bargained for an illness curse from an auracle, intending to strike down your mother with you still in the womb."

"No," I whimpered.

I grieved my mother with new understanding. The beautiful, soft-spoken nixie from Thalas's memory was already becoming sick. Auracle magic was powerful in a way that couldn't compare to other fae races— the curse would be undetectable and incurable unless she was taken to another auracle. And it wasn't as if they were around every corner, waiting to provide assistance. Most auracles were known to be reclu-sive, fickle, and cruel.

"That hateful fucking female," I seethed between angry sobs. "There was no reason...no point to any of this."

Fal wrapped me in a hug as my mourning and fury became a mael-strom, an incomprehensible whirl. It was easier to be a little feral, to scream until I was hoarse and claw at his clothing. He was immovable, a rock to break apart upon and hold me upright once I sagged. It never took long for me to cry myself out. Cymora had taught me not to enter-tain such weakness where she could exploit it.

Fal wiped my face dry, chasing the swipes of his thumbs with feath-erlight kisses as delicate as mist after a brutal storm. "You never have to see her again," he murmured. "Say the word, and I will see about expe-diting her execution."

I cleared my throat to answer in a strong voice. "No. I do." But I could see the disbelief written across his face. He'd thought the truth would dissuade me. "I know you're just trying to care for me. But she has to answer for what she's done. She's going to tell me why, even if I don't do a good job giving her a piece of my mind." As senseless as my parents' deaths seemed, there had to be *something* going on in Cymora's head for her to have ended their lives the way she had.

Fal cradled his forehead in his free hand. His slit pupils resized as he looked me over, and something he saw drew forth a glimmer of something new, something I couldn't put a simple name to. "All right, *mo stór*. But I refuse to consider a future where I send you to this talk unprepared."

<h1 style="text-align:center">36</h1>

<h2 style="text-align:center">LARK</h2>

BUT FIRST, Fal held me in the semidarkness of his bedroom for a while longer. He busied his mouth with kisses and gentle nips, paying special attention to the sensitive spots on my neck and jaw. The occasional nuzzle layered his sunshine and grass scent over mine.

He didn't ask for more. He could've come knocking, as he put it, and I would've said yes. Yet I was glad he didn't. His warmth, the press of his body against mine, and the harmony of our purrs calmed me like nothing else could. Because of him, I was ready to face the day ahead.

I had a light, bland breakfast before Marius and Tormund joined us. Both alphas were milling around in the hall outside, looking at a loss before they spotted me. I led the way, crutching to Thalas's workshop. My reserve of essence felt low, probably because of my ceiling wakeup, so I didn't attempt to fly.

All three males were in the middle of a tense discussion in Serri. Now that they knew I understood them, they'd dropped their voices to an angry masculine murmur. It made me feel small, like they had to be furious about my secret-keeping, though the much bigger issue of the day was my stepmother.

Before I did anything with Cymora, I had two more apologies to make. They were nearly as important as mastering my unknown magic before it activated outside and I floated away without a ceiling to save me.

The workshop's door was already open when we arrived. The alphas split off to continue their talk while Thalas greeted me with a smile. To my relief, he was as calm and friendly a presence as ever, barely batting a lash when I spoke in sluggish Serri throughout our visit. He corrected my occasional misused word and slowed the cadence of his speech as we discussed this morning's event.

"You used wind magic when we released you from the *olcanus*. I thought it was a backlash effect at the time," the king mused. "Kellam was a wind sprite. It seems you took after him a bit."

I melted at the thought. Maybe I was more Unseelie than I'd ever imagined, but I still had something from my father other than my pixie wings.

However, I did end up apologizing to Thalas when he revealed that my unleashed magic had resulted in a tipped-over table and the shattering of dozens of his various knickknacks. He waved me off. "Want to know a secret?"

I nodded and leaned in while he cupped his hand over his mouth to whisper, "I don't know what most of those things even do. They came with the workshop. I think they've been hanging out for generations for exactly that reason."

I laughed in disbelief. "What?"

"They might be priceless, but I don't know what they're for," he said, shrugging. "So, they're actually useless."

"You could put them in a box or something?" I suggested.

"Then I'll definitely never find them again!"

He flew to one of the upper-level balconies and returned with a thesaurus of magic abilities. He started at the back to look up wind sprites, and we spent a couple hours seeing what kind of wind I could— and couldn't—summon in a flash of essence.

Halfway into the process, the air shook with a roar. I startled and looked over at the alphas. Fal and Marius were grappling while Tormund watched and laughed. The dark elf was making himself hard to hold on to, but he was soon tossed on the ground.

"Should we do something?" I whispered to Thalas.

The king shrugged. "Best to let them get it out of their system."

Marius wrestled Fal into a headlock. "Take it back," he demanded.

"No," Fal growled. He escaped the hold without trouble. It seemed one of their arguments had finally spilled over into something physical. My racing heartbeat started to calm as I saw they weren't hurting one another.

After Thalas prompted me to pay attention to my magic, I continued failing back-to-back spells. Maybe this morning's magic was a fluke or even some kind of freak accident. My enthusiasm for having some of my father's wind magic waned one disappointment at a time.

Thalas announced that we were going to try the last spell in the wind sprite repertoire, called vortex. He eased backward before teaching me the hand motion and twist I needed to give my essence.

I mimicked him and muttered under my breath. A sudden force of air shoved under me, shooting me up twelve feet in the air before I could draw breath to scream. My crutches clattered to the ground, dropped halfway. I flapped my wings, loosing an alarming amount of pixie dust and steadily falling despite my best efforts to remain in the air.

Thalas looked up at me, adjusting his glasses as he did. "Interesting. Looks like you have access to a single wind sprite spell."

"I've got you, little bird," Tormund said nervously. In Serri, he didn't struggle to say *little*, and I already missed the quirk. He was directly under me with his arms lifted, getting covered in purple sparkles for his trouble.

I floated downward with all the grace I could muster until Tormund pulled me from the air by catching my hips. "Don't scare me like that," the big male mumbled.

I was of a completely different mind about what'd happened. "Did you see that?" I practically squealed. "I have wind magic!"

"Oh, I saw it, all right." He made an attempt to remove the tousle the wind had left my hair in. Our eyes met, and I smiled at him hopefully. He petted my hair one last time and said with affection, in Theli, "Li'l bird." My heart leapt.

"It'll take some practice, but you'll be happy to have the vortex spell for emergencies," Thalas put in, interrupting our moment. He handed me my crutches. "We'll work on control today and practice some other time, when you're not in danger of breaking your cast."

"Couldn't it come off now?" I asked as innocently as I could.

"Nay. I won't consider removing it until I see Kauz awake and standing next to you."

Well, it was worth asking. He had Tormund place me in a seat, and we discussed strategies for control so I didn't summon another accidental vortex. It was like learning how to retract the membranes between my fingers but involved a mental muscle rather than a physical one. I followed Thalas's directions and promised to keep up the series of meditation-like steps to maintain my control.

This way, I also wouldn't accidentally end up in someone else's dream. Too-crisp memories of entering Cymora's dreams haunted me as I practiced. She'd always been furious if my powers catapulted me into her mind at night. I'd had no idea why it happened so often, since I'd only been a kid hoping each time that it was *my* dream and that I'd conjured a kinder version of her. No matter the punishments she delivered by day, before the silencing band, my sleeping mind had sought scraps of compassion where there were none.

She could've chosen to be kinder. She had so many opportunities, I reminded myself, shaking off the memories before I could get emotional.

I said goodbye to Thalas with a hug and made my slow way out of the workshop. Marius and Tormund kept pace at my sides while Fal roamed ahead of us.

"I'm sorry I kept this from you," I said, speaking Serri.

Marius answered without looking at me. He was keeping a watchful eye on our surroundings instead. "A female is entitled to her secrets," he replied in Theli. "Though this one was guaranteed to come out sooner rather than later."

"I'm glad," Tormund put in, though he also spoke Theli. It seemed they'd all decided to continue on with speaking the language I was most comfortable with, which I appreciated. "About your decision..."

Marius turned his gaze away from the hall for just a moment, fixing his brother with a strict look of warning and causing the redcap to taper off. "We support you. So, we're all going to help you prepare," the kelpie said.

I dry swallowed, wondering what "preparing" me could entail. We headed back to my suite as a group. Jani and Lon greeted us cheerfully past the door and went to get refreshments.

Fal motioned for me to head to the table in the dining nook. We all sat, and there was an expectant air as they turned toward me. "What are you going to say to Cymora? It's time we devised your strategy," the dark elf said.

My gaze darted between them.

"Will it be a pointed questioning? Does she get to speak, or are you going to be chewing on her hide the whole time?" Fal asked.

"I was just, um…"

My handmaidens came over and set up a tea service. I fidgeted with the cup they gave me, sliding it around its saucer. Tormund angled his hand over his mouth as he said in a loud whisper, "We go over important conversations like this all the time."

"Too much." Marius added a feral noise behind what he'd muttered, a grumble I understood. "*Too many words.*"

I giggled into a sip of tea. It was sweet and fruity. But when I placed it down, I took in my audience again and shifted in my seat. "I wasn't really thinking about a strategy. But I do want a conversation."

"A conversation or…"

Fal motioned to Marius, who picked up on the cue. "A *conversation?*" The kelpie put a menacing growl behind it.

I pointed at Marius. "Well, I can't do that." But I tried anyway, summoning up a high-pitched, shallow growl. *Grr conversation, so scary.*

Tormund's face fell. "She's too cute. This isn't going to work."

"Good thing there's zero chance this conversation will be just Cymora and Lark in a locked room," Fal put in. "Lark can be her usual self, and we'll plant Marius in the seat next to her for intimidation."

"I'm fine with this," the kelpie said.

"I'm not. Cymora's already seen you flinch," Fal answered. Marius chuffed angrily but didn't argue.

"Really? You're going to be there with me?" I asked. They replied in a chorus of "aye," and I tilted my head, considering. "All three of you?"

"That depends. Our parents are involved, and they have a bone to pick with her too," Fal said. "They're setting the terms. When and where it will be, and how many fae will be in the room. It will still be your moment to say what you need to say. Whomever is there with you will help protect you and control the environment."

"The environment. Right." I chewed on my bottom lip. While I wasn't opposed, there was a deeply personal element to this conversation.

Who was I kidding? Fal had already told me that the entirety of Pack Serian had witnessed Cymora's interrogation. Privacy was hardly an option anymore.

"No matter what, you need to know what you want from this beforehand," Fal said.

That was where we started. I wanted answers, so it was to be a pointed questioning. But the problems arose when we worked toward what I was actually going to say to Cymora. It was private enough that I didn't want to speak the words aloud so they could be dissected by committee.

I tiptoed into the process and cut a couple glances too many at Marius, prompting Fal to turn to him. "Stop scowling. You're making her nervous."

The kelpie snorted. "That's just my face."

"And those lips have a proven track record of saying judgmental things to her."

"It's fine," I said, a little mortified that Fal was turning this into a confrontation. Yet he was right. I was uneasy about being vulnerable in front of all of them, Marius included. He had predatory instincts to contend with, which could drive him to latch on to any weakness.

"P'nixie." He met my gaze, and determination reflected from those yellow eyes. "I would find ripping out my own fangs preferable to hurting you again. I'm only here to support you for this difficult conversation. Please don't send me away."

Fal and Tormund exchanged a surprised glance. I gave Marius a reassuring look and murmured, "I wasn't going to send you away."

"That would be Fal's next course of action if you continue to struggle," Marius replied.

"Well, you can stay." Sending anyone away wasn't going to help. I reached over and put my palm in his, feeling the strength in his callused hand as he gave mine a squeeze.

I just had to knuckle down and talk, even though it was going to be difficult. There was value in planning what I was going to say and do. I had to be calm and composed in front of Cymora, else she'd eat me alive regardless of who was in the room with us.

If he could keep a hold of his voice rather than fall back into feral silence, Marius could be a good coach for how to put up a stony façade. He did it all the time.

"All right, Lark. Let's try a new angle." Fal drew my attention back to him. "Pretend Tormund is your stepmother. Give him a piece of your mind."

The gentle giant pointed at his chest with raised brows.

"You're furious with him," the dark elf prompted.

Tormund's expression shaded with alarm. "Um, aye, very angry. Let me have it, li'l bird."

"Cymora, I am cross with you." There was an element of fae honesty that let us talk about theoreticals and pretend to be in the mindset of others, as long as it was clearly stated to be the truth of another. Cleverer minds than mine could bend their words to breaking this way.

"I am the worst," Tormund agreed. He pitched his voice an octave higher, not that it made him sound any more feminine. "I'm your evil stepmother who talks for hours about the money my remote farm town produces. And I'm definitely exaggerating every single number."

My composure broke, and I snickered. "Wait, really?"

His eyes widened. "*Hours.*"

Fal propped his chin on his fist, watching us go with a sigh as I tried —and failed—to speak with any kind of anger at Tormund. When it was apparent that this wasn't working, the dark elf had me speak to Marius as if he were my stepmother.

"Don't slouch," the kelpie growled. "Don't cower. Look your prey in the eyes, and let her see how unbreakable you are."

"Next advice you're going to give is for her to tear out Cymora's throat with her teeth," Fal remarked.

"She understands the analogy."

"C'mon. She's not feral, Mar."

I did understand the analogy, but I still struggled. Fal took over as Cymora, but first, he began to scrub his face with both hands. He hushed us and muttered to himself. He called it "getting into the mindset," and I watched him, puzzled.

"He does acting on the side," Tormund told me.

"Stars, not 'on the side.' Whenever I can get time away from this starsforsaken palace," Fal muttered.

I held in my questions so I didn't interrupt his process. Well, he still had the temporary tattoos from his role as the Prince of Winter. It wasn't a surprise he was an actor in his free time; it just hadn't really come up in conversation.

Fal mussed his hair so it more closely resembled Cymora's usual style. She liked her hair with volume so she could give it a windswept tousle as if she'd just emerged from the sea and it'd dried that way.

"Well then, Lark, you have something to say to me?" His tone was spot-on in mimicking how she spoke to me. A melodic voice turned to acid, condescension hidden as an undertone to mermaid sweetness. I tensed like he'd reared back to slap me.

"Maybe you just want to return to Osme Fen. I'm sure there are a few fae there that'd be happy to see you." He even simpered like her.

My hands balled into fists under the table, and my claws dug into the meat of my palms. He didn't mention Pack Ellisar by name, but that was who I pictured. I trembled, furious. Misty-eyed. My lips parted to tell off Cymora. What emerged was what could be called a screech of rage.

"Maybe a little feral," Tormund said in an aside to Marius. The kelpie looked proud, then alarmed as tears rolled down my cheeks. He reached over and swiped one away.

"I'm angry, I promise." I dried my other cheek with my knuckles. How embarrassing to burst into tears right in front of most of my future mates. "This always happens when I get mad."

Tormund watched me with open worry, his expression mirroring the same one he'd made when he'd last said, "This won't work." And if I couldn't keep it together, he was right.

FAL'S CYMORA impression drew out my emotions, both good and bad. We worked through potential avenues of where this conversation would go after I calmed down. I was building a fake persona, a strict and implacable omega for the course of the talk, rather than my usual soft and shy personality.

They collectively had several good ideas about how to steer the talk toward where I wanted it to go: explanation and contrition. When they weren't suggesting new ways to phrase my questions, Marius and Tormund echoed successful deliveries with praise. My inner omega fluffed herself up each time. *My alphas support me.*

It was still exhausting to verbally shadowbox with the potential of my stepmother. Hours later, we stopped to eat. I fluttered to the bathroom to take a break from everyone and splash water on my face.

"*Please* stop flying," Marius said gruffly when I returned. "You bob around like a drunken butterfly."

"It's cute," Tormund added. He met Marius's glare with his usual broad smile. "What? It is."

"It takes some of the pressure off the bruises." I sat down, eager to tuck into the bowl of salad I'd asked for tonight. It was full of veggies and fruit, with chicken for protein and a light dressing...

Marius was staring at me, unblinking. I stopped stabbing my fork into my dinner and nearly whimpered at the intensity of his gaze.

"What bruises?" he growled.

"You know, from the crutches." I lifted my arm and circled the sore area around my armpit. His feral stare was becoming uncomfortable to meet, so I turned to Tormund. He was nodding in understanding.

"I know exactly what you're talking about. Crutches can make you feel really uncomfortable. Remember when I—okay." Tormund cut himself off as Marius pushed abruptly to his feet and left the suite. "Rude. Fal, you remember when I broke my leg?"

The dark elf smacked his lips. "Mmhmm. Forget not being able to walk. You were inconsolable for *days* about embarrassing yourself in front of Theodred's friends."

"My future clan mates," the redcap sighed.

"And do they even remember it now?"

Tormund's gaze darted around before he breathed a sheepish, "Aye."

"Oh, the indignity of it all," Fal teased.

I munched on my salad while I listened to them. Little could compare to the bright flavors of fresh fruit and vegetables. Maybe it was a farm town girl thing, but I'd missed the simplicity of a salad made from ingredients that'd mostly been in the ground mere hours ago.

Marius returned with two wooden pots and offered me one. The herbaceous scent wafting from it matched the magical wound salve that he'd had on the train. "Use this before you go to bed," he instructed.

"I'll be okay. I think I'm getting the cast off in a couple days."

"And reapply it as often as once a day," the kelpie continued, ignoring my protest. "If it pleases you, I'd be happy to assist. I've been trained in physical therapy. That includes joint and wound care."

"He gives a mean massage," Fal put in. "Emphasis on *mean*."

Marius's ear flicked. He didn't glance away from me, though his tone turned brisk as he addressed his brother. "When you randomly ask for one, that's true. The same doesn't apply to my mate."

Cymora demanded I rub her feet often enough, so I'd never ask something like that of another fae. "I can handle it," I said.

Marius didn't reply, yet he did. A soft growl communicating what he wouldn't, or couldn't, put to words. *"But I want to care for you."*

His various growls and grunts hadn't had meaning to me before. I could've been imagining it, but he kept inspecting me with a speculative air. Like he was wondering how to say what I'd already heard from his feral side.

Once dinner was finished, we strategized further, and my focus went back to Cymora. *She's not going to know what hit her.*

A house moth came in well after we'd dismissed Jani and Lon for the night. He bowed while balancing a plate stacked with letters in his palms. "Good evening, Prince! I have the daily correspondence for your pack," he said to Fal.

The dark elf smiled. "Hello, Villi. I see that duty has found me."

"It always will, Prince," Villi sighed playfully. He distributed the pile of letters. Most of them were for Fal, though a few were passed to Marius and Tormund. Two, he set aside for Kauz, which Fal slipped next to his stack. "And one for the new princess!"

The three alphas turned to watch as he set a letter in front of me. Whoever had written to me had placed "Lark" on the front, which narrowed down who could've written it to only a handful of fae.

"King Rennyn requests an immediate response," the house moth said to Fal, pointing out a specific letter.

"Of course he does," Fal mumbled. He opened the envelope and picked up the quill still resting on the plate.

I opened my letter and gave it a quick scan. Who would write to me? Well, who else but Laurel. Her handwriting was a shaky sprawl compared to the practiced neatness I was used to seeing from her.

Dearest Lark,

I need your help. They have me trapped in this room now, so I can't come talk to you in person.

I know Mom isn't the kindest fae. You and she never really got along. But—

I stopped reading there. Stars, I wanted to cast this note in the nearest fire.

"Well? Who is it from?" Tormund asked.

When I sighed my stepsister's name, Marius's lip curled. "Give it to me. I'll get rid of it for you."

"I'll burn it right now," the redcap put in.

"It's all right. It's not all that inspiring." I skimmed the rest, unmoved by what Laurel had to say. There wasn't a chance I was going to speak up for Cymora, no matter what she wrote. Maybe it was my new change of mindset, but I didn't find her plea all that strong.

Fal cleared his throat. "So, the conversation is scheduled for tomorrow evening in the moon parlor. Besides Cymora and Lark, there will be one representative from Pack Serian and one from Pack Sorles in the room. Who do you want there with you, *mo stór?*" He circled the quill to encompass the three princes.

That was an easy decision, though I spent a moment glancing at each male to disguise how quickly I'd come to an answer. Tormund gave me a pleading look, Marius shook his head, and Fal smiled with his usual confidence.

"You, Fal." He'd stayed through the whole interrogation, after all. He'd heard the worst of what my stepmother had to say already.

He tossed his hair. "An excellent choice," he said with Cymora's signature simper. I cringed immediately. "Sorry. Now I've got her mannerisms in my head."

"That's all right." I was just sensitive to anything that reminded me of her at this point. As soon as I folded up Laurel's letter and set it aside, Tormund reached for it. I had him promise not to set it on fire before letting him read it.

Fal sent Villi off with his response and turned to me as soon as the house moth left. "From the top, then?"

I put my fingertips to my forehead and set my mouth just so when I felt a whine coming on. *You have to do this. You have less than a day to get it right.*

The strangled whine still made enough of a noise that Fal tilted his head. "Ah, yes," he said in his impression of Cymora's acidic tone. "We did go through a phase of training away your omega noises. In your youth, I ordered you to pinch yourself if you made any sound of pain."

I glanced away, shoulders hunching with humiliation. She had done that, only revoking the order once the clusters of bruises on my thighs were more obvious than how I'd learned to suppress myself. But this was news to the other alphas.

A burst of heat kissed my cheek. Tormund's hands balled into fists on the table, tucking in his lengthening claws. His growl was full of redcap menace.

"Lark had to stay under my control until she was old enough to legally sign over her inheritance. She couldn't go around sounding like a kicked puppy every time we were in public together. Honestly, Tormund, think like an abuser," Fal simpered.

I wanted to say he was going too far, but he wasn't. If I lost control of tomorrow's conversation, she could be this nasty or say even worse. I had to be prepared to shut her down rather than rely on someone else to do it.

Kind of like what happened next. Marius snarled at the dark elf. His feral side stared out of his eyes, in complete control. He stood, and the next thing I knew, I was up in his arms and carried away from the table.

"Wait—fuck, don't just run off with her," Fal said behind us.

37
LARK

MARIUS DIDN'T STOP until he set me upright on the edge of my nest's bed. Fal was right behind us, trying to get his attention. Wrath crossed Marius's face the moment his brother passed the boundary into my nest. He turned, fists balled. "That was too much. Leave," he demanded in a feral rasp.

Fal put up his palms. "Can you make an attempt to think logically—"

"*Leave*," Marius barked. I suppressed another whine at the force behind it, even though I wasn't on the receiving end. He glanced over his shoulder, nostrils flaring. Oh stars, hearing the strangled hint of my distress had only made him more furious.

"I'm leaving." The dark elf nudged Tormund, who stood behind him. "*We're* leaving." He closed the privacy curtain, and they both slipped away. It was probably the first time I'd seen them back down to Marius like this.

Fal had barely scratched the surface of what Cymora had done to mold me into her perfect little servant, yet Marius had lost it. Now we were alone, and I could still sense the anger radiating off of him.

I used to think the only thing that'd predict Marius's mood was the flip of a coin. But even before he looked me in the eye, I knew what I was about to see: a male willing to lower himself in apology. And he did what I predicted, dropping to his knees and baring his throat in a quick flash.

He took my hand and placed my fingers on his unscarred cheek. Though he remained below me, his dilated gaze met mine rather than averting in submission. "No one speaks to my mate that way," he growled.

"It was just practice. He didn't mean it," I assured him.

His brows pinched. "No more... Not tonight."

"What do you want to do instead?" I traced his cheekbone with my thumb, taking advantage of being able to touch his face while Niall was in control.

He lidded his eyes and didn't reply. Now that the surprise had worn off, I was grateful for his outburst. I could worry about what Cymora would say tomorrow with a fresh mindset. The rest of the evening could go to something else.

Like practicing with him accepting my touch, if he could stand much more of this. I explored his face with my fingertips. His strong, stubbled jawline, the waves on the edge of his ear, and finally, the thick, frizzy length of his blue and green hair.

He'd show me someday that he was truly ready to bond when he let me acknowledge the damage done to him. I avoided his scar for now, so he wouldn't pull away. He purred all the while with a soft chuff marking the end of each exhale.

A little groan escaped him when I gave his scalp a tentative scratch. Oh, he liked that. I gave him more, using both hands.

"Around every turn, we keep ending up in this same place." His voice was the rich timbre of his princely side. "With you comforting me."

"I'm glad I get to remind you that you're not alone anymore." I echoed Kauz's wisdom because it'd always resonated with me. Hopefully it did with him too.

When he opened his eyes, they were back to normal. "Allow me to care for you in return. Let me take away your bruises. Please. I want to show you that you can rely on me as your mate."

I was learning, one action at a time, that this was how he showed his loyalty. I nodded and let my hands drop into my lap.

He shook out his hair as he eased to his feet. "I'll be right back. In the meantime, take off your shirt and lie on your front."

He left my nest, and I followed his instructions, only because I knew he wouldn't have access to my armpits otherwise. I left my breast band on. A hum of masculine voices drifted outside of the nest, and Marius reentered several minutes later with annoyance etched across his scarred face. He'd retrieved the wound salve and the other wooden pot he'd brought to my suite.

"Fal and Tormund say good night. They're really leaving this time. They were just eavesdropping to be sure I wasn't going to have a wild fit."

"Oh, so they heard…"

"Everything." He sighed and worked off his boots before removing the shoe on my left foot. "That's pack life. Very little privacy." He was softening his voice again, as I was coming to prefer from him.

He climbed onto the bed behind me, his knees on either side of my hips. Catching a floating faelight, he leaned over my back and inspected the skin under my arms.

Honestly, it wasn't so bad, not compared to the pain of the silencing band. But he cared for the bruises as if they were the most serious of wounds. He worked the salve into my skin, his touch businesslike, then gave the opposite side the same thorough treatment.

As the tingles faded, along with the soreness, I murmured, "All healed. Thank you."

"I've only just gotten started." He put the lid back on the salve and uncapped the other, spreading an unscented lotion between his palms. I made an "eep" of surprise when he started massaging my back. I'd just said to myself that I'd never ask for this, but maybe he'd noticed that I needed it.

Certain muscle groups hurt, especially at first, but the pain wasn't something he created purposefully. He worked with a firm touch and enough patience to focus on problem areas until there was no pain at all. I made the occasional hum of enjoyment, and he answered in quiet sounds, along with a rekindling of his purr that vibrated through his fingers and across my skin.

I snuck a look over my shoulder. He was relaxed, somewhere between prince and feral, content in a way that seemed new. The tenderness in his expression echoed other loving looks I'd witnessed between mates and now experienced with a lover.

The tingles spreading through my chest had nothing to do with the wound salve. While I knew he wanted me to claim his one kelpie bond, I hadn't realized how deep the change in his emotions ran. He was hardly recognizable as the snarling male I'd done everything to avoid on the train ride here.

And since he had me lying facedown, I didn't think he intended for me to notice. That seemed like a quintessentially Marius thing to do. I stopped peeking back at him, though my wings gave away how I was feeling. They started opening and closing slowly of their own volition like they belonged on a perching butterfly.

Marius shifted away with a confused grunt.

"That means you're doing a good job," I whispered. *It means I like you. A lot. See, I can hide my feelings in plain sight too.*

He made a wordless murmur and worked around them. By the time he was done, I was a boneless heap. Painless. And I couldn't move even if I wanted to, which I didn't.

"A really good job," I mumbled into my pillow.

He nuzzled my neck, then rested his body atop mine. All that muscle made him a heavy male, but my nest's cushioning protected me from getting crushed. I was pinned, again. "*Mate,*" he said with just a low noise.

The weight of his arousal pressed against the swell of my ass. I shifted, my pussy warming at the intimacy of this pin. His mouth brushed my shoulder, the softness of his lips pillowing a hint of fangs. The promise of a bite made me slicker than I'd have expected.

I lifted and rolled my hips, notching his erection between my clothed thighs. His growl stuttered with the trembling of his body. Then he nipped me hard, drawing out my gasp. "I didn't ask to care for you with an ulterior motive," he rasped.

"Consider it a reward?" I pressed against him again with a needy trill, which he answered with a rumble that shook me to my core.

Oh yes. More of that.

"No." He eased off my back. "Turn over. I need to see you."

Though he'd made my legs shaky, I flipped over, and he loomed over me with one arm braced under my wing. Heat blazed from his eyes as he took in my expression.

All he was sure to see was yearning. I wanted to relieve the need tenting the front of his trousers. And I would've reached for it to finally see an alpha knot for myself, but he'd already said no.

His expression shifted to disbelief. "I want you. So fucking badly. But I'm here to please you, not the other way around. I don't want you to think I'm trying to take advantage—"

I risked another nip by placing my finger over his lips. "I know. It's okay. You said no, and that's the end of it."

This gave him pause for a moment before he licked my finger. I took it away from his face. "If your desire for me survives the light of day..." Though he had a doubtful slant to his mouth, he murmured, "Perhaps tomorrow."

"Nothing about how I feel will change tomorrow," I said with surety.

A moan escaped his lips. "Tell me you mean it." He trailed his fingertips up my leg to my waistband. That predatory gaze fixed on a distraction, the modest swells of my breasts through their thin covering. They rose and fell with my panting breaths.

"I mean it. But...tomorrow, you're going to have competition. Your brothers will be around."

"Good."

I fluttered my eyelashes with surprise.

"I'd be happy to have them close if you chose to mate with me." He brushed his fingers over my shoulder, showing me a smear of blood. "I may wear the trappings of a prince, but I'm an animal, p'nixie. A beast. Someone has to look out for you if I lose control. Someone has to protect you before I become dangerously obsessed."

"You're not going to hurt me," I said with the same level of certainty. "No matter if it's Marius or Niall in control."

"Yet I already have," he murmured. He picked up the wound salve and dabbed a bit on the twin pinpricks he'd left on my shoulder. Then he kissed me, making it a slow and sweet brush of our mouths.

I longed for more even as he pulled away. "Tomorrow, then." I sighed. He dipped his chin in agreement. "Dangerously obsessed?"

"Your attention is a thrill, and your touch"—he took my hand and rested it over his heartbeat—"addictive. No, it's more than that. Your warmth, your *skin*, against mine. That's what I'm starting to crave."

My pussy clenched with a pulse of heat. Oh, he shouldn't say such things while my pre-heat was more active.

"As for danger..." He hesitated, then shook his head. "I don't know how far my cravings for you will go once we mate."

"What do you mean?" I asked gently, sensing that wasn't the full truth.

"It would be better if you didn't know about my newest argument with Niall. That's all I want to say on the matter."

Well, he is entitled to fight with himself occasionally. I decided to let it go and reached back to unhook my breast band.

"If you take off your shirt, we could sleep with your skin against mine." As my breasts rolled free and his attention sharpened, all the moisture evaporated from my mouth. Perhaps this was a step too far.

"Aye," he breathed. "I would like that." He sat up and pulled off his shirt. I tried not to gape, but wow. If Kauz's chest was a map of strength, then Marius had topography, his muscles defined in every line of his abs. I'd caught a glimpse of him shirtless from above, but that'd been before I'd come to view him with any kind of interest.

His skin wasn't a uniform blue below his collar; speckles of green covered his chest like irregular freckles. He noticed my admiring perusal and posed with his chest lifted. The gold bars piercing his nipples glinted under the faelights.

He crooked his finger. Stars, what a surreal moment, to see Marius smirking and teasing. "Touch me a little. Then we should rest for tomorrow."

I didn't hesitate to explore his sculpted chest, down the soft texture of his skin and ridges of old scars I felt rather than saw. He didn't have much give to him under the surface.

He cupped one of my breasts and pressed enough to see that it was just softness and give. I knew he was untouched, but his perusal turned almost playful as he bounced and squeezed my modest orbs. "*Nice*," he chirped.

I sputtered a laugh and nearly fell off the bed as my mirth deepened. He had to catch me. "These are nice," I echoed in the midst of giggles.

He whistled to dim the faelights until they were just a hint of illumination. To hide his embarrassment? Maybe. But after he snorted at me, I could feel him laughing too, until the fit faded. "You understand Niall's nonsense," he murmured.

"Sometimes."

"Nice," he practically drawled.

He pulled me into him until we lay skin to skin. I tucked into the line of his body, sighing in contentment. *This* was safety, resting in the arms of my protector. He released one of Niall's softer growls and spanned his hand over my back, pressing us closer together.

I BLINKED awake in the dark of night. I was still in Marius's arms, his limbs heavy around me. The heat of his body and the smell of mint and waterlilies put me straight back to sleep.

Sometime later, I woke again on my own, tucked into a patch of body heat where the kelpie had been. I glanced around, feeling like something was missing, other than the alpha. I whined, but he soon returned, still shirtless, shortly after I'd wiped away the bleariness from my eyes.

He slid back under the covers with me. "Good morning. I gave the moonbloom water. It's getting some sun right now," he told me. That's what was gone—I'd kept his gift on my bedside table.

"Good morning," I whispered back, snuggling up to him again.

We shared an unhurried kiss; then we didn't speak for a while. He lay there and admired me, his pupils adjusting as he shared the moment with Niall. He sifted my hair between his fingers, and we both purred in contentment.

I explored his body with my fingertips, glad he didn't shudder with oversensitivity. He breathed the occasional moan instead as I found where he was most sensitive along his chest and back. The air was tinged with his aroused musk, though he kept his hips canted back.

I hesitated at the line of his trousers. It was tomorrow, after all. He took my hand and pressed it below his clothes, to a spot along his hip. His breathing quickened as I rubbed a raised line on his skin, like a scar if one pulsed with the drumbeat of his heart. "My mark. For when you claim me."

I circled my thumb over this section of his mark. He bit his lip, tensing with pleasure. Just seeing his desire sent a thrill of heat through me. Emboldened, I reached for his erection next. We shifted together, and I ended up on my back, fingers ghosting over his length while he braced above me, fangs pressed to the curve of my neck. He growled low. "*Mine.*"

The next moment, he was gone. He disentangled from me with lightning speed and whipped his head toward my nest's privacy curtain. The tone of his growling sharpened into pure aggression as the fabric swished from the touch of someone on the other side.

"Stars," I muttered, ready to shred one of my blankets in frustration. My pussy practically wept at the interruption.

But then the newcomer spoke, and my heart leapt. "Lark?" That was Kauz's voice! Marius's growling faded into an annoyed chuff.

My dreams from last night were a smudged memory, but I recognized that this was partially my doing. I'd visited his sleeping mind and shared news of my upcoming conversation with Cymora. He'd done *something...*

"Hi, Kauz. Should you be awake?" I replied.

"Good morning, sweetheart. May I come in?"

"Not yet," Marius growled. "She's not dressed." He handed me a shirt, and I slipped it on, sleepy enough not to realize it was his until his scent enveloped me. I stood and adjusted the dark cloth, which fit me like a loose, overlong tunic. The kelpie looked entirely too pleased with himself as he took me in.

I was just as happy with my view of him. The first floor of my nest was dim and enclosed. The light of day drifted down from the second-story windows, enough to caress the bare planes of Marius's chest. He was never getting this shirt back.

"She's not?" I wished I could've seen Kauz's face; he sounded shocked. He'd missed a lot while he was asleep.

"Come in, please. You've invited," I said.

Kauz slipped inside the nest. Though his silvery eyes still lacked the starry nebulae I was used to seeing, he looked healthy enough to be awake. The shadows under his eyes were receding, and the gray pallor of depletion was giving way to his usual purple hue. He'd washed, changed, and combed out his white hair, which had grown just long enough to part.

I was so thrilled to see him up and active that my wings quivered. He closed the distance between us, sweeping me up to meet his lips. A tingle of Always danced along my tongue. Looping my arms around his shoulders, I clung to him as we kissed.

Kauz broke the lip-lock to ask, "Where are you going?"

I glanced up, only noticing Marius heading for the nest's exit because of Kauz's question. "Privacy," the kelpie answered.

"No need," he said in his serene way, plucking at my borrowed shirt. "It seems I'm the one intruding."

Marius worked his jaw. "We haven't mated," he said in an undertone.

He could've left the assumption unanswered. With his scent and shirt covering me, I was marked as his. Besides, there was still an impressive bulge in his trousers as evidence of what Kauz had interrupted.

"Really?" the dream warden asked.

I nodded and said, "Really. Outside of my dreams, I'm still untouched."

This drew a disbelieving laugh out of Kauz, and he held me a little tighter. "What? Why? Wait, no, let me guess. All three of my brothers have hardly left your side since you woke up."

"It's a little more complicated than that. But, um, yeah."

"For her protection, I'm open to the idea of sharing her—"

Marius cut himself off when the privacy curtain shifted. Fal poked his head into the nest. "Discussing sex? Without me?" He smacked his lips playfully.

"When did you get here?" I practically squeaked.

I was already picturing what "sharing" might actually entail, and my core was heated at the images it conjured. As an omega with four mates, I would need to take the pack. And when I was in heat, I would *need* the pack.

He tilted his head, pointing with one of his elfin ears. "I was in the next room over. Tormund and I are by drafting potential 'fuck off, fishling' letters for you to choose from."

"Good morning, li'l bird!" the redcap in question exclaimed, drawing the curtain back more to reveal him beside Fal.

"Well, we were," the dark elf hedged. "Then, to my *infinite* disappointment, I heard a certain someone is still untouched."

Marius snorted. "What did I tell you, p'nixie? Not much privacy in pack life."

I was pulled into said pack life in what felt like an instant. Kauz's pair of house moths came and went from my suite, moving in a portion his things. He'd been the first to say he'd sleep in my nest nightly, and he'd meant it. But as Tormund predicted, the moment I said yes to him, suddenly, the rest of my mates wanted the same privilege. I wasn't about to say no to them. They also had their house moths moving in some of their belongings.

While the mothkin bustled about, we sat in my dining nook together and resumed preparing me to see my stepmother. Kauz spent some time listening and catching up before he spoke. "If you come to this talk angry, Cymora has already won." His silvery gaze met mine. "There is a place of hurt within you, Lark. A hint of a small child that remains frozen in time after she made an ill-fated deal. And do you know what she wants now that the deal is broken?"

I swallowed thickly. "Answers."

"Closure," Kauz corrected. "You may catch a few glimmers of it with the right strategy. Cymora will expect a few things when seated across from you. Your accusations, anger, and pain. Everything she hasn't allowed you to be. I recommend that you put her off guard with the one thing she won't expect."

I knew he was right. She'd always managed to get the upper hand in any argument when I'd been young and angry, until she'd wrung the fight out of me one order at a time.

"Apathy?" I guessed.

"Something close. Something we all would reasonably fear in her shoes. That nothing she could say or do will change the course of her life. Her death is certain. She will die if she is nasty to you. Or she will die kissing your feet." He set his mouth in sympathy of the pained sound I made.

"I've kissed her feet enough." Now, I was ready to see her sweat.

38
LARK

THE DIFFERENCE between yesterday's preparation session and today's was night and day. Kauz's arrival back into the waking world brought the sunshine streaming in behind him. But he tired visibly past noon, his voice becoming a flat wisp.

Fal exaggerated a shudder. "It's the old Kauz. Why don't you take a nap before the big moment?"

The dream warden said in a mumble, "Then I won't wake up again. And I'm not missing this."

"I'll figure out how to wake you up," Tormund offered. Kauz still shook his head.

"Suit yourself. Dinner should be interesting." Fal's gaze flicked to me. "I realized we're going into the perfect setup for a 'spontaneous' kings' dinner. Protocol restored. Step one, presenting you to our mother." He ticked it off on his fingers. "Step two, we court you. Step three, you meet our fathers in a formal dinner. But since you've already met them and they're prone to meddling if given half a chance, we're going to be swept into the kings' dinner tonight."

He was saying this like it wasn't a big event, but I went rigid in my seat. "How formal is it going to be?" I asked nervously.

Kauz gave me what was meant to be a reassuring smile, though fatigue pulled it back down. "I sincerely doubt our fathers will give you a hard time. The kings' dinner is meant to be a test for us. How well do we know the future Queen of Serian?"

"Well enough to know not to call her that yet," Marius growled. "Don't panic, p'nixie."

I was trying not to. I had fond, if fading, memories of all four kings. It wasn't just the formal environment of a dinner; they would also be seeing me again as the future Queen of Serian. A role for which I clearly was not suited.

"We won't be expected to take the thrones for another fifty years at least," Fal said almost directly to the fearful thoughts spiraling through my mind. "It's customary for the next queen to apprentice to the current one for at least that long. No one expects a new princess to be ready to rule right away. That would be fucking disastrous for all of Serian."

I sighed, going nearly limp with relief. "I was worried about that."

"We're going to do a better job of communicating." He stood and pushed in his chair. "Starting now."

His expression had an intent edge as he crossed the table to my side. Something unspoken passed between the princes. It had to be over their pack bond, as I didn't feel anything except for the rapid shift in tension through the room.

I swallowed. "Did you have something in mind?"

Fal's smile spread to show his fangs. "You're coming with me. Now that you've figured out tonight's conversation, I'm going to give you the confidence special."

The what? I made a confused squeak. Marius scowled, Kauz rolled his eyes, and Tormund sighed wistfully.

Fal plucked me out of my seat much like Marius had done yesterday. "Give us a bit of privacy, would you? We'll be in her nest," he said over his shoulder.

"Ten minutes," the kelpie said, but it sounded like a warning.

"Why so generous? You should've given him five," Kauz commented.

Marius growled in agitation.

"Ah, ah. He said ten," Fal sing-songed, carrying me away quicker.

"What's happening?" I asked in an undertone.

His demeanor shifted as he put a door between us and his brothers. He wetted his lips, eyes hooding as his feline gaze dropped to mine. "I wanted to get you away from that table for a bit. There is such a thing as over preparing, even in the short time we have."

Oh, that's all he wanted? No, it couldn't be, not with how the other princes reacted.

He took me back to my nest and placed me on the edge of the bed. "Communication time," he said in a soft voice. "I love how this room smells already."

My nostrils flared. I rarely noticed my own scent, but with a deliberate sniff, I caught hints of chocolate and honey crackers entwined with Marius and Tormund's pheromones and...*oh*. An undertone of my sugary arousal. His sensitive alpha nose must've homed in on it.

"Your turn," he said.

"Hmm?"

"We're communicating. Tell me something I need to hear." He slid onto the bed next to me, putting his arm around my waist. "Sliver for your... nay, I can do better than that. Kiss for your thoughts?"

"Um. I hope I'm prepared enough for tonight."

He leaned over, his mouth brushing mine in a featherlight tease. "New rule. No Cymora for ten minutes. What else is in that head of yours?"

"If I said nothing?"

"There's always something, tricksy p'nixie. Don't be shy," he coaxed.

Our foreheads were nearly brushing, breaths mingling, as he waited for a more serious answer. Too bad my thoughts had slowed when I'd become distracted by the smallest thing—his thumb circling on my hip. It could've been deliberate or an idle movement betraying the quick thoughts darting through his clever mind.

I ended up saying my most pressing concern out loud. "I wish I could walk."

He rewarded me with another kiss, but I wasn't done. As I continued, he nuzzled my cheek and kissed a path across my face.

"I just...I want to be more normal. I've had several itches for *days* that I can't reach, and I can't start crutching around with at least one of you trying to carry me, and I *still* haven't seen the palace or the city or the stables or..." I let myself drift off with a small intake of breath. He'd licked the sensitive spot under my jaw. The merest whisper of his fangs against my skin sent a jolt of pleasure straight to my core.

He lifted his head, an odd expression on his face. "My mother, who is the fearsome Queen of Serian, lest you've forgotten."

"Uh huh."

"Also complains that her alpha mates try to carry her everywhere."

I snorted in disbelief. "That can't be true."

"Oh, aye. After the longest, most trying days, one of my fathers is guaranteed to just..." He made a scooping motion with his free hand before settling it on my knee. "They try to be subtle about it and keep it to the royal spaces. But I'm here to swear to you, carrying around a beloved omega is one hundred percent an alpha instinct. Any alpha who would tell you otherwise is either lying or hasn't met their scent match yet."

I was still skeptical, despite the ring of truth he swore to. I'd just need to see it for myself.

"And as soon as we're finished here, I'll write to Thalas about your cast," he added.

"Thank you. Your turn."

He hummed. "This is harder than I thought. I so rarely get time alone with you. And to waste it talking about myself..."

Fal could easily spend our ten minutes by talking if given half a chance. His gift of gab was a talent I admired. But his evasive answer made me think he wasn't all that interested in continuing the game-like conversation he'd started.

I reached for him, stroking the side of his face and admiring his bold, elfin features and the gleam in his sapphire eyes. His skin was perfectly smooth under my fingertips. Unlike his brothers, it seemed he didn't grow facial hair at all, as his chin lacked the roughness of regular contact with a razor.

He leaned into my touch. "How about this," he said in his low purr.

"I think you're the loveliest sprite I've ever laid my eyes upon. Delicate on the outside, strong within." Reaching over, he rested his palm over my heartbeat. My wings quivered as his fingers drifted to find the tightened bud of my nipple. He traced its outline through my clothes. "Your turn."

"Fal, what are we doing here?" I murmured.

He tilted his head in the other direction with an expression of faux innocence. "Communicating?"

I couldn't help a little giggle. "Okay. Right. I, um, wish I knew how to do this. Make you feel this way with just a touch...and a look." My inexperience seemed inescapable.

"You do, *mo stór*, though not purposefully. If you knew how to wield your charms to their full extent...that would be magnificent. I'll teach you. Then you can devastate me daily, just as fate intended." He winked.

"Is that..." I fixated on him saying that I affected him too. "Really?"

He chuckled, smiling with his usual mischief. "And you're adorable as well. I want you to know I've held back and given my brothers time with you first. Even though I thought it might kill me. In return, they've given me frustration, just as I should've known they would." He sighed and nuzzled me, cheek to cheek.

I kissed him this time, coaxing him into a tangle of tongues. His taste was strong, flooding my senses with grass, warm sunshine, and an edge of fresh male musk. He drew back to murmur, "May I have the honor of tasting you first?"

My pussy practically answered the question for me, flooding with warmth. Greedy thing. His eyes darkened as he caught a breath of my scent. With his feline gaze intensifying like he was about to devour me, I only grew slicker. "Oh, yes," I gasped. "What do I need to do?"

"Nothing. Some things are free, my dear," he teased, going down on his knees before me.

Somehow, he'd already gotten my pants undone and shimmied them and my panties down my legs at the same time. That *had* to be a talent, or some serious experience. He ended up freeing one leg and left my clothes bunched up above my cast.

I sat self-consciously, my knees pointed toward one another. Caressing my bare thighs with graceful fingers, he spread goosebumps over my skin. Nerves and excitement warred within me as he breathed in the arousal already glistening on my lower lips. Dozens of worries filled my mind, all 'what ifs' that he silenced with a low, possessive growl.

"Even the full ten minutes was never going to be enough. I could spend days down here with your flower." He met my gaze and swiped his tongue, outlining the curve of his lips and the point of one fang.

"I could be convinced to stay here for days." Especially if he kept looking at me with such a smolder. I spread my legs in invitation, and he tugged to position my hips on the edge of the bed.

In Osme Fen, females often talked about their mates, gossiping details about their bedroom habits while laundering clothes or preparing food for the evening meal. I'd gleaned that there was an imbalance of enthusiasm for certain acts. While males wanted their cocks sucked like they were candy logs at Yuletide, there was a lack of returning the favor, or it was done halfheartedly at best. Like tasting a female's intimates was less desired by all parties.

I assumed that was universal. And as was said about assumptions, I was dead wrong.

He eased my leg and cast over his shoulders. Even as his mouth greeted the heated petals of my sex, his thumbs drew swirling patterns up my inner thighs. He licked the seam of my pussy bottom to top, laving at the bud of nerves at its apex. The groan he emitted, like it was his first drink of pure water after days at sea, was nearly as gratifying as the pleasure sizzling straight to my core.

I moaned in echo, not just from how he made me feel. There was something intoxicating about watching him occupy that talented mouth with something new. With me as his full focus. If I emerged from my nest a more confident omega, it was because his enthusiasm for my pleasure was so palpable.

My fingers were fisted on either side of my knees. He freed my right hand and placed it on the back of his head. I didn't question it, just grabbed some of his long hair and tugged when another wave of pleasure threatened to leave me breathless. His answering gasp leapt straight to my core.

Heat and need quickened within me. I spurred him on, my heel digging into his back, each flex silently begging for more. The promised peak was coming so fast. Too fast, it seemed, as he pulled his mouth off me to blow cool air over my folds. My sugar-kissed scent swirled around us. His purr vibrated through my fingertips, mirroring the enjoyment on his face after he inhaled.

He replaced the sudden chill with the warmth of his mouth. I trembled with a mix of sensations as his heated breath washed over me. A lusty trill escaped my lips. No matter what, I was primed to desire his knot inside me next. The scent of his arousal was leaking from him, twining with mine to make a perfect match of sunshine and melting chocolate.

Another rush of cool air. Goosebumps spread over me from crown to toes. "F-Fal," I gasped.

He breathed a soft growl in reply. His expression was tight with desire, mouth glossy from my slick. With his hair and clothes disheveled and a savage kind of satisfaction on his face, he was all alpha in a way counter to his usual primped and polished manner. My omega instincts quivered. He was my mate, *mine...* I should offer him more than just a taste.

He replaced any lingering chill with his warm tongue, delving into me with firm strokes. Then he closed his lips around my clit with just the right amount of pressure.

Sparks of light danced before my eyes as I came. I thought for half an incoherent moment that I'd died and seen the stars. Pleasure coursed through my body in waves of sensation. My fingers clenched in his hair for some anchor once my soul decided it hadn't fled my body.

I went from being as tightly drawn as a bowstring to limp with bliss. "Wow." *What a ride.*

He glanced up while licking my pussy clean. "Now for the confidence special," he said huskily.

"That wasn't...?" I managed.

"Oh, no. That was just for fun." He pressed a kiss to my inner thigh. "I have an offer for you. If you demolish Cymora in your conversation today, as we've planned, I'm going to bring you back here tonight and...I won't be alone in celebrating your victory with pleasure."

He faced the privacy curtain as he added a little louder, "Isn't that right?" A growl answered him, which could've been from either of his alpha brothers.

"That needs to be a door," I muttered, flush for a new reason.

Pack life had embraced me, all right, along with its lack of privacy. Fal noticed me scrambling to fit my leg back into my clothes and helped me get them back in place.

"Is she decent?" Kauz asked on the other side of the curtain.

Stars, are they all out there?

Fal stood, putting me at about eye level with the erection straining his pants. He angled his body away from the nest's entrance. "Aye, get in here."

To answer my question, yes, all three of my other mates were waiting right outside the nest. And in similar states of arousal, which only intensified when they came in and scented the air.

"Here's my plan, Lark. I'm going to celebrate your victory by dousing myself in chocolate sauce as your dessert tonight. But you know what's better than one delight? Four of them."

"That's true," Tormund put in.

"Is chocolate sauce a metaphor for something?" I asked.

Fal grinned. "Oh, goodness me. Would you prefer fruit sauce? No, really. It's about time for pack love. Marius and Tormund don't trust themselves otherwise, and someone's got to help Kauz stay awake."

"He doesn't always speak for us." Kauz made this pointed remark at Fal, who spread his palms in a languid shrug. Marius grunted in agreement, his predatory gaze fixed on me, unblinking.

Tormund stood back from the others, smoke and heated vapor streaming from his mouth. His struggle was apparent, the fires in his eyes igniting and dimming even as I watched. I tried to ignore the tension in the air and fluttered my wings, flying the short distance to him to clasp his palm between my hands to help calm him. An overheated blast of air washed over me. His gaze fixed on my face, and those eerie flames danced in his pupils, growing hotter…

Callused hands snatched me by the hips, pulling me away. Marius clutched me to his chest and aimed a warning snap of his teeth at the redcap. Tormund answered with a growl full of fiery menace. I whimpered, stuck between them as their aggression rose.

"I'll give you both nightmares if you start fighting over our mate *in her nest*," Kauz hissed.

Despite everything, they took a step away from one another. "Honestly," Fal sighed. He hadn't moved other than to massage the back of his neck. "Maybe I'll keep her to myself, then."

"Nay," Tormund rumbled.

"No. She's *mine*," Marius growled nearly in the same breath.

Kauz rested a hand on the kelpie's arm. "She's ours," he corrected in his usual calm tone. Though he chuffed in warning, Marius relaxed his snarl and placed me on my feet. He eased back for Kauz to wrap his wing and arm around me.

Fal said, "Marius, Tormund, you've told me that you want the support of the pack while exploring your attraction to Lark. I have a deal for you."

"Aye, I don't want to hurt the li'l bird," Tormund agreed.

"What's the deal?" Marius asked, sounding far more wary.

"You can have exactly that. I just want to knot her first. In return, I would be willing to move my date with her to last," the dark elf said.

Kauz nuzzled me, his brow pinching. "That sounds like Lark's decision."

"Are you saying that we mate...all at once?" I asked, trying to wrap my head around what Fal was really saying.

"As it pleases you, p'nixie," Marius answered. "I only want the pack to pull me off of you at the first sign of danger."

Not that there will be danger, I thought, though I kept it to myself.

"Same. If my monstrous side comes out, I want the pack there to act in your best interests, li'l bird." Tormund had a rumbly edge to his voice, as if his fiery form was still trying to break loose.

"And I saved a little something for you," Fal said.

I gestured for Kauz to close his other wing around me, sealing me into his embrace. He ducked into the circle of leather and stars, looking at me curiously as I whispered in as small a voice as I could, "I trust them. They don't need to do all this."

He tipped his chin in agreement, tapping his forehead and then under his eyes. "See for themselves," he mouthed.

"What are you two doing?" Tormund asked.

"I'm conferring with my Always," I answered.

And, as always, he was taking his brothers' oddities in stride. I read Kauz's lips as we continued our more private conversation. "You'll be okay. You know how alphas are. They think their strength is earth shattering. They see the reality of your size and strength and default to pack protection."

I giggled, nodding. I did know how alphas were. It was nice to have someone to commiserate with.

"It'd help if two of them weren't virgins," he added. "They'd at least know their limitations."

I hugged Kauz around his torso, saying, "Thanks."

He was halfway through murmuring the promise of Always as a couple other things happened all at once. Fal asked, "So, do we have a deal, then?"

There was a clatter in the next room over. "Princess, um, and Princes, you have visitors," Jani squeaked.

I heard this for myself, muffled by a couple walls. "Yoo-hoo," Rennyn called in Theli. "I'm looking for my missing lads! Has anyone seen them?"

39
LARK

As one, the princes cursed. The mood in the room chilled so fast it was as if a bucket of ice water was dropped in our midst to splatter everywhere.

"Why is your father here?" Marius growled at Fal in accusation.

The dark elf threw his hands up. "Why are you asking me?"

Kauz released a heavy sigh. "Okay, it's not the best timing, but there's no need to panic. We'll talk to him. You clean yourself up, Fal."

I nodded. I'd probably die of humiliation if he didn't scrub his face thoroughly before he saw his father.

None of my mates seemed all that surprised that Rennyn was here, though. *Maybe he often comes by unannounced.* That seemed to fit the dark elf king's style.

I made it about two flutters of my wings toward the privacy curtain before Tormund scooped me up. "I've got you. Let's see what's happening."

Well, this particular alpha instinct was alive and well. I reminded myself that Fal had described it as a need to carry around a "beloved omega" and relaxed into Tormund's arms.

Just out of our path stood Jani, wringing her hands. She reported that there were three kings waiting for us.

"Wonder who's missing," Fal remarked on his way to my bathroom.

The rest of us moved to my receiving room as a group. It was a good thing we had a small army of mothkin lingering in my suite, as most of them were already bustling to move seats and prepare refreshments.

The three kings waited just inside the room. Rennyn, with a gleam of impatience in his ruby eyes as he worked his lucky coin between his fingers. Thalas, who had his hands laced before him, waiting serenely. And behind them both, an absolute mountain of an alpha.

"Hi, Dad!" Tormund exclaimed.

Instead of just Theodred answering him, all three did, saying hello at nearly the same time with varying levels of enthusiasm.

Rennyn elbowed Thalas. "It worked! I found our missing lads." It seemed the kings had chosen to speak Theli for my benefit.

Thalas slanted an amused look his way before stepping forward. "Kauz, you're awake," he said. The two of them crashed into a big, wing-tangled hug.

I motioned to Tormund, trying to get him to take me to my crutches, which were propped against a nearby wall. He gestured back. He wanted me to say hello to his father first.

Fal rejoined us on cat-silent feet. His voice announced him before he stepped around Marius. "To what do we owe the pleasure?" He'd fixed his suit into immaculate lines and cleaned away any evidence that he'd just had his face between my thighs.

"Maybe I just wanted to see you, sunshine lad." Rennyn ticked off the possibilities, tapping his coin against his fingertips as he went, gaining momentum. "Or annoy you, wild boy. Or watch this reunion between Serian's calmest bats. Or maybe! To get my spine realigned by Tor-Tor, except his arms are already occupied by the omega I'm really here to see. Hi, Lark."

"Hi," I giggled.

"Guess what," he said brightly. As I drew breath, he answered himself. "We're getting you out of that cast."

Thalas raised one of his fingers, turning away from Kauz for a moment. "Maybe. I can't guarantee her wounds are healed."

"We're getting you out of that cast, at least momentarily," Rennyn amended. He tilted his head back to look up at Theodred, who raised a brow. "Are you going to say anything, or just stand there all intimidating-like?"

"Only if you're finished prattling." His voice fit his size, a deep rumble that reminded me of a rockfall.

"He who controls the air…"

"*Ach*." Theodred made the scoffing noise extra guttural.

"…controls the narrative," Fal was supplying.

"I've done such things much quicker with a weapon in hand."

Rennyn puffed out his chest. "Aye. Big sword. Hit good."

The redcap king pushed him. Laughing, Rennyn caught his stumble with a dancer's grace and headed for the refreshments. The mothkin had set up a hasty selection and a tea service on the coffee table nestled between the pair of couches in my receiving room.

While most of the group followed his lead and moved toward the couches too, Theodred remained in place, and Tormund carried me over to him. I was thankful of the boost my mate gave me, as I was able to look the king in the eye where otherwise it would've been impossible.

Tormund was the largest male I knew…but his father had him beat, as he was built like a wall of solid muscle. He hadn't changed much, actually. Age hadn't softened a single line, only lengthened his forward-facing horns by a fraction and faded some of the red vibrancy in his hair to orange shades.

He wore a sleeveless shirt and knee-length shorts, showing off the pairs of blood-red knot tattoos that circled each limb in helix patterns. They matched the color of his irises. As a child, I hadn't been unnerved by the miniscule yet eternal white flames in his pupils and had even complimented his fiery stare. His rage had to be a breath away if he wanted it, yet here he was, untransformed.

He dipped his chin in acknowledgment. "Daughter."

He recited a few lines of Serri poetry, which Tormund joined in on. They had a ring of something I'd heard before in the distant past, probably from Theodred himself. I understood about half of it. Dewdrops on morning blooms, the kiss of a summer breeze, and the nature of butterflies to alight on a peaceful perch if only for a moment.

"And now in what feels like a moment, the butterfly I knew has grown," he said.

I shook off the nerves threatening to steal through me. He had a dangerous presence. But I remembered how safe I'd felt with him as a child, and as a sensitive little omega, I'd known instinctively which alphas were safe and which ones weren't. I smiled at him and said, "It's nice to see you again, Dad."

"And you as well." The redcap king drew a knife from his belt and offered it hilt-first to Tormund. "I shall let my son do the honors of freeing you." With a jerk of his chin, he motioned for us to join the rest of the group.

We headed for the empty seat on the couch, between Fal and Marius. Tormund set me down gently. Thalas stood to the side, while Kauz and Rennyn waited behind us.

I tried not to sound nervous as I said, "I hope I get to walk after this."

"You all must've been reading my mind. I was just about to request a peek under the cast," Fal said.

"Most of us wanted to see Lark step into her meeting today on her own two feet," Rennyn remarked. When I glanced up at him, grateful for the sentiment, he flicked his lucky coin over, and I caught it. I circled my thumb on the flat gold surface, hoping some luck rubbed off on me.

Tormund knelt and repositioned my cast so my leg was extended. He showed me the knife. It was shaped for opening casts; no thicker than my knuckle, with a dull side to protect skin.

I nodded with a smile of encouragement. Fal took my hand, pressing the lucky coin between our palms. Marius covered my knee with his palm.

Kauz leaned over to rest his hand on my shoulder. The softest of growls lifted from him when Rennyn mirrored the movement on my other side, and the dark elf king laughed, sounding genuinely amused.

The cast parted with minimal sawing, and Tormund eased it off my leg. I held my breath as it slid away to reveal an intricate wrap of condensed essence. It was black with silver sparks, Thalas's magic, and the winged fae nudged Tormund out of the way and knelt to take his place.

"Moment of truth. If there's any hint of essence bleeding from you, you'll need to go back into a cast." He took hold of the edge of his magic.

Thalas slowly unwrapped my leg. Itchiness hit my exposed skin, which was visibly dry. Those itchy spots prickled with pain as I forced myself not to set my claws upon them immediately.

The dream warden king tugged when he reached the top of my ankle, revealing a new scar shaped vaguely like a diamond, or the first spike of the silencing band. He leaned in to inspect it before continuing to unwrap my foot. My chest froze each time he stopped to look more closely at me.

"Breathe, kid," Rennyn said, squeezing my shoulder.

More encouragement rose from the group as my foot came free inch by inch until I was wiggling and spreading my toes with a sigh of relief. My ankle looked...well, not like the swollen mass I'd been tricked into thinking it resembled. A pattern of scars looped around my foot and ankle.

I undid the shoe on my left foot, comparing the size and shape of my ankles with a hum. Marius growled softly as he inspected the differences too, however slight they were.

"Your wounds are sealed. Try putting weight on your feet," Thalas suggested.

My palms were damp with nerves as he motioned for me to stand. The room seemed to hold its breath. Thousands of instances of agony flashed in my mind's eye from moments just like this one, when the *olcanus* dug in and restricted my ankle.

But that awful chain was gone, and so was the pain as I stood. I took a step and wobbled. Then I took another and another, my gait smoothing out. I wanted to skip and jump and run around like I hadn't been able to do in years. I was truly free, mind and body alike.

It wasn't as pronounced, but I still limped. Maybe it was a learned reaction from years of pain, or maybe it was permanent. I cupped my hand over my lips to muffle a sudden sob, all too aware of my audience watching. There was no helping it, as joy and fear for what this meant for the rest of my life clashed.

"Keep going," Fal encouraged. "Do a couple laps, maybe."

I made to do just that. Marius joined me, putting an arm around my waist and walking with me toward the fireplace at the back of the room. "Slow and steady. No rush."

"I'm limping," I murmured.

"You're going to need therapy. We'll work on restoring as much of your mobility as we can. Don't worry, p'nixie," he murmured back. "Every scar and flaw is a reminder that you've survived the worst life has offered so far." He smiled with lopsided charm. "Or so I've heard."

I admired his expression for an infatuated moment. *Handsome beast.*

"You're going to help," I said.

He answered like I'd asked a question. "Every step of the way." He winced as he realized what he'd said. "If you'll excuse the pun."

I stopped walking and fluttered my wings to get a boost of height. He was too tall for his own good, though he caught my hips and slanted his mouth over mine with a familiar growl. "*Mate.*"

"They've had an extended moment. Time to steal her," Rennyn announced.

Marius pulled away and scowled over my shoulder. "Steal her for *what?*"

Rennyn exaggerated a gulp. "No need to bite, wild boy. She's got to walk to her meeting."

And what a lot of walking it was. The moon parlor was on the opposite side of the palace, within the private halls dedicated to the royal pack. I found it a privilege to exercise my stiff ankle, and I was surrounded on all sides by supportive males, who walked at my pace.

When I caught a glimpse out a window upon starting this journey, I thought we were leaving my suite too early. But by the time we arrived, the sun was an orange ball on the horizon. It was impossible to miss the moon parlor, as the door off the main hall was painted silver blue, with etchings of the moon's phases covering it vertically.

A female voice, loud enough that I heard her furious tone through the wall, came from inside. It sounded like Nemensia. I cast a curious glance at the nearest king, which was Rennyn. He cupped a hand behind one of his elfin ears. "Oh, did I fail to mention that my beloved has a meeting with our mermaid guest too?"

There were several chairs lined up outside the parlor, and he gestured for me to sit. "I didn't realize. Has she been in there long?" I asked, lowering myself into one.

"Who's to say? They have a lot to go over, and my queen has no shortage of ire." He shrugged with both arms out and went to sit next to Theodred. He poked the redcap's dense arm. "Hey, about that kerfuffle in my least favorite courtyard today…"

They lowered their voices, so I didn't find out what constituted a "kerfuffle." I sighed, nerves bubbling in my belly. This was it. Very soon, I'd be seated across from Cymora again. I made a stern face, as I'd practiced. I looked over at Fal, who'd settled in the seat next to mine, and he recoiled and made an expression of dismay back. My composure fled as I cracked up.

"We might be here for a while, *mo stór*. If only someone with better hearing than mine could tell us what's being said." He cast a meaningful glance over at Kauz, who had his head leaned back against the wall in the seat between Marius and Tormund.

The kelpie elbowed Kauz, and he startled with a "Huh?"

"Let him sleep," I murmured while Tormund repeated the question.

Kauz closed his eyes. I thought he may have just started dozing again when he mumbled, "Mother is talking about the importance of family ties. It sounds like one of her wind-ups."

Tormund eased to his feet. "Going to use the lad's room," he announced before leaving.

Fal nodded and turned to me. "Cymora might be a bowl of fish soup by the time you get your turn. Mother's anger is like the tide. It ebbs down, and she just talks. You think she's done lecturing, then no, she's just set up an anecdote for how much you've screwed up and how disappointed she is—and then she's yelling again."

Nemensia was, in fact, yelling again.

"This can go on for a long time. I wish you were in the room now to take notes," Fal continued. "It's a good strategy to have."

If this whole ordeal had taught me anything, it was that I needed a way to express my anger without it getting tangled up in other feelings.

It'd be easier when the recipient wasn't my stepmother. Despite all the preparation we'd done, there was a part of me that still shook like a chastened child at the mere mention of her name.

As the minutes dragged on and conversation lulled around me, I fidgeted with my fingertips and occasionally pressed them to my queasy belly. Marius came over and sat cross-legged before my seat. "Let me see your ankles. I figure we'll either be here for a while longer, or Mother will finish as soon as you take off your shoes."

I was hoping for the latter, but no luck there. Instead, Marius inspected my right foot and ankle, occasionally comparing it to the left. He poked and pressed, moving up my leg. "This is probably going to hurt," he warned before pushing his thumb down the side of my calf. And stars, did it ever. I whimpered and nearly fell from the chair, as it felt like he'd opened a line of fire inside the muscle.

Fal caught me and slanted a glare down at the kelpie. "Last I heard, you weren't an expert in magical wounds," he said coolly.

"Nay. But ankle troubles are common enough. I can already tell that you're probably doomed to a variety of calf and ankle stretches for the rest of your days, p'nixie."

"That's all right. It's already better than what I had," I said.

"I'll take her to the infirmary when it's time." I glanced at Fal in disbelief. He was really going to challenge his brother on this? "I know how much you hate that place, Mar," he added.

"It's fine." He caught my curious look and added briskly, "I associate the infirmary's smell with the injury to my face. I was stuck there for months."

I could imagine so, with how much work had gone into saving his life. No wonder he hated it. I didn't want to linger on the topic, since it was clear he didn't want to discuss it. So, I asked Fal, "Why do you call him 'Mar'?"

Marius snorted, while Fal perked up. "Why do you call me 'Fal'? He used to prefer it. We"—he gestured between himself and the kelpie—"used to agree on something. Our princely names were too much. We were Fal and Mar, not *Falindel* and *Marius*." He stuck his nose in the air and infused their names with pretension. I giggled, even though I liked the ring both of their names had.

"It was a phase," Marius supplied.

"I bet he'd let you call him Mar if you just did it," Fal suggested. "That's how I get away with half the shit I say."

"We know," the kelpie deadpanned.

"Confidence," I agreed. It'd been what I'd admired most about him before I'd gotten to know him more.

But that word had Fal slanting a meaningful look my way and wetting his lips. Such a simple action still had my thighs pressing closer together. His nostrils flared, and he sighed wistfully. "Oh, if we weren't interrupted..."

The beautifully carved door into the moon parlor opened. We all looked up, save for Kauz, who was snoring by this point, as the queen stepped into the hall.

40

LARK

Nemensia arranged her skirts and went into the arms of her pack. Each king took time to comfort her with kisses and strokes of the gossamer fins on her back.

I glanced away to give her privacy. This was how I'd expect any omega to act after such a long and charged confrontation. It wasn't right to see her as *just* the Queen of Serian. She must've had extensive training to suppress this part of her instincts around those outside of her family.

Maybe with fifty years of training, I'd be able to do the same. I hoped so. In the meantime, I put my shoes and socks back on. Rolling my stiff ankle, I said to myself, *I'm going to walk in there whole and strong.*

Someone else stepped out of the moon parlor. It was the last king I had yet to meet again, unmistakably Elion. His yellow gaze went from the queen to the pack of princes. A smile quirked his lips as he took in his son still sitting cross-legged before me.

Elion had a politician's practiced poise, not a thread on his dark suit out of place. A crown resembling golden maple leaves growing from a gilded circlet rested on his brow. Despite the finery he wore as the leader of Pack Serian, the firstborn king of the Unseelie, he still reminded me of a noble animal. He had dappled gray skin and the half-shaved hair of a mated kelpie, with gold rings pierced into his nose and ears. His long ears sported a wavy outside edge, and angled subtly toward the nearest sounds. The cuffs of his suit were tailored to accommodate the jagged fins tucked against his forearms.

His long blue-green hair had three braids spaced through it. The first was thicker, woven with a length of curly, darker blue hair. The middle braid had several jeweled rings hanging from it at even intervals, and the last one glinted with small silver charms.

Elion waited by the door until Nemensia was finished seeking comfort. They came over to us together, and we all stood. Even Kauz, who, judging by his groggy squint, had barely wrested himself from the jaws of unconsciousness for this moment. Tormund skidded around a corner and rushed over to join us too.

Nemensia stopped a few paces away, beckoning. "Let me see you walk, *mo stóirín*." Now that I had a better grasp of Serri, I knew she was saying "my little darling."

Her gaze fell to my feet as I came to her. Her lips pressed together when I limped, but she didn't remark on it. Instead, she cupped my face and pressed her forehead to mine, purring briefly. "I'm glad you're able to walk on your own two feet. We've worn her down for you. How long was it?"

"Four or five hours," Theodred answered.

"Ren got bored and rousted the kids to wait with us," Thalas added.

My eyes rounded in surprise. She'd been yelling at Cymora for that long? That was beyond impressive.

Rennyn scoffed. "You could've at least given poor Elion a break."

"Oh aye, so you could take my spot. No thank you," the kelpie king said. He spoke Theli with a precisely formed accent, his lilt smooth.

"You're going to have plenty of time with—" Nemensia broke off with a gasp. "And whose idea was it to wake up Kauzden? My poor boy."

He said hello in a wispy voice, and she released me to bustle over to him. *Stars, he's about to be smothered.*

While she visited with him and the other princes, Elion and I turned to one another. "I can't tell you how overjoyed I've been to hear of the p'nixie's return." His voice also carried an undertone of alpha authority; a subtle echo of his emotions tickled my senses. I could've chosen not to accept it, but it felt like being enveloped in a warm hug. I perked up under his attention. "I wish I could've visited with you sooner. It seems there's much we have to catch up on."

"Were you really in that room for so long?" I asked.

"I received lunch and a comfortable seat from which to view my heart's ire, if you're feeling bad for me. In my experience, it's a treat to see an omega put another in their place, and I'm eager to see you do just that too."

I shifted on my feet and laced my fingers together, hoping to hide my nerves. Hopefully I'd rise to the challenge as he was expecting.

"My li'l brother was ready to fight me for the spot, but I figured you wouldn't be able to get in a word edgewise while seated between both the family's dark elves," he added mildly. He lifted his chin to indicate I look over my shoulder. Rennyn was sliding closer to listen in on our conversation.

"I'm still her favorite bonus dad. She said so herself," Rennyn remarked.

Elion gave an indulgent hum. "Just wait until she knows you as an adult. Loyalty defeats charm every time."

The dark elf king rolled his eyes. "That's the *kelpiest* thing you've ever said."

"And yet, not untrue. Now, *mo stóirín*, bring me up to speed on the strategy you'll be using. How can I assist you?" Elion asked.

I explained what I'd been practicing with my mates, only interrupted by the occasional question from the kelpie king. Rennyn, to his credit, looked as if he wanted to make a dozen suggestions as I spoke, but he aired none of them. Pressure whitened his lips as he kept himself contained.

By the time I was finished, my audience had expanded to include my mates, the queen, and all four kings. I cast a grateful glance over at

Fal. Without him pushing me to practice, I would've been caught flat-footed in front of everyone. He winked back.

Once Elion was satisfied, it was time. I set my shoulders. *Whole and strong,* I reminded myself.

The kings wished me good luck in their own ways, while my mates had kisses and a few last-minute reminders for me.

"Remember that you're not alone," Kauz said.

Marius nodded. "Your pack is with you."

"And we'll be here to support you afterward, no matter what," Tormund added.

A warm glow lit in my chest. They believed in me, and that made it easier to walk into the parlor with my head held high. I paused for a moment to take in the stunning space.

The domed ceiling was painted the same silver-blue hue as the door, with shining pinpricks of light overhead providing lighting, resembling the night sky and its many stars. Lines of essence connected certain constellations. There was The Dancer and The Guardian Fox, though the latter had the suggestion of multiple tails rather than the single one I was used to seeing.

My nose wrinkled as the room's scent hit me, a ripe fishy stink under a layer of dirt and other leavings. Its pungency was enough to make my eyes water. It had to be coming from Cymora, who sat shackled to a seat furthest from the door.

A table set with four carved chairs dominated the center of the room. The squared expanse of dark wood was bare, save for a perfume bottle that Elion picked up and began to generously spritz. A mist of scent blocker swirled through the air, dulling the odor.

Cymora was hunched over and didn't look up at our entrance. Her hair was only adorned with mats and dirt, and the unkempt mass shadowed her downturned face.

Fal cleared his throat and said with practiced ease, "Announcing The Wave King, Elion of Serian; Crown Prince Falindel of Sorles; and Metalark, Lady of Osme Fen."

Cymora released a little gasp when she heard my full name. Her chin rose, and for a moment, our gazes met. My heart leapt straight to my throat with a cold shock over my skin. I could hardly breathe.

The phantom of pain encircled my right foot as I placed it down. Even though the silencing band was long gone, I remembered the restricting feeling of it and how every spike jabbed my skin. She had done this to me, ensured that agony would follow me with every step I took.

My brows furrowed as I bared my teeth in the beginning of a snarl. I lowered into the chair across from her. Fal pushed it in and ghosted a kiss over my hair.

Cymora's attention flicked left and right as Elion and Fal took the remaining seats. We'd boxed her in, enemies on all sides. A huff of air escaped her lips as she looked at me once more, those eyes glossy in a feverish kind of way. Her chest heaved until she made a proper wet cough.

Dirt was smeared across her skin, outlining patterns of mermaid scales on her cheeks and neck. Brown crust marked jagged patterns on her bare arms. *Those look like knife wounds.*

Her baggy eyelids and sagging shoulders spoke to the kind of exhaustion she'd experienced on the train ride here. Kauz had plunged her straight into nightmares from the moment he'd uncovered what she'd done with my temporary nest. It was like those had continued to plague her.

Before she even opened her mouth, I put the details together. This meeting *had* been set up in haste. I was sure Cymora had already experienced Unseelie torture. Her poor condition had no other reasonable explanation.

To see her so humbled made her look like a different mermaid entirely, a beggar lifted from a street corner rather than a dignified lady. And I didn't feel sorry that she was finally receiving her due. If anything, I hoped it hurt. A murderer deserved no less.

As she met my practiced, stern expression, her face crumpled. "So, this is the finishing blow!" She wailed as only a mermaid could, hitting a discordant pitch that dragged talons over my nerves. *"They've turned you against me!"*

"Stop screaming," I gritted out.

Tears left clean tracks down her dirty face. She shook as she wept great heaving sobs, which transitioned to more heaving coughs.

Fal turned to me and lifted his brows. Yes, we'd talked about this.

He'd led me through how Cymora would press on every weakness I had —first and foremost, my empathy.

"If you think this display will garner any sympathy, you're mistaken," I said coolly.

If anything, she cried a little harder. "You're like a daughter to me. I raised you from when you were a small child. You could've been one more baby in the orphanage—"

"And yet, we were never family. Were we?" I didn't wait for a lull in what she was trying to say, speaking over her instead. "Cymora, I am cross with you, to say the least. I have a few questions for you that you will answer in full, and then we will go our separate ways. Understood?"

She closed her eyes and took great gulps of air to calm herself.

"The lady asked you a question," Fal needled.

"Yes, I heard *the lady's* question," she replied with a hint of her usual acidic tone. "I don't see why I must be forced to answer anything asked of me by my stepdaughter. Who, I remind you all, legally signed the rights of Osme Fen to me. I am the lady here, *not her*."

I hid my hands under the table so she couldn't catch them trembling. I was free of her compulsion, but years of fear couldn't be erased so easily. *You knew she wasn't going to make this easy for you.*

"In accordance with Theli law, all vows made by fae under the age of seventeen must be re-sworn once they come of age," I said, putting faesteel in my tone and the rigid set of my spine. "You have been a criminal, not a lady, for the last five years."

She opened her glassy eyes to stare at me for a long moment, but I didn't look away. "Who are you to speak to your stepmother this way, foolish girl?" she demanded.

My insides twisted, filling my belly with queasy nerves.

"The future Queen of Serian," Fal said when my silence was held a moment too long. "My beloved mate. So mind your tongue, mermaid, because I could easily have it removed once we're done here."

Her face turned a shade of pale blue. "Go ahead, then. Ask what you're going to ask. It's not as if I can stop you," she said to me.

"No. You can't stop me anymore." After so long under a compulsion to tell her yes, a thrill shivered through my wings to say no. "First question. Why did you murder my mother?"

Her expression had fallen to a drawn look, and she wavered in her seat. "Did these Unseelie try to tell you I did such a heinous thing?" She was too exhausted to sound outraged, so the deflection fell flat.

"Why—" I heard the emotion crackling in my voice and stopped to clear my throat. "Why did you pay an auracle to place a fatal illness curse on my mother?"

"One only bargains with an auracle," she corrected. "And I ended up with the better end of that particular deal."

"I don't care."

"Well, if you are to be a *lady* now, you must know the proper terms," she said scornfully.

Frustration was already starting to bubble in my throat. "I've asked you a clear question and want a straight answer."

"I doubt the truth from my lips will do anything to change your mind. These Unseelie have poisoned you against me...haven't they? Here you are, repeating their accusations. Wearing their clothes." She sneered as she gave me an obvious once-over. "Warming their beds. Can't you see that it's a lie?"

"The only one trying to spin a false story here is you," I replied as evenly as I could.

A ripple of fish scales marked her dirty skin. I didn't peek under the table to check, but she looked to be shifting to mermaid form, trading legs for a fish tail. Another wet cough wracked her body, and the scales disappeared. But not before a new wave of overripe fish filled the air. Fal and I gagged, while Elion wielded the scent blocker to offset the stink.

While I was occupied with not losing the contents of my stomach, Cymora said, "Can't you *see*? Once I'm gone and they tire of you, it'll be you reduced to rags and a hole in the ground. They are playing a game and moving you around like a piece on their board. *Think*, you stupid child. No pack of princes wants a filthy little serving girl for their mate. No matter what they seem to be saying to you, they're not going to put *you* on a throne."

"That's enough," I snapped, letting my anger loose. It flowed free without any tears to follow it. "I demand an answer! Why did you murder my mother?"

Cymora cocked her head, smiling like she'd had a victory. "She was in my way."

"In your way. What do you mean by *that*?"

"Undoubtedly, the next question will be about your father. Same answer. In my way. Everyone who has inconvenienced me has met a bitter end. Remember that." She smiled a little wider. I'd seen plenty of her expressions, but the lack of regret, even now, was unsettling.

I glanced at Fal briefly. This was a terrible time for an "I told you so" moment, but he had predicted this. Her answer was less satisfying than his explanation of her deeds.

"Is that all?" I asked. "That's your *entire* reason for murdering them?"

"Yes. Next question?" she simpered.

There were no answers here because there were none to begin with. Just a monster who'd been stripped down to her rotting soul. I saw that now. A burning hot fist of emotion closed around my chest, making it hard to sit here and look at her. I despised her so much.

I'd deviated from my strategy the moment I'd raised my voice. The idea had been for me to remain calm and apathetic of her fate, but it seemed I couldn't. I had to be strong in my own way.

"Why did you write to Queen Nemensia with the lie that I'd died?" I asked, even though I knew this answer would hurt.

She laughed, hitting a pitch that caused the hair on the back of my neck to stand on end. "Kellam took you here to visit before we mated. He came back unsettled. 'The royal Unseelie wanted to steal Metalark away,' he said of the experience. Your godfamily kept pushing boundaries, sending letters and gifts with the post. I convinced him not to entertain such things. He'd gotten lucky with Dorei—she had a sweeter nature—but most Unseelie are wicked malcontents. As I have tried *very* hard to teach you."

That was true. She'd taught me many lies the princes had helped me see beyond.

"A letter from the queen happened to arrive right after your father's demise," she continued, smirking. "It was convenient timing. I wrote back about Kellam's funeral arrangements. The body was, in fact, left in a field of wildflowers before it dissolved into stardust, for example. And just like Kellam, your so-called godfamily vanished out of my way."

I bit the inside of my cheek, letting the sting distract from the emotion welling in my chest. "You could've told them the truth. They would've taken me off your hands."

"Ah, but Kellam's will was clear. You were the Lady of Osme Fen, and I merely your guardian until you came of age. Did you think I would trust a pack of Unseelie to do *me* a good turn if they whisked you away to be their plaything early?" Her scoffing laugh echoed her last one, rising and falling like a swelling tide. "I had to act in the best interests of myself and my true daughter. That meant keeping you until you were old enough to sign Osme Fen over to me."

When Elion spoke up, the alpha authority underlying his voice had turned to pure ice. "Such harm you've caused, all for a parcel of land no one cares about."

Cymora shuddered violently. "Yet it worked. No matter what you say, I am the Lady of Osme Fen. Even if you restrain me in these." She grunted as she hefted the set of manacles around her wrists and clunked them on the table. "When *my* queen hears of how I've been treated, you will regret everything, *Unseelie scum.*"

Elion's lips quirked, though there was little amusement on his face. "You don't strike me as having seen a third century of life, Cymora. That kind of racism is a relic of the past."

"And there's no need to deride the 'parcel' of land I've worked so hard to earn. One town becomes two or more with the right matings. It's hard to understand the trading-up mindset when you're born to such blinding privilege," she spat at him.

"She acts as if she's deserving of another mate she'd undoubtedly murder," he remarked across the table to Fal.

"To her credit, she's full to the brim with delusion anyway. She thought she could push her daughter into Pack Sorles," Fal said with a tsk.

A weak ripple of scales passed over Cymora's face as she twitched with impotent rage. "Laurel is too good for you. I see that now."

Fal laughed mockingly. "Truly? She's more than free to mate with a different pack. Lark completes us in a way no one could compare to."

"Yet she doesn't carry your pack mark. Because she never will, right?" Her voice was a verbal blade coated with poison. "Because you're just toying with her, aren't—"

She's just trying to hurt me and steal my joy. Like Fal predicted.

"Cymora," I interrupted. "It wouldn't be right to execute you. You should see many tomorrows."

As I'd wanted, she looked at me with her mouth hanging open, her poisonous blade dropped.

"In fact, you should be placed in a quiet room with the bare minimum for survival to dwell on your many mistakes." I relished her change in expression, resignation replacing the meager spark of hope in her gaze.

"Maybe it was foolish to think you'd give me any explanations rather than more of your caustic reasoning." I stood as I spoke.

Strong and whole, I repeated to myself as my new mantra, crossing the table to loom over her. If I limped, I didn't feel it.

"I understand now. You needed me. You've only ever endeavored to steal what's mine. Just look at where you've ended up without me."

As she craned her neck to fix me with the full weight of her hatred, I got in her face and lowered my voice. "When your soul joins the stars, it's going to get lost in the darkness. You do not deserve another life, not when you've taken so many for no real reason. Not when you've abused someone who only strived to please you before she realized who you truly are."

"You *really* think you're a princess now," she breathed.

"Goodbye, Cymora. Even if it takes you a thousand years to feel regret, this is our last conversation. We shall never speak again," I said firmly, straightening and turning my back.

"Guards," Fal called, recognizing my cue.

There was a second entrance to the moon parlor, behind my former stepmother. As it opened, she raised her voice to another awful wail. "Wait. Wait! I'm not done with you yet! Have you forgotten you agreed to mate with Pack Ellisar? Unhand me, you brutes!"

I didn't turn back to see the "brutes" handle her, though I quivered from the effort. I'd said goodbye. I meant it.

"You signed a contract!" she screeched. "And they will come for you! You're not escaping—"

The guards dragged her past the door, and it closed with a thud and sealed off all but the muffled sound of her continuing to scream.

Fal drew me into his arms and held me tight while I quivered with

Cymora's words still reverberating in my head. "You did brilliantly. That went about as well as we could've expected," he murmured.

I nodded and hid my face against his chest, not trusting my voice. I was a wrung-out dishrag on the inside; in the process of holding in my reactions, all happiness had been squeezed out, leaving me limp and aching.

"You were right," I mumbled. I didn't think I needed to specify.

He stroked his fingers through my hair. "Nay. I knew it'd be unpleasant, but I'm glad you did it now. When she's gone, you won't wonder about what she could've said had you not heard it for yourself."

"I'm only worried about..."

He slowed his touch when I drifted off. "Hmm?"

"Never mind. I'd rather not talk about it." Pack Ellisar was where they belonged, in the past. They were probably still waiting fruitlessly for me to return to Osme Fen.

"Look at me, *mo stór*." I lifted my face toward his. He cupped my cheek, gazing at me with his usual mischief-lined affection. "You're going to be a part of Pack Sorles when you're ready. As far as I'm concerned, you're already a princess." With us pressed so closely together, he only mimed a courtly bow.

"I can hardly wait." I rose onto the tips of my toes to try to kiss him. Why did all my alphas have to be so starsdamned tall? My lips landed on his jawline. "I want to know what it's like to have a pack bond and feel you just a thought away."

He tilted his head to kiss me properly, but Elion cleared his throat before it was more than a brush of sensation. Fal sighed and released me from his hold with one last squeeze.

"I'd like to follow up about something else Cymora spoke of in error," Elion said. He stood as well and rounded the table. "Concerning your first visit, when you were small. There was never a moment we planned to steal you. Nothing nefarious was planned."

"I believe you. I know she was just spouting hate," I assured him.

"Mmm. Well, I'll admit that we spooked your father, something I look back on with regret." He stopped a pace away, hands laced over his middle. "Nemensia's desire to keep you was not masked in the slightest. You're the only child of her dearest friend, and at the time, you were a tiny thing that called her Mama."

"She put a lot of pressure on him to stay." It was a halfway informed guess, based on a distant memory at the train station.

"She did, but she wasn't the biggest problem. My brothers and I echoed her desires, as we always will. I fear he perceived my pack as competition. Kellam was *not* happy about you receiving so much attention from four bonus dads. I must apologize on behalf of all of us. If we had held ourselves in check, perhaps he wouldn't have pulled away and would have instead brought his new mate, her young merchild, and you back to Serian for a second visit. We would have seen Cymora for who she was." A muscle jumped in his jaw while he clenched it. "I'm sorry, Lark. I wish we could've had that future."

My eyes started to water. I opened my arms, and he obliged with a hug. "What-ifs are dangerous. I'd rather have four bonus dads than none," I said.

"Not that you have much of a choice there. Nemensia's heart has not moved in regards to you. You're still her child." He patted my back before releasing me. My wings flicked, a hint of levity returning after the weight of this conversation. "And you've had my kelpie loyalty somewhere between hello and telling me about my grain-eating cousin, Meya."

My old horse? Oh stars. I *had* told the firstborn king of the Unseelie about her after mentioning how horse-like he looked.

"You remember that conversation?" I practically squeaked.

His smile was broad. "Of course. It was refreshingly candid. We'll make up for lost time eventually, but for now, let's have dinner. I believe the rest of our family has been planning something special while we've been occupied."

"How special? Do I need to change?" Fal brushed nonexistent dust off his lapels.

"Not that special. Just a dinner with your parents. You might even call it a kings' dinner," Elion said meaningfully.

Fal gestured to the ceiling in a grand flourish. "I *knew* it!"

41

LARK

I LEFT the moon parlor as I'd entered it, with my head high. Everyone was clustered around a seated Nemensia, and they turned my way with an expectant air. In my mind's eye, I saw the smothering of affection that was incoming between my godmother and Tormund especially and held up my hands.

"Cymora released some fish stink, and I'd like to freshen up first," I said.

"Rotten mermaid," Nemensia remarked.

Fal took me to a restroom down the hall. I retreated inside and locked the door with haste. As soon as I had a moment of privacy, I wilted, wings sagging toward the ground. Blood rushed through my ears, along with the frantic pulsing of my heart.

Seeing Cymora again had been so many layers of awful.

I knew it'd be a difficult conversation. She hadn't had an incentive to offer me closure. Maybe I'd look back and see that talking to her wasn't a mistake, though it felt like one now.

I hardly had time to mope, not when I needed to be as fresh as possible for the formal dinner ahead. I was in the nicest restroom I'd ever seen, consisting of two separate rooms.

The first was carpeted, with a fainting couch and side table stacked with a random assortment of entertainment. To my relief, a basket full of heat supplies was nestled in the corner, so I grabbed sanitary wipes and a bar of scent-blocking soap.

I headed into the second room, the actual bathroom, which was a beautiful marble area lit by a few fluttering faelights. I went to the sink, ran water, and cleaned my exposed skin of any lingering fishy odor.

The brightness of the room seemed to intensify as I scrubbed. Another phantom spasm of pain squeezed my right ankle.

"Curse Cymora. And curse her nonanswers too," I muttered.

She'd done everything in her power to ruin my life. I'd bear the marks of her treatment for the rest of my days, a fact that heated my veins until I could've rivaled the beginnings of Tormund's rage.

No matter how much lather I worked into my skin, I still smelled fish. This *disgusting* mermaid. Even after living with her and Laurel for so long, I had no idea they could produce such a stench.

My arms pinkened from my rough treatment, and when I reached up to wash my face again, the skin was hot to the touch. *Uh oh...*

My belly fluttered, and I met my own gaze in the mirror, eyes widening in realization. I whimpered in denial a moment before the heat cramp seized my stomach.

"No," I groaned, hugging the sink to keep me upright through the sudden spasm of pain.

I hadn't had one of these in a luxurious amount of time, enough to almost forget how debilitating they were. *Stars, no. Not now. This is a terrible time to go into heat.*

A tentative knock sounded from outside the bathroom. "Lark, is everything okay?" It was Kauz.

My response was a keen. Under other circumstances, he might've been proud that I hadn't suppressed the sound of my distress. He did something that flipped the lock open and came in without hesitation. "How can I help?"

"It'll fade in a couple of minutes," I managed to say, turning my head his way.

His expression pinched with worry. "Your skin's so reddened. You look like you're going into heat."

I shook my head. "Just a cramp. I hope."

Kauz turned off the faucet and took a few hand towels off the rack by the sink. As the pain eased and I released my hold on the basin, he dried my arms.

"Now I'm more of a mess than when I started," I murmured.

"You don't smell like fish."

He just didn't have the ultra-sensitive nose of an alpha.

"I do," I sighed. I could still scent it lingering on me. Oh stars, it was probably on my clothes. If this wasn't one of my nicer ensembles, I would've considered burning it.

He cupped my cheek, searching my face. As far as I could tell, he wasn't using magic, yet the lingering pain in my middle vanished. "You smell fine, sweetheart. Really. And now that you're cooling off, you have a rosy glow."

"That's just a nice way of saying I'm sweating."

"You're more radiant when you sweat? Now that's just unfair," he teased, stroking my cheek with his thumb. I leaned into his touch with the stirrings of a purr.

"Kauz!" It was half laugh, half complaint. "I can't go to the kings' dinner like this."

He dropped the damp towels to the side and wrapped me in his wings. I put my arms around him, and slowly, a real purr warmed my chest.

"You did great. I'm so proud of you. You spoke firmly and didn't let Cymora see you flinch," he murmured. "Elion shared everything with Mother over their mating bond as it happened, and she told us."

I took in the faint glimmer of stars in the whites of his eyes. I could've stayed here for longer, just admiring him, but... "I'm keeping everyone waiting, aren't I?" I groaned.

"Not in a bad way. It'd be unusual if you *didn't* need a moment after such a hostile conversation. Take the time you need."

I sank into him gratefully. It took me a few more minutes of comforting before I stirred, and I let my fingertips drift down his chest. What I wouldn't do for another shared dream of pleasure, to lie skin to skin with him. "After dinner, do you want to... I mean, if you're awake..."

"Whatever it is, if it's with you, aye," he answered.

"Making love," I clarified.

"I'd answer more enthusiastically if I had the energy."

My wings quivered from the electric thrill that traveled down my back and straight for my core. Thank the stars; finally, a yes. He'd shown me pleasure, and I'd chased it ever since. Each "no" from his brothers had had the tone of "not yet." I knew part of that was me and my own inexperience. Maybe we would resolve some of it tonight.

The promise of intimacy had me eager to see the kings' dinner through. As we left the bathroom hand in hand, I took another sniff of myself and didn't detect any fishy odor. I'd let Cymora get too far into my headspace, but no longer. It was time to let her fade into a distant memory.

We sat down to eat in a private dining room connected to Pack Serian's quarters. When I'd visited as a child, I'd sat in Nemensia's lap during mealtime and asked how they'd gotten such a long table. Rennyn had joked that it'd been made from an extra tall tree. At that age, that'd sounded perfectly logical to me.

A tablecloth in Serian's colors, dark blue and silver, ran the length of the massive table. Piles of paperwork lined one end, and an unfinished jigsaw puzzle, which was big enough to be thousands of individual pieces, was scattered across the other side.

It could've sat thirty places comfortably, but we occupied the middle section with complicated place settings. There were repeat pieces of flatware before me, and plates so fine I could practically see through them.

The room had a large hearth and a collection of paintings that ringed the room. Most of the art was abstract, filling the spaces between portraits of the royal family. Several portrayed Nemensia with great love and flattering attention to detail. Thalas caught me admiring one and proudly shared that they were his work. "In one of the traditions of my line, most existing art of any queen was created by her magician."

"It's really unfortunate when the talent skips a generation," Rennyn remarked.

Thalas chuckled. "The couple of times it's happened, they hire more skilled artists."

"Look me in my eyeballs and tell me that the portrait of Queen Drania was created by someone with talent."

They both leaned back in their chairs to look at one another. Thalas let the moment draw out before he said, "It absolutely wasn't."

I muffled a giggle behind my hand. We'd arranged ourselves in a particular order. I was sitting across from the queen, and we had two mates to either side of us. To my right, it was Marius and then Kauz. To my left, Fal and then Tormund. The kings also sat in the same birth order, but Elion and Rennyn were at Nemensia's right, while Theodred and Thalas sat to her left.

I wondered why my mates were reversed. My best guess was so Marius could see me.

A set of house moths bustled in and started pouring water and wine for all of us. Nemensia received a separate pour of what smelled like fruit juice. I took a cautious sip of the wine. It didn't taste like it had fae fruit in it, but I was going to be careful since it was still nice, a sweet blush.

Kauz had previously described this meal as a test for my mates and how well they knew me. That became more apparent when the first course was a bowl of fresh salad, veggies and fruit with a light dressing, just like I'd scarfed down the other day. Fal whispered to me behind his hand, pointing out which fork was the salad fork.

Elion and Marius were served bowls full of what looked like miniature lobsters. The kelpie king took one between his fingers and twisted, separating its tail from its body. "All right, tell us how you all met. We're eager to hear the whole story," he said.

Fal started the tale, talking about their plan to infiltrate the Omega Masquerade. I munched on my salad and listened in, curious since this was far before we'd actually met. "We grew up hearing about Mother's best friend mating a Seelie male, so I ventured that we might be missing an opportunity, even if the Theli have never allowed Unseelie at their annual matchmaking ball."

"I should write to Queen Alora about this," Nemensia murmured with all the air of taking a mental note.

Fal narrated how there had been some careful planning around setting their affairs in order and sneaking out at the right time, when they'd be least missed over the course of their long journey. "But I wanted to see Marius happily mated, so I made the arrangements," he said.

The kelpie snorted. "To see Tormund happily mated, you mean."

The redcap looked up from his salad, brows raised. "Is this where I keep the chain going and mention Fal or Kauz?"

"Yes, yes. You all, understandably, wanted to see each other with a mate and happy," Rennyn put in.

Marius popped a strip of meat from one of the mini lobsters in his mouth. His ear flicked as he narrowed his eyes over my head at Fal for a few moments longer before glancing at me. He took another shellfish and twisted it apart, peeling the tail open and offering it to me.

"No, it's yours," I said under Fal's continued narration.

"I insist," he murmured, holding it further out.

"Is that baby lobster cooked?"

He chuffed a laugh. "It's a crawfish. And aye. Nothing's served raw at this table while Mother's pregnant."

I took it and tried the bit of flesh inside the shell, brightening at the sweet and salty flavor mixed with a spicy blend of herbs. He fed me more crawfish tails, sucking the meat out of the other half of the shellfish.

"These were my favorite food growing up. Got to be a predator early." He twisted another in half with a playful little growl.

"Cute."

"You are," he said without missing a beat.

I opened my mouth to correct him, then stopped. *Oh, he's flirting.* "Well, you have become quite the predator," I replied, lowering my voice so the remark was for his ears only. "And a handsome beast."

His lips tilted upward. "I do have a response. For later."

"Later," I agreed. I was keeping some attention on Fal's story, which was getting to the point where he and I crossed paths at the Omega Masquerade. There was time for one more kelpie fact before I'd probably need to add in my side of the story. "Why is your diet so different? Is it because you're a shifter?"

He shrugged. "Something like that. If it's not from the sea, or protein, bread, or potatoes, I probably won't enjoy it. Like *salad*." He gave a small shudder.

That was kind of a shame, but more salad for me.

After Fal shared my balcony jump and the table stopped laughing at the absolute absurdity of that moment, Nemensia asked how we'd gotten to that point. I went back in time to the plan Cymora had started when she'd had the local apothecary make a fake version of my pheromones. I shared how I'd worked around her scheming so I could illusion myself to fit in at the Omega Masquerade and steal enough to fund a new life elsewhere.

In the meantime, we tucked into the main course, herb-and-bread-crumb-stuffed chicken with a side of mashed potatoes. Another repeat of a meal I'd loved and enjoyed just as much a second time.

"I love the classically Unseelie thought patterns of making a plan within a plan, plus the stealing." Rennyn put up a finger. "For the right reason."

"I'm more amused Fal and Lark attended this event with their identities both hidden and revealed in the same way. That's fate," Elion remarked.

"Well, great minds do think alike," Fal said. He and I exchanged a fond look.

"Seems more like dumb luck to me," the dark elf king remarked. Fal rolled his eyes. "Lark's plan was doomed for reasons she didn't even know about, and our kids went *way* out of their way for a shockingly half-baked scheme."

"Not everything has to be an elaborate multistep event, *li'l* brother," Elion said.

Rennyn threw up his hands. "Aye, and we're talking about hare-brained plans, not making cracks at my height. Which is the same as yours, I might add, if you add in my horns."

The kelpie king grinned. "No one does."

Fal stopped eating and covered his mouth, shoulders shaking as he tried not to laugh aloud. I had no such restraint, surprised as I was to hear such casual banter between the kings.

"Our mate does. Don't you, sugar blossom?" Rennyn wheedled.

She put up a palm. "Oh no, don't drag me in the middle of this."

"As the queen insists. Lark, do you factor in the horns?" He clasped his hands under his chin.

I wasn't expecting to be called upon next, so I gave him a flat-footed answer. "Um, you're already taller than me, so no?"

Rennyn snapped his fingers. "That's right, I'm not the shortest at this table. Thanks, Larkie." It seemed he'd already had a nickname for most everyone else, so I beamed to receive one too.

Theodred murmured to Thalas in his rumble of a voice, "The entertainment doesn't stop." The dream warden king nodded in agreement.

"All right. Anyway," Nemensia said, circling her fork, "you all were telling us a story. What happens after the balcony jump?"

Tormund eagerly took over narrating his part in things. The queen put her hand to her heart as he talked about calming me down. "*Mo leanbh*. Always the gentlest lad," she said.

I shifted in my chair as Kauz talked about visiting my dream, and then it was time for Marius to talk about following me to a pawn shop. The kelpie didn't mention my heat scare, to my relief.

"I haggled the pile of her stolen goods up to nine hundred fulls," he was saying.

"He kind of bullied the shopkeeper," I put in.

Marius snorted. "He was taking advantage of you. He probably turned the lot around for five thousand."

A house moth started distributing dessert. I looked down at my plate and made a candid squeak of delight. A pair of fresh apple tartlets awaited.

"I *told* you," Kauz said victoriously.

"I could've sworn the berry trifle was your favorite dessert, li'l bird," Tormund said.

All four of my mates looked at me expectantly. "Oh, I probably would've had the same reaction to a berry trifle. I just really like my sweets," I said.

"That's my daughter," Nemensia said, beaming.

Elion's gaze went from her to his brothers. Nods were exchanged. He cleared his throat. "I have an announcement to make. Sons, this will be about as surprising as if I told you that the sea is wet, but it doesn't change the joy we have that you've found your fated mate. You have our blessing to complete your pack with Lark as your omega."

I did have the sense that no one was particularly shocked, but I still had misty eyes as we received a hail of congratulations from the rest of Pack Serian. Fal hooked his arm around my shoulders and pressed his cheek to mine. Marius mirrored him, holding my waist and nuzzling me. Kauz joined in and Tormund, not to be left out, squished all of us together into a big group hug.

I was still buzzing with happiness when we returned to our seats. The rest of the meal broke off into smaller conversations as we lingered over this final course. It might've lasted longer had Ambriel not burst into the room, little face creased with distress, with an exclamation of, "Daddy!" All four kings turned nearly as one.

Rennyn intercepted her and lifted her up. "Oh no," he gasped. "*Un*happy Fins? This will not do!"

She was already giggling when he passed her to Elion, who murmured in an undertone, clarifying which dad she wanted. By the time he passed her to Nemensia, she was her usual bubbly self and giving the remains of the queen's dessert a covetous look. Her nixie fins swished with joy, as hinted by her nickname. Ambriel ended up in Thalas's lap, the dad she was here to see, who received a puppy-dog look and a request for a bedtime story.

"Seems you've survived our parents," Fal said in an undertone to me. He drained the last of his wine as Thalas got to his feet and bid us good night, meaning to carry their pack's youngest to bed.

The rest of us stood, and we started the long process of saying goodbye.

"It was so nice to see all of you together," Nemensia said. She gave me the big, smothering hug I'd expected after finishing up in the moon parlor.

Rennyn mimed swiping a tear from under his eye. "Now our lads are going to go missing again."

"At least they'll be somewhere in the palace this time," Theodred pointed out.

"Hah! That's what they want you to think."

Nemensia patted my back. "Treat my sons well, all right?" she murmured in my ear.

"I always will. I swear it," I whispered back, my voice carrying a ring of truth for my four beloved mates.

42
LARK

I RETURNED to my suite pressed up against Kauz's side, giggling, belly full and the buzz of a couple glasses of wine warming my veins. He shrouded me with a half-unfurled wing and let his hands roam, shaping my curves with the occasional squeeze.

Despite how long a day it'd been, I had an eager bounce to my step. I hadn't forgotten about the confidence special, and today was so full of victory that it *required* a celebration. Kauz was awake, I was walking on my own two feet, I'd survived my confrontation with Cymora, and we'd even had the kings' dinner, mostly according to protocol.

The moment the door closed behind the alphas, who trailed Kauz and me, I drew the dream warden into a kiss. It became a whirl of color tinged with stars and the sweet promise of Always. He'd dipped me playfully, but we teetered, off balance together.

Tormund caught us and tugged me away from Kauz. "My turn," he announced.

I squeaked in surprise when he lifted me, claiming my lips next. He walked while we kissed, coating my taste buds with smoke and the sweetness of caramelized mallows.

The redcap sat and plopped me in his lap. We arranged ourselves around the couches. There was a new charge to the air, something electric; the attention from all four males was nearly a physical caress over my body. Fal's gaze was darkened with desire, while Marius was fixed on Tormund and me, his tense stance radiating jealousy.

Tormund was pleasantly hot, and as I scooched in to get comfortable, his arousal twitched against me. I nearly trilled at him but suppressed it at the last moment, unsure of what would happen if I made such a blatant cue of need right now.

A light fragrance wafted through my nostrils. Sweet lavender, elevating the usual aroma of clean linens in my rooms. Someone had left us a bottle of champagne set in glowing, enchanted ice, fluted glasses, and a covered tray.

I hummed to myself. Tormund *had* been gone a suspiciously long amount of time while we'd been waiting for Nemensia to finish up in the moon parlor. He must've come back here and set something up.

Fal cleared his throat. "Any room left in your belly, Lark?"

"A little," I said. "Dinner was a lot."

"It was. This whole day has been, in more ways than one. Yet you still have that lovely smile. I'll drink to that," he purred.

He popped the cork on the champagne bottle and started pouring. The bottle produced four glasses, which was perfect since Marius was disinterested in the sweet alcohol. Mist wafted from the tray when Fal lifted the cover, revealing a selection of fruit frosted with a spelled chill.

The redcap fed me nibbles from a peach slice while I sipped my champagne and purred as it added to the pleasant warmth in my belly.

"I just want to say, I got what I needed from Cymora. We don't have to worry about her anymore." I was ready to put her name to rest for good.

Tormund sighed with relief. "Good. I did not like her."

"Understatement," Marius growled.

"All that matters is that you're satisfied, sweetheart. Our feelings truly echo yours," Kauz put in.

"Well said. And now that we're all here together in blessed privacy, we have a couple things to discuss," Fal added, taking a leisurely sip of his drink.

I finished the last bit of chilled peach Tormund was holding for me. A growl shook his large frame when I licked off the juice on his fingers. It vibrated through me too, spreading pleasant warmth through my core. My heart ticked faster as extra heat spread along my wings, radiating from Tormund's interest.

"If you want to celebrate with pack love, I'm here," Fal said, full of his usual unshakable confidence.

"We all are," Marius said.

The dark elf held up his finger. "But first, we need to discuss protocol."

Everyone else groaned, myself included.

"Ah, ah. We'll get back to what we all really want in a moment," he teased, smirking. "Lark, the protocol for courting our princess dictates that we take you out on individual dates so we get to know one another better before you join our pack. Personally, I think you should leave the palace for a while and see our country. My date is probably going to take place here in the capital, so I wouldn't mind if you saved the best for last, so to speak. No deal required, and no need for me to knot you first. Though"—he flashed his fangs in a smug smile—"it would be nice."

"It's still Lark's decision," Kauz insisted.

"Of course. That's why I wanted to talk first. All of this is your decision, Lark. There's no need for anything tonight, if that's what you'd prefer. Don't feel as if you need to bend any of your boundaries for our eagerness."

I tilted my head back to read Tormund's expression. He gazed back at me with desire, tiny flames shimmering in the gray depths of his eyes, though he nodded in agreement with what Fal was saying.

I did want all of them. And if the only way two of them felt comfortable was if the pack was there to support them, then that's what we'd do. I'd been considering how to make this work and shared my conclusions. "I do want pack love, but I'm not comfortable with all four of you in the room at the same time." Excited smiles vanished around the circle of males, only to be replaced by speculative looks as I made my suggestion. "Why don't we do two and two?"

Kauz tilted his head as a few looks were exchanged. "Completely reasonable. It could be Fal and Tormund, and Marius and me," he said.

The kelpie shifted in his seat. "Do you have enough magic to handle Niall?"

"Aye. And make no mistake, it'd be the most unpleasant stunning spell of your life if you harm my Always." He said it in his usual mild tone, though his expression was as hard as faesteel.

"I'd expect nothing less," Marius muttered.

"I'm okay with this too," Tormund put in.

"Agreed. Which pair is first, though?" Fal asked.

"Answer something for me." I took a bolstering drink of alcohol as his feline gaze turned expectant. "Why is knotting me first such a big deal?"

I expected Fal to laugh and say it was some alpha thing, but instead, his expression turned serious. "Well, we did have to discuss this at some point. I've built up a bit of a reputation while waiting for you."

I glanced away, embarrassed heat rising on my cheeks. Oh, this was about the last thing I'd wanted to bring up. My every insecurity threatened to bob to the surface of my thoughts. How many females had come before me? How would I measure up in his experiences?

"What you need to understand is that they were dalliances. A way to pass the time. I've never had much tolerance for loneliness. Our fathers went much longer than we have before they found their mate... and I took their example to heart. I knew it could've taken sixty to seventy years, or maybe even longer, for us to meet our perfect omega. But my past lovers have been all betas. I swear it."

Just like that, he'd drawn me back in. I knew from my memories that he was thirty or thirty-one, the tired eldest child of his huge family. Not committing to a relationship in all that time must've been lonely in its own way. But he was also implying something else. An alpha that forwent sleeping with omegas had also never knotted anyone, as only omegas were built to take a knot.

His smile was nearly shy as he spoke to me as if I was the only fae in the room. "It's a compromise I made with myself when I came of age. I saved something for my omega fated mate, and it happens to be my knot. Romantic, I know."

"It is," I murmured. I wouldn't have expected him to put any experience on hold, yet he had anyway. For me. Before we'd even known each other.

"Suffice it to say, I have had many experiences, but you will be my first—and only—omega. I have no female to compare you to because you are incomparable, *mo stór*."

Stars, I fell more for him by the moment. "I hope I've been worth the wait." I patted Tormund's arm before I stood and crossed over to where Fal was sitting. He drew me into his lap, meeting me halfway for a champagne-flavored kiss.

He nuzzled my cheek and said, "You absolutely have been. Never doubt that."

Echoes of agreement sounded from his brothers. *My mates.* I was overwhelmed in the best of ways, my chest full to bursting with emotion.

The redcap cleared his throat. "You know, I've been saving my knot t—"

"Tormund," Marius interrupted. "Let him have this."

He sputtered in surprise. "You're not going to put your two slivers in too?"

Marius shook his head. Well, that was certainly something. A moment of kelpie loyalty for Fal, I assumed. I spoke up quickly, "So, that means Fal is last, with the knot."

The dark elf grinned. "And I will honor the terms of my deal, as previously stated. Relax, li'l brother," he said to Tormund. "You get to go before me. In more ways than one. Third is better than fourth. And as for first...I suppose that's between our favorite book nerds."

"Still Lark's decision," Kauz sighed out.

"Why did you *immediately* assume she isn't my most favorite book nerd?" He snuck another kiss on my cheek as I giggled behind my fingertips.

"Most favorite isn't..." The dream warden let the thought drift off and shook his head. "Ready, sweetheart?" he asked me instead.

"Almost." I took the last sip of champagne to empty my glass, hopped to my feet, and turned to Tormund. I hadn't missed the way his desires had been pushed around by the group. "I just want a moment alone with my gentle giant first." It didn't feel right to see what I assumed was his handiwork with anyone else.

He perked up and stood too as I offered him my hand. I tugged him toward my study, discovering a path of pink rose petals scattered past the threshold.

"Did you do all this?" I whispered, pointing out the flowers.

As soon as there was a wall between his brothers and us, he said, "Aye. I ran back here to do something special for you. Sorry it's not much."

The trail of petals continued to the first bedroom, forming a heart on the end of the massive pack bed. The pink popped against the gray bedspread, fitting in with the little red flowers stitched into the fabric. The air carried an undertone of sweet lavender that he'd applied with a light touch.

"In Serian, we believe it's bad luck to put anything on an omega's bed without permission," he continued at a nervous speed. "And I would've drawn you a bath, but it'd be cold by now. Do you want a bath? I brought a bottle of the bubbly soap. There's a lot of bottles, actually. I put most of them in the corner, except for the champagne—"

"You did a great job, Tormund," I put in.

He paused with his lips poised. His expression had a clear question, an "I did?" written in his worrying expression before it morphed into his usual jolly smile. "I just want the best for the li'l bird."

I was seized by the desire to kiss him all over. "I know." I fluttered my wings for a boost of height and hooked my arms around his neck. He cupped his broad palm under my rear to support me. "You've been comforting and looking after me from the moment we met. You've helped me feel secure in my own skin, and I've been meaning to say...I love you."

He gasped, then crushed me in a big hug. "I love you too! I was waiting for the right moment to say it."

"Me too," I said on a wheeze.

He relented some of the pressure but still held me close with a broad grin. "Maybe it's dumb to wait for just the right moment. I'll say it all the time. I will never get tired of reminding you."

"We're going to be one of those couples," I joked, though I couldn't wait. If any of my mates wouldn't mind being unbearably lovey-dovey with me, it'd be Tormund.

"We are," he agreed. He set me on the foot of the bed, in the middle of the heart of flower petals, blew me a kiss, and left the room. "She loves me!" he crowed, and I covered my face with a laugh. It was such a Tormund thing to immediately announce it.

"Congratulations!" came Fal's muffled reply.

I made to stand and invite Kauz and Marius in but caught a hint of a hushed conversation occurring in my study. The interplay of a calm tone through a deeper growl was unmistakable. My wings flicked as I considered whether I should be eavesdropping on their discussion.

Whatever they'd had to say, it was brief. They arrived while I was still weighing the temptation and shut the door behind them. "...and you show those feelings with your body. How you touch and move with her," Kauz was saying.

"I can do that," Marius murmured.

They stopped short when they spotted me at the foot of the bed. Kauz tilted his head. "We're not going to your nest?"

"Here's fine. We might as well put this bed to use. I might get rid of it soon." Depending on how well we actually shared my nest. I still had my doubts all five of us could be comfortable on one bed, no matter how large it was. But I'd have to see it for myself.

They sat on either side of me, and I went languid, soaking in the heat of their bodies so close to mine. "Do you have an idea of how you'd like this to go?" Kauz murmured.

"I was hoping to ease into it." Yet even as I said it, my gaze landed on the most obvious sign of his fatigue, his wings drooping behind him.

His silvery eyes still twinkled with dancing stars. "We can go slow," Kauz said, his calm tone reassuring.

The kelpie shook out his mane of hair, speaking with a feral rasp, "How about a massage too, p'nixie?"

He watched my expression with Niall's unblinking intensity. And a massage sounded really nice after this long day. The memory of his hands roaming over my back and soothing out any hint of pain had me shifting with an eager flutter of my wings. He was on his feet, heading for my nest, before I even responded aloud.

"Hey," Kauz murmured, putting his wing around me in the kelpie's absence. "After hearing Fal's confession, I feel the need to tell you something of my past as well."

"Something about lovers?" It hadn't escaped my notice that Kauz had experience in the bedroom too, but my inner omega craved more of *us* and less about the past. But I didn't complain. When would there be a better time to mention it and put it behind us?

"Aye. I've had three. The first bedded me out of gratitude. I'd done her a favor with my magic, so she did me a favor in return, so to speak." His mouth tilted at an uncertain angle. "As for the other two, well, one was just as short lived. She truly wanted Fal and thought she could use me to get to him instead."

I winced in sympathy. "Oh, I'm sorry."

"She was very unsuccessful. She left the court completely after being chastised by both of us at the same time," he assured me. "The last was a longer-term relationship. I knew it was temporary, as she wasn't a match for the pack."

He brushed a lock of hair out of my face, his knuckles brushing my cheek in a tender sweep. "She ended up leaving me because she'd found her Always. While we were happy together, I never brought her the same kind of joy I'd witnessed in her when she met her fated. After that, I yearned to find my Always too. And now that I have, I understand. You're everything to me."

My breath caught. "I love you." My belly tingled with effervescence. If I figured out how to relive memories in my dreams, "you're every-thing to me" would be a nightly star.

"I love you too. Let me show you how much."

He drew me into a kiss. It deepened from a brush of our lips into a meeting of our mouths, with his tongue greeting mine alongside the taste of Always. He slipped his hands around my waist and undid the buttons securing the slits in my shirt around my wings. I pawed behind him until he guided my hands to the right spot to show me that his tunic had a similar design.

We parted briefly for air. He took his tunic off, and my admiring gaze lingered on the flex of his muscle. This was still the Kauz I'd loved in my dreams. Nothing about him seemed exaggerated from sleep to waking. There was no need for him to distort the truth about his body.

When we came back together, I trailed kisses down his throat and over his light purple skin. He murmured suggestions of where he was most sensitive, and his wings shivered when my lips and tongue found those spots.

I paused only to let him free me of my shirt, with my breast band following shortly after. He teased and rolled the soft orbs of my breasts. I was sensitive to every brush of his fingertips stoking the heat in my core with an artist's skill, my body his canvas.

Each touch was worshipful, slow and loving. I mimicked him, caught in his gaze as wordless meaning passed between us. We were still building something together, intimate partners as fate intended. This time, it was real in every definition.

My hands shaped his body, memorizing the smooth softness of his skin and the unique curves of his wings. He eased us further back onto the bed at a tempo of coaxing kisses and squeezes. After heading toward the top of the massive pack bed, he twisted so I ended up on my back. He braced above me, his wings hanging loose to shroud us from the outside world.

Sparkling dust rose from me as my wings flicked. Kauz flashed his teeth in a slow grin and slowly undid the front of my pants. He didn't just rip the rest of my clothes off. He eased them down, exposing my lower belly and the curves of my thighs one inch at a time. The scrap of my panties followed. Without the magic that usually covered his irises, I caught every nuance of him admiring my bare figure.

"You're a beauty, my Always. You take my breath away." He switched to speaking in Serri. The effortlessness of his native language, mixed with its earthy lyricism, made it sound like a flow of poetry from his lips. "A flawless form of stars and wind. Why else would I have been made with the magic of dreams and grown wings to fly alongside you?"

"Perhaps it's the other way around," I suggested in more painstaking Serri.

His eyelids fell into a smolder. "In the spirit of Always, both are true. We were shaped for one another."

"You were just the right size last time."

"A perfect fit," he agreed.

He drew his fingers through my folds, tugging lightly. I tensed when I felt his fingertips at my entrance, and he murmured for me to relax. He wiggled a finger inside my channel. Dusting my face with kisses, his keen ears perked as I gasped, "More."

"Patience, sweetheart. We have to get your body ready first." He teased the innermost rim of my pussy before pushing that single finger in and out. I made a little begging whine, and he added a second finger. When his thumb circled my clit in a burst of electric pleasure, my legs drew up as a cry escaped my lips.

"Just like that. Let me hear you," he coaxed, echoing my memory of our dream together.

With his encouragement, there was little chance I'd learn to be a quiet bed partner. I was open with my pleasure because I could tell how much he loved it. His wings shivered. Lust darkened his gaze. And he had to stop and free his cock before it burst from the front of his pants.

He searched my face, and a knowing smile quirked his lips as he moved his length through my slick folds. The heat of him was an intimate tease that had me trembling for more. "Ready?" he asked.

I lifted my hips, chasing the sensation of him so close to where I needed him most. "Yes!"

His gaze softened. "You're sure you want me to take your virginity... twice?"

"Of course. I still want it to be you," I said.

With a nuzzle and a lingering kiss, he pulled my hips forward and entered me, pushing inside in a long, slow glide. My body adjusted, pleasure edged with a bite of soreness as he stretched my pussy for my true first time.

He trembled with restraint. Those silvery eyes held mine for the intimacy of the moment until he was sheathed to the root. "You're no longer untouched. How does it feel?" he asked.

In truth, I was remarkably the same. But he'd been the one to suggest that "untouched" had multiple definitions, and I'd left it behind some time before now.

"Full," I answered, tipping my head playfully. "One could say perfectly so."

He grinned and withdrew, just to return with enough force to curl my toes. "That's how you feel, too." Another thrust, rocking my body. I tipped my head back, mouth popping open for a breathy moan. "Perfect."

All I could do was make a noise of agreement. I wrapped my legs loosely around him, rolling my hips into each drive of his. He started strong, but even as my pleasure soared, his energy and pace flagged before either of us found completion.

"Want to try something new?" he offered. Hoping it was something I could do to help him, I nodded.

He clutched me to him and rolled so I was on top with him still seated within me. He shifted, propping up his torso on a pile of pillows. I knew what to do from here, in theory, but I felt split at this angle, straddling him.

"I'll give you a few pointers along the way, all right?" He offered like he'd taken a peek in my head and noticed my worries, sure I was going to mess up in some unforeseen way. Hopefully while he was busy reading my mind, he also noticed that he was the mate I'd most prefer to make a blunder with.

"Okay."

He beckoned until I leaned over and met him for another, sloppier kiss. We didn't part until I shifted and resettled my weight in a way that felt more natural. "Ride me. Or as you're sure to hear soon...*fuck me, princess.*"

I flushed with heat all over. He'd bid me to fuck him in Serri, the coarse words like a firm nudge. As I lifted up, my body adjusted, practically mourning his absence until I pressed down again. He moaned as I got used to the motion, and once I was, he urged me to roll my hips in a circle rather than going straight up and down. We cried out together when I tried it and felt him stroke new, sensitive spots within me.

There was only the feeling of rightness to be joined with my mate and Always. His wings were spread like an extra blanket over the bed, twitching, shifting, and lifting on their own accord each time I did something he liked. He left me to ride him as I willed, running his fingers over my lower wings instead and swirling my dust into my skin.

Everywhere he touched tingled faintly. Maybe it was magic, though I was more certain it was just...*him.*

He sat up, meeting my momentum with his own. We matched thrust for thrust, skin to skin, though my pleasure seemed to quicken first, speeding along to a lofty peak. I arched against his chest and screamed, my greedy pussy pulsing and squeezing, locking down on him.

It was only when he joined me that my eyes rolled back. Liquid heat bloomed in my core, and I ground to push him deeper as the sensation felt like it was extending out my bliss. Once he was finished filling me with his come, I relaxed, languid atop his solid chest.

He put an arm around me and murmured, "You're radiant."

I peeked at him, giggling. "So, I'm sweating."

"Still unfair that it makes you prettier." He muffled a great yawn, eyelids drooping. "Talk to me. I need to stay awake a little longer."

I hummed, a little concern breaking through my post-peak haze. "That was better than a dream," I said, nuzzling up under his chin.

"Very true. But I can show you so much more without the bounds of reality. A bit of Never doesn't hurt in small doses."

"There's more? Really?" I asked, already excited to see it all with him.

He shifted to be more upright on the pillows piled behind him and dipped his fingers over my wing again. He eyed the smears of dust he'd left on my skin and chuckled, wiping most of it away with his wrist. This time, he painted purple sparkles on me in deliberate lines and strokes.

"Mmm. Always," he teased.

He hummed as he spread my dust down my arms. Eventually, he inspected the heat suppressant tattoo inked on my wrist. Hairline fractures showed damage through the pattern. "The more sex you have, the faster this cracks. And the more broken it is, the more you're going to crave your pack. When it's completely gone..." His tired smile still had a gleam to it. "Then you can complete Pack Sorles."

I nodded, no longer seeing a reason to dread my heat or push it back. Except... "What if I don't survive it?" I whispered. It wasn't exactly common for an omega to suppress a heat for as long as I had. As I'd experienced during my brushes with the end of my pre-heat, the internal temperature felt more intense each time it was delayed.

"Your heat won't kill you," he said immediately. "I'll need to do some research, but there has to be information on long-suppressed heats and how to handle them."

"That's a relief. Hey, Kauz. After you gave me your essence, my wing scales changed color. It was like they were half silver." At this point, most of his essence had filtered out of me, and those scales were slowly darkening to their natural indigo. "I loved it. I mean, wearing a part of you like that. Can you give me some of your essence again to change them back?"

"There's a much easier way to mark your wings with my magic, though I'll have to show you later. I won't be casting any serious spells for at least a few more days."

"Okay," I said cheerily.

"It would be permanent, though," he warned.

All the better.

He'd reached my arms, treating them to less detailed patterns, while the more artistic swirls emphasized my breasts, belly, and thighs, showing them off for... I grasped his wrist, eyes widening. "Where's Marius?"

He shrugged, less than concerned. Stars, this was the second time today that I'd taken my eyes off one of the princes, who'd then disappeared.

43
LARK

I WENT to the bathroom to grab some towels. Though we'd used what'd seemed like a good portion of the pack bed, once I turned back to look at Kauz, I saw the truth. We'd covered maybe a fourth of it, disrupting the bedspread into multiple waves of fabric and scattering the rose petals. He sat at the epicenter, his chin drooping toward his chest before he shook himself awake with a little gasp.

I ran some water and wet a washcloth to clean between my legs thoroughly. Then I took a moment before the mirror. My lips were kiss-swollen, and my hair was in a hopeless tousle that I attempted to straighten anyway. Patterns of purple pixie dust practically glowed on my arms, torso, and thighs. I loved how they emphasized my modest curves and pert breasts. I let Kauz doze for a moment or two longer to pose and admire my reflection.

That done, I brought Kauz a clean washcloth and a fluffy towel.

After he tied the towel around his waist, I tried to revive him further with a lingering kiss. "Go get him. I'll be okay," he murmured.

I nodded, though nerves churned in my belly. I asked myself why they were there, past the obvious: that I was about to walk into my nest and greet Marius naked and shimmering with my own dust.

It's tomorrow. He wanted to be here.

But he hadn't agreed to anything. He'd said, *"Perhaps tomorrow."*

Perhaps. Maybe it was complicated; part of him wanted me, and part of him did not, because I'd gotten the impression it was both. This "tomorrow" could become another until tomorrow never actually came. My instincts quailed at the idea of offering myself up for another no. But that was the risk I ran, wasn't it?

I strode for the curtain sectioning off my nest and slid it partway open so it didn't brush off Kauz's handiwork. Marius hadn't gone far at all. He sat on the edge of my nest's bed, fully clothed. He'd left bunched fabric on either side of him where his fists had been clenched.

He looked at me and stilled. I didn't think he was breathing. The weight of his attention was like a caress, starting at my breasts and tracing a path downward.

"Hello, Marius." I eased into one of the poses I'd just practiced before the mirror.

He worked his jaw and his throat bobbed, but nothing emerged. My smile started to drop. I hoped it was just this first look at my unclothed body that'd left him dumbstruck.

He finally took another breath, and a growl emanated from him like a roll of thunder. *"Sweet prey. Look at you. Irresistible."* It was practically a purr from his feral side.

He shook his head a moment later. "You're gorgeous," he murmured, sounding more like himself. "Do you know what's unfair, p'nixie?"

"What?" I murmured back.

"Whatever force it is that shaped us went in two vastly different directions. It matched our souls and paths, yet it made me a brute." He stood as if to emphasize his point. With him drawing my attention to it, he was still over a head taller than me, not to mention the broadness of his honed strength. "And you...so delicate."

I took a step toward him, and he eased to the side, maintaining the distance between us. I tried again, to the same result. It seemed we were the wrong kind of magnets, repelling each other. I whined, caught somewhere between confused and hurt. "I thought you wanted me."

"I do. But...I...." His gritted his teeth with a frustrated growl.

But he can't really explain. His feral side is getting in the way.

"Niall," I said. Marius's stance changed, his darkened gaze fixing on me with feral intent. His fingers balled into fists again as his form quaked with self-restraint. "I want you to rest. I need to talk to Marius. We can have a moment together later, all right?"

He tensed further, and I worried that hadn't worked. But when he spoke, it was in the deep, rich tone of his princely side. "What did you do?"

"Marius?"

"Aye."

"What's the last thing you remember?" I asked.

His ear flicked. "Being feral doesn't mean I have memory loss. I was just saying that I want you. Then you silenced Niall." I listened with growing wonder. There was no hint of his usual grunting and growling. "That doesn't change the fact that you're fragile. Like a walking work of art. I'd pull the fangs out of my skull if I harmed you again."

I sucked on the inside of my cheek. He'd been so sure he was going to hurt me, practically from the moment we'd met. How would we mate when I was so tiny and frail? The wording and the emotion behind it had changed, but the sentiment had not.

"I know fate is not your favorite topic," I said slowly. His response was a derisive snort. "Okay, look at it this way. You cultivated your strength with the intent to protect the future princess."

"In part."

This time, when I eased forward to close the gap between us, he didn't back away.

"Well, that's the role you've taken on as the second-born prince," I said, continuing to inch toward him. He dipped his chin in agreement. "You're the protector of the pack. I think you're very good at it. After your apology, I've felt safe every moment I've been with you. And that's been most moments, hasn't it? You've been there every step of the way, just like you've promised. You've even slept on a bare mattress to be closer to me."

"That's kelpie loyalty," he replied.

"Seems like more to me." I closed the rest of the space between us. His lips parted, then he shut his mouth with a shake of his head. We were nearly touching, and something unsaid was right there, if only I could coax it out of him.

"Talk to me. Please," I murmured.

"You're going to think I'm pressuring you," he said in a low voice.

"I just want to understand. Is it yes, or is it no?"

"It's yes, but—" His ear flicked again as he stopped mid-thought. "Listen to me, about to say it's both. It's a kelpie thing."

"Saying yes and no?"

He chuckled almost nervously. "Casual sex is unusual for my kind. It's common for our mates to not realize their kelpie won't tumble them into bed unless they're ready to forge that permanent bond and mate for life. It usually results in the nixie thinking he's too intense and the kelpie getting his feelings hurt. Drama follows." Marius eyed me, his mouth slanted in a doubtful line.

"We started this conversation talking about your fear of hurting me," I said.

His expression shuttered in an instant. "We don't have to start the bond now."

"No!" I caught his hand, pressing it between my palms. Meeting his startled gaze, I tried to beseech him with my expression. "No," I repeated more gently. "How are these two things connected?"

"Isn't it—" He cut himself off, sighed, and began again. "It's not obvious, is it? You weren't raised Unseelie. And I haven't told you..."

I squeezed his hand in encouragement.

"Forging the bond is a process. You start it by biting my alpha mark. That's the claim I've been waiting for. When I accept it, I'll begin to sense your thoughts and emotions as if they were my own. It would be like the loyalty I feel to you right now, one-sided. But I could sense your limits and mate with you more safely."

He cupped my face with his free hand. An ache bloomed in my chest at the longing in his softened gaze and how he smiled down at me. "And I should say ahead of time... not that I think it should color your decision. There's a possibility I'll be more stable if we bond. But I haven't wanted to turn wild since you forgave me, and I can wait if—"

"It's okay. What's the rest of the process?" I asked, purposefully interrupting him. My mind was already made up as I smiled back at him. I knew the kelpie bond was a big deal, but not that it was *this* important and would help him so much.

His hand drifted until he was sifting my hair between his fingers. "Next, I take you to the nearest body of water. You ride on my back while I'm in my kelpie form, which strengthens the bond to the point you feel my thoughts and emotions too. Then I claim you in return by sinking knot-deep in you. It's why I didn't give a shit about knotting you tonight. I won't have a knot until then."

I opened my mouth, ready to tell him my decision, but he wasn't finished.

"I know it's barely been a few days. You don't have to bond with me now. Make me earn it. I... You're precious to me. I'd rather drag myself through broken glass than have you think I'm—"

I reached up and stroked his cheek, deliberately brushing the dense end of his scar. He drew in a sharp breath and hesitated only briefly before angling his face for more. I stopped at the ridge of his nose, satisfied. "I'd be honored to bond with you," I said.

"Right now?" he murmured.

"Of course."

"You're too good to me, mate." He straightened, his lips stretching into a lopsided grin, fangs bared and all. "Here's my mark." Not about to waste time, he worked to free himself from the confines of his pants.

I'd cooled off enough from my encounter with Kauz to blush anew as Marius flicked open his pants and swept them away along with a hint of dark underclothes. A silvery gleam at the head of his cock caught my eye.

"You're pierced...*there?*" I squealed.

He was halfway through shrugging off his shirt. He paused and glanced down, like he'd forgotten about it. "Oh, aye. There's a story."

It looked like he had a bar all the way through his tip, with a stud marking the top and bottom. I immediately wondered what it would feel like inside of me. That had to be the point to it.

He tossed his shirt aside and kicked away the rest of his clothes, now just as naked as I was. It was my turn to be dumbstruck. His thighs were thick with muscle and patterned with more irregular green speckles. Past his waistline, his body formed a sculpted V, and his cock... Foregoing the distraction of his secret sixth piercing, it was proportionate to his size, and he was a big male.

Was there a saying in Serri, hung like a kelpie? No wonder he'd been so worried about hurting me.

"You can look at it all you want later," he said, nearly playful.

"Sorry." I glanced up at him instead. He wore an excited expression so pure I wanted to take the apology back. No negativity should've tried to taint this moment.

He beckoned, angling his side toward me. "Bite my mark hard enough to draw blood." He patted right above it.

The tails of Marius's alpha mark wrapped around his hip, leaving most of it in an intimate spot right up against his groin. I knelt in front of him and inspected it in fascination. This was the first time I'd seen the sideways loop that darkened on an alpha's skin when they manifested the traits of their designation.

The whole thing was barely bigger than my palm, slightly upraised from the rest of his skin. I pressed a kiss to where the lines of the loop crossed, and his groan was my immediate reward. It smelled like him, the floral bite of mint and waterlilies.

I nosed into his mark and licked it for a more concentrated taste of him. He threaded his fingers through my hair, applying light and encouraging pressure. "Go on, p'nixie. I'm yours. I'll be yours until our final breath, because I will not exist in this world without you."

I took my attention off his mark for a moment. "I love you too." I smiled against his skin when his eyes widened, before fierce affection creased every line of his scarred face.

This was the reversal of a moment I'd been preparing for since I understood the function of designation marks. As an omega, I was supposed to be the one who received claiming bites. Once my heat overwhelmed me, it'd be him sinking his teeth into my mark to strengthen our pack bond. But to bite him first, that was special. Unique, even.

I bared my small fangs and sank them into the top of his mark, around where it was thickest. His skin parted with unexpected ease, and my mouth was flooded with a concentrated burst of his pheromones. He tensed with a gasp and a muttered "*foc.*"

He held on to the back of my head like it was an anchor. Though he didn't come, he panted and shuddered like he felt some kind of orgasmic pleasure from my claiming bite. My slick threatened to drip down my thighs just from seeing how much he enjoyed this.

I released the pressure and took in my handiwork. I'd left two small punctures behind, which started leaking thin trails of blood. He didn't let me inspect his mark for long, as he hauled me up and into his arms to slant his mouth over mine, kissing me like he was ready to devour me. My pussy clenched, my body replying to *devouring* with *yes, please!*

"You're mine now," I said once we surfaced for air.

"And I accept your claim," he growled.

His acceptance triggered a tickling sensation at the back of my mind. He set me back on my feet, his hands roaming up my belly, leaving behind a trail of goosebumps smeared in pixie dust. Tilting his head, he narrowed his eyes in concentration as he reached my breasts. He bounced and squeezed them, adjusting the pressure until it was pure pleasure.

"That was fast?" I asked. I reached out to touch him, just for him to shake his head.

"Overwhelming," he grunted. "Don't be worried. I just need a few minutes to adjust."

I closed my mouth. I *was* a little worried. But if he was feeling everything both of us felt, of course that would be overwhelming.

He bent to layer nips over the curve of my neck. When he found the extra-tender spot under my jaw, he released a purr at the same time I did.

"Let's go back to the other room," he murmured. "I still owe you a massage." I made a sound of denial. I was about ready to try to take his cock, size concerns or not. "Ulterior motive this time, mate."

I peeked past the curtain first, but to my surprise, Kauz was still awake. Barely. I didn't have a chance to warn him of the naked kelpie behind me. Marius scooped me up. His nostrils flared as he carried me into the room and placed me on the far half of the bed, where I hadn't been rolling around with his brother.

"I've got that stunning spell ready," Kauz said, his gaze tracking me.

"Good. On your front, Lark."

I did as he said, exchanging a glance with the dream warden as I lay flat on my belly. "Is this awkward?" I asked in a lowered voice.

Kauz shrugged and flashed a reassuring smile.

Marius applied lotion to his hands, and they fell first in a place I didn't expect—my right calf. I whimpered as he squeezed and kneaded.

"I know. It's going to take some work to loosen these muscles," he said.

Once he worked away some of the tightness in my calf, he made his way up my body. It was a quicker treatment than last night, and the difference in the way he was touching me was obvious. *Ulterior motive, indeed.* He caressed the backs of my thighs and the globes of my ass, lingering with every hum, sigh, and moan I uttered.

Once his questing fingers moved over my wings and found their sensitive inner curves, I jolted beneath him. He circled his fingers and growled, "No one outside of our pack gets to touch these."

"Possessive," I murmured into the bedspread.

"Problem?" He pinched the edges of my lower wings, and pleasure rushed down my spine.

I caught my breath. Maybe it was just my omega instincts in the back of my head, but I liked his possessiveness. Yet I couldn't help but remember how he was saying something about a dangerous amount of obsession last night.

"Oh, about that," he said.

I stilled. "Can you read my thoughts now?"

"Only the direction of them. You're thinking about last night and my ongoing argument with Niall."

I nodded, glancing over my shoulder at him. His lips shifted, guilt in their uneasy set. "I should've told you before you claimed me. I argue with my instincts often, but it's unlike Niall to bulldog on one thing as much as..." He shook his head and made a twirling motion.

I shifted onto my back. His knees straddled mine, and my gaze was drawn to his erect cock. Its blue skin had traceries of purple from his veins, and the slit at its head wept a droplet of precome. What really caught my attention was the darker ring at its base. His knot, not yet inflated.

He bent over me, cupping my cheek, caressing, gazing intently at me. This didn't feel much like a massage anymore.

"You went into heat when we met," he said, direct to the point. I flushed at the heated gleam in his eyes. "You came very close to having my child in your belly. Niall hasn't let me forget. Every day since, I've smelled your pre-heat and…"

He drifted off, searching my face.

"I smell fertile?" I murmured. I must, to his sensitive nose.

"Potent," he agreed. "Feral alphas can supposedly smell when their omega is ready for more than one child. If you wanted to be bred, I think your next heat might produce a litter."

"Oh *no.*" An omega's litter was one baby from each of her mates. It was an exceedingly rare event that was also the last thing I wanted. The idea of becoming pregnant now, let alone with four babies at once, was terrifying.

Marius put his hands up. "I agree. I'm not ready to be a father. This is all my overactive alpha instincts that just…" He rumbled with an aroused growl. "You smell breedable. And I imagine…"

He hesitated, eyeing me again. I gave him an encouraging look and a nod. As alarming as the litter comment was, I knew Marius was a male who valued actions over words. When given a chance to breed me, he'd plopped me in front of Kauz instead so I could receive a suppressant. He hadn't pressured me into sex. The opposite, in fact, even while tangling with his instincts over it.

What a male. I smiled softly, more enamored than ever.

"I imagine you round with my child. And that mental image gets me harder than faesteel. I want to fill you with my seed. And do it again. And again. And *again.* Don't you understand? If we didn't have a bond to finish, you wouldn't leave this bed."

My eyes widened as he leaned in with the force of the question. I understood, all right. My pussy rippled to a phantom rhythm while I imagined us coupling again and again. That was about the hottest thing one of the princes had said to me yet. His nostrils flared, and disbelief and pure lust clashed in his expression.

I fought off a lusty trill to speak. "I'm wearing a fertility blocker. What's the harm?" I bent my legs, freeing them from between his knees, and spread them wide. "Breed me, Marius."

If I was expecting him to continue overthinking this, I was wrong.

Snarling soundlessly, he lowered between my thighs and nudged his cock inside me with no other preamble. He braced an arm under my wing as our bodies aligned. My mouth dropped open when he pushed in several inches and stretched me for another wave of pleasure edged in pain.

I'd thought the length of him was impressive, but it was his girth I noticed now. Plus the hard nub of his intimate piercing rubbing my inner walls in just the right way to make my every thought scramble into incoherency.

He withdrew far too soon. I grabbed him, trying to pull him back.

"This...okay?" he gritted out.

"Not so shallow. I can take more." I held onto his strong shoulders, still tugging in encouragement.

He thrust a little deeper this time. My belly quivered as the piercing found a spot within me that felt like pure, electric bliss.

"Oh. Fuck. I felt *that*," he said, halting his momentum to pull back and hit that spot again. I moaned loudly, my eyes practically crossing.

He trembled as he thrust again, sinking another inch deeper. When his piercing found the spot a third time, he made a breathy sound at the same time I did. Feeling the pleasure from both of us at once...now that was something to envy. He adapted, his shaky movements growing steadier over time.

He took me with the kind of patience I once would've thought was unlike him. Something I appreciated, especially when he started stretching my pussy in ways it hadn't been tested before. By the time he was buried in me to the root, we were both sheened in sweat.

"See." My breath came in short pants. "You didn't hurt me. We fit together." Yet I was *very* full as he paused for my body to adjust. He had found my body's limits.

His response was a soft noise from Niall. "*Mate.*" At some point, the prince had been overtaken by his instincts. His feral side's dilated eyes and loving expression were unmistakable. It was time for the moment together that I'd promised this side of him.

Our lips met, mouths melding. He adjusted the pressure until it was just right, the kind of kiss I could spend hours savoring alongside the taste of his waterlilies and mint. The air smelled strongly of him, but with an additional musky undertone where his arousal mixed with mine.

He layered love bites down my chin and jaw as he started a purr that vibrated my body inside and out. My toes clenched each time it thrummed through my core.

His lips brushed my neck, lingering on the ticking of my pulse. It only fluttered harder as an edge of fangs joined the softness of his kisses. Gentle. So gentle. Nothing like the breaking force he feared his feral side would unleash on me. I lifted my hips, working myself on his cock, trilling softly for more.

A deeper rumble cut through his purr, followed by a chuff. *"No rushing. You're finally mine."* He nuzzled up under my jaw, and then our cheeks met for a tender brush.

"Yes. And you're mine too." I cupped his scarred face. A touch he leaned into, though he didn't shutter his intense gaze. The dark, dilated moons in his eyes reflected the animal desire on his face. Anyone else would hear a dangerous pitch in his answering growl, but he was simply agreeing without words.

He caught my wrists, holding them over my head with one hand, the other still braced under my wing. My pussy fluttered and clenched on his length with a new rush of precome to have him pin me.

"You won't leave this bed without my colt inside you," he said through an intense rumble.

I bit my lip. *Do not laugh,* I hissed at myself. It was just the absolute worst time to learn that kelpies apparently called their boy children "colts" as if they really were the meat-eating cousins of horses.

My feral lover sensed and responded to the burst of mirth in my chest, even though I kept my giggles contained. He dimpled the side of my neck with his fangs and rolled his hips, *finally* taking a full thrust. My breasts bounced, and I suddenly forgot what was so funny as I loosed a breathy cry.

He worked his pace up until he was moving without pause, dispersing my thoughts yet again with that intimate piercing. I was already primed for a release, and it roared up on me.

As I teetered on the edge of completion, he pulled out completely. I squirmed and bucked, still pinned. He watched me, a slow, predatory smile curving his lips. Was he about to toy with his prey?

"Marius, please," I said, breathless.

His eyes hooded as he relished the moment. But he didn't leave me wanting long, instead flipping me without warning. I landed on my knees and newly freed palms, wobbling jelly-limbed. He caught my hip to right my balance and drew me into a pose my instincts recognized. Shoulders and head down, ass up. Presenting myself for my mate.

He mounted me again from behind, thrusting with the kind of force that drove any remaining breath from my lungs. I fisted the sheets, puncturing the gray comforter with my claws to hold on. He sank even deeper inside me at this angle.

Dark spots flared at the edges of my vision and I shut my eyes tight, surrendering to sensation. The urgency of his movements was changing. He wrapped his arms around me with a few staccato drives of his hips. Like he'd mentioned, there was no knot—even as he unleashed a hot burst of his seed deep in my core. The sharp points of his teeth dug into my shoulder.

I came on a gasp, fine trembles emanating from within with each new rope of his come. He held me closer until we were as flush together as this angle allowed. An affectionate noise escaped his lips as I quivered beneath him.

Everything was slowly muffling, like I was sinking underwater. I couldn't seem to catch a breath. My eyelids were too heavy to lift; my limbs weighed double. I sagged in his arms as darkness closed in around me.

44
LARK

I sprung back to wakefulness like nothing happened. Some time must've passed, as I was on my back, legs tucked. Cool tingles from a touch of wound salve marked the spot where Marius had bitten my shoulder. My wings fluttered as I giggled, thrilled after receiving the breeding treatment from Niall.

"—not a sign of your sexual prowess if you knock her out," Fal was saying in a tight tone. I turned my head, spotting him leaning his head into the room past the door to my study.

Marius was prowling at the foot of the bed, tearing at his hair. "Spare me the lecture, pack lead..." He paused mid-snarl and looked over at me just as I was piecing together that something was wrong.

Kauz entered my line of sight upside-down and winked. "She's awake," he reported belatedly.

"P'nixie." Marius rushed over and helped me sit up. I put my arms around his solid torso, letting him support my weight, as I was still feeling jelly-limbed. Burying his face in my hair, he breathed, "I'm sorry. I didn't mean to—"

I interrupted him with a murmur, "I'm fine. Really. Don't apologize for blowing my mind."

He drew back enough to look at me, disbelief and hope warring in his expression.

"We should do it again soon," I added, giggling.

He released a relieved sigh. "Thank the stars."

Fal cleared his throat. He hadn't left yet, and his feline gaze gleamed as he looked past Marius. I didn't feel a tug of modesty that he was seeing at least part of me naked. It'd be normal once we lived together for longer. "I'm going to call for a healer, just in case."

"Nay. I don't sense anything amiss. I think she really is fine," Marius said.

The dark elf's brows rose. "Is this insight from a kelpie bond?"

Marius hugged me closer, nodding.

"Congratulations," Kauz said.

"Happy for you, Mar. Are you going to go wake a barber to shave half your hair now?" Fal grinned, running a hand over one side of his head. "Hmm. He might take the wrong side off out of spite if you did at this time of night. What do kelpies do if they get the wrong half cut?"

Marius didn't look up at him as he answered briskly, "Cut the other half too and let the correct side grow. You'll be wanting your turn, aye? Just give me a few minutes to hold her."

"Take your time." The dark elf glanced away, his lips tugging downward.

As often happened when the less-than-subtle tension between them became frosty, I felt badly for Fal. I'd watched him try to connect with Marius more than once, often just to be rebuffed. It also wasn't a good time, when the kelpie was intent on basking in whatever after-glow remained between us.

But he was watching me, and presumably sensing what I felt, as Fal turned away. "Wait," Marius sighed, finally shifting to acknowledge the dark elf. "She has the breeder's delight. You should know that for when you knot her."

"Oh, really?"

"It's...nice," he stated awkwardly.

I blinked in surprise. I'd known about "the breeder's delight" but not by that name. The vile pack I didn't want to think of had called it something else, making it sound incredibly dirty. Not every omega had it. But now that I'd experienced it for myself, it was "nice" for certain. Incredible, even, to shake with bliss each time a partner finished inside of me.

Fal flashed his usual smile. "An understatement, I'm sure." He considered his brother before adding, "If you change positions too quickly and don't give her a chance to catch her breath, that can lead to her passing out."

"I'll avoid doing it again," Marius said.

"You tell her about how you got your extra piercing?"

The kelpie's expression shuttered. "I don't know why you're bringing that up."

"Why, someone who's not a kelpie has to help explain your race's many intricacies. This one is particularly confusing, and Kauz is asleep," he said lightly.

I glanced over my shoulder. He was right; Kauz had finally succumbed to his exhaustion. He'd cocooned himself in his wings, peacefully snoozing.

Marius sighed. "When I turned eighteen, I received my tags," he said, bringing my attention back as he pointed to the two eyebrow studs and nose ring on the right side of his face. I tweaked the bar through one of his nipples. He released a soft, aroused growl. "After my tags were in, the piercer asked if I wanted, and I quote, the 'lady pleaser package.'"

"Package. Like, more than one?" I asked.

"Mmhmm. We made it to one before I swung at him. So, I did not receive the whole package," he said, shaking his head.

"You punched him?"

"I missed. I didn't realize it would hurt like a sonofabitch even with the numbing cream. Violent kelpies get thrown out, though, and it was already a miracle I'd gotten through all my tags without biting the piercer." He shrugged as if it wasn't a big deal.

"Theodred sent me to look for him the next day since he'd missed training. He was still in bed, groaning like he'd caught the winter flux. He looked at me and went, 'I think I'm fucking dying.'"

Fal deepened his voice into a fairly spot-on impression of his brother.

Marius glanced away with a resigned sigh while I muffled a laugh.

"And I'm eyeing his face as I say, 'It doesn't look *that* bad' before he flings his covers aside. It was very purple and very swollen, and not in the good way."

I winced in sympathy. "Oh."

The kelpie grumbled, "I asked my dear older brother to tell Theodred something to cover for me for a bit. You know what he did?"

"Told him the whole truth," Fal said.

My eyes widened. "Why would you do that?" How embarrassing for Marius.

Fal mirrored my expression back at me. "I didn't know what else to do! I was *baffled* that Mar had gotten pierced there. I still am. He's always said it's just a kelpie thing."

"If you heard her scream, you'd understand," Marius said dryly.

Fal purposefully crossed his eyes. "Uh huh. Way to assume I'm deaf and that Tormund is too. He's still cooling off."

"What?" I put in.

"He's fine. Just lost his shit a little bit. As I'm sure Mar will when it's not his turn with you anymore."

"If he burns her..." Marius drifted off with a warning growl. Fal leaned further into the room to sweep his arm toward him in a gesture of 'you see?'

"I'm sure it'll be fine. Just like it was with us," I said, petting Marius's chest to soothe him. I had no doubt that Tormund would do everything in his power to remain cool and in control of himself.

But first, I was a mess. Sweaty, vaguely sparkly, and sticky all in between my thighs.

"Could you give us some privacy?" I asked Fal, who ducked out of the room without another word.

Marius immediately began to lap at the sweat and pixie dust under my collarbone. "You're not a mess. You're perfect," he murmured against my skin.

Having him able to sense the direction of my thoughts would take some getting used to. But I enjoyed the other benefits to the kelpie bond as he made his way down to my breast, swirling his tongue around my nipple and flicking it just right.

"When we fully bond, I want a few hours just to explore your body," I said.

"Done. I intend to swim with you as soon as possible. It'll be a big part of our date."

"Oh, um. About riding your kelpie form..." I pictured us both underwater and shivered with fear. Cymora had repeated and layered her orders to avoid water after I'd proven a better swimmer than Laurel. The feeling clung to me like a foul odor, even now.

He stilled halfway into nuzzling between my breasts, brows knitting. "You're afraid? Why?"

"Cymora ordered me to fear open water. She reinforced this one enough that I still feel it. It'll go away in time." *Hopefully.*

He kissed the skin over my heartbeat. "The sea represents freedom for us water fae," he murmured. "She cannot take that away from you."

"I'm only half water fae," I said hesitantly. "And it's been over a decade since I last used my gills. I'm not so sure they're *going* to open."

Marius answered with a rumbling, "We'll figure it out. Later." He pressed his mouth to mine and lifted me from the bed while we kissed. I purred in approval as we found the perfect lip-lock and lingered with it.

When he placed me down, it was in the rain room for the shower I'd been considering taking between seeing the pairs of my mates. "Don't worry about Kauz, I'll get him into your nest. And I'll be close by if Tormund loses control of himself," he said.

"Okay, thank you," I murmured. "Oh, Marius?"

"Hmm?"

"Baby kelpies are called colts?"

He chuckled, which set me to giggling, finally releasing the pressure of holding in my surprise. "It's an affectionate word for a shifted young kelpie. My kind begin shifting practically before we start walking. Colts are wee and playful. Mother will assure you that I was the cutest colt in existence."

"I'm sure you were," I said, beaming.

He aimed a halfhearted snort at me. "You're not supposed to agree. Anyway, take your shower. Love you." He strode off before his words sank in.

I covered a thrilled little squeak with my fingertips, even as my fanning wings covered the bottom of my shower with a layer of sparkles. Turning on the water for a quick rinse, I erased the visible signs that I'd been mated so thoroughly. My cleansing found some tenderness, especially along the inside of my thighs and just inside my folds.

When thinking about the logistics of the confidence special, I'd expected my energy to be flagging by now. In this quiet moment, I did feel the tug of fatigue, but the excitement stirring my heart pushed it away. I still had an opportunity to make love to my gentle giant and see whether Fal was serious when he said he'd douse himself in chocolate sauce.

I donned a bathrobe and peeked into the bedroom. There was no sign of Kauz or Marius. Tormund was in the process of straightening the comforter, and Fal was waiting right beside the door. "All done? Trade you," he said, heading past me into the bathroom.

I shrugged and closed the door. Tormund glanced up, his brassy cheeks darkening. The little flames in his pupils left sunspot-like lines in my vision as he looked me up and down. I flushed, knowing where his mind was with a look like that.

"Hello again, li'l bird."

"Hi, Tormund. Are you okay? Fal said you needed to cool off," I said.

He scratched behind his horn. "I heard... Well, I heard." He gestured vaguely to the room with his other hand. "I was mad when you passed out. But I'm all right. You're okay too?"

I nodded and headed around the bed to him. "I'm fine. No harm done." And glad to have a moment just with him, as Fal was taking a shower, by the sound of falling water from the other room. "Do you want to get more comfortable?"

"Aye. By the way, I tell Fal he has no good judgment for food." He stooped and picked up a pair of squeeze bottles. One was half full of chocolate-colored syrup, and the other was topped up with purplish liquid that had flecks of berry skins suspended within. "Chocolate for the sweet omega. Fruit for the male that smells like the outdoors. It'll pair better on the tongue."

"What about for you?" I asked, cocking my head.

Tormund loosed a belly laugh. "I've got too much hair! Let me show you." He loosened his shirt and tugged it off.

I took a couple steps back to look at him properly. "Could you sit down? So I can touch you?" I suggested.

He nodded and, after setting his spectacles aside, made his way toward the center of the pack bed. Drawing me closer with one broad hand, he lifted his chest for my inspection.

He had a scattering of red hairs across his torso, forming a trail down the generous curve of his middle. It seemed that he had freckles over his whole body, as the brown speckles continued unbroken across his skin. His alpha mark had manifested on the right side of his upper chest, and within it was a knot-like tattoo.

I rested my hand just under his collar and followed the path of hair down his chest. His weight cushioned the alpha redcap muscle he carried, giving him that enticing softness I loved so much. I went slowly, my touch reverent. It was Tormund, after all. I admired him for who he was, broad and strong yet comfortable and inviting.

Without his spectacles, he squinted at me like he used to. "Do you like?" he whispered.

"Of course I do." I brushed my cheek against his shoulder affectionately. "You're strong and handsome. My snuggly bear of a male."

His breath caught. "Yours," he echoed.

"Tell me a redcap fact. What does this mean?" I traced the knot tattoo on his chest and accidentally brushed his alpha mark in the process. His muscles swelled with sudden growth. I petted his arm, trying to help him calm down.

A hint of deeper red stained his cheeks above his beard as any changes receded. "I transform a li'l bit when I get excited," he said in his loud whisper.

I tilted my head. "How much?" It was clear the other princes were worried about him taking his monstrous form completely during mating. But I'd helped him keep it at bay before. It might even be easier to do with us joined together.

"I don't know. I've scared off a couple females before we got too far. But I feel more in control when I'm touching you." He skimmed his fingertips over my curves ever so carefully.

I inched closer, pressing myself into his hands. "Then you'd better keep touching me," I invited.

His eyes held extra glimmers as he smiled in his broad, toothy way. He took one of my hands and rested it over his alpha mark and knot tattoo. "My tattoos are from the Bloodhunter Clan. Many generations ago, the first Queen of Serian chose her redcap from my clan and elevated him as her king. This tattoo means I'm a member in good standing."

He moved my hand to rest it on the left side of his chest as I listened. His heart made a powerful drumbeat against my palm. "Once you join the pack, I'll place a knot of promise here. A symbol that I am taken for life."

"Should I get one too?"

"Nay. It's a redcap thing. Something I'll do for you."

I hummed and straddled his thigh, leaning up to press my lips to the line of his neck, under the edge of his beard. I explored his chest further with my fingertips, tracing paths where I wanted to kiss next. His moan was deeper than I expected, with crackling fire lingering in the throaty sound.

It's still Tormund. He can't help it. I didn't let the hint of his fiery form spook me into stopping.

"I'm going to unwrap you. Okay, li'l bird?" As he waited for my reply, he spanned his big hands over my hips and waist. He asked respectfully, like my body was a present I would allow him to reveal. My wings fluttered as I nodded.

He undid the cloth tie and pushed the bathrobe off my shoulders. It didn't even have buttons to tighten it around my wings, so they sagged for a moment until he tugged the garment the rest of the way off.

I was fully revealed, my skin flushed pink from the warmth in the room. The temperature seemed to rise by another few degrees as Tormund took me in. His attention was like a caress of heat anywhere he looked.

"You are very lovely and perfect. May I touch you?" His other form entered his voice, lowering it to a gravelly rumble.

I nodded, purring softly as he spread the heat of his palms down my arms first. As much as he was causing the room to swelter, the direct heat of his skin against mine was bliss. He touched me everywhere in slow sweeps. Curls of smoke escaped his lips as his breath quickened.

He adjusted the straining front of his pants. *Oh stars.* Just the size of his hands against the modest swells of my curves was a reminder that he was my biggest mate, and if he was proportional too...I didn't know whether he'd fully fit inside of me. But I was more than willing to try.

I leaned in while he mapped my body, giving his alpha mark a lick and enjoying the taste of his smoke and mallows pheromones. He growled, deep and fiery.

"Calm," I said a bit nervously, petting his chest in faster strokes.

The warmth coming off him lessened, and I took that as a sign to keep going. I pressed kisses to his upper chest and laved the buds of his nipples. All the while, he squeezed and kneaded my ass, his touch unpracticed but enthusiastic.

"I think it's time for this," he mused. He reached over and took the bottle of chocolate sauce in one palm.

"What are we actually going to do with that?"

He squinted at the bottle, then at me. "Turn around. I have an idea."

I faced away from him. Tormund practically giggled as he placed a bit of liquid chocolate on my upper left wing. I tried not to flick the drops off as if they were rain. His warm breath had the sensitive membranes quivering before he licked the chocolate away and immediately loosed a purr. "I knew it. Tastes like you smell. So, so good. And sweeter. Must be the sparkle dust."

"Pixie dust," I corrected, also near giggles as he added more chocolate to my wings.

The wet swipe of his heated tongue turned my mirth into moaning. No one had licked my wings directly like this before, but it sure felt as if he was laving paths up and around my intimate folds instead. They wept slick moisture that started to roll down my thighs in hot droplets.

The dessert mixed with my natural scent and made it richer, bringing out its cocoa tones. Tormund feasted on my dust and the chocolate sauce like I was a fine dessert, his deep purr thrumming through me while I squirmed with growing need. He'd moved on to my top right wing when the shower shut off.

Fal stepped into the room, toweling his hair. He was otherwise nude, casually showing off what had to be the wellspring of his eternal confidence. His clothes had always been tailored to emphasize his athletic, elfin build, but it was something else to see his leanly muscled form unclothed. Those trim hips and flat stomach were male perfection, with his alpha mark nestled right under his belly button. He didn't have so much as a curl of body hair.

He lifted his feline gaze to mine, winked, and looked past me to Tormund. With a chuckle, he smacked his cheek. Such a motion would rattle his earrings, but he'd taken them off, leaving his long ears bare too. "The chocolate's for her body, not her wings."

"Oh, like..." The redcap reached around, resting his hand over one of my breasts.

"Mmhmm."

"You have to try it on her wings. They're so sweet."

"I would prefer to make love to her over denuding her of pixie dust."

Tormund lifted his head further, making a confused *ach*. "What is that word?"

Fal dropped his towel and prowled up the bed. "Which one?" he said playfully.

"Denude?" I guessed.

The dark elf switched to speaking Serri. "The only one yet to fully denude is you, little brother." He stopped in front of me and pressed a featherlight kiss to my nose.

"*Ooooh*. I'm going to do that," Tormund said in kind. He shifted out from behind me, sending quakes through the bed as he wrestled with his pants.

Fal swiped the bottle of chocolate sauce before it could tip over. "Lay back, *mo stór*," he purred in a mix of languages.

"I'm going to make a mess. My wings..."

"So? We'll clean up later." He grinned. That energy was infectious, so I went onto my back, wings spread to either side of me.

Fal drew patterns on my lower belly with the chocolate, then nestled his torso between my thighs to start lapping up the sweet treat. My belly quivered with each stroke of his tongue. Swiping one of my lower wings with a fingertip, he sampled my dust with a lick and an approving hum.

His nostrils flared from scenting the air. When he growled with interest and his lust-darkened eyes smoldered up at me, my breath hitched. I made a soft, needy trill. He looked past me, murmuring, "She's ready."

I sat up after Fal finished cleaning the chocolate from my belly. He moved away and lay casually on his side. His cock had jumped to fully erect, and he gave it a stroke when he noticed where my attention had drifted to. Out of curiosity, I'd been looking at his knot. The ring of darker flesh at the base of his member was already just a bit thicker than the rest of him.

Tormund caught my chin between two fingers, tilting my head so I'd look at him instead. He was bare, his cock jutting out from a thatch of red-brown curls. I swallowed. Yes, he was proportional. *Huge.*

The transformation was taking him, turning his eyes to flame and elongating his nails and teeth. I tried stroking his chest and belly, but this time, the monstrous form didn't fully recede. I leaned up instead, meeting his lips despite the hot gusts escaping his nostrils. Our mouths melded for a moment. He tasted strongly of smoke, with just the barest sweetness of mallows underneath.

While we kissed, he swung us around so I was on my back again and his knees rested between mine. I parted my legs, even though he seemed impossibly large as his body rippled with new muscle. Sweat sheened me from the heat pouring from his body.

"I'm yours. Take me," I invited anyway, eager for *him*, Tormund, past the way his body was changing.

"Mine. I like the sound of that." His monstrous side had a voice deeper than Marius's, hitting a tone I felt down to my core. *Ooh.* My pussy clenched, greedy for more.

I lifted my wings so he could brace himself by sliding his arms underneath the top pair. He kept his entire weight off me, but that wasn't what I needed from him.

I cupped his face and leaned up to kiss him again. Ever so slowly, he relaxed his stiff stance and rumbled deep and low. He was purring, actually, and keeping his pointy bits at bay, though he trembled with restraint.

I forced a purr too, thinking he might be self-soothing. It stuttered away into a gasp when he nudged at me and missed, his hard length sliding through my folds. I sank down and reached, earning a crackling growl when I wrapped my hand around him and guided him to the right spot.

He kissed me gently. We gazed into one another's eyes as he sank within me this time. His mouth parted, revealing sharp teeth, while I moaned and tipped my head back. As his length went deeper, my pussy was full of the sensation of a pleasurable burn. Part intimate stretch, part heat from his body.

I clung to his shoulders, dimpling his skin. Inch by inch, it seemed he was going to fit. Somehow. He purred all the while, working his own kind of magic to help me accept all of him. Once he was fully seated, his trembling worsened as he took great gulps of air through his mouth and leaked smoke.

I smoothed my hands down the span of his back. It didn't seem to help. His muscles jumped under his skin, just about to burst free. His control was at its end, seemingly at the point where we were joined.

"Tormund," I whispered.

"I have it," he gasped. "Just...give me a second."

"It's okay. You can let go," I urged.

His eyelids peeled open, those fiery pupils dancing with worry. This was clearly something he needed. The monstrous form was as much a part of him as Niall was a part of Marius.

The only thing we could do now was embrace it, even if the idea of Tormund unleashing himself had my heart pattering at double the intensity. Fear and desire mixed well together, and the combination was heady as I made my offer. "What kind of mate would I be if I didn't take you in your other form?"

His jaw clenched. "I don't want to hurt the li'l bird," he gritted.

"You won't." I put my full confidence into it.

Something like relief lit his expression before he lowered to pepper my face with kisses. After a single, lingering press of his mouth to mine, he let the transformation go. The full-fanged maw of his monstrous form emerged, as did the claws he had folded in his fists underneath my wings. He vented extra heat from his back as his chest expanded and glowed molten with fire from the inside.

His form swelled with exaggerated muscles, and his cock... I made a strangled scream and bucked as it thickened and pushed the absolute limits of what my body could take. I writhed and left scratches down his front, not that my claws could penetrate the hide of a transforming redcap. As the moments passed, he was only inching up in size and heat.

He still hadn't moved from where he was buried in me, but now his blazing gaze threatened to recede with concern as he watched my reaction.

"Please," I moaned and made a whistling sound of need.

And as much as I thought I was ready for him, his first real thrust had my eyes rolling back. Without the sensation of stretching around him, it was pure bliss to be filled to the brim. He coated me with a sauna's worth of heat inside and out.

"I'm okay." My breath rushed out of me when he took the reassurance and rocked into me again. "Better than okay."

"Better?" he echoed in a core-shaking rumble.

My thoughts were in shambles. I'd brainstorm how to get the giant to talk to me mid-mating later. When he wasn't rocking my entire body with the slam of his hips against mine.

"Uh huh" was about all I managed. I hooked my legs around his ass and held on tight as he threatened to ruin me for any other male. His transformation made him look dangerous to the touch, but most of his heat was venting from his back to halo us. His panting breaths expelled smoke and steam, which he aimed away from my skin to avoid any burns.

All the while, his mouthful of deadly fangs remained close to my exposed throat. This was the ultimate act of trust, and I hoped Tormund never doubted how much I loved him after our coupling was over.

He could've hurt me at any point. But he didn't, just as I knew he wouldn't. He did, however, find sensitive points deep within me that had me mumbling encouraging nonsense for more.

His knot began to inflate with each thrust. It was a new sensation that my instincts recognized immediately. A little voice at the back of my head wanted me to urge him on, so he'd tie with me and breed me properly.

The expanding ring of flesh kept catching and rubbing my folds and the rim of specialized muscle just past them, designed to seal in an alpha's knot. His knot grew too large to enter me, so his last thrusts were a couple inches short. His panting breaths shuddered as he came, grinding and bucking the swollen flesh against my clit.

I came too, as soon as his liquid heat bloomed in my belly. The breeder's delight prolonged my pleasure, and as he tapered to a finish, I fell limp with bliss beneath him. I had to acknowledge a dirty fact about myself: much as I didn't want babies right now, there was nothing nearly as satisfying as being stuffed with fresh come from one of my mates.

Tormund's transformation receded, and he gathered me up, the two of us nuzzling. He pressed a soft kiss over my throat. "You're okay," he whispered.

"Better," I echoed, breaking into a big grin. "That was *amazing*."

45
LARK

I cuddled Tormund afterward, the two of us purring in harmony. It became difficult to ignore how hot he was to the touch, though, and he was making the room feel like a sauna. We separated, and he donned his clothes, promising to be back after he'd cooled down.

This left me with Fal, who'd been uncharacteristically quiet, though he still lay on the bed nearby. His sapphire gaze was keen when it met mine. "Well, that went better than I expected. Be right back," he said.

I peeled myself into a sitting position, then stood on shaky legs and fanned my wings to try to cool off. My sweat-covered skin chilled from my efforts. Stars, back to being a mess, it seemed. But I still had a head full of pleasant fluff after successfully taking my biggest mate. Fate had shaped me for my males after all.

Fal returned with a carafe of ice water and offered me a tall glass full of clinking cubes. I downed a few healthy swallows before pressing the cold edge of the glass to my forehead. "Thank you. I, um, need another shower."

"Well, not yet. I got clean for the chocolate sauce experience and everything." He gestured to encompass his bare, perfect body.

"You're unfairly attractive." The thought fell from my lips, unbidden.

His face creased with amusement. "Unfair?" he echoed, sliding a little closer.

"I don't know how I'm supposed to function like a normal fae after tonight." My voice lowered to a respectful hush. I set the glass of water on my dresser, and he placed the carafe next to it, not letting more than a few inches of air come between us.

"I've felt the same way for a while. But..." He tilted his head with an impish smile. "What is normal anyway? If it requires me to trade this moment away, then I don't want it. All I want is you."

I was breathless to hear his desires spoken aloud. "I want you too."

"Well, then I have one pressing question." He turned toward the pack bed, which was more rumpled than ever. "Where *haven't* you fucked on this bed yet?"

Oh stars. I'd completely lost track of that. He chuckled at my expression as I tried to remember. He went ahead and patted the foot of the bed before easing onto his back.

"Bring the sauces. I'm wondering if I really taste better with berries. You can be the judge," he said, grinning.

I retrieved the bottles and gave them to him before downing the rest of the glass of ice water. He held the underside of the chocolate sauce, shaking his head. "That lad's too hot for his own good."

"He is," I agreed, but with a loving lilt.

Fal affected a swoon before he smeared a few drops of sauce on his upper chest. Chocolate on one side, berries on the other. "Come get me, tricksy p'nixie," he purred.

I straddled his lower chest, leaned down, and inhaled the warm scent of sunshine and grass floating off his skin. The first taste of chocolate also included a hint of those notes on my tongue. Sunshine and melted chocolate were a pleasant combination. I purred a quiet approval, then lapped up the purplish smear of berry sauce next.

"Hmm."

"Mmhmm?" he echoed.

Tormund might be wrong about this one. They both worked well. The berries mingled best with the hint of earthiness from Fal's scent. It just depended on my mood, really. "Berries," I decided.

"All right. I thought food play would ease you into this, but now I'm going last." He set the chocolate sauce aside and started drizzling sweet purple lines on his upper chest, smearing extra around the tight buds of his nipples. "So, how about we play as you like, clean up, and see what happens from there?"

"As long as seeing what happens is you knotting me," I murmured. I began to trace the planes of his chest, slowly licking every inch he'd covered. The taste of him was nice, but I also enjoyed learning where those tender spots were that caused his breath to hitch.

He stroked his fingers through my hair, eyes lidding. "Finally, you're losing that untouched modesty."

"It's died swiftly tonight." And as I swirled my tongue over one of his nipples, I didn't really miss it. I was having too much fun.

"Oh, really?" He switched to speaking Serri. His wicked tone left little to the imagination, but my limited vocabulary did. I flushed, skin tightening with desire as I pieced together that he was describing, in intimate detail, what he wanted to do with me next. "But first, more berries?" he concluded in Theli.

I nodded but I could feel the pulsing heat of his erection close to the swells of my ass. I got off him so he could leave little patterns of berry sauce on his abdomen, this time rubbing extra over the sideways loop of his alpha mark.

"While I don't know everything you said, yes." I traced the lines of his abdominals with my tongue and tasted the hint of musk on his skin. It only grew stronger, nearly overpowering the berry sweetness, as I laved his mark and restrained a grin to feel him shift and growl beneath me.

He took one of my hands and placed it on his cock. It kicked in my hold as I took the hint, rubbing his shaft as I cleaned the rest of his abdomen. Thankfully, he wasn't about to break me out of sheer size. The base of his length had a different texture, denser where his knot would inflate.

I continued to lick his alpha mark past calling it clean, savoring the way he tensed from the attention. "Careful, *mo stór*. When you have a mark of your own, I will be returning the favor." His tone was roughened with desire.

I raised my head and deliberately turned my attention to his cock. "Speaking of returning the favor..."

"I was hoping you'd pick up the idea. Especially if I did this." He gathered his legs under him and rose to his knees. Waggling his brows, he tipped some berry sauce onto his shaft.

"I might not be very good at this," I prefaced, finding my nerves.

Fal brushed the backs of his knuckles across my cheek. "Don't worry, it's not difficult. And you've got four eager volunteers to help you practice."

He started giving me instructions. I cupped my lips over my teeth as he demonstrated and ran my tongue over the tip of his erection. Male musk and his grass and sunshine hit my tongue at the same time, melding in harmony with the sweetness he'd coated himself with.

My mind hazed pleasantly as I licked the underside of his shaft and was rewarded with a drop of his precome to savor. I took him into my mouth inch by inch, sucking on as much of his length I could fit.

"That's it. Just like that." He guided my hand to stroke the rest of his cock and firmly grip the denser flesh of his knot.

I found a rhythm, coordinating my hand and mouth to stimulate all of his length. His moans were encouragement that I was pleasing him just fine, even if my attempt seemed wet and messy. He rocked his hips into my bobbing mouth, his shaft absorbing my every noise.

He hadn't stopped talking or stroking my hair to soothe my omega side, though he mostly murmured disjointed praise. "Such a good fucking omega," he growled. "You look so beautiful with your mouth stretched around my cock."

My wings fluttered. I really was trying to move past my blushing shyness, but a bit of it remained to make me flush all over. Even with him filling my mouth to the back of my throat.

His knot was expanding, distracting me from the heat of his hooded gaze. It swelled with every frenzied pulse of his heart.

I sucked a little harder, eager to see him undone.

"If you don't take the knot, it's polite to squeeze." His voice broke at the end as he spilled in the back of my mouth. Though I couldn't get my hand around it fully, I squeezed his knot and shivered with secondhand pleasure as his breathing stuttered. He flooded my mouth with his seed. Rivulets of it escaped the seal of my lips despite how much I'd swallowed.

He pulled himself free and swiped up some of his come from my chin, teasing my lip until I sucked it off his finger. "Well, now I'm properly dirty. Let's clean up together once I can walk."

"Okay. Um. Is this going to go down?" I pressed on his inflated knot gently, yet he gasped and growled.

"Aye," he said with some strain. "Since we're not tied, it should take a couple minutes. But not if you do that."

"Oh, sorry." I pulled away, and he caught my elbow, tugging me closer to meet his lips. He ran his hands over my curves and wings, petting and caressing until I purred and melted into his sunshine-filled kiss.

After a few minutes, he drew back and rested his forehead against mine. "I adore you. I just want you to know that."

My breath caught. "I love you, Fal. I loved you first, you know."

"Oh, first? I would've expected it to be Kauz," he mused. "That lovestruck lad chased you where I couldn't, in your dreams."

"Yes, but..." I searched for the right words. "You saw me. I mean, you looked past what I showed you when we first met and...and *cared* when you didn't have to."

He mimed a bow. "When you asked for help, I couldn't say no." I wracked my brain, trying to think of when in our first short conversation I'd asked for help. "Your body did. The shadows in your eyes, the tense set of your wings. Your limp, your exhaustion, and your sticky fingers too. You didn't *ask*. You went to the event thinking you'd save yourself and ended up with my pack falling over ourselves—as I warned you we would—all trying to save you at the same time instead. Clumsy love."

I was trying not to get teary, in the good kind of way. I cherished Pack Sorles's clumsy love. They really had saved me when I couldn't save myself. It was striking how much he'd read from me and responded to after our fateful meeting.

"Besides. To be seen is to be loved." He placed a clawed finger on his chin and cocked a mischievous smile. "Or is it the other way around? Either way, once I saw you, I couldn't look away."

"You did save me. Brought me here, listened, noticed something off about my stepfamily, and made me feel like a princess," I murmured.

"Lark, get used to hearing this," he said, then paused meaningfully for a few heartbeats. "You *are* a princess. You *are* a lady. You're *my* lady."

He picked me up, carrying me to the rain room. "Fal," I laughed.

The rain room was big enough that we could've probably fit another fae in here. Fal turned on a shower of cool water, chuckling when I nudged him out of the way and turned so the downpour would cover my back and wings. I released a sigh dramatic enough to rival one of his.

He wetted his hands with soap and began to wash my body. I took the soap bar and did the same, muffling a yawn behind my hand as I did. "Tired?" he murmured.

I was flagging a lot more than the last time I'd taken a quick rinse. I glanced up and took him in, mouth poised to reply. His feline eyes gleamed in the bathroom light as he performed so domestic a task as washing my belly. His long hair was damp and clung to his neck and shoulders. A little imperfect to balance out the polished charm he was taught to show the world.

I couldn't lie, but I could answer him indirectly. "I wish I could stay in this moment longer." Just us, stripped down to the basics. So, despite my fatigue, I lingered. Instead of following the urge to lean on him and close my eyes, I polished his body instead.

After he gave me the same treatment, he set the soap aside and rested his hands on my hips. He sang to me, softly at first, adjusting to the acoustics of the bathroom to keep his voice between us. And stars, what a voice it was. Not too high or low, and smoother than the brush of silk.

He sang a slow Serri love song, pulling me closer so we stood just out of the direct spray of water. I looped my arms around his neck, and he bent so I wasn't up on my toes to do so. We swayed together to the pace of the music he made.

If only we'd met more honestly at the Omega Masquerade. We

could've caught a song and come together in a dance that would've looked something like this.

Yet I preferred what we had now, as I felt his arousal growing and pulsing between us as we pressed together. He finished his song, letting it taper into a melodic hum.

"That was beautiful," I said earnestly.

A hint of a smile pulled at his lips, some deeper emotion flicking over his expression in the moment before he kissed me. Slow and sweet to start, then becoming a passionate duel of our tongues. He fumbled blindly before shutting off the fall of water. We hit the wall of the rain room together, with his arm braced over my head.

He slid his other hand further up my leg to brush his knuckles over my clean pussy. His thumb found my clit and circled it ever so carefully. My answering moan seemed much louder in this room.

He nipped my bottom lip, then trailed kisses along my jaw. "I think it's time I claimed my treasure," he purred. "Don't you agree?"

"Yes. And knot me." I ached to know what it felt like.

"That's right. A *full* claim."

We toweled off briskly, then he lifted me for a short walk to the bed and sat on the closest edge. My belly quivered with anticipation as I spread my legs, more than eager to accept his cock. The angle of his hold changed, drawing me in until there were mere inches between us, and he tilted his head. "I still have your almost full trust?"

I grimaced at the reminder of our conversation on secret keeping. Something we'd both worked on since then. "You have all of my trust," I corrected.

He grinned. "Let me show you a real trick." His voice held a subtle thread of alpha authority, the enticing whisper of his bark that he layered on just thick enough for me to sense it. "Listen, Lark."

I rested my weight back into his bracing hands and waited, an attentive audience.

"You are safe here with me. Nothing else matters. No worries, no fears, no doubts."

As I accepted and let in his dominance, my mind emptied of lingering static. I was damp, full of desire, and aware just how poised I was to be full of him. Shifting in his hold, I made a soft trill of need.

"You're not going to come until I tell you to. Okay?"

"Okay," I said, though I was of half a mind to push back on that direction.

"Good omega." With his trick still winding through his voice, the praise felt like a stroking hand of pleasure down my spine. My wings practically quivered with delight.

He took in my reaction with a gleam in his feline eyes. Instead of dragging me onto his cock, as I expected, he stood and switched places with me. He slid his grip to my thighs and pulled me into a thrust of his hips that seated him in me in one long push. "Fuck," he groaned.

I made a breathy cry of agreement. He started off slow, getting me accustomed to the size and shape of him in a measured slide. Fresh out of the shower, I wasn't soaked with slick yet, so I felt each inch and the grind of his pelvis at the apex of every thrust. Starting this way didn't immediately overwhelm me with pleasure. It was more of a slow, sizzling burn or the first steps to an intimate dance he'd invited me to learn from him.

"You feel perfect. Move with me. That's right. So fucking good," he murmured. I let out a moan at how amazing his praise felt, nearly as incredible as each meeting of our bodies.

With my head emptied of my most negative thoughts, I could focus on being present in the moment. I admired his lean body and the view I had of his cock sliding in and out of me. My belly quivered. It was all the more intense to watch his claim in motion.

He flashed that wicked smile and reached between us, pinching my clit and rubbing it between two fingers. My legs locked up as I anticipated the shattering pleasure of an orgasm. But it didn't arrive. Instead, I tensed on the edge and drifted down without reaching it. I whimpered in denial. *Come back.*

"Lark." He had my attention immediately, especially when he pulled out. "Get on your hands and knees."

He helped me turn over, and I crawled further onto the bed with him right behind me. He cupped and kneaded my ass while my wings flicked in enjoyment. After a few squeezes, he stopped, merely holding my hips. I looked over my shoulder. His eyes were lidded, and he took deep breaths through his lips.

"Fal?"

"You feel too good. I need a moment to pace myself."

"Okay."

He rumbled low in his chest and I dripped slick with a needy whine. "Okay, what? Who am I?" he coaxed.

"Mate. Alpha. Pack lead," I answered breathlessly.

One of those was the right answer, as he closed the space between us and rubbed his hot length through my folds. "I love how eager you are. So greedy for your pack lead's cock." Ah, that was the winner. I trembled as he teased me for a few more moments before slamming home in one quick jerk.

"Yes!" I yelped, bracing harder when he jolted my body.

"Mine." With his claim, he rode me in earnest. Hot breath ghosted over my wings as his breaths started to sound like the snarly cadence that'd come from the other two alphas as they'd hit their stride. I couldn't see his face but imagined his pupils rounded out of their feline slits and his expression tight with lust.

With his claim intensifying, I found the pressure and need for completion roaring up on me. But I'd already agreed to push off this feeling, so it faded again even as I cried out as if I'd just come.

The next thing I knew, I was on my back, and he was lining up to re-enter me yet again. We were face-to-face, and he was an alpha possessed. He took hold of my left leg, testing my flexibility by bending my knee toward my shoulder. His cock drove as deep in me as it'd felt when he'd taken me from behind.

"And you know it," he growled. "That you are mine."

"Yours," I gasped.

He rewarded me with a sloppy kiss and a particularly powerful drive of his hips. We were seconds from his knot tying us together. The hot, dense flesh had expanded enough that it pulled at the ring of my pussy as it entered and left.

"Sweet, perfect omega," he said with effort. "You may come with me. Delay to feel the breeder's delight, if you can."

His knot caught inside me, and instead of pulling it free, he ground his cock as deep into me as it could go. I dug my nails into his back, aching from the new sensation as his knot continued to swell with each frenzied beat of his heart. That specialized rim of muscle in my pussy locked around his swelling flesh.

"Fuck, fuck, fuck," he chanted, sputtering as he rocked his hips without going anywhere. He spilled, filling the ache in my core with his seed. The rush of hot come felt like utter relief, or maybe that was all the tension in my body snapping as soon as it had permission. My pleasure soared with his and kept climbing. I really could see stars if I came hard enough.

He groaned as my channel squeezed his knot further. The liquid rush from him, which had been abating, became another heated flood instead, though less than the first time he came. We spiraled down from the pleasure high with smaller spikes of mini orgasms until I lay limp and he was doing much the same on top of me.

"Wow," I said in a daze.

So *that* was what taking a knot felt like. I was now touched in every sense of the word, because I definitely wanted to do this again. Every night—multiple times, preferably. Though when I shifted my weight and accidentally tugged on his knot in the process, the freshly tested muscles in my pussy supplied plenty of pain to encourage me to stay still.

Fal purred, which only grew in intensity as he recovered enough to lift his weight off me and slide us onto our sides. The comforting vibrations helped ease any lingering ache where we were tied.

"Looks like you're stuck with me," he said playfully.

"Or you're stuck with me," I giggled.

"That was special. I'm glad I saved my knot for this moment." He caught my lips for a more leisurely kiss while I hummed in agreement.

Once that was done and we'd taken a long gaze into one another's eyes, I asked, "What now? How long are we going to be tied?"

"Guess you'll just have to talk to me." He tweezed his tongue between his teeth for a moment. "Also, I've heard twenty minutes. But if you come again, that time resets."

I muffled another yawn, settling in more comfortably against him. "I didn't take you for such a possessive male," I murmured, closing my eyes.

"I'm still an alpha. You're doomed to hear this every time we fuck." Clearing his throat, he said with a full growl, "*Mine.*"

My pussy fluttered in response, and he came a bit from the squeeze, setting both of us to moaning until the pleasure subsided again. "And now I know how much you like that," he remarked.

"Twenty minutes starting now?"

"Aye. Let's talk about something not sexy." He exaggerated a thinking pose.

Try as we might, though, there was no topic that could distract us from the intimacy of being tied together. I eventually fell asleep in his arms.

46
LARK

I woke abruptly, already in the middle of a screaming keen. The high *"eee"* pierced the pitch darkness around me.

Restraining hands. Male voices.

They're here! They came for me!

I elbowed a hard, muscled torso and wrenched my arms free. Those hands were still trying to hold me down, but Pack Ellisar had only known me before I had full use of my magic. I summoned a whipping vortex of air in a ring around my body. A male hit the floor with a thud and a groan.

I darted to freedom with a few frenzied beats of my wings. My bare feet hit plush carpeting. I ran blindly, straight into another fae.

Someone whistled, brightening the faelights in my nest. Tormund's belly jiggled as I rebounded off him. He caught me before I could fall, while his head whipped around.

"What is it? What's wrong?" Fire burned in his pupils as he bared a mouth full of sharp teeth.

"Tormund!" I exclaimed tearfully, jumping up to cling to him with all four limbs. I'd never been happier to see him than this moment.

Stars, he was burning up. I let him go with a yelp, shaking off the heat lingering on my skin. Well, if Tormund was here, that meant...

Glancing over my shoulder, I spotted Fal sprawled on the floor of my nest with wild tangles in his windblown hair. Marius was still on the bed, squinting against the sudden influx of light. Both eyed me with sleep-dazed concern.

I flushed in mortification as reality sank in. Stars, just let the ground open up and swallow me whole.

I hadn't woken everyone at least. Kauz was still fast asleep on my nest's divan, one wing drooping down to the floor.

"I'm sorry." I cleared my throat, trying to dislodge the fearful clog strangling my voice. "Um. Go back to sleep. Please."

I fled my nest at a slightly more controlled pace, narrowly edging around Tormund's bulk. I hid in the bathroom, back pressed to the closed door. My breathing was too fast. I couldn't get a good lungful of air.

I clapped to awaken the essence lamp over the vanity and focused on taking deeper breaths, which became great gulps to try to calm my heart. It pounded against my ribcage as I tilted my shoulder forward in the mirror.

The nightmare lingered in my mind with full clarity. The three barkfolk alphas of Pack Ellisar had claimed me, sinking their fangs into my mark where it'd manifested on my shoulder. Except there was nothing there except two faint pink lines from when Marius had bitten me and then healed the punctures with wound salve.

I had no corded marks on my wrists or neck from vine-like restraints. The only lingering scent on me was from Fal, who must've taken me to my nest once I fell asleep and his knot had deflated. That explained why I was naked, though my skin's hue was shaded an unhealthy gray from terror. I was trembling from the inside out.

Just a dream. Just a really bad dream, I told myself, repeating it like a mantra.

I splashed some water on my face and opened the door. I was ready to dress in something comfortably baggy and curl up with a book until a more reasonable hour. There was no way I'd be heading back to bed, but my mates deserved to rest undisturbed.

Except the three alphas definitely had not gone back to sleep. They were lined up outside of the bathroom. Tormund stood a safe distance away, his monstrous form only half leashed. He wore a rumpled full outfit, while the other two males had pulled on their underclothes. Marius had his arms crossed, scowling at whatever Fal was whispering. Their attention turned toward me all at once.

"I didn't mean to wake you," I mumbled, my shoulders rising.

Fal tsked and strode over, sweeping me into a hug. I accepted it rigidly, tilting my head away in discomfort when he bent as if to kiss me. He arrested the movement, bowing his head over my hair instead. "It's all right. That had every sign of a night terror. There's no way we'd leave you to suffer through the aftereffects alone."

I hugged him back with a sob. Here was my pack lead, who observed my every boundary. *This* was real, no matter how much the night terror had felt like reality in the moment.

Fal started a comforting purr while Tormund said, "You need something warm to drink, Lark. Would you like some tea? Maybe some hot chocolate?"

I made a little squeak of interest at the idea of hot chocolate. Something warm and sweet to chase away the bitter fear still lingering within me.

"I'll get that right away," the redcap said, striding off with new purpose.

Fal straightened and eyed me with concern. "Is it all right if I carry you?"

He hadn't asked that in ages. I was feeling fragile enough to deny him, except I didn't know where to possibly go from here. "Okay," I murmured.

The dark elf scooped me up and carried me to one of the couches in my receiving room. The other smelled strongly of Tormund's smoke and had a rumpled sheet half flung off it. Fal set me on my feet, and Marius pushed a folded bundle of cloth into my hands. My pajamas, I noted with relief, brushing a fuzzy sleeve against my cheek. I donned the sleeping clothes and eased a little closer to the kelpie.

He sat and held his arms out for me. I snuggled into him, feeling small and tucking in my limbs to be smaller so he could maneuver us into the kind of hug I'd been hoping for. We were stretched halfway along the couch, my back to his front, his bulk shielding me from the outside world. He held me firmly while his legs caged mine. His chest thrummed, comfort I absorbed without purring back.

Fal claimed the rest of the space on the couch. "Has Kauz told you what night terrors are to a dream warden?" he asked. I shook my head, and he sighed in his most dramatic fashion. "They're nightmares enhanced by magic. Worst fears come to life. All li'l dream wardens are plagued by them right around the time their hair bleaches white."

"It took Kauz months to sort out his magic and make them stop," Marius added.

"He was what, thirteen?"

"Something like that. I made a habit of checking on him in the morning. Half the time, I'd find him curled up in his wings, shaking and gray as a fucking ghost."

"Poor Kauz," I murmured. I didn't want to imagine having routine nightmares so vivid and terrible. One had been more than enough.

"Aye, well, poor Kauz will be training you on controlling your dream warden magic as soon as he isn't dead asleep," Fal remarked. "With the *olcanus* removed, your full essence is only starting to flourish. Luckily, we all know what it's like to recover from a night terror."

It occurred to me belatedly that when Kauz threatened nightmares, *this* was the kind he meant. *This* was the level of terror he'd inflicted on Cymora as revenge. Such realistic, visceral fear could drive anyone to madness if exposed to it long enough.

Tormund thumped into the room, announcing himself with, "I have the hot chocolate!"

I unfolded myself, hopeful that he had somehow cooled off. I could use my gentle giant right about now. Not that Marius was doing a poor job, and I snuck a guilty glance at him since he could now sense the direction of my thoughts.

He met my gaze, ear flicking as he growled, "Get your fire under control so you can comfort our mate."

Tormund came up behind the couch and offered me a mug that was too hot to hold. The kelpie took it and set it on the side table to cool off, wafting the sweet scent past me as he glared at his brother with a rumble of warning.

Some of the redcap's cheer dimmed. "I...can't. I'm sorry, li'l bird." He managed to look sheepish even with glowing eyes and sharpened teeth. "I don't know what's wrong."

"Well, stay right there," I murmured. Most fae would run from a half-transformed redcap, yet here I was warming my arms off the halo of heat wafting from him.

"The best way to overcome a night terror is to talk about it," Tormund offered.

Fal watched him for a moment before shrugging. "That's true. We usually talk through it while it's fresh, to pick it apart so you know it's not a real memory."

I stilled. Pack Ellisar and their contract had, to this point, been the kind of presence in my life we hadn't directly discussed. It was a problem in the past, where the barkfolk should've firmly stayed. But I didn't want the night terror to grow roots and anchor in my mind like a rotten weed, either.

"How much do you know about Pack Ellisar?" I asked. The question was for Fal, but all three alphas answered with equally aggressive growls. I mewled and curled on myself further in the face of such concentrated alpha rage.

Fal held up his hand. "I probably know the most. Cymora mentioned them a few times, in regard to your past. She took glee in forcing you to sign a breeding contract with a trio of alphas she knew wouldn't treat you well. You've kept them waiting on your heat for four years. A testament to your strength and willpower that hasn't gone unnoticed. Pack Ellisar will face immediate execution if our paths ever cross."

"That...that's all you know?" I managed to ask.

"Aye. Plus the fact that Kauz sent a spy back to Osme Fen to look into the contract situation. I'll remind him that he should double-check on that information," Fal answered.

A hand tipped with sharp talons waved close to my head. Marius chuffed in warning. "Don't hold her so hard," Tormund said in his loud whisper. "Pet her. It's better comfort."

I expected a defensive response from the kelpie, but he immediately loosened his hold around my torso. He brushed his fingertips over my cheek, and I leaned into the touch.

"Thanks," he said gruffly.

I soaked in the attention for a few minutes, until he rubbed and rotated the base of my ears, and I practically melted with a tired sigh.

I glanced over at the mug of hot chocolate with longing. Marius reached over and touched it before delivering it to me. The hot, sweet sip I took doused the worst of the chills still causing me to tremble from the inside out.

"The males of Pack Ellisar are barkfolk," I began. "Three brothers. Ellisar, Dalstin, and Floris. They came to Osme Fen from Etalenza because..."

I drifted off, realizing I'd lose them if I started referencing places and groups they weren't so familiar with. Holding the mug in one hand, I shaped a flat illusion of Thelis's island over my other palm, big enough for them all to see.

"Are you familiar with the Dragon Wars?" I asked.

"From a history book," Fal answered dryly. His gaze roamed over the map. "Okay, where the fuck is Osme Fen?"

I added it to the map, a tiny dot in the western wetlands. All three alphas leaned in to study the map more closely.

"The Dragon Wars ended up creating a blighted strip of land between the Seelie and the dragons. It's called the Pixie's Lament, or just the Lament," I narrated. For once, I was the one explaining the oddities of different fae cultures. "All alpha- and beta-designated fae who come of age in the Eternal—the giant rainforest, right there, see—are drafted for a decade to cross the Lament and fight the forces of the scaleborn. Those are the scale-bearing races that serve the dragons."

"I thought there weren't any more dragons," Tormund said.

"Well, there aren't. And there aren't too many scaleborn left that want to fight Eternalans, either. The draft is an ancient tradition at this point. Pack Ellisar moved to Osme Fen right before the youngest, Floris, came of age so he didn't have to go through the decade of training and keeping watch. He was, um…"

I stopped myself from speaking ill of one of the barkfolk, then shook off the impulse. Cymora had ordered me to be polite to them, but I no longer had to do as she said.

"He was liable to get himself killed with the business end of a spear. When they showed up, it was Floris who was always at the market when I had to go there. I was also nearly of age at this point, and he tried to get handsy a few meetings past hello. He'd follow and corner me whenever he could. I was an easy target."

Marius tensed. I glanced up at him, and it was Niall looking back at me, lips partway peeled into a soundless snarl. He hadn't moved from his protective curl around my body, though his comforting purr had faded to a vibration I felt more than heard. "Show me his face," he said in a smoky feral voice, indicating the illusion I was holding.

"You don't have to. Perhaps that's reliving the past too much," Fal interjected.

"It's fine," I murmured. I had no doubts that Marius's feral side wanted to hunt down Pack Ellisar and tear them to ribbons. There was also next to no chance he'd meet the barkfolk in the first place. They were on one island; we were on another. And that was how I wanted to keep it.

I changed the illusion to show Floris's simple face. Barkfolk had faces like carved wooden masks, and his was the smoothest. He had vacant eyes and no magic to his name. The most notable thing he'd done, other than harass me, was his draft dodging.

Marius took in the illusion with unblinking focus. "And the other two?" he growled.

"This is Dalstin." I altered the illusion to reveal the middle barkfolk brother, who had a face covered in cracked wood grain and green eyes a shade darker and meaner. Short tendrils of vines formed his hair.

I took a deep sip of hot chocolate and let its warmth chase away the fear creeping down my limbs to see him again. It couldn't mask the hitch in my voice. "H-he was the forceful one. Always bragged about his accomplishments in the militia. Killed twenty alpha kobolds, or so he said. He enjoyed fighting and would've kept doing it if it weren't for Floris."

Fal rolled his eyes. "Excuse me while I weep for that tragedy."

I mustered up a faint smile and let the illusion drop. My fingers trembled even as I gripped my mug with both hands. "Then there was Ellisar. He named the pack after himself, obviously. Their farm had the most bountiful crops we'd ever seen because of his magic. The land grew and shaped itself to his command."

"I'll set him on fire for you," Tormund said, all earnestness. "And I've never wanted to kill anyone before."

"It's in the past. He's long gone," I mumbled. Yet another clog of fear made it hard to breathe, let alone speak. "He was kind on the outside, but only for long enough to convince Cymora to agree to the breeding contract. He wanted to buy me, like property. And once he succeeded, he wasn't shy about reminding me how I belonged to him and his brothers."

Marius shifted, nosing into my hair. He cradled me as close as we could come. "*No. Mine. My p'nixie,*" he said in a feral growl.

"I know it's not true," I whispered. "But I saw them all again in my night terror. They repeated all the terrible things they've been saying for four years as they waited for my heat to overwhelm me. That I belonged to them and had signed a contract...and they went further than that, biting my mark...and...and..." With a keen, I trailed off and started sobbing.

Someone took the mug from my hand. Marius eased back just enough for Fal to fit in front of me. To squeeze me between them, there was a measure of the brothers hugging one another, but I hardly noticed that miracle. They combined scents, warm sunshine and cool greenery mingling perfectly, and joined forces to comfort me with double the purring. Tormund thrummed just out of reach, though the heat rolling from him was also welcome.

"It wasn't real, *mo stór*. You belong with us," Fal said.

"They won't touch you again. I swear it," Marius snarled.

"We love you," Tormund added. "And I'll burn their stupid contract, too, so all they have is ashes."

Their presences seeped into me, banishing my lingering worries one at a time. I finally purred back and nuzzled Marius, then Fal. All of my fears were quieted, except for one I couldn't face: Ellisar himself. Hopefully Marius hadn't noticed that I hadn't mustered the nerve to summon an illusion of the eldest barkfolk.

I didn't want to run the risk of the magic looking at me with his cruel mossy eyes. The nightmare had made him seem too real, like he could still be coming for me despite everything to the contrary.

MY MATES stubbornly remained awake with me. When I considered faking rest so they could catch some, Marius answered the stray thought aloud. "Don't even think about it. We can miss some sleep."

"Okay. But I'm just going to be boring," I answered. I picked out one of my comfort reads from the books in my study and curled up between him and Fal.

"Book nerd," the dark elf whispered with affection, resting his chin on my shoulder. He asked about the book and why I'd picked it off the shelf first. Dangerous questions to ask a reader, as it coaxed out a much longer conversation than he was probably expecting. I really loved this story.

Marius and Tormund listened in too as I read a couple of my favorite scenes aloud. Fal grinned and tugged the book from my hand when one started to get heated. "Did you think I forgot about reading the saucy bits to you?"

Most of me heard that and went *oh no*. But my omega instincts perked up with a cheer of *oh yes!*

Fal had me blushing and squirming by sunrise. "There are a *lot* of saucy bits in this book," he mused, finding another after a quick skim.

"There's a pack. She has to build relationships with everyone," I said.

He glanced at me askance with pure, impish amusement.

"Okay, you tease the li'l bird. I'm going to work," Tormund said, grumbling as he looked out the window at the rising light.

"Aw. Bye, Tormund." I reached for him, grasping at air.

"Come back when you get control of yourself," Marius said.

Tormund's glowing eyes rested on me for several moments. I gave him a worried smile. It seemed unhealthy to be running as hot as he was for this long, but it could just be an ill-timed redcap thing.

"I'll try everything I know to cool off," he promised.

As soon as the door closed behind him, Fal lowered the book and frowned after him. "I'm going to ask around about his condition."

Marius snorted. "All right. I'll stay with Lark."

The dark elf brushed some hair back from my face, leaning in slowly. I raised my face to his, but he still kept his kiss to a chaste brush of our lips. "See you soon, my lady," he purred.

I bid him farewell too, though he needed a few minutes to put on his earrings and a clean suit one of the house moths had moved into my closet. Well, *our* closet. Several varied outfits had appeared in it while I hadn't been paying attention.

"Your handmaidens should be here any minute. Let's eat breakfast, p'nixie," Marius said. He went to the bedroom to get dressed too. I was glad, because I might get territorial if anyone saw more of him than they should. Even my sweet handmaidens.

The pair of mothkin came in together as distant city bells chimed the hour. "Good morning, Princess!" they exclaimed.

Jani came over to where I sat, a letter resting on her palms. "The mail moth had this for you, Princess."

My smile for them dropped as soon as I recognized Laurel's handwriting on the front of the envelope.

47
LARK

Two or three letters had arrived from Laurel each day, and I'd been too distracted to open them. I picked up a stack of loose papers on the desk in my study; each were different drafts of letters, the "fuck off, fishling" suggestions from Fal and Tormund. Next to them was the tower of sealed letters from my stepsister.

If I were being honest with myself, I didn't feel bad about letting my stepsister be an afterthought. The last few days had been blessedly Laurel-less. She hadn't stolen my things or expressed jealousy over my change in fortune. All she could do was write these letters. I was still of half a mind to throw them into the nearest fire.

I took the papers to the dining nook and went to the window to look at the moonbloom on the sill. The silver flower was angled to one side, growing toward the sun, now fully unfurled with a second bud forming on its stem. It was thriving, just like my relationships. I used its pot as a paperweight with the mass of letters so I could keep admiring it.

First, I read the potential responses my mates had written. The first one I picked up was an absolutely scathing message penned in Fal's looping script. *No. Way too mean.*

The thud of boots announced Marius as he came up beside me. He ran his thumb down the side of the stack with a muttered, "What the fuck."

"I think she's a little worried," I remarked.

His answering growl rattled with the kind of irritation I felt. He remained standing until my handmaidens arrived with a platter of breakfast foods, far too much for two fae. Jani paused, her antennae flaring upward, when he beckoned her over and murmured instructions down to her. "Yes, Prince! Right away," she exclaimed, leaving the suite.

"Stay there, Lark. I'll serve you," he said.

That was an unexpected pleasure. He loaded my plate as I asked, with fruit, pastries, and, since he insisted I have variety, some sausage and sliced hardboiled eggs. He slid it over and added a glass of ice water and another of reddish juice.

His plate was pure protein, compared to mine. Thankfully, no raw meat in sight. As we ate, I picked up the next suggested message to Laurel, this one written by Tormund. I tried to read it, then brought it closer to my face.

"Giant male. Tiny handwriting," I giggled. It was also penned fully in Serri. I might've understood the spoken language well enough, but in writing, it was just as foreign as it'd been on the train ride here.

Marius tugged it from my fingers and started reading it to me. "Fuck off, fishling" was more how Fal felt about Laurel, which was evident from his words. Tormund seemed mildly annoyed with her by comparison.

I shook my head. "I'm going to compose my own message to Laurel."

"Seems like an unnecessary bother."

I nodded, and the two of us ate quietly for a few minutes. A random thought popped in my head. "I've kind of noticed... what about your job?"

"What about it?"

"Not that I'm complaining, but surely there's more to it than spending time with me."

"I technically haven't returned to my job." He shrugged. "I left a trusted friend in charge of my duties before we went to Thelis. I don't intend to go back to work until you have a full retinue of guards, and that's not happening until you're claimed. Also, why do I sense that you're surprised? Wait." He held up his hand and tilted his head, concentrating. "Is it because I mentioned having a friend?"

"I didn't mean anything by it," I mumbled. But yes, him talking about a trusted friend was a surprise.

"She's a mated female kelpie," he clarified quickly. "I'd be happy to introduce you two sometime. She'd be an excellent member for your guard, if you don't mind her tongue. Mother has twelve guards, and you're supposed to have eight, myself included."

"Eight?" I practically squeaked. "That seems excessive!" I wouldn't be able to go anywhere if I was constantly under guard by eight other fae.

He snorted in amusement. "Not all at once."

We chatted more about guards as we finished breakfast. I shuffled the suggested responses aside and faced the stack of unopened letters.

As I started reading, I expected a progression of emotion. From begging to anger. Fury to pleading. Sadness to resignation. But I scanned the third letter and put it down, half read, and did the same with the fourth and fifth.

"Huh."

Marius made a curious noise, but I didn't say anything until I glanced at each letter again to confirm. "They're basically the same," I said, passing a few to him.

All variations of: *Please help me. I'm stuck in a palace room, and all I can do is send you letters. Mom's life is in danger, and I think you're the only one who can do something about it.*

He took a moment to read before snarling, "She's fucking with you."

"Maybe."

His ear flicked. "The girl has no manners to speak of."

"You don't know her like I do. This is..." I waved my hand over her letters, a troubled frown tugging at my lips. "Really strange. Laurel and I used to be close. I learned that from my memories. You would think she'd, you know..." I shrugged, unable to find the right words. But she should've known from the first letter that I'd have no sympathy for her mother.

His unamused expression didn't change a flicker. "All she's interested in is using you. Again. She's not even disguising it. This female is not family to you."

"She's leaving soon, right?" I asked.

"Very soon. The next train to Thelis."

"Well, I'm going to send her the kind of message that I know will annoy her most." I swept the papers into one big stack and straightened them. "No reply."

"A fitting goodbye to the girl who pestered me all the way here," he muttered. That, we were definitely in agreement on.

I got up and went to change into something for the day. Springtime outfits were sneaking into my wardrobe, just like the extra clothes from my four males. I didn't know where they were coming from, but they were tailored to my size and wings, so it could only be the doing of one particular male.

I picked a loose pink blouse with short sleeves and a long pair of fawn-colored shorts that cut off just above my knees. It was suitable springtime attire, and I was ready for mild, sunshine-filled days.

I checked my reflection in the bathroom mirror, just to cringe. My skin was shading back to a healthy tone, but my lack of sleep was apparent from the darkening hollows under my eyes. I reached for my makeup and had a brush in hand when male voices approached the bathroom.

Marius was laughing at something a brown-hued kelpie was saying as they came around the corner. The unfamiliar male had a barber's kit in hand and short, straight black hair combed to one side in the half-shaved style of a mated kelpie.

He glanced up at me and stopped short. "Is that your mate?" he asked in Serri.

"Aye. Get your own," Marius replied in kind.

"I did! She's delightful!"

Rolling his eyes, Marius nudged the other male aside as I left the bathroom. "I'll give you two some space," I said.

"It won't take long!" the barber called behind me.

Wasn't that the truth? Hair always took forever to grow and just moments to cut. I went to settle on the couch where Tormund had spent half the night, folding the sheet he'd used before giving it a good sniff. His smoky scent was still soothing in his absence.

I leaned my head back against the couch and dozed for however long Marius needed to get his hair cut. It felt like a long blink before he and the other male passed by the couch, still carrying on like friends. Marius came over as soon as the door closed behind the barber. I turned toward him, hands clasped in anticipation.

The kelpie posed for my perusal, chin lifted proudly. He hadn't gotten exactly half his hair shaved off. It was more like an angled undercut that left a fuzz of blue stubble, with the rest combed over to form the pseudo kelpie mane that shadowed the right side of his face.

I admired the effect, hoping he could sense how much I approved of the look on him. With his other asymmetrical angles, the hairstyle just emphasized his more savage beauty. "Handsome beast," I purred.

His slow, predatory smile was all Niall. "Yours." His gait was a fluid prowl as he came over to me. He tilted his head, eyeing me with concern.

"What is it?" I murmured.

He settled cross-legged before me and started unlacing his boots. I watched, confused, as he placed them aside, his socks following with a haphazard toss. He tugged the sandals off my feet next.

Without warning, he surged to his feet and tossed me over his shoulder. "Caught you," he said.

I protested with a mewl and a few flutters of my wings. "What are you doing?"

"We're going to go do something fun, sweet prey. I insist." He carried me out of my suite. My handmaidens watched, mouths hanging open. Lon elbowed Jani, and they both waved farewell belatedly.

I waved back. "And I don't have a choice in this matter?"

"You could've fled," he said in a musing tone. "But I still would've caught you."

"Next time you take off my shoes, run. Got it."

"Don't threaten Niall with a good time," he said in a low growl. "By the way, I intend to take you out for our date as soon as possible. There's nothing to stop me from stealing you away to the sea."

Nothing was in the way of that, other than the unwelcome tug of fear in my gut at the mention of the sea. I took a deep breath to ground myself before saying, "At least give me a chance to say goodbye to your brothers."

"Deal. Then we're leaving."

Not even five minutes passed before he heaved a sigh that had me bouncing on his shoulder. "Speaking of my brothers," he grumbled.

"Well, look who got half his head shorn at the earliest opportunity," Fal teased. I flapped my wings for balance and looked over my shoulder, catching a glimpse of him and Tormund. They stood in Marius's way, and he stopped. His hold on me tightened.

"I need to talk to Lark." The gentle giant sounded a little confused.

Instead of putting me down, Marius turned around so I was facing the other two males. I gave my full attention to Tormund, whose skin was flushed red.

"Is everything okay?" My stomach filled with queasy nerves at his expression. It wasn't right to see misery pulling at his usually jolly face.

"If you don't tell her, I will," Fal said, raising a brow at the redcap.

"Could you put her down?" Tormund asked.

"No," Marius stated.

Tormund shifted on his feet. "I need to say goodbye, li'l bird. My dad is stealing me away on one of his hunting trips," he said with a hefty sigh.

"It seems akin to torture," Fal added more lightly. "They catch and kill poor woodland creatures to eat and then sit and chat while watching the sky, as far as I understand it."

"We roast and season the meat now, at least." Tormund rubbed the back of his neck. "I don't know how long this one's going to be, but I assume you'll be on your date with Marius or Kauz by the time I get back. So, um, goodbye."

"What's wrong?" I blurted, sensing some unspoken awkwardness between us.

"I can't control myself," he said miserably. "They say a mate's touch soothes the rage, but it's been out of control ever since...since we..."

My heartbeat quickened as I put together the evidence right in front of me. "*I'm* triggering your rage?" Tears pricked the corners of my eyes.

Marius cast a glare over his other shoulder. "You're upsetting her. We're leaving."

"Wait. Don't be sad, please. I can't stand it," he said, though his words were punctuated with a menacing growl. "I'm going to figure it out. Promise."

"Telling Theodred what's going on would be a good start," Fal suggested.

Tormund's expression tightened with stress. I couldn't blame him. I, too, wouldn't want to talk about this with Theodred. However... "If anyone would know what you're going through, it'd be him," I said in agreement.

"He's never struggled like I have," he practically snarled. "It's not fair. I just want to hold my li'l bird and be at peace. Is that so much to ask?"

"Sometimes you have to fight a war before you get peace," Fal answered.

"*Ach*. It's not fair," he repeated. "I need to go before the rage gets any worse. Bye, Lark. I love you." Even though his teeth were pointed in the beginning stage of his monstrous transformation, he still made a forlorn expression that just about broke my heart.

"Goodbye, my gentle giant. I love you too, and I'll see you soon." I mirrored him with a pout. I couldn't help but think this was my fault.

Marius stepped aside for them to head past us, shaking his head as he turned and proceeded to carry me further into the palace. "It's not your fault, p'nixie. He's struggled to control his magic for years."

"But the timing..."

"He'll be fine. Let's focus on you. I really want to wipe away those worries."

At this point, it'd take a pretty hefty distraction to get me to place my concerns aside.

He carried me to a stairwell and descended. The air changed, weighed down by humidity. My nose twitched as I picked up notes of fresh water and the tang of mold and moss underneath it. "Where are we going?" I asked.

"We call this the sea corridor, for water fae to have a bit of home despite how far away the sea is," he explained.

I glanced down, noting the damp floor carved from rock. "Your feet," I said.

"Are fine. I make this walk all the time."

"Make this walk...to where?" I narrowed my eyes, already having my suspicions.

Marius ignored the question and carried me down a narrow, rocky hall lined with shopfronts. A handful of fae called out to us, as each stall had at least one fae working inside. There was a shop with art made of sea glass and driftwood, another selling fresh or cooked fish, and, at the end, the familiar face of the kelpie barber. He grinned as he watched us walk by.

We passed through a pair of doors into a cavern of rough-hewn rock steadily sloping downward. Essence lamps pulsed at regular intervals. The scent of fresh water, mossy greenery, and wet stone was only getting stronger as we descended.

"We're not going to open water, are we?" A nervous quaver entered the question.

"You'll see."

"That's basically a yes."

"There's nothing to be afraid of. I'll show you," he said gently. "You trust me, right?"

"I do." And because of that trust, I decided to see what he intended.

He walked us over a stone bridge. A stream wide enough for two or maybe three fae across trickled underneath it. A young nixie floated by while I was watching, waving as the current carried her into the maw of a square-cut cave.

Marius splashed through a few errant puddles. "I bet you didn't know the palace has a few underground pools and an undine-blessed river that circles them. Each is different."

He pointed out each doorway and the shape of the pool within. The first was for non-water fae, long and shallow for kids to play and adults to swim laps. The second, deep and circular for diving.

The next two were also shaped for aquatic fae, while the fifth... Marius stopped before a metal door and placed his hand upon the knob. "We'll have Kauz add your palm to this spell, too. Those four pools are free use for all fae. This one's only for our family," he said.

He finally shifted me off his shoulder, carrying me cradled to his chest so I could see the royal pool for myself.

Small essence lamps lit the carved ceiling, twinkling like starlight. The rectangular basin was gigantic, with a sloped bottom that gave it shallows on one end and a shadowed far corner. My belly fluttered with nerves when I couldn't see the bottom. The single underwater lamp, in what I assumed was the middle of the water, didn't quite illuminate it all.

The closest wall had a carved nook full of towels. It overflowed with colorful toys meant for use in the water, some scattered along the ground alongside many tiny pairs of shoes that were probably Ambriel's. Reed chairs, reclined for lounging, were angled toward the pool.

Across the room was a second door with a spell sigil engraved in the wood. Marius pointed to it and said, "That's the royal pack's private entrance. I'll take you through it when we leave so you know how to find it on the other side."

"All of this is for us?" I murmured.

"Aye. My father has to make use of it a lot, as he's too busy to venture to the sea most days. Kelpies need water and to stretch our second forms sometimes," he explained. "There's an emergency exit, too, that will flush you, along with all this water, into a river tributary. I'll show you where the latch is."

"Wait." I realized too late what he was about to do, as we were heading straight for the placid surface of the water. "I'm not dressed for this! Marius!"

He tossed me in. I had enough time to shriek before I hit the pool with a solid splash. I flailed as the water enveloped me and I sank.

The water churned as Marius jumped in behind me. He swam through the liquid separating us and wrapped both arms around my torso. Now we were both sinking further into the pool, face-to-face. His hair fanned out above him, waving in the wake of the bubbles escaping his open gills.

The essence lamp cast half his face in shadow as he watched me struggle and run out of air. I wiggled in a panic. My gills were stuck! I needed to get back to the surface.

Marius held up one of his hands and unfurled the webbing between his fingers. He gave me a meaningful look. I curled both my hands, and air flooded into my chest as my webbing unfurled too. A dull ache bloomed on either side of my neck as my gills flared wide in the fishy equivalent to a gasp. *Thank the stars. They still work!*

He flashed his fangs in a lopsided grin before releasing me. I hung suspended in the water, my earlier panic fading like it'd never happened. Why had this been so scary? I was half water fae, after all. Most of my Unseelie traits were only useful while I was fully submerged.

This wasn't just Cymora and Laurel's domain. It was mine, too.

Marius tapped my shoulder after I had that realization. He swam away like a darting fish, then turned to look at me. That had all the energy of an invitation to play. I tried to swim after him but only succeeded in spinning in place.

Two purple, glowing tendrils wrapped around my side. Those were my *wings*. I glanced over my shoulder, watching four fins swish behind me when I twitched my flight muscles. *How surreal.* They'd softened considerably and thrashed about with little control.

I closed my eyes, trying to remember what it'd felt like to use my wings as fins. I used to undulate them to steer my body underwater during fun afternoons in Osme Fen's lake. Back when I'd been a better swimmer than my mermaid stepsister.

I twitched my wing-fins about until they rippled in the right motion to propel me along. Just like walking, my body remembered how to do this after all. Marius was watching, floating just out of reach as I got the hang of it. In his fae form, he treaded water with limber rippling motions of his abdomen and limbs.

Gathering my wing-fins, I sprang at him, tagging his leg. I didn't dart away, though, so he caught me in moments, the two of us whirling through the water. Up was down, and nothing limited our motions except for the rapidly approaching sanded wall of the pool. Marius caught it with his palm and pushed off, letting me go.

Dizzy but giggling in a heavily muffled way, I caught my bearings and chased him, this time relearning how to slow down, as I nearly collided with the floating lamp. Something cool slid over my eyes, clarifying the darkest shades of the pool and giving everything definition. They were my nictitating membranes, eye protection that would've locked into place earlier if we'd jumped into seawater.

Marius motioned for me to follow and swam toward the shallower end of the pool. He pointed at a handle fused into the rock and a heavy chain attached to it. It looked like it'd be far too weighty to lift unless it was enchanted in some way. Once I thought that, he pointed at me and exaggerated a nod.

I nodded too, then lunged at him. He swam away, his teeth a flash of white in the depths of the water. I chased him, but as I got re-accustomed to my nixie side and sped around on my fins, he pursued me. He peppered my neck and arms with love bites each time he caught me. I squirmed and laughed, not that the water let the sound spread.

We played until I tired out, then retired to the undine-blessed river to float together. I learned that the blessing was for water flow, as there was no slope to logically create the circuit the water followed.

Marius acted as my raft. I lay on top of him, my fins spilling into the water on either side of his torso to occasionally steer us away from colliding with a wall. "I was thinking we'd head for the sea tomorrow," he said, using a backstroke to propel us through a section with a weak current. "An early morning magirail to Laculi Point should get us to the water by midday. That'll give you a chance to say goodbye to my brothers tonight."

I nodded and shifted to get a better view of his face. "Perhaps," I said lightheartedly.

"Hmm?"

"Perhaps tomorrow."

He sat up a bit in the water, slowing our momentum as he narrowed his eyes at me. "What do you mean, perhaps tomorrow?"

I giggled. "Maybe we'll do that tomorrow."

He snorted in amusement. "That's not how this works." Then he took shameless advantage of me lying atop him and tickled my sides and wing-fins. I wiggled in a ticklish fit, which only set him off to do the same. "Yes or no, p'nixie?"

"Stop, stop! I can't..." *Splash.* I rolled off him and submerged fully. My gills opened, so I spent a few waterlogged moments along the riverbed, overstimulated, before bobbing to the surface. I emerged and floated alongside him as I caught my breath. "Yes. Let's go tomorrow."

48
LARK

I SAID my goodbyes to Fal and Kauz that night. It was strange to leave them behind, even though it was temporary. Fal, I wouldn't see for a couple weeks, but Kauz would be spending most nights in my dreams to train my magic. He'd been aghast to hear about my night terror and promised to keep any more at bay until I learned how to do so myself.

My date with Marius began early the next morning, as scheduled. Jani and Lon had packed the essentials for both of us in a waterproof bag with a long strap, designed to be worn over the shoulder while I rode astride my kelpie's back underwater.

The magirail ride to Laculi Point was four hours long. We headed south and spent the whole time cuddled up in the back car, which was the least crowded. Marius explained some of the mechanics of riding his second form. The directions came between long stretches of time where he surrendered to his feral side. He'd bury his face in my hair, inhaling with a deep, rumbling purr I melted into.

I managed to pick up the basics: I'd hold on to him with my legs as if I were riding a wild stallion. Kelpies had a reputation for drowning non-water fae, as their manes would cling hard to their riders to help hold them in place. Most of those deaths were accidents. Allegedly.

We disembarked at noon, emerging into a wave of humid sunshine. Marius took me through the outskirts of what turned out to be a port city. We ate street food—fried, cheese-stuffed potato puffs for me and dubiously cooked shrimp skewers for him—and wandered without haste toward the rocky beach beyond the piers.

There were some purposefully placed stone ramps designed for kelpies and their riders further down the beach, shaped from boulders. They were out of the way enough for some privacy, which I appreciated since he needed to strip down before shifting.

He paused before a ramp and picked me up, lifting me to meet his lips. He adjusted his mouth to make it a perfect lip-lock and carried me up a steep incline that would've tested my ankle. When we parted, we were standing on a rocky outcrop overlooking the sea. "Is this dive safe?" I asked, peering over the edge that jutted several yards past the waves.

"The platform wouldn't be placed here if it wasn't safe."

I started taking off my clothes, hearing Marius do the same. I had swimwear on rather than underclothes, a tight top and shorts that left my midriff bare.

I started folding and placing our extra clothes in the waterproof bag. He kept stripping until he was only wearing a pair of swim trunks. These, he eased down slowly for my admiring gaze. His shift took hold as he dropped the trunks and toed them to the side, and the magic altered his body so fast that I only caught a glimpse of my favorite piercing, the lady pleaser.

I watched him transform with my mouth hanging open. It was a quick transition, but it sounded so violent. His bones and cartilage snapped and popped back into place as magic forced him into the form of an animal. I secured his swim trunks before sealing the bag and slinging it over my shoulder, scrambling in eagerness to meet his second form.

Kelpie Marius was nearly as large as a horse, though shorter at the shoulder and longer with his fish tail. It curled around him, lined with sharp fins to match the ones on the sides of his horse-like front legs. Unlike a mermaid's tail, his ended with a bundle of smaller fins that'd resemble hair once wet.

His coat was the same color as his skin, a rich blue with speckles of green down his chest and back. It gleamed with a sheen of health. I approached his head, which he tossed with a snort.

Even with the jeweled tags glinting on his chest, brow, and nose, his most distinctive trait was still the scar that crossed his muzzle. His yellow eyes were forward-facing and predatory, full of pride when they met mine.

"What a beautiful beast you are," I said in admiration. I stroked his muzzle, and as my fingers approached his ears, a lock of his mane magnetized to my wrist, wrapping around it tightly. The cerulean strands had a mind of their own and gripped harder when I tried to tug away.

Marius jerked his neck to free me and stamped his hoof, motioning to the sea with another toss of his head.

"Okay, okay," I giggled. I faced the drop and swallowed, fidgeting with the strap across my chest.

I sprung from the boulder and landed feet-first in the water. Bubbles circled around me as I floated downward and shuddered at the sudden embrace of chill water. My gills opened instantly, and my nictitating membranes slid into place over my eyes.

Marius dove in soon after, cutting through the water and leaving a torrent of churned silt in his wake. He reached out to nudge me before shooting away far faster than I could dream of swimming. Oh, I was never winning this version of our chase game from yesterday. I still swam after him. He let me tag the end of his tail and then vanished into the murky depths where the sunlight wasn't strong enough to reach.

When he reappeared, he swam literal loops around me while I scowled playfully. He was swift and graceful in his element. *Show-off.*

We frolicked for a while, but eventually, I stopped to tread water. Marius swept around me, slowing until we were nearly face-to-face. He tilted his equine head in a clear question. My heart pounded as I nodded. I was ready to take the next step to complete our bond.

He dove further into the sea, just to execute a turn and rise under me. My legs bumped his torso. His mane wrapped around my right arm, and several tendrils anchored around my hips to hold me to the welcome heat radiating from his back. Without the strong grip of all that hair, I probably would've been swept away the moment he moved.

I gripped his mane just as hard as it held me for balance. Marius tilted so we were heading further out to sea, kicking up bubbles with a snort. His tail undulated slowly at first, but he accelerated as I moved with him and leaned over his neck to help us cut through the water. We descended until the sunlight was halved, and my ears popped from the pressure around us.

At first, our bond was a tickle of static in my mind. It became more intense as he carried me along. The back of my head went numb. I gripped my forehead with my free hand, hunching over Marius's back.

Essence poured into me along a previously invisible tendril. I pictured it as a cord of braided magic stretched between us, formed and anchored by my mate. He'd shared that kelpie magic, past the shifting, was specialized in creating bonds. Now I felt it in motion, connecting us mind-to-mind.

As the numbness faded from my head, in its place was a magic-formed connection. His fierce joy filled my chest, and my excitement echoed it.

Then everything else he felt and thought tumbled into my head, mixing up with what was already there. It was immediately overwhelming to be two fae at once. I sank into who he was, leaving myself behind until I figured out what we were experiencing.

Through Marius, I sensed the tug of the tide and the currents streaming around us. There was a thread of blood in the water. Whatever it was from had died and dropped to the seafloor as a feast for the critters that skittered amongst the silt. There were sea creatures all around us, but they swam a hasty retreat from us.

Past what he sensed, I felt the movement of his mind. A sharpness of intelligence, with rapid thoughts and feral focus. Underwater and in his second form, he was the sea's apex predator.

But deeper still, he worried. Perhaps our bond wouldn't form right.

Or maybe I'd back out of the bonding process at the last moment and leave him bereft.

He corrected his own thought, and his voice entered my mind as clearly as if he'd spoken aloud. *"Nay. The p'nixie wouldn't do that to me."*

I wanted to respond and reassure him. This triggered something else, tangling our headspaces together to the point that Marius groaned, *"Oh no, what's this?"*

We glided on a current as he bowed his head and threw off bubbles from his muzzle.

My stomach churned as my thoughts mixed with his. We traded emotions and thoughts in a whirl where nothing quite made sense. Then our headspaces socketed together like puzzle pieces.

We were stripped bare to our truths. He knew I saw him as an immovable wall of muscle and feral instincts. A straightforward, honest provider of a male.

And he saw me as prey, small and fragile, but so resilient it humbled him. I was his p'nixie to cherish and protect, and he would not fail me again.

At some point, his mane detached. He coiled around me, especially with his flexible tail, and we floated, foreheads pressed together, as the sensations deepened and our connection strengthened to the point where we could exchange thoughts as conversation.

We also traded worries, fears, viewpoints, and more, much of it so fast it was incoherent. Nothing was kept secret. It should've made me feel vulnerable, but he was also exposed. I plucked out facts and concerning thoughts to talk about, and it seemed he was doing the same thing.

When the rush of information ebbed, we shared a thought. *"That was far more intense than I expected."*

He nuzzled my cheek, and I giggled, stroking his neck while his mane was floating harmlessly in the water. *"If you don't stop admiring how beautiful I am as an animal, I may never shift back,"* he thought.

"Would that be such a bad thing?"

"If you leave me behind in the sea, aye."

I sensed the hidden nerves in his statement. An instinctual fear that I would disappear again. He truly didn't want to continue on in a world where I was gone.

"I'm not going to leave you," I promised. Though I wasn't sure how I'd secured his deep loyalty so swiftly. How had he fallen in love so fast he'd already chosen to mate for life with me?

He answered my unspoken thought. And it was in the form of a memory, a moment where I'd stopped him mid-apology and kissed the throat he'd exposed to me in submission. In that split second, he'd had the surety that he would be my faithful shadow until the end of his days.

"You could've made me grovel. You could've made me suffer. *And yet, you forgave me instead, with no further expectations."* He bumped me with his snout and unrolled his tail, swimming down and around to return me to his back. His mane wrapped around my arm and hips again, holding on tight as he brought us back up to a traveling speed. *"How are you so sweet-tempered after everything you've been through?"*

"I don't know. But it's not always good." I thought of preparing for my final talk with Cymora. My inability to be truly angry, not without it getting tangled up in other emotions. *Sweet* wasn't *strong*. And if I wanted to be taken seriously as a princess, I needed to learn how to be both.

"You're plenty strong, p'nixie. Quiet, resilient strength is easily misunderstood, and fools overlook it." He had a hint of wry regret, echoing the many times he'd been forced to eat his doormat comment. *"Besides...I'll bite anyone who challenges you."* The offer sounded like Niall, even though the texture of his mental voice remained the deep and rich tones of his princely side.

"Thanks, Marius." It was a quieter thought, full of affection. He echoed his fondness back at me.

As we traveled along, I caught a hint about our destination: an underwater city and a cave he wanted me to see at low tide. He obfuscated any further details by practicing speaking through his thoughts. With the feral condition came a sensation like a tight throat and jaw, permanently rendering him less communicative, but his thoughts still flowed freely. It resulted in a flood of things he wanted to talk about and tell me.

His wit could give Fal a run for his money. *"Now you see why he frustrates me so much."* He punctuated this with the sensation of rolling his eyes. *"Maybe if I equalized..."*

His mind supplied the details. He framed the word "equalize" by it rolling off the tongues of most of his family, including members I'd never met. His mother, who spoke it with hope that his condition would cure itself one day. His father, equally loving but less sure it was possible, as he'd always known Marius had gone feral because of my "death."

Then there was his grandmother, a permanently disapproving nixie in the first stages of bending from age. She'd hurled the word at him when he was a kid, right before she'd shot a look of betrayal at Elion and clasped her chest. *"My father broke his oldest loyalty bond for me,"* he narrated. *"And banished his own mother from the Unseelie Court. She called for my execution when it was clear I was going to become a feral alpha."*

"That's terrible! Execution? Isn't that extreme?"

"It's the fate of all violent adult ferals. I'm lucky my father tolerates me."

"Tolerates? Please. He clearly loves you."

He agreed and echoed the sentiment. His feelings for his father were only further strengthened by mutual kelpie loyalty. *"I just don't really know* how *to equalize. I would've done so years ago if it was that simple,"* he admitted.

"Maybe it just happens."

"Perhaps."

We traveled quietly for a while, sharing simple joy in the freedom of sea travel. His side of the bond nudged mine, checking for any hints of fear lingering from Cymora's orders. After yesterday, he didn't find any of it within me. I also enjoyed being this far from the public as much as he did.

He showed me random points of interest along the way to our destination. Fish scattered everywhere as he darted down to circle a tiny shelf of multicolored coral. *"Serian's waters get too cold for us to have significant amounts of coral, but we have this. I've only seen Cela Reef from a distance. The merfolk don't allow kelpies close, even to this day."*

I was surprised by the spike of dislike he had for merfolk. I wondered if it was because of Cymora and Laurel.

"While they didn't help matters, I'm probably privier to the war crimes merfolk committed on kelpies long ago than you are. There's still a lot of bad blood there," he answered.

I didn't want it to taint our date by asking for details. But I was curious, and he could feel it. He steered us away from the coast and considered how much to tell me. *"Mermaids used to have a spell called the siren's song. It was fully effective on males and sometimes on females too. Those caught in the spell were compelled to do anything the singing mermaid demanded. A lot of nixies were murdered by their own mates in a ploy to break the bereft kelpies and clear the sea for merfolk conquest."*

He shuddered in fear and rage just imagining that distant past. *"Which, in turn, resulted in revenge plots that killed hundreds of mermaids who could sing the siren's song or were suspected of it. There's a very good reason our people mention the water fae first when they talk about Unseelie warring with Seelie."*

"Stars, I've never even heard of the siren's song, and I lived with two mermaids." I knew neither of them could cast such a spell, because Cymora was the type to abuse the fuck out of something like that.

"The merfolk lines that had access to that spell are gone. And good riddance."

"Good riddance," I agreed.

"Last I heard, Queen Alora was still looking for her daughter. Mother's letter detailing why we'll be executing Cymora may be buried in a pile by this point." He was concerned that that would delay the mermaid's death, no matter what the royal pack said to the contrary.

"Wait, what happened to Glory?"

"We still don't know. Not that it's our business. Probably just cinnamon girl being extra bratty."

He shared his impression of Glory as a peer from a rival nation. The queens visited with each other at least twice a year, which meant their kids mingled too. He'd found Glory to be loud, brash, and bossy, and her pheromones about as pleasant as being hit in the face with an autumn festival cinnamon broomstick.

"She can't be that bad," I protested. I lingered on my only impression of her from the Omega Masquerade, of her saving me from the male that'd tried to carry me onto the dance floor.

The vibrations of Marius's furious growl shook my legs. He didn't think the gentle warning Glory had given the other male went far enough. *"The fucking nerve. No one touches my p'nixie."*

That effectively distracted him from talk of cinnamon girl Glory.

We circled an old shipwreck. Only the broken boards that used to be the skeleton of the vessel remained. According to Marius, there were several lining the depths of the Doras, from nations I'd only heard whispers of, beyond the seas of Faerie. The world was so much bigger than I'd expected from my life in Osme Fen.

He bobbed twice, the signal that we were surfacing. We emerged up to his shoulders into the late afternoon sunlight. I stretched muscles gone stiff from the prolonged trip on his back.

Marius turned us toward land, though we wouldn't be able to get to civilization from here. Foaming white waves pounded huge cliffs of rock. The water roared and occasionally revealed jagged teeth of rock jutting out just beneath the surface.

"We're close. Look for a sea cave opening," he said.

We scanned the cliffs for a hole that, apparently, I would have to be blind to miss. We searched for a good half hour before we spotted it. It was definitely unmistakable, fifteen feet high and crumbling around the edges to become even larger. The tide was low enough that we could see the bottom curve of the cave opening. Marius rode a wave overtop it and treaded water in a small circular space.

"We should have a personal essence lamp amongst our things. We need it to go exploring."

I searched for it, cringing as I got salt water in amongst all of our things while retrieving the round lamp toward the bottom of the bag. Once I activated it and fixed it over his shoulder, Marius dunked underwater and undulated his tail slowly to take us under through a narrow opening partially blocked off by a rockfall.

Once we were past it, he said, *"Welcome to the drowned city of Telimarr."*

The essence lamp illuminated our immediate surroundings, but I had the impression we'd just entered a large, still space. We headed down at an angle, skimming over a set of stairs cut into the stone. There were hints of elegant patterns chiseled into the rock, though they'd mostly been eroded away and coated in a layer of mossy fuzz.

"Telimarr was a dark elf city back when the elves were still a subterranean race. The Doras beat up against their back door until it burst in one day and flooded all three levels of the city. I've come here a few times just to sightsee."

He knew we wouldn't be the first—or last—kelpie and nixie couple to visit Telimarr. Distant orbs of light suggested we weren't alone now, even.

We traced a path of devastation first, as the sea had poured forcefully upon the rubble of the first buildings we passed. But further along, we saw what Marius called *"a period of ancient history suspended in time."* Some of the facts he remembered, he related to me as we explored.

There was a town square, marked with a circular fountain where a cracking statue of a headless female stood with her palms extended downward. Before emerging to see the stars, dark elves used to worship the black spaces found deep in their caves. There was no darkness as complete as that found when surrounded by solid rock. Elves trapped for extended periods in the unknown claimed it was a religious experience.

"Half the time, they'd come back blinded, too. Total darkness is terrible on the body, no matter what kind of fae you are," Marius added.

"What made dark elves turn their eyes up toward the stars rather than down toward the deep earth?" I asked curiously.

"Other fae." That was a joke. He didn't really know either, but dark elf promiscuity was what held the many races of the Unseelie together, especially going back to the early days of Serian.

The surviving buildings we passed were made of stone, some occupied by small sea creatures. The architecture was curious, blocky and crude compared to modern fae buildings. Sculpted embellishments turned columns into works of art, and wall panels became optical illusions from engraved, looping shapes.

I could admire all this for hours, especially when we followed a path down to the next level. Everything was more intact here, as if the sea had filled it up gently after taking its wrath out on the floor above.

"Look at these crystals." Marius took me to a bush-sized cluster of spiky, prism-like growths on the ceiling and had me turn off our essence lamp.

Darkness closed in, but it wasn't complete. The prisms glowed with dull lime green light. Pinpricks of different colors dotted the ceiling, walls, and floor. *"They're so pretty."*

"They're a special crystal. Do you like silver?" The question wasn't as random as it seemed. Marius's next thought was that Fal preferred the color silver.

"Um, yes?"

"We should find him a silver or gray piece. Dark elves fucking love rocks."

He wanted to do something nice for Fal?

"I can play nice," he grumbled. *"Besides, this'll mean something more to him. I'll let him tell you the dark elf fact."*

"We can just take these crystals?" I asked.

Marius exaggerated a look left and right. *"I don't see anyone around to stop us. Besides, you only need a piece, not a whole formation."*

We searched for crystals of a nice silvery hue on and off as we explored the rest of Telimarr. Eventually, we found a cluster of them. Marius had to wrap some of his clinging mane around a crystal and pull with the full strength of his kelpie form, but we did wrench a prism-like chunk free.

Though most things of value had long been taken, there was enough intact here to see how the subterranean fae had lived. My favorite spot by far was a thick temple made with sheets of multicolored crystal. We floated inside the empty area where ancient dark elves used to gather.

Marius released me from the hold of his mane and wrapped around me again. He was on the cusp of doing something and only hesitated because, as his thoughts narrated, *"This is romantic, right?"*

"Yes," I answered. Rocked gently by the water, under a roof that'd survived a natural catastrophe, connected mind-to-mind with him... this was a moment only he and I could share.

He glanced at me and made the mental equivalent of clearing his throat. *"'Sea spirit, our vessel may be wrecked, but we will survive together. You've helped me understand the error of my ways, for to brave the tides alone is to perish.'"*

"What?" I giggled.

"Tides of Treason. Your favorite part," he said confidently.

"When did you have time to read Tides of Treason?" I asked in disbelief. The shipwreck scene was almost the last chapter of the story.

"Shh. You're thinking too hard."

"I think I'm thinking entirely hard enough!"

"Where was I?" he asked, nearly playful. *"Ah, yes. 'To brave the tides alone is to perish. And I intend not to die today, nor tomorrow, for that matter.'"*

"'Especially not without knowing the feel of your lips on mine,'" I supplied for him. It *was* my favorite part of this book, and I knew it well

enough to join him. "*The captain took her hand in his and tugged her close...*"

"*He could see the stars sparkling in her eyes as they leaned in at the same time.*"

"*Finally, you appreciate that we're better together,*" I said for the female's part of the scene.

"*He realized she'd been waiting years to hear him admit to such a thing. He'd been a fool not to see how much she cared for him. He would dare to say she made him the best he could be. As flawed a male as he was.*"

Marius nuzzled me, the pressure of the water slowing him. "*And he kissed her with the floating detritus of his once great ship and the stars as witnesses. Alongside the good-natured jeers of the rest of the crew when they were forced to witness too,*" he concluded. "*I'm a little surprised that wasn't the end of the book.*"

"*They had a great comeback.*"

"*They did. You were right. It was a much better book than* The Battle of Marsh Hill.*"

"*How did you know that was my favorite part?*" I asked.

He slanted over a playful look, even in his animal form. "*Consider it an educated guess. My p'nixie loves kisses. And prefers kissing scenes to saucy ones. Anyway...are you okay to leave? I'm eager to hold you in a form with hands.*"

I was content to go. I'd gotten my silvery crystal, I had my kelpie, and this had been a unique experience. Marius agreed and took me to dry land.

49
LARK

WE ASCENDED toward a circle of dim sunlight. Marius started to shift back into his fae form as soon as we passed the rockfall partially blocking off access to Telimarr. As his animal features receded, the clinging kelpie mane released me, and I floated to the water's surface.

The sun was going down, leaving our lamp the best illumination of our surroundings. Water lapped at a pebbly shore of crudely cut rock, leading up and around a bend shrouded in darkness. I emerged onto the shore waterlogged and quickly chilled by a breeze off the sea.

Marius emerged from the water, finger-combing his wet hair back in place. The intensity of our bond was starting to fade now that he wasn't in his second form, but I could still feel the shape of his thoughts. He prowled toward me, his dilated gaze intent. His muscles were taut, and his cock throbbed at rigid attention.

I felt a tug toward him low in my belly. It was the bond demanding completion, and my omega instincts were in full agreement. We could fuck like animals right here amongst the grit and pebbles.

"Not yet," he growled, palming himself and angling his body away. He cupped the base of his shaft and the heat of his knot. It'd inflate for the first time to seal our bond, but the sensation of pulsing need where it'd only been dormant was something he was trying to squeeze out.

"You're about to enter polite society. Don't think about her tight, wet... fuck..."

"You need non-sexy thoughts." I cleared my throat and listed things I knew Marius didn't like. "Loud noises. Elves who talk too much. Glass shattering. Oh! Someone needing something when you're twenty pages from the end of a book."

"That's the most frustrating thing," he muttered.

"As bad as getting tricked?"

"Depends." He shook off some of the water still clinging to his skin. "Glance away for a moment." He wasn't sure he could stay down if I looked at him right now. I tilted my head back to eye the crystal formation growing from the ceiling while I listened to him rummage through our bag.

He donned a sleeveless shirt and his swimming trunks after giving himself a brisk dry-off with a towel. I took the second towel and wiped away as much water off me as I could.

He pressed to my back, his body heat more than welcome against my cold skin. His hands roamed, spreading his warmth over my bare midriff and through the damp fabric of my top and shorts.

"Going to make you mine," his feral side whispered in my mind, and I showed him my throat. I soaked in his rumble and the pressure of his fangs dimpling my neck.

"We can do that soon. I'm going to freeze if we stay here," I said.

"So dramatic. It's usually *much* colder at this time of night." He slung our bag over his shoulder and took my hand, leading me up the rough-cut rock path leading away from the sea and the entrance to Telimarr. We'd both put on sandals for a bit of protection from sharp stones.

Marius reached up and dimmed our essence lamp. We rounded the bend that'd seemed so dark and entered a tunnel lined on either side with glowing, multicolored crystals. Unlike the ones we'd observed underwater, these had grown to hip height and absorbed the lamp's light to gleam twice as bright.

My mouth fell open, and I gasped. No wonder he wanted to visit at low tide. There were puddles here and there that suggested the sea level rose to cover the first section of this tunnel, which was set at a gradual upward slope. Prisms of multicolored light and spiky shadows danced around us as we walked.

Marius watched my reaction to the surreal loveliness around us. He felt so strongly in the moment that his emotions and mine mingled. This was it. Very soon, we would make our bond permanent.

It was as beautiful a concept as this path of light and color. I saw why it'd been created as the bridge from the sea to our ultimate destination. We *could* rush through it, just like we could grab one another and complete the bond with damp stone as our bed. But the anticipation was heady as we walked hand in hand, soaking in the moment and each other.

"You've helped me understand." He kept his voice at a hush, reverent for our surroundings. "Fate's guiding hand is the force that brought you back to me. The odds of us meeting again were so incredibly low."

"You don't despise fate anymore?" He was still the only fae I'd met with an abject hatred for it.

His ear flicked. "I will give thanks for it once. Now. But any time after, I'll say that Fal tripped over you out of sheer luck. I would've still found you if he hadn't, p'nixie. I was right on the edge of turning wild, and Niall was of a mind to abandon Ilysnor to chase your shadow."

"I was also close to getting on a train to a sanctuary city," I admitted.

"Your destiny was never there. This is your path, part of your journey. Here, by my side."

I looked up at him, smitten. He was swiftly becoming my safe haven. The close friend I wished I'd had with me all along but was more than grateful to have returned to me. "I give thanks to fate, too, for deciding that we fit together perfectly." I squeezed his hand and admired the multicolored gleam off his fierce gaze. "I love you, and I am yours."

My words set off a wave of possessive desire in him, a blend of alpha and feral intensity. "I have always been yours. And...I think you're about to hear this far too much. I love you too."

I practically glowed with happiness and really hoped there was a bed waiting for us at the end of this tunnel.

He answered my thoughts again. "Better. The cutest fucking inn. Though you'll have to wait until I let you off my knot to see it in the light of day."

"I look forward to it," I said dryly, assuming he was exaggerating for a male who hadn't knotted me yet.

He raised an eyebrow back in challenge. *Uh oh,* I thought playfully.

"We'll see," he said, low and rasping. We'd reached the end of the tunnel, where it leveled off into a dirt path. The first stars dotted the night sky as it deepened to a velvety purple-black overhead. I huddled closer to Marius as a cold breeze whistled in from the sea.

He released my hand to draw me close for a short walk around the side of a two-story structure half hidden in the trees. The windows on the second floor were dark, while a full-powered essence lamp gleamed atop a wooden porch made with fresh-smelling timbers.

Marius got the door, the hinges of which creaked mightily as he pulled it open. Instead of having a front desk and an area for baggage right off the front foyer, it looked like we'd walked straight into someone's living room. A healthy fire in the hearth provided a wave of welcome heat.

It smelled like cooked seafood and aged fabrics. The floor was wooden and scuffed in places, covered by a faded area rug in the center. Several wooden shelves lined the walls, especially over the hearth, all of them burdened with dusty items.

A wrinkled figure paused in a rocking chair, her knitting needles stilling as she took us in. "Henrik!" she bellowed at the top of her lungs. I startled, not expecting such a loud voice from a little old fae like her. "Henrik! Guests!"

"What?" called an equally elderly-sounding male voice from the next room over.

The female got up with the help of a walking stick and left her knitting behind. "Deaf as a post, he is," she muttered to herself. Fae aged, but very slowly, so she had to have seen many centuries to earn the stoop in her back and the whitish-gray hue that'd leeched away most of her coloring.

"Hello, honored elder. May we rent a room for a few nights?" Marius asked.

"Of course. Look at you two dears, so young and in love," she said, shuffling right past the Unseelie prince with his distinctive pack mark and scar without more than a single glance. "You just missed dinner, but I'll cook you up something special. New couples always deserve treats."

"Oh, no, that's quite all right," I blurted. We'd be too busy in bed to eat anytime soon, and I didn't want to trouble an honored elder.

She walked to a set of stairs and retrieved a keyring off the banister, flipping through a few of them before holding out a key dangling between her fingers. "Right up these stairs. First room on your left. I'm Illia, by the way. If you need anything, ring the bell, though it would be nice if you'd come downstairs too. These steppers don't work like they used to."

"We'll be no trouble," he assured her.

She smacked her lips and waved him off. "Ah! Such a charmer. You remind me of my Henrik. Came back from the war full of fire and verve."

Marius drew up in surprise while I struggled not to laugh.

"Did you need me?" the male in question called.

"Nay, I got it!" she called back over her shoulder.

"What?"

Illia breathed a sigh. "Why don't you two dears go get settled?" she suggested.

We started up the stairs a breath later. Marius let us into the cozy room we'd rented, turning on the essence lamps so they glowed with soft half-light and closing the curtains over the two windows inside. I skipped straight to the bed, lip caught between my teeth.

"Go ahead and nest," Marius said on his way to the attached bathroom. He leaned into the closet and tossed out a set of extra pillows, a heavy comforter, and what looked like a flat cushion.

I set up the bed enticingly, but this temporary nest wasn't more than a strategic curve of fluffed-up pillows so we could lounge together.

I folded up the comforter and the hand-knit blanket already on the bed to place them to the side. They'd be nice for sleep, later.

Marius handed me the cushion last. "I think this is a soak mat."

The soft material had a nice give and, more importantly, a faint hum of magic. Soak mats were for heat sex, to keep the fluids contained, though I sensed Marius wanted to make use of it to be polite to our hosts. I shrugged and laid it on top of the sheets. "Worth a try."

I smiled at him, still full of anticipation for what was next. His answering grin stretched his scar before he turned and headed for the door. I almost whined, but all he was doing was setting the keyring on the knob outside and locking us in the room together with a slow slide of the privacy bar.

When he faced me, his eyes immediately dilated. I'd dropped my damp top and shorts already, awaiting his return naked and eager. He prowled toward me. "Lie on your front," he instructed.

My wings quivered in excitement as I crawled onto the bed and rested on the cushioned mat. I looked over my shoulder to see him rooting through our bag and taking out two familiar pots: the wound salve and, as he unscrewed the lid to check, the lotion.

I twitched in confusion when he straddled my hips still clothed. "Someone's been hunched over a kelpie's back for several hours." He rubbed some lotion between his palms.

"But—"

"Let me take care of you." He started massaging my shoulders. Through our bond, I mostly picked up that he wanted the positive contact, to feel how warm and soft I was. His thoughts weren't crisp enough for me to figure out what else he was planning.

"Mmm." He was really talented at rubbing away the lingering stiffness in my back.

"Do you want to know what else I'm thinking?" he teased.

"Hmm." I was turning into a content puddle, especially once he applied rolling pressure between my wings. "Sure."

"I'm doing this wrong. I was supposed to give you my knot underwater."

"How's that supposed to work?" I murmured.

He chuffed a laugh. "I don't know. There aren't handholds in the sea. I imagine it'd be a disappointing fuck."

"Nothing about this is disappointing," I assured him. With him soothing away any pain, all that was left was the anticipation pulsing in my core. My chocolate and honey crackers scent was already escaping my parted thighs.

He continued rubbing my back and wings with one hand, the other slipping between my legs. His fingertips glided between my folds, gathering slick, before he pressed a single finger inside of me.

Arousal pulsed between us. I could practically sense how hard Marius was, though his attention was focused on his pulsing knot. It made his length feel hotter, and it wasn't even inflated yet.

He forced himself to focus on me as he added a second finger. He learned quickly how to curl and twist his digits to make me squirm and trill beneath him. "You seem ready."

My circling hips probably gave that impression, plus the whine that escaped me when he withdrew his hand and smoothed the other down my spine.

With a little shifting behind me, he had his clothes off and placed something metallic on the side table. "I want to bond with you as I am," he said.

I agreed with a needy sound. He rubbed his cock, free of the lady pleaser piercing, between my folds. I lifted my hips, trembling when he ground the pulsing, growing ridge of his knot right where I wanted him most. My core ached for it.

He helped me turn over and inhaled the pheromones at my neck before nuzzling and nipping the sensitive column. "Mate," he growled, muffled against my skin.

"Mate," I whimpered. He tilted his head so I could taste his pheromones too. His waterlily and mint burst on my tongue and fogged my mind with desire. I licked him again, savoring it, and opened my legs to invite him in.

His first thrust was shallow. My pussy stretched to fit his alpha size as he rocked into me deeper with each roll of his hips. The bond between us quieted until he was fully sheathed in my body.

He drew in a rasping breath, eyes shuttering. I cried out a moment later as I felt it too. The bond was tightening around us once more, merging our sensations. I had a new sense of how heated my own body felt when we were so intimately entangled. At the same time, there was pressure squeezing its way down his spine and spurring him onward. His feral side spoke. *"Claim. Rut. Breed."*

He trembled with restraint. *"Nay. Gentle. She's fragile."*

It seemed I would be privy to his arguments with himself. As he would sense my thoughts in turn. *"I was made for you. Claim me. I won't break, no matter how you do it."* I dug my claws into his back to spur him on, and he sucked in from the jolt of pain.

He met my gaze. While he seemed to be staring, his princely and feral halves were negotiating and coming to a truce. Marius would claim; Niall would breed. There were neither minced words nor any glances at my arm to confirm the fertility blocker was still in place.

He was braced under my wing with one arm. The other hand shaped my curves, teasing sensitive spots with a press of his callused thumb. My pre-heat made every touch more intense. The added sensations of how he felt through our bond was blinding. He tested this with a thrust that ended in another starburst of shared pleasure at its apex.

The last of his control snapped. He pinned me with more of his weight, grabbed my hip, and pulled me into each core-shaking pound of his hips.

I clenched my eyes closed and sank my teeth into his shoulder to hold on, knowing he would be unrelenting.

"Harder," he demanded, wanting to display the little bite wounds until they healed. And then he wanted them reapplied so everyone would know that I was unashamed about marking him as mine. He'd wear any scar I gave him with pride.

"Mine." This whisper alone was all Marius, all alpha. *"This is my claim, right here, right now. You are* mine.*"*

"Yours," I agreed. I quivered all over, on the precipice of coming, which meant he was the same way. His knot swelled and rubbed against my pussy lips. Our bond was heartbeats from completion.

I opened my eyes, and he did the same on a shared impulse. He slowed the roll of his hips, tilting his head. His feral instincts had already staked a claim on the moment of completion, and I heard exactly what Niall wanted. *"Breed her on her hands and knees. Fill her as deep as possible."*

He pulled his cock free, his muscles locking before he went far. Without him inside me, he—we—felt incomplete. I flipped over onto my hands and knees below the tight cage of his body. He rumbled deep in his chest as his thoughts said, *"Don't fucking faint on me now, mate…"*

"Still waiting for my breeding," I teased.

He grabbed and pinned me in this new position, then sank his fangs deep into my shoulder. I arched into his solid chest and screamed. His bite was full of blissful, claiming pressure. It hardly hurt even as he dug a little deeper to truly leave his mark. A small omega trait I learned as it happened—my arousal dimmed the pain of an alpha's bite.

Aligned with me from behind, he slid back inside of me with a sigh of relief. His knot remained a steady bump in and out as he slowed, savoring the way I twitched and moaned. *"My female. My prey. Mine."* This version of his claim was all Niall.

"Yours," I repeated. I was open to his bond, his seed, his love, a surrender that echoed between us. He was ready to finish giving me all three things and more. Everything I wanted. Every part of him was mine.

His knot popped into place, filling my channel and stretching the rim of my pussy. Pleasure burst between us at the same time. He came with a roar, drowning out the rest of my senses in a shattering moment. I trembled with each liquid rush as he pulsed within me. And it wasn't my imagination; he spilled a lot and tried to roll his hips without going anywhere.

"The bond isn't set." He had this distinct thought just as we started to come down from our shared high and a shred of reason peeked in. Did we do something wrong after all? We'd followed all the steps, shared our minds, and joined…

As soon as we stopped coming, it snapped into place. The cord of braided magic anchored in my essence and resonated with a *twang* that felt like pure bliss.

"There it is!" I immediately came again, just as hard as before. Sparks danced in my eyes, and Marius groaned. My squeezing pussy grabbed his knot and milked out more of his seed while he panted and shook.

Thank the stars there was a soak mat, because this would be a mess when he pulled out in twenty minutes or so. By the time we were coming down from our second peak, I was sweaty and limp, only held up by his arm around me. Our bond settled, letting us have our separate headspaces again.

He repositioned us so he was seated and I rested in his lap. *"You really think you're getting away in twenty minutes?"* he asked.

"We can't fuck again if I'm stuck on your knot," I pointed out.

He gently licked the twin wounds he'd left on my shoulder. They were starting to hurt in earnest. Maybe I wouldn't scar him with my little fangs, but the stinging punctures he'd left behind were sure to remain. *"That's not how this works, sweet prey. I caught and marked you. Now, I'm going to breed you properly."*

"Okay, Niall. Breed me, then." I wasn't all that concerned about what he'd do while we were tied.

His rumble turned into a pleased purr at the invitation. He licked the pad of his thumb and used it to circle my clit. *Oh stars*, I had underestimated him. The touch was electric, at first too overstimulating, causing my leg to jerk. He slowed until he was rubbing the side of the little bundle of nerves, coaxing out a reaction.

Just a flutter of my pussy would squeeze him enough to keep his knot sealed in place. We could be here for a long, long time if he drew out my pleasure just right. And there were few forces more determined to make that happen than the male kissing his way up my neck. I tilted my head back to meet his lips with mine, moaning when I tasted his mint and waterlily and...

My channel rippled. His fangs dimpled my lower lip as we both came a bit, and his knot pulsed with his heartbeat, firmer than ever.

"This is a heat strategy," I said, a thought I meant mostly for myself.

"Mmhmm. This is how I make sure the child is mine."

I also meant how he'd keep me from combusting from my heat. My understanding was that an omega's heat pain only abated while she was knotted.

"That too. When you're in estrus..." He drew off, confused, but only for a moment. His thought patterns shifted subtly to reflect his princely side taking over again. *"No babies yet, hmm? Niall is so disappointed."*

I released a pleasure-drunk laugh. Even though he'd returned to his senses, he'd resumed rubbing my clit after realizing where his hand was. We moaned together through another shared mini orgasm.

He worked his jaw before saying aloud, "I want a life for *us* before we go creating new lives."

"I agree," I murmured.

He cradled the side of my face with his free hand and brushed my kiss-swollen lips with his thumb. "From tonight until our end as stardust, we are bound. There's plenty of time to make more p'nixies later. Much later."

"And colts too. As handsome, strong, and blue as their father," I added.

His ear flicked. "Stop saying such sweet things while you're squeezing my knot, mate."

I batted my lashes back at him. "Maybe you should let me off of you so we can eat something," I suggested breathlessly. He hadn't stopped playing with my clit ever so slowly, and my skin was tight with awareness.

"Hmm." He flashed a wicked smile. "Soon. For now, sit tight." As he teased, he pressed my sensitive nub just right, and we came together again.

50
TORMUND

Dad had me pack for a several-day hunting trip, and I dreaded the time spent away from my mate.

As a boy, I was always excited to spend time with him and would count down the days to the next trip. We would walk out of sight of Mom and the rest of the family, and he'd put a weapon in my pudgy hand. He did the hunting and butchering for the first few years, handing me meat skewers by night that I didn't recognize as once belonging to an animal.

My first kill was a squirrel. I was six. I walloped the poor thing over the head and then cried about it for the rest of the day. I carried its limp body in my hands, inconsolable that it wouldn't return to its little squirrel family.

Dad had taken in my reaction with understanding at first. But as the day grew long, he made sounds of annoyance under his breath. "It's just a squirrel, son."

"But *I'm* the reason he died." This spurred on a fresh wave of tears.

He made a scoff with his signature *ach*. That night, he'd tried to feed me meat skewers from his kill, and it finally dawned on me where the food had come from. I decided I'd rather starve than eat small, defenseless critters.

With a heavy sigh, he admitted defeat and reached into his bag of supplies. He handed me a squished hunk of bread and some cheese. The next morning, we buried the squirrel under a patch of wildflowers.

Dad's impossibly gigantic hand had covered my shoulder as I stood over the tiny grave. "You'll learn before long that you're a redcap. Delivering death is what we do, son."

"But I don't want to," I'd said petulantly.

As the years passed, my answer to what I was *supposed* to be remained largely the same. Dad didn't push me to change as much as he could've, because Mom had stars in her eyes. She saw what kind of boy I was and didn't want to sacrifice me to make another executioner. And I had a bad habit of eavesdropping on their arguments about it.

I was the first royal redcap in the family line to be placed as the next queen's comfort, a role that had always been traded between the dark elf and the kelpie lines. Before me, the role of queen's protector always went to the redcap, regardless of birth order.

"I know my sons," Mom stated. "Marius will be the protector, and Tormund the comfort. Tradition will bow to fate."

"Tormund will change," Dad argued back. "Once he's a little older, he will thrive performing everything the protector role entails. Marius is young enough to adapt."

That'd been before he'd scarred Marius. After that, Dad didn't quite change his mind. Instead, he fought to have two protectors, as he and my kelpie older brother had bonded significantly over the accident.

Mom said no. "Watch my gentle boy become the sweetest male, Theo."

I strove not to disappoint her.

Dad's final words on the matter were "As you wish. However, you're setting him up for failure. You'll see one day."

So, while Dad didn't stand in the way of what Mom wanted, he kept moving back the day I would learn what manner of fae I was. Maybe when I was ten and started in on the tedium of managing the palace.

But I ended up loving my apprenticeship under Rennyn. I'd especially enjoyed organizing the nesting supply rooms and picking out things to make the palace omegas happy. It was all a matter of patterns and fabrics, and I recognized that every omega had different nesting needs. They, in turn, loved my enthusiasm for getting them the right things.

At age twelve, I found a bird struggling with a broken wing on one of our hunting trips and scooped it up off the forest floor. As I sat with Dad around our evening fire, he'd suggested I break its neck to put it out of its misery.

I was aghast at the thought. "It's not a meat bird. I'm going to take it to the lodge to heal." At this point, I'd come to accept that hunting was a necessity. We didn't waste the life or the body of the animal, though.

I still needed to roast the meat we caught on the evening fire. Dad ate his raw-ish. As a fully grown fire fae, he could enjoy the bloody flavors and roast it as it went down his throat. *Ach. Gross.*

"A predator will kill it the moment you release it," he'd pointed out.

I'd looked down into the beady eye of the bird, who wore the splint I'd made for its wing. It hunkered down, trembling, in a scoop of rocks and moss. Patting it gently, I'd said, "Well, first it needs a fighting chance."

He'd let out yet another sigh, shaking his head in confusion, but suggested an empty room I could use in the winter lodge.

I seized the opportunity. My set of duties was becoming increasingly outdoorsy, as managing stable hands, working animals, and hunting rights were some of Rennyn's least favorite tasks. I gathered up more small animals to rehabilitate in the newly named critter room and made the journey on horseback from the palace to the lodge often.

I learned what it felt like to hold a tiny soul and give it medicine, protection, and a second chance. The bird with a broken wing healed and flew from my hand to continue its little life. I savored the lightness in my chest as I waved goodbye to its fluttering outline. It felt like peace and life and mercy, light as a feather. And that was ten times as moving as the final gasp of an opponent or the stilling of a heartbeat.

My favorite animal friend was Balti the squirrel, who I'd raised up from being a pink, blind thing. He stayed with me for nearly two years.

He'd do flips for treats but eventually left the lodge forever for the love of a lady squirrel. I'd come to terms with it as what I deserved for the murder of his ancestor.

Soon enough, I turned sixteen and started blowing smoke out of my mouth. It was the first sign of several that heralded the rage form growing. I never developed a taste for the things that would keep the fire within me satisfied: venting, fighting, killing, and sex. I didn't yearn for the sensation of blood wetting my hair.

Maybe that was the age when my problems really started. I avoided the things that would've gotten the rage form under my control. And once something gets out of control, be it a secret or a wildfire, it was nearly impossible to rein back in.

Not finding a balance with the monster that lived inside me wasn't the only failure I experienced at that age. The molten rage erupted from me early when I was informed I was failing a test I hadn't even known I was taking. Rennyn was weighing the problem of whether I was clever enough to take over fully as his apprentice. Like Dad, he had two jobs, but the second one was the quietest secret—Serian's spymaster.

Dad and Rennyn sat me down to explain this. While the dark elf king was still complimenting my straightforward nature, I'd lost my mind and erupted.

"Are you calling me simple?" I'd asked with redcap menace. The sudden heat pouring out of me was a shock. I hadn't even known what it felt like to be a monster until that moment.

A swift blow to the back of my head extinguished me. The next thing I knew, I was waking up naked in a tub. House moths were hurriedly adding ice to the melting mound packed around my body. I'd transformed early, before my alpha designation manifested. The heat and internal pressure had almost killed me.

I nearly died fourteen times succumbing to my rage form before my induction into the Bloodhunter Clan. Each and every loss of control was an emergency. I had to stay content and not feel any spike of negative emotions, or the monster within me would boil over. A nearly impossible task for any teenager.

Dad presented me for the first time at the clan's annual meeting when I was seventeen, and I received my membership tattoo early. The tattoo activated the magical heat vents along my back and made them resemble the stylized knots of the Bloodhunter Clan.

A redcap without a clan is dead. Not just a saying, but a fact. Clans were created to give us a nonviolent outlet. In the ancient times, only delivering death until even our hair was wet with blood would make the rage recede. Redcaps nearly went extinct due to the sheer violence of that time, even with ongoing wars to be fought.

If I ever brought enough dishonor to the clan to be banished, those vents would vanish. It was the most common death sentence amongst my kind. There was a small, cruel hope of living, but as I'd experienced, that life was spent on the point of a knife, desperately balancing in an attempt not to unleash the monster within.

Only after I had my vents did Rennyn revisit the spymaster discussion. He'd said with his usual air of levity, "That was a self-improvement talk, not a 'Tormund is stupid' talk. You're not simple, Tor-Tor. You're still a kid. You just can't seem to keep a secret to save your life."

Over time, I realized he was right. I got excited and blurted out most secrets I knew. We worked on it, tiptoeing into the vast amount of work I needed to do to become the next spymaster. Rule number one...never tell anyone I'm a spy. It was so, so hard not to share that.

I had one thing going for me. Other fae liked my personality, even my fellow clan members. My attempts at being a better spy apprentice served me well during clan meetings; I fit in with them despite being the perfect example of a weakling redcap. And while weaklings weren't banished, they were relentlessly mocked in other clans.

Everything I liked, from poetry to li'l animal rehabilitation to the general scope of my duties, fell outside of the common redcap interests. I hated fighting, didn't kill unless it was for hunting, and sex, um...I had to see if it worked for me.

And now I knew it *didn't* work for me. I needed to alpha up and tell my dad what was wrong. Except I would've rather died than look him in the eye and say, "Dad, I made love to my mate. Now the very sight and smell of her is triggering my rage."

So, I stayed silent about it.

Even if he was the male who'd taught me everything I knew about being a redcap.

Just thinking about the problem had me venting while I

prepared our dinner. We'd caught two wild turkeys apiece, and I'd already spitted and seasoned the dressed meat. He and I made small talk about clan business while I rotated the birds to cook them evenly. This would ordinarily take several hours, but I breathed the occasional wave of heat overtop them to speed the process along.

Dad would never admit it, but he ate a lot more on our hunting trips once I took over preparing the kills. Could be the salt. Or the herbs. Or maybe even the nice char on the skin after receiving the double flame treatment.

Or...he could just be humoring me. He had given me his usual bemused look when I'd told him I'd started learning how to cook from the palace kitchen staff. He didn't ask why, only told me it was now my job to make dinner when we went into the wilderness. Which I was happy to do to elevate our time together, because raw meat really was sadness.

"Dinner's done," I announced. I took his turkeys off the fire and presented them to him still spitted and sizzling.

He ate them just like that, bones and all. I sat on the other side of the fire and did the same thing. Simmering with my monstrous form just below the surface was good for one thing, at least. The fangs were very helpful for tearing into this kind of meal.

I sat on a stone, shirtless, venting so hard I created a furnace around me. The evening was chill, but signs of spring were spreading. The snow was all but gone, flowers bloomed, and insects sang outside the radius of our campsite at the top of a rocky hill. Our horses cropped the grass nearby.

I watched the stars blink into being above us and wondered where Lark was and what she was doing. It'd barely been a day, and I already missed her so much my chest ached.

"So." Dad broke into my thoughts. I took another bite of my half-eaten dinner and looked at him through the ripple of heat and smoke over our campfire. "You finally had sex. I heard you had some difficulties."

I swallowed wrong and considered letting the mouthful block my throat. Better for the stars to have me than to answer my dad's unspoken question. He rarely asked questions directly. With his size, strength, and station, his every whim was answered without having to ask for anything.

"*Ach*. Don't choke, boy," he grumbled.

I coughed painfully and glanced away, my face and body turning a uniform red. But then I thought about what he'd actually said. My eyes vibrated as flames ignited in my pupils. My chest expanded with muscle and heat.

"Who told you? Fal?" I demanded with growling menace. Tongues of fire escaped my mouth. "I'll kill him!"

It had to be Fal. My eldest brother was such a meddling jerk sometimes.

Dad arched a brow. "You've been venting continuously for hours. There's obviously *something* wrong."

"Yeah, there's...yeah..."

"Don't kill your brother. Your mother would miss him. Besides, he didn't give any details." He fixed a commanding stare across the fire at me to supply said details.

I breathed plumes of smoke as I struggled with what to say next. "You've always told me there are four ways to control the rage form."

He nodded and listed them, as he always did. "Venting, to a degree. There's also a good fight, the feeling of taking a life, and sex, preferably with your mate. In an emergency, a mate can also extinguish the rage, but it's not worth the risk to a one and only."

Dread bit into my skin, and my anger cooled as I nodded in agreement. My little bird had had to call me back to my senses more than once. *Shameful, putting her in danger.*

"I heard Lark had to do that for you," he said, echoing my thoughts. I nodded again reluctantly. "For her, as your fated mate, it works the other way. She can extinguish the rage, or she can set it free even if you are perfectly calm."

"I know." Nothing else explained why I'd unleashed myself on her in her bedroom.

He breathed a heavy sigh. It was a sign I knew well. As his son, I wasn't quite as intimidated by him to prattle off anything he wanted to know. "Did you finish?" he asked briskly.

I bristled. "Aye."

"Did you have perfect control of the rage?"

I hesitated, which was answer enough for him.

"So, you didn't knot her, then." It was a statement of fact.

"I was hurting her," I mumbled.

"*Ach.* Tell me why you think that."

Well, she had reassured me that it'd been good for her, but... "She clawed at me."

He pressed his lips together. I kept talking, sure to lose my nerve if I stopped. "And she was moving around, not holding still. And, um, the noises she made. There were a lot of them, and they sounded pained."

He closed his eyes, shoulders shaking. Stars, he was *laughing*.

"Dad!" I protested.

He rubbed a hand down his face. "Did she tell you to stop? Or make noises of obvious pain, like whimpering or keening?"

"Well...nay."

"I've been remiss, apparently, by not telling you omegas are *loud*," he deadpanned.

He told me what I'd done wrong and how to fix it. I could've wilted from relief as I listened intently and asked a few questions. I wasn't broken, and Lark was still the solution to my rage. In all this time, I hadn't realized how the way my monstrous form grew to full size matched the mounting pressure of sex.

I also wasn't doomed to hurt my little bird every time I made love to her. That thought had been completely unbearable. I just had to love her right the next time, and then I'd be freer to pleasure her like she deserved.

I celebrated my newfound knowledge by pulling out chunky mallows and a couple of fireproof sticks from my supply bag. Dad watched me toast a sweet with my breath before he said, "Pass me some of those."

He speared a mallow and bathed it in flame. It was still on fire when he put it in his mouth. Once he swallowed, he said, "Tell me about Lark."

I lit up, grinning happily. "My little bird! What do you want to know?"

"Anything," he answered, his fiery gaze flashing over at me. He smiled too, in his own way, a slight curve to his craggy face. "I know how much you love little birds."

I gladly toasted mallows with him while we chatted late into the evening.

WE RETURNED to the palace after a couple of days. I was in much better spirits until I noticed Fal waiting by the stable yard. He stood out amongst the dirt and animals, primped and polished with his silver earrings glinting in the sun. The pack bond was calm, at least. Kauz and Marius were too far away for me to easily pick out what they were feeling.

"*Ach*." He was about to rope me into something. I just knew it.

After the stable hands took our horses, I hugged Dad goodbye. He lifted me off my feet, the only male able to turn around my usual affection.

"Love you, Dad," I said. He grunted in agreement, like he always did, and patted my shoulder before returning to his duties.

I went to tend to my mare, Rory, personally and took my time. Either Fal would go away, or he'd be standing right behind me in a moment, sneaking up on me like the cat he halfway resembled. I looked, and there he was, leaning indolently against a wooden beam with his usual smirk. "Welcome back, little brother. Learn anything?"

I didn't let him get my hackles up. I may have fire in my blood, but I wasn't Marius. "Aye. What'd I miss in the meantime?"

He flicked his fang with his tongue. Something was bothering him. "I'm glad you're back. It's good timing. I have news of a particular pack and a certain friend of Kauz's. When the friend couldn't gain access to Kauz's dreams to tell him something, she told my father instead. He's taken his time sharing the news with me."

Kauz's friend? *Oh*. He'd sent a spy, a fellow dreamlander he could communicate with at night, to look into Pack Ellisar. I balled my hands into fists, willing my anger not to rise. My brothers wouldn't tell me anything if I made a habit of erupting with rage.

I took a couple deep breaths and fished out a sugar cube to feed Rory. "I'll let someone else take care of you for now, my girl."

Whatever Fal said next...I wanted to be out of a flammable structure, just in case.

The dark elf left the stables and waited for me to join him at a safe distance. Then he looked up at me and whispered, "Pack Ellisar is on their way here."

"What?" I demanded. The rage kindled immediately. Billows of smoke escaped my clenched, sharpening teeth.

Fal barely blinked. "According to the friend, they're going to arrive today. How do you feel about being part of the welcoming committee?" I felt the shift in the pack bond. There was anger lurking under his practiced façade, and it was just as potent as mine. We shared the same urge to protect our omega. Her night terror had been about these males, for stars' sake.

"I would love to *welcome* them," I answered with a fiery growl.

He rumbled in agreement. "We're also giving the fishling the boot. Same train. It's going to be a great afternoon."

And that's how, a couple hours later, Fal and I ended up on a train platform with a glum mermaid standing between us. All Lark would have to know was that we took care of an issue for her. Plus, she wouldn't have to see her whiny stepsister again. Win-win.

Not that Laurel was whining now. In fact, she hadn't said more than a quiet "thanks" when we told her she was going back to Thelis today. With her slumped posture and downcast gaze, she was the very portrait of an enemy we'd defeated.

While I'd never really liked her, I didn't see a point in laying her any lower than we already had. She was returning to Osme Fen without more than a few slivers to her name. It wasn't likely that there was a warm welcome awaiting her.

A small army of police and guards were posted around the station, dressed and armed discreetly so we wouldn't scare any of our subjects. The moment a trio of barkfolk alphas disembarked, they would be surrounded and taken to the palace. We'd make it look as if they'd disappeared—or as if they'd never been here in the first place. But they would no longer have any opportunity to trouble Lark.

"Are you ready for your date?" I asked, trying to distract Fal.

The pack bond pulsed with longing that I echoed. Fal sighed wist fully. "For the most part. A lot depends on how long she's away from Neslune. How about you?"

I smiled broadly. "Her present should be arriving in a few days."

"Oh, what is it? I got her a rock."

I'd have been a little offended on her behalf if I didn't know he was making light of an ancient dark elf tradition. I told him all about what I'd gotten her, too excited for it to be a secret for much longer. He nodded along, suitably impressed with my quick and meaningful acquisition.

Laurel turned and craned her head up to look at me. Some of my excitement faded as I met her gaze. I knew that thoughtful face she was making. She was about to ask a question, most likely a dumb one.

"Is my mother dead?" she asked in her native Theli.

Oh, now that's a kick in the gut. A reminder that for as viciously as we tore Cymora down, she still had someone relying on her. "Nay," I answered in kind.

"Not yet," Fal said at the same time.

She stiffened with a disappointed sigh at my answer, just to gain a glimmer of something like hope in her eyes at Fal's. How strange. She twisted her lips. "I...I understand why..." Laurel swallowed and worked her jaw. I assumed she was choked up and braced myself for tears.

Fal watched her struggle to speak with all the sympathy of a spider eyeing a fly struggling in its web. "She is fortunate the Unseelie have moved past the 'dance to death on hot coals' method of execution. Her death will be more painless than she deserves."

"It's not..." She blew out a frustrated breath and stomped her foot like a child. Tears welled in her eyes. I shifted with discomfort as they rolled down her cheeks.

I exchanged a glance with my brother. He smirked, ready to deliver a finishing blow. He'd send her away from here with a verbal knife stuck through her loss. But I hesitated and reached out to nudge him, shaking my head. There might be something we were missing here.

"Don't you remember when Lark couldn't finish her sentences?" I asked him in Serri.

A line appeared between his brows, cutting through his pack mark. "She's just being a brat. We saw it a hundred times on the train ride here," he answered.

It'd be easy to accept his explanation, but I still had a niggling sense in my gut of something amiss. "Take a deep breath," I encouraged her in Theli. "Finish your thought. Talk to me, not Fal."

She sniffled and fixed watery sea green eyes on me. "It's not *just*—" Her voice broke on another sob. Ah, stars. I awkwardly patted her atop her head, hoping she'd stop crying.

"Why couldn't you all just—" she tried to ask, just to cut herself off again.

"Just what?" I asked quietly and shot a meaningful look at my brother. This was *just* like Lark when she'd been under Cymora's control. Our mate had experience navigating around what she could and couldn't say, though. She'd avoided choking herself on things she couldn't utter like her stepsister was doing. A hint of a troubled frown graced Fal's lips as he listened in.

Laurel couldn't seem to form a coherent thought, leaving those statements hanging as the closest magirail vibrated from an incoming train. Our hidden allies shifted, some reaching for weapons. Fal straightened with a low growl, the mermaid forgotten.

She watched the train coast into the station with one last hiss of magic as it slowed smoothly to a stop. "So, this is it, huh?" she asked after another hiccupped sob and looked at me for confirmation. "Pack Ellisar is on that train."

I squinted at her.

"You aren't exactly subtle, even talking in another language," she said in a wobbly voice. "I'm sorry about this."

She drew a deep breath and began to belt out a wordless, haunting tune. It warped through the train station, threading into the ears of guards, police, and innocent passersby alike. Everyone stopped what they were doing to listen, even Fal and me.

Still singing, Laurel bent to retrieve her bags. Tears made new trails down her cheeks as she sang and sang, and the world bent to her whims. The eyes watching the train from Thelis looked away. Fal relaxed. I surrendered to thoughtless nothingness. My eyes saw what was happening right in front of me without my mind comprehending a moment of it.

Three alphas with whorled, gray-brown bark for clothes and mossy vines for hair disembarked and took in the frozen figures around them in bewilderment. Their leader pointed at Laurel, who approached after wiping her face clean. She beckoned with both hands, and they walked away with her.

She spared us one last glance on the way by, and her song changed only briefly. A beautiful melody wrapped around me. While the station resumed its usual bustle, a trickle of warmth escaped the corner of my eye.

I dabbed away the tear, moved by something elusive, a melody that sounded a little like *It's not just Lark who suffered. Why couldn't you all just end this when you had the chance?*

I watched the drop of liquid roll off my fingertip, seized by a hollow sense of alarm as the melody faded from my mind. Laurel was in danger? But...Laurel was going back to Thelis. She'd just gotten on the train.

I turned to Fal, who usually had all the answers, just to see him frowning, troubled. "I'm wrong about...?" he asked himself.

"My princes," interrupted a female voice. It belonged to a panicked-looking winged beta, who began to prostrate herself in apology. "They've disappeared. I don't know how they did it."

Fal shook off his daze and bared his fangs in a snarl. "Well, don't just stand there," he announced to our allies. "Three barkfolk alphas, all of the same pack. Find them! Neslune is no haven for enemies of the crown."

51

LARK

Marius didn't let me off his knot until the early hours of the morning, but only because he'd fallen asleep. I promptly followed him into unconsciousness and stirred before him to the rhythmic sound of waves crashing against the cliffs near the inn. The curtains closed off all but the cheery outline of sunshine.

I disentangled from my mate slowly, not wanting to wake him from his dead sleep. I expected my pussy to be sore, but perhaps it was a testament to my coming heat that my core only ached for more.

Marius's ear flicked a few times, twitching in his sleep. He was sweating, his skin flushed a dark blue tone. While my nose picked up something different about his scent, I was unable to tell what it was while I was covered in his pheromones and warm from a flush of pre-heat.

I wrapped my torso in a towel and cracked the door open. The hall was empty, and a wicker basket full of lumps wrapped in waxed paper waited in front of the threshold. My belly grumbled as I took in the scents of seafood and bread.

Taking the basket, I went rummaging through the room for plates. Illia and Henrik had stocked us with water and sachets for tea. I was looking for a magical heating element when flutters clenched through my belly. I put everything down and held my middle, murmuring, "No no no. Not now. Not...*ugh*."

The cramp seized my middle like a squeezing fist in my guts. Marius woke with a violent snarl and a litany of Serri curses. I clenched my eyes shut. So much for surprising him with breakfast in bed.

He found me leaning against a counter and helped me upright as he pressed his nose up against my neck. The cramping pain eased as he rested his palm over my belly, soothed, perhaps, by the heat of him. He was running hot this morning, and it radiated from him, soaking into my wings and through the thin barrier of my towel.

"*Was that your heat?*" he asked in my mind.

"*Just a cramp.*"

"A cramp? *It felt like a punch to the balls.*" He took a deep sniff from my neck and rumbled a low, possessive growl. "*You smell incredible.*" Nuzzling into my skin, he parted his lips and took in air over my pheromone gland.

I sensed what he did through our bond. The sweetness of my fertility turned my scent into an irresistible call. Marius ripped the towel off my torso and pressed closer, grinding his erection against me. The tip was already wet with precome.

His changed scent became unmistakable, filling the air with blooming waterlily and mint. The cloud of his virility filled my nostrils and my mind blanked, fogged with need.

"Marius," I murmured. On the precipice of maddening lust, I looked back at him.

His expression reflected the pure, animal need to be inside me. Subtle glimmers of yellow light sparkled from the rings of his irises. The infamous "rut glow" that was one of the only visible signs an alpha was in rut.

I'd seen it often enough. Alpha males went into rut regularly, with or without companionship. Mated alphas usually synced up their ruts with their omega's heats, and I had no doubt that Marius's sudden rut was a result of our new bond.

His self-control was a tenuous thread. Mating cycles were when any fae was at their wildest. For him, any reasoning not centered on my immediate claiming was being tossed from his mind. Niall was in charge for the time being.

There was one thing left to do: tip over the edge of overwhelming desire together. *"Go ahead, Niall. Breed me,"* I invited, arching my hips.

Marius swept the counter clean. Plates shattered as he perched me in their place. He dug his fangs into my neck as I spread my thighs for him.

As the Seelie would put it, we fucked like brownies.

Marius and I spent days with our bodies twined. His rutting battered my heat suppressant tattoo, but miraculously, the magic held up despite my kelpie's passionate efforts. Neither of us caught any meaningful sleep the whole time.

Meanwhile, Illia and Henrik moved like specters, leaving food and clean linens outside our door. I reminded myself they were mostly deaf and probably couldn't hear my screams or Marius's occasional roars.

Inevitably, the rut slowed. He'd wake from the breeding haze and feel a sudden and painful twist of dismay at how roughly he'd taken me. This led to aggressively loving aftercare. He plundered his wound salve to heal the bites peppered over my shoulders and any bruises acquired along the way. The only bite mark we left to scar was the one from our bonding night.

We spent four days enjoying one another in the inn by the sea. In the between moments, we'd lie together and talk. Marius told stories through the bond. Long, elaborate tales he'd never get through in one sitting otherwise, due to his condition. They often ended with him saying, *"I never thought I'd get to tell anyone else that happened"* and another round of mating.

My stories, in return, were a lot smaller. But farm town life was baffling to Marius, who self-reported as a pampered prince. I'd tell him about the day-to-day in Osme Fen and touch him, finally getting to explore his body head to toe with our bond to learn him as he'd already done with me.

Our time together drew to a close in what felt like no time. Kauz was flying out to meet us at the inn this afternoon to start our date. I remained cozy in Marius's arms until then. Eventually, he drew me a bath, and I washed alone, else we'd end up in another hours-long knotting.

He watched me dress in my last set of clean clothes, knuckles white in the tangled sheets of bedding where I'd left him. "The rut will die down without me around, right?" I asked.

"Go downstairs before I rip those clothes off you."

"That doesn't answer my question."

"I don't know what to tell you. It should've only lasted two days."

I eyed him with concern.

"Go. Really. I'll be fine." A lusty growl rolled from him, a reminder that he was moments from tearing off my skirt.

"Okay. Love you," I said.

"Love you more."

I left the room with a giggle and a flutter of my wings, heading downstairs to meet Kauz when he arrived. Except he was already here, seated and nursing a steaming cup of tea while listening attentively to what Illia was saying. She knitted away as she rocked in her chair, and a feather duster floated a few feet above them, flicking over the contents of a shelf.

Kauz's gaze shifted in a sparkle of stars. He lit up with a broad smile. "There's my mate."

Illia didn't look up. "Ah, aye. She's been here with the strapping blue lad I was telling you about. Just like my Henrik in his prime."

I bit my lip to hold in a laugh and made a mental note to whisper "strapping blue lad" into Marius's mind when he least expected it. Kauz put aside his tea and stood, catching me when I leapt into his arms. He enfolded me in his wings, and our lips met for a long moment.

"Hello, my Always," I murmured.

"Hello, sweetheart. I've missed you." He put me back on my feet but didn't withdraw the privacy of his wings, nor the gentle brush of his fingertips over my cheek. Purple nebulae danced in his eyes as he took me in.

Illia's chuckle interrupted what I was going to say. "She already has a room, if you wish to make use of it."

His star-filled eyes twinkled in amusement. "That's kind, honored elder, but I'll be flying away with her soon."

"Marius will be right down," I added.

"Will he?" Kauz took his seat again, and pulled me with him so I was across his lap. I rested my head on his shoulder and snuggled in, placing a hand on his chest.

"Marius," Illia echoed to herself. "Where have I heard that name?"

Kauz ignored her and turned over my wrist, clicking his tongue. "I should've figured," he said under his breath.

The fertility blocker remained a bold X, but half the decorative loops marking the heat suppressant tattoo were gone. *Whoops.*

He shrugged and petted my hair while we waited. I purred like a kitten and angled my head for more. "I don't need this to tell me your heat is close. I have an idea to float by you and my brother, if he ever gets himself down here."

Illia tried to get Henrik's attention. While I'd gotten used to the elderly couple yelling, Kauz winced at their back-and-forth until the aged kelpie shuffled out of the back room to see what his mate wanted.

Marius came downstairs a few minutes later, our traveling bag slung over his shoulder. He paused for a fraction too long when his gaze tracked to where I'd settled. This time, I felt his internal clash as he considered being territorial.

"—couldn't possibly be royalty," Henrik was scoffing. "One of them would've told us."

"That's our cue," Kauz said. With a flick of his wrist, he sent the feather duster to float over to its holder and gestured for me to stand.

"Honored elders, we're leaving. What do we owe you for our stay?" Marius asked.

Kauz and I slipped outside. "He's in rut," I warned him when we had privacy.

He nodded. "I figured it had to be something like that. You haven't been sleeping much lately."

I released a surprised laugh, though I hoped I didn't have shadows under my eyes. I'd gotten as prepared as I could for our date but already knew I smelled of the sea. That saltwater tang was unavoidable this close to the Doras.

Kauz kept talking, seeming thoughtful. "His side of the pack bond is...interesting. I sense his lust and, well, *pressure*, but I'm not having a sympathetic reaction."

"Because you're a beta?"

"Perhaps. But it's still there, and I could reach out and accept some of it," he mused. "Not that I think you need two mates *this* worked up."

My core clenched as I imagined gentle Kauz in rut. Even though it wasn't part of his designation, I wanted it all the same.

Marius burst out of the inn. "All set?" Kauz asked mildly.

Those yellow eyes turned from me to his brother reluctantly. "Aye."

"I have a deal for you. Lark's heat is close."

"Very," the kelpie grunted.

"You know where I'm taking her. Follow us, just in case. She won't be in a state to return to Neslune if her heat arrives, and I can't see to her needs like you can," Kauz reasoned.

Marius didn't even blink before he blurted, "Deal."

We said our goodbyes quickly. I picked up on his hope that he'd be back in bed with me by tomorrow evening. *"As long as Kauz is willing to share. But I'm certain he will be,"* Marius thought.

I pressed up against him with a soft purr. *"Bye, mate."*

His gaze was bright with longing already, but he stepped away. *"Safe travels, p'nixie."*

I turned to Kauz, who had his wings mantled for flight. The brothers exchanged a nod of farewell before the dream warden said, "Let's fly. It's not far."

I should've asked what wasn't far before he launched into the air. I followed with a boost of speed from a vortex spell and waved to Marius until he was a featureless speck of blue from above. The bond faded the further I traveled from him until I couldn't feel anything but my own thoughts and emotions. I missed my kelpie immediately.

If only dream wardens could make similar bonds. Kauz flew much faster than I did. Though with his wing shape, he couldn't stop or hover at a moment's notice like I could. So, he did the same thing Marius had done in kelpie form, flying circles around me like an absolute show-off.

I was used to measuring out my essence for moments of flight. Without the silencing band, I had plenty of magic to do this without breaking a sweat. The height and speed we'd coaxed from my pixie wings were new, and my palms grew damp with nerves every time I happened to glance down. I checked my essence levels constantly to be sure I wouldn't drop out of the sky.

My preoccupation distracted me. I looked up, wondering when the sun had started setting, as the clouds were painted in shades of orange and purple. Kauz swooped over to fly closer to me. "Can you feel it?" he called.

I started to shake my head, but...something odd was going on. The wind whistling through my ears was quieting, the sun was setting far earlier than it should, and a magnificent spread of stars glittered in the sky ahead of us around a luminous crescent moon.

My jaw dropped, and my skin tingled before taking on the pleasant warmth that could only follow a well-deserved nap.

Oh. Oh, literal stars. We'd crossed into the dreamlands, the portion of Serian where the magic of Ever, Always, and Never leaked from sleep into waking. It was more surreal than I could've imagined. Rolling alpine hills covered the land, lit red from one side, reality, where the needles and branches were crisp and distinct. From another angle, they were outlined in blue, turned into indistinct blobs as if they were a painted backdrop.

Kauz wheeled around again, his wingbeats and momentum slowing. He coasted above me; I could take shelter under the canopy of his open wing. "Just glide. You won't fall," he said.

I stopped flapping my wings. The calm air seemed to buoy me as long as I kept them spread as if I was still manually flying. I gave the occasional flutter, nervous despite the feeling that gravity had given up on me. "What is this magic?" I asked.

He smiled serenely. "The dreamlands recognize a dreamer. Welcome home, Lark."

The stars and moon painted him in soft light, and as I smiled back, I noticed movement on his wings. I looked over my shoulder and ended up flipping onto my back with an "eep" of surprise. My momentum remained the same, and I let out a thrilled laugh he echoed.

The tattoos on his wings that I admired so much were *moving.* They glowed silver from ambient magic, dancing and glittering in waves of mist and stars on the bottom half of the leathery span.

I angled my wings so I flew lazily into Kauz, who caught me. I looped my arms around his shoulders. "I have questions." But I was immediately distracted as I looked into his eyes. The illusion of a starry night that covered his gaze was extra sparkly.

"Of course. But first…" He cupped my cheek and kissed me, drawing his wings in to spiral us through the air in a whirl of colors. I was dazzled by this beautiful place and my handsome mate, who seemed cut straight from the cloth of semi-night resting over the land. His voice dropped to a dulcet murmur as he held me close. "You want to know how things work here, sweetheart?"

"Mmm." I soaked in the ambiance and him. Maybe making sense of everything didn't matter as long as I was with Kauz.

His touch roamed my body, mapping my curves with gentle reverence as he explained, "One of the most common dreams is flight. As winged dream wardens, we can fly without trouble and bend reality to stay up here as long as we like. I get quite spoiled by endless flight when I visit."

I traced the strong lines of his chest as I listened. "Wow. And your wings tattoos are moving and glowing, too."

"I painted them under the light of the dreamlands so they'd take on some of its magic. Do you like them?" He posed his wings playfully, and without concern for a fall.

"They're gorgeous. But…how did you reach around to do that?" I asked.

His eyes creased from an amused smile. "There's a spell to lift ink that's painted on something else and apply it to skin. They're unfinished, you know."

I hadn't considered them incomplete, but now that he mentioned it, he did have the top half of his wings left unmarked. "I thought that was intentional."

He shook his head. "I left some space for my Always. And since you're a dream warden too, we could have a matching pattern."

I gasped. "That would be amazing."

"I'm glad you think so. I was hoping you'd let me start painting your wings as soon as possible." His fingertips skimmed a swirl over one of my top wings.

I barely let him finish that statement before pressing my lips to his for an enthusiastic kiss. That explained how he intended to mark my wings with his magic.

He let me go at the end of the kiss so I was flying on my own. I righted myself so my belly faced the ground and coasted through the air beside him.

"We have a ways to travel. How about a dance?" He offered his hand with a midair bow and an expectant look. I didn't ask how we could possibly dance while flying. I just put my hand in his knowing he'd lead me.

We twirled together, and I didn't feel dizzy even though I was expecting it. This was no ballroom dance, but something we invented together while gravity didn't want to drag us down. Weightless, we floated together and varied our performance, sometimes quick and looping and, as our mood shifted and we flew chest to chest, slow and intimate.

He kept us on track as we flew across the dreamlands in one another's arms.

52

LARK

WE ARRIVED before dark on the outskirts of a city lit with a scattering of essence lamps and fluttering faelights, a shimmering mirror to the stars. My ears popped as we came in for a landing and passed an invisible barrier spell.

An increasing number of dreaming minds had been soaring around us, resembling little orbs of multicolored light. According to Kauz, they usually posed no harm to dream wardens, but if they gathered in a large number, they could warp reality erratically.

"The dreamlands' thin barrier between reality and dreaming works both ways. Our people gather in settlements under special enchantments to keep us safe at night," he'd said.

The city was built with short, closely packed buildings, and no two were alike. Serian's usual A-frames and pointed roofs sat next to the flat structures more common in Thelis, or the two combined to make a hybrid. There was more whimsy in how they were made. Some were ordinary brick, timber, and stone constructions, intermingled with what looked like straw for one house and a construction of many thousands of multicolored pebbles for another.

Kauz held my hand and let me look my fill. "This is the city of Once Else," he said when I turned back to him to share in this moment.

"Where have I heard that name before?" I wracked my tired brain. Every passing mention of the dreamlands included location names like Ever Borough or After All that could slip into a conversation unnoticed.

He gave my hand a squeeze. "I asked Mother if there was any family I could take you to meet on your Unseelie side. She shared that Dorei was a foundling surrendered to the Once Else orphanage."

My mouth formed a soft O as I looked around again. "This was her home!"

"Aye, and I did find a few folks here that you should meet. How does tomorrow sound for that, though?" He tipped a tender smile my way. "I'm feeling a little selfish with your time."

"Tomorrow," I agreed quickly. "I probably smell like the sea and..." I muffled a yawn that took hold when I was about to suggest how tired I was.

"You smell like Always, as always," he teased. "I have an inn room with human plumbing and a warm change of clothes ready for you."

"And a big bed? With a handsome, naked dream warden in it?" I dropped my voice not to let any passersby happen upon our conversation. Though there weren't as many fae walking the streets as I'd have expected for a city this size, there were other dream wardens like us, and also a handful of other dreamlands races, strolling casually.

"That can be arranged." Kauz made a pained face and added, "However, perhaps we shouldn't go too far tonight."

I whined. After enjoying the journey here and having his hands on me for our dance, I was eager to have him.

"Because of your heat. I don't want to trigger it without one of my alpha brothers present. I could add to the suppressant tattoo..."

I shook my head, though reluctantly, before he even finished the thought.

"But suppressants aren't meant to put off a heat for as long as you've pushed yours. I don't want to add on to any consequences you may experience from it," he said.

I was ready to be done with suppressants, even if my incoming heat promised to burn me from the inside out. "You're right," I sighed.

"Don't worry, we still have dreams. And Marius will get here sometime tomorrow. I wanted to see if you were interested in some sharing."

Sharing. Stars, did he mean what I thought he did by that?

He tugged me toward a one-story inn constructed of river stones that spread out over an entire city block, and we retired to the privacy of our room for a date night over a meal and fae fruit wine. He only ordered one bottle, so the walls were stationary even by the time I was down to nursing my last glass.

He pulled out a sketchpad and a pencil. I snuggled against his chest and watched him form art in confident strokes of charcoal. He drew two sets of my wings, brainstorming what his mist and stardust tattoos might look like with me wearing them, front or back.

It was only while tipsy and dozing did I realize something. "Kauz," I murmured.

"Hmm?"

"Wouldn't you just be painting over my wing scales?"

He pressed a kiss to my temple. "Not with magic, sweetheart."

"Being observant isn't magic," I said sleepily. "But art is."

"When words on a page or paint on a canvas can make you *feel*, what else could it be?" he reasoned.

"That is very wise." I nodded a few extra times. "Have I told you how pretty your eyes are today? They're *so* extra sparkly. I would rather watch them than the night sky."

He abandoned his sketches to wrap his arms around me and nuzzle my neck. "That's enough wine for today." He stole my glass while I purred, distracted.

I pouted. "Hey! I meant that. I like your eyes."

"I'm rather taken by your gaze as well. Still, too much wine."

When it was clear I wasn't getting the rest of my drink back, I took his encouragement to head to the bathroom to see myself in the mirror. The same dreamlands mystique that'd multiplied the number of stars in his eyes was doing the same to mine.

I paid the rain room a visit, happy to have a shower again, and settled into bed with Kauz. "Fun fact," he said after we'd turned off the essence lamps. I was snuggled into his side, arms around his torso and eyes already closed. "You can reach pretty much anyone's dream from the dreamlands without a token of something they own. You just have to fall asleep with one fae in mind."

With countless possibilities, I still picked his dream to infiltrate. Or he picked mine. Either way, after my nightly magic lesson and a discussion on sharing, we made love until sunrise in a space without consequences.

KAUZ and I spent the better part of the next day wandering Once Else, shadowing the places my mother used to pass time in. Some of the fae who lived here still remembered Dorei, and they helped me piece together what her life had been like.

She'd been adopted by a potter and his pack, who'd raised her with the secrets of clay, paint, and glaze. One of her best works, a painted platter, was still displayed in a shop's glass case. The shop was under the ownership of a cousin who, while friendly, was a little distant as I asked questions and admired Dorei's old work.

She'd painted a metalark over that platter, rendering every feather in meticulous detail. Light gleamed off its beady eye and the little clusters of blood-red berries that decorated the outside rim. A small sign was propped next to it, declaring it not for sale.

"You could fetch quite the sum for that," Kauz said to the cousin while I admired it. He offered an amount of fulls that had me twitching. Too much money for something like this. Yet, it was one of the only things of my mother's that'd survived past Cymora's hostile takeover of Osme Fen. It was priceless.

Kauz carried the platter out, padded and wrapped twice. He explained he'd followed the breadcrumbs of Dorei's life only so far, since she'd always been a free spirit. She and Nemensia had lived under the stars and out of the back of a wagon for years, trading wares in settlements across Serian. They'd made it a lifestyle before the future queen crossed paths with her pack. Dorei had returned to Osme Fen, only to later meet Kellam and settle in a faraway farm town. The rest, as they say, was history.

After we dropped off the platter in our inn room, we went outside of Once Else's magical barrier to sit in a patch of grassland together. Sunshine and wind stirred the long blades from one angle while the ever-present purplish half-night hung overhead at another. It was odd but beautiful, and I sat in silence just thinking of what I'd learned of my mother today.

I missed someone I'd never truly met, her loss an echo in my soul that couldn't fully heal. Kauz kept an arm around me. As always, he seemed to understand exactly what I needed.

I leaned my head on his shoulder and murmured, "Thank you." He hadn't had to share some of his time with Dorei, though I was beyond glad he had. Now I wouldn't be constantly looking for hints of her as we traveled through the dreamlands.

Those glimmering eyes were gentle on mine. "Anything for you, my Always."

I gazed at him adoringly. "Consider me smitten."

We kissed for a long time under the dreamlands' stars. He'd mastered the perfect lip-lock too, coaxing a soft purr from me and a tender ache in my core. If my heat wasn't so close, I'd push for us to lie together and make the kind of love he filled my dreams with. I yearned for it, even if there were consequences in how my body would react.

Kauz pulled away first, humming. I cracked open my eyes, catching the confusion in that sound. "What's wrong?"

"It's the pack bond. I'm being summoned," he said dryly. "Oddly enough, by two brothers. They are rather insistently trying to get my attention." He shared that it was about as annoying as being poked in either cheek. Whatever it was, both Marius and Tormund thought it was important enough to signal for Kauz to come to them.

"Tormund's here?" I perked up. I missed him and his bear hugs. Hopefully he'd figured out what he needed to do to get his rage back under control.

Kauz nodded and motioned for me to follow as he took flight. We headed around the outskirts of Once Else and toward the utilitarian train station right on the edge of the city. It was like a dry gray fingernail when compared to the color and whimsy of the other buildings. There was one magirail in and two of them out of the station, at odds with the complicated tangles in stations like the ones in Neslune and Ilysnor.

"The trains don't run at night in the dreamlands, so each line is a short jump," Kauz explained while we waited amongst a small crowd for the next train to arrive. It would double back the way it'd come to a massive station called the Dreamlands Nexus.

Marius was definitely on that train. Our bond fixed back into place as the magirail began to vibrate, and my kelpie was *pissed*. I cringed away from his anger for a fleeting moment before he sent feelings of greeting and love down the bond.

"What's going on?" I asked him, trusting the shift in emotion meant he wasn't mad at me.

"I'm not mad at you," he said in echo to my thoughts.

The train pulled into the station with a groan of settling metal and the hiss of steam. It was a short thing, only four cars, with the front and back mirrored in appearance and, presumably, function. Amongst the disembarking crowd were the two princes. A storm cloud seemed to follow Marius as he prowled toward us.

"Here we go," Kauz muttered.

The kelpie walked past him to catch my face in his hands and kiss the breath right out of my lungs. He still tasted strongly of fertile mint and waterlily. Resting his forehead on mine, he murmured, "I have to get back on the train, p'nixie. But I needed that first."

I searched his gaze. "What's wrong?"

He held me closer before sharing the news mind-to-mind. *"My incompetent brothers failed to apprehend Pack Ellisar when they arrived in Neslune a few days ago. They are loose in the city somewhere."*

I stiffened so hard it was a wonder I didn't snap like a brittle branch. A keen escaped my lips. Not Pack Ellisar. Not *here*, in Serian.

Oh stars. They had to be here for me, contract in hand. They were going to try to steal me back to Osme Fen.

Whatever else he said was drowned out by the animal panic that threatened to choke me. He loosened his hold just as a sense of calm wrapped around my back; Kauz sandwiched me between them. Not to be left out, Tormund's ever-present heat joined in as he hugged all three of us. Now in the middle of all this affection with me, Marius released a testy growl.

"It'll be all right, sweetheart. You're ours. Nothing's changed about that," Kauz said.

"And you're safe," Tormund added. There was a low crackle of flames in his voice. Maybe he hadn't gotten his rage under control, as this hug was feeling awfully hot all of a sudden.

"And you will remain that way." Marius scowled as the boarding announcement for the train, outbound to the Dreamlands Nexus, echoed around the station. He eased away with slow reluctance. "I will make sure of it."

He was heading back to Neslune, then, to hunt the trio of barkfolk on my behalf. Everything they'd said soaked in as I took a grounding breath. I was theirs, I was safe, and I'd remain here, far from Pack Ellisar's reach.

"But...your rut," I murmured.

"I will endure." He left abruptly to buy passage before the train left without him. Kauz didn't release me, but Tormund did, shaking his head sharply as smoke leaked from the corners of his mouth. I shifted to hold on to Kauz tightly as he shrouded me in the privacy of his wings.

"*I love you,*" I thought to Marius. The words failed to encompass everything I was feeling as the shock continued to wear off and gratitude for my males swept in.

"*Love you more.*" He was gone again with the thrum and blast of air from the train launching back the way it'd come. I sighed wistfully.

Tormund asked, "Is the li'l bird okay?"

I blinked in surprise. I'd expected him to get back on the train with his brother.

"I'm okay." A little shaken and a lot whiplashed, but fine for now.

"Good. I need to talk to you both when we're somewhere more private."

"Aye, I want every detail," Kauz grumbled. He withdrew his wings and frowned at the giant. "Can I trust you to keep it together around our mate?"

Tormund had one of his hopeful smiles fixed in place. "I learned how to get my rage under control," he said. Stars, what a relief.

We started the trek back to our inn room. Tormund put Kauz

between us, so I held my dream warden's hand and leaned past him to ask, "So, are you going to tell us the solution?"

A blush darkened the redcap's brassy cheeks. "Such things aren't appropriate to talk about in public."

Now I *really* wanted to know. But I kept my questions contained until we reached the massive inn and showed Tormund into our room. Kauz cast a fireproofing spell over the couch in a whirl of starlight essence. I dragged over a chair to sit at a safe distance.

Tormund rubbed the back of his neck. "All right. The solution first. Sex is a known outlet for relieving the rage, but when we had sex, I didn't do it right."

I couldn't help but giggle despite his air of discomfort. "What do you mean?"

"I didn't knot you, and…" He mumbled the rest.

Kauz's sharp ears picked up what I didn't. "The full rage form?" He turned an alarmed look my way.

"*Ach*, aye. My dad said if I vent throughout, I won't burn her."

Stars, the heat wasn't so much a problem as the size of him. Even partially shifted last time, his cock had been massive and his knot even more so.

"Um, you're not going to fit," I ventured.

"I said that too, li'l bird, but if I accept the rage form as we get started, the growth should be steady enough that you adapt," he explained.

I glanced at Kauz, who was still looking at me, though his expression was shaded with thoughtfulness. "We did discuss sharing last night." Specifically, what kinds of fun things he could do as the pack beta while I was stuck on a knot. I rubbed my thighs together at the reminder.

"We did," I agreed.

"Sharing what?" Tormund asked.

Kauz tipped his head. "He needs it. Why don't we show him?"

I nodded and stood, crossing the room to ease into the space where my gentle giant had his legs spread.

"Sharing *me*."

The temperature in the room spiked as I undid the buttons securing my shirt around my wings and slowly slid the fabric off my body.

53
LARK

KAUZ CAME UP BEHIND ME, cupping my breasts through my underclothes. "But I will still have her first," he said.

Tormund made a guttural *ach*.

The winged fae hummed back playfully as he helped me work my breast band free. He caught the sensitive orbs and tweaked my nipples just right. I moaned, arching for more of his touch and the lingering tingle on my skin from his magic.

"It's a great idea. He'll get me stretched and ready for your, um, full rage form," I said a little breathlessly.

"And if Lark goes into heat from this, you're here to help her. Especially if you go into rut," Kauz added.

"Rut?" Tormund's form had swelled with muscle, his voice deepening with power and fire. "Why would I go into rut?"

I blinked. I thought rut was contagious.

"Did Marius shield his side of the pack bond from you on the train?" Kauz asked.

"Aye. I thought he was hiding something!"

"Maybe you won't go into rut, then," I murmured. And hopefully my heat wouldn't come, even if I took my redcap mate in his literal hottest form.

Kauz circled his hands down my belly, leaving tingles and shivers in his wake. His starry gaze flashed between his brother and me. "Don't just sit there. Touch her."

In answer, Tormund lifted his hands, brandishing lengthening claws that could pass for knives. I swallowed at the sight of them and the thicket of fangs poking from behind his lips.

Kauz shook his head and undid the button on my pants, helping me shimmy out of them. "How do you expect her to take you in any form if you don't try to use what you have?"

"Easy for you to say," Tormund grumbled.

I hooked my thumb into my panties and eased them down, letting the sweetened smell of my pheromones hit the air between us. His nostrils flared as chocolate and honey crackers mingled perfectly with the smoky caramelized mallows that made up his scent.

"Do you still want to try the mesh?" Kauz whispered in my ear.

"Yes." For as often as I'd been with my mates lately, there was one part of me that remained untouched save for the occasional brush and tease. He intended to change that today.

He nudged his knee between my legs and explained what he was doing to Tormund, who watched while clutching his thick thighs. "An essence mesh is made to help with ass play." Those tingling fingers brushed through my lower lips, gathering up my slick. "It sizes itself up to stretch the recipient without tearing and provides lubrication and a barrier for cleanliness."

I tried to hold still as he circled a slick-coated fingertip around the rim of my ass. The tight ring of muscle started to yield as I whimpered, wings quivering from the unusual sensation being touched there.

"Can you make something like that for her, um, lady parts?" Tormund asked.

I giggled. "You can say pussy, Tormund. It's okay."

"I want to be respectful!"

Kauz pressed his fingertip deeper in my ass, and I squealed, flapping in place. "That just—that's what it's called," I said once my dream warden held me steady against his chest. "You're very respectful, my gentle giant."

He wiggled his shoulders proudly, even as a half-shifted rage monster.

Kauz was casting the spell now, but it felt like he was twisting his finger around in my ass. The mesh supposedly started about as thick as a thread. It'd slowly expand into a cylinder of interwoven essence a little larger than the size of the average alpha cock, relaxing from there unless I took one. It wouldn't help me take a knot back there, but nothing would except for an excruciating tear in a very intimate place. Knots were only for my pussy to squeeze.

"Time to be less respectful," Kauz put in. He withdrew his finger and placed a kiss on my cheek. "Get up for a moment, Tormund. You'll want to lie on your front."

He followed directions without complaint, a hint of nerves stealing over his fanged expression. I glanced back at Kauz.

"He's still perfectly capable of licking," he said.

Oh, that he was. I perched on the armrest in front of where Tormund's chin rested, now that he'd laid stretched out across and partially off the small couch. He blew out a cloud of smoke and dry heat away from my skin before he unrolled his tongue.

My wings fluttered in delight. The rage form had something seriously going for it: that tongue was nice and long. *Stars, the things he could do with that...* I'm sure there was a practical fire fae purpose for it growing along with the fangs and all, but with some practice, I had another job for it.

"C'mere." I spread my lower lips with two fingers.

Need and pre-heat sweetened my scent further to beckon to his alpha instincts. He rumbled with a deep purr and seated his face in the cradle of my thighs. I yelped as he delved straight into me with a long lick, his fiery gaze flashing to mine. I grabbed onto his horns, elongated nicely into the perfect handholds, and tugged him closer.

"Not too hot?" I thought he asked. Hard to tell with his tongue otherwise occupied.

"Not too hot," I confirmed. I kept my legs off his back, though, as a draft of heated air tented his shirt.

His breath was a breeze of similarly heated gusts. My knees drew up in pleasure as his exhales rolled over my pussy. It pulsed as he delved the wet muscle of his tongue into my channel.

Once he loosened up and let himself enjoy my taste, he ate like I was a quality dessert served warm and fresh. His enthusiasm outstripped how he'd feasted on my pixie dust when mixed with chocolate sauce. He tossed his spectacles aside and smothered himself without placing so much as an edge of a fang on my most sensitive flesh.

"You're doing great," I moaned. "You're heating me up just right. I had no idea it'd feel this good..."

My core squeezed and rewarded him with a hot gush of precome, which he lapped up with an eager noise. The way I clenched reminded me of the last time I'd perfumed. With a flush spreading and sweat beading across my skin from proximity to his internal fire...this could be the next trigger my heat had been waiting for.

Wait. Stars, don't go into heat now. I needed my nest and all four of the males I loved to see me through my most vulnerable time. I'd try not to succumb today, even if it'd hurt later.

My gaze landed on Kauz, who'd worked his shirt off and now watched me writhe on Tormund's face. The dream warden's expression had a hint of concern, though it smoothed out as he nodded at me. He cupped the bulge in his pants and winked, scattering sparkles from his icy lashes.

A possessive growl from my gentle giant vibrated straight to my center. He lifted me, one huge hand under my thighs, the other spread across my lower back. This gave him a better angle, and his writhing tongue reached depths that had my toes curling. "Tormund," I moaned.

He slowed, eyes widening. "N-no, no, don't stop," I practically begged.

With an air of confusion, he resumed his mind-melting delving. I pulled his horns and the short fluff of his hair, grinding against his face for more until I came apart.

"I didn't hurt you." He grinned broadly, fangs all on display without a hint of his usual self-consciousness.

His giddiness was infectious. "Quite the opposite. You can take a lick any time you like."

"Don't mind if I do," he said. "What now?"

I considered, since Kauz was waiting for his turn. "Do you want to watch?" I asked Tormund. Would it set off the rage worse to see me with another male, even his packmate?

He breathed a soft *ach* and glanced between Kauz and me. "Have fun with the kinky bat. You deserve a bed. I'll cool myself off and wait here."

I snorted in surprise. *Kinky bat? I mean, it fits.*

"Better than nerd," the dream warden sighed.

"The li'l bird calls me a bear," Tormund said proudly.

"Fitting. I'm taking the bird away now." Kauz met my gaze and inclined his head toward the bedroom.

After one last glance at the still-smoldering redcap, I went in that direction, and Kauz closed the bedroom door behind us. "Is this the last time I get to have you in reality before your heat?" he asked in a low voice.

"I think so." I couldn't help a little shiver of fear.

He closed the distance between us to rest his hands on my hips and his forehead against mine.

"I know I shouldn't be afraid," I murmured.

"There's no shame in it."

"It's just—that vile pack..." I hiccupped and cursed to myself as a single tear slid down my cheek. I'd known that the news about Pack Ellisar would truly hit me later, and here it was.

He enveloped me in his wings. "You've feared them for so long that you associate them with your heat," he supplied.

"And now that they're back—"

Sparks flashed between the stars in his eyes like streaks of lightning. "Between Fal, Marius, and the royal pack, they will be dead before we return to Neslune. They will be branded enemies of the crown, if they haven't already been, with generous bounties for their carcasses. So, they are not *back* by any stretch of the imagination. They won't get within a sniff of your heat."

"Thank you." My shoulders loosened in relief.

My fingers drifted to his waistband, and he caught them. "We don't have to," he murmured.

"You don't want to?" Stars, way for me to kill the mood.

"I didn't say that. It just strikes me how selfish it is to claim you before Tormund, who's sought a way to control his rage form for years. I've made love to you plenty at night. I can let him have a turn."

"You were going to stretch me out for him," I pointed out. "Also, I haven't felt the mesh yet."

"Well, my fingers work fine for that purpose. And I haven't activated it, so of course you haven't felt anything," he teased.

He had me lift my leg and supported it around his hip while he slipped his fingers through my slick. I shuddered from the first contact of his tingling magic. "What *is* that?"

"Just me casually manipulating your nerve endings. Is it too much?"

"I didn't say that," I echoed playfully.

He smiled, though he stilled his hand, cupping my pussy. "Lark," he said, as if he didn't already have my complete attention and focus. "Once Tormund and I mate with you today, you may only need to have sex one more time to trigger your heat. You should save it for Fal."

"I agree, but I'd like to hear your reasoning."

"Ah, tell me you don't see him putting the good of the pack first." He spread his fingers and sent a jolt of magic into my ass. I yelped as a strange sort of tension pressed against the sides of my back entrance. "Give that ten minutes or so."

I nodded, breathing shallowly. He'd suggested earlier that I might like the mesh and enjoy ass play once prepared for it properly. My knees felt weak already, as the expanding magic reminded me of how a knot felt as it stretched me and locked into place.

Kauz leaned in to kiss me and circled my clit ever so slowly with his thumb, then slipped his middle three fingers into my pussy. He teased the inside edge of my ass with his pinky, treating it as gently as he did the bundle of nerves at the apex of my slit.

Our tongues twined, filling my mouth with a strong taste of Always. He didn't stop me when I went for his waistband again, freeing him from the rest of his clothing.

I ran my thumb through the bead of precome at the head of his shaft and spread it down his length, stroking with a reverent hand. Though he throbbed against my fingers, he eased off the pressure just as my breathing changed, and instead of chasing another peak, I came back down with a ragged sigh.

He parted from my lips to murmur, "I think it's time."

We emerged from the bedroom together. Tormund hadn't moved except to remove his clothes and fold them neatly off to the side. His brow drew in as he squinted at us. "That was fast."

I bent to retrieve his spectacles and placed them back on the bridge of his nose. "Kauz talked me out of it," I said.

"He...did?" Despite his puzzled frown, he wasted no time in pulling me in to straddle him on the couch. "I'm not complaining. I've mostly cooled off."

A fresh wave of warmth lifted from him as he spoke. He was tracing the outline of my hips and waist, careful of the claws starting to grow from his nailbeds again, then cast a glare at his own hands with a frustrated *ach*.

"It's okay, Tormund. I'll touch you instead." I traced the loop of his alpha mark, and tiny fires ignited in his eyes. I rubbed his padded stomach as he clenched his clawed hands by his sides.

"When I can control myself, I will hold and touch you like I used to. That's a promise."

"I can't wait," I said with longing.

New muscle stretched the skin below my fingertips, revealing the inferno burning within him. The orange tint of flame in his chest made his brassy skin glow like molten metal. He was venting dry heat through his back, so touching his chest directly was like resting my palm on a sunbaked stone.

He cupped my neck with his massive fingers, trembling with restraint. A growl rattled through him as I gave his shaft a testing stroke. It was heavy and enlarged already, pulsing with the heat of him.

"Kiss me. Trust yourself a little," I coaxed.

He met my lips, kissing carefully with a closed mouth so I didn't cut myself on his fangs. The sweetness of caramelized mallows clung to him, even with his internal fire lit and body swelling. If I waited or teased him much more, he'd be too big to take.

I held his cheek, gazing into the reflection of tenderness in his fiery eyes. "And trust me, too. Once you give me that knot, you're going to feel so much better. All right?"

He tilted his head, showing his throat in a trust display. My breath caught. "All right, li'l bird," he said in a low, crackling voice.

I angled the head of his shaft just right and sank the first couple inches onto him. He clenched his jaw with a strangled growl.

"Don't hold back," I murmured. "I'll tell you if it's too much."

"Not too hot?" he asked again.

I circled my hips as I lowered a few inches more, working his cock into me about as quickly as I could handle it. His shaft pulsed; if anything, it matched the temperature of my pre-heat. It felt perfect, and my pussy stretched to adapt to his size so far.

"Not too hot," I confirmed.

Smoke escaped in two long tendrils from the corners of his mouth. He breathed through his teeth, growling with every exhale.

The heat mounted, but he expelled most of it in a cloud that dampened my body with sweat. His muscles twitched and grew in slow increments, making him broader, especially in the chest and arms.

And his cock...*oh*. I was glad to set the pace. Once I fully sheathed him, I preferred for his length to be inside me for each jump in size. He stretched my pussy just as effectively as the mesh in my backside, and my legs shook each time he expanded my channel a little more. I moaned and writhed on him as he continued to test how much I could take.

Tormund's expression shaded from worry to confidence. He started to move with me. The impact of his hips on mine gave me a boost up his shaft. No matter how gentle he wanted to be, he'd grown to twice my size and many, many times my strength, something he didn't let himself forget even as he finally started to touch me.

The back edge of a claw tracing my cheekbone. Fingertips on my wings. I drew my nails down his chest, barely scratching his thickened hide. "More," I moaned.

"More." He hit the body-shaking tone of a powerful male, and I quivered head to toe as it passed through me.

"Talk to me," I added. "Talk more."

"About what?"

My pussy squeezed him greedily. I felt those low vibrations to my core. "A-anything. The weather. Just talk."

"It is nice outside? Half day, half night."

"Tell me I'm yours," I coaxed with a throaty moan.

Still an alpha to his core, he growled, "*Mine*," with the force of an avalanche. I barely refrained from coming on the spot as I shook with his claim.

He panted, his fingers flexing close to my hips. There was still some thread of hesitation preventing him from grabbing and claiming me harder.

"D-do it. Fuck me," I coaxed.

The flames in his gaze brightened. He placed his fingers ever so carefully around my waist and pulled me into the powerful thrusts of his hips. His heat lingered around us as his length twitched, on the cusp of release.

Each of his heavy exhales held a snarl, and his knot swelled and bumped against my ass. He seemed huge even seated below me. A mighty redcap just as he was born to be, of a bloodline of kings and ancient conquerors of battlefields.

Yet still my gentle giant. The tendons on his neck stood out with his restraint, giving him a moment to ask in the lowest rumble yet, "May I knot you?"

I swear my heart swelled just like he had, expanding just for him. "Stars. *Yes.*" I would've begged for it. I needed to feel him fully claim me.

He grinned and pulled me into it while I angled my hips, twisting so the edge of his knot slipped inside my pussy to make way for the whole thing. The great drum of his heartbeat matched the flickering of the molten flames within him.

His gigantic knot locked into place. He came with a redcap roar full of monstrous, crackling menace, but I was not afraid. Not even for a moment.

My eyes crossed as his blazing-hot seed flooded my core. I came screaming his name, and my breeder's delight was, well, *delighted* at how I could feel the liquid weight of his heated come settling inside me. I fell against his chest, boneless and trembling as we traded bliss, my channel still squeezing his knot for more.

His body shifted abruptly under my cheek, becoming smaller with a great gust of hot air streaming out from his vents. Thank the stars this poor couch had a fireproofing spell. I settled on his reduced knot, still seated firmly inside me.

He stroked my cheek without the threat of claws and made a sound somewhere between a laugh and a sob. I cracked my eyes open to look up at him, feeling like we'd reversed roles. If he was about to cry, I was going to be quite upset.

"I can feel the rage settling. It's contained. *Finally*." His eyes shone with tears of joy. He squished me in a bear hug as a pair of tears evaporated off his face with a sizzle.

"I'm so happy it worked." I was muffled against his chest.

"Thank you. Thank you so much. Knotting really did satisfy the rage," he said with wonder.

"You're welcome." I would have said *any time*, but it felt a little impersonal for the intimacy we'd just shared. Even if I meant he could knot me most any time he wanted.

He came a bit more, which had us moaning together again. I mourned that once I worked myself free of his knot, I had to somehow stay off my mates until we were gathered and ready for my heat.

Kauz shifted and cleared his throat. He'd settled on the chair I'd pulled over earlier. I jumped, having forgotten he was even there, and Tormund gave a great startle. "Ah! *Ach*. Were you watching this whole time?" he demanded.

The winged fae raised a brow. "Aye. With a stunning spell ready, just in case. Not that I doubted you for a moment, Tormund, but that's my Always who just took you in full rage form."

"I understand," Tormund replied. "I'd stun me, too. Twice. I mean, if—"

I giggled. "I'm ready for you," I said to Kauz, trying to shake my ass. He got the idea, at least, and drew to his feet.

Since I'd had a flaming hot redcap to mate with, I hadn't noticed when the stretch in my ass had stopped, but the essence mesh was a cool counterpoint to how heated my body had gotten. It'd stretched me and then let my ass relax back to its natural state. Kauz squeezed my hips while he stole a sideways kiss before striding out of my line of sight.

He returned with two full glasses of water. "First, you both look like you need this."

I said thanks, while Tormund narrowed his eyes. "What are you planning?"

Kauz grinned. "Drink up. You'll want to be hydrated for this."

I'd already downed my entire glass, then whispered with my hand over my mouth. "Trust the kinky bat."

Tormund tipped his head in acknowledgment and started drinking.

The winged fae shook his head. "Please don't call me that around Fal. I'll never hear my real name again. More water, sweetheart?"

"I'm good. Don't you want to...?"

"Aye, very much so." He took Tormund's glass when he emptied it and set the two glasses aside. He had his brother reposition us so he lay on his back and I was kneeling, still knotted.

Kauz climbed onto the couch behind me, his touch spreading familiar tingles as he cupped my ass and leaned me forward as much as I could go. "I know this is new. Tell me to stop at any time if you're not liking it."

I nodded and smiled over my shoulder, fully trusting that he knew what he was doing.

He worked a single finger into my ass, giving it a testing wiggle. My wings quivered as he tested and poked at the mesh, and my channel squeezed Tormund's knot. He came more on reflex, drawing a moan out of us both.

As soon as my core stopped clenching, I explored Tormund's body, starting with stroking the planes of his face and through the texture of his beard. He smiled, his expression softened with the afterglow of pleasure.

My wings twitched anew when Kauz worked a second finger into my ass to flex and tease. He sawed them back and forth in a thrusting motion that, once I was used to it, felt amazing. It wasn't as sensitive as my pussy, but it was a close second.

"Is this all right?" he asked.

"Yes. I think you could take me now," I said.

Tormund's eyes were just now widening in realization as the teasing around the rim of my ass triggered my channel to squeeze him again.

"Oh, really?" Kauz pulled his hand free and rose to his knees. "Tormund, you know what you should do?"

"Hmm?"

"Play with her clit." He was lining his tip up with my second entrance as he added, "Lick your fingers first."

Tormund grumbled an annoyed *ach* and did as instructed while I released a short-lived giggle. The male behind me slid his cock all the way into my ass, and my body adapted to him without pain. The sense of pressure where I'd never had pressure before had me clenching down. Tormund and I shared another blinding moment of pleasure from it.

The giant groaned and threw back his head, releasing a mouthful of smoke and steam. He didn't recover until I did, and then he pressed his thumb up to circle my clit. I was going to go crazy between the two of them, and Kauz hadn't even moved yet.

"So tight," he grunted, waiting for my muscles to relax.

Once they did, he drew back to thrust slowly. His wings made their shivery sound as he coaxed a hard moan from me. Knowing Kauz, he was going to pace himself and really slay me.

Was I going to be able to walk after this? We'd just have to see.

"I can feel you moving in her. That's weird," Tormund said in one of his loud whispers.

"Better get used to it. You're stuck, big guy." I could just picture Kauz's smirk.

My channel spasmed, and Tormund and I cried out together. I don't think he minded being stuck. Well, I certainly didn't. I imagined the two of them mating me just like this when my heat came. Maybe my other mates would take a turn so I would stay on a knot for as long as possible.

I came in earnest from the gentle circling on my clit and the unconventional lovemaking Kauz showed my second entrance. Stars sparkled at the corners of my vision as he kept going. This was so much more intense with two males, especially locked in place as I was. I cried out until my voice went hoarse, and Kauz came with a groan and one last liquid rush.

He caught me as I leaned back, boneless from being stuck between them. "Seems we've found something else you like."

"More than like," I tried to say, drifting on a hazy cloud of bliss.

Tormund mumbled something too and lifted a thumbs-up.

54
MARIUS

My leg bounced with barely leashed energy under a tavern counter.

The trap was set. All I had to do now was wait. One would think my feral impulses would grant me patience, but I'd never been an ambush predator. I came at my problems head-on, fangs bared, pursuing them to the bitter end. Waiting around gave me too much time to wallow in my own thoughts.

The rut only made Niall more extreme. *Why not hunt down Pack Ellisar where they hide? I'd tear out their throats in moments. Problem solved.*

What my feral side really wanted was a reason to return to Lark. Her absence was a fierce ache in my chest. I hadn't intended to turn our date into a days-long breeding session, but I couldn't say I regretted it. Even as I waited, poised to destroy her enemies, Niall clawed at me to continue what I'd left behind. *Why did you let her go again? What if she doesn't return?*

I shook my head sharply. Fucking maddening.

I'd last slept in her arms, in the inn by the sea. The phantom touch of her caresses remained with me. Her effortlessly musical voice and laugh, too. The softness of her body, with skin as fine and smooth as spidersilk. Chocolate and honey crackers on my tongue, a taste I'd savored and bathed my taste buds in. Who said I didn't have a sweet tooth?

It'd been what, two days? Three? This time without her blurred. I'd returned to Neslune after stealing one last kiss and paced in her rooms that night, hatching my plot to hunt Pack Ellisar as efficiently as possible.

I'd settled for weaponizing the same thing that'd robbed my reason and turned me into a lusting animal. Lark's intimate scent. I'd brought home some of her underclothes still stained with it.

To set the trap, I'd first washed with scent-blocking soap to dampen the thick cloud of pheromones I was still putting off. Then, I'd tied a satchel to my side that leaked Lark's scent, leading a deliberate looping trail through the Seelie side of Neslune, the Garden District. It was a beautifully maintained piece of land on the outskirts of the city.

I'd loosened the satchel to leave a strong impression of chocolate and honey crackers in front of a general store at the end of the district. Just beyond this store, the oversized flowers grown and coaxed into place by Seelie magic met the scraggly Serian forest.

One of the barkfolk would emerge from hiding in the wilderness and run face-first into my mate's fertile smell. Since I was seated by a window in a tavern across the street, I would see the moment it happened.

Fal was already at work in the Garden District, doing things his own way. Making friends. He'd gotten Thalas's help before I'd even arrived and had the Magician King transfer our Seelie disguises to rings.

Thalas had advised me to avoid speaking, as most mermen had melodic voices rather than my irritable growl. The Seelie were on high alert for anything suspicious. As soon as the crown announced a sizable bounty for three barkfolk, a flood of would-be bounty hunters upturned this district and harassed our more plantlike citizens. Many Unseelie had to be thrown out by the police for ruining the business of the single barkfolk who already lived here, a beta female.

Fal had approached her in the guise of a forest elf to apologize for the damage done to her greenhouse and shopfront, then paid her handsomely to demonstrate how barkfolk magic worked. She'd called it treeshaping.

A barkfolk could assimilate into the side of a tree and blend into its bark. With their eyes closed, a motionless barkfolk would be perfectly camouflaged. From there, they could listen in to the network of tree roots to learn information about a forest's surroundings and jump from tree to tree quickly.

Truly powerful barkfolk could command plant life in addition. According to Lark, Ellisar was blessed with this level of magic. *"The land grew and shaped itself to his command,"* she'd said. He was undoubtedly the most dangerous of the trio.

I assumed the bark brothers—as we now called Pack Ellisar—had seen the wanted posters going up and gotten the fuck out of the city.

Fal thought they were disguised via illusions and hiding in plain sight amongst the Seelie, waiting for information on Lark. I figured that was giving them too much credit for forward thinking. If they'd managed to acquire a disguise, one of them would use it to tiptoe into town, buy supplies, and go back into hiding. We'd see who was right.

Thalas had given us identical gadgets and explained in detail how they worked, which had been entirely too many words. All I cared about was that mine was discreet, resembling a bronze timepiece, and already attuned to the magic that'd formed our Seelie illusions.

Instead of telling time, the needle under its glass dome pointed toward the next nearest concentration of essence, presumably an essence spinner or a full-body illusion. It was currently pointed toward a boisterous olive-skinned alpha orc behind me, who pounded down beers with a group of laborers.

I was at the window by myself, by all appearances a lonely merman drinking the day away. I was into my fourth flagon of imported Theli wheat beer. The last time I'd drunk this, I'd been watching Lark limp out of a Theli inn while thinking the locals had no taste. It was absolute swill, too sweet and fruity.

But now it reminded me of her and eased Niall's anxiety about her absence, just a little. The staff left me alone to daydream and suffer with only the memory of her to comfort me.

A forest elf came up to my left side and clunked his flagon against mine. I tensed, nearly baring my teeth at him, before I recognized Fal's disguise. No longer a lithe dark elf prince, he'd been given muscles and scars to better resemble a working-class alpha. We wore the same fake pack mark, a wheel and anchor.

"Hey, brother," he said gruffly, speaking Theli. I slapped him on the back in greeting, as he would be used to if he spent more time with the kind of alphas he was emulating. He winced and drew up the stool next to mine, taking a quick glance at my timepiece-like gadget.

"Anything?" I asked in a low voice.

"Not yet. How goes this?" He couldn't help a chuckle from entering the question. I ignored his doubt. If Lark's scent had affected me this strongly, it would lure the bark brothers out of hiding. It was only a matter of time.

Fal smelled downright floral. It probably helped him fit in amongst the Seelie he'd spent time befriending. The scent change and the sheen of sweat he wiped from his forehead were the only symptoms of rut he was displaying so far. I hadn't deliberately rubbed my affliction into the pack bond, yet he'd picked it up from me immediately.

His side of the pack bond simmered with aimless lust. The rut hadn't taken his mind yet, but it'd probably boil over the moment Lark returned to the city and he caught a whiff of her mouthwatering pheromones.

She'd be nudged into estrus and sandwiched between us so fast...

"Are you going to answer the question or just drift off?" Fal grumbled.

I blinked, coming out of my dissociation. "Nothing's happened yet."

He took a long, overly obnoxious sip of his beer. His brows lifted in surprise. "It would be unfortunate to develop a taste for this."

"It's disgusting," I grunted.

He eyed the three empty flagons I'd shoved off to the side. "Uh huh."

"It reminds me of her."

He drummed his fingertips on the counter, though his illusion betrayed him by not masking the clicking of his claws striking the wood. I kept my gaze on the dirt path leading in from the forest, even as growing shadows lengthened into oncoming night outside. My leg continued to bounce.

I tipped another swallow into my mouth. Longing soured it going down.

P'nixie...

"I miss her too," Fal said heavily.

The lack of a needling remark was unlike him. Any other day, he'd ask what it was about the disgusting beer that reminded me of our mate. Instead, he hunched over his flagon. Loneliness was as disconcerting and ill-fitting a look on him as the stiff illusion he wore.

He hadn't seen Lark in over a week. A self-imposed sacrifice he'd made for me. Yeah, he'd half-assed a deal to hide his intent, but he'd opened the way for me to bond with Lark first for a reason. To make sure we *would* bond. Tormund and Kauz had fallen for her instantly, and if my older brother was ever fully honest about it, so had he. I'd been the odd one out, denying for too long how drawn I was to my p'nixie.

Fal, as pack lead, would not accept Lark as our princess unless we were all in agreement. I'd wager the crown's treasure that he hadn't confessed how much he loved her yet, dancing on a fine ledge around the words as he waited for me to stop being fucking stupid.

He may have let Pack Ellisar walk right past him, and that was a *huge* mistake, but I owed him. Upon hearing the news, my kelpie loyalty to Fal had stirred, shaking off a layer of dust. I'd felt a tug to provide my assistance.

I blamed that steadfast feeling for what I said next. "Thank you."

He raised a brow. "For what?"

"You know what," I grumbled.

His usual smirk tugged on the side of his lips, and he propped his chin on his fist. There was the brother I knew, about to say something annoying and ruin my attempt at gratitude.

The timepiece-like gadget locked on to a new target with a tiny *ping*. We both tried to snatch it, but I got it first. The line of the needle pointed toward a hooded figure pacing outside, head tilted back to scent the air.

I bared my fangs in a bloodthirsty smile. I'd been right.

Fal leaned over my shoulder. "Well, fuck me sideways."

The needle followed the path this male took to the front door of the tavern before I pocketed the gadget. Fal grabbed one of my old, empty flagons and got to his feet, heading to the bar behind the hooded stranger.

I tensed, ready to follow and wrestle this newcomer into submission. *Bite first; ask questions never.* I only held back because there was a chance he was simply a powerful essence spinner, not our quarry.

After a few minutes, Fal tapped our pack bond in a signal I'd been waiting for. He showed the hooded stranger to the stool on my left and sat on his other side.

I glanced over the rim of my flagon and suppressed a growl by sheer force of will. Floris's face was unmistakable. Even wearing an illusion, the youngest bark brother had the same smooth features Lark had shown us through her magic.

"He'd follow and corner me whenever he could. I was an easy target," she'd said.

I'd show him how easy a target he was. But my jaw tightened. I couldn't speak, not even to put him in his place. Niall seethed within me. *Kill him now! Bite out his throat!*

Not yet, I argued back. *He's one of three. We need this idiot alive. For now.*

He's a danger to the p'nixie.

If we kill him now, we'll never find his brothers.

My feral side relented after a moment. *Whatever is best for her.*

Aye, I thought back.

Floris was disguised as a dryad. Magic replaced the tree bark shingles that grew over barkfolk like a suit of armor with skin the color and texture of wood grain. His cloak was pinned down his front, probably to conceal that he wasn't wearing any clothing.

"My new friend tells me you have information," he said in a hope-filled hush.

He hadn't seemed to notice that I'd stopped blinking the moment he'd sat next to me. My fingers tightened on my flagon, trembling with restraint. As several moments passed, Floris's expression shaded with uncertainty.

He had to die in the most painful way possible. I had to lead him there, and to do it, I needed words, not growls. Niall agreed. For once, we were perfectly aligned with what had to happen from here.

The pressure in my jaw and throat receded. The bright, warped vision that accompanied Niall dilating my eyes relaxed. Clarity of thought rushed in as the breeding haze parted. At any other time, I would shake my head and snarl, but the animal impulse to do so was also gone.

I took in a deep breath, probing inside my head. My feral side was still present and watching, poised to strike at any moment. We were equal partners, working together for once. Niall had ceded full control to me when he was at his strongest, during my rut. For any feral male to have a clear head *during* a rut was a starsdamned miracle.

Fal and Floris were both looking at me. My brother's eyebrows were up in his hairline, his mouth rounded in surprise. Our pack bond had probably expressed everything he needed to know.

And Floris was still waiting for a response to a question I'd promptly forgotten.

My most violent urges were blunted, but Niall still whispered encouragement. *Toy with our prey.*

"Did you say something?" I asked Floris.

The disguised barkfolk tilted his head. There was a certain stiffness to his face, like he was stuck with his vacant expression. "Um. You have information," he whispered.

"Concerning what?" My feral rasp was gone for now, lending me the smooth voice Lark liked so much.

"I've been searching for a pixie. She was here recently," Floris said.

That's it. Kill him. My fingers spasmed with the urge to wrap them around the barkfolk's throat.

We were doing so well, I thought irritably.

"There are many pixies in the Garden District. You'll have to be more specific," Fal put in silkily while I struggled.

Floris took a deep drink of his fresh beer. "She's unique. If you saw her, you'd know it. Petite. White hair. Silvery-gray wings. Walks with a limp."

Fal signaled victory the moment Floris took a drink. We just needed to keep him here for a few minutes. As a reward for not smashing him over the head with my flagon, I'd torture this male soon. The promise of pain soothed my feral impulses again.

"Information will cost you," I drawled.

"I can pay. Have you seen her?" he pressed.

I pictured Lark as we'd first met her. The poor, weak waif in a grass-stained servant's gown, completely cowed to her stepmother's will. This male asked about the pale shade of my p'nixie. A beaten-down omega he felt so fucking entitled to that he was asking after her in a foreign kingdom.

My anger didn't fade, but calculation took its place. I could keep him occupied for the short time we needed.

"I have, actually. Helped her with her bags when she first moved here." I put my palm out, and he fumbled a few full moon coins into it.

"Tell me everything, please," he begged.

Cheap bastard. I was darkly amused he thought this was enough to buy any kind of access to my mate.

"Beautiful li'l female. Delicate but curved in all the right places." My sweet, resilient omega.

Floris practically salivated as he nodded. *He's aroused by her at her weakest. Disgusting.*

"She said she was scared of something back home. I don't make such things my business, but it sounded like she was running from some unwanted male attention." I eyed him, letting my usual scowl fall into place as I grunted, "You know anything about that?"

He scoffed. "You know females. They're fickle sorts."

"Are *you* the male she's been running from? Is that why you're asking about her?"

"She's my mate. She signed a contract." There was a hint of a slur in his words, as if he were several pints in rather than a few big gulps.

"Oh, did she now?" I bared my fangs in a vicious smile.

He tried to say, "She's mine by rights," but the poison Fal had slipped in his drink made him mostly unintelligible.

"My, my. Too much to drink already," my brother remarked, his tone dangerously close to a furious growl. "Where are you staying nowadays, *friend?*"

"Out in the forest," Floris slurred.

"Your pack is in the forest?" he pressed.

"That's right."

"Call them." His bark threaded through the order. Fal had trained extensively to turn his bark into a persuasive whisper, though he couldn't lay it on too thick. It was noticeable above a subtle thrum of encouragement.

But Floris, whose mind was already addled, was guaranteed to obey. After a few moments, he said, "They won't come. They already said I'm on my own if I get caught."

"What a shame. No matter what?"

"That's right," he repeated.

I wasn't surprised. It would just make hunting the other bark brothers more interesting once they started to feel the pain we inflicted on this male. Floris would agree to anything, including a deal to lead us to the rest of his pack, with the right encouragement applied.

Fal flashed his teeth. "Well, in that case, this has been fun, but you're coming with us. Don't put up a fuss. We have plenty more questions for you to answer."

WE PRACTICALLY CARRIED Floris between us to a carriage we'd had waiting. The barkfolk acted, for all the world, like a real drunkard, even catching a short nap on the journey. I ripped the hooded cloak off him, revealing his true form.

He seemed alien to me, an ambulatory tree fae with vines for hair. Bark covered most of his body, even forming whorls over his limbs. His face was a blank mask of smooth wood.

The shingles across his chest stuck out, though. Did he have flesh and blood under those layers of bark? I'd have to pry some pieces loose and see for myself.

We took off our disguises as well. After we eyed Floris's unique form, we exchanged a glance. "*This* is one of the males from her night terror," Fal said, nearly speculative.

An aggressive growl rose from me.

"I know," he said.

Up until now, that would've been the only thing I had to say. But not anymore. "The nightmare was about being claimed against her will."

"I was there when she talked about it."

"I mean her mark," I continued, ear flicking. "It was the first thing she checked once she realized the nightmare wasn't real."

Fal shut his mouth, his slit-pupiled eyes darting as he thought back to that night. The carriage slowed, rolling over a familiar dirt path around the back of the palace. "What are you thinking of doing?" he asked.

I snorted dismissively. "Don't worry about it."

"Worried?" he echoed with his usual flippancy. "If I'm worried about anything, it's missing out!"

"Follow me, then." I was certain he'd balk if he knew what I intended. Fal had stopped playing in the dirt with me when he'd grown old enough to learn just how important he was. This was the adult version, where my role was to commit the dirtiest deeds. He'd back out once he saw that the only way this night ended was with blood and screams.

We took Floris through a back entrance to the palace. I had him slung over one shoulder at this point, his dead weight nothing despite his alpha size.

We descended into the freezing-cold dungeon. The familiar stench of suffering rolled over us in a wave. Either the smell or the shock of cold woke Floris. He startled, jerking at his restraints. Muffled shrieks came from his gagged mouth.

"So, you intend to watch me *question* him?" I said to Fal in a heavy hint, switching to Theli for a moment. The barkfolk quieted to listen to the response.

"Certainly. I'm a big fan," the dark elf replied in kind. I counted down from three in my head. After those three seconds had passed, he added, "Of the absolute faesteel balls he must have. Coming all this way with a piece of paper as his only protection."

"How foolish," I agreed.

"You know, Mar, he probably doesn't think he did anything wrong. Shall we list his crimes for him?"

The pack bond was lit with our shared anticipation. But while I was excited for bloodshed, Fal's emotions were currently woven with a kind of hopeful longing. He wanted me to play along with his game of words. Maybe he even wanted to help me make Floris suffer.

I indulged him. "The illegal breeding contract, for one."

That was just the tip of the iceberg. We bandied back and forth the slights dealt to our mate while Floris struggled and tried to respond. There wasn't anything he could say that'd save him.

I had Fal check the first interrogation room. The sound of a female hacking her guts up floated in the air before the door closed behind him. "Cymora's still in there," he said.

He checked the second room and motioned for me to follow. We took the barkfolk inside and tied him to the single chair. I expected Fal to come up with a reason to leave at this point...but instead, he helped, even pulling the rope around Floris's ankles to make the restraints as tight and chafing as possible.

I removed the barkfolk's gag. The first thing out of his mouth was an earnest question. "You two know Lark?"

Fal and I exchanged another glance. He cracked first, but I swiftly followed, the two of us filling the chamber with a round of mocking laughter.

"She was more polite about your intelligence than you clearly deserve," Fal answered.

"And you will never see her again," I added with a low growl.

He seemed to finally notice our surroundings. "W-who are you guys?"

This room was identical to the first interrogation room. Small and bare, save for the chair and the rusting torture implements lining the walls. He'd fixated on one of them with an audible swallow.

I'd witnessed many interrogation sessions during my apprenticeship, carried out by Theodred, Rennyn, and a dozen other professionals. While I'd performed a few questionings too, none of them had felt as personal as this.

Once I started introducing Floris to true pain, I would be loath to stop. I still had the feral urge to turn his suffering into the slowest, most painful death imaginable. Over the pack bond, I sensed that Fal agreed.

I turned to him in disbelief. "Are you *sure* you want to get your hands dirty?" I asked in Serri.

He made a show of inspecting his claws. "I'll clean them off before our mate sees." Despite the levity in his answer, the pack bond told me that he was deadly serious. His desires and mine were the same—we'd do what it took to protect our most vulnerable pack member. "We're her retribution, Mar."

"We are." I nodded in approval of him. He was following up his words with action for once.

"Um, hello? Could you let me go?" Floris asked, glancing between us. He froze when we turned identical glares his way.

I went to take a pair of pliers off a hook on the wall and worked it open and closed a couple times. It was stiff with age and disrepair, but it would do the job.

Floris saw me coming with a flash of dull metal in my grip and tugged fruitlessly on his restraints. "W-wait. Maybe we could strike a deal? I have money. Or information. Um. So much information!" he blurted.

Fal waited, his cat eyes gleaming expectantly.

"Hold his mouth open," I directed.

"Oh, fuck. I see now. Well played." He grinned as he grabbed the barkfolk's head. Since Floris didn't understand Serri, he didn't shut his mouth in time. Fal held him still as he screamed and thrashed.

The dark elf watched with vicious delight when I clamped the pliers around one of Floris's fangs. I added my grip under the barkfolk's jaw and relished the fear reflected in his eyes.

"If, by some miracle, you leave this room alive," I said coolly, "you will *never* have a chance to claim our mate."

55
LARK

With how close my heat was, we decided to remain in Once Else rather than explore the dreamlands through flight. Kauz promised to show me what we'd missed out on later, when I wasn't burdened by my body's needs. "There will be more dates," he'd assured me.

We did some sightseeing in Once Else instead, interspersed by wing-painting sessions and magic lessons. Tormund stayed and became a part of my date time with Kauz. The cramps were back, and I wore heat pads to do something about the amount of slick I produced even without any stimulation.

The heat suppressant tattoo was unraveling on its own. Only a couple decorative loops remained. I had days before my heat overcame me, or one good knotting, which I craved despite my best intentions.

The wing-painting sessions were the biggest source of sexual frustration. I lay in different positions while Tormund held my neck just tight enough to trigger my omega instincts into submitting. It was the only way to get my wings still for Kauz to work his magic to make the ink set permanently. But my body reacted to the hold by making me extra wet.

My gentle giant smelled it no matter what and gritted his teeth while I made the occasional trill and whine to be touched intimately. He purred to soothe me and usually kept my head cushioned comfortably against his belly or thigh.

Kauz started this process by mixing his essence into a large bottle of ink. By the time he was finished with it, it glowed white with brilliant sparkles, as if he'd trapped starlight inside the glass.

"I'm going to teach you how to do this someday," he'd said while I'd admired the liquid, tipping it back and forth inside the bottle. "So you can paint my wings with your magic, too."

I'd stilled, flushing with embarrassment. "I can barely hold a pencil properly." There was no way I'd put a sloppy attempt at art on him for the whole kingdom to see.

He'd kissed me, though not as deeply as I craved, and promised to teach me. He wanted to wear my art however it turned out, marked as my mate just like he marked me. I'd melted and vowed to do my best to learn.

His magic made the ink smell like Always, and I caught hints of it lingering on me after it dried and my dust began to shed in shades of indigo, lavender, and silver. I wanted him to have the scent of Always trailing behind him, too.

The ink was so potent it soaked through the thin skin of my wings to show through to the other side. This ruined our original notion that I would have a different pattern on them front and back. He adapted the artwork and was due to finish by the end of the second day of working on it.

During our idle time, I practiced magic under his direction. Summoning essence and shaping illusions or wind from it was a process of mental muscle work. It kept my mind off of how delectable Tormund smelled to focus on my spells instead.

But magic couldn't distract me when Kauz urged Tormund to talk about Pack Ellisar. How had the barkfolk gotten off a train while he and Fal were standing at the station, waiting for them? My Always had him tell the story multiple times.

"Go over it again. Spare no detail," Kauz said.

I was on my front, resting my chin on Tormund's thigh. He was still holding my neck. I was perfectly still as Kauz, who straddled my knees, painted the edges of my lower set of wings.

The giant breathed a sigh but didn't complain. "Rennyn gave word to Fal late that Pack Ellisar was on the way to Neslune. We gathered up the fishling since she was leaving with the same train they were arriving on. Then we went to the station."

"Mmhmm."

"While we were waiting, the fishling asked if we'd killed the fish." He scratched behind his horn, brows furrowing. "She seemed disappointed when we said not yet. Then she started stumbling over her sentences."

"Stumbling how?" This wasn't the first time Kauz had tried to narrow in on this part of Tormund's story.

The giant shook his head slowly. "I can't really remember. I was worried about her for a little bit, though."

"That reminds me of when we first met you, Lark," the winged fae remarked. He paused to focus, the wet brush painting a delicate curlicue in a ticklish spot. I bit my lip, trying not to giggle.

"That's what I was thinking, too," Tormund murmured.

Kauz hummed in agreement. "You would stop mid-sentence if it was something you couldn't say. Or if the conversation led to something you'd been forced to forget, you'd completely blank."

I nodded, grimacing. It did sound awfully similar.

"She tried to tell us something," Tormund said. "And then, the next thing I knew, a dreamlander was standing in front of us and apologizing for losing Pack Ellisar."

A troubled silence hung over us for several moments. There was a gap in his memories, and no amount of probing was helping him remember.

"Cymora didn't order Laurel around like she did to me," I said finally. "And Laurel loves her mother. I can't imagine her being disappointed Cymora's still alive."

"I'm more concerned about what happened between talking to Laurel and receiving the spy's apology. You said Fal has the same memory loss?" Kauz put in.

"Aye. He also said he had the sense he was wrong about something but can't remember what."

"And what happened to Laurel?"

"She got on the train to Thelis."

"You're *sure*? You saw her walk onto the train?"

Tormund bit his lower lip. "Well, nay. I can't remember her doing it, but I know she did."

I wanted to turn and exchange a glance with Kauz, wondering if he was thinking what I was.

"She's still in Neslune," I said.

"I'm going to visit her mind tonight," Kauz said at about the same time.

"What?" Now it was Tormund and I speaking at once.

"This is the dreamlands. I can access her dreams no matter where she is. For some peace of mind, why not look at her memory of that day?" he reasoned. "Something obviously doesn't add up here. If Laurel doesn't reveal anything, I'll see about infiltrating one of Pack Ellisar's dreams instead. I've seen enough of them from your memories, Lark, that I could find them."

"I could visit Ellisar or one of his brothers while you're with Laurel," I ventured. Not that that would be anything other than a complete nightmare.

"Absolutely not!"

If Tormund wasn't holding my neck, I would've sprung right off the bed from the thunder in Kauz's response, followed by his soft beta growl. Tormund echoed it in a deeper, more menacing tone.

"Promise me you won't endanger yourself that way, sweetheart." The dream warden gentled his voice. "You're still a beginner in the intricacies of magic. Just the thought of you getting stranded in one of their heads for a whole night..." His wings shivered.

I tensed, my breathing coming up short as I imagined it too. "I just want to help," I murmured.

"And we want to take care of this problem for you, li'l bird." Tormund stroked my neck gently with his thumb. "If Fal got his way, you wouldn't have known they were here in the first place."

I sighed heavily. "I don't need you all keeping me in the dark, even if the truth scares me."

"It's not that at all. We know you're a grown female. It's just..." Tormund shrugged.

"Fixing things for you is practically our calling," Kauz added in. "And making your enemies disappear is an act of love from an Unseelie."

I let my negativity flow out of me like water from between my fingers. All of my mates had proven themselves enthusiastic about these things. It was their "clumsy love," as Fal put it; they'd saved me when I couldn't save myself. Perhaps it was inevitable they'd do it again.

"Maybe someday I'll make your enemies disappear," I said.

"That's the spirit." Kauz patted my ass and probably regretted it, as I released a full-blown moan. His wings shivered again, and Tormund echoed the sound with longing. I clenched my eyes closed and wished I didn't have to have a heat. It was nothing but trouble.

"Anyway," I mumbled. "I know whose dream I'm visiting tonight." Remembering the clumsy love talk made me miss Fal more intensely. It'd been too long since I'd seen his unfairly attractive face. *And body.*

Soon after this conversation, my mates let me stand and admire the finished art. I took it all in with the help of a hand mirror, thrilled at the results. My wings sparkled with beautiful silver patterns through their natural amethyst hue.

Stars and mist outlined each wing, representing Kauz and matching him as my mate. We'd settled on curlicues and comet trails for me, which originated from the base of each wing to spread in looping flourishes.

The smell of Always rose from my wings as I fluttered in delight and lifted a few inches off the ground in a cloud of pixie dust. I launched myself at Kauz, who caught me and grinned as I peppered his face with kisses. "I love it. Thank you, thank you!"

"Well, I love you." He kissed the tip of my nose. "And now everyone can see that you're mine."

He definitely won the prize for the gentlest claim amongst my mates. I nuzzled his neck and whispered back, "Yours."

56
FAL

Marius and I tortured Fangless Floris for most of the night, seized by a second wind of manic energy we shared through the pack bond. There was very little information gathered compared to the amount of pain we'd inflicted.

I hadn't realized my brother was so good at dealing agony. He was stone-cold about finding and pressing weaknesses. I took mental notes on the techniques he showed me, just in case I found myself in a different room with another of the bark brothers. Couldn't have Floris having all the fun.

My father and Theodred came into the interrogation room the next morning. Father took in the scene we'd made, with our working male's clothes stained with blood and sap. Various tools were scattered about, and the barely conscious barkfolk had his ripped-away bark mounded in a bloody pile atop his lap. His head lolled, and he made a raspy moan. It sounded a little like "Help."

The dark elf king eyed us with new wariness, at odds with his easy-going façade. It was only then that I thought, *Maybe we went too far.*

And then my alpha instincts whispered back, *Nah, he deserved it. And so much worse.*

"This is quite the scene to start the morning with," Father said in his usual chipper tone. "Who's the unfortunate Seelie lad?"

Marius bared his teeth in reply, the very picture of an animal ready to defend his kill.

"Floris of Osme Fen," I answered for both of us.

My father's red eyes widened before darting in calculation. With a growing frown, he nodded to Theodred.

"Come brief us on what you've learned," the redcap king ordered.

No one sane argued with Theodred, so we dropped our current tools of choice to step away with the two kings. Marius took Floris's fangs with him.

My brother was still in an odd headspace. Feral but in control. Taken by the rut but perfectly rational. When his condition had robbed him of his voice, I'd fallen into the role of translating his various noises. I'd become a master at reading him without us exchanging a word aloud. With a glance at him and over our pack bond, I knew he was reluctant to give any sign of his shifting headspace to our fathers.

My father, specifically. He'd run straight to Mother to crow about their wild boy finally equalizing. That had all the makings of an *absolute* disaster if Marius was simply experiencing some new feral quirk. We didn't know what him finding a balance between instinct and reason looked like, though it'd certainly felt like he'd achieved it from talking to Floris, of all fae.

I shared my intent over the pack bond, and Marius grunted in agreement. I continued speaking for us both while he pretended to dissociate.

"Floris of Osme Fen is one of the three alphas Lark signed a breeding contract with due to her stepmother's compulsion. Pack Ellisar came to Serian independently of Cymora. They were not invited. They chose to show up here."

Marius punctuated the statement with a rattling growl. I echoed it in agreement.

"When Cymora, Laurel, and Lark did not return to Osme Fen in a timely fashion, the bark brothers followed the breadcrumbs we left behind in Ilysnor. Some of the locals remembered Lark in particular as an oddly faded pixie with a limp, which is the version of her they're still looking for. They heard Lark had boarded a train to Serian with a pack of noble Unseelie and decided to pursue her. The eldest brother, Ellisar, has the original contract in hand. They have no other prospects for a mate, clearly, so they thought to push the matter to its breaking point."

Any hint of Father's good cheer faded as I spoke, revealing the calculating mind beneath. "So," he said in a low voice, "you've been sloppy. Instead of stealing your mate away from her enemies, you've left the door open for them to come along to Serian with her."

I tensed. A reprimand from Father for being *sloppy* was a prelude to one of his elaborate punishments, and we didn't have time for that right now. "I don't think we could've prepared for the sheer audacity of Pack Ellisar coming here," I said carefully.

"And where, pray tell, is the rest of Pack Ellisar?" he asked.

I kept my lips sealed on the answer he expected. We didn't know, and Floris wasn't in a position to tell us.

Father made a show of looking around and threw up his hands. "The forest somewhere, hmm? We have no chance of finding them, now that you've attacked their brother. Those two barkfolk cowards have gone to ground so thoroughly they may as well be *trees*!"

"We'll find them," I murmured.

"Son," he said heavily. "You are the crown prince of our great nation. You cannot owe a grievance to *anyone*, especially not a trio of unknown Seelie. That's exactly what will happen if Lark doesn't escape her breeding contract—her new pack lead will owe Pack Ellisar in accordance with the document she signed."

While he was right about the grievance, all contracts had loopholes. She was my fated mate, for stars' sake, and *no one* would stop me from claiming her for Pack Sorles.

"I can smell the rut on you both from across the palace," Theodred said in his deep rumble. "Your mind is compromised, Fal. I've never seen you proudly wear signs of another's pain." He swung his fiery gaze over the evidence of the gleeful way I'd joined in Floris's torture.

"Floris deserved far worse," Marius put in. He spoke without a growl or feral rasp, and Father's brows rose as he likely noticed.

"What are you holding there, wild boy?"

The kelpie spread his fingers, showing the two bloodied fangs in his palm.

Father drew his hands down his face and muttered to himself, "Did I say attacked? I meant mauled. How the fuck are we going to find the other two now? And *please* tell me you're not intending to give those to sweet Larkie." He shot a glare at Marius, who looked chastened.

"It's the rut. Neither of them is thinking clearly," Theodred put in.

"I can see that!" Father snarled.

"I have not succumbed," I said.

"*Ach.* Lie to yourself if you must."

I would, thank you very much. Heat pulsed under my skin just a millisecond behind my heartbeat, threatening to drive me mad with lust. This was the third time I'd gone into rut, and the other two times, I'd accepted it with excitement. I'd taken my pleasure and exhausted a few beta lovers while wearing a bracelet of fertility blocker charms, just in case. No ongoing consequences for slaking my alpha needs.

I teetered on the edge now, resisting the fall. Lark deserved better than her new pack lead succumbing to alpha instinct and shoving her on her back. Especially in the midst of her enemies plotting to snatch her away from us and scheming for a grievance from me. Stars only knew what they'd want, but it'd be nothing good. I'd keep my head for us all.

Father hummed, a hint of dark amusement taking up residence at the corner of his mouth. "Well, Theo, looks like we've got some trees to burn," he said. The redcap king nearly smiled and cracked his knuckles, a terrifying sight on its own. "Lads, we will be taking over solving this particular problem."

Theodred spoke, letting out just a hint of his forceful bark. "Neither of you will interfere with our forces sweeping the city or forest. Nor will you execute any more plans involving the capture of the last two males in Pack Ellisar without first running your intentions by one of the kings." His gaze hardened when Marius twitched and made a pained noise. "Your orders are to rest."

"And shower. Use a whole soap bar, for stars' sake. You both stink," Father added.

We snarled in offense together. He just gestured at us and glanced up at Theodred. "You are dismissed," the redcap king ordered.

I drew breath to say something, and the giant male speared me with a glower. Marius filled the pack bond with stirrings of warning. "As per your instructions, I wish to state my intentions," I said anyway.

Theodred rumbled like an incoming storm. The hairs on the back of my neck stood on end. "Insolence is punishable, boy."

I tossed my rather matted hair. Stars, I needed to see to my grooming. "I will continue to plot out the capture of the last two bark brothers. I *intend* to follow through on the best course of action for my omega. As I believe you mean to do the same. We need not decide on separate paths."

"What are you suggesting?" Father knew exactly what I meant. He just wanted me to say it aloud.

"That I wish to be allied with the Clever King, who is always a step ahead of me, no matter the occasion," I said smoothly. "The rut has not taken so much of my mind that I cannot be communicated with."

Father tilted his head back and forth. "We will be chatting, no matter what. If you two bumble through my plans, I will *communicate* a few things your way. As for—"

"Let us speak plainly," Theodred interrupted. "We all want the same thing. Sons, this involves your mate, so I understand how personal it is. However, this rut of yours has come at the worst time. Our decisions will not be endangered like yours. Set aside your pride and allow us to do our jobs as the Kings of Serian."

"Sometimes good decision-making includes a measure of secrecy," Father added.

Well, fuck. That just meant he was going to maneuver us like pieces on a game board. Marius, coming to a similar conclusion, snorted irritably.

I turned wearily toward the door. "No matter what, we'll get them. The queen is watching. We will not fail Lark again," Father said.

My brother stilled before swinging his attention toward my father. He inclined his head, grave in his agreement.

I WISH I could say I was productive in the following hours of forced rest. Marius and I were too keyed up to consider sleeping. We cleansed ourselves and settled in Lark's quarters. Marius paced like a caged beast while I took her old notebook and wrote in it from the back.

I jotted down countless ideas, plotting them to their inevitable ends. Unfortunately, nothing I came up with made a lick of fucking sense after a few steps. The rut was torching my logic, seeping in despite my best efforts not to think about Lark's beautiful figure and sparkling eyes and plump, kissable lips.

A whole flock of beta mothkins took care of us, making sure we were fed and as comfortable as could be expected. I recognized my pair of chipper males, and the two females were Lark's handmaidens...and those two were Tormund's...

All of our house moths were here, serving us in our mate's quarters. Most of our things had been relocated to the bedroom, including our collection of random trophies and plaques that we passed back and forth for competitions we'd invented. Most of them belonged to Tormund at the moment. They'd been placed next to a basket full of Kauz's random magical trinkets.

At either end of the dresser was part of my rock collection and Marius's seashells. We both had a habit of picking up things during our leisure time, and we were stellar examples of our races. He collected the remnants of sea bugs—that was where shells came from, I assumed— and I took shiny things off the ground.

Might as well covet my uncut gemstones for a while and arrange them properly, because I wasn't going to get anything else done today.

I'd also picked up something for him while spelunking for the perfect crystal to present to Lark. I went to my old quarters to retrieve it.

Marius had stopped pacing at some point, so he didn't catch me slipping the tiny spiral shell fossil in with his former sea bugs. Checking the pack bond, I noticed he was...passed out. *Finally.* There was hope his rut would end soon.

He was in Lark's nest. He'd constructed a mini nest for himself on the divan, cocooned in a few random blankets and her favorite fur-lined cloak. He had the right idea. I dismissed the house moths and crawled into bed, settling a few layers down where her scent was still present.

My mouth watered as I drifted off with my mate dominating my every sense. My dreams were a heated tangle of erotic fantasies. Everything we'd do when she returned and was finally *mine*.

So intoxicated by her, it was all the more jarring when I had an unwanted visitor in my dreams. The occasional intruder tested my mind, trying to access crown secrets. Hoping I wasn't trained to recognize a dream warden's probing, probably.

I was particularly furious about the timing of this intruder's interruption and began to imagine them trapped with one of the simplest yet worst childhood punishments my father used to inflict on me: *the metronome*. A few hours with nothing but the rhythmic *tick tick tick tick tick* was enough to drive me mad.

That was before I caught a glimpse of the "intruder" wandering the darkness of my abandoned dream.

"Fal?" Lark called. The real Lark, unmistakable by her pixie outline and ethereal beauty.

I realized my mistake a moment too late and ended up following her into the memory of a punishment. The gouge marks I'd clawed into the battered table and uncomfortable wooden chair were as prominent as ever. Somewhere out of sight, a metronome set to play at an awkwardly fast tempo ticked away.

I'd nearly trapped Lark with the maddening sound. I tried waving it away, then thought with force, *Fucking stop.* And what do you know, it did, giving way to blessed silence.

My mate's expressive blue eyes roved over the tiny room before landing on me. Her pupils resized as they focused, and she broke into a beaming smile. "Hi, Fal!"

It was like the sun emerging from behind stormy clouds. She was the sun, of course, heating my insides and kindling the lust hiding just under my skin. Her scent hit me: extra sweet and concentrated as we lingered in this tiny room together.

I pressed my claws into the meat of my palms. *Focus. You are still in control.*

"Hello, *mo stór*," I purred. My need made my voice huskier than usual. "You've come to visit me, hmm?"

"I've missed you." The trust and love that gleamed in her expression just about crushed me. My chest ached, echoing those feelings.

I needed to get her out of this room before I succumbed to my instincts and bent her over the table. She tested the fraying threads of my self-control by coming forward for a hug and leaning up expecting a kiss.

If I met her lips with mine, I'd snap. I caught her slight form and tilted my head, letting her mouth skim my neck in an electric brush. My fangs sank into my bottom lip, drawing blood, and the pain helped clear my head. I held her to my chest, trying to ignore how perfectly she fit against me.

"I've missed you too. You know, when you were first learning how to enter the dreams of others, I prepared a reward if you chose to visit me. Would you like it now?" Nuzzling into her hair, I drew out a shiver from her as my breath washed over her pointed ear.

"What is it?"

"Hmm. A surprise, and technically something for us both."

She hesitated. "Will you remember this dream tomorrow?"

"Bits and snatches, like any other dream." I would know I'd held the real her, and that was all I needed to remember.

"Well, I love surprises."

I smiled wickedly. "Good omega." I let a bit of my alpha authority thread through the words, just to see her flush that delectable shade of pink.

I offered her my hand with a flourish and focused on changing our surroundings. As she put her delicate fingers in mine, I tugged her deeper into my memories.

We walked my old path of self-discovery together, starting from my childhood. "As a boy, I spent more than my share of time learning the dances expected of a prince," I narrated.

I remembered strict tutors, long evenings, and my father pressuring me to learn better, faster. No son of his would be a graceless fool. I'd practiced until the strains of music and the ticking of the metronome were embedded in the back of my mind, invading quiet time and dreams alike.

"And I didn't enjoy it until later. I asked Father whether the songs we danced to had actual words. That kind of kicked off my passions, since it led me to musical theater."

It'd been a stuffy operatic soprano that'd started it all. Father had dug up an essence orb with the song saved and laughed at the way I'd scrunched my face and winced at the highest notes. Lark made a similar expression as my memory replayed the song, and I nodded in agreement, nudging her shoulder with mine.

"After hearing that, I said to myself that there had to be *other* songs out there," I whispered to her. "That's what I want to give to you, *mo stór*. All the music you've forgotten and then some. If we don't get through it all tonight...you'll just have to come back, hmm?"

I hoped Kauz didn't exaggerate about how amazing his magic was. Allegedly, he remembered everything he saw in another fae's dream with perfect clarity, so hopefully she'd do the same.

Lark regarded me with wide eyes and the beginnings of a hopeful smile. "Okay. I think I'd really like that," she said.

We walked through surreal streams of memory with songs along the way. I gave her the most popular ones, trying to fill her head with music and color. We traveled past buskers strumming their instruments and crooning about love and loss on street corners. Catchy tunes sung a little off-key in taverns. Drunken revelers swaying and mumbling those same songs.

Lark caught snatches of tunes and hummed along, just as I suspected she would. I gave her the words when she seemed to take a shine to a song. *Sing, my love. I know you were meant to sing.* She kept shutting her mouth and glancing shyly up at me, too self-conscious to try.

We stepped into a recreation of the run-down theater where I used to hide from my duties and needy younger siblings. The managers and director would pretend they had no idea the crown prince was the kid underfoot. I'd visit whenever possible to watch in fascination as the actors told stories with song and dance.

Lark and I sat on the threadbare seats in the front row. I itched to pull her into my lap, but if I did that, I'd lose my focus on what I wanted to show her. My favorite play, *A Duel of Hearts*. I'd seen it enough as a boy that it played out flawlessly onstage.

Lark rested her head on my shoulder, laughing along and sighing with the romantic overtures. During the interlude, I told her, "This play woke my love for theater. The visuals, the dancing, the music..." I affected a dramatic swoon.

"I can see why. How old were you?"

"Thirteen or so. If you watch closely, I might actually be in this version."

Mother had paid handsomely for an essence orb to record the cameo appearance I'd made toward the end, which she still let me watch occasionally. I'd basked in the radiance of her approval.

"This play became a fresh start for the Fifth Wheel Troupe. The director eventually gave me a chance to audition," I added. "He made me really work for it. Even though just having me onstage gave us enough prestige to build up a following and move out of this run-down place."

"No wonder you're so confident," she said, mostly to herself.

"I'm confident because I'm irreplaceable." I flipped my hair and rattled my earrings just so.

My brothers would've smacked the ego out of me for saying that, but Lark smiled with open fondness, admiring me for who I was. She was winding my willpower around her littlest finger as she did it, too. A first for me.

I was no stranger to *that* look. As a prince and a performer, I'd had no lack of female attention, but it was always superficial. I could tease and pleasure my lovers, but as a general rule, I couldn't return the affections they heaped upon me. Thus, I'd never invested myself in a lover *long term*.

I'd always known I would have to find my scent match and mate her along with my brothers. It was my duty to find and elevate her as the next queen to continue the royal line. She had to be a lot of things before she joined Pack Sorles, though. Resilient, determined, and loving would make for a strong start. Sweet and mild-mannered, even better, for her to get along with all four of us.

Deep down, I'd been afraid I'd see this mysterious female through a lens of duty and sacrifice. I'd thought I would find it difficult to love her, especially if I was expected to share her with Marius, Kauz, and Tormund.

But Lark had destroyed those doubts in what felt like an instant. She put a face to a concept and supplied everything my pack needed in one petite package. She fit seamlessly in with the four of us. *Our* omega.

We were a true pack with her at our center. We might even—*gasp!* —enjoy one another's company. Even though our love for each other, and her, was clumsy, it was well-meaning and always enthusiastic.

She was already ours, heat or not. I hadn't missed the elegant art Kauz must've painted on her wings or the lingering scent of Marius coming from some kind of claiming bite on her shoulder. The lack of Tormund's claim was no concern. He'd sand down his own fangs rather than put a mark on his beloved li'l bird.

Soon it would be my turn to make her mine, and it'd be the soul-bonding bite that would put my pack mark on her brow. My expression became a mirror of hers as I admired her back. It was *that* look. I wouldn't tire of looking at her face even if we lived to a thousand years together.

When we weren't in a dream, I'd tell her how I felt. *Anticipation will make it sweeter.*

I gazed into her star-flecked eyes for quite some time. We both stirred as I added to the mostly forgotten conversation, "You are irreplaceable too. Never forget that."

Her lips framed a shy smile. It was the face of "Really? You think so?" It was a travesty that I didn't kiss her then and there. But I knew my limits...and why I'd brought her to this memory.

I started remembering the second act of *A Duel of Hearts* before I got any more distracted. She snuggled closer, practically wrapping herself around my arm and purring with delight toward the end of the play.

The music and choreography only went from great to better, and by the finale, she drew up with a gasp and pointed.

There I was in the background, a lanky teen dancing my absolute heart out with the rest of the cast while the main couple had their closing duet.

"I snuck on the set," I whispered. "I convinced my mother to come to this backwater theater, stole a costume, and wedged myself in the back for the final song before I could be chased off the stage."

The memory faded out, but I had another one take its place. A string quartet played the opening notes to the starting duet for the play. I crooned the lines of the male role and then made my voice a little higher to add in the chorus too. Then I swept my palm toward her.

She thought for a beat too long, but that was all right. My heart soared as she sang back to me, her sweet voice crystal clear as it soared through the acoustics of the theater.

Gorgeous. Just like I thought. I raised my index finger with an unnecessary flourish of my hand, almost missing my cue as we counted up together. The leads were hostile to one another at first, thinking they were having a real duel before the play showed them in a competition and, inevitably, a romance.

I coaxed the full song from her, smiling brilliantly all the while. It'd be okay if I never got her on a stage with me. I could covet her singing voice and keep moments like this to myself. *Mine, mine, mine,* hissed my alpha instincts.

As we finished, I leaned forward, tipping her face up. Stars, I *was* a rut-addled fool. I was going to wake up with her taste seared on my tongue and couldn't bring myself to regret it. My lips were just skimming hers as I heard, "Fal, wake up."

I opened my eyes, and instead of seeing my mate eager for a deep lip-lock, I was face down on a pillow, my limbs tangled up in Lark's nest. Marius stood over me, already washed and dressed and flapping a piece of paper over my ear.

"There'd better be a good fucking reason for this," I snarled.

He handed me a note that I took in blearily.

Dearest Sons,

There has been quite an upset in my plans. I will require your assistance after all. How do you feel about an endurance test? Don't get too excited. You're not going to like this.

Father hadn't signed it. He didn't have to. My heart thudded at double its usual speed as I rushed to get ready for the day and whatever else was coming next.

57
KAUZ

LAUREL WAS deep in the second stage of rest when I found her mind and wandered its paths a bit. My lips twisted with wry amusement at the vacuous space in her psyche. I delved deeper still, into the area where her experiences and being were woven in pulsating strands of color.

I looked up and sighed. "Ah, fuck."

Torn, forgotten memories. They clotted her mind, shorn off with jagged edges. The tangle was a disturbing but all too familiar scene. Instead of being forced to forget countless small moments, like Lark had, Laurel suffered from the removal of a few large memories.

I reached for one and pushed past the pain that gripped my head. I needed to make sense of what she'd lost. Cymora's voice invaded my mind, rising to a forceful pitch. *"...is just a farmhand! You will obey me, you impertinent twit. Forget about him and set your sights higher. On someone you deserve, as my daughter. A male, or a pack of them, to elevate our status."*

"Okay." The response was a watery whisper.

Flashes of a young merman flitted by my eyes. He was streaked with dirt and sweat and usually dressed in muck-stained overalls. But he smiled with open affection at Laurel, a fact now stained with an echo of her regret. A male she was forced to forget. *Jerrin.*

I released the lost memory and sat down beneath it, brushing a hand through my hair. The implications of what I'd already found in the fishling's mind were staggering.

We'd missed that Laurel was in the exact same situation as our mate had once suffered. She hadn't announced her compulsion as clearly as "yes, Stepmother." Her atrocious manners had made her the most annoying fae on the train ride home.

But she'd grown up under a female who had no qualms about trapping children in cruel vows. We'd never thought to check and see whether she was all right.

I held my forehead and thought back. When Cymora gave her a direct order, Laurel said...okay. I was pretty sure the response was always "okay."

Far too easy to overlook in the tapestry of family dynamics we'd had to decipher on that train. I doubted my brothers would care much that we'd overlooked the bratty beta's suffering. However, missing even one small aspect of a complicated situation could have dire consequences. I suspected her perspective would show me those costs firsthand.

I waited for her to settle into the third stage of rest to take a peek at her short-term memory.

Don't empathize with her too soon, I tried to tell myself. If the fishling had chosen to ally with Pack Ellisar and somehow assisted their disappearance, she would have to die just like her mother.

But I was already looking back, turning over the stones of the past. What else had we missed hidden underneath Laurel's immaturity?

Her mind relaxed, and the memories of her day went zinging by me. Those threads halted when I held out my hand and gathered everything her mind was processing toward storage. Certain ones buzzed, signaling trauma or strong negative emotions. I started there, plunging into her recollections.

I VIEWED the world through Laurel's eyes, a hitchhiker in her head for the duration of her memory.

"Hurry up," hissed a male alpha next to her. Laurel's thoughts supplied his name: Dalstin. The middle brother of Pack Ellisar, wearing a hooded cloak too heavy for Neslune's mild spring weather.

I'm going as fast as I can, Laurel replied without words.

She was singing to his mind? That's what it seemed like. She couldn't carry the wordless tune, which had a heavy physical weight in her lungs, and rush through the familiar halls of the palace at the same time.

Pain radiated from her chest as she maintained her haunting song. Her thoughts were hopelessly fragmented, nearly panicked as she tried to remember where to go in the deeper recesses of the palace.

"Shut up," another male snarled at Dalstin. I recognized his voice from Lark's worst memories. It was Ellisar himself. He also wore a cloak, though he didn't have his hood drawn, revealing a dryad illusion layered over his face.

You don't see us. You don't notice us, Laurel sang. Guards, servants, and other palace officials turned their heads away or simply continued about their day as if Laurel and her companions weren't there.

Oh stars. It couldn't be. But there was only one kind of magic Laurel could be wielding. The siren's song. In our darkest days of war, Unseelie had butchered countless mermaids to force this particular ability into extinction.

Yet here it was centuries later, wielded ponderously by a beta. As a fellow beta, I predicted what history would call her: some random nobody. Not an illustrious omega or a powerful alpha. *The fishling* sang with the willpower-altering magic her ancestors had bled and died for.

Her role in Pack Ellisar's disappearance slotted into place perfectly with this information. Laurel was dangerous. I should've withdrawn from her memory and destroyed the delicate inner workings of her psyche to disable the threat she represented. Yet something about the details around her made me hesitate.

Pain pulsed down her throat and pooled in her lungs until she could hardly draw breath. It only grew worse the more Unseelie she passed and ensnared in her song. Tears streaked her face as she led the two Ellisar brothers to the prison and descended one jarring step at a time.

A firm hand swatted Laurel's ass. She stiffened from the unwanted contact. "Guess you're worth something after all," Ellisar sneered.

She quivered, bracing for him to try something else. The guard on duty at the front of the prison had his gaze averted. He didn't see or notice them, just as her song instructed.

This clearly wasn't a willing partnership. Laurel thought in her usual whiny tone, *"Don't touch me! As soon as we do this, I never want to see you again."*

She pictured her old room in Osme Fen with longing. Back when she'd had some control of her surroundings and a clear path ahead of her. The Omega Masquerade and everything that'd happened afterward had ruined her life. And that, as she thought with the mental equivalent of stomping her foot, was *"so unfair."*

"Where do you think they're hiding him?" Dalstin whispered.

Her. My mother first, as we agreed, Laurel insisted in her song. She wove a request into the guard's mind, asking where Cymora and Floris were being held. He pointed at the first two interrogation rooms across the hall.

They went to the first room, and Laurel cautiously sang at the threshold while the two alphas ranged ahead of her.

"Just your mother in here. Close the door," Ellisar said.

She passed through the small viewing area, still singing, her chest heavier with dread.

"She doesn't know. What is she going to do when she learns about the song?"

It was one of the only secrets she had, something she was proud of. As soon as she'd figured out what kind of magic she'd manifested a few years ago, she'd used it in subtle ways to avoid the worst of Cymora's rages. She didn't want to be Lark, wrung dry of her essence because she had a useful magical talent.

It wasn't that she considered how fearsome Cymora would be with the siren's song at her command. She was simply protecting herself the only way she could.

As powerful as the siren's song was, Laurel didn't understand how it worked, only that it did. Usually. And if she sang for too long, there were unpleasant consequences.

She resigned herself and walked into the interrogation room to see what'd become of her once proud mother. The barkfolk brothers were cutting her bindings as she hacked with a nasty cough. Cymora had dropped a noticeable amount of weight. The prominence of her collar and cheek bones were stark. She was dirty and unkempt.

The older mermaid still lifted her chin and beheld her daughter and her magic for the first time. Laurel didn't flinch from the hollows that darkened her face or the state of her body, but she *did* recoil from her mother's glassy-eyed stare.

She thought about Cymora's original order to save her, made shortly after they'd arrived at the palace. They'd had their last visit before Cymora's torture had truly begun. Compelled by her mother's instructions to do whatever it took to get her out of that prison, Laurel had returned with the only allies she could scrounge up.

"Why couldn't they have just killed her?" Laurel thought.

"He was worth something after all. I thought he was full of salt about the power hidden in his seed," Cymora said in a husky slur as she took in her singing daughter. "But look at you. *Magnificent.*"

Cymora's legs trembled as she put her weight on them, making to stand. She collapsed back into the chair with another cough.

Laurel rubbed a chill from her arms and watched as Dalstin lifted her mother's body while shooting over a look of warning. They had an agreement, after all. She'd saved them from death at the train station in exchange for their assistance with rescuing Cymora. But they'd pushed it off until last night, when they'd sensed Floris's capture and overnight torture. Now the agreement was a simple exchange: they would save Cymora and Floris both.

The last barkfolk was in the next room over. Laurel went first, re-ensnaring the mind of the guard on duty, plus two more that happened to be walking by. The weight in her chest increased further from disabling the guards. Yet somehow, she'd excluded Cymora and the Ellisar brothers from the effect of her song.

Dalstin shouted a warning before they entered this interrogation room. There was someone else already there, twirling a tool between his fingers. *Click click snap. Click click snap.*

It was Rennyn. Laurel pictured him as the male who'd scoffed at her when she'd whined over being confined to a palace bedroom. She swallowed nervously. *"Oh. I don't want to do this."* But she had to enter the room first, so she did. Her heart nearly stopped when the dark elf king swung to face her, before his eyes glazed over from her song.

She nearly gagged. Putting him under thrall had taken far more effort than most of the other fae they'd met.

Interesting, I thought. My nerves rose to have this many enemies near one of my fathers while he was rendered helpless.

"Fuck! Floris, look what they've done to you. We're going to get you out of here," Ellisar exclaimed.

The undisguised barkfolk in the interrogation chair rolled his head listlessly. His lips moved, just enough to reveal two gaps where his fangs should be. Laurel tilted her finned ear. Floris was wheezing, "We have to leave. We have to go *now.*"

She looked at him with a curled lip, disgusted by the state he was in. It was as if he'd been torn into by a pack of wild animals. His bark was stripped away in several places, revealing spots of rent skin surrounded by dried blood and sap. *"Gross!"*

"It's not worth it," Floris lisped.

"Did this fucker torture you?" Dalstin interrupted, inclining his hood toward Rennyn.

"Y-yes. Yes, he did. He hurt me. They hurt me."

Even in the midst of a memory, my heart threatened to stop as everyone's attention shifted to the motionless king. The barkfolk had armed themselves with daggers, and Ellisar shifted his hold into an underhand grip.

A bead of sweat drifted across Laurel's nose to join the tear tracks down her cheeks. *"I have to do something,"* she thought. She didn't really know Rennyn. But if she saved him, maybe he would save her.

Pack Ellisar fully intended to replace Lark with Laurel in a twisted echo of fate if they could not secure my pack's omega as their mate. And because she'd somehow granted them partial immunity to her song, she was vulnerable to being bitten into their pack.

Laurel hated these barkfolk just as much as we did, if not more. So, she stopped singing.

As the siren's song faded and the last notes hung in the air, she bent double and vomited up the liquid weight that'd settled in her lungs. Pack Ellisar scrambled and cursed her for being worthless, abandoning her as she threw up blood. It leaked from the seams of her gills too, drowning her in metal and tears.

I cringed but stayed with her, needing to know whether my father escaped this situation.

When she straightened, it was to come face-to-face with the dark elf king. The misty befuddlement had faded from his gaze. He tilted his head, regarding her with a blank expression. Not his usual cheerful act, the smile of Unseelie mischief, nor even the air of calculation he tried so hard to mask.

"That looked unpleasant," he remarked.

"Sorry," she croaked. Her stomach lurched, and she swallowed bile, trying not to puke on his fine leather boots a second time. That'd been a taxing song to carry.

"Why am I apologizing? He's going to kill us all. Starting with me!" Laurel knew the Ellisar brothers had to be huddling just beyond this room with Cymora. Without her siren's song, they couldn't leave the interrogation room without alerting a guard.

More tears blurred her vision before they fell. She wasn't planning on dying to spite Pack Ellisar. Not today. It was better to be a coward and survive to see another day.

Rennyn looked through her as she drew breath, and his face tightened with understanding. That red gaze pierced straight through to the truth of who she was and what was happening. She felt like a butterfly pinned to a board. Something within her, a kernel of self-preservation, warbled a warning.

She began to sing, and pain razored through her lungs anew. Before the first notes could confuse his mind, he covered one of his ears. *You didn't see me. You won't remember me,* she sang in his mind to the haunting melody of the siren's song.

His attention remained unaltered. It wasn't working! She'd messed up, just like she always did when put under pressure. She never did anything right.

A cruel smile curved his lips. "Hard to forget a li'l singing fishling." He raised his other hand, twirling the tool he'd been holding and pointing its sharp edge at her. "Cut that out and tell me where Floris went."

She edged away from him. *Wait. Wait!* Her song hit a louder note, drawing a wince from the dark elf king. *I declare that you owe me a life debt!*

Rennyn stilled as an ancient force responded to her words. The terrible pressure of governing power arrived in an instant, settling between them with oppressive force. Life debts were like grievances, granted through the magic that'd first woven the fae races into being.

The weight of a magical debt came to balance on his shoulders. Laurel trembled from the brush of sheer power even as it vanished just as swiftly as it'd arrived and rendered its judgment.

Rennyn straightened and bared his fangs with a fierce growl. She hopped backward with a squeak of fright, breaking the flow of her second song.

"The nerve of you, girl," he snapped. He gestured sharply toward the door, pivoting toward it. "Keep your life, for now. You'll rue the day you made an enemy of the Clever King."

As an outside observer, I knew his anger was a show. I'd seen him truly furious often enough to know what that looked like. It didn't resemble the calculating expression he wore the split second before Laurel whipped around and fled.

Besides, he'd just delivered his warning to Cymora and the barkfolk waiting just beyond the enclosed interrogation room. Despite sending her away, he hadn't declared his debt to her repaid.

I only lingered with her long enough to confirm that she escaped without doing any further harm. Rennyn was fine—and undoubtedly three steps into a new plan to recapture the lot of them.

When I emerged from the recollection, she was already well on her way to dreaming. The quiet of my own mind enveloped me. After experiencing Laurel's jittering nerves firsthand, it was a relief to have a sense of stability back.

I didn't need to dig into any more of her memories. Not after everything I'd just learned about her.

Her mind shaded toward dark unconsciousness. It made finding the dreaming manifestation of her body harder, since dreams always centered their dreamer in a way I intuitively understood.

I found Laurel in a corner of sorts. She waited for morning with her chin resting on the knee joint of her mermaid tail, fully unfurled in its glory of silvery teal fish scales. She'd fallen asleep unhappy, and the feeling clung to her now, lingering overhead in a cloud of melancholy.

"Laurel," I whispered, rousing her gently to the fact I was here with her.

She blinked slowly before her gaze turned toward me. "Hi, Kauz," she said, still waking up enough to talk to me. Fear marked her face with pale strain after a few more moments. "Wait, it's really you, isn't it?"

"It is," I said mildly.

She retreated further into a tight ball. "What do you want?" she asked in a sullen mutter.

"Are you sleeping in a safe place?"

Sniffling, she nodded.

"Has Pack Ellisar...touched you?"

She pressed her lips together. "Not yet. They won't bite me into their pack until..." She gave a watery little laugh. "Floris's designation is already changing. You guys defanged him for Lark, but it saved me."

Good, I thought. Alpha fangs weren't just for show. He'd change into a shade of himself, reduced to the equivalent of a beta with a severely damaged pack bond. He couldn't harm Lark *or* Laurel with his bite anymore.

"Thank you for saving King Rennyn. He's one of my fathers."

She nodded, dropping her gaze.

"I'm sorry," I added. Her attention bounced back up, and her mouth rounded in surprise. "If I'd paid more attention, I would've noticed you're under Cymora's compulsions too."

"How...?"

"I know you can't talk about it. Don't worry. I have experience with cruel vows now."

"You're talking about Lark."

"Aye."

Laurel stewed in a moment of guilt before asking, "Is she doing okay?"

"Better than ever."

She offered a fleeting smile. "I'm glad she has you all."

"You could have our help as well," I offered. She was a female in need of a change of fortune. Just like Lark had been.

I held out my hand, which she shrank away from. "What do you mean? Your pack hates me," she mumbled.

"Nay." I kept my hand extended. "It seems we've never truly gotten to know you. I may not be able to offer you friendship, Laurel. But I'd like to be your ally. You need help, and I need someone who can assist us in ending Pack Ellisar's threat for good. What do you say?"

Several emotions played out over her expression. Hope warred with fear and doubt as she had to wonder if I was being genuine. I was. Lark would do the same thing if she was the one standing here. She didn't hate her stepsister, either, despite being pitted against her for most of their lives.

Laurel unfolded herself from the lonely corner of her mind. She reached out and gripped my hand as if it were a lifeline.

58
LARK

I woke before Tormund and Kauz with a wistful sigh. Fal had *just* been about to kiss me when our dream fell apart. I closed my eyes, picturing him as he'd appeared. His artfully disheveled clothes, the tousle of his blue-black hair, and a hint of heat warming the gray tones of his cheeks.

His feline stare, gleaming and hungry. He'd been close to Marius for a few days. He must've caught the rut too, since he'd looked at me with the same burning lust I'd last seen on my feral mate's face.

I let the melodies he'd given me play through my head. It was a gift to have lyrics I could carry again. It'd been many years since Cymora forced me to stop singing. I wasn't allowed to outshine Laurel, who had a gifted voice in her own right.

I wondered what Kauz was finding in her mind. His face was peaceful at rest.

Tormund stirred first, so I flipped over to snuggle into him. We whispered together as we shook off the last vestiges of sleep. He was a little surprised to hear that I wanted to sing to the metalarks today. He'd been the one to point out that my namesake birds would come out in the morning, probably while I was still in bed. I had a new goal to collect a few of their star-flecked feathers.

"You know, they probably sell the feathers around here somewhere, li'l bird," Tormund suggested.

"We can look if—"

Kauz woke with a gasp and jerked to a sitting position. His widened starry gaze turned our way. "Oh, good, you're both awake. We need to go home right away," he said.

WE ORDERED a quick breakfast to be brought to our inn room, and as we ate, Kauz told us about the memory he'd witnessed in Laurel's mind. Something that'd happened yesterday but still chilled me to the bone for multiple reasons.

Pack Ellisar had their talons in my stepsister.

She was being compelled by Cymora.

My former stepmother was free once more.

Rennyn had been in serious danger.

And Laurel saved him? I had Kauz repeat that part of his story, blinking slowly in disbelief. She was selfish at best. And sure, saving him had saved her. But the Laurel I knew was the type to step aside for another—me, usually—to take the fall for her actions. That she'd acted decisively for another fae and put herself at risk to do so... Wow.

That didn't even break the surface of the huge revelation that she could sing the siren's song. She'd been wise to keep that detail a secret from Cymora, but stars, now my former stepmother knew about it anyway.

I walked with my mates to the train station in silence, lost in thought. I struggled to understand this version of Laurel Kauz claimed to have seen. It wasn't that I thought he was lying...

No, this is so petty. I just couldn't help but think of all the good my stepsister could've done with the siren's song back in Osme Fen. Couldn't she have sung a kinder Cymora into existence? Couldn't she have sung away Pack Ellisar when they first came sniffing around?

We could've teamed up to make life better, but neither of us had tried to do so.

I must've been too perfect a scapegoat for her to confide in. Just as she'd been the ideal daughter in Cymora's eyes and thus someone I'd never considered trusting.

The next train to the Dreamlands Nexus would be arriving in a little under an hour. I went to sit in the grass by the station to think some more. Kauz and Tormund stood nearby but gave me space to digest what'd happened.

A mournful whine left my throat. Laurel's letters must've been a cry for help. At the time, I'd thought the letters were a clear message of *Help Cymora because I've been locked in a room.*

Now I had to wonder if they weren't really *Come talk to me because I need help.*

Stars, would things be different if I'd gone to visit her? I'd even noticed the letters seemed unusual. If she'd been compelled, that would explain why she'd written Cymora's name in each. It was a shame that'd been all I'd seen, a plea for the female I despised the most.

Well, things were going to change. *I* had changed. I knew what it was like to be silenced and manipulated like a puppet with invisible strings. Even if it was Laurel...

No. No matter who she was, I wouldn't leave her to take the fate originally meant for me. If Laurel was meant for a pack, fate would bring her one. There were plenty of betas who ended up as matches for alphas and omegas and were bitten into packs as loving mates.

I'd help her. And then she could leave to go find her own way in the world. It was only right. The matter of the siren's song, though...that was dicey. But we had more pressing problems to consider first, namely that said song was currently under Cymora's control.

I held my breath as a tiny, winged shape swooped down and started pecking at the ground nearby. I released a sigh of quiet awe. It was a metalark at last. The feathers coating its back and wings were the darkest of indigos, perfect for blending into the night sky, and its belly was soft with white down. It whistled birdsong, and a few more of the birds popped out of the undergrowth.

As they hopped around, their feathers glittered with stardust. They were truly dreamlands' creatures, just like me. I cleared my throat and scattered them when I started singing a shy rendition of "Hello, Starlight" to an audience of the little birds. They came back when they realized I wasn't going to try to grab for them.

They left a few sparkling feathers behind that I took to admire on the train ride home.

WE ARRIVED in Neslune's train station by midday. Kauz strode over to talk to a beta dreamlander standing toward the back of a crowd of waiting fae. She had bat wings and skin so dark purple it was nearly black in the shade. When she bowed deeply to Kauz and bared her throat in apology, I figured this had to be his spy friend.

"...not so bad a punishment," she was saying as I drifted over to join their conversation. She bowed her head briefly toward me with a low murmur of "Princess."

"You've done your job well. Thank you for helping me at such short notice. The mistake was not your fault, either," he said.

Her lips twitched. "Joyous news. In the meantime, the Clever King wished to be made aware of your arrival. You're a day earlier than expected, so it may take some time for him to send a carriage."

"We'll wait."

As soon as she flew off, Kauz glanced at me with an odd twist to his mouth. "What?" I asked.

"He's sending a carriage." He said it as if I should know what that meant.

Tormund came to my rescue, whispering behind his hand, "That means he's coming in person to talk to us."

We settled on a bench right outside the train station, and I fidgeted with my fingertips. What did Rennyn want to tell us directly?

Kauz threaded his fingers through mine, and Tormund caught my other hand. Together, they tugged my sharp nails away from my cuticles before I could hurt myself fretting. With Kauz rubbing my arm and Tormund purring to provide comfort, I let myself relax while we waited. Before long, a team of beautiful dappled horses pulled a carriage to a stop right in front of us.

I supposed the carriage was pretty, too. It was well varnished, the ebony wood gleaming in the sunlight without being too flashy. The door opened, and out popped Eletha. "Hi!" she exclaimed.

I blinked in surprise, not expecting the librarian nixie out in the light of day. Which was silly. She had other things to do besides work and write her manuscript. "Hi, Eletha," I said.

Kauz reached out and ruffled his sister's hair, ruining her ponytail. "Hey," she giggled, ducking back into the carriage. The rest of us followed her in.

The interior was sizable, designed for three, maybe four fae to sit side by side on the plush benches. Rennyn was already seated in a corner on the right side. I inspected him for a moment, relieved to see that he was fine with my own two eyes.

"Larkie," he said cheerfully. "How nice to see you again. Sit right there."

He indicated the corner of the bench across from him, pointing with the edge of his lucky coin. Eletha settled next to me, the two of us sharing a companionable lean. Kauz took her other side, wrapping a wing around both of us, and Tormund occupied much of the free space next to the dark elf king. Rennyn tapped the ceiling, and off the carriage went with a jolt.

"We have a lot to talk about. Don't mind 'Letha being here. I stole her away from the library tower, given how nice a day it is. We were just catching up."

"We have some things to share with you, too, Father," Kauz said.

Rennyn sighed dramatically. "Probably more bad news. You might as well go first."

Kauz wasted no time delving into what he'd learned from Laurel last night, both from her memories and the damage to her mind. Eletha made a soft mewl of concern while he mentioned how her memories resembled mine before my *olcanus* removal.

When Kauz revealed the mermaid had accepted his invitation to ally with us, Rennyn inclined his head. "Well done. Glad someone in the family is still thinking strategically. The house moths are still scrubbing my favorite pair of boots clean, by the way. Truly wretched stuff."

"Can we trust her, though?" Eletha murmured.

"Of course not," Rennyn answered, then raised his index finger. "However, she now represents both the greatest strength and weakness of our enemies. I'm confident we can turn this to our advantage."

"We're going to get her away from Pack Ellisar, right?" I asked nervously.

"I owe her a life debt, so aye. She may not enjoy the fate I have in mind for her, but it involves her being safe and alive." He waved dismissively. "I didn't go out of my way today to talk to you all about Laurel. You're early. I expected you to return tomorrow."

"We were worried about you!" Tormund exclaimed.

Rennyn walked his lucky coin between his fingers as he smacked his lips. "Aw. If this isn't just a carriage full of sweethearts. I'm already on it. I just need a bit more time to work some things out. *Soooo*, Tor-Tor, your date with Lark is next, right?"

Tormund nodded, beaming.

"You two are leaving as soon as possible. Once we arrive, you'll make the arrangements. Larkie, I want a quick conversation with you. You're staying out of the palace, so I'll have your handmaidens come to you."

"I'm staying out of the palace?" I echoed.

He nodded without explaining further and continued giving instructions to the others until the carriage came to a stop. My mates left first, while Eletha and I hugged in farewell.

"Thanks, 'Letha. See you tonight," Rennyn said, reaching out to clasp hands with her before they hugged too. She left, shutting the door behind her to seal me in with the dark elf king.

"What did you just give her?" I asked.

He smiled with Unseelie mischief and swung his legs up to recline across his bench. "You may as well get comfortable for this. We have more pressing matters to discuss. Did you ever read the breeding contract you signed?"

I flushed hot and cold at the sudden change of topic. "I didn't have much of a chance to," I said in an embarrassed mumble.

"I know this is a sensitive topic, but no shame, all right?" He kept talking before I could answer. "Before Pack Ellisar took the original with them on their trip here, our spy transcribed a copy of it. I've poured over it. So have Nemensia and Elion, who have far more experience adjudicating fae law."

No shame, he says, before revealing all this. I hunched in on myself. "I signed it only because I was forced to."

"We are all *very* aware. The contract itself is illegal in Serian, as you've likely been informed." He fiddled with his coin, keeping it moving and his fingers occupied. "And because it excludes a certain clause, it turns out it's illegal in Thelis too. There is nothing written into the contract for an omega who finds her scent matches to be released from the agreement. We looked for it first."

"But it's just a piece of paper." I echoed the unconcerned way my mates talked about the contract. "Right?"

Rennyn released a sound between a growl and a sigh, full of frustration. "I wish that was the case. Do you know how grievances work?"

My mouth became drier than dust. I croaked out a small "No." After my foolish vow to Cymora, I'd done my best to dodge making any large vows.

"Brace yourself for this... *No one does.* It's old magic. Probably the same magic that prevents us from outright lying to one another. The contract has a clause that states that your new pack lead will pay a grievance to Ellisar, as the wronged party, if you are mated into a different pack.

"Now, the contract sits in a gray area of validity. You were compelled by a vow, and the contract itself is not enforceable in any kingdom. But you *signed* it, in effect giving your word as a fae. We've studied it top to bottom to see whether you joining Pack Sorles would activate the grievance clause despite all the layers of illegal we're dealing with. And the only answer we've come to agree on is that we cannot risk it."

I bit my lip, trying to stifle the sudden sob that tore from my lungs. I was so close to mating into Pack Sorles. My heat was a breath away. But the stupid contract and vile Pack Ellisar were going to get in the way at the very last moment. I didn't want to fulfill the contract. I'd rather never have a heat at all.

Rennyn cursed under his breath and sat up. "Stars, don't *cry*. I was just about to tell you the solution," he protested. He ran his hand between his horns, glancing around like someone else would materialize and comfort me as I tried and failed not to shed tears.

"Aw, c'mere. It's okay." He slid onto the seat next to me and looped an arm over my shoulders, hugging me to his side. "I'm called the Clever King for good reason, and it's not because I let my family get fumbled up in stupid contracts. I have a plan." Pausing for a few moments, he purred, and the soothing vibration emanating from his chest worked wonders to take me down from the despair that'd seized me. "I'm going to make sure all three barkfolk are fed into the nearest bonfire regardless of *anything*. Okay?"

"Okay, Dad," I sniffed, wiping my face clean. I caught a hint of his scent, something warm and floral. It reminded me of Fal and my omega instincts of the short, blissful time I'd visited Serian's palace and found family here as a young girl. Relaxing into his hug, I self-soothed with a small purr of my own.

"Listen to me. You're not mating into Pack Ellisar, and Fal is not going to owe them a grievance. Before your heat arrives, Ellisar, Dalstin, and Floris must all either be dead or otherwise unable to claim you to render the contract null and void. I suspect they came to Serian fully intending to hide until you'd been claimed. That way, they'd receive their grievance as a gambit to make themselves rich and powerful off the crown's back. They didn't expect to bumble into Laurel and thus Cymora." He rolled his eyes hard. "And I didn't expect two of my four sons to be so deep into rut that... Well, let's say they've made my job much harder lately."

My eyes widened in alarm. "Marius is still in rut?"

"*That's* the first thing you ask?"

"It's been over a week!"

"He is..." He whistled and passed his free hand over his face. "Gone. Don't worry about him. He'll get better. But right now, he's a dangerous variable for my very amazing but not foolproof plan."

"So, you're going to kill Pack Ellisar before I go into heat," I said slowly, letting it sink in for myself. "And thus, no contract."

He tilted his head with a hum. "With about fifteen more steps in between now and then, aye. Well, and also nay. I'm not going to do any killing. That's where my brother and his love affair with gigantic weaponry comes in." He grinned cheekily. "Your part in the plan is simple, but it's a big ask. You need one last heat suppressant tattoo. Thalas will touch up the one you have."

I mewled in quiet denial. I'd been *so* close to not needing to suppress my heat. Even if it was the best course of action...yes, it was a sacrifice.

"You will *not* go into the palace, as previously stated. Marius and Fal are temporarily confined to your quarters to keep you kids separated. If you cross paths, they will have...a strong reaction to your scent. They can't help it," he remarked with an annoyed edge to his tone. "You and Tormund both have to leave on your next adventure as soon as possible. I very much don't want to see sweet Tor-Tor in rut. You kids all grow up way too fast."

I giggled. "Sorry."

"Aye, do apologize. Omegas start going into heat frightfully early. You shouldn't even know what sex is until you're in your thirties, let alone be discussing breeding. As a male I know would say, *ach,*" he grumped with extra disgust. He gave my shoulders one last squeeze before he made for the carriage's exit. "Now, if you'll excuse me, I'd better go burn this shirt before those rut-addled lads smell it. Bye, Larkie."

It concerned me a bit that I couldn't tell whether he was joking. "Bye, Dad."

I followed him out after a minute, as the inside of the carriage had gotten awfully stuffy. We were behind the palace and close to a stables area, which was busy with palace workers and messengers coming and going. Nearby, a trampled circle of dirt hosted a few guards engaged in a practice bout while several more alphas watched.

The carriage pulled away, revealing Rennyn waving to the crowd of alphas and cupping his hand over his mouth, pointing back at me. The largest male glanced over, then nodded at the dark elf king. It was Theodred, and he started to stride my way.

"Princess, you're back!"

Lon swooped out of the sky, distinguishable by the brown leaf patterns on the inside of her moth wings. I brightened immediately. "Lon!"

Her oversized red eyes swerved left and right before she fluttered over, arms out for a hug. I hugged her gladly, purring since she was as soft and warm as she looked with all that dark fur. She settled her feet on the ground with one last flutter and let me go.

"I missed you," she giggled. "My sister does too! She's packing you a bag right now. I'm here early because Prince Marius wanted me to give you this."

She patted her dress and reached into a pocket to produce a letter. I unfolded it for a quick skim. Most of it was in Marius's slanted, left-handed writing, but it seemed Fal had intercepted it before it'd been placed in an envelope. He used blue ink overtop the black ink already there. He'd drawn arrows to put his two slivers in beside Marius's words and added a few paragraphs to the bottom.

I grinned as I read, enjoying the interplay of their wits. Marius was mostly reporting what I already knew—that they couldn't see me right now and that the royal pack was making decisions, as he and Fal were rut-addled. Fal drew a tiny, annoyed face with elf ears and added in massive quotation marks around "rut-addled."

They also shared that they'd been the ones to capture and defang Floris before his escape. I read that part again, brow furrowing. They'd defanged him for me? I was sure Kauz had mentioned one of the Ellisar brothers losing his fangs, but it'd gotten lost in the avalanche of information about my stepsister.

As I understood it, defanging an alpha was much worse than a simple dental procedure. Alpha fangs were the one pair of teeth that wouldn't dull, chip, or fall out under normal circumstances. Even alphas with terrible gums would lose every other tooth but their fangs.

It was part of their identity, connected to the soul in some small way. Alphas claimed their omegas with their fangs and left their scent in other bites. Without them, their bodies degraded, losing physical size and strength, as did the bonds they'd created. They transformed into the equivalent of a broken beta. Healthy betas could still have bonds, but not defanged alphas.

No matter what, Floris could never claim me. Hope kindled warm and bright in my chest. It was a savage gift, but my mates had done this for me.

I pulled the metalark feathers out of my pocket. I'd placed them carefully in an envelope to keep them pristine. "Will you give this to Marius for me, Lon?"

She took the envelope with a perky smile. "Right away, Princess," she said before fluttering off.

Instead of reading the rest of the letter, I folded it and put it away. Theodred was waiting, his fiery eyes watchful on our surroundings. "Hi, Dad," I said.

"Li'l bird." He nodded in acknowledgment. "Come with me." He lumbered into motion, heading away from the guards and stables. I had to hurry to keep pace with his long stride.

"Thank you for talking with Tormund. He's calmed down," I said.

He cracked a slight smile. "That boy. I'm still not sure how he came from me."

"But you love him anyway." I beamed up at the gigantic redcap.

"*Ach.*" Somehow, he made it sound like agreement. "I felt it was the right time to remind you that you're safe here." He extended a massive hand and covered my shoulder. "I look forward to adding three more marks to myself."

I glanced up at his arm and the spirals of blood-red knots around the limb. Each was the size of a full moon coin. "Is that what your tattoos represent?"

"Aye."

"That's a lot of lives," I squeaked out. He had to be covered in *hundreds* of them.

"Some redcaps would say I'm cheating, to carry the marks of my role as Serian's executioner. I wear them with pride because I know I've spared my son from the task. Though sometimes I wish his skin wasn't *quite* so empty.

"It is like tending to a garden." He gestured to our surroundings. Servants worked in the flowerbeds around us and coaxed growth from the soil. "We give little value to the weeds that choke life from the flowers. They must be removed for the good of all."

"That's right," I agreed quietly.

He patted me ever so gently atop my head. "That is my duty, daughter. I will keep you safe too."

Safe. A feeling I'd sought out and only recently found with my mates and godfamily. It was something so fragile at times, but worth defending by the strongest of us. "Thanks, Dad." I smiled up at him, my tone full of gratitude.

The flames in his eyes brightened. If I didn't know better, it seemed I'd just made his afternoon. "I must return to my duties now. Have a lovely day." He waved in farewell and left just as abruptly as another male I knew.

He'd guided me to a spot a few paces away from a garden gazebo, where Thalas, Nemensia, and Elion were gathered. The queen gestured enthusiastically for me to join them.

59
LARK

THE GAZEBO HAD a central table with eight sides, each with a small bench. I circled around it for hugs. Elion intercepted me first with a warm purr. After the round of hellos, I settled on the bench between Thalas and Nemensia.

"Would you like some tea, Lark?" Elion invited. His voice radiated comforting approval, underlain by his alpha authority.

"Yes, please."

I was unsure of the etiquette of taking tea with royalty. The tea set was closest to him, and he started pouring and stirring before I could move, generously dishing out spoonfuls of sugar as he spoke. "I'll prepare your cup as my mate prefers it, and we can adjust from there."

"That's a good idea," Thalas commented. He had an ink kit set next to him and regret tightening his lips when he glanced at me. "You look like you've already endured a full day's trials. I take it you've spoken with Rennyn?"

I nodded and held my arm out to the dream warden king, resigned for the suppressant tattoo. He slid closer and peered at the remnants of his handiwork, clucking his tongue.

Elion stood and placed a cup of tea before me. His yellow gaze narrowed on the spot where I'd once had intricately looping ink. "Rennyn isn't the expert in clever plans, despite the title he chose for himself." The buzz of alpha authority in his voice turned chilly with disapproval. "Surely there's some other way."

"I'll be okay. I've suppressed my heat for this long," I ventured.

Elion shook his head. "There will be consequences from manipulating your body for so long, *mo stóirín*. I'm not comfortable asking you to further the damage."

"One more suppressant shouldn't affect her too much," Thalas said. "It'll buy us time. There's value in that."

"Now is not the moment to argue about the way forward," Nemensia put in.

He released a short, refined kelpie snort. "How do you like the tea?"

I took a testing sip while Elion waited, and I perked up the moment it hit my tongue. It was more warm milk and honey than tea, with a pleasant aftertaste of spices. "Delicious!" No wonder, with how much sugar I'd seen him add to the cup.

He nodded, eyeing me with poorly concealed concern, and went to take his seat again. "Lark needs to be with our son, my heart. It's not healthy for a newly bonded couple to be apart for this long."

Nemensia and Elion gazed into one another's eyes, their expressions changing as they switched to having a silent argument over their bond.

Thalas prepared his brushes and told me in an undertone, "Suppressing your heat was a three-to-two vote amongst the royal pack. Elion believes the grievance clause Rennyn is worried about will be rendered null just by the fact that you and Marius have completed a kelpie bond. Rennyn argued he was being emotional about an unpredictable and illogical force of magic."

"Who voted with Elion?" I whispered back.

Thalas smiled and gestured to his chest. "Pack Ellisar would need to show their faces to claim a grievance if the old magic sides with them. I don't believe they possess the stones to do so; plus, Fal could make himself impossible to find. However, Elion and I were outvoted, so this is all hot air." He pointed between the queen and her lord, who were still locked in their private moment.

"I don't mean to sound ungrateful, but shouldn't I have a say in this matter? It's my heat we're talking about."

"I don't disagree," he said in a placating tone. "However, the situation has a chance of threatening the line of succession. We have to act in the best interests of the crown. Besides, anything that threatens *you* gains the immediate ire of my mate."

Nemensia turned our way. "That's right. We owe you a fresh start, Metalark, which means these males will not be skulking around with a grievance in hand. Or even without one. They pose a threat that requires elimination. There will be *no skulking*."

"As the queen demands. No skulking permitted," Elion said with grandeur. His ears were angled back in displeasure, though when Nemensia glanced his way, he regarded her with affection.

"I'm sorry about the suppressant, Metalark. Right now, it's the only way forward. You will take it and let us plan, right?" She clasped her hands and fixed me with an earnest smile.

I couldn't say no to that face. "Yes, Mom."

Thalas got to work repairing the suppressant tattoo. I privately mourned losing the feeling of impending heat as my core chilled incrementally with each swipe of ink. Disappointment replaced kindling heat, and I sighed. I thought I was past this.

The dream warden king was still working when Lon returned with a curtsy for the royalty and a box of tools in hand. "Princess, Prince Marius requests a lock of your hair."

Elion chuckled. "You'd best take two, just in case. I remember when I tried to get my braids right for the first time."

"You kept asking for more of my hair. I thought you'd leave me bald!" Nemensia laughed.

"It's harder than it looks, my heart, and I was too proud to ask for help."

I leaned into the house moth and whispered, "Did he like the feathers?"

"Yes, Princess," she giggled. "Prince Kauzden is going to help him keep them nice with magic." She brushed my hair while humming a cheery tune. With a zing of excitement, I recognized it and hummed it with her.

"Dad, um…" I glanced between the two kings.

"When there's two of us, just refer to us by name. It's easier," Thalas said.

"Elion, what's the significance of the things you have braided in your hair?"

After learning about Theodred's tattoos, I figured it was time I asked why the kings styled themselves the way they did. Rennyn, with all his tricks and misdirections, was an ongoing enigma, but my other bonus dads were more straightforward in their choices.

Elion beamed and lifted the first of his three braids. "Ah. Well, there's the classic, a lock of Nemensia's hair braided into mine. The next one is a selection of her rings."

The queen sighed fondly. He rested his hand over hers as they exchanged a tender look.

"My heart has many differently sized rings that she wears throughout her pregnancies," he continued. "And our quarters had a ring explosion when she was carrying Tormund."

"My fingers swelled so much during that pregnancy," Nemensia bemoaned. "Also, he's holding my favorite ring captive in the middle of that braid!"

"It won't fit on your finger right now." He seemed to rethink this statement when she crinkled her brow in the beginnings of a scowl. "I've been meaning to get it resized for you."

She lifted her nose. "Hmph."

"And finally, Lark, the third braid is symbols. If your handmaiden wasn't taking a lock of your hair, I'd have you come look." He lifted it. A set of silver charms was woven into his hair, each the size of my thumbnail or so. "One for each child, from Fal's guiding star at the top to a ray of sunshine at the bottom for my li'l Happy Fins. Though it upset my mate for a time, I never removed the p'nixie wings." He felt his braid with his other hand and flicked the third charm from the bottom, just above Tormund and Ambriel's.

My lips started to get wobbly. I hadn't even realized he'd included me so casually with his pack-born children.

"Now I'm glad he didn't," Nemensia added, giving me a gentle smile.

"Okay, all done," Lon put in cheerfully.

"I'm done as well," Thalas said. "It should hold for two days or so. And that's without doing anything to damage it."

My eyes widened. Only two days? And that was with no sex? My heat was coming with a vengeance no matter what, it seemed.

"We're running out of time." Elion took a long sip of his tea and shrugged. "Fewer hours for our children to suffer as my li'l brother makes his overcomplicated plots. Let's see who's right in the end."

Jani came to the gazebo about thirty minutes later with a backpack for me. "For your rugged outdoor adventure, Princess," she'd announced in a joyful squeak. I hugged her too, happy to see the perpetually sunny house moth.

Tormund was not far behind my handmaiden. He seemed subdued as he said hello to the three royals.

"Please limit your time to two nights. She needs to return before her suppressant breaks," Elion said.

"Okay, Dad," Tormund answered, flashing a brief smile his way and resting a hand on my shoulder. "I'm taking my mate away now."

I said my goodbyes and glanced anxiously at my gentle giant as we walked back the way I'd come with his father earlier. He seemed to be heading straight for the stables. "Is something wrong?" I asked with a hint of a whine.

He blew a curl of smoke from the side of his mouth. "Our date is getting rushed. I'm just disappointed, li'l bird. I know I crashed your date with Kauz, and that wasn't fair to him, but I wanted you to spend some time here with...you'll see." He gestured to a paddock beyond the stables and angled toward it. "It's a surprise."

Poor Tormund. He'd seemed so excited about what he'd planned for our date time earlier. We also needed to go out on another date when everything settled. "Oh, I love surprises!"

He stopped at the fence to pick up a bucket full of pieces of fruit and carrots. He clicked his tongue until a huge, shaggy-furred mare trotted over with an eager toss of her head. "This is my girl, Rory. I already have the stable hands socializing her with the new arrival," he said while feeding her a chunk of apple.

My fingertips tingled as I leaned past Rory to catch sight of this new arrival. There were a couple other horses in the paddock right now. One was of the same breed as Rory, while the other...

Oh stars, she was gorgeous. She was visibly a few hands shorter than her companions, built with finer bones due to her unicorn heritage. I forgot how to breathe when I noticed the short silver horn poking from her forehead, no more than four inches long.

Full-blooded unicorns were small and frail creatures. They had horns the length of swords and would only allow beautiful virgins to ride them. As a kid, I'd dreamed of riding one, but as an adult, I was probably too big. And now I wasn't a virgin either.

A half-unicorn, as this mare had to be, was an excellent middle ground. She had a coat as pure a white as fresh snow and hooves that sparkled with silver glitter. Her mane and tail were lavender and looked silky soft.

I turned a gleeful look toward my mate, who was grinning broadly, and latched onto his arm. "*Tormund!*"

"I told you I was going to buy you a half-unicorn horse," he said.

"That's the most beautiful horse I've *ever* seen! What do you mean? You really bought her for me?"

"I did! I got her here as fast as I could. Her former owners couldn't maintain her upkeep, and...oh, hello." He was momentarily distracted as the second shaggy mare approached us. Rory wandered off, content with the treats she'd received.

He passed me the bucket, and I happily fed her. "This girl belongs to Kauz. He's going to be shadowing us."

"Really?" I glanced around, but there was no sign of my beloved kinky bat. I supposed "shadowing" didn't include him riding with us like a chaperone.

"It's only fair, and he'll help keep you safe," Tormund continued. "And I'm sorry, but you'll be riding with me. Dad wants me to get you out of here right now, but there's no rushing the adjustment process for an animal. Your new horse needs to get used to you first."

"Aw." I knew he was right. My last horse was Meya, and she'd already been used to me since she'd been my father's mare first. "Well, I'd still love to feed her a treat and say hi before we leave. Where are we going on our rugged outdoor adventure, by the way?"

He winked. "You just told me you love surprises."

I tingled with excitement and held up a carrot. I tried wiggling it at the half-unicorn from a distance. To my surprise, she crossed the paddock and came right up to me. Each fall of her hoof sent up silver sparkles of magic.

She munched through the carrot and waited patiently for more. "You are such a pretty girl," I cooed, offering her the last dregs in the bucket. Once she'd eaten it all, she remained by the fence. Those soulful, liquid dark eyes inspected me.

She didn't seem like a new, skittish horse, unsure of her spot in the herd. When I reached for her, she remained in place, flaring her nostrils to take in my scent.

"I wouldn't—" Tormund stopped with a gasp as the half-unicorn eased a little closer and pressed her muzzle into my palm. I stroked her velvety face.

"How old is she?" I whispered.

"Five years."

An adult, then. She was experienced enough to know what she wanted. I wondered if unicorn blood gave her more intelligence too.

"Would you like to go on an adventure with us, pretty girl?" I asked. As if she'd understand.

She pawed at the ground and neighed, which I took as a yes. I turned my head to give Tormund a hopeful look, not realizing she was mirroring me and doing the same thing.

He scratched behind his horn. "We could see if she'll let us saddle her..."

The half-unicorn kept pace on the other side of the fence as we walked toward the stables. Once we were past the paddock, he told me in a low voice, "Her last owners said she was trouble with a capital *T*."

I huffed, offended on her behalf. "What did they mean by that?"

"Unicorn offspring are usually too smart for their own good. You should be fine, li'l bird. She seems to like you. But we're coming right back if she gives you any problems."

"Of course." My wings practically vibrated with excitement.

As we came back with the proper equipment, he said, "Her old owners called her Stella. You can rename her how you like."

She apparently heard him and whinnied in sharp protest.

"Stella it is," I remarked.

Stella posed prettily so her lavender mane and tail flowed in the wind. Oh, she *was* trouble—but in the good way.

Tormund was leery and led me through a proper introduction to Stella, as he probably would between any horse and its new rider. She remained relaxed and gave the occasional snort of approval until he admitted that she seemed ready to go with us. "But I'm watching you," he whispered to her while gesturing to his eyes.

Stella accepted a saddle and let me mount her without a single nicker of complaint. Her stride was a jaunty bounce as Tormund led us through a few exercises and double-checked my technique and riding knowledge. Once he was relatively sure she wasn't going to rebel, he gathered up Rory and led us into the forest.

I took in the trail lined on either side by tree branches full of tiny green buds. As we left the bustle of fae life behind us, the forest came alive with the singing of insects and the call of animals back and forth. I took a deep breath, savoring a lungful of fresh air marked by the barest bite of pollen. Serian didn't seem to burst straight into bloom with spring, but I still had the sense that the change of seasons was here around us.

"I remember someone mentioning racing," I said, looking way up at Tormund as we rode side by side down the trail. Rory's height, plus his, put him way above me.

"Once you train her! I'm not ready to lose yet. Neither is my girl." He patted Rory's neck affectionately.

Stella snorted loudly when he mentioned training. Stars, she understood that too?

"Okay, okay. We'll just win later," I giggled. My horse tossed her mane in apparent agreement.

Tormund scoffed. "I don't lose. I have the trophies to prove it."

I asked about the trophies, which launched him into a story. He and all his siblings started having annual tournaments they'd made up, with "suitably grand" trophies and plaques. It'd begun out of sheer boredom with the card game Liar Liar well before any of them had manifested their designations. It'd slowly grown to include every game that could be halfway competitive and every sibling, down to little Happy Fins.

"No wonder you all were so competitive about Liar Liar when we were traveling," I mused. "When is the next tournament?"

"The autumn festival! We all have time off during it. Just know I'm not going to take it easy on you because you're my mate."

"What? I don't..." I didn't expect that I'd be included in the tradition. "I was just going to watch."

"No need," he said cheerfully. "I'm inviting you right now."

"Okay, but that means you're teaching me every competitive game and at least *some* tricks."

He glanced at me with his version of Unseelie mischief, which was his big smile. "Is that a deal?" He offered one of his broad palms to shake, and I did without hesitation. "We'll start right away!"

I grinned back. "Looking forward to it." I just wanted to be closer to his enthusiasm.

We lapsed into a companionable silence for a brief time. I appreciated the beauty of the outdoors and the forest as we traveled further into the wilderness. In this quiet space between moments, Pack Ellisar crept back into my thoughts. With the innate talent of barkfolk to assimilate against trees, the trio could be anywhere in the woods, watching us and waiting to jump out of the bushes.

Don't be ridiculous. They wouldn't try anything. Not while I rode beside Tormund, who could set them aflame in one deadly breath. Still, I couldn't help but inspect any irregular shadows or twitch at unusual noises like it could be *them*.

"Hey, Tormund," I said, not wanting to dwell with my worries.

"Aye."

Though it seemed we were past his original feelings of disappointment, I felt this needed to be said. "I'm happy to be out here with you, even if we have to cut the date short this time. You know there's going to be so many more dates, right? Especially with how excited Stella is to be out with us."

His expression softened, and he nodded. "I'm sorry if I came across negatively. I'm glad I get to have time with you, no matter how long or short it is, or how rushed. What matters is that you're safe and you're..." He hiccupped and coughed up hot steam. "Mine," he added in a raspier tone.

My eyes widened. *Was that...?*

"And I get to share my home away from home with you and Stella," he added in his usual bright tone.

"That's right. Um, did you talk to Fal or Marius earlier?"

Tiny twin fires flickered behind his spectacles for a moment, then he rolled his eyes, which extinguished them. "Just Fal. He wanted to make sure I knew a few things. But he mostly wanted to exaggerate what he'd do if something happened to you."

"Did you—"

"You know I'd never let anything bad happen *ever*, right?" he continued overtop me with an air of alarm. "And not because Fal said, um, inappropriate things for me to repeat to you."

I started to smile despite myself. "Tormund, it's—"

"Not okay. Don't say it's okay to curse in front of you. You're a princess," he proclaimed.

"Tormund," I sighed.

"What?"

"Did you shield your pack bond?"

"Oh! Of course I did. We disagreed about your suppressant, and that was about it."

I eyed him, worried he was also upset since our time together would have to remain chaste. "I don't want to go into heat if it leads to a grievance. I'm sorry. The timing... My body won't let us delay much longer."

He beamed with his usual cheer. "No worries. We have plenty of other things to do. By the way, on the trail is the best time to talk. Do you want to practice your Serri?"

"That's a good idea." I was getting spoiled by the royal family all speaking Theli to me. It was about time I returned the favor.

There weren't any other quiet pauses between us. Tormund mostly filled the air, telling me stories. We spoke in Serri, which required some pauses for translation and correction, but I was engaged in what he had to say. He had no qualms about sharing embarrassing information about his siblings, and I tried not to bend over giggling too much. Stella tilted her ears back to listen.

We rode until sundown, arriving at a massive hunting lodge just as the shadowy shapes of flying house moths lit the essence lamps lining its eaves. "I'm here so often it's like my second home," Tormund said with a grand gesture of his arm. "The winter lodge."

"Why so often?" I asked curiously.

"It's mostly managing the hunters. Something always goes wrong with them, no matter the season. This is one of the hubs that serves the hunters that keep us city folk fed. I've got two permanent rooms here."

I admired it as we approached. The first level was built with decorative stonework, while the upper levels were wood paneled. A pair of stable hands came to take our mounts, and Tormund led me up the front steps.

An alpha mothkin bowed deeply by the door. He was a hulking male, his sheer size and prominent fangs seeming an exaggeration from the little house moths I knew. He still had a mothkin's oversized red eyes, and fuzzy antennae naturally curved backward over his head. The dark green tunic and pants he wore strained to hold his midnight-black fur. "Good evening, Prince Tormund. We have the kitchen and your quarters prepared for you," he said.

My mate thanked him and introduced us. This was Head Moth Wirr —his name was more of a mouth noise—the steward of the lodge. Wirr puffed with pride and bowed to me as well. "Welcome, Princess. We aim to deliver the best hospitality this side of Neslune."

I smiled back, sure I would see more of him and his staff's hospitality. The lodge was familiar in a way the palace couldn't match. Hunters, with their kills and trophies, had a particular earthy scent, and it lingered. I'd smelled it plenty in Osme Fen.

Two fae sat in the common area; a beta dark elf with an unstrung bow and a quiver resting at her feet, and a grimalkin alpha hunched over a bloody meal. The alpha glanced up, and his slitted cat eyes dilated in a telltale way. He released a chuff in our direction and went back to tearing into his undercooked food. *Feral.*

Tormund greeted them by name as we walked to the stairs, passing under the glassy stares from dozens of various impressive beasts. The mounted heads lined the second-story railing from the entranceway all the way to the crackling stone hearth at the back of the lodge.

Tormund took me up to the third floor. He slowed his stride as I climbed the stairs stiffly, feeling my hours on Stella's back. *Fucking stairs...*

He let me into his room, a corner suite overlooking the forest. It was sure to be a beautiful view, come morning. "Feel free to use the rain room, li'l bird. I'm going to get dinner started." After stealing a quick peck on my cheek, he ducked out of the room.

It was a small space by the standards of a prince, with enough room for a bed big enough to fit a giant, a dresser full of clothes, and a couple boxes of toys that looked as if they were for pet cats or dogs.

It was only when I was standing under a weak stream of water in the adjoining rain room that I wondered, *Did he mean he was going to make dinner himself?*

60

TORMUND

I INSPECTED the spread of spices and raw ingredients on the kitchen counter.

"Is everything to your liking, Prince?" squeaked one of Lark's handmaidens. I'd had her house moths fly ahead of us with a parcel of these items. The pair had waited for us to arrive, standing out in their palace uniforms amongst the more subdued hunter green Wirr preferred for his eclipse—as any large group of mothkin were called.

"Aye, thank you. You may go. I thought I told you to take the rest of the day off?"

The handmaidens exchanged a glance. The one with streaks of white in her antennae said, "We can help. We were in the Red Eclipse before the queen reassigned us."

There were several subgroups of mothkin servants within the palace, color coded to their tasks and which alpha mothkin they reported to. The kitchen moths from the Red Eclipse had taught me how to cook, so it was a tempting offer.

"I appreciate it, but I want to show off my skills to my mate. You really can go and relax."

The handmaiden with a brown pattern inside her wings said, "Okay, Prince. Before you get started, will you please introduce us to Head Moth Wirr?"

"Did you want to be reassigned again?" I asked in surprise.

"No way! We love serving the princess."

What they were asking really sank in. "Oh, you want to be *introduced.*"

Their fuzzy antennae shot straight up in either shock or embarrassment. "No, Prince!" they squeaked at about the same time.

"I want to learn how to be a head moth," one squeaked.

"No, *I'm* going to be the head moth," said the other.

I glanced between them, brow wrinkled in confusion. *Wirr can figure this one out.*

I took a moment to locate the big alpha. One of them whispered their names to me as I waved him over. "Wirr, this is Jani and Lon. They've proven themselves to be hard workers and excellent handmaidens for my mate," I said.

Rennyn had taught me that you *always* compliment a house moth's work ethic, especially to an alpha mothkin; otherwise, you've wounded their pride. They held grudges, and their gossip spread like wildfire after a drought. But they were excellent allies for a spy wanting to know who was sleeping where and plotting with whom in as busy a place as the palace. He kept his thumb on everything going on just by listening to the head moths, who sorted through their eclipse's gossip to offer him the juiciest details.

While the pair of betas peppered Wirr with questions, I headed back into the kitchen to start cooking. I got into a groove of chopping, slicing, and seasoning, only interrupted when Kauz tapped the pack bond to let me know he'd come inside. He'd remained at a polite distance but within range of our bond the whole day.

I sent him the equivalent of a thumbs-up to ask if everything was still okay. He sent back a yes, and I relaxed, getting back to work. I wasn't a master chef by any means, but I enjoyed the tasks, especially the bespoke-level roasting I could offer with my fire. I'd packed enough food for everyone to eat well off my efforts.

Lark poked her head into the kitchen. Oddly, I'd smelled her coming, her sweetness wafting ahead of her and arrowing straight into my nostrils. Her white hair was still damp around her rosy-cheeked face fresh from a shower. *Adorable, as always.*

When she spotted me, her eyes widened in surprise. "Tormund? Are you *cooking?*" she asked in Theli. We'd switched to speaking the language she was most comfortable with after a few hours of practice. I hadn't wanted to strain her mind, even though hearing Serri from her lips had been a treat.

I blocked her view of my work by covering her star-flecked eyes. "Aye, li'l bird. I'll bring it out to you when it's done."

"It smells really good."

"You smell really good."

"Oh?" She tried to peek around my hand.

A flush of heat raced over my skin. Was it my rage? *Already?*

Stars, no. I thought we'd finally fixed my problem. "Go sit down, please," I said.

She left and took her sweet pheromones with her. I was still feeling a little warm in her absence. It wasn't the rage after all, just something new. Lark was still in my thoughts, but they'd taken a decidedly sensual twist, focusing on the last time we'd mated and she'd taken my knot like a champion.

My cock jumped to full life. I scowled down at the tent in my pants. *That's not very chivalrous,* I chided it and thought about unpleasant things until it relented.

I rushed to make sure the meat didn't burn. Then, I finished roasting the potatoes one long exhale of flame at a time across their metal pan.

I peeked into the common area before doing my final plating. The house moths were at a table, chatting together. Kauz was sprawled in the middle of a couch with a stack of books on the floor beside him. One of his wings was curled around Lark. She rested her head on his shoulder, gazing up at him adoringly as she giggled at something he'd said.

A spike of jealousy skewered me. Kauz glanced up and looked straight at me with his unusual eyes, brows rising in surprise. His expression smoothed into a knowing look. I squinted back. *Smug, overgrown bat.*

I went back into the kitchen to split the food fairly. There was plating, covering, and finally, cutting the bread. I loaded everything on a platter to carry out with me.

"Dinner's ready," I announced with my usual cheer. "Good news. Kauz and the li'l moths aren't going to starve today!"

Jani and Lon's wiggling antennae showed their obvious confusion when I slid a covered plate toward them.

"You're feeding us, Prince?" Lon, I think, asked. Jani framed her fuzzy face with her hands in glee.

I nodded, beaming. "It might not be as good as something from the palace kitchens, but I made it with love. Lark, I was thinking we could eat in my room."

She turned to kiss Kauz—briefly, I noted with some satisfaction—and stood as I slid him some dinner too.

"Be careful," my brother murmured in an undertone as Lark headed for the staircase.

"*Ach.*" I had plenty of practice with my self-control. Two days of being by Lark's side without mating with her would be fine.

"Um, small problem," she said once we were both in my room and I'd kicked the door closed behind me. "Your desk only has one chair."

The desk was a scarred thing in one corner. It had slim poetry books lined up facing the wall and the remnants of a wood carving project lying forgotten under a thin layer of dust. I'd tried more than once to take up carving—it was a nice masculine activity I could do at clan meetings, if I were good at it—but all I got from it was splinters and cuts on my fingers.

I should've tidied up in here before rushing off to make dinner, but I'd been so excited for this meal. The fact there was one chair was something I'd already been aware of. It was a blocky fireproof monstrosity I'd sat in so much the wood was soft and pitted to the touch.

With a thrill up my spine, I said what I'd been daydreaming about since I'd first come up with the idea for this date: "I was thinking you could sit in my lap while I feed you."

I took great joy in providing for my omega. But I wanted to go further still, to have her sit in my lap and accept a meal from my hand.

She nibbled on her lower lip as she considered the tiny room. The winter lodge didn't have any spacious suites. This room was only big enough for one of us, so if she didn't want this...I guess we'd need to go back downstairs.

"It's not a bother?" she asked.

"Nay," I said, probably too quickly. "I mean, I would love to share this moment with you. If you're okay with it."

She smiled up at me, her eyes twinkling with many sparkling reflections from the essence lamp overhead. The sight made my heart skip a beat. She was straight from the dreamlands. A gift from the stars that smelled like one of my favorite things in life, a sweet dessert.

"I'd like that."

Me too, li'l bird.

I set the platter down at the foot of my bed and swiped aside the failed wood carving and the knife that went with it. "Okay, I saved us some of the best stuff," I told her as I arranged all of it on the desk.

The main dish and dessert, I kept covered under appropriately sized cloches, but the goblets for wine and water, the bread and butter, and the salad were in plain view. I'd prepared a lot more salad than necessary, just in case she didn't actually like my cooking.

I stashed the wine bottle under the desk and sat, patting my lap, excitement kindling within me. She sat across my thighs and rested her slight weight on my chest. "This looks really nice. You're helping me eat all that salad, right?"

"We don't have to eat all the salad." I'd heard plenty about "overfeeding" her by now. As if having a round and happy mate was a bad thing!

I dished some up for both of us and speared a few bits of lettuce on the fork I guided to her mouth, my other hand under the tines to catch any spillage. She chewed demurely, crunching into the fresh greens. "Bread? Water?" I asked.

"I want you to feed yourself too."

"I will. Just tell me what you want, and I'll get it for you first."

"More salad, please."

She munched through another forkful of salad, and I ate some as well. The tart lemon vinaigrette added a good zing to the meal staple.

I watched her expressions for little hints as to what she'd want next. In the meantime, I told her about my wood carving experiments at this desk, explaining the many scars it'd received from my frustration.

She bent to pick up my failed project and inspected it. "Oh, that's the problem. This isn't the right wood for carving."

I blinked in surprise. "Huh?"

"See the grains? They're too far apart. That's why they're splintering." She pointed at the offending split in the wood, where I'd given up in frustration. "You need wood with a tighter grain, and then you'll get further."

"You know how to carve wood?"

A touch of pink lit her cheeks. "Just some of the basics. There's not much to do in a farm town, so I learned things here and there growing up."

"You're so smart, li'l bird," I said cheerfully.

We ate buttered bread, and soon, it was time for me to reveal the main course. Palms tingling, I pulled the bigger cloche to reveal my handiwork in a cloud of fragrant steam. I'd prepared boar with an apple reduction, served with caramelized onions. To the side were hills of roasted potatoes and root veggies dusted in rosemary and thyme.

She inhaled, and a purr thrummed through her. I drank in her expression and the feeling of her delight vibrating my heart at just the right frequency. The best sound in the world was still my mate's purr.

I traded plates around and poured the wine. "This is a berry wine. No fae fruit involved."

"Thank the stars for that," she giggled. "This looks amazing. Let's try it."

"First, wine." I gave her a sip from her goblet and tried it too. Oh, aye, that was going to be the perfect compliment to the dish. Now for the moment of truth, cutting into the meat. Nothing would ruin this meal faster than if I'd cooked the boar too much or too little. With my dad, cooking over a fire, it didn't matter either way. Too little, and we could just bathe it in flame on the way down. Too much, and it just received an *ach* and some extra fire anyway.

Lark deserved a perfectly cooked, juicy boar. I cut into one and *phew.* It was the correct color inside. I fed her a cut of meat with some of the apple reduction dabbed on top and waited breathlessly for her reaction.

Her face was a moment I'd picture forever. The flavors hit her tongue, earning a soft sound of delight. Her expression lit up, and her eyelids lowered from the simple pleasure of good food. There really was nothing like the first bite of any meal, when anticipation met satisfaction.

"Wow, Tormund. This is delicious." Absolute music to my ears, and not just because of her naturally melodic voice. After I fed her a potato and carrot, plus another sip of wine, I tried my own handiwork and nodded in approval.

"How did you get the apples so concentrated? I never thought to pair fruit and meat quite like this," she said. I paused my chewing to adjust my spectacles, though I squinted at her anyway.

Right. If she knows wood carving, she likely knows how to cook too. I told her about how I'd made the reduction, and she nodded along without needing much clarification.

"You know what this means, right? I'm going to make dinner tomorrow."

"You don't have to," I said immediately.

The twinkles in the whites of her eyes danced with her amusement. "No, I want to. You already learned the secret. Cooking is fun. And I bet we have access to much better ingredients than I'm used to." When I opened my mouth to protest, she added, "We could cook together."

That could be a lot of fun, but I still wanted to hand-feed her whatever we made. Call it alpha instincts—or just a me thing—but it was immensely satisfying. "Okay."

I looked forward to having more dates like this. Without there being a rush to hustle Lark out of the city, I'd catch a protein of her choice and make something more elaborate, start to finish, from my labor. Now *that* would sustain my pride for months.

She filled up before me and rested her head against my chest, right over my alpha mark. It tingled with awareness. All marks, regardless of designation, were a manifestation of our souls, and mine resonated just from having her close. She traced idle patterns on my belly as I ate, and fire pooled toward my groin.

No. Think chivalrous thoughts.

My member stirred anyway, tapping her hip as it plumped up. With her in my lap, smelling so much like a treat, it was inevitable. "Sorry," I whispered.

"I want to. So badly," she murmured back. "You deserve something for this lovely dinner."

"Just being with you is plenty reward."

As was the expression she made, looking up at me with love in her eyes. She'd just been looking at Kauz the same way. Starsdamned bat. Why did he need to be here too? I was plenty worthy of defending my mate on my own and…

Wow, where did all this jealousy come from? It wasn't as if I was uninformed about sharing my perfect female with the rest of my pack.

"I love you, my gentle giant," she said, effectively waving away my negative feelings.

"Love you too." I kissed her hair and decided I'd had enough to eat. *Gentle giant* was a nickname with its own kind of magic, putting my oddities as an admittedly weak redcap under a different lens. It was my identity now, something Lark loved.

She leaned up to get a real kiss. Her concentrated chocolate and honey crackers taste lingered on my tongue and definitely didn't help my self-control. *Be careful*, indeed. The next logical step would be to strip and make love on the bed until sunrise. But I did have one distraction left.

I broke our kiss and asked huskily, "Are you ready for dessert?"

"There's dessert?" She sounded a little throaty too.

"Of course!" I reached over and lifted the smaller cloche, revealing a ceramic bowl of custard still chilled from its time in the lodge's cold storage. She perked up. As an omega, she had mighty sugar cravings. I'd tried to observe what sweets she liked the most, just to discover she enjoyed every single dessert placed in front of her.

"I love custard. Thank you, Tormund!"

"Ah, it's not done," I said playfully. "Close your eyes for a moment."

I leaned away from her with the bowl in hand, then breathed a superheated burst of flame over the custard. The top caramelized, bubbling into a crust of dark brown. Lark startled with a yelp, though by the time she peeked between her fingers, it was done.

"Whoa," she murmured.

I placed it down and handed her the spoon. "Here, give it a tap. It's the best part."

"Not the taste?" she teased, tentatively tapping it until its shell cracked. Then she scooped up a modest amount and held it up to my lips.

"It's for you," I protested.

"It smells too delicious not to share!"

She didn't have to work all that hard to convince me. I loved caramelized cream and happened to be perfectly suited to making it. I was glad to share the dessert and this moment with her. It was the best part of a very eventful day.

I woke to a feeling of flames under my skin. I was harder than faesteel, pressing into Lark's belly while she woke groggily with the rising of the sun. Her intoxicating sweetness was branded on the inside of my nostrils.

We lay entwined in my bed. At some point during her rest, she'd kicked off most of the layers she'd settled under to reveal a tempting triangle of skin where her sleepwear had twisted askew. My mouth watered to taste the soft swell of her breasts, but my fangs...

I probed them with my tongue, snapped out of my thoughts. I had a mouth full of regular, flat teeth, other than my alpha fangs. Lark nuzzled my neck and inhaled as I lay there puzzled. "Your scent is changing," she murmured.

She laved an approving lick on my neck. It felt like she'd licked my cock directly, and I rumbled with interest. I took her soft curves in hand, pulling her up to kiss the breath from her lips. She mewled just right as I rubbed my hardness into the damp fabric over the apex of her thighs.

Wait, no. What am I doing?

I startled away. Heat pulsed under my skin just behind the frantic beat of my heart. I couldn't draw my gaze away from her kiss-swollen lips and the way they'd parted.

"You *are* going into rut," she said.

I sucked in a breath to keep from cursing aloud in her presence. *Aw, fuck,* I thought as I got out of bed and backed away from her. This wasn't happening. It was my only full day with her before we had to return to Serian Palace, and I didn't want to spend it staring longingly at her ass.

"I'm going to take a shower. Why don't you head downstairs...get some tea. Or something. Wirr's staff will help you."

She nodded slowly. "Okay. Sure. Tea."

She dressed and left while I showered under a thin stream of the iciest water the lodge could provide. The scent of soap and the shock of cold helped give me my senses back.

Fal must've given me the rut when I'd seen him yesterday. While he'd spoken with most of his usual polish, he was not as perfect in his physical appearance as he usually was. He must've been using scent-blocking soap, because he hadn't been surrounded by a cloud of pheromones.

The biggest sign he couldn't hide were his eyes, which were emitting the rut glow, reflecting facets of light not too unlike dreamlander stars. Females were apparently entranced by it, especially omegas in heat. I should've known he was able to pass it on despite us shielding our sides of the pack bond.

Good thing Lark and I hadn't had sex last night, else I'd already be succumbing to the pressure to mate nonstop until my alpha needs were satiated. I'd never been in rut before. I knew what to expect in theory, yet it'd still hit me hard and fast. It hadn't even been a day!

But I had my self-control. Regardless of anything else, I'd held my rage at bay fairly successfully for years and regulated my emotions so I didn't erupt into flames as often as I wanted to. I would bend this to my will, too, and only let it out once it was time to claim my mate's heat.

I owed her a nice, angst-free day, and that was what I was going to give her. *Not my knot.*

Before I went downstairs, I checked the room at the end of the hall. Technically, it was mine, since I paid an annual fee for its upkeep. It'd been an unused broom closet, too small to house most fae with its slanted roof. I had to stoop to fit inside.

It was my critter room. The house moths cared for the woodland creatures when I wasn't around to do so. The occasional hunter brought in an animal that needed care, and they received it in this wee room that was probably a palace for a wee creature anyway. I'd fit in a cat tower, a scattering of small toys, bowls for food and water, and a box of medical supplies. I checked the supplies, noting what needed to be restocked.

Then I found the newest critters hunkering down in a section of the cat tower. I held in an unmasculine sound of delight with considerable effort. "My mate has to see you. Later," I whispered to them. Lark was definitely going to make the noise I'd just barely suppressed when she did.

I headed downstairs and held in another growl. Kauz was already awake and had an arm around Lark as she nursed a steaming mug. At least now I knew where these negative emotions were coming from, though my brother didn't deserve to be a target for them.

He glanced over his shoulder and asked whether I was all right over the pack bond. I signaled back a yes and forced myself to relax.

"Good morning," I said.

Lark made a sleepy noise into her tea, and I went to sit on her other side. One of her handmaidens brought me a mug of snownettle tea. I took a drink and shuddered. That sour-sweet tang was *stimulating*, to say the least.

"Wait. Why are you still here? You have time off," I said to the house moth.

"Always happy to help the princess and the princes. Jani went up to clean your room. We thought you wouldn't mind," she answered cheerfully.

House moth work ethic was something else.

"Thank you. We did leave a mess last night."

Lon glanced left and right before gesturing for me to come with her. I got to my feet and followed as she led me into the kitchen. "We heard about what you wanted from Wirr's eclipse and made it better for you." She pointed to a wooden basket on the counter with a telltale white and red checkered cloth sticking out from one side. "Do you want me to sneak it into your horse's saddlebags?"

She regarded me with an earnest smile, hands clasped before her.

There was only one appropriate response to the two handmaidens going above and beyond. I scooped her up into a hug, squeezing delicately since she was such a tiny thing compared to me. "Thank you."

"Thank you for dinner, Prince. It was very nice!"

Oh. Stars, I should've realized what was going on earlier. I was so captivated by Lark that I'd forgotten I'd given Jani and Lon part of last night's meal. Serving a house moth was an overture of friendship in their culture, and they'd obviously accepted it.

I trotted the wee moth back over to Lark and Kauz to see what they wanted for dinner. I only put her down after she wiggled with excitement to hear we were preparing something else tonight. She promised to fly to the palace to get the ingredients.

"Don't you want breakfast, Princess?" Lon asked.

She shook her head with a giggle. "I know Tormund's going to feed me." And she was very right about that.

But first, we had to wake her up more. I ended up with a deck of cards for us to start fulfilling yesterday's deal and roped my brother into helping.

Kauz was an absolutely shameless cheater. Since he used illusion magic instead of sleight of hand like Fal, I could never *quite* prove it. But I squinted at him after he won most of our games, while Lark learned and winced over every sip of her snownettle tea.

While she went to use the restroom in preparation for us leaving for the day, he said, "So, your scent is changing, hmm?"

"I'm trying not to think about it."

"Well, her upcoming heat is about all I've been focused on lately." He nudged his stacks of books so I could read the spines. They were all related to unique heats and fae breeding habits. "I promised Lark I'd research long-suppressed heats."

I sat straighter. "Learn anything important?"

He tilted his head back and forth. "Things we could've guessed. There's evidence she's going to need constant care and her heat is going to last longer than the usual two days."

A chill creeped down my back, winding around my vents. I was gladder than ever that we'd found Lark before her heat arrived. It was rare, but omegas could perish if they didn't have assistance during a heat, and a lengthy one would only multiply the danger.

But she had us, and once she was in the pack bond, we'd sense her needs and care for her no matter how long she stayed in heat.

"You can cast blame for your impending rut on biological factors. Alphas in the same pack tend to sync up their rut cycles to their omega's heat," Kauz continued. "And finally...if she were interested in having babies, she's at her most likely to emerge from this heat with a litter."

"*Terrible* timing!" I exclaimed. Lark had barely started enjoying her freedom. The last thing she needed was to be weighed down by four babies now.

I also wasn't sure any of my brothers were ready for kids. Well, except for Kauz. He had a wistful look on his face before he nodded in agreement. Glancing up, he lowered his voice. "If you don't want to test yourself tonight, have her rest in my bed. Once you succumb to the rut, I'm going to be the last voice of reason in our pack."

"Ready to go when you are," Lark said a moment later, coming to stand behind the couch with an eager smile.

"Not until you kiss me goodbye, sweetheart," he said.

As they took a moment to say farewell, I pushed the resulting jealousy away again. It was different this time. I was a little resentful because Kauz was "just" a beta and thus immune to the push-pull of instincts the rest of us had to deal with. He was such a lucky bat...because I already recognized that Lark should sleep in his bed tonight. Just in case I was tempted to ruin the plan by pushing her into her heat early.

But until then, she was *mine*. To have a lovely date with, I mean.

WE RODE FURTHER AFIELD on horseback. Stella had whinnied with excitement when she'd seen Lark and was still extra bouncy on the trail. I *completely* understood wanting to prance around in my mate's presence. It seemed the half-unicorn had chosen Lark in the way some horses did.

I showed Lark my old haunts from years of familiarity with this stretch of forest. We practiced her Serri again, with me teaching her some words for the plants and animals we spotted. She loved seeing the small animals as much as I did, which didn't surprise me.

By high noon, we approached the sound of rushing water. This was about as far from the lodge as I'd take her. I slowed Rory as we reached a stone bridge arching over a relatively calm section of river and stopped halfway across to dismount. Lark followed suit, the two of us holding our horses' reins as we looked out over the rippling sheet of clear water.

"Do you know what this is?" I asked, grinning down at her.

She raised a brow back at me. "A river."

"Aye, the Sorles. Surprise! Our pack is named after the largest river in Serian."

"Oooh. But why?"

I shrugged. "Tradition. The Sorles River is the lifeblood of the kingdom, just like the heirs of the royal pack are the blood of Serian."

She nodded along, leaning over to take another peek into the depths of the water. "You know, I never thought to ask. I thought it was a family name. But I like the symbolism so much more."

Sunshine gilded her skin and drew out the bright highlights in her hair. Instead of looking out over the water, I drank her in instead. Her wings sparkled with shimmers, loosing purple and silver dust. They opened and shut contentedly behind her as if she were an overgrown butterfly.

Stars, I could just live in this moment. She eventually turned her gaze up to meet mine, cocking her head at whatever she saw. "Sliver for your thoughts?" she murmured.

"Do you ever wish you could take a memory and put it in a bottle? So you can look inside the glass and see it again? I want to do that with this moment. To see a free, healthy Lark in the sun." *One just a little extra pink with pre-heat.* "My sweet li'l bird where she belongs."

She slid forward, putting her free arm around me and purring. I did the same happily. "You have such a nice way with words."

"Now, I'm not sure about that. Maybe only when I'm talking about you," I teased. While I read plenty of poetry, not much of it seemed to stick. Unlike my brothers, who could recite songs and whole passages from the books they'd read. That was why I had one of my favorite poetry books secreted in Rory's saddlebags, to get the words right. "Shall we have lunch and head back? I figured we could have a picnic... over there."

I pointed back the way we'd come, toward a stand of trees and flowering bushes. There was a clearing in the shade where we could sit for a while and let the horses crop the grass and rest.

Lark agreed, and we crossed over to the clearing. I pulled out the picnic basket from my saddlebags, unfurled a blanket, and set out a light meal of bread, cheese, and fruit.

The mysterious "improvements" made by the house moths were hidden to the side: napkins, sealed jars of lemonade, even more food, and a ring toss game with brightly colored rings. The latter seemed like the kind of thing only a house moth would think of.

I dragged the blanket closer to a tree trunk and sat with my back against the bark. We ate to the music of nature: the whisper of wind through the leaves above our heads and the burbling flow of water.

"Do you ever want to go back to Thelis?" I asked her.

"Someday, maybe. I saw so little of it, but it was my home for most of my life. I can't imagine traveling without you and your brothers, though," she said.

I smiled at the idea. "It'd be an adventure. I'd love to go with you."

She scooted closer, lying down beside me, half in the grass, her hands folded over her middle. She rested her head in my lap. I stilled for a moment, as if an actual bird had alighted on my thigh.

It was the perfect moment to pull out my poetry book. I opened the little dog-eared volume to its first page. "Before we head back, I wanted to read to you. I haven't been able to share my favorite poems." They were all written in Serri, so she'd either understand them okay or I'd figure out how to translate their meaning.

"I'd love to hear them," she said, turning an expectant look at me.

The poet had been a similar age to us when he'd penned these words. At first, I hadn't understood why he mused about living in his mate's shadow. But I read them to Lark and chuckled to myself. Now that I had her, the words held new meaning. I'd choose to live in her shadow in a heartbeat, if only to emerge at the first sign of potential danger.

And to love on her, of course. I tamped down the warmth threatening to heat my blood, too entranced by the way she soaked in every poem and gave it a minute or two of thought before voicing her opinions. I did the same thing, lingering on the prettiest and most insightful turns of phrase.

I would think *relatable* and uncover a tiny insight into my soul. Now, I shared bits of myself with Lark in every verse, entrusting her to keep each revelation close.

61

LARK

Tormund and I returned to the winter lodge just past sunset. I felt closer than ever to my gentle giant after the day's adventure. He'd shown me his introspective side, and now I knew he had a mask too, which slid back into place with his beaming grin and raised voice.

We went to the kitchen and were joined by Jani, Lon, and, eventually, a curious Kauz. I'd asked to make a humble favorite for dinner, meat pies. The whole process took hours, and the house moths and I did most of the work at first. Tormund chased his brother around with flour until Kauz, laughing and white-streaked, found a safe perch up in the rafters.

My gentle giant returned to being helpful after that. He added in his fire to cook our meal quicker. The pies themselves turned out delicious, and I'd smiled so much by bedtime that my face ached.

I had another rough time finding sleep, worse than the night before.

A pain deep in my belly was making itself known. I'd shifted around trying to find a comfortable spot, just for there to be none. Kauz had been half asleep when he'd finally brushed his finger down the ridge of my nose, mumbling about my heat, and sent me into unconsciousness for a couple hours. I'd slept in his arms since Tormund was swiftly succumbing to the rut.

Stars, my heat was really coming. The suppressant I'd just gotten from Thalas was fading, even though we'd been chaste throughout this trip. The physical signs of pre-heat hadn't fully returned, but the emotional ones hit me with debilitating force.

Before we left to journey back to the palace, Tormund had a surprise for me. He took me to a tiny room and told me a bit of the story of the critter room through the doorway. He directed my attention to the little cat tower in the corner, and I squealed as a small face peeked out at me.

I emerged with a hedgehog baby cupped carefully in both hands, its body still pink and hairless. He'd been snuggled up to his mother with his other spiky siblings. The mother had suffered some kind of wound to her side that'd been neatly bandaged.

A few tears leaked from me out of joy. "Look at him," I whispered, overcome by the miracle of life.

I want one. The hedgehog, I told myself, though my instincts were in full mood swing. I'd just been cursing my omega neediness with the sunrise. *Stupid heat.*

Tormund's brows rose as he took in my expression. "Are you okay?"

"It's just so beautiful." This teeny tiny life, new and fragile.

He eyed me with concern. "You should probably go put him back," he suggested in his usual loud whisper. "I thought you'd like the critter room, li'l bird."

"I *love* the critter room," I sobbed.

I don't think I convinced him, even when I put the little creature back with his mother and came out to hug and nuzzle against Tormund. His scent was still changing, deepening, and it was intoxicating to my omega instincts. He'd lost the sweetness of mallows, smelling of smoke and a woodsy cologne, as if he'd set fire to a pile of exotic kindling. I wanted to be covered in his scent. *Soon. So soon.*

We saddled up and left for Neslune shortly after that. It'd been nice to get away from the crush of strangers in the palace and disappear into nature, but I was ready to curl up in my nest with the comforting scents of my mates all around me. I wanted to take sweet Tormund and steadfast Kauz straight to bed with me.

But I needed Fal and Marius too. I missed them so much.

Kauz rode with us on the return trip and added in occasionally to Tormund's ever-present storytelling. He didn't question the way Tormund and I switched languages back and forth until we understood one another completely. The gentle giant had a talent for making sure there were never awkward pauses, because there simply wasn't much quiet between thoughts. His voice helped keep me from dwelling on my yearnings too much.

I would say he wasn't one for introspection, yet I'd seen how moved he'd been as he read to me from one of his poetry books yesterday. He thought plenty and felt deeply, but he didn't let just anyone see past his jolly exterior to know that about him. That he'd shown me was a blessing. I was grateful we'd gotten to eke out some time together.

But I still wilted with relief when the woods thinned, and we made our way to the palace stables. *First things first, a nap.* Hopefully no one intercepted me on the way to lying down.

Kauz cut into my daydreams of rest. "We should check in before you head inside, sweetheart."

"Do you think...maybe they're dead?" I couldn't say *Pack Ellisar* right now. Bile threatened to rise in the back of my throat.

"There's always that possibility. Let me go ask first."

I couldn't help but whine. Tormund added in, "The li'l bird should come inside. She hadn't been home in ages."

"It's not a good idea," Kauz said gently, earning a growl full of redcap menace that barely made him flinch. "Give me half an hour."

"Sure. That's not too long," I said before Tormund could get any angrier on my behalf.

We had Kauz head out while we took care of the horses. I took Stella to her stall and saw to her needs for a while.

My ears perked when Kauz returned and spoke to Tormund a few stalls away, their voices too low for me to hear. Except for the fiery "What!" the redcap crackled after a few minutes of conversation. "Tell him..."

I huffed. I could've cried from frustration, and that was the pre-heat at work again, making everything much worse. *He's never this quiet any other time, except when I want to know what's going on.*

"You tell him," Kauz said louder. "I'm going to escort Lark."

I poked my head out of the stall. Stella did the same thing with her equine face above mine. "Escort me where?" I asked.

Kauz turned a smile my way that didn't quite meet his eyes. Something was definitely wrong. Tormund was wafting visible heat around his body as he stomped out of the stable, hands forming clawed fists at his sides. "Your nest. The royal pack wants you to rest up for tonight."

"What's happening tonight?"

He didn't answer. I patted Stella in farewell and rushed over to him, my wings pinned to my back with nerves. "Kauz, what's going on?"

He put an arm around me with a sigh. We walked together up to an entrance to the palace. "Nothing's wrong. Everything is nearly as we left it," he assured me in his calmest tones. "Your date with Fal is happening tonight, and you should rest."

"What aren't you telling me?" I asked in a small voice.

He bared his teeth. "I've given my word that I would let another tell you what to expect tonight."

"Will this person talk to me soon?" I asked.

"Aye."

"I trust you."

He stopped walking. We'd entered the palace through a less-used hallway, so no one bumped into us as he swung to face me. "Your trust is not misplaced, Always."

"My Always." I reached for him, and he obliged, drawing me into the embrace of his arms and wings. He rested his forehead against mine, and our breaths mingled.

The uncertainty creasing the planes of his face was an upsetting change for my inner omega. *My mate is in distress.*

"I'll be okay," I assured him.

His breath hitched, and he hugged me tighter. Determination hardened his expression. "You need to sleep. It's going to be a long night."

I didn't doubt it. We let one another go and completed the trek to the royal wing. My nostrils flared in the hall leading up to my room. Notes of sunshine and wild mint twined in the air and lingered. The ache in my belly only grew more pronounced; I was about to have the worst cramp of my life if I didn't do *something* about it soon.

I said goodbye to Kauz at the door of my suite, holding my middle as soon as I was inside and the door closed behind me.

"It's the princess!"

"Princess!"

I startled and straightened. My receiving room seemed to be swarming with house moths. They gathered and bowed or curtsied, massing into a gaggle of ten mothkin. There were eight males, plus Jani and Lon, who happily made introductions. The males were assigned to the princes, relocated to serve us all here. "We're cleaning everything in preparation for your heat, Princess," Jani reported.

"That includes everything in your nest. Please don't be upset," Lon added. "Most omegas want to redo their nest right before their heat anyway."

It was impossible to look at this flock—eclipse?—of earnest house moths and be angry. However, I'd wanted to lie down in my nest, and fatigue weighed me down just at the idea of redoing it.

"Don't let me interrupt your work. I'm going to the rain room," I said.

"I'll get your favorite soap!"

"I'll get your bathrobe!"

Jani and Lon bumped into one another in their haste. I scrunched my nose and giggled, fluttering by them. "It's okay. I'll be fine. Thank you, ladies."

The rest of the moths split up to return to what they were doing. When they said they were cleaning *everything*, they meant it. Yet I still picked up a strong whiff of Fal's grassy scent in the study and saw my old journal was upside down on the desk. I flipped it up, noticing the number of scribble marks on the pages before any other details.

I thumbed through it while standing, as one of the male house moths was wiping down the study's armchairs. Fal's handwriting marked the back of the journal. I'd recognize the looping script anywhere, even though most of it was unreadable since it was written in Serri. Still, it was a rare peek into his mind, and apparently, it was chaos in there. There were so many things crossed out on the first page alone.

Deeper into the journal, there were arrows pointing every which way. Then he'd started doodling in the middle of an idea or a thought. He wasn't half bad at drawing, either. When I saw the barkfolk shape surrounded by a plume of fire, I had a better idea of what I was holding. Brainstorming. Fruitless, by the marks of his frustration.

I turned one more page, and my breath caught. He'd sketched a full page spread of, well, versions of me. *"Mo stór"* was written at the top next to a heart. There had to be a couple dozen doodles, and they were increasingly naughty and detailed.

The top was a progression of him getting my face, body, and wing proportions right, plus sketches of a few expressions. Excited, blushing and shy, annoyed, and coy seemed to be his favorites. Then there were full-body doodles. Me wearing outfits I knew he liked and then just without clothes at all, posing in bold and sexy ways I'd never had the confidence for.

I blushed and flipped through the other pages. More plotting and scribbling until he seemed to give up mid-thought. I turned back to the sketches and studied the poses carefully. For reasons.

A tickle of static began at the back of my head as the kelpie bond fell back into place. Marius's voice was a deep growl in my mind. *"Mate."*

I got a little slick. *Just from that? C'mon. Bad Lark.* To be fair, I was already stirred up from the peek into Fal's mind, and my body was reacting accordingly.

"Where are you?" I asked.

"I came running. Almost there."

I tingled with anticipation. The door into my suite slammed a room over. I put the journal down as he rushed into the study and over to me in a few long strides. He crushed me into a hug, burying his nose in my hair, and I sighed happily as his scent hit me. His scent of fertile waterlilies and mint was enough to make me weak at the knees.

"P'nixie." His voice was smooth and clear.

When I tried to pull away to see his face, he wouldn't budge. A high level of anxiety was easing out of him as he held me.

"I missed you," I said through our bond.

He made a feral sound, a gentle murmur of agreement.

"Are you all right? I've been worried."

He nipped my ear before nuzzling my neck, breathing in my scent intently enough that he stirred the little hairs on the back of my neck. "Worried? Why?" He tasted my pheromones with a quick swipe of his tongue.

I held in a moan with a sharp inhale. "You're still in rut. I thought it only lasted a couple days. You know we can't—"

"I know. Don't remind me," he said in a hush. "I've been holding on to it."

"You wanted to stay in rut without me?"

"Not without. I wanted it for your estrus." He shook his head. "Your heat, I mean."

"Marius..."

"It's so close, p'nixie."

"You didn't have to put your body under that kind of pressure." I could sense the echo of how painfully tight it'd become in the days we'd been away from one another. It was a full-body experience, though most intense in his back and groin. He absolutely should've let himself relax rather than endure this.

He released me with a snort. "Pain and I are close friends. This is nothing. The worst part was being separated from you."

Catching my chin between his thumb and forefinger, he inspected my face while breathing shallowly through his mouth. As his eyes roved, they threw off shards of light. I was immediately caught in the spell of the rut glow as I gazed back at him with affection, blinking sluggishly.

He broke eye contact first, and I refocused on something new—a braid where my white hair stood out starkly when woven into the blue and green of his.

"You're in pain too." His expression set into a worried frown. I was about to tell him all I needed was a shower and a nap, when he rested his palm over the ache in my abdomen. The discomfort reacted to his presence, its dull throb fading like magic.

I layered my hand over his. "All I need is a shower and a nap." *And him.*

His feral side finally emerged, dilating his eyes and turning his voice into a resonant growl. "If you get naked now, I'll be putting a colt in your belly."

My skin flushed from head to toe. "But I smell," I said in weak protest.

His ear flicked, and his gaze returned to normal. "Apparently, I do too. How about just a nap?"

I tilted my head, a little confused at Niall's quick retreat. He mirrored the movement in sympathy. The new braid slipped over his shoulder, and I gasped when I saw the end. It was capped with a silver bead and two metalark feathers, the filaments still starry and pristine.

"I had a bit of help and bought a spell to keep it nice. Do you like it?" he asked.

"I love it. But it's prettier than anything I'd imagined you'd put in your hair."

His candid laugh spellbound me just as efficiently as the glow in his eyes. "The tradition is to show off a reflection of you as my mate. Of course it's pretty." Nuzzling me again, he breathed a frustrated chuff. Over our bond, we knew we couldn't kiss right now and expect to stay off one another. "Come on, it's time to rest. This is going to be a long night."

A chill crept over my skin. That's what Kauz had said, too.

We headed to my nest, which was clean and nearly scentless. Stacks of neatly folded bedding and pillows were piled beside the mattress. I whistled unhappily at the sight, and Marius delved into the piles to find my favorite blanket and pillow for me. "We'll redo the nest later," he suggested.

I agreed and giggled when he bundled me up in the blanket fully clothed. He only paused to take my shoes off and tuck my feet into the wrap of fleece. He untied his boots and left his clothes on too as he climbed onto the divan to cuddle me as the big spoon. The only thing likely holding him back from re-unleashing his rut on me was the bulky barrier of fabric and his considerable discipline as the protector heir.

With his purring bulk angled over my back and his hand resting over my belly despite all the layers, the pre-heat pain faded enough that I dropped straight to sleep.

I STIRRED from the darkness of rest with the vibrations of Marius whispering, "If you open that big mouth and wake her, you and I are going to have a problem."

I cracked my eyes open and blinked away the fog that'd filmed over my sight.

"It's almost dinnertime. The li'l bird needs to get ready for her next date." That was Tormund's loud whisper.

Yawning, I stretched as much as I could in my tight blanket wrap. "Now you've done it," Marius muttered.

"He didn't wake me," I said groggily. I tried to get my bearings. Marius was still behind me on the divan. Tormund stood just inside the nest. The woodsy note in his rut-enhanced scent twined perfectly with the green fertility of the kelpie's, threatening to send me into heat right then and there.

Stars help me.

The kelpie lifted me, blanket and all, and offered me over to Tormund, who swept me up. "Did you have a nice nap?" my gentle giant asked.

He carried me into the bedroom attached to the nest and helped me out of the blanket wrap. When he saw I was still in my wrinkled traveling clothes, a line formed between his brows.

"It was really good. Um, I need a shower first. And what kind of date am I preparing for here?"

He smiled, though for once, it was a forced expression on him. "Just dinner for now. Fal wants you to wear something comfortable to eat with him in his rooms."

I hadn't missed the *for now*, but I gave my head a shake and put on a forced smile too. This was supposed to be fun. It was a date!

"Okay. I can take it from here," I said.

He stepped aside, and I made my way to the rain room, finding my bathrobe on a hook by the door and a new bar of lightly scented soap waiting to be used. The suite was quiet of house moth squeaking. I wondered if Tormund dismissed them as I showered off the trail and the lingering slick between my legs.

I scrubbed myself thoroughly to obscure the extra-sweet note of my deepening pre-heat. It was probably futile. My folds were tender to the touch, and the pain in my belly had transformed into an ache deep in my core after a couple hours of Marius's presence.

"Mate," the male in question said over our bond while I was inspecting my sex with gentle fingertips. Ah, stars, did he feel that or something? *"Do you remember taking a crystal from Telimarr?"*

"Yeah, for Fal. Do you have it?" I'd definitely lost track of it.

"Aye, p'nixie. I've been hiding it for you."

He and I talked about smuggling it along with me. He didn't explain why, just that I should keep it a secret and under an illusion. When I emerged from my closet, dried off and dressed, Marius was waiting with a decorative box resting on the pack bed outside my nest. I peeked inside, and there it was, the prism-shaped crystal we'd stolen. It was a cloudy white with generous veins of silver, nestled in a bed of velvet.

"You're going out of your way for this," I mused aloud.

He shrugged. "Most omegas unlucky enough to mate with a dark elf know this tradition. It'll mean a lot to Fal."

Unlucky, I repeated to myself, lips twitching in amusement. "It's sweet you're doing this for him."

His ear flicked a couple times. "Don't mention me at all," he grumbled.

I bit my lip. Fal was going to figure this out so fast. "Okay. Lean down so I can kiss you goodbye?" I was already going a little crazy without kisses from my alpha mates.

"That's a terrible idea."

"On the *cheek*."

He gave me a knowing look but still bent his knees and tilted his unscarred cheek in my direction. I pressed a kiss there, and his chest thrummed with a brief purr before he said, "You should go, sweet prey. You smell too tempting."

I thought this meant goodbye, but after I gathered up the crystal in its box and placed an illusion over it, Marius trailed at the end of my shadow. I acquired Tormund too, who waited in an armchair in my study. He fell into step with his brother.

As I crossed the hall toward Fal's suite of rooms, I thought of Tanith and her snark right before nixie night. *"Did it really require two of you to escort her over here?"*

Kauz was also out in the hall, standing sentinel at the entrance to the royal wing. He turned his starry eyes toward me and winked. Marius went over and tugged on his wing, which Kauz extended to smack his arm playfully. They spoke in hushed Serri, drawing in Tormund too, while I knocked on Fal's door.

62

LARK

A house moth answered. "Princess!" he exclaimed. "Come in."

The small eclipse of house moths had moved here, as several of the fuzzy betas were cleaning the receiving room when I stepped inside. I'd been in Fal's rooms before, but I'd been severely hungover, so I took in the area with new eyes. The front was very...*princely*, all dark colors and orderly lines. A gigantic painting of an outdoor scene, with a handful of unknown fae posing on it, hung within line of sight of the door.

"I'll let the prince know you've arrived," the house moth squeaked.

I nodded and headed toward a carved coffee table situated between several comfortable-looking seats for guests. I slid the box with its crystal underneath the table, changing the illusion on it so it resembled part of the furniture.

After I straightened, Fal emerged from the next room over. He wore a short-sleeved shirt and pants that framed the graceful lines of his legs. Shadows lined the hollows under his eyes. His nostrils flared, and he gave me a smile full of Unseelie mischief. "*Mo stór*, you're here. And early. Eager to see me, hmm?" he asked in a husky purr.

"Always." The answer tumbled from me before I'd given it any thought. The full truth. He could tease me if he wanted, but I was always at least a little giddy to see him. My inner omega would giggle and kick her feet, saying, *"That's my mate!"*

And his scent... Oh stars. I was in trouble. He smelled strongly of sunlight and something more, something *compelling*. I went weak at the knees from the moment it threaded through my nostrils and took me to another place entirely. Breathing in deep as I crossed the room toward him, I felt as if I was skipping through a field of wildflowers.

I was a kid again, laughing, carefree, rolling through the greenery until I had smears of pollen and crushed flowers on my dress. My father would put me in white to see how many colors my clothes would be once I was done playing. Those were the best days of spring.

Strong hands framed my hips, and in a blink, my memory was gone, replaced by Fal's curious face. "Where'd you go?"

I gazed up at him, entranced. His feline gaze sparkled with gemstone fractals in this well-lit room. The rut glow danced with every movement of his eyes. After each blink, it reformed to dazzle me again.

He covered his eyes with one hand, and I startled. "Sorry," we said at the same time.

Good going, Lark.

"A great start, I know. I'll blindfold myself." He didn't sound like he was joking.

"I'll just look somewhere else. Like, um, this big painting you have."

He uncovered his face and glanced at it. "Ah, *The Knighting of Sir Rennick of Daraleth*. A classic. You can just *smell* the history."

All I could scent right now was Fal. If he didn't have a hold on my waist, I'd probably be pressed all the way against him for more.

"I don't prefer this room," he added. "It's more comfortable over here."

He took me back the way he'd come, into a room with multiple varied seats around the perimeter and a few cabinets nestled in the corners. The walls were full, mostly of drawn posters advertising various plays, and the center was empty except for the rug underfoot. He could easily have a dozen fae seated in here.

"The middle is by design. Get a bunch of performers drunk, and this becomes a stage." He pointed at the rug and nudged me playfully. "Can I get you a drink?"

"Something without fae fruit, please."

He rummaged through one of the cabinets, clinking bottles as he went. "Siora ruined fae fruit wine for you, huh."

"I just don't want to hallucinate again."

"Okay, so she did. I understand," he chuckled.

I opened my mouth, then closed it with a shake of my head. I wandered the room, looking at his posters instead. When I found the most recent one, I gasped. There Fal was in glossy color as the Prince of Winter, just his head, shoulders, and a gloved hand holding a rose made of ice. His slitted eyes and smirk gave him the sinister edge the character was usually depicted with. He was the villain in this play, while the child main character and a few other fae posed on the other side of the poster. I wished I could've seen the performance.

"How'd you hold that rose without it melting?" I asked over my shoulder.

"Let me show you." He went into his bedroom and emerged with the rose's stem in his mouth. Its fan of petals and leaves were glinting, icy blue crystals.

Fal lifted his brows at me suggestively and made a muffled roll of his tongue. A blush warmed my face. Taking it out of the clamp of his teeth, he leaned down until the crystal bloom was the only thing between our mouths. "My director let me keep it because my fangs put too many marks on it between takes."

I took it to admire with a laugh. *He would do that on purpose.*

His expression softened as I tilted the rose and took in the sparkles it put off. I noticed him a moment too late and held my breath in anticipation of a kiss. He whipped his face to the side abruptly. "I have control of the rut by my claw tips," he said in a low growl. "I'm going to put a bit of space between us. Okay?"

"Okay," I echoed, eyeing him with worry.

"Good omega," he said huskily. "I'll send a mothkin off to retrieve some food. In the meantime, I have a wine I think you'll like, if you want to get comfortable."

I picked a seat on one side of a loveseat. It squashed under my weight, suggesting that it'd received a lot of use. Fal retrieved a bottle and two wineglasses, serving us both a measure of the blush-colored liquid, then sat next to me, angling so we didn't touch.

We clinked glasses and drank. It was sweeter than I expected, and I took another sip immediately, following up my swallow with a wistful sigh. If things were different, I'd crawl in his lap and bury my face in the curve of his neck to enjoy his concentrated pheromones.

"Well, tell me about your dates," he invited.

I perked up and started from the beginning, which was the train ride to Laculi Point with Marius. I talked about the landmarks on the trip to Telimarr and some of the cool things preserved in the old city after the flooding. Eventually, he went, "Hm." It was a loving little sound, and I glanced up to see him watching me intently.

I doubted he was listening to a word I said, just soaking in the sound of my voice.

"Then you two fucked underwater like a pair of passionate wild animals?" he asked after a moment.

I nearly choked on my wine. After I was done with my coughing fit, I croaked out, "Phrasing, Fal."

His mischievous grin only grew. "Is that a yes, then?"

Heat suffused me. "Yes. Well, not quite. We weren't sure it would work underwater."

"Not sure of *what* working underwater?"

"Like, sex. You can't really thrust... The water prevents fast movements..." I let the thought fade as Fal wheezed, tears beading at the corners of his eyes.

He put down his wineglass and held his side as he continued to laugh. "No, please, go on. Tell me why you and my water fae brother didn't have sex in his element."

"Fal," I groaned.

"Are you going to say you two didn't even *try* it?"

"We didn't."

"Stars. It's called friction, *mo stór*. Sounds like we are taking a trip to the sea to rectify this gap in your experiences," he said playfully.

I was glad I was wearing a heat pad. I got rather slick imagining entwining with him in the shallows. "Looking forward to it."

"Anyway," he prompted.

Spurred on by the touch of a buzz warming my blood, I said, "We went to a cute inn by the sea and fucked like animals in a *bed*. We finished the kelpie bond."

Fal retrieved his wineglass and sipped, nodding with what seemed like approval when I mentioned the bond. "At least someone's been having sex."

"Sorry," I murmured.

He waved me off. The heat in his glowing gaze was full of promise. "Soon, lovely. Tell me the rest first."

I nodded and told him about my midair dance with Kauz and our more introspective journey through Once Else. "Kauz painted my wings. The outside edges represent him, with the stars and mist. But the inside pattern is for me."

"They're gorgeous. And my favorite color, no less." He reached out before halting just inches from my wing. With a frustrated growl, he retrieved his hand.

"He wants me to paint the rest of his wings once I feel confident enough," I added with some nerves.

"Dreamlanders do tend to view their wings as a canvas to be filled. That's an honor." He topped up our glasses with more wine and toasted, "To be a swirl of ink on your skin."

I drank to that with a giggle. He did the same, then hummed. "Though I would pick a more intimate location. Your thigh, perhaps."

"You would. Anyway, then Tormund arrived and stayed for the rest of our time in Once Else. I, uh, fixed his condition with his rage."

"Don't get shy on me now."

I flushed a bit more. "I took his huge knot and the fieriness of his full rage form without getting hurt. He stopped losing control after that."

"Oh, good. And then you returned home just long enough for my father to scare you off again and went on a date with Tormund."

I nodded and told him about it too.

"Food, poetry, and the great outdoors. That's my li'l brother," he said, shaking his head.

"Yeah." I loosed a fond sigh. "What have you been up to?"

"Daydreaming of you, mostly." He made an echo of my sigh. "I don't know how you've done this for four years. I'm not going to be able to hold back from being completely rut-addled for much longer."

"It was easier not to go into heat before I met you and your brothers. And I had suppressants." I eyed him, not sure if he had one too. The only essence spinner tattoos he seemed to have were the fading ones on his face.

"Alphas can't suppress ruts. It's either find a partner or suffer." He shrugged.

"Well, I'm here with you now."

He licked his lips, outlining the point of one fang. Then he shook his head sharply. "Let's change the subject before I..." He cleared his throat. "I've waited a long time for this moment, and this starsdamned rut won't steal it from me. Put your stuff down." I placed my wineglass and his crystal rose on the ground, and he did the same.

He eased to his knees before me and caught my hands in his. Because I didn't want to get mesmerized by his glowing eyes, I focused on his lips and the flash of his extra-sharp fangs as he spoke. I didn't want to miss what he had to say.

"I know I'm not a perfect male. I've been insulted in many ways for being the way I am. One simple word has stuck with me the longest." He squeezed my hands. "A female once likened me to a tomcat because of my grimalkin blood. She said I'd never be satisfied or know true love. Of all the things, a jilted lover's accusation was what I'd dwelled on. *Tomcat.* Ugh."

An irrational fear rose in me that he was about to say I hadn't satisfied him either. I held in my reaction, though, letting him talk.

"I'd feared she was right. At that point, I'd never invested myself long term in any female. My duty in finding the next Queen of Serian was too heavy a burden. I've always known, from the moment I was old enough to understand my place as crown prince, that my mate had to be very special indeed. Until we met, I was afraid I wouldn't know what to do when I finally had my mate in front of me. What would it even be like to be drawn irrevocably to one female for the rest of my life? And her to me?"

He blew out a heavy breath. "And the rest of my pack to her too? There has never been an omega that's captured all four of our attentions at once. Yet you did that. *Effortlessly*. It's as if the hand of fate just..." He cupped our hands together. My fingers trembled.

"As for what it feels like to be drawn to one female..." He drew my quivering hand to his mouth to kiss the back of it. "I have not been so much as tempted by another since we met. I helped release you, a shy, sweet songbird from her cage, hoping you would let me keep you anyway. I wanted you to see my kingdom as your home, my bed as your nest, and my pack as your refuge."

He reached up to cup my cheek, and on reflex, I met his gaze and the tenderness that reflected in those sapphire pools. "And finally, my heart as yours to keep," he murmured. "With my pack in consensus about who we want for our mate, I can *finally* say it: I love you. I want you by my side now, tomorrow, and every tomorrow after until my star and yours sparkle next to one another in the sky."

"I love you too," I said, full of joy to hear him say it at last.

He stroked my cheek, his smile warm and genuine. "Can I tell you a dark elf fact?"

I perked up but probably not for the reason he expected. Maybe I would find out what was going on with the crystal from Telimarr after all. "Of course!"

"We have a ritual dating back to our time underground. A male would go deeper into the tunnels and search for a specific kind of mineral—it gleams to dark elf eyes. He'd present it to his intended female to ask for a mating bond. If she accepted, she turned it into jewelry unique to them. In modern day, it's called a stone match, and it's practiced to show permanence in a relationship," he explained.

"Do you want to have a stone match with me?" I asked in a hush.

"I'm supposed to ask you that," he teased. He stood and reached under a different couch, pulling out a box that looked remarkably familiar. When he came back to where I was seated, he returned gracefully to his knees. "My lady, I have traveled to a cave and spelunked for an arduous period of time to bring you this."

He opened the box and took out a squat and fat prism-shaped crystal. I gasped as he pulled it free and it caught the light. It was a blue-purple color with no hint of imperfections, truly a gorgeous shade that merged our coloring. He assumed a pose of supplication, offering it up to me.

"By that, I mean an incredibly difficult journey of…three hours or so through a well-lit tunnel. And though the trip was long and the choices sparse, I have returned to the surface with a cool fucking rock. Should you accept it and we make stone match jewelry from it, you will make me a reformed and happily claimed tomcat." He flashed a grin up at me. "What do you say?"

I reached out to Marius mentally. He'd suggested I'd know exactly when I would want the right words for Fal, and he was right. The kelpie responded immediately and after a pause for a quick back and forth, I continued the ritual. "I say that no stone match is complete without the efforts of us both."

Fal's slitted pupils rounded out as his lips parted in shock. "What?"

"Be right back."

I got up and rushed to retrieve the box I'd hidden, returning to find the dark elf prince still on his knees and not yet recovered from his surprise. "Um, I don't know what to do next," I admitted.

"Lark, you're killing me. How do you also have a rock for this?" he asked.

"Do you want to see it?"

"Aye!"

"Look at this cool fucking rock," I echoed. I slid onto my knees beside him and opened the box. "It glows in the dark!"

"Oh, you mean it's phosphorescent? Or fluorescent?" He took the silver-veined prism from its velvet bed, inspecting it closely.

"I'm not sure."

"Easy test. We can do it later." He placed it next to his crystal, beaming. "They'll make beautiful jewelry together. I was thinking of replacing my earrings." He flicked the largest eight-pointed star hanging off his earlobe. "You would look nice with some guiding stars of your own. Or maybe a ring."

"Or both?" I suggested.

He put his hand to his chin in an exaggerated thinking pose. "Hmm. We'll figure it out. I have one more thing to ask you, but I can't do it alone."

I was about to ask what he meant when he plopped me in the middle of the loveseat and pushed the crystals to the side. He must've sent a signal over his pack bond, as his brothers piled into the room.

"Hey, Tormund. She loves me," Fal said.

"Congratulations," the redcap replied cheerfully.

Marius raised a brow as he slid to his knees next to Fal. Kauz followed suit, then Tormund. They made a semicircle around me. My heart thudded faster in my chest to see all four princes bowing their heads in submission and holding the pose for a few seconds before they looked up.

"What's happening?" I murmured.

Fal spoke up first. "In many ways, our courtship has been unusual. Yet I've never been more grateful to fate for how we beat some incredible odds to cross paths. You've become a dear part of my life, and I can't imagine continuing it without you. The rest, I've just told you privately." He nodded to Marius.

The kelpie considered before he spoke, and I felt the swift river of his thoughts through our bond. As he gathered the words he wanted and kept them partially shielded from me, I caught on to what was going on. "Fate is a construct we've created to explain the unexplainable."

Tormund turned his head and squinted at Marius. He trembled with restraint but kept his lips sealed.

"I've come to accept that when we refer to fate, we mean the choices we've made and the chances we take. That which leads us into the unknown," Marius continued. "And I am grateful fate led us to reunite with you, p'nixie. I'm here to serve you until my last breath."

"You are both dear to me, too." I clutched my hands to my chest, trying to keep myself contained. I was fit to burst from a surge of pure happiness.

Kauz spoke up next. "You've brought color to my life, my Always. I've been ready to serve since we met. Fal can attest that I was ready to personally escort you to Zemosia."

The dark elf exaggerated a shudder. "He woke up and *demanded* that we help you. It was the most emotion I've seen from him in years. Not so eerily calm anymore."

"I saw that you needed a champion, and seized the job under my brothers' noses." The dream warden lifted his shoulders and wings with pride. "I wanted to be the one to free you. I put every bit of myself into the task, and now I'm here to elevate you further."

I nodded, a lump forming in my throat as the corners of my eyes pricked. They were joyful tears, but I didn't trust myself to speak. I didn't want to ruin the moment.

Tormund mirrored me, his eyes shining with emotion. "I just love you so much, li'l bird!" he exclaimed. "You gave me back my control. It's the best gift anyone's given me. I'm so glad we freed you, and now...can I ask her?" He turned to his brothers.

They switched to speaking Serri. It was a habit, I think, even though I understood them now. Amongst their murmuring, Marius said, "Let him have this." And the other males agreed.

With a big grin, Tormund turned back to me. "Join your soul to Pack Sorles and be our princess, Lark. We want you to be ours forever."

I drew in a breath to fix my composure. It was really happening. I was truly about to be theirs. "I love you all and would be honored to join Pack Sorles."

Fal tugged me off the couch and into an embrace with all four of them. I purred deeply as they smothered me and I lost myself in the press of affection and their intoxicating scents. My head swarmed with need at the heady combination of sunshine, fertile blooms, and fragrant, burning wood.

Their kisses came just short of my lips, except for Kauz, who cupped my face and sealed his mouth to mine. We shared in the taste of Always as his brothers growled in jealous tones.

Their restraint reminded me that there was still a sword looming over my head, and the words *Pack Ellisar* were etched into the blade. Shivers traced paths over my skin, putting a tremor in my wings. Kauz drew back to look at me.

"It's time," he said to Fal.

"Aye, I suppose it is," the dark elf sighed. "Are you hungry, Lark?"

I nodded, even though my stomach was threatening to sour. He got up to signal to the house moths. The small eclipse traipsed in and set up a table in the center of the room with a platter of finger foods and a few berry trifles in decorative jars. I latched on to the sight of them. Maybe I could eat after all.

Marius insisted on retrieving my plate, and Tormund gave me a hopeful glance. I ended up between them on the floor, accepting food from the gentle giant's hands. We chatted idly while we ate.

Once we were finished eating, Fal's expression turned serious. "I wanted to tell you everything about tonight and give you an option. Even if it does ruin my father's plan. My brothers and I are in a rare consensus about hating his fucking plan anyway. It is very risk-reward. The reward is the deaths of Pack Ellisar, and hopefully Cymora too."

"But the risk?" I asked.

His face smoothed into a disapproving mask. "Is potential harm to you. Listen carefully. If you want to do it, we'll do it. If not, we'll push you into heat and claim you. *Right now.*"

While I was flush with heat and anticipation, I tried to clear my mind enough to listen to the plan. Fal talked and talked, to the occasional interjection from one of his brothers. His only omission, that I could tell, was that we were going to a mysterious "event." But the rest...

I gulped an audible swallow. I was glad they'd told me and given me a choice. The amount of danger the plan could put me in was terrifying.

"Using her as bait continues to be unacceptable," Marius grumbled.

"Illusions don't cover scent." Kauz used his patient tone, which suggested they'd already discussed this. "The bark brothers will notice if 'Lark' doesn't smell like an omega almost in heat."

The kelpie snorted in derision. "If I were to replace her under an illusion, they'd be dead before it matters," he deadpanned.

Fal pinched the bridge of his nose. "As hilarious as it'd be to see *anyone* mistake you for Lark, it won't work. It has to be her."

"All of this for a life debt," Tormund muttered.

"No, it's for all of us," I said quietly. "If Pack Ellisar is dead, then the contract doesn't matter. There'll be no chance of a grievance." The fact that we would save Laurel too if everything went as Rennyn had planned it was a bonus.

It'd push the limits of what I could take as a violence-averse omega, but it was a sound plan, and the reasons for every move made sense to me.

"I'll do it," I said, unable to raise my voice from lingering fear. "But I want a weapon."

Fal and Marius exchanged a glance. "You'll have the best one in our arsenal," the dark elf promised. "Now, let's go back to your rooms. The mothkin have been preparing another surprise for you. I think you'll love it, *mo stór*. Everyone else, get dressed. We're going out."

63
LARK

Fal and I stepped into my rooms, and I spotted the next surprise. Giddiness tingled over my skin. We were still going to have fun tonight.

A cluster of female house moths, with Jani and Lon at the front, waited beside a small boutique. There were clothes still hanging in protective wrappings, then shoes, makeup, and jewelry on display in their boxes.

Fal soaked in my reaction. "Remember when I got your measurements? These are all yours. The dresses are audition pieces from several designers who want to be your personal tailor. The prompt was to make a pixie dress for a Serian princess. They've included accessories to complete the looks, but no one would mind if you mixed and matched." He winked at that.

"All this is for me?" My lips wobbled with emotion. Stars, he had to have been planning this since he'd first gotten my clothes measurements.

He stroked his fingers through my hair and nodded. "I can't take it anymore. Kiss me with closed lips, like we're fumbling teenagers," he invited.

I was more than willing to do that. I tilted my head up to meet his lips but couldn't help a giggle. It felt purposefully awkward not to taste one another's pheromones. He drew back and licked his lips anyway, growling in a way that was more alpha than refined prince. "Enjoy picking your outfit. You have plenty of time. Remember, this is our date, and I'm going to show you a great time."

"I can hardly wait."

I watched him leave and pushed my worries to the side as I turned to the gaggle of house moths. Jani and Lon introduced the new mothkins as the handmaidens that served the other princesses. The group waited as I inspected the dresses first.

"You should try them on, Princess. See what fits and feels best," Jani suggested.

The handmaidens provided several extra hands to help me in and out of each dress. There were eight garments in total, all fashion statements in their own right. If Fal hadn't mentioned pixie dresses, I wouldn't have immediately thought that was the inspiration.

I didn't have to be tied into any of them, though one did have a bold slit up both sides that showed flashes of my undergarments. It was an automatic no. I inspected each dress when it was on my body, and narrowed down to the right selection one by one. Once I picked the best dress, the handmaidens swept me up in a flurry of activity.

There were appropriate accessories to find and makeup to apply. I tried not to giggle as one determined house moth painted my face while another asked if I wanted the undergarments with extra lift or extra support. A third suggested I forgo heels for a pair of slippers. And those shoes she was waving around were *very* cute.

"One at a time, ladies! Also, extra lift." I wanted to look sexy for this event. Whatever it was, I was attending by Fal's side.

Despite my request, there was a lot of work they needed to do to get me ready. A fourth moth tiptoed behind me with brushes, combs, and flash curlers for my hair. Lon took my right hand, and Jani my left to file and paint my fingernails with shimmery pink-purple lacquer. I started to feel like a posable doll with so many hands preparing me at the same time.

The house moth with the shoes returned, showing me each pair one by one. I decided on the slippers anyway. They were a dark purple cloth, cut and shaped for support while also designed to look as if I'd wrapped my feet in indigo leaves fresh out of a Seelie forest.

I saw the inspiration reflected back at me in a full-length mirror once we were all done. My chosen dress left my shoulders bare, with floaty sleeves that ended in a bell shape around my wrists attached to the bodice. The fabric hugged my torso and formed a design of layered feathers on my upper chest.

The gravity-defying undergarments pressed my breasts up and out to make an alluring crease. The handmaiden that'd helped me into it nodded in approval. "Siora always says an omega's décolletage should cause alphas to break their necks. I think yours will," she said sweetly.

Siora would absolutely say that, I thought, picturing the voluptuous nixie in something far more daring than what I was wearing.

I smiled brightly and thanked her before swishing my skirts around. The best part about this dress was the layered skirts that tinkled from multiple tiny bells with every movement. The back of the fabric hit my knees, so there was no danger of sitting on any of the silvery bells that'd been sewn all the way around each skirt. To finish off the pixie dress inspiration, this garment came with a braided silver belt, from which hung more bells that chimed gently with every sway of my hips.

It was perfect. My dust clung to it the longer I wore it, giving it the kind of sparkle it needed to really pop. I completed the look by putting on a pair of amethyst hoop earrings. They glinted while I adjusted my hair to frame my painted face just right. I'd grown my hair out enough that, even curled, the white strands brushed my bare shoulders.

"You look beautiful, Princess," Jani said.

"There's one more thing. A gift just arrived," Lon added. The house moths squeaked excitedly as they gathered around to see what was in the box she handed me. We gasped together when the light hit the bracelet within. It was a solid chain of gold with amethysts and diamonds glittering upon it.

I knew what this was before I even read the note folded up in the box.

Larkie,

This is a special bracelet that's been treated with multiple layers of magic. While you're wearing it, it will completely change your scent. <u>*Please wear it!*</u> *Otherwise, your pre-heat smell is going to start a hundred fights tonight.*

Love,

Your Favorite Bonus Dad

I put it on. The first thing Fal had explained was about Rennyn and his involvement in orchestrating what would happen tonight. *"My father knows what he's doing. He's acting in his position as Spymaster of Serian. Aye, surprise, he's got his fingers in thwarting every treasonous plot, murder, and kidnapping attempted in and around the palace. He has almost a hundred years of experience outmaneuvering alphas with more brains than the bark brothers combined.*

"With that in mind, your role in his plan is to lure the bark brothers out of hiding. They have to have a reason to act recklessly, and they will. Your perfume could cause any unbonded alpha in this city to think with his cock, let alone three males who already know what you smell like. But we're going out in public, so you cannot go around smelling breedable until the right moment. My father is going to give you some shiny bauble layered with questionably legal spell work his spies use to obfuscate their scents. And he's going to do the same thing to Marius, Tormund, and me just because he thinks we stink. You must wear it."

So far, Fal was completely right about how tonight would go. Some of what he'd told me had been based on his intuition, as he'd been benevolently manipulated by Rennyn countless times to avoid being in the wrong place at the wrong moment.

"Should I tell the princes you're ready?" Lon offered, cutting into my thoughts.

"Yes, please." I practically vibrated with anticipation for my mates' reactions when they saw me all dolled up. In the meantime, I thanked the gaggle of handmaidens for their help. They curtsied happily and rushed off to go help the other princesses.

I was only alone for a few minutes before Kauz slipped into the room. He froze three paces in my direction, and his eyes widened, exposing more purple-threaded nebulae. "Wow, sweetheart. I think you stopped my heart for a moment. You're a vision."

"Thank you." I wiggled my wings with joy. "You look great as well."

I didn't think I'd seen him in a suit before. His jacket was a deep plum color, and his pants and undershirt were black rather than his signature gray. He wore a set of dark gloves with intricate stitching along the back that glowed the same silvery white as his magic.

He came over, pulling at his jacket sleeve, lips parted. Whatever he was going to say went unaired. By the shape of his eyelids, he was definitely looking at my décolletage. "Kauz," I prompted with a giggle.

"We have to dress you up more," he said, giving his head a shake. "I'm here to place a tracking spell on you before we go."

He pulled on the top of my dress so he could pinch the edge of my undergarment and leave the spell on it. "This looks uncomfortable?" he ventured.

"It's the extra lift version."

"Aye, it's lifting all right." He flashed his blunt teeth in a grin.

"I was wondering whether I should have all this showing tonight. You're the voice of reason right now, and even you're distracted."

"I have eyes, my Always." He rested his palms on my hips, and I swayed in his hold to make my skirts rustle and ring with tiny bells. "Don't cover a thing. I can't wait to see everyone else's reactions."

We shared a conspiratorial look. "Let me see if anyone else is ready through the pack bond," he murmured. His gaze was intent on mine as he stepped to the sway of my hips, drawing me into an impromptu dance in the meantime.

As we moved together, he wove an illusion over himself, transforming into a second version of me. This was part of the plan too. With his magic and wings, his role tonight would be to sow chaos and spirit me away from danger.

His lips eventually twitched as he said in a higher voice, "Marius isn't dressing up. He's guarding you tonight."

We parted, and he mimicked my pose, hands laced over his belly, as Marius walked into the room. He'd cleaned himself up, but he was in plain, dark clothing with a pair of axes tied to his hips. He glanced between us, brow raising.

"Who wears it better?" Kauz asked.

"Try mimicking a flute. You sound like this right now." Marius spoke at the top of his register, which wasn't very high, considering his deep alpha voice. He came over and put his arms around me, murmuring, "I see I'm breaking some wrists tonight."

"Better than necks," I mused.

"That's a good idea. Thank you, p'nixie."

I nearly protested, but I could sense through our bond that he wasn't serious. He sniffed me, his lips twisting to the side with a chuff of displeasure. I had a similar reaction, since he smelled faintly of moss rather than his rut scent. But maybe that was a good thing for us both.

"A gift is more enticing when it's wrapped with a bow," he said.

"And meant for another male?" Kauz added. His mimicry was slightly more feminine.

The kelpie's ear flicked. "Aye, I suppose that's how that saying goes. And not inappropriate for what we're about to do to the bark brothers." He released me with reluctance but went to pace the length of my receiving room with barely leashed energy.

Kauz let his illusion go and put his hands on my hips again. This time, we swayed together with him behind me, and I leaned my head back on his shoulder to admire him. I was glad one of my mates was unaffected by all these pheromones flying around.

And as if I'd summoned him with my thoughts, Tormund came into the room next and poorly concealed a growl. I sighed inwardly. The redcap seemed to find me every time I was having a moment with Kauz. He probably thought I just sat around staring wistfully into the dream warden's eyes—not that I would be opposed to doing exactly that.

Kauz gave me his knowing smile and a wink before letting me go. "Hi, Tormund," I said. He and I took each other in across the room.

Over time, I'd noticed Tormund had similar clothing tastes to an omega, preferring the feeling of certain fabrics over wearing the newest fashions. Tonight, he wore something that was unlike him, more like armor.

Leather sheathed his broad chest, tooled with an elaborate set of redcap tribal knots in the center. He wore a heavy belt for securing a weapon he currently didn't have, dark pants, and thick-soled boots. An elaborately embroidered red and orange cape hung from his shoulder, a flashy distraction from the way he was dressed for war.

"Tormund is the bark brothers' worst enemy. He knows our forests,

breathes fire, and, despite his gentle ways, would gladly kill another fae if it meant protecting you," Fal had said.

At the time, I hadn't seen it. But the decorative armor was a message of his intentions. While he wore this, I could picture him bathing Ellisar, Dalstin, and Floris in flames.

My gentle giant burst into his usual sunny grin and exclaimed, "Li'l bird! Look at you, you're gorgeous." He picked me up by my hips to whirl me around with a merry peal of bells. "Straight from springtime. We should've gotten you a flower crown."

I giggled, nodding in agreement. "Oh, that would've been cute. Next time."

"Next time," he agreed. I wiggled a bit so he'd put me down, but he pulled me into his chest for a bear hug instead. He smelled, oddly enough, like roses. His nostrils flared and squinted. "Did Dad say you smell bad too? You don't have to wear something that changes your scent into lavender. It's weird."

"He said I was going to start a hundred fights, smelling like my heat." And he was probably right. "You seem very redcap-like tonight. The armor looks good on you," I added.

"Do you want to know a secret?" he asked in a loud whisper.

"Yes," I whispered back.

He finally set me back on my feet. "This is my ceremonial clan attire. My father's probably wearing his version too. It means we're serious."

"When are we *not* serious?" Fal put in.

I startled, not realizing he'd arrived soundlessly, as he so often did with his sneaky feet. The reformed tomcat needed to wear a bell. Thankfully, I had a few he could borrow.

Most of my snark dried up in my mind, along with the rest of my thoughts, when I saw him.

"New suit. How do I look?" he practically purred, adjusting the flawless set of his collar. His shirt and pants were a shade of gray that complimented his complexion. He'd layered on a jacket in his signature navy, with silver embroidery bright at the shoulders and cuffs.

There was only one answer to his question. "Unfairly attractive," I said with full conviction. Rennyn had gotten to him too, as he smelled faintly of frost and ink. Taking away the springtime meadow of Fal's rut scent should've been a crime.

He came over to cup my cheek. "You clean up so well. I just want to make you dirty again." Though I couldn't smell his natural scent, the rut was obvious in his glowing eyes and lusty smile. I flushed hot from how intently he gazed at me, until his nostrils flared. His expression shifted to unamused. "Is that lavender?"

"Aye," Tormund said.

"For fuck's sake. He color coordinated our new smells to match our hues," he muttered under his breath. "I have one last thing for you before we go, *mo stór*. Before you get excited, it's a knife."

I had perked up, before retreating a step as he held up a blade sheathed in a leather strap. *This is what you asked for,* I reminded myself. My inner omega, closer to the surface than ever, wanted to recoil as if he was holding a hissing snake instead.

He waited for me to muster myself before he carefully unsheathed the knife. "This is treated with faebane poison. Smell it."

I took a sniff in the weapon's general direction and gagged. The faebane was so bitter and concentrated that its taste coated my tongue.

Fal sheathed the knife with a nod. "You never forget that scent. It's death. A small wound infected with faebane will kill even the heartiest alpha in ten minutes flat."

He beckoned for me to come closer and waited again as I unstuck my feet from the floor. Once I was listening, he showed me how the small gemstone in the pommel unscrewed. A powdered version of the antidote was inside its hollow shell. The sheath had a locking mechanism that kept the deadly blade secured, which was the only reason I held my left arm out for him to hide the knife up my sleeve.

Once he had the leather band secure, but not too tight, he bowed over my hand and kissed it. "Promise me you will use it if you have no other options." His lips grazed my knuckles, and despite all of our scents being thrown off, I was still slick between my thighs as if he'd kissed a more intimate location.

My wings remained flattened to my back. "I promise," I said faintly.

"You promise what?" he coaxed. He doubled back over his kisses, running his mouth over my littlest knuckles.

A fae promise was not easily broken, even if it wasn't quite a vow. He had to feel my fingers tremble as I imagined the worst-case scenario, where I had to fight for my life and pack on my own. "I...I promise I will use the faebane if I must."

Fal's sigh of relief gusted over my skin. "Good omega," he murmured. "All right. Let's be off."

"Where are we going?" I asked once we were moving together down the hall.

Fal rested a possessive hand at the small of my back. He smiled with a hint of mischief. "Oh, just an event."

"Tormund, where are we going?" I asked over my shoulder.

The big male chuckled. "An event. You'll like it, li'l bird."

Fal gestured to the ceiling with one of his dramatic flourishes. "Stars, do you hear that? He's learning!"

If even Tormund wasn't going to tell me, I'd have to find some patience. I noted other dressed-up groups heading in the same direction as us. Whatever the event was, it had to be big. And we were going as a pack! The first time Pack Sorles would be five members rather than four, even if my forehead remained unmarked for now.

We headed outside to a carriage already waiting for us. The inside was large enough for Fal and me to sit on one side, with the rest of my mates across from us.

"Hey, Lark," Kauz said.

"Guess what," Tormund burst out.

I giggled, my wings fluttering a bit. "What?"

Marius's gaze was on Fal, narrowed in a subtle warning. "It's time for another tradition," the kelpie said.

Fal reached around me to drape a strip of cloth over my face. He tied it behind my head while I whined. What was going on?

"What self-respecting pack of Unseelie doesn't steal their mate away?" Fal proclaimed. "Consider this a well-meaning relocation, *mo stór.*"

64
LARK

I MADE myself cozy against Fal as we rolled toward the event, resting my eyes since I couldn't see anyway. Our disguised scents mingled in the air, smelling of a different pack. I was growing used to it, secretly glad no females would be chasing my mates' real scents at the event.

Fal laced his fingers through mine. "We're all celebrating that you're joining our pack tonight, Lark. Everyone else attending the event is too, even though they don't know it."

"It's not like we've kept our infatuation with Lark a secret," Kauz said.

"Then they can all release the fakest gasp of surprise together when we announce her as our princess at the autumn festival." I could practically hear the dark elf rolling his eyes. "Anyway, Lark, I'm claiming your first and last dances."

"Okay." With that detail alone, I had a good idea of what kind of event we were about to attend. There'd been a few hints.

"We'll leave a little early. How does moonrise sound?"

There was a murmur of agreement around the carriage.

"All right, good. I want our omega home and claimed by the midnight bells."

I pressed my thighs more tightly together. I yearned to be theirs by the end of the night. My mates' attentions were on me, their gazes a caress I could practically feel.

"Finally," I breathed. *And forever.* The next few hours would set the rest of my life on course. I had one night to preserve my fate with these males as my pack.

There was a charged quiet for a while, before Fal broke it again. "Oh, before I forget. Thank you, Marius."

"For what?"

"You know what."

The other male made a sound halfway between a grumble and growl.

The carriage came to a stop shortly afterward. Fal's breath skimmed my ear. "We're here. I'm going to carry you out of the carriage for the big reveal."

I was up and pressed to his chest before I could agree, giggling as he tucked me under his chin to duck out of the carriage. We bounced down a couple of stairs before he placed me on the ground and whipped away the blindfold. I covered my mouth with my fingertips as I took in the estate before us.

The front gates of a palatial residence were thrown open to a steady stream of well-dressed fae. The estate appeared to be coming to full life as darkness descended. Lamps sparkled in every window. Faelights shaped like insects darted between flowers in a lush garden full of blooming flowers.

Fal made a sweeping gesture. "Duke Revantee's spring revel. Delayed by a few days, unexpectedly. Pack Revantee received a generous donation from the crown for their difficulties." He winked, then offered his arm. "I thought you would want to be seen in the more traditional sense, *mo stór*. With me."

I made sure to shut my mouth so I didn't gape as a sense of awe filled me. The dress, the spring-themed event... "We're redoing how we met."

He nodded, grinning. "With a different ending, I hope."

Surely my eyes twinkled with excited stars as I took his arm. I'd been a frightened soul back then, a depleted ghost of myself with a painful limp. Fal had been a shock, something *other* I'd been trained to fear.

We had a chance to smudge the lines of the past. Replace the fear, pain, and uncertainty with love and new beginnings. And *pack*. We entered the event with my other three mates right behind us.

"Pack Sorles," Fal said to the servants at the gates. He barely broke his stride. Instead of checking the guest list for our names, they simply bowed and gestured us on.

As we passed through the gates, the gardens seemed to grow three times as large. Blooms gilded with essence opened our way, and the faelight insects buzzed like real ones. Trees unfolded from out of nowhere. More faelights shaped like owls hooted amongst their branches.

I admired the magic. "Whoa. Look at these illusions."

"Pack Revantee is a kitsune family. They make a point of having impressive illusory work at their events," Fal explained.

As he spoke, a cluster of flowers grown to about shoulder height unfurled their petals. Each contained a glittering letter on the inside to spell out "Welcome, revelers!"

We made our way into the mansion and were greeted and pointed in the right direction by house moths and guards wearing the white and red of Duke Revantee. The flow of revelers slowed in the narrower halls, leaving me to do the same thing as many others. I admired the art on display. Antique paintings, vases, and collections under glass cases were set out for us along the way.

I chatted idly with my mates as we shuffled toward the main event. They'd come to surround me amongst this crowd. Marius in particular stayed alert of our surroundings, and our bond thrummed with his protective instincts.

We reached the party, and the crowd dispersed into the vast, open space of a ballroom. I tilted my head back with a coo. The ceiling had to be another illusion, as it seemed there was no roof, only a night sky with stars to rival the dreamlands. There was a real ceiling up there somewhere, to provide support for the golden lanterns and hanging garlands of flowers. Their floral fragrance colored the air.

"There are so many fae here," I murmured once I was done admiring the decorations. Here and there were full packs, but also clusters of gossiping omegas with their mates in other corners, catching up over refreshments.

"Remember, they're celebrating us. They just don't know it." Fal patted my arm. He was the only mate that'd stayed with me. At some point during my gawking, the other three had disappeared. "How about we dance? It's early, so the floor isn't too crowded."

Hmm, this felt familiar. "I still don't know how," I answered.

Tilting his head, he echoed what he'd said the fateful night we'd met. "Is that so? It's not difficult." After a moment's pause, he added, "It shouldn't be long before the next song."

We waited at the edge of the dance floor. Stars, I was still in trouble. I really wanted to kiss that mischievous smile. I already knew he'd taste like wildflowers, sunshine, and every lusty thought I was keeping tamped down. *No, bad Lark.*

The music rose to a peak before fading out. He led me onto the dance floor and bowed over my hand. Our gazes met as a new song began, and despite the other couples around us and the murmur of many voices all at once, my focus narrowed. I saw only Fal—the grace of his form, the eternal confidence in his expression, and the way he looked at me that had my heart threatening to melt.

He placed my hand on his shoulder and cupped my lower back, drawing us into a dance together. There was not a foot of propriety between us. Maybe three inches, as a generous estimate. Just enough space that our clothes didn't brush.

Without the silencing band crippling my foot, this was easier than I remembered. The rhythm of the music matched the cadence of our steps. I was light as air. I was *dancing.*

My excitement spiked, filling my blood with effervescent bubbles. I could see why Fal loved to seek more challenging ways to express himself through song and dance. Maybe with a lot of practice, I could join him. Until then, being pressed up against him, moving in sync, was blissful. As soon as the first song ended, we went straight into a second.

"Feel like being shown off more directly, lovely?" He looked over my shoulder and lifted his chin toward a few male voices calling his name. "As long as they don't try to touch you, I think I could introduce you to some of my friends."

"You're going to know a lot of the fae here, aren't you?" I asked.

"Aye. You tend to amass acquaintances when you talk as much as I do." He winked at that.

The song came to a close, and we stopped. I nuzzled under his jaw, marking him with...well, I wasn't sure what scent. He did the same back to me without hesitation and didn't leave any pheromones behind at all.

He swept me away to meet his friends, introducing me as his mate. With a group to catch up with, he really perked up. I let him talk, staying a quiet observer on his arm as the group discussed several fae I didn't know and possibly would never meet.

This could go on for a while. Not that I'd attended many parties before this, but every festival and celebration inevitably became clusters of fae idly chatting. I was used to being a wallflower or escaping the moment no one was paying attention to me.

After a while, Fal pointed out a nearby stone column where Marius stood. "Why don't you explore the event a bit? I'll catch up with you," he offered.

"Okay. See you soon." I was happy to leave him to his socializing.

Marius stood with Theodred, who was a hulking shadow also standing with his back to the column, though facing a different section of the ballroom. They were amongst a handful of armed and watchful royal guards.

I walked into Marius's arms, and he tucked me into the line of his body. "You're not supposed to notice your guard, p'nixie."

"But what if he's my handsome beast?" I murmured back.

He didn't answer, just held me a little tighter.

"Daughter." Theodred's sudden rockfall of a voice startled me. "You're distracting him from his duties."

"She's safe right here," Marius said.

Heat brushed my cheek as Theodred turned our way and took in how the kelpie was holding me. "I'll keep watch, then. Go enjoy the party," he stated.

Marius unstrapped his weapons and left them by Theodred's feet.

The redcap king was wearing ceremonial clan attire, just like Tormund had guessed. The knot at the center of his leather chest armor was more intricately tooled, and the cloak that hung at his side was embroidered with a symbol I couldn't quite make out in the folds. He stood rigid and alert, turning to watch the crowd instead of us.

I followed where his gaze pointed, which was toward where Nemensia danced with Elion. She sashayed to the beat, her fins undulating behind her with weightless grace. It was a surprise to see her, because that likely meant all of Pack Serian was here.

We found a peaceful spot to stand together. Marius stood behind me, his arms around my middle. *"Do you want to dance?"* I suggested over our bond so we didn't have to shout over the orchestra's music.

"Nay. This is Fal's date with you, and he's getting almost no time, compared to how long I had you at that inn."

I glanced over my shoulder at him, brows raising. Was this some kelpie loyalty for Fal?

"Maybe." He answered my thought with a brief dart of his eyes. That had to be a yes, then. *"I'm content to hold you."*

The current song drew to a close. Nemensia called a hello to us and bustled over, Elion on her heels. They interrupted the prolonged stare Marius and I were having as we spoke over our bond.

The queen whispered something to Elion. He glanced our way and smiled warmly before whispering back to her. They settled next to us in a similar pose, with the kelpie king cupping his mate's baby bump.

"Look how beautiful you are in that dress, *mo stóirín,*" she said, beaming. "Give those skirts a shake."

"Oh, thank you!" I shifted my hips, and the bells pealed gently.

This started a trade of compliments. I admired the jeweled coronet her hair was up in, and her glinting dress too. I trailed off as the orchestra played an odd, repetitive string of notes. Most of the dance floor was emptying, and the fae gathered in clusters around those that remained.

"A dance challenge." Nemensia sounded excited for it.

"There are always a few at Unseelie events. It's a chance to show off your dancing skills against another fae, sometimes with a boon for the winner," Marius explained. He nudged me forward so our view of the dance floor wasn't completely obscured by the crush of the crowd.

We joined the cluster around Rennyn and Tanith, who were circling more like sharks than dancers as the anticipation for the challenge thickened in the air.

The music changed to an up-tempo piece. Rennyn nodded along before bursting into dance first. Tanith watched with her hands on her hips. He seemed to be making up something new, moving his body with uncommon precision. His feet barely skimmed the ground. I joined in with the rest of the crowd, cheering and clapping.

He danced for maybe a minute before the music restarted from the beginning for Tanith's turn. This was the first time I'd seen her outside of nixie night. She wore a dress that curled around her tall and slender form, its satiny fabric hugging her modest curves tightly. Her dancing was just as quick, though her motions were as fluid as if she was underwater. Her red and gold fins moved with her to exaggerate each ripple and sway of her body. The wavy mass of her unbound scarlet hair flew about her head as she tossed it.

"The second part is what you really watch for. Now they have to imitate one another's dancing style," Marius said.

Rennyn cracked his neck and stretched while the song changed and the tempo slowed for the second round. His red gaze flashed over to Nemensia, and he winked at her. He danced slow and sensual, mimicking Tanith's flowing movements with boneless grace. The fae around us whooped, while I could've sworn I heard her sigh longingly and Elion growling under the crowd noise.

When it was Tanith's turn, she slicked back her hair and held her fins mostly stationary as she mimicked Rennyn's earlier dance. Her heeled shoes hit a few angles that had me wincing in worry for her, but she didn't so much as stumble.

"How do we know who won?" I asked.

"Crowd noise. It's not a perfect system," Nemensia answered.

I saw what she meant. The music gave us cues, and the crowd roared elsewhere for other dancers. Rennyn raised his arm first, grinning as he was surrounded by a wall of noise. The queen cheered for him, while Elion, Marius, and I raised our voices for Tanith, who still had a quieter crowd around her. She bowed her head in defeat, and Rennyn went to her side to pat her on the back. His lips moved, exaggerating the words, "That's my girl!"

Nemensia went to them, which gave Elion a moment to lean in and whisper to me, "I've noticed your heat must be very close. If you want to leave early, feel free to take my carriage back. I don't want you to experience any more discomfort, *mo stóirín*. You've been through enough."

Marius pulled me a step away with a warning growl. Even if it was his father murmuring in my ear, my mate's continued rut said that was too close for a rival male. Elion chuckled and straightened, starting after the queen. "Think on it," he said over his shoulder.

Another of Fal's predictions had just fallen into place. *"Elion will offer you some way out of the plan. He'll disguise it as concern and offer you a different carriage that will remove you from any danger. Usually, he and my father are thick as thieves, but in this case, he's going to be the only royal willing to sabotage everything in the eleventh hour."*

But if I was going to take him up on his offer, I may as well have stayed in my nest. I smiled up at Marius. "How do you feel about refreshments?" I asked.

"I'm sure there are some at our table. Let's go find it, and I'll return to my duties."

We found a few family members at a table in a quieter corner. Siora, artfully draped over a chair in a beautiful dress, licking her lips and making come-hither gestures at males that interested her. Thalas, who was quietly enduring the evening. And finally Eletha, writing away in a notebook while tapping her feet to the orchestral music.

"Of all of us, Eletha is only coming to the event because my father included her in the plan. He calls her his secret weapon," Fal had said.

She lit up when she saw us. "Oh, hi!"

"Hi, Eletha. How's the book coming along?" Marius asked.

"Still working! I'll have another chapter for you to read soon."

I could feel through our bond that he was eager to read it. "Can't wait." He nuzzled just behind my ear in farewell, then headed back to his post.

I sat and sighed as the pressure on my feet eased. Someone had taken a generous amount from the refreshments for us to graze on, and I filled a plate with things that looked good.

"How are you holding up?" I asked Thalas, who was covering one of his bat ears with a free hand.

He nudged his journal so I could see it. Across both pages, he'd made an elaborate ink drawing of a tree at sunset. Each individual leaf had texture. "I'm keeping myself occupied. When the magic show starts, I might sneak in a few measurements. You know how it is."

I nodded like I understood what he'd be measuring. I would've asked about the magic show, but a cramp struck my middle like a punch to the guts. Sucking in a breath, I hunched over in my chair.

Eletha gasped. "Oh no, are you okay?"

Siora straightened. Her chair legs clacked on the floor as she leaned over to rub my back. "Looks like one donkey kick of a heat cramp."

"It is," I groaned. The room seemed stuffy all of a sudden. I was certainly sweating.

Someone else rested a hand on my shoulder, the familiarity and pressure soothing. "Is it time, sweetheart?" Kauz asked quietly.

I didn't answer for a moment, fighting a surge of emotion. I'd endured plenty of cramps just like this one, but I'd never gotten such an immediate embrace of support. "Not yet." I took in my mate's concerned face. "There's going to be a magic show."

He pressed a kiss to my temple. "So I've heard. We're taking measurements." He gestured between him and his father. Siora moved seats to make room for him and he sat down by my side.

"Measurements of what?" I whispered.

He wiggled his fingers to send up silvery sparkles. "Magic. Kitsune illusory magic always has my father's attention. They can do some visual feats that dream wardens struggle with."

We were still chatting about illusions when Fal said behind me, "Ah, I thought I'd find you here." He reached past me to pluck a little cucumber sandwich off my plate and popped it into his mouth. After he'd chewed it, he propped himself on the back of my chair, resting his chin atop my head.

"It's the book nerd table," Eletha said cheerfully.

"Hey, you said it, not me," he chuckled. "Seems I might fit in here better than ever. Lark's convinced me to pick up the habit, for the pleasure of reading to her."

The librarian nixie brightened, while I covered my face to try and hide my incandescent blush.

"On a completely related note, I need recommendations for the sauciest books in the library tower," he added in an undertone.

"Fal!" she exclaimed in shock.

"Don't be like that. I know the type of books you like," he teased.

"Fine," she conceded, blushing in a shade of darker purple. "I have plenty of recommendations."

"You could just have them delivered to our suite. I'll remind you—"

He drew off abruptly and straightened at a familiar two-toned whistle behind us.

"Yoo-hoo," Rennyn called. He came up to the table, holding something bubbly in a long-stemmed glass. "If it isn't my son and all my favorite nerds in one place." His gaze alighted on me, and his smile faded to concern. "You're looking a little warm there, Larkie. No one would mind if you disappeared a little early with the lads."

There was a tap on the back of my chair from Fal. *"When a pair of fish take our bait, my father will come by to encourage you to leave early,"* he'd said earlier.

I took a deep breath to calm my nerves. "I think we might leave after we see the magic show," I said.

"Ah! An excellent choice. I hear wily old Duke Revantee will be showing off. Better hurry outside to get a good spot." With that, the dark elf king waved and faded back into the crowd.

"Tormund's saving us a few spots on the balcony," Fal said, offering me a hand up. He read my expression and quirked a brow. I nodded back, still sure of the plan, even with my reservations. I took his proffered arm and walked with the rest of our table toward the back of the ballroom. Several sets of glass doors were open and letting in a light breeze.

"Do you know what a dream intermediary spell is?" he'd asked earlier. I hadn't at the time. Most dream warden magic was still a mystery to me.

He'd nodded to Kauz, who explained, *"Eletha is very good at it. She joins one fae's dream with another so they share the same headspace as long as she's there. Rennyn loves to use this trick to observe an intended target before he makes himself known. He wants to see how that fae reacts to an omega as sweet as her before coming face-to-face with the Clever King."*

"Who was the target for his plan?" I'd asked.

Fal was the one who answered. *"Laurel. He approached her in her dreams with a bargain that she accepted. Because of Eletha's magic, she hasn't forgotten a word of his instructions. If Cymora and Pack Ellisar take the bait tonight, it's because Laurel arranged it."*

I had to acknowledge that the impossible was reality. Circumstances had twisted so much that we were relying on *Laurel* to step up on our behalf.

"I'm not sure Lark's going to make it to moonrise. Perhaps we really should make our exit once we see this," Kauz murmured to Fal while I came back from my wandering thoughts.

The dark elf felt my forehead. The backs of his fingers felt cool against my skin. "You're burning up. I think he's right."

I made a soft whine. It felt like we'd just gotten here.

We stepped out on the balcony, and Fal snickered as he tipped his hand. "Here are the stairs, my lady, in case you wish to escape me tonight." They curled around and down from the balcony.

I wrinkled my nose at his teasing. "My wings work perfectly well for that task, my lord."

"I would be uncouth if I didn't at least point them out to you," he said, catching his tongue between his teeth playfully.

"Li'l bird! Over here!" Tormund announced, his waving hand emerging overtop the heads of the growing crowd.

We squeezed our way to the front of the balcony, where he'd saved as much space as his arms could reach. That meant I fit in next to him, with Fal beside me and Kauz on Tormund's other side with his wings tucked in tightly. The dream warden took out a couple small magical tools from his suit pocket.

"Duke Revantee's in his fifth century. You can tell because of the tails," Fal whispered in my ear. He pointed out the kitsune in the middle of the patio below, a white-haired figure wearing an elegant robe. Five snowy fox tails tipped in orange waved behind him. "A kitsune fact for you. They're an Unseelie race that integrated with dreamlanders early and thoroughly. Most of their bloodlines have illusion magic because of that."

"But they continue to develop their essence reserves over time, unlike most fae," Kauz added. "My father would love to study with a nine-tailed kitsune, when they reach their full potential, but we don't know any that've reached such a venerated age."

I asked plenty of questions, eager to learn more about one of the rarer Unseelie races. We had time, as Duke Revantee didn't start casting any spells for a good thirty minutes. I sweated on and off, but my mates kept me talking and distracted from my creeping pre-heat.

Marius eventually shouldered through the crowd to join us, standing just behind me like a protective shadow while I leaned companionably against Fal's side. No more cramps came for me while I was surrounded by my alphas, which I was grateful for.

When the illusions started, they exploded into life. I yelped at the sudden burst of red and pink light appearing overhead. It unfurled into the petals of a flower, becoming a delicate bloom that was a solid fifteen feet wide. A few fae cheered around us, accompanied by a hail of polite applause.

That's the most impressive illusion I've seen, I mused. The size, movement, and flashy colors were all things I probably couldn't match.

Several more illusions launched back-to-back, forming more gigantic flowers and the image of a red and white fox above them. I cooed in awe and latched my free hand onto Tormund's arm to share the moment with him. He looked as equally awestruck by the sight as I felt.

"My father's having a great time with this," Kauz murmured. He hooked his thumb toward the patio below.

Amongst the faces turned up to the sky was the whole of Pack Serian in a cluster. Thalas had his wing around Nemensia while he gestured animatedly at the magic on display. "She probably understands a third of what he's saying but loves to listen anyway," Kauz said.

"Do you love magic that much?" I asked.

"I love you that much. You could talk to me about anything."

I giggled. "Love you too."

Fal smacked his lips. "So sweet I can practically taste it."

Kauz nudged him. "Try it sometime."

"And step on your toes, Kauzden?"

"You might find it suits you well, Falindel."

I enjoyed the show while they had their back-and-forth. They were both plenty sweet when they wanted to be. And so was Tormund, effortlessly so, and Marius, who was coming around to the idea. I ached to return to my nest and have them all.

The need nestled deep in my body was the sign that my heat was upon me. There would be no pushing it back again.

"One last dance, everyone. Then we leave," Fal said once the show was over.

Tormund nodded and lifted me, parting the crowd with ease. He took me back inside to wait for the next song, the two of us cuddling in the meantime. The heat of my body practically matched his.

Fal caught up to us after a few minutes. The orchestra went silent and stayed that way for an extended period. My mates exchanged a glance before Tormund released me and stepped away.

I hugged Fal next, and he held me close as I buried my face in the front of his suit.

"The minute of silence is a sign that they're going to play a slow song. Lovers and mates are grabbing one another for it as we speak," he narrated.

I inhaled and mewled quietly. He didn't smell right.

"It's time, isn't it?" There was a sad hush to his question.

I blinked, a little lost where I stood. What was it time for?

A slow tune started to play from the orchestra, and Fal tapped his foot along to the melody. He held my hips and encouraged me to loop my arms around his shoulders, leaning in as I reached up.

We swayed, pressed together, nearly forehead to forehead. The only thing I wished for in that moment was for us to be wearing fewer clothes. But my thoughts were winking out one by one. There was only Fal and the warmth stoking in my core, a raging fire that wouldn't be contained for much longer.

"Stay with me, Lark," he said, threading his subtle bark into the words.

My heat. No. No no no. Not in public. I need my nest!

His voice was without extra influence as he said urgently, "As the lord gives his queen a portion of his will to make her spine unbreakable, I need to reiterate a few things before your heat overwhelms you. Tell me that's all right."

"It's all right." I agreed readily.

"Listen, Lark."

I smiled back, already an attentive audience. I submitted to his dominance with full trust.

He whispered lower than the music and the general hush of conversation around us. "You have no reason to fear the enemies you may see within the next hour. You are stronger than Cymora, Ellisar, Dalstin, and Floris. They've always been bullies, controlling you by keeping you small and alone."

"But I'm not alone anymore," I said without any prompting.

He nodded. "That's right. You will not be sweet nor submissive. You will be a queen someday. There is no force in this world that you bow to. No shadows you fear. Nothing alpha, beta, or omega in nature. Do you understand?"

"I understand."

"And finally, if they get close enough to touch you." He patted my arm, reminding me of the slight weight of the faebane-treated knife secreted under my sleeve. "You use this. As you have promised."

This was the only part I resisted. I *had* promised, but violence never came easily to an omega.

"I—I will," I said faintly.

He pressed his lips together as his nostrils flared. "Such a good omega. I still can hardly believe the stars blessed us so. And to—" He cut himself off, jaw tight. I whined, sensing the misery hiding just under his skin.

"I wish you hadn't agreed to the plan, *mo stór*. Letting them think they've won you, even for a moment, is unbearable. That they even get to smell your heat—fuck. They don't deserve it, nor a chance to get close to you." His hold on me turned protective. "I know why you said yes, and I will honor it. But you are *mine*."

"Yours," I echoed.

My alpha is in distress.

But what could I do to ease his worries?

My instincts pushed me to say something to reassure him. "I love you. I want you in my nest every night," I said, sweet and lyrical.

He smiled sadly. *Oh no. That'd just made it worse.*

"I'd let you give me a baby?" Maybe he wanted one of those.

"If you weren't in heat, you would've never said that." He stopped dancing with me to hug me, burying his face in my hair. He hid a small intake of breath in the white strands, as well as a couple of tears. I wouldn't tell anyone they were there. "I love you too. So much it scares me."

"It's not supposed to scare you," I whispered.

"It's not that. It's knowing I have to let you go."

I clutched the front of his nice jacket. "Not yet."

"Not yet," he agreed. "I swear to you now, I will do everything in my power to ensure you come to no harm tonight."

He held me until the end of the song. As the music's cues softened, he cupped my face with his clawed fingers. The rut glow in his eyes seemed all the more dazzling with the lingering wetness filming them. This was the moment, the signal Rennyn was watching for.

As the last notes of the slow song rang through the air, he swept me off my feet into a dramatic dip and kissed the breath from my lungs. Our tongues twined in a desperate dance of their own as we swapped our real pheromones. My eyes rolled back as I tasted pure sunshine, floral sweetness, and the pollen-like way his fertility bloomed on my taste buds.

And he, in turn, knew I wasn't in heat yet. He'd be able to taste it. I teetered on the edge of it, and while we'd talked, I'd leaned toward my instincts and needs. But the incredible taste of him reminded me that I couldn't fully fall. Not yet. It would be so, so easy. But I didn't want Pack Ellisar to know the scent of my full heat either, not after I'd fought to hold it back for four years.

What was one more hour if it meant I never had to suppress myself again?

Fal righted our balance, his pupils completely rounded. His tongue darted out to taste his lips and his brows rose in genuine shock. "You're so strong. I am in awe of you." He bowed deeply before offering his arm. "Let's go find our carriage. It's time."

65

LARK

WE LEFT the crowded ballroom and filtered past others leaving the revel early, all heading to their own carriages or inn rooms. Fal reached into his pocket and scratched his ear.

"Looks like your earring is loose. Let me fix that for you," he said.

We paused for him to sweep my hair away and tug my earlobe long enough to sneak a plug inside my ear. It was made of essence and activated, creeping down my ear canal to expand and block out any sound. I twitched and whimpered. This was not a pleasant feeling. However, it would dissolve within an hour and give me back my hearing with no negative side effects.

There was one big unanswered question in the plan, and it concerned Cymora. She was a dangerous variable as long as she could command Laurel's song. But we could neutralize the song's effects with these plugs, and reasonably assume my former stepmother was weak and afraid.

"When backed into a corner, all fae revert to their base instincts. They will fight, flee, or freeze. Your stepsister's job was to convince her mother not to run from Neslune until she's used you for her benefit one last time," Fal had explained earlier.

I'd known immediately that Cymora would do it. She wouldn't question how Laurel knew which carriage was ours; she'd take the bait, and they'd be waiting for us to finish our time at the revel to snatch me.

We stopped outside the carriage to signal to the chauffeur—Villi, Fal's steadfast mothkin attendant, who was earning a generous bonus tonight—and Kauz, who crouched on the rooftop of the nearest building. The winged fae saluted to show his readiness. Fal climbed the couple steps up the coach, deliberately rocking it, and opened the door.

A blast of wordless music escaped the threshold. It was beautiful in a way that made my heart ache to stop and listen. With one of my ears blocked, I heard the melody and the mental command of the siren's song as two separate things rather than one ultra-compelling spell.

Put Lark in the carriage. Do not resist. The words felt almost like my own thoughts yet sounded like Laurel's voice.

Fal pretended to be enthralled and backed away, lifting me gently by the hips. As he moved to place me down in front of him, a second set of hands seized my upper arms and pulled with desperate strength. I clamped down to suppress a whine when my right foot banged on a step and my slipper slid off. Pain shot up my leg, radiating from my weaker ankle.

Cymora slammed the door behind me, but not before I caught a glimpse of Fal's face creasing, fangs bared in fury. He held my glittery bracelet of diamonds and amethysts hanging from his fist.

Drive now. Go fast, Laurel prompted through the siren's song. The carriage window was open, letting the order filter to the house moth chauffeur. Even though he had one of his ears blocked too, he pushed the horses into motion as swiftly as possible.

Hi, Lark. Don't talk. She'll know I don't have you under my control, Laurel wove into her song. Cymora didn't seem to notice that Laurel was using it to communicate.

A dim essence lamp was activated over our heads, letting me take in the two mermaids sitting across from me. Laurel was propped against the side of the structure, her open lips pointed toward the window. She looked exhausted, her teal and blue skin washed out with gray tones. Nearly depleted. Her clothes were matted with dirt, threads coming loose in some places.

I never expected to feel this worried for her, but if she continued singing much longer, she'd exhaust her essence and fall unconscious. She was being pushed too far.

Next to her, Cymora had never looked worse. The odor of unwashed skin and filth wafted from her. It threatened to overpower my nostrils and gag me, which would ruin the ruse that I was enthralled and pliable before it even began.

She regarded me back with a bright gleam of something like madness in her eyes. The laugh that escaped her rose and fell discordantly. "Sweet, sweet Metalark. Everyone loves you." Her sweet mermaid voice held that familiar, acidic edge. "Yet you're so helpless. Your mind belongs to the song now."

Marius pushed a single word through our bond. *"P'nixie."*

"I'm okay. Cymora thinks I'm enthralled."

"Don't underestimate her. We're right behind you."

"We're not going to hurt you," Cymora was saying while my attention was diverted. "We're even going to give you back, along with that trio of barkfolk trash. You just have to do one more thing for us and spend the night."

I watched her, oddly detached. Even without Fal's influence, I wasn't afraid of Cymora like I used to be. All that training to confront her, just to end up pitying her instead. Ransoming me and Pack Ellisar back to the crown was a terrible plan, one she would've never made if she weren't so desperate and misled.

As Fal explained it, *"My father had Laurel do what she's good at. He had her tattle different things to Cymora and the bark brothers to pit them against one another. Cymora expects them to kidnap Laurel and flee to Thelis. She's acting to stop them, with a side of saving her fins. At the same time, the bark brothers think she's planning on murdering you tonight to prevent them from gaining their coveted grievance. If you're confused, don't worry. They are too. They'll take the bait because they're already paranoid about being fucked over."*

"Soon, we'll be free," Cymora muttered. "Hopefully I never meet another starsforsaken Unseelie." She continued to talk to herself as the carriage transitioned to a road of hard-packed dirt.

I clung to my connection with Marius like a lifeline as each minute passed one eternity at a time. He supplied soothing waves of reassuring emotion and remained a steady presence at the back of my head.

We were heading deep into the woods, where the mermaids had been sleeping. According to the plan, the barkfolk were made to think I'd be murdered here. They'd assumed Cymora wanted to stash my body in the middle of nowhere until it dissolved into stardust.

"No. I will show her. I will show all of them. She deserves recognition under the waves. She has the song. The *song*," Cymora whispered in an increasingly frantic cadence. "Which means *I* have the song. We will be great. Greater than them."

Stars, what was she even talking about? Laurel and I exchanged a glance. My stepsister's expression was pinched with misery.

Another heat cramp hit me, the most brutal one yet. The agony that hit me was like my guts were a pasta that'd been twirled around a massive fork. Cymora's discordant murmurings faded into a shrill tone in my ears.

I breathed shallowly through the pain as Marius called my name at the back of my mind. *"I'm okay,"* I sent back, not that he seemed to believe that. *"I just need—"*

A horse screamed as something happened outside the carriage, marked by a great and terrible *crack*. Our momentum slowed significantly. "Oh no. Oh no! Stop, stop, stop!" Villi squeaked outside.

Wood groaned and snapped as something heavy bashed to the ground, shaking the whole carriage. It had to be a fallen tree. The whole team of horses panicked, snorting, jerking, and neighing as we came to a stumbling stop.

In the full dark of night, it was impossible to know what flicked against the carriage, dropping something inside before slamming the window shut. A bulbous glass bottle hit the floor and exploded, wreathing the air with greenish-gray gas that smelled of pepper and vinegar. It assaulted my senses immediately. My eyes watered, and I choked on my next breath. Cymora hacked violently.

But Laurel...she stopped singing to cough and then gagged. She dropped to her knees, bent double and vomiting.

The carriage opened from the outside, and through watering eyes, I saw something snakelike emerge from the darkness. Dirt clods rained from it and a second creeping form before they struck, wrapping around Cymora's arms and throwing her outside.

All Marius heard from me was a panicked, *"We're stopped. Smoke bomb. Tree roots!"*

At least, I thought that was what they were. They made a sound like a rope pulled taut as they whipped around my arm and waist next before I was flung out of the carriage and skidded in the dirt and grass for several feet. A new scrape burned down my side.

There was an intake of breath nearby. "Stars, could it be?" asked a voice I'd relegated to my nightmares.

I tensed with a sound of denial. Of the trio of brothers, the eldest was the one who loomed over me. My wings provided dim illumination, enough to show his bulky outline and the gleam of malice in the whites of his eyes. The forest rustled behind him, at his command. For one all-important moment, I froze in fear.

Smooth wooden fingers closed around my waist, dragging me further away from the carriage. We disappeared into the all-encompassing darkness of the nighttime forest. Dread shrilled under my skin, setting every nerve on edge.

"No! Let me go!" I cried out. I squirmed and pushed against the plates of bark that covered his chest like armor. They were thick and mossy, and my fingers slipped on the grassy texture of them.

"Shut up. I'm not going to hurt you," he hissed. One of his hands gripped my shoulder, forcing me toward him. The little hairs on my nape stood up as he scented me.

This is still the plan, I thought with rising panic. It crept up my throat, cutting off my air.

Roots slithered and whipped around us. "I'm just going to put you here—" Ellisar cut himself off with a lusty growl. "No, fuck it. You're in heat, aren't you? My brothers will handle Cymora while I—"

I drowned him out with a screaming keen, signaling my distress at the top of my lungs. Pain exploded across the side of my face. The force of his blow whipped my head to the side. "I said shut up. Stupid omega," he snarled.

My bond with Marius quaked with his fury. The pain from Ellisar's slap reverberated between us. I held on to the feeling of feral rage originating from the kelpie, letting it mute my first reaction to the eldest barkfolk. I didn't need to panic; I needed to *fight*.

Ellisar's grip on me tightened, and something new wound around my head. The taste of dirt and wood forced its way past my lips as the binding root muffled my distress.

Oh stars, oh fuck. It was too close to my night terror. He was too strong, and his magic would hold me down for him. All he had to do was bind my limbs next...

"You owe me this," Ellisar was saying. More roots slithered up my body as I struggled and pushed against his hold. Fabric tore against his jagged bark. "You signed that contract. Did you really think running away to Serian would get you out of it?"

Something flexible and dirt-covered closed around my bare ankle. *No, I'm not going to allow this to happen.* I had another recourse, and I'd promised Fal I'd use it. I reached up my sleeve and unlocked the knife from its sheath, drawing it in a bitter, wafting trail of faebane.

With all of my might, I jammed the knife between the plates of his bark. He howled in pain and tossed me away. His slithering roots slammed me against the unforgiving line of a young tree's trunk. The bark crushed a diagonal line across my wings and back. My head missed bashing against the tree by inches, whipping through empty air as my spine bent backward.

I began to slump toward the ground, dazed by how quickly I'd been injured. Ellisar's outline approached, his teeth flashing in the glow off my wings. He grabbed my root-covered neck and hauled me up with an irritated growl. I saw another opening to buy myself more time.

Though my back seared with pain, it didn't stop me from reaching up toward the wooden mask covering his face. I pressed my index and middle fingers into the hollows under his eyes.

Kauz and I had practiced the spell I unleashed, though I'd never cast it on another fae until now. It would afflict Ellisar with disorientation, most likely. A more practiced dream warden could use this spell to create severe hallucinations even in a waking mind. I put as much essence into the magic as I could, hoping to overcome inexperience with sheer force.

Ellisar released me abruptly. The root around my neck and jaw tightened and I clawed at it as it closed off my air.

Light bloomed nearby. The glare made the dark spots invading my vision all the more apparent as I choked. *Thwump!* The pressure around my head abruptly eased, and I crumpled to the forest floor.

I gasped for air and spat out the root, unwinding it by its newly cut end and kicking away the other root around my leg. Kauz offered me a hand up. I rasped out a sound of sheer relief to see him.

A couple paces away, Ellisar was clutching at his face, his eyes covered in a pitch-black film of magic. "This trick isn't going to save you. All you've done is piss me off," he growled.

Tree roots, branches with jagged ends, and vines twitched and rose from the ground, pointed all around him. They writhed and jerked in a way I'd never seen from Ellisar's magic. I'd seen him make bushes walk and crops dance. The way he unleashed the greenery at his control now was more akin to a blind frenzy.

Kauz mantled his wings over me protectively. Strings of silver essence wove between his fingers as he spun up a spell. A shell of essence appeared around us, shaped like a massive egg. Several vines and branches snapped against it and bounced off, but a sharpened stake of jagged wood pierced through while he was still reinforcing the spell.

Droplets of blood spattered my face. I shrieked to see a bundle of roots protruding from a hole in Kauz's wing.

"Gotcha," Ellisar mumbled. The bundle started to unwind into three separate points that pointed toward our torsos.

Kauz didn't stop moving his glowing hands. At the end of his spell, he snapped his fingers. The shell around us flashed, and the roots sagged, severed cleanly. He pushed the sharp edges back out of his wing, a grunt of pain escaping his gritted teeth.

My heartbeat quickened. His *wing!* All I could see was the stream of crimson gushing down the curve of it. "It's all right. We have to move," he murmured, nudging me out of my horrified stupor as he pulled me to my feet. "Get to the carriage."

The carriage. The plan. Right. My bruised wings gave a halfhearted flutter as I stumbled a few steps. The dim star of the carriage's lamp formed a beacon through the underbrush. Ellisar hadn't dragged me too far. The carriage was a short sprint from here. It'd stopped mere feet from the bulk of a fallen tree. Villi's fuzzy outline showed that he was on his feet, still trying to calm the team of horses.

"—you overreacting bitch!" Dalstin was shouting. He and Cymora were also nearby, standing in a ditch by the road, a couple yards between them. She held her fists in front of her, while he gripped a wooden spear with both hands, waving around its sharpened tip to emphasize his words. "You've ruined everything!"

"You were going to kidnap my daughter!" Cymora screamed back.

"So you were going to *kill* our meal ticket? That grievance is going to give us a king's ransom! We were going to share it with you. But no! Not anymore. I'm going to skewer your ass, and we're going to have a fucking fish fry instead."

Eyes wide, I turned stiffly to look at Kauz. His body rippled with an illusion that he formed carefully. He transformed into a second version of me, mimicking smudges of dirt around my mouth, a rip up the side of my dress, and a missing slipper.

He motioned that he would step out first and distract them while I made for safety. I would have to run. I'd bruised my wings before; they'd crumple under my weight if I tried to fly. Either way, as long as I got to the carriage, I'd be in a defensible location and out of the way of any fighting. My mates could handle the rest.

Movement caught my eye. Floris emerged from the carriage, pulling a gray-looking Laurel out of the lingering smoke. He had a knife to her throat.

"No," Cymora gasped.

Both barkfolk whipped their heads around as Kauz burst from the tree line. "Hey!" he shouted in his best impression of my voice, high and wispy. Floris and Dalstin exchanged a glance. The latter even shrugged.

But Cymora's gaze narrowed in suspicion as Kauz approached them. "Let my stepsister go!" Stars, we should've worked on his delivery.

I counted to three in my head, then went to the road and started running. The barkfolk would sense my movements in the undergrowth. Even without Ellisar's more advanced magic, they were attuned to the natural world in a way that'd give away the deception.

Cymora's gaze flashed from the fake Lark to me, and she rushed to intercept me. I flapped my wings on reflex, but couldn't achieve much lift or speed to slip around her. She drew a knife from her belt and jammed the cool, sharp edge under my chin. I held on to her arm, trying to wrestle it and the knife away from me. But she was a female possessed, holding on to me doggedly. "Be still," she hissed.

Dalstin's nostrils flared as he caught a whiff of my scent. "What the —don't move, Cymora, or my brother slits her throat," he said, gesturing to Floris and Laurel.

My stepsister had a trail of blood leaking from the side of her mouth and down from her gills. The whites of her eyes flashed in fear. I tried not to focus on her, considering how close I was to panicking once more. If Cymora was forced to choose between saving Laurel or cutting my throat, she'd kill me in an instant.

The male behind Laurel muttered something nearly inaudible. His fingers twitched occasionally, which was terrifying while he had a hostage.

"Don't hurt my daughter, or your precious omega dies." Cymora sounded more caustic, now that she had some control over the situation.

Breathing shallowly, I saw one opening. I focused my gaze on the knife Floris held and wove an illusion over it, working my magic as fast as possible.

"Release Lark, and we release Laurel. No one has to get hurt," Dalstin said slowly, though his grip shifted on his spear. He was slipping into a ready stance as he spoke. "I might even forgive you for trying to pull this stunt—"

Ellisar burst from the trees, the tips of dozens of tree roots slithering around his feet like living creatures. More uprooted as the moments passed, big, small, sharp, and splintered alike. There was still a film over his eyes, but it was fading, revealing the cold, green malice hidden underneath. "Stop wasting time. Kill that imposter," he ordered, pointing behind me.

Glancing down, Floris shrieked like a small child and flung his knife away. He'd finally noticed the flame I'd illusioned on its blade, creeping into the bark over his fingers and hand. Laurel jerked away from him, groaning as she slumped to the ground.

Dalstin sighed and lowered the spear, charging past us. "That's Kauzden, isn't it?" Cymora breathed in my ear. "Hope he survives, just to see me slit your throat. He deserves to watch you die."

"You wouldn't," I whispered back, all bluster. We needed more time. Where were my mates? We couldn't win this fight without all of them.

"I see what's happening now. This is a trap. Well, if I cannot have my freedom, *no one* gets to have you."

My blood turned to ice. I breathed shallowly, unable to turn and see whether Dalstin successfully struck Kauz. Sharp metal bit into my skin. I despaired that I couldn't do anything else to help him. Though I swore I heard the thud of hoof beats in the dirt.

Laurel shifted, her legs melting together. She grew a mermaid tail under her skirt, and its iridescence shone like a thousand silvery teal gems. She sucked in a huge breath. Rennyn had taught Laurel *something* about her siren's song, but Fal hadn't known what it was. We all learned it firsthand as her siren's song emerged in a forceful shockwave.

Stop!

Cymora and the barkfolk froze for several heartbeats. Tree roots collapsed to the ground with brittle snaps. A trickle of blood flowed down my neck from the tiny cut Cymora had inflicted.

A redcap's fiery roar split the air. *Tormund!*

He wasn't the one who snatched the knife from Cymora's hand and pulled her away from me. Fal flung her to the ground and turned toward me, his pupils retracted to panicked lines. He jerked his chin, mouthing one word: "Go."

I stumbled into a run for the carriage. Laurel and Floris were between me and safety. But the fangless alpha wasn't paying us any mind, looking over my shoulder. He trembled before putting faesteel in his spine. His voice emerged with a lisp. "*You.*"

"If it isn't fangless Floris," Marius taunted. He emerged from my shadow with his weapons drawn and fangs bared.

I did my best not to look back as I bent over Laurel. "C'mon, shift back," I muttered, hooking my arms under hers as I tried to drag her toward the carriage. Her tail undulated, helping her along.

She opened her mouth to reply, only to scream. Magic wrapped around her suddenly, ancient and humming and *terrible*.

I whipped away from her on reflex. The weight of a grievance, as I instinctively felt down to my cowering soul, settled around her. *A debt owed.*

"I remember..." Laurel gasped. I didn't understand what was happening, only that Cymora must've died. Laurel pulled at her matted hair, her eyes rolling back. Her forgotten memories had to be assaulting her mind.

"You can't pass out here," I said urgently, pulling her along again. Why did she have to be so starsdamned heavy? We were so close to safety, the open door of the carriage just a couple yards away.

Another set of hands dug under Laurel's tail. "Thanks for saving my life," Kauz said to her. He still looked like me.

He hefted up her weightier half. I got behind her and lifted under her arms, and together, we got her up and onto one of the benches inside.

She mumbled, trying to look in his direction. He shook off his illusion, and I inspected him, not seeing anything amiss besides the bleeding rip in his wing. Thank the stars. He flashed what was meant to be a reassuring smile before leaving and shutting the door behind him. He'd seal the door shut with a sigil.

We were safe.

I exhaled, though none of my tension escaped. I was still wound as tightly as a drawn bowstring. Our surroundings stank of vinegar, blood, and vomit. The sounds of fighting were only intensifying outside, punctuated by shouts and a bloodcurdling scream. I shrank in on myself with a fearful whimper.

Laurel muttered again, incoherent. She held her head in one webbed hand, the other flopped toward the floor and twitching occasionally. With her full shift, she was too long for the bench, and the pretty, teal fan of her caudal fin sagged over the side. Her breathing was jagged but slowing.

I knelt beside her, taking her hand in both of mine. "You're okay. You made it. Everything's going to be all right." Now that my adrenaline was fading, fear warbled through the words.

Stars, we'd almost died. My mates were still out there, fighting. There wasn't a guarantee they'd escape this uninjured. My only role was to be the bait, and I'd gotten a beating for it. Scrapes, bruises, and cuts were already making themselves known with dull throbs over my body.

"La...Lark?" Fright made her sound like a little girl.

"Yes. It's me." I rubbed her arm, trying to soothe her.

"She's gone." Relief broke across her face. She looked at me and smiled, tears welling in her eyes. "We're free, birdy."

Now that was an old nickname, from a long-lost time where we'd been friends, even sisters to the true depths of that word. My sight swam as I joined her, crying from the sheer weight of what we'd just endured.

"We're free, fishy," I agreed.

"Do you...remember..." Her voice faded, her eyelids falling.

"I do," I assured her softly. "It's okay. Rest now. Eletha's waiting to help you."

Her lips parted before she was gone. Her body went slack, fingers loosening in my hold. I gave her hand one last squeeze before placing it over her belly. I wiped my tears and sat on the other bench to wait.

The sound of fighting continued outside of the carriage. Stars only knew what was going on out there. I picked anxiously at my cuticles, struck by how helpless I was in this oversized box. If Pack Ellisar won the battle against the princes and broke the seal keeping us safe, I would be the only one able to protect Laurel and myself.

If it happened, I'd fight to the bitter end. I'd learned a valuable lesson when I'd struck Ellisar with the faebane-laced knife. When pressured, I *could* fight back. Even on the precipice of my heat. Even after taking a beating.

When the fighting stopped and the silence outside set my ears to ringing, I slid back into a place of instinct. My vision warped. I was a cornered creature, ruled by my feral side as I waited for what came next. There were no voices outside, no sounds of victory from either side. Just a brush of static in the back of my head. Easily ignored.

I wound a vortex spell halfway and let it go. It kept the stale air in the carriage circulating. In my limited magical training with Kauz, we'd learned that if I wound the spell fully, it would snap out of my hands with little control. But I could stop casting it halfway and finish it if I needed to.

Like when the carriage rocked as someone ascended with heavy steps. Panic gripped me as the door started to open, no longer sealed by Kauz's sigil. I finished the vortex spell and shot it straight at the male who opened the door.

66

FAL

FEAR and I had an uncanny relationship. I so rarely feared for myself anymore. I had the words to escape most situations unscathed and the agility of an elf with grimalkin blood when sweet-talking wouldn't suffice.

But for others? Most of my life, fear set in when fate intervened to change the paths of those I cared about. When an event was too big, or the variables too out of control, those familiar lumps in my gut made themselves known. I would lie awake, staring at the ceiling, thinking and plotting multiple ways out of poor circumstances for my friends and family.

With my impending rut, I'd done very little sleeping lately. I'd pathed out my father's plan for Cymora and the bark brothers and found no alternatives for what we had to do. That didn't stop ice from forming over my nerves from the moment Lark agreed to act as bait.

Cold moved in and took residence in my gut, only spreading at the end of our time at the revel. Once I surrendered my mate to Cymora and Laurel, my heart struggled to pump an icy slurry through my veins. I knew a terror for Lark so deep that it'd be a miracle if I warmed again. Willingly setting her inside the jaws of a trap would haunt me, no matter what happened next.

Tormund brought the horses as soon as the carriage carrying Lark and the two mermaids disappeared into the nighttime gloom. My brothers and I gave chase in careful silence, only interrupted by the occasional muttered reaction. Kauz used our pack bond to signal his location as he flew over the carriage. Marius shared how Lark was doing, informed by their kelpie bond.

The briskness of the wind on my face drew further shivers from me. I was as free of the mind-addling effects of the rut as I could get, with the scent of the night forest shoved up my nostrils.

We held steady until the bark brothers made themselves known. Kauz didn't quite panic, but he tapped the bond frantically to say he'd lost sight of our mate.

Find her! I signaled back, an icy fission darting down my spine. We spurred our mounts into the branch-lined maw of the forest, Tormund in the lead with flames wreathing his horns.

Marius's fury was an explosion in the pack bond. "One of them slapped her," he told us in a low growl. His emotions flared a second time like she'd been hurt again.

No, this couldn't be happening. We'd set everything up so she wouldn't be hurt at all—Cymora would want to ransom her, and the bark brothers would lose their minds to lust once they scented her. Kauz's only job was to protect her. Starsdamn him. If she was hurt again under his watch, *I'd* give *him* a nightmare...

We came upon the carriage, now stopped by the bulk of a fallen tree. Tormund rode out the furthest, announcing himself with a crackling roar. He dismounted and moved into the trees. His role was to transform and circle around, to be a fiery presence at our enemies' backs.

I got a look at the fight we were joining as I slowed my noble steed. My heart just about stopped and crystalized over with ice. There were two Larks, and both of them were in mortal peril. A bark-folk charged down the dirt road toward one p'nixie, a wooden spear aimed for her heart. Cymora held the other, a knife to that Lark's throat.

Kauz signaled over the pack bond to identify himself. He was the closer Lark, wearing an illusion of her. On second glance, he was frantically weaving a spell while the point of the spear surged toward him.

Stop!

I shook my head, startled by Laurel's sudden scream of a song fracturing my innermost thoughts. I wore a plug in one ear, as did my brothers, so we didn't obey like our enemies did.

Kauz breathed out a tense sigh, the point of the spear inches from piercing his chest. He stepped out of the way and completed his spell, tossing it toward a more distant figure and haloing him in silver light.

He could handle himself, so Marius and I rushed for the real Lark. He may be stronger than me, but I was always the faster sprinter. My vision blurred as I got there first. I had the knife flying away from Lark's throat and Cymora on the ground in the next blink.

My chest heaved. Through a tunnel of darkness—my pupils had shrunk and shut out what meager light there was—I met my mate's frightened gaze. "Go," I breathed, jerking my chin.

Lark tore away from us. Her scent lingered, its sweetness robbed. The bitter chocolate of her fear was just as efficient at suppressing my rut as the cold air had been. My heartbeat calmed enough for me to refocus on the mermaid slinking across the ground toward her discarded weapon. I vibrated from sheer hatred as she picked up the knife and faced me.

I growled, hand already halfway up my sleeve and unlocking the secret blade secured to my arm. The bitter scent of faebane followed in its wake as I brandished it in front of me. I'd given Lark my best poisoner's blade, but I always had a similar one on hand for self-defense. It was a cliché weapon for a dark elf, poison, but a prince must always have the means to defend himself.

"Falindel." Cymora still had the acid-edged tone that she used to hide so well under melodic sweetness. She was a mere shadow of herself, dirty and haunted by the punishments she'd endured for her crimes. But she was still *breathing* and possessing enough faculties to nearly kill my beloved treasure. It was time she met her end.

"I challenge you to a duel!" a familiar voice shouted nearby. I glanced up for a moment. The lisp was new, wholly from the defanging Mar and I had inflicted.

"I'll fight you. With pleasure," Marius answered. He spun one of his twin axes. "I'll even let you take the first shot."

The other barkfolk, the one holding a spear, offered it to Floris. He must've been Dalstin. A third male stood near the tree line, his mouth open in a soundless scream. Unearthed tree roots and jagged branches beat at a nearly invisible barrier, slowly creating cracks in the magic. Until he broke Kauz's spell, Ellisar was sealed in place.

A blur of metal flashed, going straight for my face. I ducked back. Cymora's blade came just short of grazing my cheek. All of my drifting attention shifted back to her as my lips curled in a vicious snarl.

I shoved her, setting her to stumbling. "Ready to die on your feet, hmm." I swiped my knife toward her. She moved out of the way at the last moment.

"What if I surrendered? What then?" she asked with a discordant laugh, setting my chilled nerves on edge.

"Perhaps you should've considered that"—I aimed a lazy stab at her, testing her slow reflexes—"before committing the capital offense of attacking a prince."

"If you harm me, you'll owe me a grievance," she practically giggled. She wasn't even trying to sidestep me, and had I not pulled my strike, I would've successfully pierced her arm. "Or have you forgotten? I released Lark from her vows, and in exchange, you promised not to physically harm me."

I smirked at her. "Why would I have forgotten that?"

She expected to wear my vow like armor, but we'd already accounted for it. I was free to do as I wished, as long as I killed her in one blow. Her eyes widened, showcasing the gleam of madness lurking just under the surface of her skin.

The ground rumbled beneath us, accompanied by the whipping sound of dozens of roots passing through the air. Fire ignited with a sizzle of heat. *Fuck.* The bulk of the fighting was happening without me while Cymora tried to pull her usual shit.

I purposefully glanced away from her, waiting for her to lunge. This time, I caught her arm and twisted, sending her to the ground again. I kicked her knife away, planting my knee on her chest and my forearm across her collarbone to secure her. She kicked and squirmed, but she had a fraction of an alpha's strength. She couldn't budge me.

"Any last words?" I asked coolly.

I expected her to surrender or spit in my face. Some clarity of thought entered her gaze, and she murmured a final message for Laurel. Then she delivered a glob of spittle to my chin, recognizing that was all she had left.

I had the chance to twist the knife and tell her that the fishling was the reason she'd fallen into a trap tonight. But I knew what sometimes happened when one lingered over their victory, be it in cruelty or just plain gloating. It could still be snatched away.

So, I nodded, then slit her throat. I watched her choke and didn't flinch from the sight of her life draining away. She was the first fae I'd killed, and I expected to feel...something. My emotions moved sluggishly under the chill of my worries, emerging as a rush of relief. This female would no longer twist every opportunity into a way to torture my mate.

I wiped the lingering spit off my face, along with a smear of her blood. I waited for the light to leave her eyes, anticipating the wrath of the old magic. It appeared in an instant and gathered just above us, its presence a physical weight that shrouded me, jerking my shoulders back in punishment.

They say the act of taking a life made the resulting debt heaviest. The grievance for it could be a request for *anything*. Now that Cymora was dead, the grievance went to her next of kin, Laurel.

The responsibility flung off me abruptly. I wheezed, filling my lungs with the stench of death.

"If I, as the crown prince, am not allowed to owe a grievance, surely you as a king should avoid it as well," I'd said to my father during the private meeting we'd had after he woke me from my dream with Lark.

He'd given me one of his favorite looks, a mix of affection and exasperation. I was never quite sharp enough for him, but who was? *"I've danced with the old magic many times before. It likes me."*

"I didn't realize it has emotions."

"That is such a rut-addled thing to say, sunshine lad. I've repaid plenty of grievances without losing too much. I already know what it's going to want for the fishling, and it's something you can't do."

"Which is what?"

"Why don't you make sure you're the one who kills Cymora and find out?"

I'd see what that clever old male had up his sleeve soon enough. I looked up from Cymora's body. "Fuck," I muttered. The rest of the fighting had descended into chaos.

Marius was circling with Floris, still taunting him. The defanged alpha wielded the wooden spear clumsily, but that didn't matter so much. My brother was doing what I'd just forced myself not to do with Cymora. Giving in to the impulse to toy with a weak opponent. Lingering over his inevitable victory.

Meanwhile, Ellisar was steadily uprooting the forest, as several tentacle-like roots followed in his wake. He was approaching the carriage one step at a time. His natural weapons were burning, but that didn't stop him from whipping fire-coated roots at Kauz, keeping him on the defensive. The barkfolk held a makeshift shield of dirt held together by vines, lifting it to block a gout of flame from Tormund.

Where was the third bark brother? My gaze roved for any sign of Dalstin as I screamed, "Mar, what the fuck are you doing? Kill him!"

The kelpie was sure to give me one of his ugliest scowls. I'd put my bark into it, delivering an order as pack lead from across the clearing. I closed the distance between us when I finally spotted Dalstin. Well, part of him.

He'd assimilated into the branches overhanging the duel. His face appeared on the tree, followed by his head emerging from the bark. It *peeled* from the wood, actually, plumping up from flat into the usual dimensions of a fae's head. That was a grotesque sight I was ready to scrub from my eyeballs.

Marius lifted his axes, unaware of the second barkfolk taking shape above him. I lunged and knocked him aside as Dalsin fully formed and plunged down, knife-first, where the kelpie had been standing.

He corrected his balance with a water fae's liquid grace while Dalstin tried to pull his weapon from the dirt.

"Get back," Marius growled. I leapt out of the way, assuming he wanted the space to properly split a barkfolk this time.

He used the flat of an axe to shove aside a stab of the spear, taking advantage of Floris's poor form. The defanged alpha fell forward with his momentum. Marius flipped his other weapon around and beheaded him in one strike.

"Killed him, pack lead," he said dryly, kicking the body that slumped at his feet.

Dalstin grabbed the fallen spear and stood, backing away from us both. He held the weapon properly, his chest heaving as he wavered between pointing it at either of us. "How dare you joke about my brother's death," he gasped out. He had to be in agony from the sudden severing of a third of his pack bond.

Marius rumbled and twirled his cleaner axe. This only pushed Dalstin further back. My brother and I saw the fiery giant turning and taking notice of how close the middle bark brother was coming to him.

Dalstin lifted the spear and went to hurl it when flames ignited at the back of Tormund's throat with a distinctive *whoosh*. He bathed the barkfolk in fire as the weapon went flying. Marius and I threw ourselves to the ground to avoid the smoldering projectile.

Dalstin screamed in agony. He, too, dropped to the ground and rolled, but he was *made* of wood in all the ways that mattered. His armored body burned until he stilled.

Three threats down, one to go. I stood as Ellisar turned our way, a choked scream escaping his mouth from an influx of secondhand pain and severed bonds. Through the patches of flame burning between us, I spotted a subtle detail: the hilt of a knife caught between the plates of bark where they met his side.

"He's already dead," I stated with a surge of bittersweet pride. My sweet mate had stabbed him. While I was proud of her, fuck him for pushing her into a situation where violence was her only recourse.

Even if he evaded us and fled, the faebane would deliver a swift but agonizing death. He had to be feeling dizzy and weak by now, especially with the amount of magic he'd been wielding.

The last barkfolk had activated the sigil Kauz had placed over the door of the carriage by getting too close. Kauz stood just within the semitransparent shield of silver magic, his glowing palms attached to it as he fed it essence. The dome of magic included the skittish team of horses and Villi's fuzzy blob of black fur. My house moth had posted himself on the carriage's roof and squeaked threats at Ellisar. He had a crossbow pointed at the barkfolk.

Villi had promised not to discharge the weapon, of course. He didn't actually know how to use it. After reporting that he'd acquired a crossbow for this job, he'd made a special request: that I put in a good word for how hard he worked tonight with his crushes, Lark's handmaidens.

Ellisar took in how outnumbered he was and changed his stance. I couldn't see his expression under the wooden mask, but one could assume it hardened with determination to deliver one last *fuck you* to us all.

He lifted his hands and pulled at the air with all his magical might. Hundreds of roots, big and small, erupted from the trembling ground. The woods around us groaned at the abuse. Trees shook, then began to tip over, to surprised shouts from us all.

"He's going to bring the forest down!" Marius delivered this in motion, making a desperate dash for the barkfolk. I was still eyeballing the angles of the afflicted trees, frozen with fear that one of them would come down right on top of the carriage.

Kauz unstuck his hands from the sigil. Its shield turned mostly transparent, rippling as he stepped through it. He walked up to the last barkfolk, calm as a summer breeze. He jerked the dagger free from Ellisar's side and stabbed it into his face.

The barkfolk crumpled. The ground tremors stopped and the falling trees halted.

Kauz reached back, and the sigil on the carriage burst. The shield disintegrated outward in a shockwave of essence that pushed every afflicted tree back with a groan of straining wood. We held our breath, but everything around us remained upright except for Kauz. He fell to the ground like a limp doll.

Discarding his axes, Marius bent down to nudge him. Tormund and I arrived next. The redcap was relaxing from his rage form and gave me space to kneel.

The dream warden groaned. I could've wilted from relief to see him still conscious and moving, albeit slowly.

"We did it," Kauz whispered. The magic coating his eyes had faded halfway, revealing the outline of his silvery gaze amongst all those stars.

"You overdid it," Marius grumbled. He helped the dream warden sit up, supporting his wounded wing. "If you'd just done the fancy magic trick, I would've killed him."

"Now, now. You got to kill Floris. No need to be greedy," I teased. I took a moment to put my knife away, locking it into place in its sheath.

The kelpie's yellow gaze flicked my way.

"*Ach*. This isn't the time," Tormund put in.

Marius's ear flicked. "Thank you," he said gruffly, with a nod toward me. "I got caught up in the moment. You saved me from a serious injury, if not worse."

Stars, where was Mother? Seeing her kids getting along would be one of her dreams come true.

"You're welcome," I replied. "Shall we present our accomplishments to our mate?"

We split up for the moment. Kauz snapped his fingers at any lingering fires to extinguish them before they could catch in the dry underbrush. The rest of us hauled the weight of the dead bodies.

As we worked, the cold fist of fear that'd taken up residence in my chest finally began to thaw. Savage joy sang in my heart. We'd done it—these four were gone, returned to the stars or wherever wicked souls went once they met their end. There was no possibility of a grievance from the contract Lark was forced to sign.

We tended to our wounds next. Kauz was the most battered, while the rest of us desperately needed a visit to a rain room. I wrestled with his wounded wing, trying to hold it stead for Tormund, who applied patches of woven essence to either side so the puncture wouldn't tear further. Kauz kept jerking from damaged nerves and hissing in pain.

Once the wing was cared for and properly folded behind him, he put his calm demeanor back on as if nothing had happened. "Right. Remember that Lark was hurt too. One of us should carry her down," he said.

Marius volunteered practically before Kauz could finish his sentence. The rest of us clustered to the side of the carriage, concern and anticipation growing between us in the pack bond.

The kelpie opened the carriage door and was flung away violently. He flew back six feet before hitting the dirt and sliding. A breeze blew my hair to the side.

"Are you okay?" Tormund blurted.

Lark poked her head out of the carriage with a dismayed squeak. Her eyes were two dark, feral moons.

Groaning, the kelpie raised a thumbs-up. "I'm fine," he called back.

I started to snicker, which edged toward full-blown laughter. "The great protector heir, unscathed by battle, just to be knocked on his ass by his own mate. Nice shot, Lark."

Marius raised a different finger in my direction, then got back on his feet and made soft, low noises up at Lark, who responded with a whistling whine. They spoke in that secret feral language until she let him lift her from the carriage and place her on the road. He stroked her hair as she clung to him tightly.

"She says she's bruised across her back and wings. Ellisar slapped her face too. Nothing some wound salve couldn't fix," Marius reported to us. His pointed tone said it all. *If we'd brought wound salve.*

It was a relief to hear she wasn't hurt worse. The royal guard would be here soon, and they always had a medical kit on hand. I'd take it from them and then chase them off.

Her scent was threading through my nostrils again. The notes of bitterness were fading, replaced by indulgent sweetness that made my mouth water for a taste. My thoughts slowed, and my cock stirred, the rut rising in me now that the threats were gone.

"Sweetheart, do you remember me telling you that making your enemies disappear is an act of love?" Kauz asked.

"I do," she said, a feral rasp sneaking into her response.

I pinched myself and took in shallow breaths through my mouth. "We have something to show you." My husky tone suggested I was going to be showing her something that wasn't a set of dead bodies.

Later. Our lovely omega deserved clean mates and her nest before we finally pushed her into heat.

Marius nudged Lark toward the lineup we'd relocated for her to see. We presented her with her enemies like a pack of cats with a well-meaning gift of dead rats. If this was exclusively an Unseelie thing, our more plant-like cousins were missing out. I swelled with pride as she took in the sight without flinching.

I moved to stand behind Cymora's still form. Marius was beside me with his kill, then Tormund with the charred remains of his. Kauz snuck a kiss onto our mate's temple before he took his place behind

Ellisar, who still had her borrowed knife jammed into one of his eye sockets.

"They're gone," she murmured, exhaling with relief.

"Soon to disappear into stardust," Marius said.

"It doesn't...bother you? That you had to do this?" She seemed to be asking this question of all of us. Her expression was still haunted by her brush with danger.

I checked the pack bond at the same time my brothers did. It was like we'd all narrowed our eyes at one another, searching for any hint of doubt or weakness. There wasn't a single flicker from four different souls.

"Nay, *mo stór*. It was our honor," I said for all of us.

"You can finally join our pack," Tormund added a moment later. He opened his arms, and she went straight to him for a hug. She yelped a moment later, and he murmured an apology as he loosened his hold, carrying her carefully by the hips away from the bodies. We followed, leaving those four to dissolve. An afterthought.

A horse whinnied in the night. I turned, baring my fangs. The clop of horses' hooves preceded a group of royal guards on horseback. If we'd still been fighting, this would've been the moment our people intervened in numbers. Marius lifted a hand, signaling to the guard captain, and went over to ask for a medical kit. I relaxed again as Tormund set Lark down close to the carriage.

"Oh, before I forget." I reached into my jacket pocket and pulled out the slipper she'd lost. "Lark, I can hardly believe your feet are this small. Look how tiny this thing is. Either that, or I have cloddish alpha feet."

I lifted my foot to put her slipper's sole against mine in comparison. She giggled briefly and came over to me next. "At least something from my outfit survived." She looked down at her dress with a pout.

"I'll buy you five more dresses just like it." I knelt and dusted off the dirt and clinging grass from her foot before slipping the shoe back on for her. "In different colors. With matching itty-bitty shoes."

My ears perked as she rewarded me with a single musical laugh. I straightened and kissed the tip of her nose, then reached up her sleeve to get the leather strap off her arm. She didn't seem all that bothered to have it removed. I went back to retrieve the matching knife from Ellisar's skull.

Even in my rut-addled state, I cringed at the sound and accompanying gore. I wiped the blade as clean as I could get it on Cymora's clothing before locking it in its sheath.

"I hear another carriage," Kauz reported. His sharp bat ears picked up the sound of wheels in the dirt several moments before I did. Tormund put himself in front of Lark, releasing a testy growl.

"I'll handle it," I sighed.

I'd recognize Pack Serian's carriage blindfolded. It stopped in a stretch of clearing where it wouldn't be too challenging to turn around. Right now, it couldn't be a less welcome sight, and I rode a wave of aggression at the thought of any other males close to my mate, even my fathers.

Theodred exited first with a lit essence lamp bobbing just above his shoulder. He glanced my way and jerked his chin in greeting. "We'll make it quick," he rumbled.

The carriage rocked, and out of it emerged my father, then Thalas, and finally Elion. My alpha instincts threatened to go berserk. I shifted my posture, blocking the way to Lark, tensed for another fight. "Fathers. Do you need something?" I asked coolly.

My father ambled over in his usual carefree way, while my instincts screamed that he was a rival male. A low growl stirred in my chest. Elion reached over to grab his horn, jerking him to a stop. "We're here to confirm a few deaths," the kelpie king answered.

Father finally seemed to really look at me, and his mouth formed a ring as he recoiled. "I also need to retrieve the fishling I owe *so* much debt too," he added, speaking more gently than usual. He jerked his head, trying to dislodge Elion's grip on his horn to little avail.

My sight darkened as my pupils narrowed to suspicious slits.

"We're not going to look at your mate," Thalas added.

"Not even a sniff in her direction," Father said in agreement. "Where's Laurel?"

I walked him and Thalas to the other carriage. Elion and Theodred stopped halfway there to inspect the bodies we'd lined up, murmuring to one another.

My brothers had relocated Lark to the rear of the carriage. Tormund and Kauz stood together, blocking sight of her. Her distinctive smell mixed with herbaceous wound salve. The side of Marius's head was visible, bent to the task of applying it to our mate.

I added myself in the way and waited in the grass. Thalas, I let past me. He received a warning chuff from Marius. "Oh, don't worry. I can't even smell her. Are you all okay?" Thalas asked. It sounded like Kauz answered him from there with a quiet report on what'd happened.

My father went up the steps and entered the carriage. "She's really a fish!" he exclaimed from inside, laughing. "Why is she in mermaid form?"

"She used it to empower her song," Lark answered.

Father poked his head back outside, brows raised in surprise. He opened his mouth to say something to her, just to stop from a chorus of growls from Marius, Tormund, and me. "Rut-addled," he muttered.

Ducking inside once more, he retrieved the mermaid and stepped down with her blue and teal form thrown over his shoulder.

I gave the unconscious girl a grudgingly appreciative look. I'd have to thank the brat later. She had saved Kauz, after all. And upheld her end of the deal to make tonight's plan possible in the first place.

Father tilted his head back and announced, "I declare my life debt to Laurel of Osme Fen repaid!" There was no shift in the air around us, but he sighed as if a great burden had fallen from his shoulders.

"*Now* will you tell me how you're going to repay her grievance?" I asked.

"Not while you and your brothers are eyeing me like I'm a rival male," he answered. "Will wild boy bite my head off if I ask why I smell wound salve?"

"Aye."

"She's all right?"

"She will be," I said stiffly.

"All right, I'm leaving now. Bye everyone. Early congratulations on your mating!" He called before carrying Laurel off. I pressed my lips together to hold in a snarl as I watched him go.

Thalas and Elion followed after him, waving in farewell, but Theodred remained. He gestured to Tormund, who pointed toward his chest. The redcap king nodded and made another come-hither motion. I took his spot so he could go over to his father.

Marius was kneeling in the grass by this point, tugging on one of

Lark's bottom wings. She bit her lip with a soft whimper of pain. "Is it supposed to wrinkle like this?" he asked in an undertone. My eyes widened in alarm.

"It'll flatten when it heals," she whispered back.

I turned my back on them and took up a protective stance.

"Son," Theodred was saying, grinning. "Your first honorable kill." He clapped Tormund on the shoulder, earning a crackling growl. The level of pure fatherly pride on the redcap king's face only grew. "I'm so proud of you. Can't wait to apply the tattoo at our next clan meeting."

My face creased in amusement at the uncertain second growl from Tormund. His father had so many tattoos from his honorable kills. Where, exactly, did the first one go? It seemed we'd find out together.

They parted ways, and Tormund returned to us. We clustered around Lark until Marius emptied the last of the medical kit's salve and lovingly rubbed it into her cheek. "All healed," he said.

She took us all in, her mended wings giving a single flutter. Her voice was little more than a raspy whisper. "Let's go home."

67
FAL

THE CARRIAGE'S tiny window didn't help filter out the reek of blood and the potion one of the bark brothers had lobbed in here. Worse than either of those things was the sheer unpleasantness of bitter chocolate still lingering from Lark's terror. We took off the scent-changing trinkets Father had given us, trying to drown out the bad with our collective rut scent.

Once the carriage door closed to give us relative privacy, she whined and went to sit in Kauz's lap. He showed her the patches of woven essence placed on either side of the wound through his wing. The magic held everything together for now.

"Just a few stitches, and I'll be fine," he murmured.

She put her arms around him and buried her face in the crook of his neck. I thought she'd stay there for the whole trip, but she eventually nuzzled him and reached for Tormund, who gladly held her next. Him, she licked, and his side of the pack bond sizzled with lust.

Holding back my instincts was swiftly driving me mad. It was becoming a more acute need because some kernel of me that was all alpha was pinging around in my mind, sure she was about to perfume. *It's time. It's finally time.*

She lifted her head to glance between Marius and me. He made some kind of inviting sound, and she cuddled up to him next. They made feral noises back and forth, which further riled up my own alpha instincts.

Omegas descended into something similar to a feral state when they went into heat. It was an unpredictable time. My mated friends talked about "types" of heats and how each one was different.

Sweetheart omegas like Lark could turn very angry and bitey for the span of a heat. Or they could beg for babies after stating beforehand that they didn't want a pregnancy. Or cry the whole time from the pain in their abdomen. The possibilities were endless, and most of them made me glad I hadn't been born an omega.

And I was also maybe a little bit terrified of what kind of heat Lark was about to have. Not that I would tell *anyone* that.

She tapped my arm while I was in the midst of my worrying. It was my turn with her, thank fuck. I gathered her up to my chest. She inhaled and purred, shifting so she was breathing in close to the curve of my neck. I couldn't help a smug smile. "She thinks I smell best."

"I'll remind you she perfumed for me first," Marius said.

"Aye, and you mishandled it. I'll get her to perfume this time," I said.

His eyelids fell to make a smoldering look at her. Whatever he said in her mind must've been lusty, as her body temperature warmed. Still no perfume, though.

She tugged at the lapels of my jacket, then mewled. I took it off and teased, "First my mask, now my jacket?" I draped it over her shoulders, and she pulled it around her body, purring rustily as she inhaled and made a blissed face. *Aw, stars.* She could absolutely keep it. "I'll give you the rest of my clothes too. Just say the word, *mo stór.*"

She didn't respond, and my brothers rolled their eyes at me. It was worth a try.

The rest of the ride home passed in a blink. Of course, when I got the chance to hold our purring omega, it went quick. I left the carriage last and carried her out. Since she didn't make so much as a peep of complaint, I carried her all the way back to her suite. Kauz went to the infirmary for his stitches and Marius and Tormund split off to clean themselves in their own rooms.

I took Lark to her rain room and finally set her down. I stripped us both naked and started cleansing her skin. This felt familiar, except I wasn't able to hide how faesteel-hard my erection was. My blood was high from the fight, and she smelled so starsdamned amazing.

Her gaze tracked my movements and watched my face, but she still hadn't formed a word since we left the forest behind.

"Are you all right?" I hoped we could at least do simple yes or no questions.

She smiled slightly and nodded.

"Are you in heat?"

For a moment, she had that same lost expression she'd worn during our last dance. Then she shook her head. It was incredibly close, then. This might be a taste of caring for an omega in heat, except she wasn't in the pack bond yet for me to sense her needs.

Once I toweled her off, she went to her nest. What echoed out from that room could only be described as a squeal of outrage.

I came running, just to see her standing with her hands on her hips, staring at the unmade bed and piles of clean nesting materials next to it, along with some heat supplies. She turned to me and gestured at the scene with absolute pique.

"I *know*," I said in exaggerated agreement. She could blame my father, who had the house moths cleaning up everything Marius and I touched to get rid of our "stink."

Lark started in on the sheets, picking out one from the middle and scattering the folded pile in the process. She unrolled and whipped it flat before laying it on the bed. I watched her go until she turned my way and made a questioning squeak. She picked up a pile of pillows and trotted over to me, placing them in my arms.

"Got it. I'll help." I went and placed a pillow at the head of the bed. She was in the midst of folding a cushion into her creation and looked up, scowling at what I'd done. She came over to pick up the pillow and tossed it to the far side of the room. "Stars, okay. That was a very offensive pillow placement. I apologize."

She dove into her pile of blankets and emerged with another one, then turned her gaze toward where I'd placed another pillow in the center of the bed. I was curious to see what she'd do this time. She stomped her foot and snatched it up, going to place it where I'd put the first one.

Hmm, puzzling. But all I knew about an omega's nest was...well, nothing. I watched her work, increasingly baffled by her frenzy of folding, kneading, placing, tossing, and nodding in approval before she went back to get more fluffy stuff to add.

Marius rushed into the room a few minutes later. She made a sound of relief, and they had a brief feral back-and-forth. He stripped off his newly donned shirt and handed it to her. As she tucked it into her nest, he turned to me. "You don't know how to nest-build. Get out."

I smacked my lips. "Rude. I could always learn."

He tilted his head when she made a soft chatter. "She says you can stay after you go get your jacket," he translated.

I put the pillows down to do just that. When I returned, he'd lifted a good assortment of her nesting supplies, and she was rifling through them. She paused and rubbed a blanket's fabric over her cheek with a purr of approval. She tugged it free to add to the nest. She took the jacket from me and added it to the nest too. Well, I guess I really wasn't getting that back.

"Your only job in nest-building is to offer her things. She decides what goes in and what doesn't," Marius told me.

"Was that so much harder to say than 'You don't know what you're doing'?"

"I could just throw your ass out. Help or leave." He flashed his fangs in warning.

I opted to help, holding armfuls of heat supplies and pillows that she occasionally investigated. Lark was kneading on a pillow with a determined furrow between her brows when she paused, blinked hard, and pawed at one of her bare breasts. "What...?" She looked around in a daze.

Marius pulled her into a hug. "It's all right. You're in your nest," he whispered over her hair. "Fal and I are here helping you. You're safe."

She clutched his chest with both hands. "Where's Kauz?"

"Getting stitches and cleaning himself up."

"Tormund?"

"Should be here any moment."

"Laurel?"

He snorted dismissively. "Taken care of. Probably in the infirmary."

She nudged out of his hold and looked over her half-created nest, panting and fanning herself with her wings. Her skin was turning a rosy hue. Marius and I exchanged a meaningful glance behind her.

She wrapped her hands around her middle and keened, flopping atop the nest. I winced as the shrill noise skittered over my nerves. That *sound*. It was agonizing to my alpha instincts, just like she had to be suffering from acute pain as her body clenched.

"Don't fight it. It's okay. Let the heat come," I coaxed.

Lark sprang up and dodged my reaching hands. She fretted over the half-built nest before turning to the nesting materials and tossing fabric every which way with a frustrated growl. "No no no. It has to be perfect," she mumbled.

Marius jerked his chin at me. "I'll take care of her. You should intercept Tormund."

That was smart. I went into the adjoining bedroom to wait for the redcap, drawing the privacy curtain in the meantime.

When Tormund finally arrived, he took one look at me and started shedding clothes, folding them neatly to the side while I explained that Lark was building her nest. We waited, both of us uncomfortably aroused by the scent of her in the air.

I figured the nest was done when Lark peeked around the curtain. Her expression lit up when she saw Tormund, and she chirped at him.

"Your pants," Marius translated from somewhere behind her.

"You want my pants, li'l bird?" the redcap asked, puzzled.

She bobbed her head and snatched them from his hand when he came over, ducking back into the nest as he leaned down to kiss her. I had to chuckle at that. "Bet you she asks Kauz for his underwear," I said offhandedly.

His brows clashed into one long line. "Why?"

"She has pretty much every other article of clothing in her nest now. And I don't think she wants socks."

I perked up as the curtain was pushed to the side. It was just

Marius, who looked at us, sighed, and disrobed the rest of the way. "She kicked me out," he said.

"Aren't we just the pent-up lads club now?" I remarked.

I strode toward the nest, ignoring Marius's chuff of warning. Lark was pacing the length of the room and had one hand resting on her belly. I watched her in concern, unsure of what she needed, but I inched forward until she looked at me and slowed her stride.

"Fal, it's stuck," she said in a roughened voice.

"What's stuck, *mo stór?*"

"My heat. It won't come." She stopped a couple steps away from me, sounding increasingly panicked. "I could've just gone into heat earlier. Or earlier still. Back and back, I pushed it. Now it's stuck. When I want it, it's not here, and you're all waiting and—"

I closed the distance between us and slanted my mouth over hers. She parted her lips immediately, and her sweet taste coated my tongue. I rumbled deep in my chest. The rut haze pushed in on my mind. But I did the same thing she was doing. I had it wait just a little longer. As we kissed, I nudged her back. One step, two. I petted her hair and down one wing until she started to purr. Three steps, four.

With a gentle push, she toppled back atop the fluffy nest she'd just made. I caught her legs and pulled them open, crouching between her thighs until I was at eye level with her slick-coated slit. It was a rare moment when I didn't want to say a starsdamned thing, so I simply tapped the pack bond in the signal for *come here.*

Then I buried my face in Lark's pussy and started eating with abandon. Her breathy, desperate moans were music to my ears. She rocked her hips, chasing my tongue and lips. I lapped up her slick, just like a tomcat for her cream.

Marius and Tormund entered the nest to see her arching her back and screaming as she came fast, drenching my face and the soak mat beneath her. I only eased back to her inner thighs as she came down from her pleasure high with panting breaths.

The other two alphas sat on either side of her. Marius grasped the back of her head to pull her into another kiss. She hummed and flicked her wings as he poured several days of loneliness into the passionate lip-lock. Tormund cupped and teased her breasts, plucking at her nipples and running his broad hands over her curves while Marius swallowed her sounds of delight.

I waited a minute before giving her seam a testing lick. When she didn't seem overstimulated, I delved back into her pussy. Her taste was blissful, and I could drown in how sweet it'd gotten. Since I was nestled between her thighs, it was easier to feel the warmth coming off her core. It seemed to be mounting as she lost herself in us.

If her heat came, great. If it didn't, we'd at least coaxed her to come anyway. I just wanted her to fall apart in the good way after the stress of tonight. She was still my princess and one of the strongest females I knew. She was still *mine*.

I moved my mouth to her clit, giving it a gentle pinch between my lips. She jolted, threaded her fingers into my hair, and pressed down to demand more. As I worked a single digit into her channel, crooking it to stretch her, she stopped kissing Marius for a moment.

"Where's Kauz?" she whispered before she grabbed Tormund and drew him into a kiss next.

All three of us immediately started poking the pack bond. Kauz probably jumped a foot wherever he was as he was hit with dozens of insistent signals to *come here*. We were so annoying about it that he poked back at us multiple times.

"He's on his way," Marius rasped.

She didn't have much of a chance to reply. Tormund kissed her deeply while I flicked her clit with the tip of my tongue. Her legs tensed as I continued to stretch her, fitting in a second finger. I started drawing the Serri alphabet over her little nub of nerves with my tongue, complete with a careful flick with each accent mark.

Sweat sheened her as she writhed between us. Her channel squeezed my fingers tight in a pulse that shook her from the core out. Could that have been one of her cramps? It wasn't so bad with the three of us touching and playing with her. Her pussy felt hot around my fingers, becoming more so by the moment.

Her body wound tight for another detonation. My gaze flicked up to watch her face. I got an excellent view of my brothers pleasuring her too. They cupped her pinkened skin and caressed her curves. Tormund eased off from kissing her, as we all wanted to hear her scream as she came. Marius layered love bites over her shoulder, his fangs dimpling her skin with just the right amount of pressure so he didn't draw blood.

The privacy curtain was drawn aside while she teetered on the brink of her release. Her star-flecked eyes danced as her lips framed Kauz's name. Then she came with a scream. *Fuck,* I loved hearing her come apart. My brothers echoed my thoughts aloud, and Kauz's wings rustled. I lapped up more of her come as she fell limp, only held up by Marius and Tormund.

I was glad Kauz made it. He discarded a hastily tied bathrobe with a dismissive flick. His short hair was still spiky and damp, but he was clean, and white bandages peeked from the folds of his injured wing.

Lark panted and exhaled with little moans, her eyes shutting tightly. "Look," Tormund said in his loud whisper.

I followed the line of his pointing finger. Right above her left breast, particles of magic formed the distinctive horseshoe-like shape of an omega mark. It was no bigger than the size of my fist. It filled in and darkened rapidly until it was an unbroken black ribbon.

For a moment, we stared at it in awe. Here was our triumph: our mate ready to be claimed. Her perfume gusted around her in a cloud of dessert. Chocolate and honey crackers, sweetened and lush. I double-checked the inside of her arm before anything else. The fertility blocker charm was still inked on her skin. No babies—not yet. That was a big step for another time.

We eased her into her nest, and everyone backed away, except for me. I climbed up with her and skimmed her omega mark with my fingertips. Her eyes shot open with a gasp.

"Sensitive, isn't it?" I murmured. There seemed to be more nerves in a designation mark than anywhere else, as if we were really touching a piece of another's soul.

Her gaze found mine. She was an open book, vulnerable in a way that still seemed a little lost. A hint of recognition glinted amongst the fever overtaking her from the inside out. "Fal."

"I'm here. *We're* here." I wanted to reassure her one last time before the breeding haze shrouded her mind. "I'm going to bite you into the pack now. Then we're going to see you through this heat, no matter what."

It was probably superstition, but no one else would touch her until

I'd fully claimed her with fangs and knot alike. Nothing could get in the way of the process. She was too precious to all of us.

"Yes." She reached for me, parting her thighs. "I need you."

My next breath seized in my chest. Stars, I needed her too, so much I ached with it.

I lowered my weight carefully overtop her, bracing under one of her wings so I didn't crush it. She shivered as my breath ghosted over her new mark. I pressed my lips to it, then laved its shape. Her mewl and moan accompanied a tremor through her whole body.

I wanted her very soul to know pleasure from my touch before I claimed it for Pack Sorles. As I traced her mark's curve with my fingertips, I took in her expression again, fully expecting her wits to be gone from her heat. Instead, she was still gazing back at me. Another testament to her strength. Trust and love and *need* glittered amongst the stars in her eyes as she gave a little nod.

I returned my lips to her mark and lined up where I wanted to place my permanent claim. My fangs sank into the very top of the omega symbol, and an ultra-concentrated burst of her pheromones coated my mouth. Closing my eyes, I focused intently. Our pack formed an incomplete circle, woven together with strands of essence, the bonds of family, and magic nearly as old and unknowable as the forces that'd shaped the fae races.

There was a gap in that circle between me, the founding member, and Tormund, the newest. Lark's essence fit there perfectly to complete the pack. Gasps sounded from my brothers as she joined the pack bond at last. Her unregulated emotions flooded in—pain tightly entwined with lust, wonder, love, and surprise, and the sensation that she was hot. She was *burning up*.

She squirmed beneath me as I pulled my fangs free. The complicated mix of feelings in her winked out, save for the strongest two, pain and need. "I need you," she mumbled, shifting, pawing at her overheated skin. "Please, I need you."

"I'm here," I assured her and practically fumbled to get inside of her as quickly as possible.

I guided my length through her lower lips, hissing as my intimate flesh felt the heat pouring from her pussy. She was soaked with slick and took my cock to the root in one long push.

"Yes yes *yes*," she hissed. She undulated her hips, grinding against me.

One thrust, and I was gone, too. I finally let the rut haze have my mind, now that I had my mate pinned beneath me. Her scent clogged my senses. She was all I wanted, all I needed. And with that fertility blocker on her arm, I could breed her for days without consequences. I'd take great joy in feeling her tremble from the breeder's delight as I stuffed her full of my seed.

I lifted and bent one of her legs to rut her deeper and harder into the softness of her nest. It *was* well constructed; it cushioned her body just right to hold her in place for each thrust. Again, her unfiltered feelings hit the pack bond, and I shuddered as her pleasure and mine combined. If it was always like this, she was rarely going to have a chance to leave this bed. She felt too fucking perfect.

She came a third time and howled her bliss even while she continued to move with me, rolling her hips into mine for more. She was going to be insatiable during this heat. The muscles in her greedy pussy clenched and jerked around my cock.

It was impossible to pace myself. I stroked the hair out of her face, wanting to watch her reaction when I spilled. My knot throbbed to the pace of my heart and inflated until it no longer pulled out of her smoothly. When it was big enough to catch the rim inside her pussy, I ground myself deep and savored how she locked down on my knot.

"*Good* omega," I growled out with effort.

The tension between us tightened into that exquisite moment when my knot could no longer expand and the pressure was too much. I came like a breaking dam, flooding her with days' worth of pent-up come. Her mouth parted as her body fed her bliss from the hot rush filling her core. She went slack—wait.

She went slack completely? Lark slumped straight into unconsciousness before I was even done breeding her. I reacquired a few of my wits, enough to understand what was going on.

Another outline was appearing on her skin. The crown of Pack Sorles, shimmering into place between her brows.

68

LARK

I was submerged in a dark lake, the water's embrace warm and all-encompassing. I descended headfirst into the silt, and my body settled in a sprawl, too heavy to move.

All I wanted was to lie there in the peaceful blackness, but I knew deep down I couldn't. I had to wake up. To do so, I had to give my feral side control. It was the only way to survive the heat. Even now, fiery need coursed through my veins and brought my blood to a rolling boil.

I needed my mates. But what would happen once I succumbed? Would I become a different female completely? Would I lash out? I didn't want to lose control and end up doing something that'd make my mates regret their claim.

"Nonsense." Marius's strong voice carried over our kelpie bond. Was he here with me? *"No, you're just not quite unconscious. I can still sense your mind moving."*

"Sorry."

He responded with one of his gentle snorts. *"You have no reason to fear the heat haze. Let go, p'nixie."*

"I don't know how."

"You do."

My instincts did. But if they led me to the surface of this dark lake, then I would wake feral and unpredictable.

"All you're doing right now is fighting yourself. Don't be afraid. I've just spoken to your feral side. I love her. She's small, shy, and sweet. A little prey animal in need of protection. Sound familiar?"

That was how he seemed to see me, as a predatory feral alpha.

"Exactly. Because she is you, my sweet prey. Just like how Niall is me."

"Oh." I had an undercurrent of understanding all in that little sound. I aired my biggest worry to him. *"You don't think I'm going to be violent and angry when I wake up, do you?"*

He laughed, deep and rich. *"Nay. I know you. You want to submit to us. You want to be fucked and knotted like we're trying to breed you."*

It wasn't possible to blush right now, and even then, I wouldn't. He'd so succinctly described my carnal desires.

"Come and take what you need…"

I followed him up through the muffling sensation of deep water. As consciousness returned, so did the pain deep within my core. I was so *empty*. That had to be fixed as soon as possible.

My eyes shot open. I was hot, hot, *hot*, my skin reddened from the pulsing, burning need that'd sunk its talons in me.

Most of what I knew about heats, I'd read in books. They were always beautiful in fiction. The swooning omega would take her chosen mate—or mates—to her nest, and they'd make sweet love for exactly two days. The heat haze was a graceful veil between her and her body's actions when her instincts took over. And she never felt the encroaching fog that marked her descent from a thinking, reasoning female into a breedable creature of insatiable need.

I felt creature-ish as I eased to a sitting position and folded my legs under me. My sight came back into focus slowly, along with my hearing and the pulse of my heartbeat in the twin punctures right above my breast.

Together, my mates smelled incredible. Their combined pheromones were a spring evening by the lake, with fragrant wood smoking in the campfire. It was graced by the elusive sprinkling of stardust, the promise of Always.

Standing at the bedside, Marius and Tormund were locked in a dominance match, nearly nose to nose as they stared one another down. Their postures weren't quite aggressive. Fal passed them, humming and grinning as he sauntered to the foot of the bed with a stack of towels in his arms.

There was a gentle touch along my ass before a finger pressed into my rear. It was Kauz, slipping an essence mesh spell in me while I was still gaining my bearings. I felt pressure in my ass as it started to slowly expand.

I turned toward him, my heart pattering with eagerness. *He's the one.* Though my tongue felt heavy in my mouth, I managed to ask, "What's happening?"

Kauz sat next to me. I pressed to his side, rubbing against him with a loving purr. "The second most dominant alpha, behind Fal, gets to knot you next," he explained in an undertone. "We've always assumed that would be Marius, but Tormund's never challenged him. Until now."

I growled softly. "That's silly." I would decide who mated me next.

He smiled and inclined his head in agreement. "Don't get caught telling alphas their posturing is silly."

An odd thing happened as I regarded Kauz with the full measure of lust burning within my core. I sensed four echoes of emotion. This was something new, something anchored in the horseshoe-shaped strip of flesh above my heart. Maybe it was the pack bond already taking root in my soul.

What I felt only encouraged me. I hooked my legs around Kauz's waist. I had surprise and a bit of leverage on my side as I grabbed his undamaged wing. With a determined pull and a twist of my hips, I rolled him onto his back and straddled him.

His eyes widened. "What're you doing?"

I rubbed his length through the wet seam of my pussy, making a pleased trill that he was already erect and throbbing.

"Lark, I...fuck. This isn't a good idea. I don't have a knot," he said.

Didn't he see? I loved him. I'd chosen him to be next. "I need you."

"You need an alpha's knot, sweetheart."

I shook my head, frustrated. "I need *you*," I repeated. Despite his mild protests, he hadn't lifted a finger to move me off him.

"Stop arguing and give her what she wants," Marius growled. It seemed they'd determined a winner, as he shoved Tormund back a step when the other male bowed his head briefly. Dominance and need rolled off the kelpie through our bond.

I shivered in delight and made another trill, inviting him to join us. I needed him too. He bared his fangs in an eager smile but murmured something to Tormund first.

I turned my attention to Kauz, inspecting him for any signs of unwillingness. He reached up to stroke his fingertips down my cheek. "Well, if you insist I'm what you want, I would never deny you."

"Need. I need you," I corrected. I sank onto Kauz's shaft with a sigh of relief. *Not so empty anymore.* I rested my palms on his chest and rolled my hips to take more of his cock. He left tingling warmth in the wake of his fingers. The magic drew immediate shivers from me while I was already feeling so exquisitely sensitive. When he brushed the side of my new omega mark, I nearly came on the spot. That strip of flesh was like a second, much larger clit. Pleasure resonated through me every time it was touched.

The nest dipped. "Is the mesh ready?" Tormund asked. His voice was roughened with need. *Oh, sexy.* I loved when he talked in the deep tones of his monstrous form.

Kauz caught my hips to still me. I contemplated biting him for that and chose to play with myself instead, stroking my clit and folds, which were stretched around the base of his cock. He turned his starry gaze to watch, just proving he was still my kinky bat.

The gentle giant came up behind me, covering my back with radiating redcap heat. His hands framed my torso, and his hot breath skimmed my neck.

"Should be. Prep her a little first, and start slow," Kauz answered.

My head felt heavier as I tipped it back. I leaned to give Tormund a sideways kiss. The thick tip of his finger circled the rim of my ass while his lips parted. We deepened the kiss, twining tongues in wild abandon. My mouth filled with his rut pheromones, which had solidified into a heady mix of smoke and dark, fragrant wood. I needed *more* of him.

I practically vibrated with my need to continue riding Kauz. He drew tingling swirls over my thighs and wings while he waited for Tormund to finish prepping me. The attention was great in its own way, but I was burning up during this pause.

The redcap wiggled his finger up my ass and tested the inner walls. They flexed for him, already made ready by the essence mesh spell. My eyes rolled back just from the tease of one finger. My wings flicked impatiently. *Stop playing around and fuck me. I need to be filled.*

Tormund worked a second finger in my ass, and I made a higher-pitched noise into our kiss at the stretch. I trembled and tried to roll my hips to get some friction between the three of us.

"I think she's ready," Kauz said.

He was right. I was so ready.

Tormund pulled from my lips and literally smoldered as he looked at me. He'd stashed his spectacles somewhere, and the tiny flames in his eyes darted over my face, lingering on my forehead. "I'm so glad you're finally ours, li'l bird." He kissed the space between my brows. "I'm going to lean you forward. Okay?"

I nodded. He repositioned me along with two more sets of hands, as Marius joined in. The kelpie guided my head to the side to face him where he'd settled beside Kauz's wing. Together, all three males angled my torso down and tilted my hips. I was still seated on Kauz's cock, but now Tormund had access to claim my ass, and my head was in line with Marius. He presented his erection close to my lips. I licked them and leaned forward, mouth already watering.

"*Wait. Them first,*" he instructed. He stroked my hair and the point of my ear, regarding me with fierce affection. I tilted my head into his touch.

Tormund slid his heated length ever so carefully into my second entrance. As before, my ass was a close second to my pussy in terms of sensitivity. All claims were sorely wanted, and I would've straightened to start pushing back against him and Kauz both, but they were stubbornly holding me in this position.

A high-pitched growl escaped me. They still weren't really *moving*. "*Oh, so menacing,*" Marius teased in my mind. "*Do that again. Show me your teeth.*"

"*Bold words.*" I turned my gaze pointedly to his cock.

"*You wouldn't.*"

He'd distracted me. Kauz and Tormund were gesturing and whispering, coordinating how they wanted to take me. Once Tormund was fully seated, he made a rumble edged with a redcap's crackling power. They lifted my hips together to hold me at the correct angle and found a rhythm. Where one entered, the other withdrew. At no time did I lack the sensation of being full of one of my mates.

I trembled, finally receiving almost everything I needed. Marius eased forward and nudged my lips with the crown of his cock. *"Get me wet, mate. I'm going to be knotting that pretty pussy soon."*

I moaned in agreement. I needed a knot right away. That didn't mean I regretted picking my Always to mate with next. It didn't even occur to me that he was a beta. He was simply, well, *mine.*

I opened wide to accept as much of Marius as would fit in my mouth and sucked on him messily. He rolled his hips to slowly pass his cock through the seal of my lips. While I had one hand on Kauz's chest for balance, I lifted the other to squeeze the base of the kelpie's shaft. He rewarded me with a stream of his precome. Blooming waterlilies and mint tingled on my tongue.

The pressure in my body was tightening all over. No wonder, with five hands covering most of my sensitive spots. Kauz continued spreading tingles over my thighs and hips. Tormund's warmth enveloped my breasts and belly. And Marius petted me one-handed down my back and wings, with his other hand closed around a glint of silver. The lady pleaser piercing, which otherwise could've hurt my mouth.

Pleasure overwhelmed me for a few blissful moments as I came. My thoughts slowed to a halt. I was suspended in dark water again, caressed by a current. *Whoa.* I returned to my head to find only a few moments had passed, and my body was still moving on instinct.

I'd regained my awareness as Kauz spilled his seed in a liquid rush deep in my belly. My toes curled, the breeder's delight feeding my core pure pleasure. I was consumed by the blinding need for more. This heat would extinguish if only I had *more.*

Marius pulled free of my mouth, easing back on his heels. Kauz withdrew from my pussy as he softened for now. I shot him a look of pure promise, sure to return to him again soon.

Now that it was only Tormund inside me for the moment, I

straightened and looked over my shoulder. My gentle giant was holding on by a thread, in the best of ways. The rut glow was intensified in his eyes, throwing off flame-like sparks of light. I met his last couple thrusts before he spilled as well. His seed felt overheated in my second channel, slightly removed from the intensity of the blaze at my core. His knot pulsed, grinding against my ass cheeks.

He remained hard and seated within me, even once his shaft was done pulsing. Once he pulled himself free, he hugged me from behind, purring deeply. I rested my head on his shoulder and purred back. What a fantastic mate.

I soaked in the soothing vibrations but couldn't find much contentment. I still needed to dampen my heat before I could lounge around.

"It's my turn to claim her," Marius prompted, reaching for me.

Tormund tightened his hold for a moment before releasing me with a nod. I went straight to straddling Marius's lap, demanding, *"I ride you."*

"Aye, mate. Soon. And I'll show you what your short absence has done to me." He added a reassurance that I would like the results.

I nearly bit him too when he pushed me back from his throbbing length. He bowed his head and licked my omega mark, tracing its whole curve in one hot glide. It filled my mind with incandescent pleasure. The kelpie rumbled as he felt its echo. Doubling back, he took his time in licking it thoroughly again, then paused to take in my blissed-out expression. His pleased smile pressed to my skin.

He nuzzled in, letting me feel the edges of his teeth. I gasped and tugged on his hair. *"Do it."*

At this point, he was merely returning the favor after I'd bitten his mark to start our bond.

"Allow me to welcome you into the pack properly."

He sank his fangs into the arch of my mark, toward the left. We were already tightly interwoven with the kelpie bond, but the magic that passed between us was something different. I could picture the pack bond in my mind's eye. It was like an unbreakable circle, each of us a stone set in the foundation to complete it. Fal, and now Marius, anchored me into it permanently with their claiming bites.

My awareness of the pack bond faded to a dull hum in my omega mark. The whole thing tingled as Marius withdrew his fangs and covered it with kisses. "Mine," he said aloud.

And in my mind, he added, *"I knew your mark would be here."* Somehow, he had. Niall had traced this spot the first time I'd come face-to-face with him.

He spun me to face Tormund. "Now you claim her for the pack," the kelpie growled.

Kauz had stood and was in the process of refolding his hurt wing, though he watched intently. Fal got up and came around to help with the wing. His feline gaze was extra intense when it met mine. He licked his lips at me, his cock kicking just from my attention when I noticed that he was already—or still—fully aroused.

I gave him a lingering look. He was definitely next.

But for now, this moment belonged to Tormund, and I focused on him as he settled in front of me. "You're okay with me biting you, li'l bird?"

I nodded enthusiastically and lifted my chest toward him. Instead of bending down, he lifted me with a grip around my waist and brought my mark closer to the heat of his breath. He covered it in more kisses and the pleasantly scratchy texture of his facial hair.

"Mine," he murmured. When he sank his fangs into my skin, he'd chosen to mirror Marius, so his bite landed on the right side of the mark.

My back arched, and I gasped from the hot pressure of his fangs and the sensations digging deep in my soul. His claim finished setting my place in Pack Sorles, firmly nestled in with my four mates. Bonds of magic tied me to them, permanent loops that connected our souls together.

"Ours," Fal said huskily once the transfer of magic was complete. The other males echoed him, and I blushed somewhere under the heavy mantle of the heat haze. I'd feared this moment for so long, then longed for it with my proper mates. Now I was claimed, loved, and about to be knotted. Life was good.

I stole a quick kiss from Tormund before I turned back to Marius, pointing and saying the only thing I could muster. "I need you."

He made a lusty growl and gestured for us to go to the head of the nest, where I'd made an inviting backrest worth of pillows. He reclined, and I followed, facing away from him as I had a seat on his throbbing shaft. At some point, he'd put the lady pleaser piercing back in its place.

I rode him eagerly, trembling each time his piercing glided through the ultra-sensitive intimate patch hiding along the walls of my pussy. Without him holding me still or helping pull me into his thrusts, I rolled my hips up and down his cock at my own pace. I could practically feel the heat of his gaze focused on the way my ass bounced.

I fondled my breasts, tipping my head back to moan as the pack bond echoed with the pleasure Marius and I shared. It probably wasn't *supposed* to be this strong, but I had the sense I was leaking all my feelings into it. Not that anyone stopped me.

Fal slid onto the nest in front of me, replacing my hands with his to pluck and twist my nipples just right. He skimmed his lips over my face as I panted with need. His kisses lingered over my forehead and between my brows.

We nuzzled one another. "You know," he purred in my ear. "When I first started going into rut, I pictured you between Marius and me."

Oh, really? I knew where this was going. I pointed at my mouth and raised a brow.

He hummed in agreement. Marius caught my hips and helped reposition me on my hands and knees. He covered my back while he waited, inside me to the root, for Fal to guide his cock into my mouth. Instead of alternating, they thrust together, setting a brutally fast pace.

I had nowhere to go except up. Or I supposed down was the better term. The heat haze had been light so far, letting me see my mates in full clarity, but it filled my head like a fog as I shattered.

I would surrender to my instincts once they found their completion. Now that I was fully claimed, there was little to fear. I trusted my mates would take care of me. If I did end up more of an angry, lashing feral than I wanted to be, Marius would keep me in line. It felt natural after letting him rut me with abandon in that inn by the sea.

Fal was a different male under the influence of the rut. There were no fancy overtures and fewer charming words. He'd threaded his fingers through my hair, keeping my head steady for the way he thrust into my mouth. At some point, he'd toweled off the excess come that'd coated him from our first joining. He still tasted of us and left behind an impression of wildflower pollen and chocolate on my tongue.

This was the alpha that lurked behind his courtly image. If I had my voice, I would see if he still became extra growly when I called him pack lead.

Marius's pace changed with urgency. His knot bumped my lower lips as it swelled. He teased me with an extra thrust, so the swollen ball of flesh made a wet pop in and out of my pussy before we were locked together.

My screams were muffled against the cock in my mouth. If I thought Fal would let up while I trembled with electrified pleasure from taking a knot in full heat, I was wrong. He grabbed a fistful of my hair and fucked my mouth harder. It was more bliss for me as my breeder's delight went crazy.

I felt what my short absence had done to Marius. Nestled deep in my core, he unleashed a torrent of seed. My heat dampened, if only by a fraction, but the little drop in temperature was noticeable when I was burning up.

My limbs felt like jelly while the kelpie and I traded aftershocks of pleasure. My pussy wouldn't stop spasming, milking him for all he was worth. Which meant my hand was hardly steady as I reached for Fal's growing knot. Once I had a hold of his shaft, I squeezed, and he spilled immediately. His irresistible rut-augmented pheromones coated my tongue as he flooded my mouth.

I couldn't possibly swallow it all, but I tried and gripped his knot harder for more. Thank the stars for soak mats. Once he was done, Fal went to retrieve a towel to clean his release off my face and neck. I blinked at him appreciatively.

It was time for my surrender, and I let my instincts creep in. The fog filled my head, softening the edges around my senses. I was floating, painless. All I needed was to sate the burning need inside of me.

I pointed at Tormund while still panting from the intensity of my last release. "I need you."

69
LARK

There were a few things I learned about experiencing a heat that'd never graced the pages of the books I'd read. In fact, I was of half a mind to go burn the novels that implied heats were clean, quick, and relatively painless. They were *wildly* inaccurate.

My heat was not, as some would put it, a magical time. After I'd suppressed it for four years, it was truly brutal. Omegas were built to experience their most fertile and vulnerable time for two days twice a year. So, that was eight total heats that caught up to me, and my body was keeping count.

Day one was the most painless. The heat haze settled over me, and I was either constantly fucking one of my mates or sitting on one of their knots. I needed them, they knew it, and they met me kiss for kiss, passion for passion, and thrust for thrust.

Day two—and I marked the days by the instincts guiding my nesting habits—started with me kicking my mates out of the nest and inspecting the bedding. Even with the soak mats, we'd soiled a couple layers, so I tossed those into a corner and rearranged the bedding for the day of breeding ahead.

I came out of the nest to invite my mates back in. They were prepared for me. Marius wrestled me into the rain room, though I stopped struggling when I realized he wanted to cleanse my body. Fal groomed my hair and inspected my skin, which he smeared with cool cream in a few places. I wasn't a fan of this. But I still rubbed against him, prepared to forgive him if he knotted me again.

He growled with interest but steered me from the bathroom, saying, "You have to eat first."

I most certainly did *not*. It wasn't logical, but I didn't want to chew anything. Marius had passed out in the bed outside my nest and wouldn't be roused even when I tried to tug on the kelpie bond. So, I had no way of telling Tormund I didn't want what he was trying to offer except to refuse it. He had cubes of meat and cheese, crackers, and other easy-to-eat items.

No food. Only fuck.

Fal ended up knotting me so I'd be stuck and forced to at least eat *something*.

Throughout all this, Kauz had the water and offered me a drink any time he could. He kept his head and made sure I didn't shrivel up from ignoring all my needs except for the burning one in my core. At some point, he acquired fruit juice too, and sips of the sugary liquid kept me going.

By the end of day two, when I was supposed to fade out of heat and back into my own wits, I'd instead exhausted Fal and Kauz. They went to sleep while Tormund alone remained in rut and kept me occupied through one exquisitely hot night between us. I howled and screamed each time he took his monstrous form. With my coaxing and enthusiasm, that was more than once, and he was too far into his rut to be hesitant about it.

Day three...I fixed up the nest again and left Tormund resting in a cocoon of clean fabric. I was the only one awake in the pack and endured the rising heat in my body for as long as I could. Eventually, I curled up in the rain room, under a steady fall of freezing water.

I still hadn't slept. The heat haze lifted enough for me to think, *As fun as this has been, it's time for it to be over.* Then the pain truly set in.

I found out firsthand that the two-day time for heats was a natural limit for omegas to mute their pain in a heat haze and for all but the deepest of alpha ruts to play themselves out. The easy part was over. Now it was time for suffering.

Marius finally woke up and found me in the shower. He sat down and held me while I cried. The pain in my belly was worsening by the minute. Instead of being chilled by the cold water, I was just soggy and miserable.

Not much fucking happened on day three. Truly the low point of the whole experience. The rest of my mates woke swiftly when the gut-twisting heat cramps came. They didn't ease or stop, either, no matter if I was knotted, snuggling up to a purring alpha, or just curled into a ball and weeping in someone's arms.

We exhausted almost all the options that could've soothed me, just for there to be no relief in sight. I whimpered with guilt when all my mates ended up crying with me at one point or another. We spent the day cuddling, kissing, and enduring the ravages of my body together.

Kauz had me in his lap when it was his turn to hold me. It was surreal to see tears in his eyes. They made the pinpricks of light gleam all the brighter.

"This is not your fault." His calm voice was layered with fatigue. He wiped my face clean with the soft, damp cloth he had pressed to my forehead. "We can all feel your pain. Not being able to stop it is the definition of torture."

I whined before my breath hitched as my insides twisted again. I hunched over, my keening adding to the chorus of cursing and snarling from my mates.

If only I could get my connection to the pack bond under control. If I closed it off, they wouldn't feel what I was feeling. But I'd floated the idea to Marius over our kelpie bond and received a hard no and an "it's out of the question." If I suffered, we would suffer together.

"Won't you let me put you to sleep for a bit?" Kauz coaxed. I'd refused this offer multiple times before, since I hadn't felt tired. I still didn't feel my fatigue yet. But now it was a way out of misery.

The only words I'd managed to utter since going into the heat haze were still "I need you," so I just nodded.

He sent me into unconsciousness and gave me dreams of the Serian winter. I laid myself down in a snowbank and melted a Lark-shaped hole in it.

Even a brutal Unseelie winter can't cool me down? Unfair.

Day four...I woke up rosy hued and sweltering, tucked in a light blanket atop my nest. My mates snoozed around me, splayed in exhausted sprawls. The bedding was still somewhat clean, considering how little sex we'd managed to have yesterday.

I was already slick and ready to turn the lack of intimacy around. It was time to sit on a knot. I climbed atop Tormund, who roused slowly to me licking his neck and rubbing my body against his. He slept nude and uncovered. His venting turned hotter as I kissed a path down his neck.

My mouth watered as my lips found his alpha mark, the sideways loop high on the right side of his chest. I licked it, tasting the sweet note of mallows. It'd been burned away briefly by his rut scent, but now it was back. Tormund held himself still as I purred over his mark.

Mine, I would say if I could. My jaw was still tight. I nibbled on him and savored the heat radiating off his skin. I bared my fangs to press a claiming—

No. What? I curled my lips back over my teeth. Tormund *always* asked for permission, even for small things. Here I was, about to give him a permanent claiming bite without even attempting to mind his boundaries.

I met his gaze, making an apologetic mewl. Those twin fires in his pupils burned bright in the enclosed darkness of my nest. He gave me one of his wide, toothy smiles. "It's okay, li'l bird. I know what you want to ask," he whispered. The pack bond stirred from a mental touch that felt like him. Big, steady, jolly, and still a little sleepy. He must've been able to sense me in the same way. "I want you to claim me back. It's only right."

I nodded in agreement. He was mine as much as I was his. I needed the intimacy of a complete bond with him, though I didn't know what to expect. It wouldn't be like my bond with Marius, augmented by kelpie magic. Tormund and I would have to explore our connection for ourselves.

I lowered my head to his mark again, kissing it one last time before I sank my teeth into the top of the loop. The pack bond shifted between us, entwining our souls even tighter. His emotions came through more clearly, a rush of love and affection that I matched with a happy sigh.

I was *almost* content to lie there and gaze in his eyes, but he undoubtedly sensed the need I'd woken up to. He rolled me over and mated me enthusiastically. *Yes yes yes.* In the absence of pain, I yearned to be intimately tied with him, just as we were magically bound.

This, of course, woke everyone else. Rumbles of interest came from the other two alphas while I howled my bliss.

"Maybe we should pace ourselves today?" Kauz suggested.

We didn't pace ourselves. I took Tormund's knot, and we saturated the soak mats again. It was sometime later that the males decided that I needed care. Shower, grooming, water, then...*sigh*. Food. Marius had the plate today.

"You know how I feel about this," I griped.

He rolled his eyes and pushed a morsel toward my mouth. *"Don't fight. Eat."*

This time, it was a few flakes of fish. Cooked, sweet flesh. I batted my lashes and opened my mouth for more. That was actually good.

Marius's emotions surged with triumph. *"I thought it might be a texture thing."* Then he handed the plate to Tormund, who brightened and patiently fed me fish and scallops. My mind kept wandering to who I was going to take back to the nest next.

I rested against the redcap affectionately during the tail end of the meal. Instinct had me getting up and entering my nest again, to find that I hadn't refreshed the bedding yet. That was important!

I tossed aside the whole thing and started building anew. Partway through, Fal lay down and folded his hands behind his head. He was naked and as unfairly attractive as ever, but also in the way. I growled in displeasure and pointed for him to get off the bed.

"Oh, you want me to leave?" he purred.

I nodded.

"You're going to have to use your words, *mo stór*. Tell me to get up."

I worked my tight jaw. I still couldn't. Until my heat passed, communication was optional.

But Fal, who'd fallen out of rut two days ago, set his mouth in concern when I remained quiet. "I miss you. Talk to me…please," he murmured.

How could I reassure him that I would if I could? I settled for winking at him. And when he still didn't get up, I started folding him into my nest. He was part of one of the middle layers. He ended up getting enveloped in fabric up to his chin. He didn't complain, only grinning in amusement as I packed in cushions, added a pillow for his head, and tucked the blankets around him.

"All right, now I'm part of your nest. What's next?" he teased.

Too many words. I sat on his face so he'd put that mouth to work for something else. He almost drowned in my slick. No complaints, though.

Marius walked in on me enjoying the dark elf's talented tongue and made a suggestion. The kelpie ended up knotting me right next to him while Fal tried to escape the nest to join in. I'd folded him in too well for a quick exit.

This kicked off hours of group sex. I was more comfortable than yesterday, but the heat had kept my body too hot for too long, and my joints ached. Eventually, we took a break, and during it, I had another heat cramp and gritted out a rough "Fuck!"

Fal gasped. "Did you just say 'fuck'?"

"No." My tongue wasn't quite cooperating with me, but I was determined to speak anyway. "No more fuck. Too much fuck."

There was a hail of masculine laughter. "Now, I don't know about that," Tormund chuckled.

Kauz tilted my face toward him and pulled at my lower eyelids before checking my temperature with the back of his hand. "Her fever hasn't broken yet. Maybe it's about to." He sounded hopeful, and I agreed with that. I was ready to cool off.

My body's needs returned shortly afterward. I was hungry, thirsty, exhausted, sore, and unbearably horny all at the same time. Couldn't an omega catch a break?

"Fuck, I'm hungry," I muttered.

Tormund's head and shoulders popped up from the other side of the nest. "Is it time for a real dinner?" he exclaimed. "What do you want, li'l bird? I'll have the house moths bring it."

I worked my jaw. "More fish," I managed to say. My tongue was getting used to this whole speaking thing a bit at a time. "Wait...house moths? No. We dismissed, right?"

"They've been coming by twice a day. How do you think you've gotten so much clean bedding so fast?" Fal teased. He was beaming over at me. "Are you sure we're doing 'no more fuck' or...?"

"Maybe a bit more," I hedged.

I felt my days' worth of exertions when I parted my thighs for him and whined when he knotted me. The rim of muscle that locked around knots was tender from overuse. And by the groan that Fal uttered when it latched on to his pulsing knot before he spilled, maybe there was some bruising going on.

"Worth it," Marius said privately, in answer to my thoughts. *"We ran out of wound salve. We knew your heat would be a lot, but we weren't prepared for how intensely you'd go after our knots."*

He was speaking in the past tense, but my heat wasn't past us yet. But the fact that I was thinking again suggested the worst was behind us. At least, I hoped so. I ate a real dinner—a side of buttered fish and some root vegetables—and asked Kauz to put me under again. Sleep seemed like the key healing component I still needed.

Day five...I woke with a mild fever and a groan. Too much fuck, indeed. My mates helped me again with my basic needs. I walked stiffly through the motions until Marius had me lie face down on the bed outside my nest. "Tormund, come over here," he said.

"Aye?"

"I'm going to teach you something."

The pack bond vibrated against my omega mark with the twinging of Tormund's nerves.

"I had the mothkins deliver this for you. It's massage oil. You have to heat it first," the kelpie continued. I looked over my shoulder to see him handing a bottle full of amber liquid to the redcap.

"Oh."

Marius cleared his throat. "I figured someone else should know how to tend to her body. You know, if I can't."

"Aye, of course." I could hear the grin in Tormund's voice. And I hid my face in the comforter, trying not to show that I was making the same expression. Marius was smart and skilled, but this was the first time I'd heard him willing to teach and share what he knew.

Plus, I was getting a massage. Tormund's broad hands moved over my skin as he followed the kelpie's instructions. They talked about muscle groups or something. The gentle giant was always extra warm, so the oil he spread down my back lingered pleasantly. I relaxed for the first time in days and purred like a kitten all the while.

Tormund started over from the top as he demonstrated what he'd just learned. As he worked, he said, "Hey, Marius."

"Hmm."

"Have you ever seen a shark? I've always wondered if that was a problem for kelpies."

"I've seen plenty of sharks. There's more than one kind."

My wings twitched nervously. I was probably envisioning the same kind of shark Tormund was when he asked the question. The big toothy gray ones that looked like they could swallow an omega in two gulps. There were more sharks than that? "Like, how many?" I asked.

I turned my head to look at Marius as he replied and joined my gentle giant in fascination. There were apparently a lot of sharks. Small, spotted ones, shallow-water ones, bottom-feeding ones, and toothy ones all included.

"Be careful. He's going to start showing you his sea bug collection next," Fal put in. He was fresh from a shower and brushing his hair as he leaned against the wall.

Well, it was nice to have peace while it lasted. I glanced at Marius, expecting annoyance. He raised a brow instead. "Seashells," he corrected. "Also, if I start showing them my seashells, then you're going to start talking about your rocks, and we're going to be stuck here for hours."

I was curious about both collections. "For later, then. You're teaching Tormund how to massage our mate, and not me?" Fal shook out his hair, then flipped it over one shoulder with his usual flair.

I saw the ear flick I'd been expecting. "When have you ever shown an interest in learning something from me?"

Fal rolled his eyes and twirled the hairbrush. "I'm sure I could teach you something in return."

"Whatever you were doing with your tongue earlier that drove Lark crazy."

"Deal."

I exchanged a glance with Tormund, who shrugged with both palms out.

Either way, I got massaged twice, so it was a victory for my sore body. *"Next lesson time is with Kauz and me. I want to know how to do this too,"* I said to Marius privately. I was eventually going to get the kelpie to let me return the favor after he'd rubbed away my muscle pain so often.

"In exchange, I want to take you back to the sea. Apparently, someone told Fal we didn't fuck in the water."

I giggled aloud. *"Sorry. And deal."*

After we were done with massage time, Fal asked for a moment alone with me. We sat side by side at the foot of the pack bed. I tucked myself up against him. "While you're still in heat, I wanted to ask for something," he said. He took my hand and pulled it toward his groin.

He was aroused, but I'd learned it was an automatic reaction to my perfume. I'd been putting off *fuck me* pheromones for five days. We'd need to do a deep clean of my nest to get rid of the potent smell.

I expected him to put my hand on his shaft, but instead, he placed it on his alpha mark. It was right under his belly button, a somewhat intimate place I'm sure I'd brushed dozens of times during the lusty frenzy of the early stages of my heat. My own mark tingled, especially in the healing spot where he'd bitten me.

"Will you claim me too?" His smile was without its usual mischief as he drew my hand up to his lips next. He kissed my fingers and looked at me with devotion shining in his eyes.

My heart skipped a beat, then pattered extra hard in excitement. "Oh...yes, of course. I would love to claim you back."

"You've already bitten Marius and Tormund, and now you have them both around your li'l finger. I'll take the next one, the ring finger." He wiggled my fourth finger playfully. "This is where I want you to wear my ring."

He distracted me for a moment. "Our stone match?"

"Aye. It's the first place a dark elf looks for the particular shine of stone match jewelry. I want all of my kind to know you're mine. The world, too. But other dark elf males, especially." His sharp fangs flashed as he took a more possessive tone.

"Then that's where I'll wear it," I said.

"Such a good omega," he purred, adding in a bit of his alpha's influence so I felt the words like a stroke of affection on my skin. He lay back on the bed so I could easily access his mark.

I stood and leaned over his hip, pressing a kiss to the darkened sideways loop on his skin. Fine trembles stirred over his skin. He seemed to hold his breath as he waited for me to line up my little fangs with the top of his mark, to bite him in a mirror to how he'd claimed me. We exchanged magic the moment after I broke his skin and his sunshine and grass pheromones flooded my mouth.

The rings of magic that bound Fal and me together in the pack bond shifted and tightened, our souls also entwining further. I released the bite and nuzzled against his mark, filled with euphoria. I'd already learned what to expect from claiming Tormund yesterday. We might not be able to speak mind to mind, but we were still connected just as intimately, able to sense one another's needs and emotions separately from the general pack bond.

"I love you," I sighed, climbing on top of him to hug him. I needed to feel his skin against mine and his heartbeat under my palms.

He tilted my face up to kiss me. "I love you too, *mo stór*." And the warmth of his emotions in my chest echoed his words. We lay together in an emotional afterglow, wanting to be close without pushing our sore intimate areas unless my heat spiked again.

Eventually, he asked, "Have you looked in a mirror lately?"

I shook my head, and he ushered me into the bathroom. I nearly climbed onto the vanity to see myself closer, gasping as I poked the three-pointed crown between my brows. "When did that get there?"

"Oh, you know, when you joined Pack Sorles. Five days ago," he said playfully.

No wonder the four of them had been kissing my forehead so much. I'd been too occupied by horniness to ask. But I had a pack mark! I did a little happy dance, and he joined in.

"You're going to teach me how to use the pack bond, right?" I asked.

We went back to the bed and talked about pack bond basics. He helped me figure out how to close off all but my strongest emotions from entering the circle of our bond. This way, I wasn't constantly shoving my feelings directly into my mates' heads at all times. I started practicing tapping into it. It was supposed to be as easy as a thought.

Kauz, fully dressed, walked into the bedroom while I was still getting it down. I turned toward him, clutching my thighs. "How'd it go?"

He extended his wing. The wound that'd cut through it was reduced to a crescent-shaped patch with the shadow of stitches. "It's going to scar, but I'll wear the mark of protecting you proudly."

Fal put his hand over his mouth to whisper aside to me, "Bite his mark next. He'll wear that scar proudly too." He winked and got up, walking into my nest while whistling a tune.

"Would you be okay with that?" I knew Kauz's bat ears had picked up what Fal had said.

Kauz smiled, his eyes twinkling. "I thought you'd never ask." He started taking his clothes off to rejoin the pack in our shared nakedness. I went over to help him with his shirt. "I ran into Laurel as I was leaving the infirmary, by the way."

I paused at the change of subject. Stars, I'd forgotten about her. "How's she doing?"

He ran his fingers through my hair in soothing strokes. "She's fine. Eletha helped her through regaining her memories. They may have become friends while we weren't looking."

I nodded, happy to leave it at that for now. "Can I see your mark?" I murmured.

He lifted his healing wing, angling to show me the B-shaped beta mark nestled just below his shoulder blade. There was a healed scar in the center of it, from Fal biting him into the pack. His wings shivered audibly when I kissed his mark with a purr. I ran my tongue over the long tail at the end of it, enjoying seeing his stance tense and hands flex in reaction.

"Claim me," he said in a huskier tone. "I don't need to be an alpha for other fae to know I've claimed you too. They only need to see your wings for that."

They fluttered behind me in awareness. The beautiful patterns he'd inked on them would remain with me forever. I'd practice until the brush fell from my hand before I painted the rest of his wings, too. Until then, I bit the trailing tail of his beta mark and hugged his side while he gasped and flapped his wings on reflex, nearly toppling us both over.

He didn't taste of anything other than a hint of blood. We wove closer in the pack bond too. As a beta, he didn't have the same kind of claim as an alpha, so it felt more like I was drawing him in with warm tendrils of magic. His emotions were a subtle weave: the calm, compassionate melody amongst the more pronounced feelings of his alpha siblings.

He twisted and pulled me into his arms, kissing me with open-mouthed passion that I met with a burst of warmth blooming over my skin.

"Love you, sweetheart," he murmured once we parted for air.

"Love you too." I tilted my head toward the nest. "Shall we?"

I ended up coaxing all of my mates into one last group fuck while I was still feeling heated and squeezed some bruised knots. My heat burned itself out shortly after. To my great relief, I descended into a deep, dreamless sleep untouched by the all-consuming need that'd ruled me for the better part of a week.

70
LARK

I SLEPT DEEPLY and woke up on my own with a big, full-body stretch. I spent a while in a bleary daze, regaining my senses a bit at a time.

"Welcome back, p'nixie," Marius murmured.

He'd filched one of the armchairs from my study and placed it at the foot of the nest's bed. A book rested open-faced in his lap as he turned his good eye my way. He was showered and dressed, smelling of waterlily, mint, and clean cloth. My mind thought, *unfortunately*, and my pussy twinged at just the concept of mating even one more time.

"What are you reading?" I murmured back.

He showed me the spine. It was the comfort read I'd picked up after my night terror. He was reading the Theli version, straight from my bookshelf. "Someone I love recommended it."

I giggled sleepily. "How do you like it?"

"It's very saucy, but in a good way," he remarked. "Stars, am I glad you're awake. It's been nearly two days. Mother's fretting."

Well, we couldn't have that. I sat up, scattering a couple layers of bedding. I huffed with effort. Two days of rest hadn't erased all the soreness from what I'd just put my body through.

Worth it.

I went over to sit in his lap and snuggle up to his warm chest. The air around us was cool on my skin. What a blessing, to be heat-free again.

"I think I've equalized." He spoke in an undertone, like it was a great secret he didn't want to spoil. "You're here, safe, and we're bound by pack and mating bonds. Niall can rest on a job well done."

I searched his face while I probed the murky blur of my memories. When was the last time his pupils had dilated with Niall's influence? It *had* been a while, even under the effects of his rut. His thoughts were a calm stream on his side of the kelpie bond. His feral side was a part of that river, but where it'd once created jagged rapids, it was placid too.

"Congratulations," I said, nuzzling him. I would say I'd miss Niall—except he was still in the room with us. Marius gazed at me with the open affection I'd once taken as a sign of his feral side. "Have you told anyone else?"

"Nay. I wanted you to know first. It's not perfect, you know?" A hint of a troubled frown teased his mouth. "I'll always be feral, just with more control. The family has always wanted a miracle, and I don't want to disappoint."

"Nothing about you is disappointing, mate."

He responded with an aroused growl. "Say that again," he coaxed.

I patted his chest. "Now I'm the one who's going to disappoint. I'm so sore."

"Me too." His thoughts mirrored my own. No regrets. "Glad you're not grabbing me by the knot anymore. We can do other things together. Perhaps you'll want to wash and get dressed? I'll send for Mother, who'll be here within the hour once she hears you're awake."

"Good idea." I didn't move, though, looking at him hopefully. He stood, carrying me up with him. "Wait. Before you take me to the shower, there's somewhere else I want to go."

He raised a brow, confused.

"Take me up the stairs?" I giggled, pointing toward the back of my nest. This whole time, it'd been a two-story affair. But I'd been given this suite while I'd had a cast, and once it was off, he'd spirited me away to the sea. The mysterious, unused second story of my nesting space was one I wanted to see with at least one of my mates first.

"You and stairs," he teased. He shook out his blue-green mane and the braid of my hair woven in it. The braid and the hanging metalark feathers had somehow survived my heat untouched.

"If it gets my protector to carry me…"

"Please. I would carry you anywhere, stairs or no."

With the way my legs and core felt, we would test that statement shortly. He took me to the top of the staircase for a rather anticlimactic reveal. The second floor of my nest had a high roof and was overall larger than I expected, with two windows facing the gardens. The wood flooring gleamed with a recent polish. But it was completely empty.

"I was thinking we could make it like a second library nest. Or, um, something," I said uncertainly. "Somewhere you and the rest of the pack would want to be."

"Whatever you want for it." He smiled with lopsided charm. "The pack wants to be where you are, p'nixie. Don't stress over it."

One less thing to worry over was a relief. I nodded, and he took me downstairs and headed for the rain room.

"I love you," I said. Before he could put me down so I could wash, I looped my arms around his neck and kissed him.

"Love you more," he answered in my mind since his lips were occupied.

I wondered why he usually responded that way. He set me down and closed the clear door to the rain room. He leaned on the edge of the shower casually and answered my thoughts. "Because I love you more than my next breath. I don't want to irritate you with my devotion if I use too many words."

My own breath caught. "No such thing."

"I'm trying not to give doubt a place in my life anymore. I can't be a very good best friend for you if I allow a rain cloud to follow my every step."

Well, it was a good thing I was taking a shower, because I could cry with joy to hear that. "You're doing a great job," I told him.

His teeth were a flash of white through the fog on the glass door.

"It's easy right now. Hard to be sad about anything after feeling how passionately *you* fucked *me*."

I muffled a groan in the stream of water. He echoed the sound and straightened. "Sorry," he chuckled. "I'm leaving."

I took advantage of the warm water and soaked. It'd been a while since I could enjoy increasing the temperature and really turn my skin red. I emerged from a bank of steam and dressed myself...then redressed myself into something less tight. The fabric had to feel just right, as my skin was extra sensitive.

In that private moment, I sniffed myself as thoroughly as I could and purred. My pheromones were already changing. As a mated omega, I represented my pack by carrying a touch of my alphas' scents in combination with my own. I was claimed by my mates in every way possible, and it felt amazing. I wore that joy openly on my face as I headed for my receiving room and found my mates sitting around, waiting.

Our whole mini eclipse of house moths fluttered around, serving tea and little pastries. They greeted me with extra enthusiasm. "Welcome back, Princess!"

"We missed you, Princess!" This was from Jani.

"Yay!" And this, delivered with a happy bounce, was from Lon.

"Thank you," I giggled.

Tormund put in, "I missed you too, li'l bird!" He gestured enthusiastically for me to come sit with him, which I did. We cuddled up to wait. I chatted idly with Fal and Kauz about what they'd been doing while I'd been resting.

As Marius predicted, it didn't take Nemensia long to arrive once she received the message that I was awake. A house moth let her in, and we all stood as she entered in a bustle of iridescent skirts and went straight over to me. Rennyn followed in her wake.

"*Mo stóirín*! Look at you. My heir at last." She caught my head between her hands, tilting my face this way and that as she stared at my new pack mark.

Rennyn made a playful gasp. "Would you look at that. It's a crown." He stood beside his mate, inspecting my forehead too.

"Hi, Mom. Hi, Dad," I said.

"Your heat was quite extended..." she started to say.

"My sugar blossom hasn't been worried *at all*," Rennyn added with irreverence.

"Hush."

"Only if you make me."

Fal cupped his hands around his mouth to announce, "Oh no, they're going to kiss!"

Rennyn rolled his eyes. "For that, I'm stealing your mate for a few minutes. C'mon, Lark. There's someone in the hall who wants to talk to you."

"Oh?" I glanced at Nemensia, who nodded and motioned for me to go.

The dark elf king headed for the door, which a mothkin hurried over to open for him. I felt my mates' curiosity growing over the pack bond. Fal tapped it as I stepped outside and spotted who was waiting out in the hall. The threads of the bond thrummed with a question, one syllable at a time. *Fish-ling?*

Yes, I signaled back. That, at least, wasn't beyond my nascent understanding of what the pack bond could do.

Laurel twisted her fingers together in worry, her shoulders hunched. After knowing her almost all of my life, she looked different on a level I hardly recognized. The haughty airs she'd emulated from Cymora were gone. She seemed smaller after her ordeal, slight and unsure in a plain dress.

"Hi, Lark," she said.

For a moment, I wasn't sure if I wanted to hug her or ask her to leave me alone. Truly, I wanted to do a little of both. Wasn't that how it always was with siblings?

"Hello, Laurel. How are you doing?" I asked gently.

Her eyes started to water. *Stars, already?* "Good, I think."

Rennyn shot a long-suffering look my way. I wondered how much of her crying he'd been subjected to. He hadn't seemed all that comfortable with tears when he'd caught me crying. But he stayed quiet, letting her lead the conversation.

"A lot's happened while you had your heat. With me, I mean," she began. "Congratulations, by the way. On joining the royal family. That's really amazing."

"Thank you," I murmured.

Laurel sniffed and swiped at her nose. "How do I even begin? My mother made me forget some big things. She wanted to shape me to be like her, I think. I slept for a few days and just *remembered*. I used to not be, um, like I am. Does that make sense?"

"It does," I assured her.

"I thought you knew I was under a vow of obedience to her," she added.

"Well, I used to think you knew about my vow of obedience to her too. The 'yes, Stepmother' thing wasn't very subtle."

She shrugged, shifting her weight anxiously. "I guess I had my own things going on. I followed Mother's lead and tried to be happy with the life she built for us. She never let me have freedom to be my own person, and I just...I never questioned why we treated you the way we did. It always was just how it was." Her eyes overflowed with tears as she sobbed and burst out, "I'm so sorry!"

I'd given an effort not to cry too, but at that, wetness marked my cheeks. "Oh, come here." I wrapped her in a hug. We clung to one another for a few minutes, letting the emotions flow.

Rennyn shifted restlessly on his feet. "For stars' sake. You two are making me tear up too," he said, as cheerful as always.

"Sorry, sorry." She sniffled and let me go, drying her face on her sleeve. "Anyway, um, I understand if you don't forgive me, or even hate me. I want to be better. But I know I haven't earned anything yet."

"I don't hate you," I said readily. "And I accept your apology."

She exchanged a glance with the dark elf king. He smiled and inclined his head. "You get to stay, fishling. My brother surely felt you fulfilling your end of the deal."

"King Elion didn't want me to live in Serian unless I did two things," Laurel explained to me. "Apologize to you with all my heart, and let him bind my song. It was hurting me anyway."

I nodded, imagining the kelpie king wasn't all that thrilled to leave a mermaid alive that could sing the siren's song. Let alone one who wanted to stay in his kingdom. "The blood vomit?" I guessed.

"A not-so-fun history fact for you both," Rennyn put in. "The mermaids of times past who used the siren's song too much ended up permanently damaging their voices. The song *became* their only voice."

Laurel shuddered. A fate meant for her, I imagined, if Cymora had had more of a chance to force her to use the siren's song.

"All right. It's time for me to be the villain here," the dark elf king continued. Laurel put on a brave face, but uncertainty tugged at her lips and weighed heavy on her shoulders. They sagged as he spoke. "From this moment forward, you two are no longer sisters. Not even stepsisters. You'll need to be separated because, no matter how much you don't want to, you *will* fall into old patterns if you remain in close contact. And the future Queen of Serian is no servant."

She nodded, shooting me an apologetic glance. I did as well. I agreed with what he was saying. He'd just helped us define our new relationship in a healthier way.

"Laurel has said she's well aware that there's no warm welcome waiting in Osme Fen. So, since she needs a place to live, she'll stay here, in Neslune. But not in the palace. A certain eavesdropper is very excited by this."

The door into my suite opened, and Fal leaned his head out. "How'd you know?" he asked.

Rennyn tsked. "It was either you or the world's calmest bat, and probably both."

Laurel froze the moment my mate stepped into the hall. She fumbled into a belated curtsy. He put an arm around my waist and pressed a kiss to my forehead. I thought he was going to ignore her, but he turned his feline gaze her way. "You know, 'fishling' used to be an insult."

"I'm not surprised," she said in a shy mumble.

He twirled his free hand. "Don't let me interrupt. I've been curious for *days* about how he was going to solve the grievance he owes you."

A familiar smirk played at Rennyn's mouth, a mirror to Fal's mischief. "Must I explain everything? The grievance is for Cymora's death, signaling the end of Laurel's old life. The old magic has already agreed that I've repaid Laurel in full because I've set her up with a new life. She'll be going to live with some of my Seelie friends in the Garden District."

"I'm going to be a baker. I mean, I'm going to learn how," Laurel said.

"In translation, she was infantilized by her own starsdamned mother and needs to learn a trade and some life skills," Rennyn said without a shred of mercy. "She and Cymora built their lives on scraps they've stolen from Lark. So, she will be creating her own path."

Even though Laurel hadn't shaken that fearful gleam from her gaze, I was happy for her. Truly. She wouldn't figure out who she was until she took some difficult steps away from the life she once knew. "It's going to be hard but so worth it," I said to her.

She nodded but pressed her lips together. More tears were coming on, and fast.

"Don't worry, we'll visit. I love bread. We'll order a lot of it," Fal teased.

"Oh, do you think they make sweets? We could order muffins," I said. Actually, I was going to ask my handmaidens for muffins for dessert tonight. I was still starving from refusing food during my heat.

Laurel started to smile. "I'll make sure to suggest muffins. Triple berry, right? Anyway...I guess this is goodbye."

"For now," Fal agreed. He reached into his pocket, producing a letter folded in half, which he offered to her. She took it, brow drawing in confusion. "Open this later."

"Okay," she said with absentminded obedience.

He cleared his throat, masking the edge of discomfort clear from our connection to one another. "I appreciate what you did for Kauz and my father. Perhaps I was wrong about you."

She clutched the letter to her chest, lips moving to frame one word. *Perhaps.* It was an easy one to overthink, but she had the opportunity to make it real. Rennyn had given her the rare opportunity to start all over again.

"Bye, Laurel," I said, parting from Fal to give her a hug farewell. She held me tight, but neither of us lingered for too long. She left with Rennyn, and I rejoined my mates, who were still visiting with Nemensia. Kauz glanced up with an approving smile as we came back in.

"A routine heat will seem like a breeze after this," the queen was saying.

Stars, I didn't want to think about going into heat again. Even though I knew, logically, that no heat would compare to how difficult this one had been.

"Anyway, welcome back, Metalark. I came here with a gift. Something I think you sorely need. It was the biggest one I could find." She picked up a squat box wrapped in a bow as I came over and took the open seat next to her.

I lit up and untied the bow. After peeking inside, I pressed my lips together and closed the box. The pack bond was full of taps, sending little vibrations over my omega mark. All four males were trying to get my attention with a reaction like that.

"Thanks, Mom," I said, trying desperately not to laugh. *Sorely* needed, indeed. It was a pot of wound salve. Something expensive, scarce, and in high demand, I'd learned.

"You are most welcome. By the way, you're invited to dinner tonight. We have so much to talk about," she said brightly. "I'll let you tell your fathers the news, my wild boy."

"We don't have to talk about it tonight. Maybe it's not equalizing. I don't know for sure," Marius said. I was glad to hear he'd mentioned this to her.

"Nonsense! I knew something was different before you told me. Elion is going to be over the moon. You two are going to have so much to talk about." She turned a warm smile my way. "And we can work out your tutoring schedule and duties, Metalark."

Tutoring? Duties? Well, I'd been warned this was coming. Being a princess was hard work, especially at first, but I'd do my best to meet the challenges ahead. My mates were counting on me.

"Okay, Mom. I won't let you down," I said.

"I know you won't, *mo stóirín*. You're here by fate, and fate doesn't make mistakes." She patted my shoulder with an approving nod.

The queen stayed a while longer, making a point to share affirmations with each of her sons. I needed to follow in her example one day, as I felt how much this visit meant to them over our bonds, even if they'd never admit it aloud.

However, once she left, I had their full attention. "Well? What was in the box?" Fal prompted.

I took out the wound salve to show them. "Maybe we should go use this," I suggested.

"Thank the stars!" the dark elf exclaimed. He plucked the pot of salve out of my hand and started for the bedroom.

Kauz kept pace, murmuring something that had Fal grinning. They both turned impish looks back at me.

The pack bond stirred with a signal I didn't know yet. Marius tilted his head before smiling too, while Tormund laughed and reached for me. "Let's go, li'l bird!"

I'd find out what was going on soon enough. Tormund pulled me into his arms, stealing me away like a true Unseelie for whatever mischief my mates had decided on next.

I HOPE you have enjoyed Lark and her pack's story! Thank you for reading.

PLEASE REMEMBER TO REVIEW! Reviews help other readers find stories they may love. Consider leaving a review for Fated or Knot on Amazon and other websites.

ABOUT THE AUTHOR

Ella Hendricks is an author of romances with dark roots and steamy twists. She loves getting lost in fantasy worlds, especially if the monsters are naughty and the lady saves the day in the end. When Ella is not writing about swoon-worthy men, she's off collecting video game achievements. She holds a master's degree in journalism and lives in Texas with her family.

Find out more about her books at: www.ellahendricks.com

www.ingramcontent.com/pod-product-compliance
Lightning Source LLC
Chambersburg PA
CBHW061528190726
48289CB00004B/971